Book III

GAMADIN™

Distant Suns

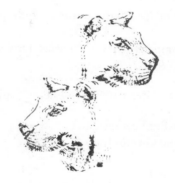

Tom Kirkbride

Publishing

Published by Wigton Publishing Company
16611 S. Melrose Drive, Suite A214
Vista, CA 92081-5471

For ordering information or special discounts for bulk purchases, please contact:
  Wigton Publishing Company, 1611 S. Melrose Drive, Suite A214, Vista, CA 92081-5471, (760) 630-2181

Design and composition by Silvercat™, San Diego, California.

Publisher's Cataloging-In-Publication Data
(Prepared by The Donohue Group, Inc.)

Kirkbride, Tom (Thomas K.)
  Gamadin. Book III, Distant Suns / Tom Kirkbride. -- 1st ed.

    p. ; cm. ISBN: 978-0-9840643-1-1

1. Extraterrestrial beings--Fiction. 2. Space warfare--Fiction. 3. Surfers-California--Fiction. 4. Science fiction. 5. Fantasy fiction. I. Title.

PS3611.I75 G263 2011
813/.6

Printed in China
10 09 08 10 9 8 7 6 5 4 3 2 1

First Edition

For Francesca

Acknowledgments

Many successful projects require irreplaceable advisors and supporters behind its creator. My works are no exception. I dedicate this page to those friends, colleagues, and family that have made this Gamadin book series possible.

I would like to thank my two boyhood pals, Dennis DeHaas and Dave Zatz, for their lifelong friendship and their teeth-gnashing, straightforward frankness. Thanks for being there.

I will always remember and appreciate my writing family: Pulitzer Prize nominee Frank Gaspar and the Long Beach City College Writers Group (Darlene Quinn, Evelyn Marshall, Sid Hoskins, Bob Telford, Susan Posner, and Kathy Porter) for picking apart my earliest manuscripts and contributing to my evolvement as a writer; Antoinette and Jared Kuritz of the La Jolla Writers Conference for turning this story into a marketable product; Richard Gerson and Gary Harmatz for their business approach and savvy; Bob Goodman of Silvercat for his hard work and attention to detail with the editing, book format, and design; and Lisa Wolff, Bonnie Wicht, and Linda O'Doughda for their copyediting skills, making the manuscript the best it can be, thus making me look good. Art Roscoe (1935-2009), I thank you for your early critiques and for taking the time to read my very rough manuscripts. Rest in peace, my friend. A special thank you to Bob Van Epps for his edits and insightful tweaks that added some cool touches to a better ending, and to Suzanne Wishner for her dogged persistence in keeping "Lu" alive and the manuscript clean and appropriate for young readers everywhere. I owe a great deal of gratitude to Lisa Haynes, who saw the potential of an unknown author early on and who has remained a staunch supporter of my series.

Lastly, I thank my daughter, Lara, the inspiration for Leucadia, for her awesome assistance in guiding me through the language of today's young characters; and Francesca Romero, for her love, patience, encouragement, and determination to see this endeavor through with me, which continues to this day. (In other words, she hasn't left me yet!)

I thank you all.

Who were the Gamadin?

Many, many thousands of years ago, when the galactic trading centers of Hitt and Gibb were the cultural elite centers of the Omni quadrant, the Gamadin ruled the cosmos—not in an authoritarian way, but as a protective force against the spreading Death of evil empires and their acts of conquest and domination. A wise and very ancient group of planets from the galactic core formed an alliance to create the most powerful police force the galaxy had ever seen. This police force would be independent of any one state or planet. They were called "Gamadin."

Translated from the ancient scrolls of Amerloi, Gamadin means: "From the center, for all that is good." The sole mission of the Gamadin was to protect the freedom and happiness of peaceful planets everywhere, regardless of origin or wealth. It was said that a single Gamadin ship was so powerful, it could destroy an empire.

Unfortunately, after many centuries of peace, the Gamadin had performed their job too well. Few saw reason for such a powerful presence in their own backyard when the Death of war and the aggressive empire building were remnants of an ancient past. So what was left of the brave Gamadin simply withered away and was lost, never to be heard from again.

However, the ancient scrolls of Amerloi foretold of their resurrection:

For it is written that one day the coming Death will lift its evil head and awaken the fearsome Gamadin of the galactic core. And the wrath of the Gamadin will be felt again throughout the stars, and lo, while some people trembled in despair, still more rejoiced; for the wrath of the Gamadin will cleanse the stars for all; and return peace to the heavens....

OUR GALAXY

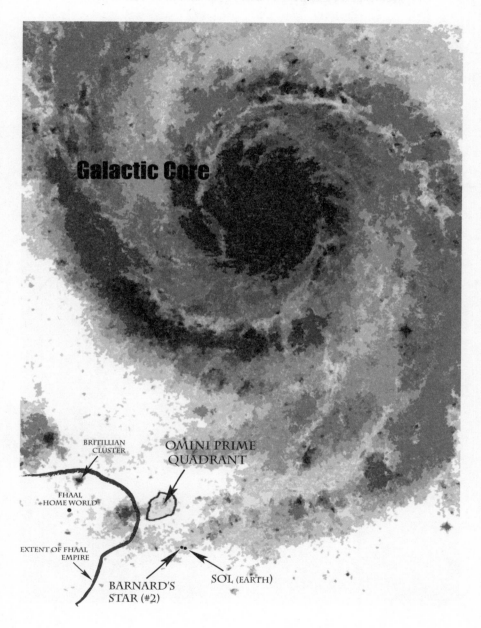

Galactic Core

BRITILLIAN CLUSTER

OMINI PRIME QUADRANT

FHAAL HOME WORLD

EXTENT OF FHAAL EMPIRE

BARNARD'S STAR (#2)

SOL (EARTH)

SOL to BARNARD'S STAR
(DISTANCE BETWEEN = 8 LIGHT-YEARS)

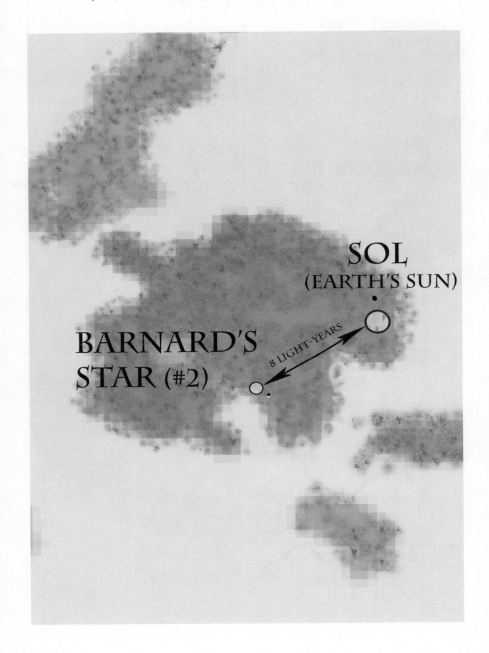

OMINI PRIME QUADRANT

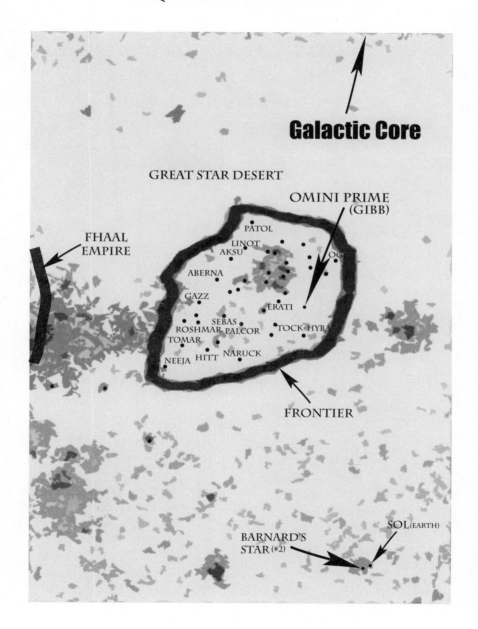

Part I

#2

...It's not a place you can get to by a boat or a train.
It's far, far away...
Beyond the moon.
Behind the rain.
Somewhere over the rainbow...
— Dorothy, *The Wizard of Oz*

1

Cruisin' on In

EIGHTEEN-YEAR-OLD Captain Harlowe Pylott sat at ease in the center command chair of his utterly cool and sleek Gamadin saucer as if he had been born to the task. The journey to Earth had been uneventful, almost routine, and now they were nearly home. As he looked out of *Millawanda's* massive forward windows, the blue oceans of Earth were in clear view. *Waves*, Harlowe dreamed, beautiful tubes of glassy waves, all waiting for him. From here he could taste the salt air and feel the warm, squeaky sand at 42nd Street between his toes before he dove into a rip that would carry him out to his first set of happiness.

They drifted low over the silent desolation of the moon. The magnificently barren and pockmarked surface of green cheese, deep craters, and tall, sawtoothed ridgelines seemed like a giant Ansel Adams photo of stark contrasting shadows. Copernicus, the giant meteor crater, floated under them, its jagged mountaintops threatening to scrape the bottom of the center hatchway if they came any closer.

"Beautiful, gentlemen," Harlowe commented in awe to his skeleton bridge crew of two.

Systems Officer Monday Platter agreed. "Aye, Captain, a beautiful sight she is."

Science Officer Ian Wizzixs checked the final landing coordinates for their touchdown site in Nevada. "Good to go, Captain..." His

1

voice trailed as he turned to a blip on the screen that suddenly caught his attention.

"What is it, Mr. Wizzixs?" Harlowe asked, his face shining with pride over the console of colorful lights dancing to a silent orchestra. Jewels, his robob servant, handed him the chocolate shake he had ordered moments ago. "A problemo?" he inquired, trading a confident wink of fun with Monday.

Ian's fingers flew over the screens with the deftness and discipline that his months of training had given him. "I'm not sure," he replied, his focus never leaving the displays in front of him. "It's a broadcast on an unusual frequency . . . an emergency broadcast," Ian stressed.

Harlowe thanked Jewels and eyed the two empty stations nearby with a whimsical smirk. The one to his immediate right belonged to his second-in-command, First Officer Matt Riverstone, while the other seat at weapons control belonged to Mate Simon Bolt. For personal reasons, the two crewmen were relieved of their duties that evening. He reviewed the heading, the speed, and the long-range sensor readouts on the overhead holo-screen before he leaned back and took a long drag on his shake. It had been an anxious morning preparing for the trip home and he had forgotten to eat. "What's so rad about that, Wiz? We get emergency broadcasts from Earth all the time," he pointed out.

Their flight plan had brought them on a leisurely course through the Jovian system. It had been the long way, but a necessary deviation. Once *Millawanda* passed Jupiter, they turned for home, on a direct path to the inner planets, waving at Lu's Place along the way. A trip that would normally have taken years in any earthly spacecraft took only a few hours of travel time for the perfectly round and sleek 54th-century golden ship from the stars.

And that was just "idling" speed, according to Ian.

At this point in their young careers as Gamadin soldiers, they had not tested *Millawanda's* hyperdrive. If they needed to push it, they knew the hours could change to seconds with a touch of the throttle.

But not now.

Now they only wanted to be simple earthbound young dudes again, cruising along Pacific Coast Highway with the smell of the ocean, laughing and playing under a hot yellow sun with the Dave Matthews Band blaring loudly all the way to the beach. What could be cooler? After their trip home, when they were done visiting with friends and families, after a date with a real doe, after catching a few waves off 42nd Street, and after stuffing their bellies full of "real" In-N-Out Burgers—animal-style with heaps of fries—and giant shakes, after they had done all the things they had dreamed about for over a year in isolation, surviving on lifeless worlds and battling Dakadudes, after all the normal stuff they yearned to do, they might think about putting their pedal-to-the-metal and going to hyperdrive just to see if Millie still had it in her.

For the present, however, Harlowe's main concern was Millie and his crew. It was still a very dangerous solar system out there, Earth included. Returning home had always felt uneasy for him. Returning to the favorite places where he and Lu had gone so many times together would be especially painful. Though no military force on Earth could harm the Gamadin ship, it was her crew that gave him concern. With the government always looking for ways to capture the ancient vessel, his crew would be in danger whenever they stepped beyond the protective confines of the ship. His crew had to be right every second of the day they were on the planet. Those who sought them harm had to be right only once.

Ian swung around in his chair and locked eyes with Harlowe. "I know, Captain, but this broadcast didn't originate from Earth."

Harlowe stopped sucking on his shake, his joyful mood suddenly tempered by the off-world contact.

2

Welcoming Party

TINKER PYLOTT AND Leucadia Mars waited with a mixture of nervous excitement and guarded hope at the bottom of the red carpet gangway for the next President of the United States, President-elect Peter "Digger" Delmonte, to exit the Mars corporate jet. The Nevada night was clear and crisply cold at the super-secret Mars science facility three hundred miles northeast of Las Vegas. The Milky Way appeared like a creamy highway across the heavens as the moon, a smiling crest peering down on them, hung a warm and bright 30 degrees above the horizon. It was a perfect night for an extraterrestrial landing.

Both ladies were stunningly beautiful in the latest fashions from Milan, courtesy of Leucadia's personal clothiers, who had designed them for this special occasion. Leucadia had on a long, knee-length, white fur-lined parka, with black slacks and a matching silk blouse and scarf. Her honey-blond hair glistened softly under the bank of 30-foot-high white lights spread out along the desolate runway. The cuts and bruises on the women's wrists and arms were nearly gone. Only a couple of tiny scars were left from the torture they suffered from Quentin Cribbs, the rogue government agent who had tried to kill them.

Leucadia bent down and picked up a football that had rolled over to her foot.

Harlowe's younger brother bolted across the open tarmac in an imaginary open-field pass play. "Over the middle, Lu!" Dodger cried out.

The Marine guards dressed in desert camouflage and carrying loaded M-16 assault rifles across their chests smirked at each other, wondering how the beautiful socialite would handle the ball. The captain in charge of the security squadron dutifully offered to take the football to save her the embarrassment of tossing a football in her twenty-thousand-dollar outfit.

"Don't worry, Captain," Tinker told the officer. "Ms. Mars can make the play."

The captain saluted. "Yes, Ma'am."

Handling the ball like a pro, Leucadia let fly a perfect spiral. Dodger snatched the ball out of the air and dashed across the imaginary goal. "Touchdown! Lakewood wins!" he yelled, spiking the ball and jumping up with a victorious fist toward the sky.

Jewels looked over at Leucadia and Tinker, grinning proudly. "I believe young Dodger is a first-round draft pick."

The ladies laughed approvingly at Jewel's assessment.

Behind them, a few hundred yards from the long runway, a hangar of corrugated steel and wire windows was illuminated by yellow sodium lights. It was the only building for miles on the desolate desert surface. Inside the hangar was the entrance to the massive subterranean world of the secret Mars testing facilities. Its underground system of vast vaults and levels made its governmental counterpart, Areas 7 and 51, seem like minor players in the world of high-tech secrecy. Every morning a fleet of Mars corporate 727s brought two thousand top-secret employees from Las Vegas, Reno, and Lancaster to the underground facility. After a ten-hour day, they were taken back to their respective cities.

"Maybe I should have stayed away," Leucadia whispered to Tinker.

Tinker saw how anxious she was over how Harlowe might react when he saw Leucadia alive. She had let him believe she had been killed by the aliens over a year ago. "Listen, Hon, you did what you had to do. If you hadn't, Harlowe would have swum through sharks to find you as sure as I'm standing here. If that ship had been destroyed or ended up in some government place because he tried to get back here, you would really feel sorry for yourself." Tinker nodded at the new, dark blue Boeing 787 Dreamliner with the distinctive "M," the Mars corporate logo, painted bright blue on the tail. "When Harlowe sees your plane, he'll know it's you waiting for him. He won't need an explanation." She looked at Leucadia's nervous hand petting Mowgi and added, "He'll be the happiest person on God's earth to see you. He'll pick you up in his arms and the world will be right again. Trust me on that one, Hon."

They came together and held each other for a long, tender moment.

Mowgi trotted next to Leaucadia, caressing her legs like a cat wanting attention. The moon was in her eyes as she lifted the undog in her arms and said, "I won't steal him away for long, Mom."

"I just want one long hug, and then you two go right along and find a beach somewhere with good waves and Harlowe will be in heaven. We'll worry about the big stuff later."

Leucadia leaned over and kissed her on the cheek. "Did the President-elect ask you to go with him after the homecoming?"

Tinker smiled, a little embarrassed. "Well, he hinted at taking me and Dodger back to Washington with him. He wants an escort to all the silly parties he has to attend before the Inaugural."

"And did you accept?" Lu inquired with a not-so-subtle slyness in her tone. "You two seemed to hit it off very nicely at the Victory Ball on election night."

"I think there's some interest," she replied modestly.

"The next President of the United States taking you to dinner every time he comes to California, Mom? I'd say there's interest."

"It's a tough job. I think he likes a woman's opinion now and then."

"With a military edge, no doubt."

"He finds it refreshing."

"I think there's more going on here than you want to admit, Mom."

Tinker's lips pressed together slightly as her eyes turned worrisome. "You don't think it's too soon, do you Lu? To see someone since, since Buster..."

"Buster would want you to go out. He loved you too much not to see you happy. You have a full life ahead of you. You're still young and beautiful. So put a cork in it, Mom," she winked, giving back some of Tinker's own medicine. Leucadia touched Tinker on the shoulder as if she held a magic wand. "From this moment on, I release you. You are free to live again, Tinker Pylott."

As if the spell had been granted, President-elect Peter "Digger" Delmonte emerged from the hatchway and stepped spritely down the stairway with his small entourage behind him: General Ivan Branch, Chairman of the Joint Chiefs of Staff; Linda Nelson, Secretary of State; and Jefferson Braxton, the soon-to-be Special Counsel to the President of the United States.

Delmonte's face lit up like that of a schoolboy seeing his first love, the instant his eyes found Tinker waiting for him at the bottom of the stairway. Tinker's face returned the glow. "Doesn't he look handsome?" she cooed, trying to keep her enthusiasm controlled.

Delmonte extended a big, friendly hand to Tinker first. "So happy to see you again, Mrs. Pylott. You look..." His mouth suddenly stopped working, appearing to have lost his breath momentarily "...ravishing," he finally proclaimed, grasping her hand as if he didn't want to let go. "This is a great moment for all mankind," he told her. She saw in his eyes that he meant every word. "You must be very proud of your son."

Tinker placed her other hand warmly over his. "Yes, Digger— I mean, Mr. President, very proud. It is an honor to see you again."

Delmonte turned slightly toward his entourage, who had gathered around them. "On behalf of my staff and the incoming administration, the honor is ours, Mrs. Pylott."

In order not to look too obvious, they released their warm handshakes. The rumor mill was already getting out of hand about their budding relationship. The President-elect turned to Leucadia, taking her hand in a different, less enduring way, the way a brother takes a sister's hand. "Ms. Mars," he began, bowing slightly, "so nice to see you again."

"Thank you, Mr. President."

Delmonte laughed. "Now, now, Lu. Don't jump the gun. 'Digger' will do just fine." He looked over at her Dreamliner. "New ride?"

"Last month," Leucadia replied as if it was just another necessary purchase for business.

"Lovely. It will make Air Force One appear a little dated."

"Sorry, Mr. President."

Delmonte let her misstep slide this time with a forgiving smile. Did it really matter? "I understand he's almost here. Let me say hello to everyone first and then let us talk," Delmonte said.

3

Stylin'

THEIR CUSTOM-FITTED clothes from Gieves & Hawkes of London fit as perfectly as a SIBA. "You're sure this is the color, brah?" Riverstone asked, touching the long-sleeved silk shirt with the back of his hand.

"Dude," Simon replied, buttoning up the front of his own tailor-made shirt that Millie had fabricated per his English clothier's instructions. "Black is totally cool."

It had taken time to style, and being out of the loop for over a year, Riverstone and Simon needed the leave Harlowe granted them while they took the long way home around Jupiter. Simon's room was decorated with his old movie posters of Captain Julian Starr, *Distant Galaxies* marquees, and his favorite photos of his present life exploring the solar system. His most prized possession was the exclusive Mons Bungee Club photo with Harlowe and Riverstone standing together after they had returned from one of the many aerial clips leaping off the side of the 20,000-foot Olympus Mons escarpment.

"Twenty-three minutes to touchdown, Ladies," Ian's voice rang out over the ship's unseen com.

"Roger that, Señor Wiz," Riverstone replied, with a terrible Mexican accent. The big blue Earth took up the entire observation window as they looked down on the night lights of the major West Coast cities of San Diego, Los Angeles, and San Francisco. Two hundred sixty miles east were the bright lights of Las Vegas, and three hundred miles north of that was their landing area, which looked like a vast black hole. "Look, Rerun! Home sweet home. Isn't she wonderful?" he asked, as he gawked at the tiny specks of the Hawaiian Islands and the blue Pacific still in daylight from a hundred thousand miles away.

Simon zipped up his black wool slacks as he strolled over to Riverstone. He stared for a long moment, leaving half his shirt untucked as he gazed reverently at the planet where he was known by millions of movie fans. "Sweet, and we're going to have our pick of the babes toooonight, my Gamadin buddy."

Riverstone sighed. "I only care about one…Phoebe Marleigh."

"Don't worry, my man. Saul's got it all arranged. Phoebe will be there looking hot, dude. From what Saul says, she's excited to meet you, too."

"Really, Rerun? You think we'll hit it off? That would be so cool, brah."

Simon stepped back, eyeing Riverstone's appearance with pride. "A Gamadin stud like you? Dude, you're all-in."

"Thanks, Rerun."

Simon reached out for Riverstone's shoulder, flicking off a few stray hairs left over from a recent haircut. "Hey, do me a favor, bro. Don't call me Rerun when we get to the party. You know…the fans. They might not understand."

Riverstone winked. "Aye. Just between you and me, Rerun."

They congratulated each other with a big high-five and a body slam, then Simon showed off his quick dance routine by twirling his chiseled six-foot-six frame as if he were standing on air, stopped, then shuffled backward the way a tall Michael Jackson would perform onstage.

"That's cool," Riverstone beamed. "Can you teach me how to do that?"

Simon pointed at the window where the Earth was growing larger by the moment. "Not enough time. We'll be landing soon, and I still have to pick out my shoes."

They started walking toward the closet.

"Did Saul get the flight tickets for my family?" Riverstone asked.

Simon flashed Riverstone a big thumbs-up. "All taken care of, mate. He's got them all set up with a suite at the Bellagio, top floor, right below the Mars penthouse..." He stopped suddenly, remembering the story Riverstone and Monday had told him about Harry and Sook Mars.

Riverstone closed his eyes, trying to forget that awful night when he and Monday discovered their bodies. If Mowgi hadn't held off the Daks long enough for them to escape down the service elevator, he and Monday would have ended up the same way.

"Hey, it's cool, Rerun," Riverstone said, helping to defray the sadness. "My parents will love the suite."

"You're sure?"

"No worries."

The door of the closet swished back. Simon returned a nod of thanks before he asked, "What do you think Dog's going to do when we get there?"

Riverstone wasn't about to tell Simon that Lu was waiting at the landing site. The secret that she was alive wasn't for him to reveal. He had known for a week that she had planned to be there. He had given his word that he would never tell unless she released him from that promise. Until then, it would always be his secret.

"The only thing Harlowe will be doing after he hugs his mom is surfing down at 42nd Street," Riverstone replied with absolute confidence.

"I can set him up with a movie star," Simon offered.

Riverstone smiled. "Trust me, a wave is all Harlowe needs."

"No babes, huh?"

"Nah."

"I guess after Lu . . ."

"Yeah, she's a tough act to follow."

Simon turned to Riverstone. "I loved her too, you know."

"Everyone loved Lu."

Simon fought off the sting in the back of his eyes. "She was easy to love."

"Those legs."

"It hurt me to see her with the Captain."

"Hurt me, too," Riverstone confided.

Simon wasn't sure if Riverstone was being straight up. "Really?"

"Sure. Listen, as good-looking and cool as I am," Riverstone said, pointing a thumb to his chest, "he gets the richest, most gorgeous girl on the planet. Now I ask you, wouldn't you be just a little steamed over about that, brah?"

Simon saw his point. "Yeah, it ain't fair."

"No joke."

"Does he always get the chicks?"

Riverstone peeled his lips back, appearing annoyed. "Always, and what's even more a slam is the ladies are always a zillion steps above his pay grade, too. Doesn't make sense."

Simon looked at Riverstone intensely. "So how does he do it? You know him better than anyone. It can't be that complicated."

Riverstone agreed. "It's not. I've been watching his act since day one. The only thing I can figure out is that they feel safe with Harlowe. Somehow, some way, he gives them a sense of security."

"You're living in a tree, Jester. That doesn't make sense."

"I know, but that's it, I tell ya. Security. What else could it be?"

"Maybe you're right. He doesn't have any money, so that must be it. If he had money, I could understand."

"Listen, money is a false promise because as you can see," Riverstone said, looking at Simon eye-to-eye, "security can be gone quicker than Millie can leave the planet. The good ones don't care about money, brah. That's a fact." Riverstone started to laugh again, then continued: "Harlowe gives them the real thing. When they're with him, they feel secure. It's no more complicated than that."

Simon shook with doubt. "That's against nature. Women are screwy."

"You got that right."

After bantering back and forth about the flaws of the opposite sex, Simon wondered about themselves. "You think we'll ever find someone, Jester?"

Riverstone lost his cheeriness as he turned to the stars, looking for an answer. "Yeah, somewhere between Saul's party and the bottom of the loneliest, darkest corner of the galaxy."

Simon joined in his lost gaze. "If I ever find one with meaning, it will be love at first sight."

"You believe in that?"

"Yeah, I do. It was that way with Lu," Simon confessed. "Then Harlowe came along. Things might have been different if…"

"Get over it, Rerun," Riverstone insisted. "Harlowe doesn't lose. I keep telling you that. The odds can be a billion to one he wouldn't survive the next nanosecond, and he'll still find some way to win."

Riverstone leaned into Simon's space. "How many times do you have to learn that lesson, brah?"

Simon sighed painfully. "I know. For the longest time all I wanted to do to Harlowe was…" He stopped, and met Riverstone with helpless eyes.

"Slam him?" Riverstone replied, completing the thought.

Simon shook his head. "No, worse. I wanted him to suffer like I did. I wanted him to hurt so bad he wanted to kill himself. It was the worst pain I've ever known when Lu fell for Harlowe."

"It wasn't his fault," Riverstone said.

"Easy for you to say. You're his friend," Simon replied.

"He's yours, too."

Simon nodded like someone does who's found religion. "Yeah, he'd die for us. I know that now."

Riverstone leaned back, sympathetic. "So, you still want to hurt him?"

"Of course."

Riverstone looked surprised until Simon broke into a smile. "But I'd follow him to end of the galaxy if he asked me to."

Riverstone's face went slack. "Be careful, brah. Don't say that too loud."

"Why's that?"

"Because Harlowe just might ask you to."

4

In Sight

"LOOK!" A SOLDIER shouted from the perimeter. "Over there!" Then everyone's attention focused on a bright star-like object dropping down from the heavens.

A Mars systems engineer walked over to the entourage and said to Leucadia, "She's right on schedule, Ms. Mars."

"How far away, Glenn?" Leucadia asked.

"About 100,000 feet, Ma'am," the engineer replied.

Tinker watched proudly. "It seems so big," she said, awed by the sight of her son's ship.

"It is, Ma'am. She's over fifteen hundred feet across and nearly a mile in circumference. A very big ship, Mrs. Pylott."

"Amazing," Tinker replied.

Delmonte whistled in astonishment, taking Tinker's hand. She let him. "Is that a fact?"

"Yes, sir. With the mass of six *Nimitz*-class carriers."

"Shouldn't it be glowing or something as it enters the atmosphere?" Jefferson Braxton asked.

The scientist kept his eyes on the disk as he laughed slightly, not from arrogance of knowing the answer, but from mere awe of what the answer was. "Power, Sir. Her immense power seems to defy the Earth's gravity."

Braxton returned his eyes skyward with a renewed sense of wonder. "Fascinating."

"That's my brother Harlowe's spaceship, Mister," Dodger Pylott said, looking up at the tall Washington, D.C. lawyer. "Isn't it the coolest thing you've ever seen?"

Braxton knelt down beside Dodger, coming to eye level with the freckle-faced eleven-year old. "I bet you're really proud of him."

Dodger's face glowed. "He knows Captain Starr. They're pards," Dodger bragged.

"Well, that is something. Do you think I can get his autograph?" Braxton asked.

Dodger nodded with a confident grin. "Sure, mister, I'll get one for you." Then Dodger took off with Mowgi, their combined energy unable to stay put for longer than a few moments.

Braxton turned and caught the troubled look in Luecadia's bright green eyes.

"Ms. Leucadia?" he said to her.

At first Leucadia didn't respond, her focus was so intent on the descending ship. It was now large as a full moon and growing larger.

"Ms. Leucadia," Braxton said again, "are you okay?"

This time Leucadia heard him, but her eyes didn't leave the ship for a moment as she replied dismissively. "Yes, Jefferson, I'm fine."

But she wasn't fine. He watched her move away from the small crowd, wondering if he should follow her. She drifted away from the bright sodium lights and the small gathering. Braxton took one step to follow her before deciding against it. If she wanted his company, she would have stayed with the group.

5

Contact

MILLAWANDA DRIFTED DOWN in a steady descent through the Earth's upper atmosphere as Harlowe bent over Ian's shoulder for a look-see. "You're sure?"

"It's definitely coming from out of our solar system, Captain," Ian informed him.

"Change of course, Skipper?" Monday asked.

Harlowe thought the possibility of governmental involvement was extremely high. He didn't want to alarm anyone at the landing site until he was sure that in fact it had an extraterrestrial origin. "Not yet, Mr. Platter; continue on course. Let our homecoming party know we're here."

"Aye, Captain," Monday replied. He passed his hand over a bright orange bar, following Harlowe's command.

Ian then jumped over to Simon's empty communications chair and verified the origin. "Millie says it's not a gomer, Captain. It's real and a little over eight light-years away, near a small red dwarf called Barnard's Star," Ian said, pointing at the computer screen above. The overhead displayed a star map of all the local stars three parsecs out. There were several points of light, but the red flashing star in the upper right corner of the map was the one he was concerned about.

"Barn's star?" Harlowe asked. "And it's eight what?"

"Barnard's Star," Ian corrected, "and it's eight light-years from here, Captain."

Ian slid his hand along a lighted bar and brought up the broadcast on the overhead for everyone to see. At first there was nothing but static noise and interference. At various intervals between the unobservable discharges, a quick glimpse of a tall, undefined form came through on the holographic viewer. They had all speculated about what other life in the galaxy might look like when and if they ever ventured out beyond the solar system. Millie had explained to them that many pockets of intelligent life did exist in the galaxy. So the idea that someday they would meet beings from another world was not an exaggerated expectation. They had already met the Dakadudes and the four attack ships from an unknown origin. Since both introductions had been near-death experiences, the first thought that raced through their minds was that this contact might be another Dak. How would they handle that?

So far they hadn't had a lot of good luck meeting beings from other parts of the galaxy. The ugly being that came out of the shuttlecraft with the killer black beasts was still fresh in Harlowe's mind. If it wasn't for the bad history behind them, they might have let out a few wild yells of *we-did-it* upon making contact with other life-forms. But they were jaded pros now. They had already experienced enough alien beings for a lifetime that wanted to kill them and take their ship. They hoped this time would be different. They were overdue for somebody friendly.

With anxious hope, Ian's skilled hands fiddled with the console trying to produce a readable image on the screen. Then right before their eyes, was a *real* live being from another world. For them it was another attempt at friendly contact, another chance to meet another being from somewhere other than Earth. It was mind-boggling!

So they waited.

And they watched.

They watched the image on the screen so closely and with such eagerness, one would have thought they held the five winning lottery numbers out of six with the sixth number about to drop down the shoot. Then it happened. The ball fell and the number materialized before their eyes as they learned the most astonishing thing of all was that the being was hardly tall and green, or short and fat, and most certainly no Dak. It was quite human-looking. There was still interference, but the image was unmistakable. It was not only human, but also a very human-looking *girl*...

6

A Call for Help

THE INSTANT HE saw the girl's image, Harlowe sat straight up in his center chair. She looked no older than they were, perhaps younger. It was difficult to tell without knowing squat about alien women; except for Lu, but she was only part alien. The woman's hair was long and black and fell past her waist in rolling waves like calm, gentle breakers coming to shore. Her large, dark eyes matched the coal blackness of her hair. Her delicate skin was flawless and creamy, her mouth small and thin. The golden jumpsuit that she wore fitted her lean, tall figure. Besides her graceful beauty, Harlowe found something more, something that stopped his breathing as if she were reaching inside him and grabbing his soul. What was this hold on him that he didn't understand? All he knew was that he was not a casual observer anymore. In the briefest moment, his mind had suddenly and unalterably changed forever. He *believed* he was somehow linked to this woman; for what purpose, he didn't know. He had to find out or die trying, that he *did* know.

Her speech was like nothing they had ever heard before. It was a mishmash of clicks and high-pitched utterances that no one understood.

"She's in trouble," Ian responded, still working to keep the picture clear.

"Stay with it," Harlowe encouraged.

21

"I'll redirect the focus array, Captain," Monday added.

"Do it quickly, Mr. Platter," Harlowe replied.

"Aye, sir. Working."

It wasn't necessary to know what she was saying. The girl's eyes spoke to them, pleading for someone to hear her. The place where she stood looked like a ship's bridge much like their own, except that it was smaller, with few lighted panels. Other uniformed beings were slumped over in their chairs or lying on the control deck. They appeared unconscious or dead. Others were working feverishly to put out the fires and stabilize the controls. Suddenly a man entered the picture. He was dressed in a silver-grey uniform. He was injured, and dark blood was flowing from a gash over the left side of his face.

Interference broke the picture again, bringing Harlowe out of his chair. "Get it back, Wiz." He had to see her again. "How's that array coming, Mr. Platter?"

"Almost have it, Captain," Monday replied.

While Monday was adjusting the outside array, Ian's hands deftly adjusted the dials and lighted bars as he struggled to get back the sound portion of the transmission.

Just then, a thunderous explosion rocked the alien ship's bridge. The girl held onto a vertical beam and tried to keep herself balanced before she turned back to the screen and spoke in a desperate voice.

"What's she saying?" Harlowe murmured under his breath.

The alien officer tried one more time to pull her away. She wouldn't leave. And, in that instant, the screen went blank. Not even static was left on the overhead. It was as if someone had suddenly pulled the plug.

Harlowe turned to Ian. "What happened?"

Ian's face was a blank. He returned to his console and did everything he could to bring the girl back, but his efforts were ineffective. She was gone. "She went dark, Captain."

Harlowe turned to Monday, looking for hope.

"Nothing, Captain. The link is gone," Monday said.

A long hush fell over the bridge as Harlowe stared at the overhead, struggling with the obvious. The girl's ship had been destroyed.

Ian shrugged. "Maybe we can pick up more by translating what she said."

Harlowe turned to Ian in a depressed funk. "Millie can do that?"

"I think so."

"The girl wasn't from Earth."

"Neither is Millie, yet she does it routinely when we listen to non-English broadcasts from Earth."

They had discovered that all languages, at least the ones from Earth, had certain fundamental patterns in common. The computer took those patterns and compared them within its vast database of languages. Presto! Translation, and it was English. Since Millie was a ship from the stars, it only stood to reason she would have a shot at knowing the girl's language.

Harlowe brightened. He was all in. "Do it!"

"Aye, Captain."

Ian brought up the girl again from the beginning. This time, however, her speech was quite understandable.

"Tock-hyba," she began. "The Consortium has intercepted...cannot reach you..."

"This is where the dude comes in," Ian pointed out as they watched the bleeding officer come to her side.

"Quay...escape pod..." the officer pleaded, "Come, the ship's breaking up..."

The girl resisted. The ship rocked like before when the bright yellow light struck. She struggled valiantly to keep her footing and fell to her knees against a bulkhead. Her lips moved but no words came out.

Then exactly as before, the screen went blank.

Harlowe kept staring at the overhead even though the girl's image was gone. He did not need an image to see her standing with beautiful dark eyes of doom as she faced Death, asking for help. The longer he stared, the more she touched him, and the more he was drawn to her crusade for assistance. He shook suddenly, feeling a chill. He felt his chest tighten while his breathing became erratic.

Monday saw Harlowe's eyes move crazily. "Are you okay, Captain?"

Harlowe fought for control, gripping the sides of his chair to steady himself. "We have to do something."

"She's light-years away, Captain," Ian pointed out. "It took eight years for us to receive that transmission."

Millawanda was still drifting down to the put-down area, passing through the 70,000-foot mark. There was only a sliver of outer space left as the Earth took up all three large windows of the control room. Harlowe's long face focused on the tiny lights of space that were still left up on the screen, while he reconciled with the hard facts of time and distance. "Eight years, huh?" he questioned in a low voice.

"We were in junior high when she called for help," Ian explained, his sobering reality draining all hope of assistance.

"Play it again, Wiz," Harlowe ordered.

Ian tried to protest. It was a waste of time.

"Just do it," Harlowe insisted.

Ian dutifully followed orders and replayed the scene again. Nothing changed.

"Again," Harlowe said two more times, and two more times Ian repeated the scene.

"What are you looking for, Captain?" Monday asked.

Harlowe slumped back into his chair. "Anything." He was heartbroken. He desperately wanted to help her. Not giving up, still thinking he might have missed something, he rose from his command chair and stood behind Ian, his eyes never leaving the overhead. "Play the last five seconds."

Appeasing his captain, Ian followed orders and played the final five seconds of the scene. The girl fell against the bulkhead as her lips moved in silence. There was nothing new they had not seen in the previous playbacks.

"What's she saying?" Harlowe asked.

Ian and Monday exchanged pointless glances as they stared at the last frame of the scene before it went blank.

"Nothing, Captain," Monday replied.

Harlowe wasn't buying it. "She's talking."

Ian's brow wrinkled as he backed the scene and played it again for himself this time. "Almost like she's praying."

"Millie," Harlowe called to the overhead, "follow the girl's lips and tell us what she's saying."

As the last five seconds slowly replayed, the screen read: HEAR ME, PEACEMAKERS. SAVE US FROM THIS EVIL, PEACEMA—

The bridge was stunned.

"I think she was praying," Ian said, turning to Harlowe.

Harlowe nodded. "Yeah, for Peacemakers to save her."

"Who are the Peacemakers?" Ian wondered.

"Gods?" Monday asked.

"Does it matter? She needs help now, Mr. Platter," Harlowe replied.

As loyal officers, there was no glossing over the fact there was nothing they could do to change the reality of what happened years ago.

"She's still gone, Captain," Ian said, being sensible. "Nothing we can do about that."

Monday added his twist, trying to turn the conversation light. "She was hot, Captain. Not many like her even back on Earth. Rerun would have given her a part in his new movie."

Ian agreed. "The dude pulling her away called her Quay."

Harlowe's mind raced along as if he were threading his way through the Noctis Labyrinthus back on Mars. "Quay... Peacemakers? How would she know about us?" he muttered as if speaking to a dream.

Ian reflected how they all felt. "Maybe it happened a long time ago, but she touched a part of our lives today... if only for a brief time. None of us will ever forget her courage."

"Aye," Harlowe mumbled, still thinking, still churning alternatives as he exhausted every possibility in his mind, trying to defy the forces of nature.

There was a somber silence in the control room until Ian turned around in his chair and informed Harlowe, "Time to start braking, sir." The Earth was dark and huge against the backdrop of stars. "We should keep Millie under the sound barrier before we past through fifty thousand, Captain."

Harlowe nodded, half-aware of his order. "Do it, Mr. Platter."

"Aye, Captain."

As Monday began the braking process, *Millawanda* began cutting back her speed as she descended through the upper stratosphere, fully immersed inside the dark side of the planet.

Harlowe's eyes flew open. "Wait!" he cried out, leaping from his chair. "Quay said 'Gamadin.'"

Ian kept his eyes on the screen readouts displaying their rate of deceleration and course as they drifted over the Montana Rockies, coming in from the northeast. "Who?" he asked.

Harlowe looked at Monday and Ian almost simultaneously, his face determined as though he had an answer for the impossible. "The girl needs our help," he repeated.

"That still doesn't change the laws of physics, Captain," Monday pointed out.

"Millie goes faster than light," Harlowe countered.

Ian almost agreed. "We think so, Captain, but we haven't tried it yet."

"Yes, Mr. Wizzixs, but you said yourself, we've just been moseying along in the solar system at idle. What if we stepped on the gas? From what we know so far, if we put our pedal to the metal, do you think we could go faster than light?"

Monday's face had an uncertain fear, and he became silent at the thought of going faster than light. Sub-light travel was plenty fast for him. The thought of his atoms going past light speed was unsettling. Ian, on the other hand, had no uncertainty at all in his reply. "No doubt, Captain."

"If we can do it, other beings can do it too," Harlowe envisioned.

"Aye," Ian replied, though his tone and facial expression remained doubtful. "Maybe it is possible to travel faster than light, but she wasn't doing it in a ship, she was sending a message. As far as I know, radio signals only go light speed."

Ian lifted his hand to activate another course correction as they were still floating down. Harlowe stopped him before his hand hit the button. "Think out of the box, Wiz. Check it out with Millie first before we fold our cards." Holding his hand up, he ordered Monday, "Hold us steady here, Mr. Platter." Then back to Ian, he directed, "Analyze the transmission, Wiz. Let's see what Millie has to say."

"Aye, Captain," Ian replied, returning dubiously to his screens. After a moment, his eyes went wide.

"Do we have an answer, Mr. Wizzixs?" Harlowe asked.

"Aye, Captain."

"Well, put on the screen if you please."

Ian's mouth hung open in stunned silence as he gazed up at the overhead screen. Harlowe's face, however, was a face of hope.

"27 MINUTES, 18 SECONDS," the overhead screen read in large blue letters while the seconds kept ticking, never stopping.

7

Hyperlight

IAN STARED AT the readouts as if they were a practical joke. He asked Millie to recheck her findings. The screen blinked twice, indicating she had completed her check and all was in order.

"I can't believe this communication went eight light-years in twenty-seven minutes!" Ian exclaimed.

Harlowe bent down to Ian. "Stop thinking twenty-first century tech, Wiz. We're fifty-fourth century wiz-bang Gamadin cool, don't forget." He turned to Monday. "Reverse course, Mr. Platter," Harlowe ordered, determined to reach the girl before it was too late. "Prepare for hyperlight, Gamadin."

"But Captain, we can't just go to hyperlight like it's nothing," Ian warned, and looked to Monday for support.

Harlowe remained steadfast. "We've wasted too much time already, Mr. Wizzixs. Give me a heading for Barn's star."

Ian persisted. "But, Sir, with all due respect, there are a lot of unknowns out there. What about the landing site? The President-elect, your mom and L—" He almost said *her* name, but caught himself in time. "Well, they're waiting for us, Captain."

Harlowe leaned forward. "Give them our apologies. You have ten seconds. She needs a Gamadin and that's what we're going to give her."

The fear in Monday's eyes was obvious. "We've never gone past light speed before, Captain."

Before he addressed Monday, Harlowe locked eyes with Ian. "Tell them."

With a great deal of reluctance, but never one to defy orders, Ian jumped over to Simon's station to relay their apologies to their parents, friends, and the new President-elect of the United States.

Harlowe knew full well Monday was about as far away from a coward as anyone could be. There were too many times on Mars that, despite his gut-wrenching fear of flying, he had pushed himself off the cliff and flown. Even though Riverstone had been with him every step of the way, he had taken the risk. He had pushed himself beyond his limits, farther than anybody thought possible. As frightened as Monday was, Harlowe knew he would follow him off a cliff if he asked him to, regardless of the outcome. Harlowe understood that, but he also knew at times his crew needed a little hand-holding to rise to the next level. Harlowe looked over to Monday and gave him a comforting nod. "We'll be okay, Squid." Monday forced a small grin of appreciation as he returned the nod with a go-ahead.

"Ready, Captain," Monday replied, shaking in his boots.

"Ready, Mr. Wizzixs?" Harlowe asked.

Ian tapped a lighted yellow bar on the console before returning to his original chair. "Message sent, Captain. We're good to go."

Through the giant forward windows of the control room, they watched the Earth slide away off their portside window as *Millawanda* pivoted on her axis. The moon reentered the scene in the upper starboard window while a heaven of bright stars replaced all that was left of the Earth. Harlowe pointed straight ahead. "Barn's star, Mr. Platter," still mispronouncing the star's name. "Light speed, if you please. We're wasting time."

What did they know about anything really? Harlowe wondered. Aside from their own solar system, they knew nothing about what they would find once they reached this distant star system. They had never ventured farther than their own star system. What would they find when they arrived? Who would they see? Who would they be helping? Would they make the situation worse for her? *Never mind that, son,* Buster countered, *just do the right thing. I trust you, son.*

The girl had called for help. Was that reason enough? To Harlowe that was all it took. They were Gamadin. This was their calling, to help those who needed their services. Even though they had no idea what they were getting themselves into once they arrived at their destination, they were going anyway.

Harlowe rose from his chair, facing the bright expanse of stars. Before Ian plotted the course, he thought about another piece of the puzzle being laid into place. How everything fit now. That's what the General was doing all along. He wasn't training them to go back to Earth. He was training them to use *Millawanda* to protect others in the galaxy, not just Earth. That's what it was all about. Harlowe's eyes fluttered, awakening from the disbelief. The old soldier knew all along the course they were headed on...and it wasn't Earth.

He remembered back at Lu's Place, discussing this with Riverstone as they left the entrance together. Riverstone thought he had never heard anything so ridiculous in his life. "There's only five of us, Dog. What can we do? When it comes down to it, we're just high school dudes who happened to find a spaceship in the desert, remember? Come on, we're not warriors from a distant past. We're surfer toads from Lakewood, California who happened to get caught up in the wrong place at the wrong time. All this fifty-fourth century space-ship stuff was an accident," he emphasized.

Harlowe remembered turning to Riverstone with an all-knowing grin. "It wasn't an accident, pard. You know it and I know it. We've been down this road too many times together to think this way: Simon's yacht capsizing, saving Lu, rescuing Sam's little girl from the bad guys in the desert, all that isn't coincidence. It's like we've been doing this all our lives. Sure, we didn't sign up for this one. Who in their right mind would have? But life isn't about sure things. It is about risk and responsibility, riding the big waves when no one else is doing it. Most of all it's doing the right thing. We have a ship that we can use to help others. She's powerful, pard, more powerful than we know. The way I look at it we've been entrusted with her to help our galaxy. So that's what we have to do. We have to go out there and make a difference with this power or someone else will, and they may not be as cool as us." Harlowe marveled at *Millawanda* with his mouth wide open as if he were seeing her for the first time. He went on, "The General, Lu, Mrs. M, and Harry all saw our Fate. They knew what we must become."

"Gamadin," Monday announced from behind as they walked along.

Harlowe looked at them both. "That's right, Squid." He gave the big guy a high-five. "Gamadin, dude!"

"So when do we make our first house call?" Riverstone joked.

Harlowe laughed. "The shingle's already on the door, Mr. Riverstone. We're just waiting for our first patient."

* * *

Well, that moment was now, Harlowe thought. Their first patient was ringing the doorbell in a panic. He could see in Ian's face that he wanted to say something more. His duty to Harlowe, however, to *Millawanda*, and to a long-ago intergalactic force would not allow him to say anything more. They were "all-in," and there was no turning back on their first house call. The months of training and preparation had prepared them for this moment.

Ian slowly raised his head and asked, "We're not going home, are we?"

Harlowe leaned down and squeezed Ian's shoulder. "We're it, Wiz, the only ones available."

Ian turned back to his console of bright lights and screens. He didn't share the sudden chill that swirled around Harlowe's body. Harlowe didn't understand it either. He gazed out at the vastness. The source wasn't there. He turned around, looking back over his shoulder. The chill had come from behind.

Ian displayed the coordinates of the course changes Harlowe would need to guide *Millawanda* to their stellar destination. "Course change in, Captain," Ian acknowledged, his eyes straight ahead, focused on the readouts. Overhead, the tactical, three-dimensional map displayed Barnard's Star, as well as other nearby stars, six parsecs out from Sol. It was a stunning graphic.

"Good to go here, Captain," Monday confirmed.

"We should clear Earth's atmosphere first, Captain," Ian cautioned. "Let's not rip a hole in the universe while we're still so close to home," he added.

Harlowe agreed that waiting until they were well past the orbit of Jupiter was prudent. "Caution noted, Mr. Wizzixs."

Millawanda's beautiful blue pulsing beacon next to their own sun, however, did little to calm Ian and Monday's thoughts of sublimity, thoughts they'd had moments before Harlowe slid his fingers over the throttle, sending them into hyperlight for the first time in their lives.

A moment later, a hundred thousand miles from Earth, Millie's response was instant. The moon disappeared in a blink. They had just gone hyperlight.

8

Be Safe

LEUCADIA TURNED FROM the bright disk as it seemed to suddenly slow its forward motion, coming to a stop ten thousand feet above the Nevada landing site.

She knew.

She knew at that moment Harlowe was not coming home.

The disk remained there for a long, heartbreaking moment like a brilliant star before it began to move away, not from where it came, but in another direction, away from the planet, away from her. Streams of tears fell down the sides of her flawless cheeks. She could do nothing to stop him as Fate seemed once again to intervene in their lives. Would she ever see him again? Only the stars knew for sure. She thought back, remembering the very first time they met. His blue eyes watching, so concerned for her as they floated in a churning sea, and he held her in his strong, weary arms that day so long ago. He had just rescued her from Simon's sinking yacht after it had been swamped by a giant wave. Harlowe had found her still trapped inside the overturned boat. She knew then she could never love any other man but Harlowe. She smiled, proud of what they had accomplished together in such a short time. With a face full of tears, she waved goodbye and called to him, *Goodbye, my dearest hero. Be safe. I will always love you, Harlowe Pylott!*

She would have loved him no other way.

Then the golden saucer winked away, and *he* was gone.

9

Faster

THE GAMADIN SAUCER was now traveling at point nine the speed of light. After the sensations had quickly dissipated, Harlowe placed his cold, dry hand on the outer bar; the same bar that would take *Millawanda* past the threshold of light.

"Careful, Captain," Ian cautioned. "Not too fast to start. She hasn't gone this fast for eons."

Monday agreed, his face displaying his anxiety. "I second that, Captain."

"Position?" Harlowe inquired.

"Halfway between Jupiter and Saturn," Ian replied.

Harlowe nodded reassurance, swallowed hard, and slid his right-hand fingers down the acceleration bar with delicate precision. He made all the right moves along the bars, yet it appeared that nothing had happened. With so many months of training, he knew everything he had done was correct, down to the tiniest manipulation. There was no feeling of a sudden lurching motion one would expect from an added increase in speed into the realm of hyperlight; no tugs from the back of the seat or sensation of a forward movement indicating they had passed such a significant threshold.

Ian turned back with a look of *Go ahead, do it! Get it over with!*

"I did," Harlowe replied, looking at Ian and Monday, confused. "I slid my fingers across the bars. Something should have happened."

Monday looked out the window at the stars and thought they did seem a little different. They were brighter than before, but as he viewed them around the edge of the side of the starboard observation window, they started to lose their glow. From a sparkling white, they dimmed to a pale yellow, and then changed to a dull orange-red when he viewed the starscape on his rear projection screen.

"I didn't feel a thing," Harlowe mused, wondering if they had done all the right things.

Ian touched the panels and read his console. His readouts said everything was working fine. Then Monday pointed to the overhead and cried out, "Oh, my God! We're ten times light, Captain! Look!"

The takeoff may have been instant, but the aftershock of going into hyperlight for the first time was hardly electrifying. If they expected fireworks, loud gyrations with their bodies pressed against their chairs like a drag racer accelerating from zero to two hundred miles per hour in three-point-five seconds, it didn't happen. What they got was anticlimactic. A slight increased throbbing hum, a light pressure to the back of the seat, and that was all they felt.

Their first foray into the realm of hyperlight travel had been a serious bummer. Monday made the comment that he felt more acceleration from his ninety-year-old grandmother pulling away from the curb in her twenty-year-old Buick La Sabre.

Going faster than light was all well and good, but Harlowe wanted to know how long it was going to take to get there at their present velocity.

"Nine or ten months," Ian calculated.

"Nine or ten—too long!" Harlowe responded sharply, pressing his fingers across the acceleration bars further until he was past the halfway mark on the bar. "How long now?" Harlowe asked, looking for a better time.

A worried frown shadowed Ian's face as he stared down at his screens and saw the saucer racing across the overhead star map. Every time the pulsing light blinked, Millie had moved to a new position on the graphic.

"One thousand light!" Ian exclaimed. "We'll be there in a matter of hours!"

"Can she go faster?" Harlowe asked, as he was about to slide his fingers to the limit.

"Aye, Captain, a lot faster, but—" Ian replied, swallowing hard.

"No time for buts, Mr. Wizzixs," Harlowe said, as Monday shut his eyes. He didn't want to look. Harlowe figured they had wasted enough time already, so he pushed *Millawanda* to the power of seventeen times the speed of light. They would be there in less than an hour. A short jaunt for a ship built for the stars.

10

Surprise

TWENTY MINUTES LATER, Riverstone and Simon came bouncing off the blinker onto the bridge, like models from a *Gentleman's Quarterly* ad. "Check these threads out, dudes," Riverstone beamed, turning around for all to see. "What do ya think, Captain? The latest from London." He pointed to his shiny black Italian leather shoes. "You like the fresh kicks, Squid? You won't find these on Rodeo Drive."

They were so full of themselves, they didn't see the blank expressions on everyone's faces.

"The color is called crimson and corn," Simon added with a pompous smile. He did a three-sixty turn, following Riverstone's example. "Classy, huh? It's the thing now. Hey, there's plenty for every..."

His voice trailed as he suddenly realized Harlowe wasn't in as festive a mood as he was the last time he saw him. "What's the matter, Captain? You don't like the choices? Maybe you'd prefer something a little more beachy."

"Take a seat, gentlemen, if you please," Harlowe offered.

Riverstone hesitantly came forward. He had seen that look on Harlowe before and knew something was up he wouldn't like. He closed his eyes briefly, took a deep breath, and didn't take the offered chair. He wanted to hear whatever bad news was coming his way standing up. He glanced out the large observation windows and said, "Where's Earth?" hoping the answer was something he could

39

swallow. He looked at his watch. "We should have touched down by now, as in landed and stepping down the rampway."

"We've been delayed." Harlowe pointed to the empty chair to his immediate right. "Sit down." It wasn't a request.

"Delayed?" Simon quickly picked up the outside scene through the bridge's observation windows. "Why is that, Captain? What's with the stars? They don't look right. They're white. I mean really white. Where are we?" He pointed at the window. "That's not Nevada!"

"We're on our way to Barnard's Star," Ian explained. "It's eight light-years from Earth."

Riverstone glared at the window. "You missed the turnoff, Platter!"

"Take your chair, Mr. Riverstone. That's an order," Harlowe directed more forcefully. He didn't have time to be understanding. "We didn't miss the turnoff. We got a call for help and we're answering it."

Riverstone looked out at the vastness. "Oh, yeah. What happened? Somebody run out of gas?"

Harlowe quickly shot out of his chair and faced crimson and corn. "Listen, you're trying my patience. I'll have order on this bridge. I know this upset your plans, but we have more important things to do right now. There's a ship out there that's hurtin' and whoever did it is probably still out there."

"So if it got blown away, why are we here?" Riverstone asked.

"Because someone could have survived, that's why." Harlowe pushed Riverstone into his chair. "Go back to your rooms. I need you back here in ten, locked and loaded and ready for bad guys," he ordered as he stood defiantly, glaring at them both to warn them not to test his patience further.

Like scolded puppies, Riverstone and Simon blew a stream of hot air as they reversed course for the blinker, and returned to their rooms. Apparently Simon's cache of hot babes and Riverstone's date with Phoebe Marleigh have been put on an indefinite hold.

11

Barnard's Star

LESS THAN AN hour later, everyone was in uniform and at their duty stations, including party animals Simon and Riverstone. One could still fry an egg on both their foreheads as Harlowe brought the Gamadin ship to a near crawl a billion miles out from Barnard's Star. When Ian finished taking his deep space scans of the surrounding star sector, he displayed the findings on the overhead holographic screen. Like their star system, Barnard had planets revolving around its center star, but only half as many as Earth, five in all, ranging in size from as small as Mercury to a planet greater than Jupiter. Ian quickly pointed out that with such a small, low-intensity star, the only chance of life would be found on the second planet, which the long-range scans verified.

"That's where we should start, Captain," Ian suggested.

Slowly heading toward the inner planets, they slid past a Jupiter-sized planet on the portside observation window. Thirty minutes later, they approached the second planet and started taking detailed sensor readings of its surface. A quick search came up empty. No ship had landed or crashed anywhere on the planet's surface. Readings showed the planet to be extremely old. There were pockets of humanoid life, but no advanced civilizations. There were no signs of wreckage on the first planet, either; the Jupiter-sized planet they scanned coming in was negative as well. They were beginning to think they might

42

have come to the wrong star system. Ian rechecked his course calculations while Monday, with Simon's help, continued their needle-in-a-haystack search of the system.

Then the sensors jumped.

As they drifted out, extending their search to the far side of the system and away from the red star, they discovered high levels of radiation coming from a small planetoid that was no larger than an asteroid. Something on its surface was sending their sensors into hysterics. The planetoid was too small to hold an atmosphere and too far away from the small red dwarf to get any heat. It was a dark, cold world, devoid of life.

As Harlowe brought *Millawanda* closer, the overhead screens laid out a complete three-dimensional topographical map of the planetoid's surface, highlighting the infected area. From the detail of the landscape, something was down there all right. The readouts confirmed it. They had found the debris field of a recently crashed ship that was spread out over a hundred square miles of frozen desolation.

Flying low and slow over the debris field, they passed silently over rising smoke and exploding pockets of fire that flared up hundreds of feet into space. Between the pockets of fire, there were hundreds of stiff and very dead bodies scattered about on the ground. They felt helpless to do anything about the disaster and could do nothing more than shake their heads. Harlowe felt awful that he hadn't reached them sooner.

Ian informed Harlowe the sensors indicated that no one seemed alive on the surface, a fact Harlowe needed no probes to see.

Suddenly, Milliwanda's protective shields snapped on. Before Harlowe could ask why, a tremendous explosion rocked the saucer, sending both Simon and Ian out of their chairs. Harlowe somehow held on and quickly gathered his wits. As he fought for control of the ship, Riverstone grabbed Ian and Simon off the floor and helped them back into their seats as another explosion sent them all to the floor a second time.

"What the...?" Riverstone cried out as he struggled back to his chair.

Harlowe held on and shouted, "Strap yourselves in!"

By the time they had both secured themselves in their seats, the next energy bolts struck.

"Where, Mr. Platter?" Harlowe shouted as *Millawanda* left the planet in a wink.

"I have it, Captain," Monday came back, his eyes fixed on his sensors. "There!" He stopped mid-sentence, looking down at his screen in awe. He turned with a worried stare and pointed up at the overhead. It was another spaceship a thousand times greater than *Millawanda*'s mass. Its long, cylindrical hull measured a mile in length, while its outer two star drives connected to a nine-hundred-foot diameter center. The rod-shaped cylinder was attached to a spherical ball at the front end while its opposite end flared outward like a cone.

Riverstone's mouth dropped open in awe while Simon's face went straight to terrified. How could they stand a chance against something as large and powerful as that?

"Time to leave, Captain?" Riverstone queried, hoping for agreement.

Riverstone's question fell on deaf ears. "Find a weak spot, Mr. Bolt," Harlowe ordered.

"A weak spot?" Simon questioned. The alien ship looked invincible. *Was he nuts?*

"Find it now, Mr. Bolt," Harlowe said again.

"She's starting to move, Captain," Monday warned as the giant ship lumbered forward, matching their speed.

"Hurry, Mr. Bolt."

Harlowe turned the ship around and headed for the backside of the small planetoid. As *Millawanda* moved away, a beam of yellow light shot past the front window. Luckily, they were secured tight in their seats when the near-miss jarred the ship like never before.

"Shields?" Harlowe asked.

"Holding," Monday responded, "but we can't take too many more of those, Captain."

"Understood, Mr. Platter," Harlowe replied.

Within seconds the Gamadin saucer vanished behind the small planet, keeping the planetoid between them and the monster. There was little time to think.

Harlowe stared at his tactical readouts as *Millawanda* swept around the backside of the planetoid. "Weapons?"

Simon glanced up at his weapons array. "Good to go, Captain."

"All right, gentlemen, we're coming around. Be ready," Harlowe said, deftly moving his fingers forward on the throttle bars.

His plan was to come around the underside of the planetoid. With the ship's shields at full power, they would fire their light cannons, striking the alien ship before it had time to react. If the shot missed, he would try again from another direction.

That was the plan until they found the enemy had already anticipated his move, firing a yellow bolt of plasma across their bow the moment they came around the backside of the planetoid.

Riverstone turned to Harlowe, his eyes shouting, "Now what?"

"HOLD ON!" Harlowe yelled as the bolt struck their forward shields head on. Their brains rattled. Harlowe directed, "Now, Mr. Bolt!"

An instant later, a salvo of blue bolts struck out at the attacking ship. Shaken, but firmly in control, Harlowe ordered more shots again and again as they came around from the opposite axis. On and on they fought with deadly hot blue and yellow streaks crossing the blackness of space like a Lazerian rock concert. One side fired, then the other, trading lethal shots back and forth. Unrelenting, the golden saucer fought the giant praying mantis. Then without thinking, in a Gamadin-trained response, Harlowe turned Milliwanda hard about and came at the alien craft from below, giving the alien vessel everything they had. The attack ship had shields protecting it from *Millawanda's* light cannons, but the warship of the 54th century had the advantage of maneuverability and power. The monster's mass was unable to match the rapid directional changes of the saucer. The slower, more massive ship was unable to react quickly enough as it fired its secondary and less powerful weapons from the aft end of the ship.

"Did you find that weak spot yet, Mr. Bolt?" Harlowe asked calmly.

"Three," Simon replied, placing the targets on the screen for Harlowe. "Take your pick, Captain!"

Harlowe left nothing to chance. He ordered Simon to fire at all three points simultaneously, scoring direct hits.

The result was not immediate. It was difficult to tell if any one of shots had been effective until Ian's sensor readings showed a significant energy drop emanating from the giant ship.

Riverstone nearly came out of his chair. "We did it, Captain! Their shields are down. She's a sitting Dak!"

Harlowe's gut, however, told him it was too soon for revelry. Wounded animals are more dangerous than healthy ones, he reminded himself. He discreetly held the ship at a cautious distance while Ian kept a watchful eye on the sensors, probing the monster's interior power levels. Meanwhile, Riverstone brought the light cannons back to full power, ready to deliver the final blow if it was necessary. They hoped the aliens had enough sense to surrender.

One of the giant's engine pods was shorting out, throwing great arcs of energy out into space between the torn-off mounts where the Gamadin light cannons had ripped a long gash in its side.

"The ball's in their court," Harlowe replied coolly. "Let's see what they do."

They didn't have long to wait. The nose of the alien craft began to rotate toward them in a slow, threatening way, like a tank turret rotating its cannon before firing. This was hardly a case where they could wait to see if the enemy had good intentions. Their own shields were strained. Harlowe wasn't in the mood to test their limits any further. Another blast from the alien warship could damage them to a point where they might be as helpless as their alien attacker.

Ian watched his readouts jump. "All power is being diverted to their forward weapons, Captain."

That was all Harlowe needed to hear. "Take it out, Mr. Bolt."

Simon gladly placed his hand over the firing bar without hesitation, placing the crosshairs directly over the main sphere of the vessel, dead center. From ten thousand miles out, the *Millawanda's* blue light struck the sphere with deadly precision, slicing through the center and exploding out the backside. An instant later a tremendous explosion sent a blinding blast of white light throughout the entire sector of space.

It was over.

They had won, but at what cost? They looked at each other in the silence that followed, wondering what they should do next. For a long, tense moment nothing was said. Unlike a football game where one cheers and dances in the streets after winning the game, this victory felt hollow and disappointing. Destroying beings, regardless of their origin, had no emotional payback. Instead, they felt a mind-numbing, gut-wrenching exhaustion that made even the simplest movement difficult.

12

Flash!

RIVERSTONE WIPED HIS lips of the sour aftertaste as he collapsed back in his chair. "How come we're still alive?" he wondered out loud,

Ian's face was still trying to find its color. "We were lucky."

Harlowe breathed in a deep sigh of agreement before issuing his first directive. "Check the star system, Wiz. There could be more out there."

"Aye, Captain."

Harlowe turned to Simon. "Weapons, Mr. Bolt?"

Simon wiped his face to clear his eyes. "Not the best, but good, Captain. Let's hope that was the only bad guy in the neighborhood."

To Monday, he asked, "What do we have on your end, Mr. Platter?"

"She's a little banged up, Captain," Monday replied. His hands were shaking but so were everyone else's. "Shields down twenty-seven percent. Her insides are shaken, too. We've got to check her out before taking any more light jumps through space, Captain."

Harlowe was a mess on the inside, but on the outside he was cool and steady. "Okay. We're going back to the debris field," he commanded.

"What if that wasn't the only ship out there?" Riverstone asked, feeling stressed. "If another hits us like that last one, we're sprouting wings, Captain."

Harlowe hadn't traveled this far just to turn around and go home. "The mission isn't finished, Mr. Riverstone. We're not done checking the area."

Riverstone leaned close to Harlowe. In a low voice, he said, "The probability of anyone being left alive on that rock is a zillion-to-one against, Dog. You saw the close-ups. No one could have survived that crash."

Harlowe agreed but, "It doesn't matter, Mr. Riverstone, we're all-in." He turned to Ian. "Give us a course, Wiz. Best speed, Mr. Platter."

"Aye, Captain," Monday replied.

Then to Simon, Harlowe added, "Crank those weapons to full power, Mr. Bolt."

"Aye, Captain."

* * *

Coming within sensor range of the planetoid, *Millawanda*'s sensors refocused on the surface around the crash site. The incinerated bulk of what was left of the crashed ship still smoldered with sparks here and there in the darkness of the pockmarked planetoid. The superstructure of the wreckage was in two large sections. A large gaping hole with jagged edges of hot metal still glowed from where the heat of the alien weapon had struck the ship.

Harlowe kept looking for any signs of survival. He knew that what Riverstone was saying made all the sense in the world, but he remained committed to the rescue. He wouldn't give up yet. *If Riverstone had seen her courage and force of will, he would know she's still alive!*

"Anything?" Harlowe asked Ian from the edge of his chair.

Ian shook his head. Nothing yet. "Sensor power is low. We need to get closer, sir."

Harlowe passed the steerage controls back to Monday. "Take her in, Mr. Platter."

"Aye, Captain," Monday replied calmly.

Harlowe saw the nervousness in Riverstone's face. "One pass. If we don't find anything, we'll leave." *Maybe...*

Riverstone nodded an okay. He didn't like it, but one pass couldn't hurt them any more than what they had already been through.

When the saucer drifted closer to the wreckage, Ian's sensors picked up an object coming up from one of the twisted sections of debris. On the center overhead screen, they watched a parabolic dish rise from the rubble.

"Identify, Wiz," Harlowe ordered.

"I don't like it," Riverstone commented, his eyes glued to the overhead screen readouts.

"I'm getting a moderated power surge, Captain," Ian replied.

Harlowe didn't feel the need for an engraved invitation and quickly had Simon dispose of the energized dish with one short burst of blue cannon fire.

"It must have been some kind of auto-defense. I didn't detect anyone around it," Ian informed the bridge.

After a tense moment, Harlowe asked for an update from the sensors. Ian's fingers danced over his lighted bars, fine-tuning his probes. "That's odd. I didn't see it before. It's real faint. Whatever it is, it's alive and inside an air pocket in the larger section of the superstructure. I should have seen it earlier."

"Never mind that. You did good, Wiz!" Harlowe exclaimed.

Monday plotted the putdown area on the screen. "That should put us within a couple hundred feet of the opening, Captain."

"Close enough."

Millawanda made a gentle touchdown at the edge of the largest section of glowing hunks of jagged metal and dead bodies. It was a tragic nightmare. A silent hush filled the control room as they stared out at the grim devastation. They had seen the results of war on their television newscasts at home, but none of them had ever seen so much death this up-close-and-personal.

Their stomachs lurched as their mouths went dry.

"You're with me, Mr. Riverstone," Harlowe said, leaving his chair. To the other Gamadin, he said, "Gentlemen, keep a sharp eye on things. Any readouts even hint at another ship out there, we're back in a heartbeat." Harlowe pointed to his seat. "You have the chair, Mr. Wizzixs."

"Aye, Captain," Ian replied. "We'll keep the porch light on."

* * *

Inside the utility room they suited up in their spacesuits of the same material as the ship herself. The outside temperature was a balmy twenty degrees above absolute zero. Way too cold for even SIBAs. The suits had more bulk, but not by much. They were easily slipped on (entry was automatic) and quite maneuverable. What distinguished them most was the headgear. The spacesuit had no bugeyes. Its helmet was one big eye and didn't rely on small power packs for energy. The helmet itself was a power source, fully charged. It would last a year of space walking if necessary.

Riverstone thought it made them look like anemic Mechwarriors since they had no rocket launchers or big, Frankenstein boots. Part of their gear was a tool bag containing a cutting light, a small winch that could lift several tons, and a few other minor tools for extraction, plus the enviro-bag to transport the person whom they hoped was still alive. Without it, no living being could last a second in the extreme temperatures of the airless planet. Harlowe also traded his pistol for a stunner, since whoever was alive in there, might not appreciate their Good Samaritan efforts.

Examining the stunner brought a slight twinge to his gut, recalling how Lu had used it on him that day she left him in the utility room out cold before she went after Riverstone and Platter on the night the Daks attacked Harry's Casino in Las Vegas.

Women!

Confident they had everything they needed and their suits were properly fitted and working, they loaded their gear in the rover and drifted down to the ground for the trip past the perimeter to the location where they would try to enter the ship. Time was critical. The opening in the ship was only a few hundred yards from the perimeter edge. With a body in tow, however, every second counted. The rover would cut the time back to the ship down to a fraction.

They drove through the perimeter shield and parked a few feet from the jagged opening of what was left of the main body of the ship. The alien ship was huge, but not nearly as big as *Millawanda*, nor as sleek and cool, either. It was bulky and massive, unlike the saucer's efficient, 54th century design.

As they stepped out of the rover, sparks were still flying from the fragments of power surges emanating from the dying ship.

Harlowe lifted the enviro-bag out of the back of the rover. "I'm going in alone."

"Why alone?" Riverstone asked.

"Because the most dangerous job is you looking out for me in case something happens."

Riverstone handed Harlowe the tool bag. "Good point. You go." He surveyed the wreckage. "This isn't a good neighborhood, Dog. Reminds me of the back alleys in Downey."

Harlowe stared at the twisted, burning metal. "No doubt."

Riverstone tapped Harlowe on the helmet. He was ready. They exchanged a thumbs-up and Harlowe headed for the opening. A small screen on the inside of his helmet displayed the direction to the air pocket, and hopefully the living body that was left in the wreckage. His helmet visor compensated for the darkness, illuminating the obstacles in his path as if they were in broad daylight. He took one deep breath before plunging through the gaping hole in the side of the ship. His suit was capable of stopping an armor-piercing bullet or a micro-meteor, but the razor-sharp edge of alien metal was an unknown. A thoughtless miscalculation might easily tear a hole in his suit if he wasn't careful. He remembered the General saying to think of your suit as being made of tissue paper. That way you wouldn't get careless. Good advice. A tiny hole in his suit and he would be dead before he could react to the penetration. Such was life in the cold vacuum of space.

"What do you see, Dog?" Riverstone asked over the helmet communicators so that the others in the ship could also hear.

"Death," was Harlowe's only reply.

As Harlowe's helmet transmitted the devastation, they all could view on their screens what he was seeing: charred lumps of the dead spread around the interior. It was difficult to tell what kind of beings they were or if they had been human. They were all burned beyond recognition.

Harlowe took another deep breath and moved on, trying to keep his stomach in check as he stepped cautiously over bodies and ducked around and under jagged infrastructure beams.

When Harlowe climbed up two more levels to the main deck, the corpses there were clearly human forms. Instead of showing radiation burns, they had all been killed when the atmosphere was sucked out by the blast. They now remained freeze-dried at absolute zero right where they stood at the time of the blast. The sight was grisly, sending dagger-like chills down Harlowe's neck. When he came to an impassable point in his journey, he took out the light cutter and literally sliced his way through the metal, creating his own path. Finally, he came to a bulkhead where the door to the other side was sealed shut from the inside.

"Captain," Ian's voice called over the com, "sensors indicate that whatever the life-form is, it's behind the wall in front of you. There's an air pocket, but it's dissipating fast. You need to hurry. The life-form is freezing in there and its vital signs appear to be dropping."

"Can I get through without breaking the seal?" Harlowe asked.

"Look to your left, Captain. There seems to be a double doorway."

Harlowe glanced in the direction Monday indicated. "Right, I see it. It's a doorway, but it's blocked by two massive girders."

"Hurry, Captain. I've lost its vital signs."

"Understood," Harlowe said, moving quickly to the door.

It was impossible for him to move the girders on his own. There wasn't any place for him to set up the small winch until they were cut. He had to use his cutter and melt the beams. That was the only alternative he had. He just had to be careful not to cut any further than the girders or he could rupture the air pocket.

With a surgeon's touch, he sliced through the beams and attached the dura-wire line from his winch. Next, he switched on the servo-motor to the winch and pulled the pieces of steel out of the way. He now had a clear path to the door. When he reached the panel that activated the door, he found it inoperable. It had either lost power or it was jammed shut. Wasting no time, he took his cutter and sliced a hole through the panel.

The door moved.

It was only a few inches but enough to show it wasn't jammed. He pushed aside more debris and with all the strength he could muster, pulled the door aside wide enough to step through. He immediately saw the other door. It made sense. The double doors were a stopgap against a potential breach in the ship's outer hull. A hull within a hull for protection, and it was the only thing that had saved the life of the being on the other side.

He closed the first door behind him, making sure it was as properly shut as he could make it. When the second door opened, he needed enough time to get the being and secure it in the enviro-bag before it froze to death.

Harlowe jumped to the second panel and quickly pulled the door release. The door opened slightly, only breaking the latch that kept it closed. Without power, it would slide no farther without assistance.

He poked his head around the crack in the door and saw a closed-in, dimly lit room. There were no other exit doors that he could see. As far as he could determine, this was the only way in or out. He also saw no bodies lying anywhere on the floor. Beyond thirty feet, he could see nothing and nothing moved.

"Wiz," Harlowe whispered over the com. "I'm looking inside the room. Is it still alive?"

"Yeah, Captain," Ian replied in a hushed tone. "To your right. I think it knows you're there. It moved when you opened the door."

Harlowe's stomach lurched. *Sweet...*

Harlowe felt like a perfect target with a bull's-eye painted with lifeguard orange across his forehead. He wanted to call out to whoever was inside that he was here to help, but how could he communicate anything without opening his helmet? For all practical purposes he figured the being on the other side wasn't in any kind of shape to hear him anyway. He remembered how cold he was that time back on Mars when he was lying on the ground, stiff and cold. when he was a hundred yards from the ship's perimeter and trying to nuke the General's face.

He shivered.

He still didn't know how he pulled himself through the perimeter force field and lived to fight the General to take *Millawanda* back.

The being inside had been in there for some time with little air or heat. *Don't be stupid, Dog. This being could be like you. As cold and helpless as it appears to be, it could still shoot you through the head then ask questions later, toad*, he said to himself as he cautiously grabbed the edge of the door and began to slide it gently to one side.

FLASH!

He had opened it only a few inches when a bolt of bright yellow plasma shot through the opening where his head should have been.

Why did he have to be so right?

The sound of escaping air turned his head. When he looked back at the first door, he saw a white-hot hole the yellow bolt had left behind in the bulkhead. Now he didn't have time to be diplomatic. The air pocket would last only seconds. He had to act fast.

With his cutter in one hand, he pulled his stunner from his utility belt with his other. Wasting no time, he slashed the door with his cutter.

FLASH!

He kicked the door open.

FLASH, FLASH!

Harlowe dove through, firing three shots at the muzzle flash into the darkened corridor. He rolled once and was ready for any counterattack. He wasn't sure if he hit anything as he waited for any sound or movement to indicate whether his action had done more harm than good. Then a small slumping sound came through his outside audio pickup.

He tossed a piece of debris over to the far corner. The clank would have awakened Simon after a night of partying, but nothing fired back.

Harlowe took that as a good sign and came to his knees, his stunner pointed, ready for anything that moved. As he did so, he spotted a humanoid figure lying face down on the floor. It wasn't moving.

He quickly moved to the body. He kicked its weapon away from its hand before he bent down and turned it over.

The humanoid's body was burned beyond recognition.

13

Burnt Remains

"Is it alive?" Ian inquired from the ship.

For a short, horrifying moment Harlowe stood motionless over the repulsive body. It was so horribly burnt, he didn't know whether it was a man or woman. "I don't know," was all he could say.

"Is it Quay?" Ian asked.

"I don't know, Wiz. I can't tell. The body is too badly burned."

"Who's Quay?" Riverstone's voice questioned in the com.

"I'll fill you in later, Jester," Ian's voice replied.

Harlowe looked at the charred skin, oozing blood between the cracks. His face twisted with revulsion. How could anyone stay alive after such burns? He didn't want to think about the pain the being was suffering. If it had been an animal, he would have put it out of its misery.

Harlowe fought off his light-headedness and sprang into action, quickly unraveling the enviro-bag. "Riverstone! Get in here, and don't bother with the door! Blow it open!"

Riverstone responded instantly. "Aye, Captain!"

Sections of charred uniform and skin fell off the body and stuck to Harlowe's gloves as he carefully rolled the body into the bag. A loud bang announced Riverstone's arrival. By that time Harlowe had already sealed the bag and was turning on the warm, oxygenated air inside. Riverstone took the feet and Harlowe the head as they went straight through the door that Riverstone had blown open.

The return path was also clear. When they arrived at the side of the ship, they lifted the enviro-bag onto the back of the rover and raced for the perimeter safety of the ship.

Baaluuweeee!

What was left of the alien ship suddenly exploded, sending sparks and debris miles into the air. The rover sped through the barrier not a second too soon. Ian and a medical team of robobs were already waiting at the bottom of the rampway the moment they arrived.

Without a single command from anyone, the robobs extracted the body from the back of the rover and raced it up the ramp to the nearest sickbay. It wasn't far. There were many sickbays strategically placed throughout the ship near the outside exits. The ancient designers logically figured a medical unit would be necessary at every entry around the ship.

The surgical team of robobs was there, waiting for their patient. By the time Harlowe and Riverstone entered the med room, the being was out of the enviro-bag and placed on the long, thin table in the center of the room. It was in the clickers' hands now.

Harlowe watched the illuminated walls come alive with bright diagrams and glowing graphics of the alien's body as more robobs came out of the wall and sprang to life. There were eight around the table now, working at impossible speeds. This was more clickers than he had ever seen around a table. As crowded as the mechanical surgical team was around the body, no elbow or pincer clanked against another robob.

Riverstone and Harlowe felt like potted plants and moved back out of the way, closer to the open doorway. They had seen the robobs perform many times before. The way they had saved Lu's life and removed Ian's throbbing heart was nothing short of incredible, but it was never like this. Never had so many clickers paid this much attention to one being. Their thin mechanical arms moved with such precision and haste, cutting away charred hunks of clothing and blackened skin while others connected the being to life-support systems that filled its arteries and veins with life-stabilizing fluids.

The being's features were unrecognizable, burnt beyond identification. They couldn't tell what color hair or skin or even what sex it was as dark red blood oozed out of its neck and shoulders and dripped in heavy droplets onto the blue-carpeted floor. When Harlowe looked down at his own hands and feet, charred bits of blackened flesh covered his suit.

"Think it'll make it?" Riverstone asked Harlowe. He removed the helmet from his head, showing the obvious strain of holding back his nausea.

Harlowe bit his lower lip. "The clickers will have to go the distance to pull this one off."

Ian agreed as he stepped between them and looked at the walls of graphs displaying the life-form's moment-by-moment condition.

"You really look like you know what all this stuff means," Riverstone said to Ian, referring to the graphics inside the med room.

"Unlike you, I've studied them."

Harlowe wasn't in the mood for banter. "Just give me an answer, Wiz."

After a quick study, he shook his head doubtfully. "It's not good, Captain. Look at these areas where she's been fried." He pointed to several areas of her upper body on one of the graphics. "There are massive radiation burns over ninety-six percent of her body. She has no blood pressure to speak of, no pulse...Her whole body has shut down." He shook his head again. "I don't see how she's lasted this long." He turned back to both Riverstone and Harlowe. "She should be dead."

"You keep saying 'she,' Wiz. How do you know she's a she?" Riverstone asked.

Ian shook his head again, frowning at the stupidly obvious. He pointed to the large graphic on the wall. "What's that look like?"

Clearly on display was a three-dimensional graphic of a female, in plain view for anyone with half a brain to see.

Harlowe and Riverstone traded embarrassed glances.

"Oh, yeah, we knew that," Riverstone replied, fingering a yellowish crystalline rock he had pulled from his utility belt pouch.

Harlowe slid out of his headgear, his haggard face a duplicate of Riverstone's. He hadn't slept now for thirty hours. "She'll make it," he declared confidently. He then led them out the sickbay door. "Let the clickers do their thing. We've got to get out of here and find a place to hide. Those toads we nuked will have friends." The rock Riverstone held in his hand caught his attention. "What's that?"

Riverstone tossed it over to Harlowe. "They were all over the crash site. Looks like that ship was carrying a load of it."

Harlowe tossed the crystal over to Ian. "Have Millie check it out."

"Aye, Captain."

"Think it means something?" Riverstone asked.

Harlowe didn't care if it was the secret to the Holy Grail. He was hungry. He couldn't remember the last time he had a bite to eat. To his unseen servant, he yelled out, "Jewels! A double-double cheese and double order of fries, animal-style, if you please!"

* * *

A short time later they were in their chairs and lifting off the small planetoid's surface. Harlowe took his food break in his command chair. He was on his second double-double and nursing a chocolate shake when *Millawanda* drifted away from the planetoid. Ian explained it was necessary to check out the entire extent of the damage before going to hyperlight. The sub-light drive seemed to be okay, as was the hyperlight drive, but they couldn't go anywhere until Millie's shields were up and running at full capacity. There were also a couple of large gashes in the outer hull that needed repair before they went too far. The lack of shields was the bigger problem, however. Traveling at high velocity without proper shielding, even at sublight, was suicide. Impacting anything no bigger than a grain of sand could damage Millie. Staying below light speeds with the shields on low power, they could travel safely if they kept a watchful eye on the sensors.

Harlowe looked up at the overhead screen, barely able to raise his head without spilling his shake. "Where are you taking us?" he asked Ian.

"The second planet," Ian replied. "At least we can breathe the air. It's warm too, like Earth. If we're lucky, maybe whoever comes looking for those guys will think we slammed out of here."

"Do it," Harlowe said, and motioned for Simon to push the ship's throttles up a notch. He needed some sleep. The sooner they got to wherever they were going, the sooner his head would hit the pillow.

Fifty-three minutes later they made their first surveillance orbit around the second planet in the Barnard system. Long-range sensors had not detected anyone entering the area yet. For the moment, they were still the only ship in this system.

After Monday completed his sensor probe, he announced the planet devoid of any cities or advanced civilizations. They wondered why intelligent life had not taken root on the planet when it had plenty of water, mild temperatures, and a good atmosphere of oxygen, nitrogen, and carbon dioxide, and a vast variety of animal life. Maybe there was a reason, but from their two-hundred-mile orbit, it wasn't apparent.

Regardless, they had to land. They were all exhausted. If they didn't get rest soon, they would pass out at their stations. Simon was already gonzo. He had slumped off twenty minutes earlier. Riverstone gently laid him on the control room floor and took over his station.

Ian wanted an opinion on a place to land. Harlowe didn't care. "Find us a beach, Wiz," he said, half-jokingly. They would worry about the particulars later.

Twenty minutes later, *Millawanda's* three landing struts touched down on the planet's surface.

Outside, it was night. At this position on the planet the red dwarf primary, Barnard, was hours away from rising. When it did rise, Barnard would appear larger than their own sun, but it wasn't. Sol was many times greater in mass and much hotter. It was also five times farther away than this sun, which is why Barnard's looked so big. It would also look rather unearthly to see a sun that wasn't yellow. The world would look eerily strange. Not as bright, and the sky would have fluffy orange clouds floating above them. It was beautiful but quite different from what they were used to. If they weren't so tired, they might have thought more about the giant shadows moving in the jungle behind them...

No one cared.

The Gamadin crew snapped on *Millawanda's* protective force field and dove into bed. Harlowe never made it to his bedroom. He passed out in his control chair, dropping a half-eaten animal burger and a half-empty blue shake onto the floor. The robobs would clean it up later.

14

Finding Heaven

TWO FULL DAYS passed before anyone stirred. Harlowe was the first to rise. During his eighty winks, he dreamt they were parked on a deserted planet with a long white beach. It was warm and full of interesting life. Best of all...the beach had waves! Nice four-foot waves, with glassy tubes coming onto shore and no one on them. *Hot, Dude!* He couldn't remember the last time he had been on a wave, riding the face, tasting the salt as he crashed downward, tumbling over before righting himself and swimming back out for another set. Then a giant beast broke through the jungle and his eyes shot open, bolting him upright out of his dreamlike state of paradise. *Wow, that was rad.* He looked around, unable to remember how he had made it to his bed.

He sighed, wanting to return to his dream of glassy tubes. Sadly, he was the Captain. He had responsibilities. He wasn't allowed to lie around all day in bed like a couch potato. He stared up at the ceiling portal above his bed. The sky was clear—not quite blue, maybe more pink than blue—with high, wispy clouds drifting across the window. *Whatta day!* He had to yank himself out of bed and check on the condition of his ship before he did anything fun. Duty called. "The buck stops with you, Dog," he groaned, peeling back his sheets.

As he looked around, everything appeared as it should. Nothing had changed. His chairs, his bed, the clothes that he'd worn before falling like a cut tree into bed. He took another deep breath. He was fine. Millie was okay and so was his crew. If anything had gone wrong while he was asleep, he knew Jewels, his robob servant, would have awakened him. He stretched his arms to the ceiling and twisted, cracking the kinks out of his neck. After that, he popped out of bed and went to the nearest window to see for himself what the world where they had landed was all about.

His mouth dropped with amazement the instant his eyes saw the landscape.

That's so sick, Dude!

He felt like Dorothy opening the door of her house that fell on the Wicked Witch of the East and seeing all the brilliant colors of Munchkinland for the first time. Instead of little people and a yellow brick road, though, he cast his eyes on the miles and miles of white sandy beach. He clenched his eyes shut, rubbing them hard, and opened them again just to be sure he wasn't still stuck in a weird dream. He breathed a sigh of relief. The beach was still there! A beautiful tropical beach...with surf! Glassy, too, like the ones he'd pictured in his dream. Small perfect tubes rolling into shore every few seconds.

There is a God! You can keep Munchkinland, Dorothy, I'll take this!

How long had it been? A year and a half since they had left Earth? Joyful glee shot through his brain. The thought of feeling a warm breeze on his face and wiggling his toes in the sand drove him crazy. He had to get his feet wet right now! No waiting required. Every curl had his name on it.

Suddenly a thought struck him like an ice-cold wind.

The girl!

His expression turned grave as he pushed thoughts of the beach aside and called to an unseen entity. "Millie, what's up with our patient in sickbay?" he asked.

A graphic readout materialized before him. Several graphs and charts flashed by. To Harlowe, they all looked the same. During times like these, he wished he had spent more time with Ian on the science of a 54th-century ship than duking it out with Quincy or blasting dancing balls of light to subatomic dust at the shooting range. What he could comprehend, though, was that the girl was still alive.

"Scale of one hundred. Will she live?" he asked the screen.

"51.012," the screen read.

His heart sank. He didn't like the odds. *Still, better than 50–50,* he mused, thinking positively. He figured she shouldn't be alive at all. The glass is half-full, he kept telling himself. To have the odds in her favor had to mean something. For the time being, until he could confer with Ian, it was good news that she was alive. The day remained positive.

Harlowe walked though the holo-screens on his way out the door. "Thanks, Millie."

Faster than *Millawanda* could go to hyperlight, he burst past his bedroom door with Jewels standing to the side, handing him a pair a blue trunks and a towel as he ran by. Charging through his cabin doorway and into the control room, he made a beeline for the blinker, still holding his trunks without a stitch of clothing on. He hit the sub-level short corridor, still running, and out the extending ramp to the soft white sand of their tropical paradise.

It was even more beautiful than he had hoped.

His first stride off the ramp wasn't a step, but a leap. He dove out onto the sand and rolled over and over in its warm grittiness, completely covering himself with handfuls of warm, white sand. For long, wonderful moments he waddled, oozed, slid, and wormed himself across the surface like a two-year-old playing at the beach.

If this isn't heaven, it ain't far away!

Still flat out on the sand, his gaze turned to the underside of *Millawanda's* golden hull. His face winced at the sight of a hundred-yard-long scorch mark left over from their recent battle in space. Other similar but smaller marks crisscrossed the hull in several places. His eyes followed one line to a large rip in her skin. He winced again, recalling how fortunate they were to have survived. It was comforting to see the small army of robobs hard at work repairing all her cuts and bruises.

He sighed, glad that he wasn't the one hanging there upside down.

Since the clickers appeared to have everything under control, he turned his attention back to the shoreline. He got up, stepped into his trunks just in case the beach wasn't as deserted as it looked, and walked the long seven hundred yards out to the perimeter of the ship and into the sunlight.

Millawanda's force field was turned off, which meant that if he had made it past the perimeter, the air was breathable. Come to think of it, he thought, if the environment were hostile in any way, Millie would have stopped him cold before he walked through the barrier.

As he ventured toward the water, the sunlight felt warm and penetrating on his back. He turned around to the big red disk with his eyes closed and let its wonderful rays fill his body with energy. When his tank was full he looked back, away from the ocean, and marveled at the abundantly large plant life. It seemed as if they had landed in a world of giants. Where the sand ended at the edge of the jungle, three-hundred-foot coconut-like palms bent their shafts like giant fingers to the sky. Below the giant palms, large round pods, two feet in diameter, dangled in bunches like their earthly counterparts. On the sand at their six-foot-diameter bases, the fallen seeds basked in the afternoon sun. Even the smallest seeds were three times the size of normal coconuts found on Earth. Farther back into the jungle, nestled under the shade of the tall palms, sweeping ferns completed the dense foreground scenery. Life was so colossal here it made Millie seem small in comparison.

The lush jungle was home to a riot of animal life as well. Beautiful jungle birds, not unlike those on Earth, fluttered in the branches while long-armed critters swung about in a playful game of tag. Like colorful pinwheels, the birds were beautifully bright and pompous, and talked incessantly like chattering women as they moved in short bursts from branch to branch. Their chirps and screeches echoed throughout the jungle, adding to the wonder of their new landing site. Harlowe didn't realize how much he missed the noises of nature, because on Mars, even at Lu's Place, no sound ever accompanied its surrounding beauty.

He turned around again and drank in the ocean air, smelling the familiar salty spray coming from the breakers while the warm surge of water flowed around his ankles, soothing his insides even more.

Wow, how long had it been since he felt the sun on his shoulders without a skin or spacesuit protecting him? Sun lamps were their only substitutes. They were artificial. This was real. Even the 54th century had no substitute for *real* sunshine!

He closed his eyes again, letting the heat of the red sun soak his face, the top of his shoulders, and his neck. Like the jungle palms, the red sun was incredibly large, taking up much of the morning sky already. It wasn't as intense as the yellow light of Earth's sun, but he wasn't complaining. At this moment he couldn't tell the difference. It was all beautiful and fresh and alive.

Then there was wind! Never had the real movement of air across his skin felt so wonderful. It was like a thousand delicate fingers caressing his face.

He shook with pleasure as he took in another lungful of humid, tropical air, smiling contentedly from ear to ear. For the first time in years since he had left Earth, he felt free; free to live without the confines of the ship, free to enjoy the outdoors with nothing around his body to protect him from the elements. He felt released, like some fairytale prince caught in a spell. He had been kissed by a beautiful princess and set free to live again amongst nature's wonderful smells, melodic sounds, and gentle winds. The spell was broken.

A moment later, he dove headfirst under a rolling breaker. Harlowe had found heaven.

15

Almost Breakfast

"Hey, Dog," Riverstone called out, knocking on Harlowe's door. "Yo! Captain Pylott. Wake up, Doggy. Time to rock and roll, brah!" Still, there was no reply from Harlowe. He hit the door activator and the door slid open. "I've got hot French toast on the menu..." Riverstone's voice trailed off as he realized Harlowe wasn't in the room. Jewels was making his bed and another stickman was removing Harlowe's dirty clothes from yesterday from the floor.

No Harlowe.

Riverstone then checked the bathroom and he wasn't in there, either. Where could he be? He was nowhere to be seen. A little dumbfounded, he walked past the large window and caught a glimpse of someone off in the distance, sliding across the face of a three-foot wall of moving glass. That could only be one person, Riverstone reckoned. Harlowe was twisting and cutting up and down the face of the wave like a playful dolphin, having the time of his life.

Figures, he thought. *Get Harlowe near a beach and it'll be dark before he gets out of the water.* Riverstone watched Harlowe catch another wave and bodysurf it all the way into the shore before he swam back out and lined himself up for another incoming breaker.

Not wanting to let Harlowe hog all the fun, Riverstone was about to join in when Ian came bursting through Harlowe's cabin door.

70

"Glad I found you, Jester! Where's Dog?" Ian asked. He had a worried look on his face.

Riverstone pointed outside. "Out catching a few tubes."

Ian face went rigid. "He's what?"

"He's out there slidin' across some nice tubes, dude, and that's where I'm going to be in about five seconds. Come on," he urged on his way out the doorway.

Ian caught Riverstone by the arm. "Don't be stupid. This isn't Earth!"

"You noticed?" he replied, continuing out the doorway and onto the bridge.

"Listen up, Jester. I found some footprints near the ship that you could park the rover in." Riverstone suddenly lost his grin. "I checked the sensors this morning. There are creatures as tall as a two-story house out there."

"As in dino big?" Riverstone asked.

"Bigger!"

Riverstone went to the window. "We'd better tell Dog."

At that moment, something large and slithering leaped out of the water a mile out on the glassy ocean. It was headed straight for Harlowe.

Ian slapped his sensor console to life and began taking readings. "Why didn't he check to see what was out there before he went screwing around in an unknown ocean?"

There it was on the overhead, one thousand yards away and coming fast. From the closeup it had all the characteristics of a prehistoric ichthyosaur. And ichthyosaurs, Ian reminded Riverstone, were the deadly predators of ancient Jurassic seas.

The beast's length measured forty-seven feet without the tail as it swam just below the surface in the shallow waters coming into the beach. Harlowe was breakfast if they didn't do something quick!

They watched helplessly as Harlowe caught another wave into shore. He was oblivious to any danger heading his way.

"Come on, Dog," Ian pleaded, staring worriedly out the window, "get out of the water!"

Riverstone shook. "It won't happen. He's just getting started, Wiz. He's having too much fun."

As Riverstone predicted, Harlowe was too eager to catch the next tube that was forming on the outside. He turned around, dove through the short break, and started stroking back out to catch another tube, completely unaware of the prehistoric predator.

"Come on, Dog, look up!" Ian urged.

"Do something, Wiz!" Riverstone cried out.

"The light cannons are offline. I shut everything off two days ago to stay dark. Even if we had the power, it would take too long to bring them back online to save him."

"We can't just sit here!" Riverstone cried, stunned at the size of the beast breaking the surface with Harlowe dead in its sights.

*　*　*

In waist-deep water, Harlowe hopped up and down, bouncing off the ocean floor to position himself in just the right spot to catch his wave. The wave had perfect form. When it curled over, he thought he might go left this time and try rolling into the curl with an underwater launch, a trick he had perfected four summers ago at the Wedge in Newport. To him there was no greater thrill than being locked inside a wave, its power lifting him up, soaring like a bird, gliding effortlessly into shore until its kinetic energy was expended, depositing him alone on the beach.

Suddenly, the wave transformed into a giant, flesh-eating creature! The beast's jaws opened wide, displaying rows of sharp, jagged teeth.

It had stalked its prey and Harlowe was the next meal. Harlowe tried desperately to move, but he was too deep. He was stuck. He couldn't jump or run anywhere. There was nothing he could do but wait out his final demise. It would be over in an instant if he couldn't find an escape. His body guillotined!

From out of nowhere, a brilliant flash of blue light surrounded the beast in mid-flight, vaporizing its entire length before his eyes. Before he understood what had happened, a wave smacked him broadside, dragging him down underwater in a violent torrent. Was he alive? Was he dead? He didn't know for sure. An eternity went by before he finally broke the surface and was able to breathe. Somewhere between blacking out and tumbling onto shore, he hurled salt water and spit while trying to get his lungs to function again.

He was alive! How, he didn't know. He rolled face-up onto the beach. After a terrible strain, he was finally able to take in a breath of air without a mouthful of water.

Another moment passed before he rose to his knees and looked up. Coming toward him on the beach, Riverstone had an angry scowl on his face, carrying a plas-rifle he had used to vaporize the beast.

Harlowe coughed between his dry heaves. "Good shot, Jester. You've been practicing."

Riverstone reached down to give him a hand. "Are we off the clock?"

"Yeah. Sure."

"I was aiming at you, toadface!" Riverstone said bitterly.

Harlowe rolled over, spat, and blew a gallon of mucous from his water-clogged nose. Riverstone's face twisted in disgust as Harlowe used him for a post to stand up. Harlowe then put his arm over Riverstone's shoulder and said, spitting up more, "I'm lucky you're such a bad shot. How did you get here so fast, anyway?"

"We dropped a blinker from the perimeter; went from the bridge to the supply room down to here in a few seconds," Riverstone explained.

"Your brain figured that out?" Harlowe wondered.

"No, dummy. It was Ian."

"Now that makes sense." Harlowe pushed him away, striking his shoulder. "You had me going there."

They made it to the shade of the ship before they stopped and sat on the sand together to rest and watch the perfect waves rolling into shore with no one on them.

"That was really stupid, Dog," Ian said, joining them.

Harlowe agreed. "But..." he said, smiling like a kid about to pull another prank.

"No buts!" Ian responded sharply, like a scared father who had just seen his son nearly killed. "This is a dangerous place. We've got to check out the area before you go gallivanting out there like you're on a Sunday stroll down 42nd Street."

Harlowe looked out at the waves and grinned. "But the waves, Wiz. You can't believe how good they are. Look at them! They're perfect tubes, like they were made in a factory."

Ian's jaw hardened as he looked out at the breakers, nice and glassy and like Harlowe said, perfect, as if they were factory-made.

Riverstone put the stock of the rifle down in the sand, leaning on the barrel as his face began releasing the fear of nearly losing his best friend. "How was the water?" he asked Harlowe.

Harlowe looked up with a whimsical grin. "Warm, like the Wedge in August."

"In August?"

Riverstone licked his lips like he was about to wolf down a fish taco. Harlowe gave him a friendly tap on the shoulder with the back of his hand. "Come on, Jester. Just like old times, Captain's orders."

Ian cut in front of them. "Maybe you didn't see what just happened . . . Sir. That thing almost ate you! Trust me, there's more like that out there!"

Harlowe looked past Ian as if he weren't there. "Yeah, but I know you'll rig up something to make it safe. You're good at those kinda things, Wiz."

"Yeah, Wiz," Riverstone chimed in. "Rig up something to warn us if anything gets too close."

Ian thought for a second, looking out across the wide beach, and pointed. "Maybe we could station a couple of clickers off the point over there with rifles."

Harlowe nodded his approval. "That's the spirit! I knew you'd think of something. That's why I pay you the big bucks," Harlowe said, walking past him.

"I still don't like it," Ian said.

Riverstone removed what little clothes he had on, down to his bright red boxer shorts. "Ah, don't worry, mate. You know as well as I do that Millie's sensors could pick out blue-eyed hermit crabs a hundred miles away if you asked her to."

Ian shook his head, knowing he had lost the argument. "Just to be careful, someone should stay here with the rifle until I can set up the grid."

"Give it to Betty," Harlowe said, running toward the water.

Riverstone handed the rifle to the made-up girl-bob who was clickity-clacking up at that moment with three other stickmen behind her. "Here, girl. Keep a sharp eye out," he told the girl-bob. He bolted after Harlowe, both of them yelling and screaming like they were about to launch themselves off the side of the Mons.

Rex

16

The Babe

TWO WEEKS LATER they were tanned and rested. Harlowe and Riverstone had ridden over a thousand waves. The red sun made their hair a little lighter, too. The crew looked like five beach bums on vacation. The events of weeks past, not to mention Earth, seemed a century ago. Riverstone's and even Simon's feelings of home had been put on hold for the time being. A sunny paradise with warm, consistent waves had a way of seducing their minds into forgetting the unpleasantness of being so far away from home. But like all good times, these days didn't last forever. It was time to begin thinking about their departure and what they were going to do next.

"How's Millie doing?" Harlowe asked Ian, thinking of how nice she was looking lately with her newly repaired golden hull. She was all bright and shiny again, beautiful as ever. His first officer was alone, eating breakfast at the round galley table. Harlowe routinely stopped in at the galley to pick up something to eat before he went outside for his usual two hours of waves before doing anything constructive. "I haven't noticed any clickers out and about lately. Union break?"

Ian continued to savor his eggs before he answered calmly, "Good news or bad news first?"

Harlowe's blue eyes turned toward the floor. He didn't like the choices. "Forget the sugar. Just give it to me straight."

"Millie's good to go."

Harlowe's face went slack. "It's the girl. She's . . ."

Ian shook his head. "No. You should know; you stick your nose in there twenty times a day. So I'll ask you: how's she doing?"

"The odds are better; over eighty this morning. I think she's going to make it. Is that how you see it?"

Ian took a bite of toast, nodding. "I'm down with that. Have you seen her?"

Harlowe breathed a sigh. "*Nada*. They keep it pretty dark in there. I would need a SIBA to see anything."

"They have her in an induced coma. She'll be that way for a while to protect her eyes," Ian surmised, putting down his toast. "Dog . . ."

"Is this the bad news?"

"Not really. I just wanted to tell you not to expect much. I mean she had third degree burns, Dog. I've seen victims like that before. They don't look the same after that. Like Freddy Krueger without the mask."

Harlowe nodded. "Yeah, not so cool, huh?"

"So what are we going to do with her?" Ian asked.

Harlowe shrugged, "I haven't got past that she's alive yet." He grabbed a piece of Ian's toast to nibble on and added, "She can't be too far from home, right?"

Ian stuck a forkful of French toast in a pond of sticky syrup. "What if she lives a thousand light-years from here?"

Harlowe stopped Ian from lifting his syrupy fork to his mouth. "Then it will be a little farther than I thought." Changing the subject, he asked, "So what's the bad news? Millie can't find Jester a date for Friday night? He's stuck with Rerun again?" He was a little more upbeat, now that there was some agreement that the girl was going to make it.

Ian pushed his plate away, suddenly losing his appetite. "Long-range sensors picked up spacecraft entering the system."

That got Harlowe's attention. "Spacecraft? Why didn't you tell me earlier?"

"I just found out," Ian replied as Monday came yawning through the galley door. He lumbered past them and took an empty chair at the table. A red-haired robob waitress clacked over to Monday and waited patiently for his order.

Monday stared sleepily at the girl-bob dressed in a pink-striped apron like one would see at a neighborhood diner. "You know the drill, Betrice. Coffee, black, thick as glue, extra large, extra heavy on the caffeine, lots of cream, lots of sugar." A moment later Betrice returned with a steaming fresh cup of sweet black goo, just the way Monday liked it.

Harlowe and Ian twisted up their noses as Monday took his first sip as if it actually tasted good. "Now that's coffee! Just found out what?" Monday asked after draining half the cup.

"We've got visitors," Harlowe replied straight out.

Monday's eyes bolted open, like a cat startled out of a sound sleep. "As in bad guys?"

"Don't know, but that's my guess," Ian replied.

"Looking for the toads we nuked a few weeks back," Harlowe figured.

Monday put his goo down. "We'd better get out of here while we can." He looked at Ian. "Is Millie up to it?"

"She's ready, but if we try to slam out of here they might detect us," Ian explained. "I'd like a little more time to check out the power drive before we stomp on the hyperlight."

"Too late. We'll have to chance it," Harlowe countered.

"If we stay here, they'll get us for sure," Monday pointed out, picking up his coffee again.

"Maybe," Ian said calmly, as Betrice refilled his orange juice.

"You're acting rather calm about the whole situation," Monday said. "That's unlike you, Wiz."

Harlowe saw Ian had thought things through. "So what's your plan?"

"If we stay dark another week, we can sneak out the back door."

Monday looked at Harlowe, confused. "What back door?"

Ian pushed his plate to the middle of the round table, then placed his juice cup on the opposite side of the table. After that, he borrowed Monday's mug and placed it 180 degrees opposite the juice glass, with the plate in the middle. "The plate is Barnard. The juice is us in six days. Your cup of mud is where they'll be concentrating their search around the small planetoid where we found the girl. With Barnard shielding us from their sensors, we should be able to make it out the back door and into hyperlight before they know we left."

"But that's not the way we came in," Monday pointed out.

"Yeah, but we can change course later once we're outta town."

Monday was dubious. "How far outta town are you talkin'? The next galaxy?"

"Two parsecs should do it," Ian replied confidently.

"I hope that's two New York City blocks," Monday grunted.

Harlowe slapped his fork down. "Sounds good to me, but we'd better be on our toes. Put the sensors on max."

Ian nixed that idea. "We can't. We have to put all power to the shields to mask our presence here or they'll pick us up for sure. Everything but sickbay will be on standby."

"We'd better use ear coms when we're away from the ship then," Monday suggested.

Ian agreed. The small ear communicators would do the job. They fit like a small hearing aid inside the ear. The crew had used them many times at Lu's Place when they weren't wearing the SIBAs. They could even swim with them on.

"By the way," Ian said, "I found fresh dino tracks this morning. Rex is getting braver."

Rex was the name for their adopted tyrannosaur that came around at night, sniffing and depositing his spores around the perimeter of the ship. *Millawanda* was all his. The ship's sensors had kept a constant eye on the giant carnivore 24/7. A couple of times Rex had ventured a few hundred yards from the perimeter during the day, but that was out of visual range and deep on the jungle side of the ship. For the most part, he kept a discreet and safe distance away. One time in the beginning of their stay, when they were all inside the safety of the perimeter, Rex came right up to the barrier. It was an amazing sight to see a beast so large and up close glaring at them with its big, narly eyes and jaws full of foot-long teeth and only the barrier between them. Ian speculated that *Millawanda's* sudden appearance might have frightened him at first, but now that the ship was a familiar slice of the landscape, Rex was getting used it. Before the big guy left in search of his next meal, he lifted his massive tail in the air and anointed the force field before going about his merry way, back into the jungle. Other than an occasional visit from Rex, the nights were peaceful. The Gamadin crew slept easily, knowing that with or without the shields, once Millie was closed up for the night, no animal on the planet could harm them inside of their 54th century fortress.

"Rex got a little too friendly yesterday. Take one of the stunners and give him a little on the snout if he gets that close again," Harlowe ordered.

"I'll put a clicker on it," Ian replied.

"So where's Rerun today?" Harlowe asked, looking at Monday, who seemed a little preoccupied knowing more ships had entered the star system.

"Squid," Harlowe repeated, taking Monday out of his reverie. "Where's Simon?"

"Sorry, Captain," he apologized. "He's sunning himself. He wants to be all tanned up by the time we get back to Earth for his next picture."

Harlowe placed a hand on Monday's shoulder. "No worries. I'll tell 'em." He was going that way anyway. He grabbed another piece of toast from Ian's plate on the way out and told them if any changes took place to call him immediately. He'd be doing his usual thing...catching tubes.

* * *

Wading back out between sets, Harlowe maneuvered himself in front of a three-foot pipe, looking to break left once he was locked in. Every now and then a small twinge in his stomach made him look outside for a large shadow lurking inside an incoming wave. Ian's idea of placing a couple of robob guards with plas-rifles at strategic locations along the beach had worked flawlessly. If anyone had any doubts about safety, they were quickly laid to rest whenever a slithering predator came around the point, searching for its next meal. The instant it crossed the imaginary line into the safe zone, a robob sharpshooter promptly shot the slithery beast in the snout with a stinging blast of irritating but nonlethal plasma.

On his way to join Harlowe, Riverstone asked Simon, "Did Dog give you the heads-up on our visitors?"

The girl-bobs started at opposite ends and worked their way toward the center, massaging in liberal amounts of the local coconut oil onto Simon's scantily clothed body. It wasn't long before he was as shiny as a seal. Simon gave Riverstone the thumbs-up. "Message delivered, Dog." Yawn..

* * *

Harlowe kicked hard and went right, passing Riverstone, who was stroking outside for the next set. A wave lifted Harlowe effortlessly, carrying him along as though he were airborne. One arm outstretched like Superman, he rode facedown, and then twisted a three-sixty, squeezing out every ounce of distance and speed he could eke out of the small wave.

The effort took him all the way into the beach. He didn't stop until he nudged the sandy bottom with his chin. He rolled over on his backside, his eyes still closed, and spat a mouthful of water into the air like a beached whale. He continued to lie in the surf a few moments, feeling good, letting the sun's warmth soothe his body. His thoughts of the girl, the ship, leviathans, more ships entering the system, and the fact that they were light-years away from home all seemed lost in the distant corners of his mind.

Another small wave came under him, gently nudging him back to reality. For some unknown reason he thought of Lu. Her fingers touching his like they had done many times before, walking along the shore. He sighed away from the pain, wishing they had more time together. He turned over and went on with his ritual of rising to his knees, clearing his nose, and wiping the salt water from his eyes. When he opened his eyes again, two ankles stood in the sand a step away.

They weren't Jester's or Wiz's. Their ankles were thick and hairy. Monday's were thick and dark. Rerun had bony ankles and his toes were crooked. These ankles belonged to no one from his ship. They were bare, smooth, and sculptured.

Another surge drifted in between his legs and around the new ankles. Slowly his eyes rose to a short, light blue linen dress that flowed in the wind around the tall, slender form of a...

Oh, sweet! A babe...

17

Nice Catch

FOR WHAT SEEMED to be the longest moment of his life, Harlowe just stared at the girl, without moving. He couldn't believe she was real. Seeing Rex standing in front of him would be less surprising than seeing a girl on *this* beach.

Harlowe forced clarity to his head. Either he was dreaming or the red sun had finally affected his brain. He blinked several more times and concluded she was definitely real. But where had she come from? Ian had said there were no humanoids on the planet except monkey-like creatures, and they were in small, isolated pockets thousands of miles away. This girl was no monkey. Even if she was a Stone Age babe, to think she had somehow lost her way over that much distance was a stretch. Then how did she get here?

Harlowe thought half-jokingly, *In her Land Cruiser?*

That was stupid. They didn't have the means to travel anywhere unless...

Nah, it couldn't be! That's too rad!

Yet, here she was, a beautiful barefoot girl on the beach dressed in a knee-length, soft blue sundress, appearing out of nowhere like a Greek goddess descending Mount Olympus. Her garment was airy and simple, with primitive sleeves, and tied at the waist with a thin line of dark blue cord. Her skin was smooth and reflected a creamy olive under the morning sun. She was over six foot five, he

85

judged, with proportionate narrow hips and legs that were toned in an athletic way. Oddly, her hair seemed out of place. It was quite short, no more than an inch long, and very dark. Her large, round eyes curiously studied his every move.

Wow, she's hot! Maybe he was the one who was out of place, he thought.

Suddenly he remembered what he had just done: blown his nose on her feet!

Not so cool...

A little embarrassed, he shrank back on his haunches, apologizing profusely for his ill-mannered act. A beautiful girl was standing right in front of him. *Whatta day!* The first female in two years and he had just blown snot at her feet! *Way to go, Gomer!* From here, her impression of him could only improve. She had to think he was the most uncivilized toad in the galaxy! How was he ever going to smooth this one out?

Throughout Harlowe's red-faced retreat, the girl remained cool in the ankle-deep shore break as he edged himself back into deeper water.

"Hi," he began, smiling with all his teeth. She gave him no response and remained expressionless and unemotional while continuing to watch him make a fool of himself. Obviously, she wasn't going to lend him a hand with the situation.

"Come here often?" Harlowe asked. "Nice beach, huh? Are you a Dodger fan?"

Harlowe wondered if all the natives were as hot as she was. He wasn't picky, though. He would stop right here with this one. He didn't need to see any more. If he had known there were babes like this around, he would have spent less time in the water and more time asking the locals for sugar!

"I hope it's all right for us to be here," Harlowe went on, continuing to make small talk with the girl. With his hips now underwater, he felt more comfortable that he wasn't so exposed. "We didn't think anyone lived around here." He pointed at *Millawanda*. "We needed to fix our ship," he told her. She didn't speak or nod or give any indication that she understood a word he was saying. Her eyes remained on Harlowe, as if expecting him to say something she understood. "We mean no harm," he said, borrowing an overused phrase from an old sci-fi movie he saw once.

Of course she can't speak your language, stupid. She's not from Lakewood!

Harlowe had run out of things to say and was dumbfounded as to what to do next. Diplomacy wasn't one of his strong suits. His friendly smile was getting him nowhere. Her facial expression told him nothing, either. If she was offended by his crude act, she didn't show it. After all the pain he was going through to be friendly, he figured some kind of response was in order, no matter how small.

As if she had read his mind, her lips moved, although no words were uttered.

First base! Harlowe congratulated himself. But it was more like a foul tip than a bunt. He needed to keep the momentum alive, though, and said, "Pardon me. I didn't hear you," cupping his right ear as though he wanted her to speak louder.

She stepped closer and spoke again. Her words, if that's what they were, made no sense. If it wasn't English, he was lost. Though her words did seem familiar, he didn't remember where he had heard the language.

"What's your name?" Harlowe asked, thinking that was a good place to start.

She looked even more confused than ever.

No, kidding, Nimrod. You're the alien around here!

She spoke again, slower this time as though she was making an effort to be understood. She moved closer and spoke with an even voice. Just when he thought he was getting somewhere, she suddenly appeared light-headed, as if she might faint. She started to weave and stumble forward, losing her balance.

Harlowe shot out of the water. This was no time for modesty! He caught her as she was about to drop facedown into the water.

He turned her over and felt her white, clammy face. She was running a fever. He didn't know what was wrong with her. Maybe that was why she'd found him in the first place, he thought. She had seen the ship and thought he was a god.

Harlowe, you idiot! Stop with the fairytales. Get her to sick bay!

He lifted her up and began running back to the ship. He looked like a half-naked Greek carrying off some wingless nymph he had found in the jungle.

Simon was the first to see him with the girl, his attention instantly focusing on her beauty. "Nice catch, Dog!" His mouth hung open like a starving dog seeing raw meat. He glanced out toward the surf. "Any more live ones out there?"

Harlowe, however, wasn't in the mood for jokes. "She's sick. I've got to get her to sickbay."

Simon looked around as they went through the perimeter barrier running alongside Harlowe. "Was she alone?"

"She's the only one I saw."

"Dog, she's gorgeous. Does she have a sister?" Simon asked, practically drooling over her.

"How would I know? I told you I didn't see anyone else."

Simon stopped and looked back, hoping to find a whole flock of damsels in distress as Harlowe ran for the first blinker in the sand.

* * *

Inside sickbay, Harlowe laid her out on the table. He was beginning to feel like a human ambulance, the way he was taking bodies into the various sickbays. This particular sickbay was located on the sunrise side of the ship. The girl from the crash was 120 degrees toward the sunset side of the ship.

Two robobs were ready with probes by the time Harlowe entered the room and put her on the table. Once the analysis was complete, a clicker touched her arm with a needleless hypo while a second clicker checked her again with its sensor probe. Both stickmen put away their instruments and returned to their slits in the wall. The whole process took less than thirty seconds.

"That's it?" Harlowe questioned in disbelief as Riverstone entered the room.

"Rerun said you found a goddess on the beach," Riverstone said, eyeing the vision on the table. "Dude! You scored!"

"I guess she didn't need much help," Harlowe said, studying the wall of colorful graphs displaying the girl's condition. "According to this, she's a little exhausted."

As they both stared with curiosity, Harlowe pulled Riverstone from the table. "Don't drool on her."

Like the language the girl spoke, Harlowe couldn't exactly explain why, but she seemed familiar to him. This planet was eight light-years from Earth. They had certainly never met before, not even in a dream. As his common sense spoke of the impossibility, his insides were telling him something different.

But where?

His impasse kept him staring at her, searching for clues. Her olive skin had a pinkish tint, as if she had been out in the sun too long. Her hair was short and cut in one length, as if a clicker had given her a haircut. However, it didn't detract from her beauty at all.

Besides her skin and hair, Harlowe saw something else, something that made his heart leap. In so many ways she reminded him of Lu. He could see no lies, disguises, or falsehoods. She was, like Lu, a beautiful girl on the inside as well as the outside.

Still, a nagging feeling kept telling him they had met. It might be all noise he was listening to in his head, but it was something from the past... the recent past... and wouldn't let up.

He tried again to look closer. What was it about her that he had trouble remembering?

Before he had a chance to dig deeper, Ian entered the room, interrupting his search for the truth. "I just heard. What's happened, Captain?"

"Dog found a bone on the beach," Riverstone said, pointing to the screen. "She's going to be okay, though, despite the shock."

Ian examined the screen first. "Looks human."

"Yeah, no joke," Riverstone said in awe, pointing at the girl. "Absolutely the hottest doe I've ever seen this side of the Mons."

"There shouldn't be any humans around for thousands of miles," Ian stated with near-certainty.

Riverstone laid a hand on Ian's shoulder, nodding at the ship's newest patient. "She must have taken a bus, because here she is, brah."

"She can't be," Ian uttered under his breath. He wasn't buying the bus excuse, even if it was a joke.

Harlowe squinted, confused. He looked at Ian and saw that he was holding back an idea. "She can't be what, Wiz?"

Ian went to the holo-screen on the side wall. "Wow," he said, admiring the graphic readouts.

Harlowe and Riverstone were beyond confused as Ian brought up an image of the girl called Quay whom they had seen just before her ship was destroyed by the alien warship.

Once again the scene played out as the girl pleaded for someone to save them, and once again, the bolt of yellow plasma struck the ship before the screen went blank. Ian rolled the scene back to the girl, and then froze the picture. After that he adjusted the holograph with his fingers, cropping the frame just so for a clear shot of Quay's face. Harlowe and Riverstone had already moved closer to the image with piqued curiosity. The only part of her face that was visible was her profile, and her long dark hair mostly covered it.

"Go forward slowly, Millie," Ian ordered. The image moved ahead. "Stop. Back two frames." The girl's face was now looking straight at the screen.

Ian turned to Harlowe. "What do you see, Dog?"

Harlowe's eyes went to the sleeping goddess on the table. It made all the sense in the world now. *It's her!* His sense of closeness had been right all along!

18

Mornin' Rex

HARLOWE PICKED OUT a private bedroom for Quay between Ian and Monday's quarters, figuring she would be safer there than next to the girl-crazy Simon or Riverstone. *Millawanda* had no shortage of bedrooms. No one had yet taken a count as to how many there were, but Ian guessed it was in the hundreds. Harlowe figured waking up in a comfortable room would be a lot better than seeing a clicker hovering over her with a probe. He entertained giving up his own room, but Ian was more prudent, suggesting a room of her own was more appropriate. Harlowe reluctantly agreed. How could he deny her anything? She had that kind of beauty that made men back on Earth trip over their own feet.

Simon and Riverstone would have slept out on the beach with Rex if she had asked them to, which almost happened the following day. The giant beast made his first daylight appearance at the ship's perimeter. Simon came charging into the control room, yelling at the top of his lungs as to why no one had warned him about the dinosaur in the front yard before he was about to take his morning jog along the beach.

Riverstone replied without breaking stride, "We thought you wanted a running partner, Rerun."

"The stupid dino almost had me for breakfast!" Simon shouted back angrily. "Fortunately for me, it couldn't swim."

92

Harlowe leaned into Simon's face. "Watch your mouth, Mr. Bolt. You are on the bridge. You will have respect at all times while on the bridge. This is a sacred place." Harlowe shot a sharp eye toward Riverstone and added, "That goes for everyone. While on the bridge, there is no such thing as off-the-clock." Harlowe's stern eyes circled the room to ensure his decree was absolutely clear. Then he ordered, "Carry on."

Breaking the tension, Ian reported that Rex was right outside the perimeter. Everyone, including Harlowe, was excited about seeing the giant carnivore up close and personal. They walked through the bridge hatchway onto the upper saucer deck to get a closer look at the beast. It was a bright, sunny day and not a cloud was anywhere on the muted red horizon. Barnard was fully up and brilliantly red, looking like a giant exercise ball against the greenish-blue sky. Two of #2's moons were straight overhead and dark because they were passing in front of the sun, while the third, the largest moon of the three, was coming up over the ocean. It made the long walk to catch a glimpse of the largest carnivore they had ever seen by daylight even more eventful.

Rex was so tall his massive head loomed almost evenly with the perimeter's edge of the saucer. His foot-wide, bloodshot eyes glared at them the entire way. Seeing the monster this close was like seeing Jupiter or Saturn for the first time. It took their breath away to know they could be a fast-food snack for him. They might not have been so cavalier about venturing out beyond the Ship's protective barrier if they had seen him this close from the beginning. His length was over sixty feet as he stood upright, taller than a two-story house.

"Man, is he ugly," Riverstone commented while sticking his tongue out at him. "Reminds me of a joke."

"A joke?" Ian quipped.

"You know where a five-hundred-pound gorilla walks?" Riverstone asked.

"Yeah, anywhere he wants to," Ian replied, almost bored.

"You heard it?"

"Too many times."

Harlowe looked at Rex's large red eyes and grinned. There were only a few steps between them now. Rex knew they were talking about him, too, the way he opened his seven-foot-long mouth, revealing his massive rows of wickedly sharp, flesh-ripping incisors. The huge beast then snapped at the ship, trying to bite out a mouthful of 54th century dura-steel. *Good luck,* Harlowe thought. *Millie is one tough babe, dude.*

They watched in awe as *Millawanda's* shimmering force field stopped the powerful jaws just short of her golden hull. Rex, in his frustration, screamed loudly, hurting their ears as he pounded his head against the barrier several times before he understood it was something even he couldn't crack.

Simon laughed behind the barrier. "I think he lost a few teeth on that one."

Monday looked out over the beach. "Why didn't the robobs take care of him?" he asked.

"I told them to leave him alone," Ian replied.

"You what?" Riverstone asked, surprised.

"You heard me. As a matter of fact, I told them not to shoot any more creatures. It's not their fault we landed here."

"Since when did you turn green?" Riverstone asked.

"It's okay, Mr. Riverstone," Harlowe butted in. "It was the right call, Wiz. Two more days and we're out of here anyway. Let the beasts be."

"It can't be too soon for me, Dog," Riverstone replied as they all turned back to the control room. The show was over. Rex had thundered off into the jungle in a huff, looking for softer things to chew on. "What about the girl? What are we going to do with her?"

Before Harlowe could answer, Simon chimed in with an idea. "Hey, Skipper, if we take her back to Earth, I could make her a star. With looks like that, Saul could get her fifty mil easily the first time out," Simon stated.

They would have laughed if they didn't know Simon was serious.

"We're not taking her to Earth," Harlowe stated flatly, stopping before the hatchway to the control room. "We'll take her wherever she wants us to take her." The decision was made.

"Can we talk here before we go inside, Captain?" Riverstone asked.

Harlowe could see that look in Riverstone, when the position of authority was holding him back. This was not one of those times he needed anyone to hold back. He needed answers and concerns from everyone, no matter how much he was against them.

Harlowe gave the go-ahead. "You're on, Jester."

Riverstone wasted no time voicing his concern. "What if she lives two blocks north of the galactic core, Dog?" he asked, registering his worry that maybe they were already too far away from home as it was. "Then what?"

Harlowe stood fast as his jaws tightened. "We're taking her wherever she needs to go. If that means taking her to the galactic core, then that's where we go."

"But why?"

"Because it's the right thing to do," Harlowe said with finality.

Ian put a thoughtful hand on Riverstone's shoulder to help his fear. "Let's ask Millie where she comes from. Maybe she lives a few light-years from here."

Riverstone had been down that road with Harlowe too many times for that possibility. "Fat chance."

"How would Millie know?" Simon asked, as they stepped through the hatchway back onto the bridge.

Ian's answer was straightforward. "If Millie understands Quay's language, it's possible she can make a pretty close guess as to where she lives. If you speak French, it's a pretty good bet you come from France, right?"

Simon grunted, shaking his head. "People from Quebec speak French, too, and they're half a globe away from France, Wizzy."

"Yeah, and every Canadian knows where France is, too," Ian replied matter-of-factly.

Simon didn't care if they exchanged Christmas cards; they were still an ocean away.

The group stood before the bridge overhead as Ian asked the questions. No matter what direction one looked at the holographic projection from, the screen always seemed to be facing the observer. No one knew how this was done. It just was.

Ian took a sip of hot mint tea from the cup a girl-bob had just handed him before he asked Millie if she could identify the source of the language the girl named Quay spoke.

AFFIRMATIVE, read the screen.

"It had better be close by," Riverstone grumbled.

"I'll second that," Simon added. Monday said little, preferring to keep his thoughts to himself. The way his worried eyes focused on the screen, one could safely bet his thoughts favored Simon and Riverstone's position.

"Please identify the language, Millie," Ian requested.

A DIALECT OF OMINIESE, read the screen.

"From what planet does this Ominiese language originate?"

OMINI PRIME

"What is the distance to Omini Prime from our location, Millie?"

IN WHAT FORM OF MEASUREMENT?

Ian took another sip of tea, "Light-years, if you please, Millie."

The screen blinked. "301.127 LIGHT-YEARS..."

Ian wasn't aware that hot tea was spilling on his lap.

19

Small World

ONE COULD HAVE heard a pin drop as the Gamadin moved from the sacredness of the bridge to the open forum around the meeting table in Harlowe's quarters. Simon was the first to speak, roaring his protest. "May I speak freely, Captain?"

Harlowe nodded, but with one condition: "Keep it civil, Mr. Bolt."

"I intend to, Captain, sir!" He then stood and glared at the table as if to say why were they even discussing this? "Are we crazy? We're already halfway across the galaxy!"

"Only next door in galactic distances," Ian squeezed between Simon's ranting.

Simon's chivalrous idea of sacrificing himself for the good of an alien goddess didn't seem quite as appetizing as before. "I don't care if she makes Phoebe Marleigh look like a pimple-faced teenybopper! I'm in major protest here. I'm not going!"

Harlowe leaned into Simon with a stare that could bend dura-steel. He would have order. "You do not use that tone with me or anyone else at this table, Mr. Bolt, or I swear I will tear your guts out and throw them to Rex!"

Simon saw the look on Harlowe's face and knew there was little doubt he was dino-meal if he didn't curb his temper. "Understood, Captain. I apologize."

Harlowe allowed his crewman to chill a moment before he gave him the go-ahead. "Continue, Mr. Bolt."

"Do we have to, Captain? I mean take her home?"

"You would leave her here on #2?"

It was no secret that Simon was never really convinced of the inter-galactic soldier stuff. Though he loved being a Gamadin and had never sacrificed so much in his life to become a 54th century soldier, there were still parts of him that were not "all-in," as with the others.

"Whatever the babe's problems are, why do they have to be ours?" He pointed across the room behind him. "Earth is only a measly eight light-years that way, so it shouldn't be too much trouble to drop me off, Captain. After that, you can fly all the way to the galactic core if you want, Skipper. With all due respect, sir," he added.

Riverstone had already voiced his displeasure earlier. He was against it, but whatever Harlowe's call was, he would support it as long as there was a light at the end of the tunnel, which to him meant returning to Earth as soon as they dropped her off. However, that was before he read Millie's calculation. Three hundred light-years away was pushing his tolerance level. Monday and Ian, on the other hand, simply sat and stared across the table, letting their thoughts reflect off their shocked faces.

Before Harlowe could respond to Simon, his eyes moved around the table and stopped at Ian, who put it simply: "We need to find out more about her."

Harlowe looked back to Simon. "Yes, we should." He then called up the screen in the center of the table. "Millie. Omini Prime. Is this the origin of Quay's language?"

NEGATIVE. A DIALECT, the tall blue letters read.

"Millie, you stated Quay's language is a dialect of Omini Prime."

AFFIRMATIVE.

"Then her home world is in another star system?" Harlowe asked.

AFFIRMATIVE.

"Display map of Omini Prime along with the planets and their respective dialects." Harlowe turned to Riverstone. "Her home could be much closer to us than Omini Prime," he suggested, hoping to put a positive spin on the discussion.

"Oh, how I wish it were so . . . Sir," Riverstone added belatedly, with a slight edge to his tone.

The projection changed instantly to a detailed, three-dimenional map of Omini Prime and all the star systems where the Ominiese language and its dialects had spread. They were amazed at how extensively the Omini Prime explorers and traders had reached out into space.

"Include our present position, if you please," Harlowe ordered.

The screen grew tenfold. The projection was so large it was difficult for anyone to see. On the lower right corner was a small reddish dot. Harlowe pointed. "That's us?" he asked, unable to hide his dismay.

"Scale back region fifty percent, Millie," Ian directed.

The projection reduced the view to a more readable size.

"What are we looking at?" Riverstone asked. "I mean, do these places have names? Which one is Omini Prime?"

Ian and Harlowe looked at each other. "I thought it was obvious. It's the bright yellow one in the middle," Harlowe replied, pointing.

Riverstone mumbled under his breath that he saw it. "I hate star maps," he grumbled further.

"Millie, give us the common names of the planetary star systems," Harlowe ordered. In a blink, hundreds of names were displayed on the screen. There was so many, again the star map was difficult to read.

"Filter out all non-Omini Prime dialects," Ian suggested.

The projection became less cluttered but was still crowded.

"Where is Quay's planet?" Riverstone asked, losing patience with the search.

Harlowe and Ian scanned the screen. Their eyes notched the many stars around Omini Prime, but neither could find Quay's planet. "Millie, help us out. Show us Quay's star system."

At first they didn't see it. They were expecting a small pulsing light somewhere near Omini Prime. It wasn't until they stepped back and looked in the far left corner of the screen that they were able to see a small, blinking point of light. It was a planetary system called Tomar. Harlowe put his hands on his hips and stared in frustration.

Simon pointed. "That's the wrong direction, Skipper!"

"That point at the top is Quay's home star?" Harlowe asked the computer.

AFFIRMATIVE, read the bottom of the screen.

"That's definitely Quebec," Riverstone quipped, his face deep with *I-knew-it*. No one had to ask Simon how he felt. His face said it all. Harlowe remained stoically silent as Riverstone asked the only question that was on everyone's mind. "So, how far away is Tomar from our present position, Millie?"

532.114 LIGHT-YEARS. read the screen.

The pin-drop silence returned before Riverstone wondered if they could find a halfway point to drop her off. "I say we call her dad and he meets us halfway, Dog," he suggested, reaching for a compromise as he pointed at the screen. "Omini Prime works for me." He turned to Ian. "Don't you agree, Science Officer?"

Ian decided to sit this one out as Monday spoke about the elephant in the room. "It's a long way, Captain," he said and then suggested, "worth consideration."

Harlowe kept staring at the star map as if looking for a way to change the laws of physics again from light-years to miles. Somehow his eyes drifted to the far right side of the projection, landing on a system nearly by itself. When he read the name of the system, he could hardly believe his eyes. Riverstone saw the sudden change and knew Harlowe had found another reason to continue the journey to Omini Prime.

Harlowe put his knuckles on the table and leaned into the projection, confirming that what he was reading was not a figment of his imagination. Finally, he stood straight again and calmly announced to the table, "Imagine that…" His eyes met their fearful faces at the table. "Neeja."

Riverstone's eyes went round. "Mrs. M's planet?"

Harlowe stared at the star map in disbelief. "Neeja is linked to Omini Prime, Millie?"

AFFIRMATIVE!

"They speak the same language?"

AFFIRMATIVE!

Ian pointed to a nearby star. "Look! That's Amerloi over there, the place where they found the ancient scrolls that guided Mrs. M to Earth."

Riverstone rolled his eyes. "Small galaxy."

Harlowe had Monday and Ian run a complete recheck of Millie's database from the bridge console before he pronounced the star map was indeed accurate. There could be no doubt then that Neeja was the world Harlowe had promised Mrs. M he would save before they found *Millawanda* and left Earth.

Harlowe had a hunch. "Millie, project the reach of the Fhaal Empire."

The map went off the scale. Harlowe's office, as roomy as it was, wasn't large enough to hold the entire star map of the Fhaal Empire.

"Dude—I mean Captain! These guys have influence," Riverstone exclaimed, nearly out of breath.

Harlowe was caught off guard. He hadn't expected such an immense reach of the Fhaal Empire, either. "Scale back, Millie, to the previous chart and mark the Fhaal advance into Omini Prime sectors," Harlowe said.

The screen reduced back to the original size, showing Omini Prime in the center with its outlying dialects, with their star chart identities. A jagged green line ran diagonally through the map from the upper left to the lower right of the quadrant. This was the line of the Fhaal Empire advance into Omini Prime. The line had engulfed Neeja many light-years ago but oddly, the aggressive outreach of the Empire had stalled only ten parsecs from Quay's home world, Tomar, which was right in their path.

Riverstone had seen enough. He knew what the discovery of Neeja meant: that returning home to Earth anytime soon was out of the question. He turned to Harlowe. "This is where my dad would say, 'I need a drink.'" He wanted to run outside and play in the surf all day and forget about this wretched hand Fate was dealing them again. He wanted to go home. He wanted to finish high school and watch football games with his date on Friday night. He wanted to play with his dog Molly and take out the trash without anyone asking. He wanted to hug his mom and taste her blueberry pancakes and bacon in the morning. He wanted to smell his dad's cigar in the backyard while he was barbequing two-inch-thick steaks on the grill. He wanted things to be the way they used to be without the thought of billions of people's lives on his mind.

Why me? He repeated over and over again. *Why us?*

A sympathetic nod came from across the table to everyone. "We could all use a drink," Harlowe said, as everyone now had taken a chair, unable to stand from what they were seeing on the massive holographic projection. He called for a round of shakes and animal double-double In-N-Outs, with piles of French fries and ketchup. His order was promptly delivered by Jewels and his girl-bob waitresses on blue crystalline trays.

"I'll take a triple-thick one intravenously, Jewels," Simon half-joked, his stoic face showing the effect such a journey would have on his plans of a comeback movie career.

Monday just wanted something to eat. He didn't care what form it was, as long as it was big and juicy. Ian only cared about the thick shake. Harlowe picked up a burger and handed one to Riverstone. "I will take you home first, Rerun," he promised the movie star.

Simon liked that idea and toasted Harlowe for his clear-headedness. "Great idea, Captain. I'll save you a special front-row seat at my next London premiere."

Harlowe faced the rest of the table. "That goes for each and every one of you. I can't ask you to go along on something this dangerous for a promise that *I* made. The chance of ever seeing Earth again is almost zero. That's probably a given. If any one of you decides not to go forward with me, no one will ever consider it a wrong decision. I've seen each and every one of you over the last twenty months survive in ways few would ever dream of. Each one of you is man-up in my book. Without a doubt you are the best crew a captain could have the honor to serve with. Each of you must make the decision on whether to go on or go home on your own. I will not make that decision for you. If you come with me, it will be strictly your choice. No more conscription. From here on out, it's your choice to leave or stay."

Riverstone carefully pulled back the wrapper on his animal burger and took a Rex-sized bite. The massive mouthful didn't stop him from saying to Harlowe, "You would go it alone, wouldn't you?"

Harlowe didn't hesitate. "You know that answer." There was no maybe in his reply. His commitment was solid. He was "all-in" with body and soul. If he said he would walk on water next, Riverstone would have believed him.

"No one would expect you to keep such a promise, Captain," Simon added.

Harlowe's eyes traveled around the table. He wanted to observe the thoughts of his crew, the way their muscles twitched in their faces, whether their hands fiddled. He saw none of that. Not one of his brave crew was fidgety or frightened. They had faced death too many times before to reveal such weakness on the outside. He was rightfully proud of them all. He turned to Monday next. "You've been rather quiet, Squid. Feel free to speak your mind here. Everyone else has," glancing at Simon and Riverstone.

Monday took a long gulp of his shake before he answered thoughtfully. "I'm with you, Captain. This may sound strange coming from me, because I'll be the first to tell you that going any farther from home scares me to death. I would rather jump off the Mons than go another parsec from home. But my life didn't begin until I met the three of you," he said, looking at Ian, Riverstone, and Harlowe. "No disrespect, Rerun." Simon nodded. None was taken. The movie star knew what he meant. In many ways he felt the same. "The years with you were good. No regrets there either. But this is different. This means something. I was lost before; now I'm living instead of hiding. I have fought with you all, suffered through rimmers, messed my underwear leaping off tall cliffs. I've almost died so many times I've lost count. I'm sure Simon would agree, we don't play *Distant Galaxy*, we live it . . . every day! For me, Captain, there is no choice but to stay here on *Millawanda* with you. What the four of you, my mates, have given me cannot be found anywhere but here. You all are my family, the family I never had. This is where I'll die. I'm here to the end, Captain. Wherever you decide to take us, I'm with you—" Monday stood up and saluted Harlowe. "SIR!"

Harlowe swallowed the lump in his throat. If someone looked closely enough, they would see his eyes turning glassy and red. He hadn't expected such a heartfelt response. It caught him way off guard light-year. He was grateful beyond words. "Well said, Mr. Platter. Thank you." He turned to Ian. "Wiz?"

Ian sipped his shake calmly. "Who else would take care of Millie? I'm all-in."

Harlowe looked at Ian, surprised. "That's it? That's all you've got to say?"

"Like this is something new," Ian replied, rolling his eyes toward the ceiling. "We've been fighting Daks since we were five, Dog, when our spaceship was made of sand. Whether it's the incoming tide at 42nd Street or the Fhaal armada," he said, waving and pointing to the star projection, "it's all the same, isn't it? As long as I've known you, you've always been the captain. So what's the difference, if we fight here, there, or back at 42nd Street? We're always going to be fighting someone, it seems. I'd rather have a 54th century weapon at my back than a handful of sand any day."

Harlowe nodded his appreciation before turning to Riverstone. "I guess I don't have to ask you, Jester. You're never at a loss for words."

Riverstone leaned way forward, gripping his uneaten burger. "That's right, Dog, I do. I've got plenty to say, but it doesn't matter."

"It does matter," Harlowe shot back. "This table always listens."

"You just said you're going anyway because you're committed to a promise."

Harlowe remained steadfast. "That's right."

"So there you go. It's a done deal. I have to stay," Riverstone stated firmly.

"I'll take you home with Rerun," Harlowe offered. "You know I would."

Riverstone laughed. "Oh yeah, right. I'm going to Earth without you. What am I going to tell Tinker? I lost you on some distant planet far, far away? I don't think so, pal. Trust me on this one. Earth's the last place I want to be if I have to look your mom in the eye and say I let you go bebopping around the galaxy alone. Anyone else's mom in the whole universe, and I wouldn't have a problem leaving your sorry buns right here to get your head blown off or eaten by some crazed lizard. No, not me. I'm going with you because I don't want to deal with your mom. It's that simple, Pylott. I'm going along because, as stupid as it sounds, I feel safer flying across the galaxy with you than telling Tinker her son's a whacko!"

"She already knows that," Ian cried out, laughing.

"His mom's that bad?" Simon questioned in disbelief.

There was real fear in Riverstone's eyes. "She could beat us all to a pulp, including the General. I saw her send both Harlowe and his dad, Buster, to the woodshed that night they went to the Dodger game without her."

Harlowe winced, confirming the memory.

"That's right." Riverstone unwrapped his In-N-Out and took a Rex-size bite out of his burger, speaking with his mouth full. "That's why I'm staying here where it's safe. It's self-preservation, Rerun."

"Well, there's no one back home that's going to take me down, and right now, I'd like to see them try." He knew, except for his other Gamadin mates, that his six-foot-six, 230-pound chiseled body could defend himself against anyone on Earth. "I feel I've put enough time into our little tour of duty, and done rather well if I do say so myself," Simon said, proudly.

"That you have, Mr. Bolt," Harlowe agreed. "Very fine indeed."

Simon slapped his hands, finished with the debate. "If you wouldn't mind dropping me off at the nearest habitable planet where the babes outnumber the men, Captain, and we all know where that is, I'd be much indebted to you, sir."

Harlowe stood at attention and saluted. "Permission granted, Mr. Bolt. I will be happy to meet your request. With the deepest sincerity, Mr. Bolt, you will be missed." The others, without hesitation, followed Harlowe's lead and snapped to attention, giving their highest respect to their fellow Gamadin.

The display of affection put Simon in shock. One could have driven the grannywagon into his mouth. For the first time anyone could remember, Simon Bolt was speechless.

20

Let's Party

THE MORNING WAS alive with robobs. Simon began directing stickmen to set up a target launcher at one end of the beach for tonight's shootout, while out in front, Ian and Monday were making the play area more secure, extending the force field beyond the perimeter with pods in case Rex decided to crash the party. Harlowe had three clickers digging the firepit for the big bonfire that was planned. Nearby, three girl-bobs were laying out a volleyball court and stringing up the regulation net. Finally, Riverstone was in charge of the menu. Clickers were already bringing out the coolers of beverages, finger foods and entrées, all SoCal delights from the old hometown: piles of animal-style, double-double hamburgers, dripping with cheese, thick onion, thick tomatoes, bunches of lettuce, and mayo, together with spicy Dodger Dogs, deli mustard and ketchup. Also on the menu were tacos and trays of fixings, along with a gallon of Tinker's secret salsa and a barrel of corn chips.

Rex was there too, looking like a starved puppy dog. Simon took pity on him and tossed him a twenty-pound steak through the barrier that he snatched out of the air like he was catching a bone. That turned out to be a mistake. Rex screamed at the top of his lungs for more. For a nine-ton carnivore, a hunk of meat that size barely filled a tooth cavity. He wanted it all, including the humans!

"Shut up, stupid!" Simon shouted at Rex, who had his snout plastered against the barrier. "You're lucky you got that. Now go away and leave us alone!" he yelled, firing a round past Rex's ear. Rex took a running start and smashed headfirst into the barrier with his thirty-ton mass. The force field didn't give an inch. "That's it, dummy!" Simon shouted back, kicking sand at Rex's face. "Break your fool neck! See if anyone cares!"

Slamming the barrier must have left a sour taste in his mouth. Rex picked himself up and lumbered slowly back into the jungle in a huff.

"Serves you right, toadface!" Simon called after him, watching the giant dinosaur snap trees as he plowed an angry path through the jungle.

After a final barb at Rex, Simon turned back to the launcher and slapped on the activator. With a crackling flash, eight targets jettisoned up from the sand.

He shot seven targets cleanly out the sky but missed the eighth, taking a painful sting in his thigh for the slip-up. Normally, eight was a snap, but today his concentration seemed a little off.

"That's gotta hurt," Riverstone said with a grin, walking up to the launcher. He was carrying a bright red-and-yellow surfboard on his way to catch a few tubes before the big bash.

"Not half as bad as a zillion light-years from Earth would be," Simon countered.

"You didn't get the update. We might take her all the way to Tomar. That's five hundred l-y's and some change. How does that grab you, bucko?"

"It doesn't. I just want to get back to the good old U. S. of A., traffic jams, Disneyland, and where the girls don't go clickity-clack," Simon replied, nodding at a girl-bob swaying off a nearby rampway with another tray of food. He stepped up to the launcher again, and was about to slap the activator when someone came up from behind, unannounced.

It was Quay.

"Hey, girl," Riverstone said, spellbound by her stunning beauty. Simon was no less enthralled, maybe more so, because his mouth was hung open twice as far as Riverstone's.

She spoke in a language neither Gamadin understood. Riverstone stared at her, confused. "No compréntde," he said to her, touching his mouth that he didn't understand. Without the computer to help translate, they were unable to communicate. However, with a few universal gestures he quickly discovered he could cross a few light-years of space on his own.

Quay eyed the target launcher with curiosity. She appeared calmer than before as she moved with a regal confidence toward the launcher. She was about to touch the target's activator when Riverstone hastily grabbed her arm. "No," he said, shaking his head, "it shoots back. You could get hurt," he tried to explain, and pointed at Simon's recent injury as proof.

A playful grin rose across her face as Quay pulled her arm away and slapped the activator.

The Gamadin stood by in shock, but before either of them could do anything about the stinging targets, Quay grabbed Simon's pistol from his holster and shot down six targets before any of them fired back. With the two remaining targets, she sidestepped the retaliations and blasted the dancing targets clean out of the sky with deadly precision.

"Wow!" Riverstone cried out, catching his breath. "That was cool!" The Gamadin were stunned. They could hardly believe how graceful and lethal this twelve on the hot scale of babes was with a weapon.

"Who taught you how to shoot like that?" Simon asked, his mouth still open in disbelief.

Quay turned back to Simon. With a heavy dose of what appeared to be superiority in her manner, she returned the pistol to him.

Riverstone had the distinct feeling that if they were able to communicate with her she would have said, "Nothing to it, dudes!"

At that moment Harlowe was walking toward them on his way for a dip before the sun went down and the festivities began. He was wearing dark blue trunks and had a pale blue board under his arm. Riverstone glanced down the beach. Rex was nowhere to be seen, presumably looking for his evening meal elsewhere.

"Hey, Dog," Riverstone called out, waving Harlowe over to the target area.

Harlowe didn't have to be asked twice. The instant his eyes caught Quay, his slow, sauntering stride became more like a high-stepping, I'm-the-Captain strut.

"Our pistols seems a little off, Dog," Riverstone explained as Harlowe strode up with a flashy grin at the girl. "See what you think."

Harlowe exchanged his board for the pistols. "What do you want me to do?" he asked.

Riverstone traded confident winks with Simon, their faces full of smugness. They looked like gamblers who knew the outcome of a race before it started. "Just do your thing, Skipper. Nothing fancy," Simon said.

Harlowe faced the launcher, almost bored, as Riverstone nudged the girl in the side with his elbow. "Watch this." After Simon upped the target number to twenty, Riverstone added to Quay with a confident wink, "Keep your eye on the bouncing ball, babe," and then Simon struck the activator.

Harlowe's hands were a blur.

Watching Harlowe shoot targets out of the sky was like watching a classical pianist play, an artist paint, a Major League pitcher pitch a hundred-mile-an-hour fastball. He was the best; a master. No one was better than Harlowe with a pistol, and Riverstone didn't care what part of the galaxy they came from.

As quickly as the second hand of a clock ticked, Harlowe had reduced nineteen targets to subatomic dust. With the twentieth, he added a touch of overkill by wrapping his left arm around his back and blasting the last target into oblivion.

When he finished, he traded the pistols for his board and remarked, "They seem okay to me. I think it's you."

"Yeah, I kinda thought so too," Riverstone grinned, knowing he had won the bet.

Harlowe added a couple of pleasantries to Quay before Simon turned him toward the beach. "We can handle it from here, Dog. Thanks," he told him.

Harlowe nodded a smiling see-ya at Quay before he strolled off through the barrier toward the water, his focus returning to the waves. Riverstone had the distinct impression that he would have walked between Rex's legs if the monster had been standing between him and the beach.

Riverstone was about to turn to Quay with a big, gloating smile when the look on her face said it all. Their world or hers, she was awestruck by Harlowe's performance. Her eyes didn't leave the young Captain as he put his board in the water and began paddling out to catch his first wave.

Simon had a hard time translating. "What's that mean?" he asked Riverstone.

Riverstone chuckled. "It means any thoughts we had about asking her out on a date just went to zero."

"How do you know?"

"Because I've seen that look before when Lu watched him leave the beach that day your boat capsized. It was the same goo-goo-eyed stare. It's a done deal, Rerun. Harlowe's in, we're out."

"We'll see," Simon stated coldly.

"You're wasting your time, Rerun. I tried to tell you that with Lu. Harlowe doesn't lose. Period. End of story." He nodded at Quay. "Look at those big, doey eyes. The girl is hooked, I tell ya. It's over for us, dude."

Simon's eyes narrowed. "He'll lose this time. I'll change her mind."

"Not going to happen, Rerun, but go ahead. Give it your best shot. You'll have an easier time ripping off Rex's dinner from him tonight." He stared deep into Simon's eyes. "Or you can think of it as a dream, and you just woke up. The best you can do is hope and pray she has a sister that's half the babe she is, and maybe, just maybe, you'll snatch her away before I see her first."

Quay turned to Riverstone and Simon, interrupting their small debate. She stared at them for a long moment as if wishing she could tell them something they would understand. Unable to communicate, she thanked them with a gracious nod and walked away. Not far down the beach, she sat in the sand near the water's edge, her eyes never leaving the surfer gliding across the glassy wave on his baby-blue board.

21

The Ringer

THE WARM, BURNT-ORANGE sun of Barnard had set behind them. It had been a fun-filled day of bodysurfing, volleyball, shooting targets, and playing the cello, flute, and harpsichord. It had even rained briefly, making the jungle fresh and clean again. The drops were so warm and light that playing in it was actually enjoyable. When the weather did clear, they set up the ball field outside the perimeter so any high flies they hit wouldn't strike the underside of the hull and interfere with a ball in play. The Gamadin ballgame had some minor rule changes that made the game more challenging. The pitcher was a robob they called "Mr. Heat" who threw bullet fastballs from sixty feet away. Mr. Heat could even pitch curves and sliders like a real Major League pitcher.

Monday played the outfield, Harlowe was at shortstop, and Molly, the girl-bob, was at first. Jewels stood patiently on the sidelines, ready to fetch any orders for food or drinks. Harlowe's team had a 4-to-2 lead going into the last inning. Only humans were allowed to bat, however, because the robobs never struck out and tended to hit the ball too hard. The clickers either cracked the baseball when they hit it or they hit it so far it made playing the game absurdly difficult, especially trying to cover a mile of open beach!

Simon made the first out, striking out on three straight pitches. Ian then singled, a blooper between Harlowe and Monday. Riverstone blasted the first pitch past Harlowe's outstretched hand so hard that the ball would have torn his hand off had he caught it. It was Simon's turn again and like before, he was quickly put down on three strikes for the second out.

Simon gestured toward the robob pitcher, who wore a blue Dodger jersey and hat. "That was an illegal pitch, puke!" he shouted at the stick-pitcher.

"Sit down, Rerun!" Harlowe shouted back. "Mr. Heat has cleaned your clock all day."

"Yeah, because he's throwing spitballs, that's why," Simon countered.

Then Ian knocked one through the middle, passed a diving Harlowe, who thought he had it but came up with nothing but sand. After that Riverstone promptly nailed another fastball, driving in their third run. The score was now 3 to 4, with Simon up to the plate again. Riverstone and Ian were both resigned that Simon would be the third out.

"Strike out and you walk back to Earth, Rerun," Riverstone warned Simon.

"Don't worry. I can do it," Simon replied.

The first pitch was an aspirin. Riverstone wondered if Simon ever saw the ball slap the robob's glove.

"I wasn't ready," was Simon's excuse.

"How can you not be ready?" Ian wanted to know.

"Shut up. I can—"

Whap!

The second pitch slammed into the mitt and the robob umpire held up two pincers.

Strike two, the umpire called...

"Pay attention, Rerun. At least swing the bat, butthead," Riverstone barked. He hated to lose as much as Harlowe.

Simon was about to launch his bat into the jungle without waiting for the embarrassment of a called third strike when Quay quietly stepped to the batter's box.

After watching Harlowe's shooting lesson earlier, Quay seemed satisfied watching the game from the sidelines. She had been enjoying the bonfire, munching on Dodger dogs and chips when it looked as though she wanted to join the game.

She said something to Simon, but of course no one understood a word she was saying.

"I think she wants your bat, Rerun," Ian suggested.

"Give it to her. We could use the help," Riverstone stated flatly.

Grudgingly, Simon offered her his bat. "Is this what you want, Hon?" he asked her.

Quay nodded politely and took his bat.

"Do you mind if she pinch hits for Mighty Casey?" Riverstone asked Harlowe across the field.

Harlowe returned a thumbs-up. "Go for it," he replied with a wide smirk of overconfidence.

Quay then stepped up to the plate, looking somewhat confused about how to properly hold the bat. Riverstone had to guide her to the proper position in the batter's box. Next he demonstrated the proper placement of her hands around the bat and where to hold it above her shoulder. She looked a little awkward, but that was the best he could do. Barnard was already down and it was getting pretty dark out. He didn't have time to properly train her in the fine art of hitting. He just wanted her to make contact and hope for the best.

"We need a couple of practice swings, Dog," Riverstone said.

Harlowe motioned for Mr. Heat to take a little off. Seventy miles an hour should be plenty fast for the final out. Mr. Heat wound up and let fly a soft one, hip high, down the pipe. Quay's eyes seemed to focus so intensely on the ball, Harlowe wondered if she wasn't counting the stitches on the cowhide as it came whizzing toward her.

CRACK!

Jaws dropped as the ball flew into a high parabolic orbit down the beach. The grin on Riverstone's face told the story. They had a ringer!

Harlowe nodded to Mr. Heat and the next pitch blew in over ninety.

WHACK!

The ball whizzed past Harlowe's ear, nearly taking his head off. Monday didn't even bother trying to catch it. After three more pitches, each over a hundred miles per hour, Riverstone signaled that he thought Quay had practiced enough.

"Ya think?" Harlowe cracked. His face had lost its cockiness and was replaced with deep concern. He stepped over to Mr. Heat and whispered to the clicker, "Low and hard outside, big guy. No holding back." He pointed, "That's an order." He returned to his position and readied himself. Mr. Heat let go a 120-mile-per-hour missile.

SMACK!

Harlowe and Monday stood helplessly by as the ball sailed over their heads. It was the longest ball anybody had ever seen hit on a near-Earth-gravity planet. The robob outfielder made a gallant effort to spear it out of its low orbit, but even a hundred-foot leap was yards short. Nine hundred feet later, the ball thumped into the sand. The robob umpire twirled his pincer in the air indicating it was a four-bagger. The grand slam home run made the final score 7 to 4. Harlowe threw his mitt in the sand as Quay's teammates lifted her up on their shoulders and carried her over to the firepit, where they shook up a cold soda and sprayed the suds over the top of her head.

22

Mr. Heat's Hat

"LET'S PARTY!" SIMON yelled after the victory lap around the field.

Everyone moved from the ball field to the beach, where the robobs had already built a blazing campfire surrounded by beach chairs in the sand. Nearby, the SoCal buffet was laid out on blue tablecloths, while keyboards, guitars, and flutes were tuned and ready on the moon-shaped stage. Riverstone grabbed another soda from the ice chest and handed it to Quay. "When we get back to Earth, you'll make a fortune playing for the Dodgers, girl!"

Simon then presented her with a black-and-white *Distant Galaxy* baseball jacket that was an exact replica of the one he wore on the set. She thanked him with a slight bow. Then Riverstone gave her his prized possession: his Derek Jeter mitt.

During the awards ceremony, Quay was gracious in her thanks but hardly emotional over her gifts until, to everyone's chagrin, Harlowe stepped up and placed Mr. Heat's Dodger cap on her head. As if she had been crowned Miss Universe, her large, dark eyes beamed with joy.

Simon and Riverstone were thunderstruck by it all. They traded hurt puppy-dog frowns, feeling more like gomers than winners when Harlowe said to her, "To the victor go the spoils."

Quay didn't understand a word anyone was saying, just as when the soda was sprayed over her head. She seemed to understand from all the laughter and attention that she was being congratulated; she just didn't know the reasons why. She went along with the wet hair and back slaps like a good sport, no doubt wondering why she was being treated in such a peculiar way.

As for the buffet of goodies, Quay needed no translation. Being the out-of-town guest, Harlowe jokingly thought she might require a special menu of monkey brains and seaweed pickles. However, after watching her down an animal-style double-double faster than Squid, he was satisfied her needs were being met just fine. As thick and juicy as the food was, she relished it daintily like a queen. She didn't drip a single grease bomb off her chin or use a napkin to clean her face. After two foot-long Dodger Dogs and six tacos with guacamole and salsa, she was still batting a thousand. Riverstone commented that he had never seen anyone eat more than he did, until now.

The music and laughter continued into the wee hours without a hitch until Simon tossed a dead branch onto the hot coals to stoke the fire. Maybe the branch was too sappy or it wasn't dry enough, but whatever the cause, the sparks exploded when the limb hit the flames. No one panicked. Ian and Riverstone casually lifted their Dodger Dogs to avoid getting any black bits on them. Harlowe flicked an ember or two from the surfboard lying behind his beach chair. Before Quay was fried, Monday heroically grabbed a towel and put out the fiery bits from around her feet. Everyone came away unscathed except for Simon. The crowd went wild when a hot one dropped down the back of his trunks. His screams of terror were loud enough to frighten even Rex away from the barrier. How the embers got down his pants no one was certain, since his back was away from the fire. But the gyrations and foot-stomping he went through before diving headfirst into the ocean was the beginning of a beach party none of them would ever forget.

After the dueling pianos, Rex's foot-stomping with the rock-and-roll guitars, and the food fights between Riverstone and Simon, Quay stood before the fire as though she wanted to make an announcement of her own. Of course, no one understood a word she trying to say.

Ian, however, found a solution when he had a clicker deliver a com unit to the party. With some clever tricks and a few tweaks of the com's projector, he managed to get a readable holo-screen to materialize above the fire. As Quay spoke, her words were instantly translated into English for everyone to see.

"That's so cool, Wiz," Monday said, astounded by his ingenuity. "Does it work both ways?"

Ian glared back as if it were a given. "Duuuh!" He then turned to Quay and pointed to the screen over the fire. "Go for it."

Her response was immediate. "I am called Quay," she began.

Ian sat back in his chair and licked the brown deli mustard from the end of his slightly charred Dodger Dog before it dripped onto his lap. "Yeah, we know," he said casually, "and you come from a planet called Tomar."

Quay's large, dark eyes displayed her astonishment that her name and home world were already known.

Ian assured her there was nothing sinister in the disclosure. It was only a guess, but since Millie understood her language, it was only logical that she knew where her home world might be located.

Quay looked around the campfire. "Where is Millie?"

Ian pointed up. "She's our ship."

"Yes, that is logical."

Riverstone then continued with a brief narrative on how she had come to be on their ship. When he finished, he ended by introducing everyone around the fire, starting with himself. "My name is Riverstone," he said slowly as if talking to an uncivilized being.

"She's smarter than you, Jester," Simon cracked, "Speed it up."

"Shut up, toadface," Riverstone snarled back.

Monday pointed to the holo-screen. "That made an impression."

"His mother calls him Matthew," Ian added, chuckling.

"Cool it!" Harlowe barked, stepping away from the piano. "Let Jester finish his intros."

Riverstone nodded his appreciation. "Thanks, pard."

After a couple of minor digs, Riverstone continued. "The smart one is Ian. Everyone calls him Wiz, including his mother." The joke got a small laugh from the crowd but not from Quay. She didn't get it. "Monday is the big dude over there with all the empty wrappers around him. His nickname is Squid."

Monday bowed his head, picking up his trash as he bent over. "A pleasure, ma'am," he said in his resonating baritone.

Riverstone continued: "The greasy one with a tan is Rerun. Watch out for him. He'll try to to make you into a movie star."

Simon tossed a fry at Riverstone's head. "She would be a superstar overnight, too, butthead."

Finally, Riverstone turned to Harlowe, who had now parked himself on a surfboard. "The big kahuna sitting there is—"

"A brave warrior," she uttered in awe, interrupting him.

Wearing a new red-with-white-letters Lakewood Football jersey but still in his swim trunks, Harlowe had for the most part remained quiet, letting his crew do the talking.

"Our Captain," Riverstone added. "His name is Harlowe. On his good hair days we can call him Dog. Don't let his cheesy smile fool ya: I taught him everything he knows."

She took a sip of her cookie-dough shake before she went on, her eyes always on Harlowe as she spoke. "You are the Captain of this beautiful vessel?" she asked.

"I am," Harlowe replied in a relaxed way.

"No disrespect, Captain, but you are so young. Was your commission purchased?" she asked him directly.

Harlowe's eyes never wavered. "None taken, Quay." He looked over his crew proudly, "Our places have all been earned."

She drank again, musing over his reply as he observed her manners. They were practiced and refined, those of like someone well-educated and cultured. "How many are under your command?"

"They're sitting here with us," Harlowe replied.

Quay's eyes again displayed their surprise. "For such a grand ship?"

"My crew is the best. It is enough."

"Where do you come from?" Quay asked, looking at Ian.

Ian checked with Harlowe before he answered. From the coolness in Harlowe's face, Ian understood he needed to be cautious. "Our home is far away from here."

Quay seemed to understand their reasons for confidentiality. She did not press them for an answer. Instead, she asked, "Are you soldiers?"

"No, we are explorers," Ian replied. He could think of nothing else more imaginative. Explorers seemed the only logical explanation for a ship traveling far away from home.

Harlowe dipped his head slightly, approving Ian's small stretch of the truth.

"For explorers, you handle weapons quite skillfully, Captain."

"The galaxy is a dangerous place, ma'am," Monday replied.

Quay suddenly became fearful. "As explorers in our quadrant, you may not understand our Rights of Passage then."

"Rights of Passage?" Ian questioned.

Her eyes spoke to each one of the Gamadin. "Without the Rights of Passage, the Consortium can confiscate your beautiful ship," she warned.

Simon scoffed. "Let them try."

"Do not be foolish. The Consortium is the imperial authority of the quadrant. Without the Rights of Passage, a vessel cannot travel within the quadrant. This is the law."

"It's a bad law," Simon grumbled.

"We have our own rights," Riverstone told her.

"By what authority? The Consortium is the only authority."

Riverstone's dad, Evan Riverstone, was a lawyer. As far back as he could remember—"since birth," Riverstone often joked—his dad had drilled into his head the importance of the Declaration of Independence and the UnitedStates Constitution, and what his country's founding documents meant to him. *These documents are sacred, Matthew. They are the rules our country was founded on and cannot be changed by time. They are as important today as they were over two hundred years ago. Don't ever let anyone tell you differently. Your life is your responsibility. The choices you make are yours alone. You make a bad choice, you live it. Don't blame anyone but yourself for the outcome.*

Riverstone thought about Harlowe, looking nothing like the spaceship captain that he was, sitting in his beach chair wearing dark blue No Fear trunks, devouring his second double-double with a bottle of Blue Stuff stuck in the sand by his side next to the two empties he had already downed. *Yeah, Dad, except for Harlowe,* Riverstone chuckled. *Harlowe was always the right dude to blame when things went south because he never denied anything. He always took the heat! So why not blame him?*

Riverstone always remembered one particular thing his father said to him once after a long speech about what Life, Liberty, and the Pursuit of Happiness meant. *You have the right to travel anywhere unimpeded by anyone. No government has the right to take that away from you. It is God-given, son...*

"As free travelers of the galaxy, we recognize no borders," Riverstone replied simply.

Quay almost laughed at the thought. "No one is free to travel without Consortium consent."

"We are," Riverstone stated.

"I ask again, by what authority?"

Riverstone touched the holographic edge of the screen. "By this authority!" An instant later, an ancient document materialized above the fire. It was as wide as two arm's lengths and tall as Monday. The handwritten parchment was old and yellow and written in faded ink with a flowing hand. At the bottom of the document were fifty-six names that had "mutually pledged to each other, our Lives, our Fortunes, and our sacred Honor." One signature, John Hancock's, was quite flamboyant and easily read.

Each Gamadin stood at attention and saluted the document as Riverstone spoke proudly. "This is our right. No Right of Passage is above this law."

"RIGHT ON!" the Gamadin cheered together.

Quay stared at the document, confused, studying the parchment from top to bottom. "I do not recognize the script. What does it say?"

Ian apologized. Although he had covered the spoken word, he had neglected the written part. "Translate our sacred words for Quay, if you please, Millie."

An instant later, the ancient script changed before her eyes to one she could easily read. Slowly, she removed Mr. Heat's hat and let it drop on the sand. Something more important had replaced Harlowe's trophy. For the better part of an hour, Quay remained in front of the document, mesmerized by its words and meaning, looking at every stroke of the pen as though committing each letter to memory.

When she was done, her eyes seemed glassy and troubled as if she had had a life-changing experience. Harlowe was the only one left around the campfire. All the others had drifted on to bed.

"It affects me that way every time I read it," Harlowe said. He went to the buffet table and offered her another shake. "Would you like another cookie-dough?"

"Please."

The dim glow of the dying coals, mixed with the muted blue light from Millie's perimeter barrier, cast a ghostly radiance around the campfire. Harlowe handed Quay the shake as he sat down beside her on a towel with a curious symbol that caught her attention. "I have seen this symbol."

Harlowe eyed the symbol of Millie's profile crossing in front of a star. "It's everywhere on our ship."

"Do you know its meaning?" Quay asked.

Truth was, Harlowe had never given the symbol much thought. He made a mental note to ask Millie later. His explanation was brief. "It is part of our ship."

"When I was a child, my mother would often tell my sister and me of an ancient legend surrounding a symbol much like this. It was the symbol of mighty galactic warriors called Peacemakers. Have you heard of the Peacemaker legends?" Quay asked.

Harlowe had never heard of anyone called Peacemakers. "Warriors, you say?" he asked.

Quay seemed to enjoy sharing their story with Harlowe. "Yes, they were very mighty soldiers of peace. It is said they had the power of the galactic core to give them strength." Quay's gaze turned toward *Millawanda* in admiration. "It was said that a single Peacemaker ship could destroy an empire."

"Cool. What happened to them?"

Her eyes returned to the fire to an almost dreamlike world. "They were gone eons ago."

"They sounded like pretty bad dudes."

Quay wiped the smile from Harlowe's mouth when she glared back at him. "No, they fought for the good of all," she corrected, not understanding his slang.

Harlowe smiled apologetically, making another mental note to watch his replies.

A long silence passed before Harlowe decided maybe it was time to ask his guest about what had happened to her ship.

Quay's large dark eyes turned down the long, deserted beach. "A great madness will soon overtake our quadrant unless something is done."

Harlowe stared straight ahead, without a blink. The memory of that night in Newport when the Fhaal stormed the Marses' beach house, the sight of the ugly Dakadude commander, and the wild beast he unleashed on them in the canyon in Utah was still fresh in his mind, as though it was yesterday.

He didn't need to answer the question. Quay saw the death in Harlowe's eyes.

"You have faced our enemy?" Quay asked.

"We call them Daks," Harlowe admitted. "They murdered our friends."

Quay's eyes filled with tears. "As they have mine, Captain," she said solemnly. The hate in her tone was thick. "Over many passings they have overtaken the outer frontiers of our quadrant. My father believes this is only the beginning."

Harlowe understood corrupt governments. "I fear he is right. They should be stopped."

"My father is very wise. His Jo-Li Ran is powerful."

"Why are you so far away from Tomar, Quay?" Harlowe asked.

Quay drank her shake before she answered. "It is personal, Captain..." was all that she said as her focus drifted into the night, along the shoreline.

Harlowe figured this was as good a time as any to call it a night. There was a ton of questions he wanted to ask her, but they could all wait. He was tired. He stood and yawned, kicking over Riverstone's beach chair in the process. The yellow crystal Riverstone found at the crash site dropped out of the small pocket on the side of the chair.

Quay became instantly concerned and grabbed it from the sand. "Where did you get this thermo-grym?"

"This is thermo-grym?" Harlowe asked. He already knew its qualities. Ian had come to him with the sample analysis a week ago. He'd stopped him in the corridor to explain what he had found about Riverstone's rock.

"In simple terms, Dog, it's a yellow quartz. You've seen it around in the rock shops. Earth has a ton of it. Anyway, according to Millie, if utilized properly, it becomes a highly concentrated source of energy."

"Nuclear big?" Harlowe wondered.

"Bigger," Ian replied.

Harlowe tossed the crystal back like a hot potato.

Ian laughed. "Relax, Dog, you're safe. You couldn't ignite it with a plas cannon. It needs to be processed and fed through a biochemical, thermal conducting chamber first before it becomes radioactive."

In less than a nanosecond Quay had suddenly changed, as though the crystal was some sort of toxic potion, turning her into a mindless, zombie-like creature.

"Where did you get it?" she asked, visibly shaken.

Harlowe wondered what he had said to offend her. "From your ship. Why is it so important?"

"It may already be too late."

Harlowe didn't understand how a yellow rock could affect her so easily, but then he didn't understand a lot of things about women and their emotions. She turned and without saying good night or thanks for the great food and the yuk-yuks, walked away, leaving him alone by a dying fire with a lot of unanswered questions.

He reached down and dusted the sand from Mr. Heat's hat.

"Good night, girl…"

23

CYBOF!

LATE THE NEXT afternoon, Harlowe lumbered in from the beach. After Quay left him by the fire, he curled up next to the surfboard and fell asleep. It wasn't until noon the following day that screeching birds playing in the jungle trees woke him. He spent the next two hours catching waves before hunger pangs forced him in. After a bite to eat, he slipped on a pair of shoes and a fresh Lakewood jersey, white with red lettering this time, and headed down the corridor to Quay's cabin. He still had a lot more questions about her ship and why it was destroyed.

Along the way, he had Jewels fetch Mr. Heat's hat so he would have an excuse to come knocking. He also wanted to apologize for any stupid acts his crew might have performed during the festivities, such as Riverstone's asking her hand in marriage and Rerun's promise of movie stardom, and that was only the short list.

Harlowe hesitated before knocking, remembering how Quay had broken out laughing when he, Simon, and Riverstone started playing old rock-and-roll tunes. She loved it! But it was Simon who brought the house down when he sang his Elvis Presley songs better than the King himself. "Blue Suede Shoes" and "Hound Dog" seemed to be her favorites. She didn't twitch or blink until he was done. *Man, was she gorgeous!* He wished he could sing like Simon. The movie star had a voice that would make Rex roll over and cry. In all this time together, Harlowe hadn't known he had such a talented voice. He laughed again, remembering how much Rex had wanted to join the fun. But before he got too far out of control, Millie stung him with a blue zap to the snout. That was the end of Rex for the night! The dinosaur howled halfway across the planet. He was so loud Ian became frantic, fearing they might have blown their cover.

Harlowe tried to remember if he'd had the gentlemanly forethought to send Jewels with Quay back to her room. He couldn't remember squat. The way her mood had changed after seeing the yellow crystal was certainly peculiar. He did remember that much.

He let loose a long belch, then wiped the spittle from the side from his mouth. "Excuse you, Pylott," he scolded himself.

He then gave the door a lively rap.

No one answered.

He called twice and knocked harder. Again, no answer and no Quay. He felt uncomfortable opening the door without her permission. That wouldn't be cool, he thought, especially if she was still sleeping. Girls liked their beauty rest, he knew, except Lu. She would always rise before dawn to be with him on a glassy morning no matter how long they had been up the night before.

He had to pause a moment to catch his breath. Thinking of Lu was always a little spooking. During his more lonely moments, there were times he heard her voice as he was brushing his teeth, or gliding down the face of a wave, or walking alone in the corridor of the ship. It freaked him out to hear her fun-loving laugh in his mind. On more than one occasion he had actually spoken out loud to her. Never once, however, did he tell anyone about these *silly* thoughts, not even Ian.

If Quay isn't in her room, then where is she?

He went to the nearest intercom and asked Ian to check on her whereabouts.

"She's not on the ship at all, Captain," Ian replied, after a few moments of checking. He then added, "She must be outside."

Harlowe found the closest blinker and popped down to the sand on the sunrise side of the ship nearest the shoreline. He didn't see her anywhere. He walked out onto the beach and saw no one in either direction. He called out several times for her and received a few bird screeches in reply.

Worried, he blinked back to the bridge in a panic.

"You didn't find her?" Ian asked.

Harlowe was sweating bullets as he moved directly to the sensor screens. "No, I didn't see her anywhere."

"She can't be far," Ian said, joining the effort beside him.

Harlowe's fingers deftly adjusted the controls. "Where is she, then? She's not around the ship, Wiz."

"Check farther out."

"There!" Harlowe pointed at the tiny blue dot on the screen. "That's her bio signature, isn't it?" Her movement was slow, as if going for casual stroll along the beach.

Ian's eyes went round. "After last night, you would think she understood about Rex."

"Where is he?"

Simon materialized onto the bridge, just as Harlowe and Ian were frantically scanning the surrounding jungle for everyone's favorite uninvited guest. "Who's in trouble?"

"Quay's out taking a stroll during Rex's snack time," Ian replied.

Simon suddenly caught the panic. "He never stops eating!" He slid between them, and took over the controls. Because it was his station, he knew the shortcuts. He touched a slide control and zeroed in on the giant T-rex. After a couple of quick corrections, he had his target. "There! That's Rex's sensor I.D." His finger tapped the bright yellow image of the reptile as it moved through the jungle. "He's about a mile in back of us, and from the way he's behaving, something else has his attention."

Harlowe didn't need to see more. He was out the door.

"I'm coming, too," Simon said, coming after Harlowe.

Harlowe pointed. "No! Stay with Wiz. Rex may change his focus," he ordered, just before blinking to the lower level.

* * *

Harlowe throttled the grannywagon forward the instant the rover touched down. Once past the perimeter, it wasn't long before he found her walking casually along the beach. "You should be able to see her now," Ian's voice said to Harlowe over the rover's com.

"Aye, I have her," Harlowe replied. "Where's Rex?"

"He's still occupied with another Happy Meal. Maybe he's found a double-cheese," Simon quipped.

Harlowe silently brought the wheelless rover to a stop a hundred yards from Quay. She seemed more caught up in the peaceful beauty of a shoreline stroll than what was going on around her. Barnard's large red disk was rising behind the giant palms as a delicate offshore breeze feathered the tops of the breaking waves.

He scanned the surroundings. Rex wasn't the only danger. He was just the most obvious. A triceratops and two of her young were munching on ferns at the edge of the jungle. They seemed quite content, chewing away at the greenery and not at all interested in any humans. A small pteranodon glided overhead looking for breakfast, while two brightly colored birds, not wishing to be part of that breakfast, squawked, ducking for cover under the wide canopy of ferns.

He turned back to Quay, who was walking along the beach. The gentle shore break was playing tag with her feet. He filled his lungs, relieved that he had arrived in time and all appeared normal and peaceful. Maybe she hadn't realized how far she had wandered, he thought, giving her the excuse as to why she had left the safety of the ship.

"Don't forget your communicator, Captain," Ian warned with a little motherly advice.

Harlowe patted his utility belt. "Aye," he replied, never taking his eyes off Quay.

The afternoon was so peaceful, he thought. Why ruin the moment by looking like Clint Eastwood gunning for bad guys?

He released his belt and laid his pistols across the seat before he fast-paced down the beach to get her. Along the way he straightened up a little, adjusting the white sleeves on his jersey and matting down his hair. By the time he was close enough to call to her, he had himself together. Quay was kneeling down, picking up a large conch shell. The instant she heard his voice, any doubts he had that he was unwelcome were cured by one look of her large, dark eyes. Her face lit up like the morning sun. Noticing his effect on her, he stood straight, tweaked his cuffs again, and casually walked the rest of the way with an ear-to-ear smile.

"It's pretty," he said to her, never feeling the incoming surge drench his shoes. When she looked at him, the afternoon sun cast a deep warmth over her face, shooting hot arrows through his heart.

Wow!

She spoke to him, but without the computer her words were gobbledegook. They were pleasing sounds, however, tonally graceful and melodic. She handed him the conch as he lost touch with everything else around him.

He took the shell and thanked her with an easy smile. He had the sudden urge to hold her in his arms and kiss her long and passionately.

From the look in her eyes, the feeling was mutual. How incredible it was, he thought, the way they had both traveled the vastness of space and were now sharing this moment here on this beach, their worlds light-years apart! *Go figure.* Fate had finally given him a fast-ball, waist-high, right down the middle of the plate that he could hit out of the park!

Batter up, dude!

He reached out to take her in his arms when, just like in a bad movie script, his communicator went off. With a deflated sigh, he let her go and retrieved his com. "What is it?" he asked, his tone a little short.

Ian recognized the irritation. "Well, I just thought you might like to know, Captain, that Rex is coming your way in a hurry!"

Harlowe's mind had not fully disengaged from his fantasy. He stared at Quay with a love-struck grin and asked, "Who?"

Ian's voice screamed from the communicator. "REX, DOG! AS IN T-REX DINOSAUR! CYBOF, CAPTAIN! CYBOF! CYBOF!"

Harlowe got the point. Instantly he snapped out of his love-struck fog. CYBOF stood for Cover Your Buns Or Fry. He grabbed Quay by the hand and pulled her toward the rover. She didn't resist. She saw the danger in his face. They had taken only a few steps when the giant carnivore broke out of the jungle, scattering the family of triceratops and a nest of squawky birds.

Harlowe and Quay froze, hoping Rex didn't see them.

Incredibly, Rex seemed preoccupied and unconcerned with the humanoids. The normally sure-footed dinosaur made a misstep and fell flat on his snout. It was almost comical to watch. Then, when things couldn't get any weirder, a magnificent white tiger bolted out of the jungle in hot pursuit of the giant T-rex.

Rex was on the defensive!

Logic seemed to defy why a tiger, though it was the largest tiger Harlowe had ever seen, would attack a beast the size of Rex. It didn't make sense. Rex was fifty times its size. But as hideous and loathsome as Rex was, the tiger was almost mythical in its beauty. It had deep blue eyes and snow-white fur. It was as if Michelangelo had created another masterpiece of flowing, powerful energy from a single white Carrara stone. Except for a couple of large bleeding battle lines across its pelt, the tiger's graceful body was flawless. It had a Bengal tiger's shape, but no tiger on Earth was this size. It was easily double that of any tiger he had seen in the zoos back home, and utterly fearless. Harlowe wondered in awe why it was taking such a chance. Even the largest tigers on Earth would not confront an elephant, let alone the largest meat-eating dinosaur of all time. But on this planet, this tiger, its muscles bulging, rippling behind its ivory fur, fought Goliath!

And it was the aggressor!

From Harlowe's point of view, the tiger was kicking serious booty. When it leaped for Rex's throat, it seemed that the tiger was about to nail the coffin lid on the dinosaur. Such was not the case. Rex's small claws managed to slap the tiger aside, ripping a long gash in its white coat. Green blood gushed from its side. It appeared a major artery was severed.

With blood flowing from its body in such great amounts, Harlowe figured the end was near. When it tried for another swipe at Rex's throat, it slipped. Its wounds had taken their toll. It didn't seem to have the spring it needed to leap out of the way of Rex's powerful hind legs. It wouldn't get another chance, either. Rex was merciless. When the tiger faltered a second time, Rex snatched the tiger in midair with his jaws and brutally threw it to the ground, crushing the masterpiece with its powerful snout.

Then, as if to leave no doubt that it was the victor, Rex bit off the tiger's head and ate it.

Harlowe turned away, gritting his teeth in disgust. Between hard swallows, like an egg cracking inside his throat, he looked at Quay. There was sadness in her eyes. She had cared about the tiger as much as he had. Where anyone else would have fled at the first sighting of the titans, she had remained by his side. He didn't know how to explain it. It was as if she had somehow always been by his side and would always be there, even during the roughest times. Other than his mom, Harlowe knew only one other girl as man-up as she. Quay was like Lu in so many ways: strong, caring, and stubbornly fearless.

Still licking the blood from his fresh kill, Rex suddenly looked directly at them. It had finished one meal and saw dessert a few yards away.

Harlowe reached for his pistols. *Great!* He'd left them in the rover. He recalled somewhere in the back of his mind the General scolding him, *How many times do I have to tell you soldier, you never ever go anywhere without protection!*

Harlowe looked beyond the beast. His pistols were right where he had left them: on the front seat.

Retrieving them was out of the question. When Harlowe took one step toward the rover, Rex charged!

24

Run, Puke

QUAY YANKED HARLOWE toward the jungle. This was no time for heroic last stands. Rex was making every effort to run them down. Fortunately for them, the battle with the tiger had taken its toll on the giant beast's jackrabbit start. Great quantities of dark green blood gushed out from the side of his shoulder. Rex stumbled again, allowing them just enough time to cross the beach and into the jungle. Maybe he would fall over and die before they had to deal with him. Harlowe could only hope.

"Die, toad!" Harlowe shouted back over his shoulder. That seemed to anger Rex even more as he struggled to his feet and continued the chase. Rex had other ideas, and dying wasn't one of them!

As they broke through the thick underbrush, Harlowe reached for his communicator, knowing that only his crew could help them now. He found nothing but his belt. The com was gone. Somehow he had knocked it off his belt.

Run, you stupid puke! the General screamed in his ear.

So they ran!

The Jurassic beast's thunderous footsteps pounded behind them, closing the gap with every stride, and there was no place to hide.

Out of time and out of ideas, Harlowe shoved Quay inside the base root of a giant tree. It was a reckless gamble. If he could lead

Rex away from her, she might run back to the rover for help. At the very least, her life would be saved.

She looked up at him with pleading dark eyes, resisting his gallantry. She didn't like it. She wanted to stay with him to the end!

"No, Quay!" he shouted, throwing her back a second time as he bolted into the jungle. He didn't have to look back to see if his plan was working. Splinters were whizzing by his head from breaking branches as the ground pounded beneath him.

So he ran.

He ran, pushing back the pain from the prickly undergrowth that slashed his body. He ran forgetting about last night, his aching head, the cobwebs in his mouth. He ran and leaped and ducked under low-hanging branches like he had never run before.

For every ten steps he took, Rex took one. The seventy-yard lead he had was suddenly cut in half when he tripped over a small branch in his path, something he would never have done under normal circumstances.

Rex had him.

Get up, maggot! someone shouted. The General was still with him. He looked around. No one was there. *Of course, he's rock temperature on Mars, stupid! Get up, Dog!* He let out a small chuckle. Even from the grave, General Theodore Tecumsa Gunn forced him beyond his limits.

Harlowe leaped to his feet—"Yessir!"—just as Rex fell, sliding headlong, five feet from Harlowe's backside. The misstep had only bought him a few seconds. Rex was already up and continuing the chase.

To his left, Harlowe spotted a fallen tree that was as long as a football field with a trunk as big as a house. He swerved, making a beeline for the center, where he saw a gap under the massive tree. This was going to be close. Rex seemed to anticipate his plan and leaped to cut him off before he got to the gap. Out of the corner of his eye, the gaping jaws came slamming down.

Harlowe dove.

BOOM!

Rex's giant head rammed the bottom of the trunk, just as Harlowe tumbled to the other side. He jerked his knees up to his face, not a split second before the beast's razor-sharp teeth would have amputated his legs. Harlowe turned and saw the snout continuing to snap at his feet. Small bits of blue shoe stuck between its yellowed teeth.

Harlowe breathed a long sigh. *That was narly!*

With Rex still stuck at the base of the tree, Harlowe stood up. He thought he had a chance of hustling back to the beach for Quay. For a brief moment Rex lay unmoving, his breathing labored, trying to gasp for breath. After a long silence, a sick feeling came over Harlowe. The jungle was too still. He started to wonder if Rex had something more cunning up his wretched brain. Maybe he had finally keeled over and died. *That* was a happy thought!

That option was quickly laid to rest when he looked down the length of the trunk. Rex was crawling over a smaller section of the fallen tree not more than fifty yards away. *Who said dinos were brainless?*

Harlowe ran.

He ran with nine tons of ticked-off T-rex right back on his tail. After all that, he hadn't gained a step!

Now up ahead, a small ravine appeared in his path. It was easily fifty feet across and twice that deep. The gap was too wide to leap across by a factor of ten in his condition. Along its sides, rope-like vines hung down from the thick overhanging branches. If he could grab one of those and swing across, he thought even a dying dino as smart as Rex would have second thoughts about leaping the fissure after him.

Coming to the edge of the ravine, Harlowe didn't have the luxury of testing the best vine for the job. He leaped out and snagged the first one he could and hoped for the best. Halfway across the gap, his hands held but the vine didn't. It slipped, causing him to lose a few feet of altitude. He smacked hard into the opposite side of the ravine.

The impact nearly knocked him out. Only sheer determination, and the fact that long thorny branches looking like daggers were nearby, kept him from letting go of his grip. The graveyard of dead animals below him in various stages of decay shocked him like a gallon of Blue Stuff. If he didn't hang on, he would be a part of their select company.

Fortunately for Harlowe, the vine held. He reached hand-over-hand and lifted himself over the lip of the ravine just as Rex came to a screeching halt on the opposite side. He raised his massive head and bellowed a loud roar of frustration. Harlowe could smell his hot, putrid breath clear across the gap. With his long neck and grisly snout, Rex tried several times to reach over and pluck Harlowe from the rim. Harlowe was so exhausted that for a moment, he forgot how close Rex actually was. All Harlowe wanted to do was take a normal breath again and calm his heart back into his chest. Every muscle in his body was spent. If it were up to him, he'd spend the rest of the day right where he was, flat on his back, looking at the undersides of trees. He didn't care if Rex grabbed a vine and swung himself across to get him. He was through running.

After a few well-deserved moment of rest, Harlowe managed to gather enough strength to stand and look at Rex's hideous face. "Up yours, maggot breath!" Harlowe shouted across the ravine.

After what had happened back at the tree trunk, Harlowe hadn't learned his lesson. Taunting an angry dinosaur was hardly the way to gain respect.

Rex went berserk. He was one second from launch. His side was still oozing buckets of green as he paced back and forth, almost losing his footing more than once when he tried to find a way across the ravine. Rex wanted Harlowe more than life itself. Nothing on the planet was going to stop him from attaining his goal . . . not even the ravine.

"That's right, stupid," Harlowe cajoled, hoping the stupid beast would give it a shot and try the leap. "Get a little closer and fall right down there, puke!" Harlowe pointed. "That would finish that ugly carcass of yours for good."

With another ear-shattering roar, Rex announced to the world that he had reached his limit. As he paced back and forth along the edge, he appeared to look down as though the gap was becoming less of an obstacle. He backed his massive hulk away from the lip about thirty yards as if he was going to make a run for the ravine. Harlowe stared in disbelief. Whoever said dinosaurs were pea-brained beasts was sadly misinformed. They could be smart, cunning, and feverishly tenacious when it came to tracking down and killing their prey.

"No way, dude!" Harlowe cried out. "You're not thinking about—" Before he could finish his sentence, Rex charged ahead like a steam locomotive toward the open gap, with Harlowe looking on in helpless amazement.

Rex had the speed!

Dude! He's going to do it!

Harlowe wasn't about to wait for the outcome. He bolted through the jungle, pushing and breaking branches as he went. When Rex crashed down, the force was so great and the ground shook so hard, it knocked Harlowe off his feet.

Rex landed snout first, clearing the opposite edge with plenty to spare, sliding through the thick underbrush, out of control. For a moment the T-rex appeared as stunned as Harlowe. He seemed to lie there, looking skyward at Barnard's big red sun in an astonished daze.

Harlowe picked himself up and ran.

What else could he do? He was running out of tricks. Rex made the Terminator seem languid. How far could he go? Three hundred miles in a day if he was wearing his SIBA, or maybe if he wasn't running through a thick, humid forest that sucked the energy out of him, he could do a hundred miles flat out without the SIBA. But being chased by a dinosaur that bulldozed paths through thick jungles and jumped ravines? He would be lucky to make it another hundred yards!

He needed a break!

His legs were ragged stumps. If anything larger than an ant crossed his path, he would trip and break his nose. How far could he go? he asked himself. Another fifty yards, and that was it! He would have to crawl on his hands and knees after that. All Rex had to do then was step on him like an irritant bug and bite off his head. His pain would be gone forever!

Shut up, Dog, stop thinking like a gomer!

If Harlowe thought things couldn't get much worse, he was wrong. When he broke out of the jungle and into a wide clearing, suddenly things went from bad to the end of the line. On the other side of the clearing was the rim of a canyon that not even Tarzan could swing across on his best day. It was two football fields wide and twice as deep, straight down. It made the previous ravine seem like a pothole.

Harlowe ran to the edge, hoping there was a way down off the cliff: a footpath, a hanging vine, a crack to hang from, anything that would allow him to escape. His face went slack. There was nothing! The rock face was too steep for a mountain goat. In his condition and without his claws there was no way he could grip the side of the rock ledge and live. He was trapped.

He thought for a nanosecond of throwing himself off the cliff rather than being eaten like the tiger, but he couldn't do it. He turned around from the edge, resigned to give it his best shot. Confronting the General at the Pearly Gates for giving up so easily was a far worse consequence than being eaten alive. Picking up the largest stick he could find, which was more like a flimsy twig, he faced the beast. If Rex could laugh, he would have a belly roll over his nothing-else-available weapon.

Harlowe crouched to a ready position. If he was going down, he was taking an eye or two in payment.

The ground shook as Rex burst into the clearing and stopped, his massive head dipping and tilting from side to side in a groggy sway. The giant dinosaur had Harlowe trapped. He was close to death, but he wouldn't go down, not until he got what he came for.

"Die, toad!" Harlowe yelled, flaunting his impotent stick. "Die, you stupid puke!"

Rex staggered closer, globs of green blood splotching the ground at Harlowe's feet. Harlowe swung, smacking the snout with his stick and leaping out of the way before Rex grabbed a piece of him. The massive head faded backward, drifting in and out of consciousness. Harlowe struck again and again. He went for an eye but missed. He could see the life draining from the giant head, but still he wouldn't drop. Rex caught himself again, his black irises refocusing like an auto-focus lens on a camera adjusting to light. He came back, as if he had been given new Duracells.

"Die!" Harlowe kept shouting, hoping Rex would yield to his power of suggestion.

To Harlowe's frustration, Rex held steady. His giant maws cocked to one side, Rex stared greedily at Harlowe with his devilish black eyes. There was no need to hurry. His prey was going nowhere. He would savor the long, hard chase and eat the human pest at his leisure.

Rex reared back with jaws wide open to rip Harlowe's head off, when streaks of sizzling blue bolts pierced the monster's head in rapid succession, riddling its brain with a dozen holes. Vile-smelling green blood splattered over Harlowe's face and body. It was all he could do to leap aside as the ten-ton carnivore crashed at his feet... stone-cold dead.

25

Orphans

HARLOWE BACKED AWAY as he stared at the giant head in disbelief. One second later and he would have been toast. It was the second time in as many weeks he had come within a hair's breadth of losing his head. He sighed deeply, collapsing to his knees, his pathetic little stick the only thing keeping him from doing a face-plant into the dirt.

He turned to see where the shots had come from. Blinking a salty crust from his eyes, he had trouble seeing at first. He wiped the green stench away and saw two large, dark eyes looking over at him from the edge of the jungle with extreme worry.

It was Quay.

She was standing next to the rover with both of Harlowe's pistols pointed to the ground. Her hands were shaking. He tried to get up and hold them, but couldn't. His legs were Jell-O. They gave out and he fell back on his haunches, next to the still-twitching Rex. He tried a second time and fell back again, only this time Quay was at his side, helping him rise, transferring his weight onto hers. He thanked her several times, marveling at her strength. Not only could she hit a baseball a country mile, she was strong enough to carry him bodily to the rover.

She smelled wonderful . . . like she had spent the day in a spa. He smelled like road kill and wondered how she could stand to touch him.

Returning to the ship was easy. All they had to do was follow Rex's path through the jungle. He figured that was how Quay found them in the first place. Along the way, Harlowe nearly passed out in the seat next to her. He was in no shape to drive. There were no worries though; she handled the rover as if it were hers.

Harlowe was beyond exhaustion. The cuts along his face and arms were painful. More than that, he wanted a hot shower and a bed to pass out on, exactly in that order.

With his eyes closed and his mind on sleep, he suddenly realized the rover had slowed to a stop. He wondered how they could be back at the ship so soon? They had traveled only a short distance. *Millawanda* was a lot further away. He forced his eyes open. They were still in the jungle. Why was she stopping? *Come on, girl, I'm beat!*

Quay touched Harlowe's shoulder and gave him a hard stare as if to say, *Quiet, Dog, I hear something.*

Harlowe scooted higher in his seat. Somewhere not far off was the weak cry of an animal. *So what!* He was the one who needed attention, not some whiny creature.

Quay grabbed a pistol and climbed out of the rover. Her ears tuned to the direction of the crying animal as she went off into the jungle. Harlowe's eyes rolled skyward. *Why was she doing this? Couldn't she just go back to the ship?* How he wished for an ocean to dive into!

The whining continued for a few moments longer, then suddenly stopped. Thinking she must have found the source, Harlowe sat up, grittng his teeth with anxiety. The thought of having to move again was unsettling. With a heavy sigh, he grabbed the other pistol and exited the rover like a ninety-year-old man with hemorrhoids.

He steadied himself at the side of the rover, grumbling to himself, "She just couldn't drive back to the ship. No, she had to go looking for more trouble!" He bit his lip and moved toward the direction she had gone, grumbling in pain with every step.

This sucks!

Quay was easy to find. She was on her knees under a large fern with a wounded white baby cat in her arms. Dark green blood dripped down onto her lap. Two other white baby cubs were rubbing up against her legs while she attended to the hurt sibling. The white fluffs of fur were each about two feet long and twenty pounds. No more than a week old, he figured. Obviously coming from the dead mother's lair, her cubs were the reason the mother had fought so furiously against such great odds. The other two cubs appeared unhurt.

Harlowe shuffled over to Quay's side and saw the rip in the cub's belly. Its only chance was to get it back to the ship, where the robobs could work their magic.

Harlowe, feeling sympathetic, removed his dirty, bloodstained Lakewood jersey and gave it to Quay, who wrapped the injured baby cub inside. After that, they set off back to the rover, with the other two cubs prancing energetically in lockstep behind them.

Back at the rover, Quay handed the wounded cub to Harlowe before she lifted the other two healthy cubs into the cab. Harlowe felt sheepish holding the bundle in his lap, wondering why he was going along with the rescue. The injured cub's eyes were shut as its belly rapidly pumped in and out, hungry for air. Harlowe squeezed the bundle tighter, trying to reduce the outward flow of blood, and wondered silently if even the clickers could do anything for the little guy.

Harlowe's head suddenly snapped back as the rover quickly came to speed, continuing along the trail left behind by Rex's hot pursuit of him. Quay wasn't wasting any time. Within moments, they were out of the jungle and racing down the beach to the welcome sight of the saucer. Harlowe had already informed Ian of their situation.

Everybody but Ian was waiting at the bottom of the ramp when they arrived. The instant the rover stopped, Riverstone took the bloody bundle from Harlowe's arms. "Man, you stink, brah," he said in a passing comment just before he leaped onto a nearby blinker and winked to sickbay.

Harlowe let out a string of short, four-letter comments as he labored out of his seat and stared at the long ramp extending down from the underside of the ship. At that moment, it seemed a thousand miles long. Monday helped the two healthy cubs out of the cab. When everyone was clear, Simon leaned over and pushed a sequence of buttons on the dash. Two hundred feet up, a hatch opened in the hull and a small tractor beam projected down over the rover. The small wheelless runabout rose and parked itself beside the granny-wagon inside the utility room. The hatch then closed and the seams disappeared.

Harlowe squinted, still looking up, clucking his tongue. "Cool..." After nearly two years of watching it rise and be swallowed up, he was still in awe of its operation.

He took in a heavy breath of fortitude before wobbling stiffly toward the ramp. Simon tried to help him and wanted to talk about his experience, but Harlowe wasn't in the mood for talk or assistance. Each step forward was a struggle while his head screamed obscenities that would make a longshoreman blush. Quite unexpectedly a warm arm came around his waist and lifted him up. He jerked around in protest, but when he saw that the two large, dark eyes weren't Simon's, his mood changed to instant submission. The closer she held him the more his pain faded, as if a clicker had just shot him with a quart of Blue Stuff. As they trudged along, he stared into her eyes. Without thinking, without giving a second thought as to whether she wanted him to or not, he kissed her.

* * *

Simon watched the two of them embracing from a discreet distance. He took a deep breath of pointlessness. He wasn't even a third wheel. He tried to say something, but neither Harlowe nor Quay knew he existed. His shoulders drooped as he made his way up the ramp, walking past them. Riverstone was right, he thought.

Harlowe didn't lose…

26

Sorceror's Moon

QUAY FELT COMFORTABLE in his arms. Her tall and slender, six-foot-five inch form nearly matched his height. A good fit, he thought. He only had to tilt his head slightly to look into her eyes. Though she seemed uncomfortable at first, as though the experience was new, she remained next to him, allowing him to hold her close, molding into his smelly, bloodstained arms. It wasn't long before their connection transcended worlds. It was possible she had never been kissed, he thought. Maybe they showed affection in some other way on Tomar. Maybe they rubbed noses like Eskimos, touched pinky fingers, or licked eyebrows. He didn't know. He wasn't an expert on intergalactic love customs. He was still just a gawky teenage kid, hoping that whatever he had done was universal enough to pass muster without making him some perverted gomer.

Quay cautiously followed his lead and put her arms around him. After the long kiss, of which Harlowe did have a long track record, they continued to look deep into each other's eyes, searching each other's thoughts in a universal language all their own.

Out across the sand to the sea and beyond, it was fully evening now. It had been a long day. One of #2's moons was a bright streetlight. Low on the horizon, its glowing bulb reflected off the water just below the perimeter rim of the ship. The scene was enchanting, created with care from the Sorcerer's magical brew. As an added touch, the charmer had sprinkled the heavens with a riot of glittering stars. Harlowe wondered if the moons had names. He would call the brightest one Quay, in any case, if the Sorcerer didn't mind, of course.

She laid her face on his bare chest. The fragrance of her hair, natural, fresh, and calming, filled his senses, contrasting sharply with his own stench. Was she a sorcerer's dream? He closed his eyes, praying she was not. Would the magic they had together here, this night, be lost if he opened his eyes too soon? Would she be gone forever? He trembled. Was this their fate? Would this moment be *it*? Would this be the last time they would ever be together, or would their days be long and happy like the end of a fairy-tale dream, their magic everlasting?

He shut his eyes harder, wishing it were so.

The air moved around them. In the distance, the palms sang their rustling lullabies to the wind. A bird cawed. A monkey screeched for its mate when a giant moved a tree. The sounds of the jungle returned. All seemed normal again. He felt her breathing. He opened his eyes and sighed gratefully. She was still cradled in his arms, her large, serene eyes gazing up at him, concerned. Wow, they *were* powerful together, more powerful than magic or a sorcerer's spells.

Feeling grateful again that he had survived the day, that he had a beautiful girl in his arms—a keeper, his dad would say—his thoughts turned to home because he wanted to share her with everyone close to him the way he had with...with Lu.

He swallowed hard from the sudden knot in his throat.

Lu was still there in his heart. In so many ways Quay reminded him of her—her courage, her strength, her desire to make the world right again. He missed her every day. He missed her laugh, her charm, her ability to light up a room with her presence. He missed her smell, her soft hair lying across his chest as they sat on the beach watching the waves rumble onto shore at 42nd Street. He sucked into a world of hurt and then let her go, remembering what Mrs. M had told him that Las Vegas night in the desert. *Don't be sad, Harlowe. You must go on without her.*

He blinked a tear from his eyes as he turned to thoughts of his mom and dad and how Buster and Tinker would react to Quay, his new alien friend. He had a vision of Tinker with her warm smile leading Quay away to the couch, where she would show her his baby pictures in front of all the trophies along the living room wall.

He let out a small chuckle thinking of how his dad would have reacted if he were alive. *Where did you say she came from, son? Topeka? No, Tomar, Dad. Never heard of the place. She's a lovely gal, though. Kinda tall and skinny, but wow, she's a looker all right. Good Irish stock, I imagine. Not from this planet, you say? Well, now, what do you think of that, Tink?* His mom would say, *I didn't know the Irish got there before we did.* Everyone would laugh at that, as they welcomed her into the family.

He matched her gaze. Buster would be right, of course. She was a lovely gal, her short dark hair glistening at its ends, touched by moonlight. Yes, maybe someday she would meet his mom and his little brother Dodger.

While thoughts of Lu, home, and Quay wrestled with his mind, his body odor began to intrude on their special moment together. He reeked with dried sweat, cat spit, and green dino-blood. His cuts needed attention, his face needed a chisel to remove the outer layers of dirt, and his blue No Fear trunks, well, they hadn't been changed in two days and would need to be peeled away from his skin. He was a mess!

He blushed, trying to hide his embarrassment with a disarming grin. Quay smiled back, seeming not to care about his dilemma. She was "all-in," taking him as is.

The warm breeze continued to blow across the sand and sea as the waves broke and rumbled to shore. Their sorcerer's moon, with its backdrop of magical stars, had edged its way above the rim of the ship and was out of sight. A second moon was rising behind it to take its place. Then something caught his eye, disturbing the backdrop of stars like an unwanted pest as it came around the backside of the second moon.

For an instant he thought it might have been two shooting stars blinking across the night, like an added offering from the charmer, but common sense told him that meteors don't travel in pairs, and they sure don't make radical turns like that.

The glow of *Millawanda's* defensive shields intensified as the sound of a massive power surge within her roared to life.

They were back on the clock...

27

Unikala

QUAY DIDN'T HAVE to know what Ian's voice was announcing to Harlowe over an unseen loudspeaker to sense the danger. They both grabbed a white ball of fur and bolted up the ramp as the first wave of attack ships streaked down from the heavens. Every time Harlowe stumbled, Quay was there to catch him, shoving him forward up the ramp way and into the corridor. Together they dropped the cubs and raced for the control room, meeting up with Simon along the way.

"Problem, Dog?" Simon asked, seeing the panic.

"We have company, Mr. Bolt. To your station!" Harlowe yelled, running by.

"Aye, Captain," Simon replied. He stowed his personal feelings aside and ran with them. He had a job to do and no time to wonder about "what if."

"Captain on the Bridge!" Monday called out, as Harlowe and Quay stepped off the blinker together.

Ian and Monday were at their stations, standing over the console of dazzling lights and color-filled screens, trying to do everything at once by themselves. A moment later, Simon materialized off the blinker, and then Riverstone appeared a half-second behind him. No one needed to be told what to do. As soon as Riverstone and Simon took their seats they all began working as a team. Quay didn't stand idle, either. She went immediately to the empty chair next to

Simon, helping him to bring all of the Ship's weapons to full power. All Harlowe had to do now was fly *Millawanda* and hope they could break atmosphere before they were shot down like a trapped Nintendo blip. They needed room to fight.

Harlowe slapped his restraints into place. "Status, Mr. Wizzixs?"

"All systems on line, Captain. Landing gear up. Hatches sealed. We are good to go, sir," Ian replied, calmly and efficiently.

The saucer lifted straight up, clearing the tall palm, pivoted 120 degrees, and bolted toward the heavens.

"Mr. Platter, how many uninvited guests do we have?"

"Two entering the atmosphere now, Captain, but we have a dozen more right behind them."

"Aye," Harlowe replied. To Simon he asked, "Do you have them, Mr. Bolt?"

"Aye, Captain. Locked and loaded."

"Do it!" Harlowe ordered, as his fingers danced over the accelerator bars. In a heartbeat *Millawanda* was streaking into the night heavens, headed for deep space. At that same moment, two bolts of blue plasma shot out from the ship's perimeter, vaporizing the two incoming attack fighters as if they were no more than irritant flies.

Harlowe's head screamed with pain. He wanted his shower and time to rest. He had to remember to space out his near-death experiences as he reached for reserves that were way past "E." His fuel credit was way overdrawn. How was he supposed to pilot on a bankrupt card?

Harlowe had Monday steer *Millawanda* around the second moon in an effort to give themselves a little more time to evaluate the situation. He needed some space to think and to set up a plan of action. The attackers, however, weren't going to let them. A dozen or more attack fighters were right on their tail, shooting bolts of yellow plasma as though they had infinite reserves. The attack ships were not like the large, slower moving battlecruisers they had fought before. They were maneuverable, fast, and very, very deadly.

"Where did they come from?" Riverstone asked Ian loudly, looking for someone to blame. "I thought you were watching the sensors."

"I was!" Ian shot back. "They used the moon as a shield."

"It's done, Mr. Riverstone," Harlowe said, and then added, "Find your targets, Wiz, so Mr. Bolt has something to shoot at."

"Aye, Captain," Ian replied.

Before Ian could react, Quay had already displayed the twelve attack fighters on the upper screen.

Harlowe gave her a quick nod of *nice work* before he unexpectedly, and to everyone's surprise, reversed course.

"Are you sure that's wise, Captain?" Riverstone commented, his eyes glued to the screen.

Harlowe grunted a reply. He wasn't in the mood to debate, nor did he appreciate at this moment anyone second-guessing his commands while they were in the heat of battle.

The attack ships anticipated the maneuver and tried to split their squadron into three parts, but it didn't matter. The Gamadin ship didn't miss at this range. Bolts of intense blue light streaked across space, each plasma dart focused on a particular attack ship. Seconds later a series of simultaneous explosions flooded the control room windows with brilliant balls of exploding fire.

Riverstone leaped out of his seat with excitement. "Way to go, Mr. Bolt!" he shouted as he watched the debris of three attack ships turn to cosmic dust before his face revolted, experiencing a whiff of Harlowe odor. "Please, Captain, take your shower!"

"Aye, Mr. Riverstone, I shall."

Quay spoke up, alarmed.

"Translation, Mr. Platter?" Harlowe ordered.

Monday replied, low and troubled. "More ships, sir."

Harlowe closed his eyes, doing what he could to eke out every last synapse of energy he had left in his body while Riverstone inquired as to the number of attack ships.

Quay said something that no one understood. "Thirty," was Ian's quick translation.

"THIRTY!" Riverstone shouted in disbelief. He glanced at Harlowe, who couldn't keep his eyes open if Quay had walked past him in a bikini. "Why do they want us so bad?" he asked, his eyes widening to take in all the blue dots coming their way.

"'Cause we have something they want," Harlowe replied groggily, opening his eyes a fraction.

"Plus we took out one of their warships," Monday added.

"How do they know she's alive?" Riverstone wanted to know.

"They don't," Ian answered.

"They must think she is," Simon added.

Riverstone turned around and looked at Quay's disarming dark eyes as she worked feverishly on the readouts with Simon. She was even more gorgeous under pressure. "She must be important."

With the scent of her hair still firmly in his mind, Harlowe didn't have a spare moment to wonder about those kinds of details. He had a ship to protect and a crew to keep alive.

"Three coming in from the rear," Monday stated, looking down at his screen.

Riverstone turned to Harlowe. "Can you make it?"

"Lote!" a voice responded from behind.

Riverstone looked at Quay, puzzled. Then to Ian he asked, "Translation, Wiz?"

Ian's fingers danced across a lighted panel. He glanced up. "She said 'run!'"

"She has my vote," Simon added.

Harlowe nodded. That was the best he could do. He banked *Millawanda* sharply away from the incoming squadrons and headed in the opposite direction toward the newly named moon called Quay.

The plan was short lived, however, as two more attack squadrons saw through his plan and had already moved to cut off their retreat.

The Gamadin ship wasted no time in vaporizing the first three attackers they met, but after that, the battle took on a new meaning. The rest of the attacking forces seemed to understand they were up against no ordinary ship, for no matter which direction they challenged them, they would be destroyed. After another hour of fierce dogfighting, the attack ships began breaking off their assault. Their numbers were dwindling rapidly. Half the ships were destroyed and many more were crippled, floating helplessly in space without power. Score to date: golden disk 25 destroyed, 10 damaged; attack ships zero. The Gamadin ship from the ancient past had miraculously survived without a scratch.

"I think they've had enough, Skipper," Simon stated, scanning his screens alongside Quay.

Harlowe peeked through what were mere slits in his eyes now. "They had to come from somewhere, Mr. Bolt."

"Transmission, Captain," Ian announced.

"Mother doesn't like us beating up on her kids, Captain," Riverstone said with a pungent edge.

"Put him on, Wiz," Harlowe uttered, his voice raspy and dry.

A humanoid male materialized on the center screen. From what they could tell, he was short and squatty. His hair was long and curly, reminding Harlowe of the wigs men wore in the 18th century. Whether the hair was real or fake was unclear. It was silver-white and down over his shoulders. His powdery white skin appeared to have never seen sunlight. His distinct jaw protruded defiantly. Riverstone remarked that he reminded him of the dweebs his dad dealt with all the time down at City Hall. "Fat, arrogant, and stupid," he added with disgust.

The bureaucrat wore a pukey green uniform with a number of medals across his chest. The ones down his right arm hung loosely and may have been more for decoration than marks of rank or merit. In any case, no one on the bridge believed they had meaning. His round fat face, bulging yellow eyes, and bad teeth were annoying to look at. Harlowe dreaded the idea of having to speak with the being.

Riverstone tried to swallow the vile taste in his mouth. "Ya think he's a relative of Sullivan's?" Harlowe's expression remained focused. "He's ugly enough." He turned to Quay. There was no fear in her eyes, but for the first time he saw in her a fierce, unattractive hate. She knew this being, he thought.

When the being began to speak, the lower corner of the overhead holo-screen displayed the translation like a foreign movie subtitle. "I will speak to the commander of the intruding vessel," the screen read.

Harlowe sat up, and in a commanding voice, he said promptly, "We are not invaders, sir. You are. Your ships attacked us."

"By authority of the Consortium ruling body, I demand to see your Rights of Passage immediately," the being demanded.

"Who are you, toad?" was Harlowe's brief reply.

"I am Unikala, Supreme Commissar of the Consortium fleet," Unikala replied proudly. "I do not recognize your vessel. You are not authorized to be in this section of the quadrant."

Riverstone leaned over to Harlowe and whispered, "He needs a slap."

Harlowe faced Unikala and stated boldly, "We need no authorization. We travel at will."

"You are breaking the law of Omini Prime. You must have Rights of Passage or your vessel will be forfeit."

"Come and take her," Harlowe challenged.

Unikala acted as if Harlowe's remark fell on deaf ears. "It was not our understanding that intelligent life existed in this sector of the quadrant."

"You were misinformed," Harlowe replied, far down the road of lost patience.

"Who do you represent?"

"Ourselves. We are traders," Harlowe stated calmly. "We have come to this star system in search of goods to add to our line of commerce."

Unikala almost laughed. "I demand to see your Rights of Passage."

"As I explained, we travel where we wish. We have no need of a Right of Passage, sir," Harlowe explained.

"Without Rights of Passage, you cannot enter this quadrant, or you will be subject to confiscation of your ship and cargo," Unikala warned him.

Harlowe glanced at Riverstone in disbelief. "He didn't hear me the first time."

Riverstone nodded toward the screen. "Try another language."

Harlowe was done being nice. "Come and take it, butthead!"

"That will impress him," Riverstone quipped.

Unikala hesitated. After losing half of his attack fighters, the Commissar smoothly changed the subject. "Were there any survivors of the ship on the small planetoid?" Unikala asked.

"Did you lose something?" Harlowe inquired.

"Something of great value was stolen from me," Unikala replied. "Our sensors found no trace of the item I seek."

"Bummer. You should be more careful."

"Captain," Ian said in a hushed voice, "we're being probed."

Harlowe gave a quick gesture to cut off the transmission. "Get ready to slap his hand, Mr. Bolt." Then to Riverstone he said, "Take Quay to my quarters. I don't know what he can see here but keep her hidden just in case." After Quay left the bridge, Harlowe nodded for Ian to return Unikala's image to the screen.

"Sorry, dude," Harlowe apologized, "we had a technical glitch." It was an old excuse, but Harlowe didn't care about being imaginative at this point.

"I will not allow you to leave until the item I seek is found," Unikala said. "It will be necessary to search your ship by authority of the Consortium Rights of Passage."

Harlowe nodded, giving Simon the go-ahead to send the slap. In the background, behind Unikala, several crewmen suddenly jumped up from the sparks discharging from their consoles.

Unikala turned, annoyed with the disturbance while an officer was busy directing the crewman putting out the flames. "You defy the Consortium?" Unikala questioned angrily.

"I do," Harlowe replied sharply, then went on and explained, "We have deadlines to meet, orders to fill. Good night, sir. Our little chat is over."

Behind Unikala's eyes Harlowe saw the ire. "I will destroy your ship for such insolence!"

Riverstone saw it coming first. He closed his eyes, knowing Harlowe would never be intimidated. He ate Supreme Commissars for lunch!

Harlowe glanced at Ian. "Is he getting all this, Wiz?"

"Nothing's lost in translation, Captain," Ian confirmed.

Harlowe nodded and stood before the screen, blazing hot. "We're done, toad. I will destroy what's left of your fleet and then nuke your bucket of bolts to subatomic dust if you don't leave this star system immediately."

"That's tellin' 'em, Skipper!" Simon cried out, slamming his fist on the console.

"Shut up, Mr. Bolt," Harlowe barked.

"Sorry, sir," Simon replied, sitting back down.

"You are but one ship," Unikala pointed out.

Riverstone watched Harlowe's eyes turn to slits. *Uh, oh...*

"You will not leave this system alive," Unikala warned sternly.

"Give that toad a shot across the bow, Mr. Bolt," Harlowe ordered.

A few minor adjustments and Simon was ready for the go-ahead.

"Do it," Harlowe commanded.

Simon touched the activator and instantly a brilliant bolt of searing plasma blazed across the open space toward the Consortium mothership. The bridge was too far away to get a direct visual through the observation windows, but on the upper screen optics, everyone on the bridge saw it clearly. The blue bolt cut through the battlecruiser's massive stardrive, blowing the starboard engine clean away from its giant strut.

Harlowe's eyes went round with disbelief. "I said a shot across the bow, Mr. Bolt."

Simon was as surprised as everyone else. "I aimed it across the bow, Skipper, I swear."

Obviously, his Weapons Specialist still needed a little practice.

Harlowe had little choice but to face Unikala as if the destruction was planned. "Quit wasting my time. Next to a good profit, I enjoy a good fight, Commissar. You have one engine left, shall we make it two?"

"What are you called?" the Commander asked, obviously shaken.

"I am Captain Harlowe Pylott, the Dog of War, Killer of Worlds, Destroyer of Supreme Commissars, yet benevolent trader to all who wish us friends. I am many things, Unikala, pick the one you wish to confront," Harlowe replied, his entire body spent. He was sitting upright on borrowed time.

Harlowe gave Ian the sign to cut communications when Unikala raised his hand. "Perhaps I could interest you in a deal. A powerful trader like yourself could be a very valuable addition to our governments. Your ship has great commercial value. What we could offer you are substantial tariff reductions on your Rights of Passage. You would be legal and have the backing of the most powerful Consortium in the quadrant."

For Harlowe the conversation was over. "I'll give *you* a deal. Life. If you follow us or take any more offensive threats against my ship, I will follow through with my promise. Now get out of my sight, toad!"

Harlowe motioned for Ian to cut the transmission. The screen went blank. To Simon he said, "If that ship raises an eyelash toward us, nuke 'em. You don't need my permission," Harlowe ordered. It was a gamble, but Harlowe was certain the Consortium Commissar would not risk losing his battlecruiser or weakening his forces further.

Simon turned back to his station and eagerly followed orders.

* * *

Riverstone was on his way back to his First Officer's chair when Harlowe hit the floor with a muffled thud behind Ian's station. When he came around the center command chairs, Harlowe was passed out cold on the floor.

Riverstone shook his head, wondering how he had managed to stay conscious this long. He then directed Monday to take Harlowe to his quarters, where Jewels and a team of robobs would clean him up and put him to bed. After Harlowe was taken away, Riverstone slid into the center chair as if it were the natural order of things.

"Have they made a move yet, Mr. Wizzixs?" Riverstone asked.

"They're thinking about it, sir," Ian replied.

"Aye," Riverstone confirmed, scanning the overhead logistics. He eased back into the chair and ordered Monday to bring *Millawanda* 180 degrees on her axis before they shot toward deep space like a plasma bullet.

The Consortium battlecruiser made no attempt to stop the golden disk. Harlowe's gamble had worked. With only one stardrive left on his mothership, Unikala made a wise decision. He stayed put while Captain Harlowe Pylott, the Dog of War, Killer of Worlds, Destroyer of Supreme Quadrant Commissars, left the star system.

No one relaxed until Millie moved to hyperlight on a course plotted days before by Harlowe and Wizzixs. Riverstone didn't know exactly where they were headed. Somewhere near Omini Prime, was his guess, on a course hundreds of light-years away from home. A frightening thought for them all. He chuckled as he sat there in Harlowe's chair, reflecting on the insanity of it all. Then his inner guffaw turned into belly laugh, because that's the way Fate had always treated him and Harlowe Pylott... with a laugh.

28

New Gizmo

Harlowe DRIFTED IN and out of another fairy-tale dream, only this one lacked a long white beach with glassy tubes of perfect waves, and there was no Lu. This fantasy was different. It had a beautiful, dark-haired girl caring for his wounds and Jewels, with his usual flair, standing beside the bed holding a tray of double-doubles, golden fries, and blue Gama shakes. The sheets smelled clean and fresh, like sun-soaked cotton hung out to dry under a warm sun. The reeking jungle odors, cat puke, and smelly dino-ooze were gone, washed clean from his body forever. The flowery scent of the dark-haired girl wafted in and out with his consciousness. He wanted desperately to see her face. He tried prying his eyes open but lacked the necessary strength to complete the chore. Never in his life had he felt such frustration. He felt like a casual observer, watching the goings-on from a distant perch, never able to play in his dream.

Like a rudderless boat on a river, he went with the flow, drifting back and forth between the tides of the netherworld until something soft and furry touched him on the side of his face. It was warm and cuddly like his dream. He breathed in a lungful of sweet air, determined this time to break out of his fuzzy confinement and push himself across the threshold to wakefulness.

Suddenly an abrupt change occurred. The warm, fuzzy softness turned rough and irritating, and it began to drive him up a wall. He tried to turn away from the prickly annoyance but the irritant dog-gedly followed him wherever he went. He flipped over and it scraped its raspiness along the back of his neck. He couldn't escape it.

"Get away!" he growled.

In that same moment his big right toe came under the same annoying assault. If only his mind could function long enough to open his eyes, he would nuke the puke to subatomic dust with his Gama-rifle!

"Knock it off!" Harlowe yelled.

Then miraculously his mind snapped on, like an engine cranking over and over before it finally ignites and roars to life. His aware-ness expanded around him as the familiar hum of the ship began to soothe his tormented mind. They were in hyperlight, he thought. He recognized the comforting power of *Millawanda*'s energy flow as she traveled through hyperspace. He grinned with satisfaction. He loved that sound.

His eyes still closed, he felt the soreness inside him rise to his plane of awareness. He cringed, fighting against the aching in his bones. For the first time in months, he felt on par with the first days of running rimmers back on Mars. Every move he made, even the smallest twitch, transformed into gut-wrenching pain.

He tried to slip back across the threshold to his dream. Maybe if he went back to sleep, the pain would go away. However, the abrasive demon persisted and wouldn't let him relax enough to sink back into his world with the dark-haired girl and double-doubles. The annoy-ance returned with a vengeance, digging and grinding his patience to a dangerously close nuclear detonation.

JEWELS! MY PISTOL! WHERE IS IT?

He reached out and grabbed the fuzzy fur, pushing it from his face. Whirling madly, flinging his arms about, battling the beast, he opened his eyes and found himself face-to-face with two large blue eyes, surrounded by puffs of white fur. "What the..." he tried to say as he made his eyes focus on the white ball of fluff staring him in the face.

What is it?

Gears in his head began to creak. Slowly one cog moved, then another, and another, and another until enough were working to create an energy synapse inside his brain. His head felt like a freight train had lumbered through, jumped the tracks, and lumbered off into another direction without an engineer. Brain cells crackled awake, and little by little small pieces of grey matter began to jell. He remembered the Consortium bureaucrat, his giant mothership, and the attack fighters they'd destroyed. After that, he remembered nothing. He wondered momentarily if *Millawanda* and his crew had survived. He looked around the room and saw that everything was as it should be. His baseball mitt and bat were in the corner. His Stradivarius violin with its bow was against the wall, exactly where it should be. The holograph pictures they had taken of themselves skiing on Europa, with the giant Jupiter behind them, hung right where it belonged on the wall. Next to it was the photo of them posing like tourists with the spectacular rings of Saturn in the background when they landed on Mimas for lunch and rover rides. All that was right. Pictures of his mother and father on their wedding day were there as well, along with Dodger and him in their baseball uniforms. Dodger's was Little League and Harlowe's was high school. There was one of Lu, too, during their happy days. He had found it on the Internet. Some paparazzi had taken it of them, walking together in their bathing suits off the coast of Corfu.

Yes, his room was cool, he told himself.

He rubbed a ball of fur at his side. It was one of the cubs he and Quay had found back on #2. The other one was resting comfortably at the foot of his bed. Rex! How could he forget him? The dinosaur almost had him for dinner before Quay nuked the toadface. *Way to go, babe!* After that near-death experience, he remembered how Quay had found the cubs and brought them and the third, injured, cub back to the ship. He wondered how the little critter was holding up.

Suddenly a thought made his heart skip a beat. *Quay!* He prayed she hadn't been a dream. He closed his eyes, reaching back to before the Consortium attack ships had disturbed their sorcerer's moment at the bottom of the ramp. He saw small things around the room he hadn't noticed before: a pair of shoes that wasn't his, a flower lying on the bedside table near him, the scent of her freshness lingering in the air. He smiled, satisfied his dream was real after all.

After a few more moments of jelling, he turned his attention to the cubs. With an infectious grin of encouragement, they bounced to his side and began licking his arms and face again. He didn't mind it this time, knowing who they were. But if he was going to have any skin left, he needed to refocus their attention away from him. After some calming scratches behind their ears, their throaty motors purred with pleasure from kitty heaven.

Mission complete, he left the sleeping cubs on his bed as he wandered into his bathroom and ordered the shower to full blast. It took some time but an hour later, he emerged from his room with a fresh new uniform, ready to meet the galaxy!

* * *

"Captain on the bridge!" Monday announced.

"Captain!" Ian said, pleased to see him.

Harlowe sauntered through the doorway, making his way casually to his command chair. "How long was I out?" he asked.

Ian glanced at his watch. "Three days."

"Three?" Harlowe questioned, eyeing but not really watching the starscape. "Did I miss anything?"

"Saying goodbye to Uni," Riverstone quipped, moving out of Harlowe's seat.

Harlowe sat down. "You gave him my apologies?"

"With a bouquet of flowers."

Harlowe grinned, turning his attention to the cubs that had followed him out of his cabin. "Cute, aren't they?"

Ian pushed an overly friendly cub away. "Yeah, what happens when they get big?"

"We get a bigger litter box," Harlowe replied, already resigned to the fact that they had already become part of the ship.

Simon reached down to pet a white furball on the nape.

"Watch their tongues," Harlowe cautioned. "They're like ten grit sandpaper." Remembering how Riverstone had taken the third one to sickbay, he asked how it was getting along. "I'll bet the robobs got the little fluffball up and running like one of Harry's vintage Ferraris."

Everyone on the bridge looked downcast.

Harlowe felt the dread. "What happened?"

"He didn't make it," Riverstone said for the crew.

Harlowe found that hard to believe. The robobs repaired the impossible—animal, vegetable, or mineral. It didn't matter. They always fixed it.

"It was probably gone when you brought it in," Ian guessed. "Nothing worked this time."

Harlowe picked up the other cub in his lap. "I kinda took it for granted the clickers could mend anything."

"Something to remember," Riverstone commented thoughtfully.

"How'd Quay take it?" Harlowe asked.

"She was man up, Skipper," Simon replied. "She wrapped the little guy in a nice blanket and said some kind words. They sounded like it, anyway. She then opened the hatch and let it drift into space near this bright nebula we were passing by at the time." His eyes met Harlowe's. "Real class, Captain. Just like...well, like..." He found it hard to continue.

"Like Lu would do, right?" Harlowe replied.

"Yeah, that kind of class."

"Yeah," Harlowe agreed thoughtfully. "Totally." He allowed the cub to drop and asked, "What about that toadface, Unikala? Any problems?"

Ian grinned. "Your gamble paid off."

"We'll see him again," Riverstone added.

Harlowe swallowed the sour taste in his mouth. "No doubt."

Ian removed a small plastic square from his sleeve pocket as he went on to explain in detail how Riverstone had taken over the controls and guided them out of the star system into hyperlight while Monday carried him to his quarters.

"Where's Quay now?" Harlowe wondered.

"She comes and goes like she knows Millie better than we do," Riverstone replied.

Ian wondered, "Haven't you talked to her? She's been taking care of you for three days."

Harlowe's expression froze.

"You looked surprised," Ian said.

Harlowe's gaze refocused past the forward observation windows. The stars were bright, radiating brilliantly like they did when Millie was traveling toward them at hyperlight. After a moment of thought he asked almost off-handedly, "Where are we?"

"On our way to Gibb," Simon replied, as if he had been dragged along kicking and screaming.

"Gibb? What's Gibb? I thought we plotted a course for Omini Prime."

"It's an old city in the Omini Prime system," Ian explained. "Quay said it's where she needs to go."

Riverstone added, "She also said it would save us a ton of time, Captain."

Harlowe glanced at Simon. "You okay with that, Mr. Bolt?"

Simon bowed graciously. "I have fallen on my sword, Captain."

Harlowe grunted an appropriate reply.

"She's hiding something, Captain," Ian said cooly. "I think there's more to the story than we know."

Harlowe remained silent, his focus staying with the infinite space before them while Ian went on with his thoughts.

"Unikala knows we have her."

"He wasn't too concerned about the energy crystals, either," Riverstone added.

Harlowe nodded in agreement with his officers. "Yeah, he wasn't, was he?"

"We're new at this game," Ian continued. He glanced back and forth between Harlowe and Riverstone. "Rookies, really. Unikala and his Consortium are pros and this is their backyard. They know the quadrant. We don't. He already knows where we're headed."

Riverstone chuckled. "He didn't scare you, did he, Wiz?"

Ian shot a couple of hard dagger-eyes at Riverstone. "Yeah. Plenty. We'd be wise to respect that fear."

"Alright everyone, we stay cool," Harlowe said. "I agree with Wiz— Unikala may seem like a toad, but he didn't get where he is by being a gomer. We keep playing like he's holding all the aces." Everyone agreed. Harlowe's eyes ended on Riverstone. "Thoughts?"

Riverstone reached down for a ball of white fur. "I think you have a problem."

"Oh?" Harlowe wondered.

"She likes you, Captain."

Harlowe looked over at Monday, who nodded in agreement. "The way she talks about you," Riverstone went on. "Cupid's arrow has struck right between those beautiful doe eyes."

Harlowe leaned over to Riverstone. "What do you mean talks?"

"Didn't Wiz show you his gizmo?"

Harlowe looked at Ian, puzzled.

Ian handed Harlowe the plastic square he had been toying with in his hand. "It's Rerun's idea. Give him the credit." Simon saluted from his station chair. "He said in his last movie, *Distant Galaxies*, they had this device that they implanted in their head that could translate any language so Captain Starr could talk to the aliens. So I checked with Millie. Bingo, she had them in stock."

"A language gizmo, huh?" Harlowe asked, amazed, twirling the square with his fingers.

"A language translator, 54th century style," Ian replied. "There's a tiny implant sandwiched between the plates. It goes in your head about here," he explained, pointing just behind his right ear lobe. "When a person talks, no matter what the language, you can under-stand what they're saying, and speak it too."

Harlowe's mouth dropped open, staring at Simon in disbelief. "Rerun thought of that?"

Ian chuckled, nodding his head. "Yeah, he did."

Harlowe smiled. "I guess you'll want a pay raise."

Simon flashed Harlowe the thumbs-up. "Big time, Skipper."

"It makes sense," Ian said, his tone turning cerebral. "Travelers among the stars needed language converters to communicate with other beings." He looked at Riverstone. "How's it work?"

Riverstone made a small circle with his thumb and index finger. "Perfecto."

"This one's mine?" Harlowe asked.

"It's got your name on it," Ian replied.

Harlowe continued to turn the plastic wafer around and around, trying to find the speck of Gamadin technology inside. It was so small, it appeared as if nothing was there. "How do I jump-start it?"

"Just take it down to sickbay and have one of the robobs plug it into your brain," Ian said, pointing behind the ear.

Harlowe stood up, eager to have his new device installed, then hesitated at the door. "Does it hurt?"

Riverstone's face twisted with a silly smirk. "No, oh Fearless Leader!"

29

Small Galaxy

A SHORT TIME later, Harlowe bounced out of sickbay as if he were walking on air. Riverstone had been right. The implant was painless. He touched behind his right ear where the robob medic had placed the device and felt no mark or soreness at all, nor had his hearing changed. He wondered if it was a lemon. In any case, he was eager to find Quay and try it out.

Before stepping out of sickbay, Harlowe had Millie find her exact location in the saucer. Millie was a big ship. He remembered the last time he went looking for Quay and found her out wandering around on the beach. If she was walking throughout the ship, he could spend a lifetime looking for her. For as many months as Millie had been a part of their lives, they still had yet to explore all of her nooks and crannies. During their recruit training he had lost count of the dozens of times they had become lost trying to find their way to the control room. Letting Millie do the searching of over three million square feet of rooms, corridors, and open spaces was the only practical solution to finding anyone onboard the ship.

Harlowe quickly learned that was Quay in the forward view room at the far end of the ship. It was a long stroll to get there. He wondered how she had managed to find it when it had taken them months to discover the first one. *Millawanda* was so enormous that Ian speculated they understood only a small fraction of the total wealth of Gamadin technology that was available to them. Before coming to Barnard, Harlowe had set aside one day a week for his crew to search out new places of interest throughout the ship. One of their discoveries was the Olympic-sized pool. He and Riverstone accidentally found it the night the vamps chased them into the dark room. For this reason, and because it was the common-sense thing to do, they went about in pairs because, like scuba divers, one never knew the trouble they might find alone in a 54th century ship as massive as six *Nimitz*-class aircraft carriers. Harlowe often thought whimsically, if it wasn't for Millie, one could easily get lost and starve like a castaway washed up on a deserted island. They had discovered the view room where Quay was located on one of the outings. It seemed to have no real purpose other than as a place for quiet meditation, similar to a library reading room. Not only could they find solitude, they could also enjoy the spectacular view from its hundred-foot-wide observation window.

After crossing the great center foyer, Harlowe blinked the rest of the distance, unable to wait any longer. The instant he stepped off the disk, he went directly to the view room door and pressed the activator. The panel slid silently to one side and, like a vision from a classic romantic movie, Quay was there, staring across the large room as if she knew he would be walking in that very moment. The only thing missing was the string quartet playing a Chopin nocturne. Looking like his dream had come true, she sat poised on a long, overstuffed couch beneath the massive window with a billion stars glittering white hot and bright behind her. One of the big disappointments they discovered about hyperlight speeds was that the stars did not go whizzing past them as they traveled. They were used to seeing the old *Star Trek* shows and Captain Starr movies where stars whizzed past the ship's windows as if they were standing still. It was only a

Hollywood trick to create the illusion of traveling through hyperlight space. In reality the stars of hyperspace appeared quite different. As you looked forward, the stars were bright white, and as you looked to the side they began to lose their luminosity, fading gradually from yellow to a rusty orange, then to deep red. Finally, looking directly behind a hyperlight spacecraft, you saw only darkness.

On the table next to Quay, Harlowe saw a half-eaten plate of French toast. Riverstone had introduced her to the breakfast specialty back on #2. It had become her favorite. She especially liked it with a touch of cinnamon and smothered in hot maple syrup. The cubs were there, too. They had blinked with Harlowe all the way from the control room, attached to him like baby ducks. The instant they saw Quay they bounced playfully to her side, licking her outstretched hands as if she were catnip. She gave each one a huge, motherly hug before they stretched out peacefully at her feet, motors at a fast idle, purring contentedly.

Before he opened the door, Harlowe had had a million things he wanted to ask her about herself and why she was so far from home. Now, as he saw her sitting gorgeously in the middle of the room like a Greek goddess, his mind seized up. Her short, coal-black hair and delicate skin reflected the soft light of the stars as her dark eyes, large and clear, watched him enter the room.

Why can't I remember the last three days?

When he took a step toward her, his knees began to feel like over-cooked pasta. As he fought to keep his cool, his stomach felt queasy, and for a moment his lungs found it difficult to breathe.

The fact that she wore a short blue dress with spaghetti straps over her bare shoulders didn't help matters at all.

He had visions of coming through the door like a heroic knight, shedding his battle-worn armor before sweeping her up in his arms and kissing her, turning round and round as the fireworks exploded above their heads and the trumpets played Copeland's *Fanfare for the Common Man*. All he could do now was waddle awkwardly through the doorway like a gomer and hope he didn't trip over a piece of furniture.

Say something, toad, before she throws the dish at you!

"Uh, good morning, uh, after...noon...I mean..." he stuttered.

He was sinking fast. He looked around for something that would tell him the time. He had asked Millie before, only now his mind was a blank. He glanced out the window for a sunset or a morning dawn—a thin shadow would work—but there was nothing like that in the vacuum of space. A vaporous blue-green cloud of a star gone nova millenniums ago was passing by the room's portside window. The nebula seemed to take up the entire celestial sphere. In a few hours, though, it would be just a speck of light. He turned back to her with a boyish grin, needing assistance. "I don't know what time it is," he finally confessed.

Her dark eyebrows arched with concern as her mouth parted slightly. "Does it matter?" she asked in words that were clear and understandable.

Harlowe smiled, his bright blue eyes drinking in every syllable. "No, I guess it doesn't." He touched the side of his head where the robob had placed the implant. *Sweet, the thing really works!*

"Please," she said, and motioned with a slight bow of her head for him to come and sit beside her.

As he moved toward her, he fought the urge to leap across the room and hold her in his arms.

Not yet, stupid, you'll squeeze the life out of her!

When he'd held her the last time at the bottom of the ramp, when sorcerer had touched them on #2, it was a different moment and a different place. He had just survived an attack by a hungry dinosaur. Kissing her for saving his life seemed the right thing to do. Had she changed her mind? After all, she was a woman. Time had passed, and so had the place. They were different people now. Maybe they needed time to start over again from Square One. She might feel differently about him now that she'd had time to think.

He didn't remember crossing the room or touching the floor with his feet as he came to her side on the couch. The way she carried herself, tall and regal, was like an angel sitting on a cloud. Her fresh, delicate fragrance had caught him the moment he opened the door. It was like a flower picked in a gentle rain. He took another step closer, barely able to control himself.

"You are the most incredible warrior I have ever known," she told him. He didn't speak. He couldn't speak. All he could do was nod and let her talk. "Unikala's fleets have killed many thousands in the quadrant. The Consortium has never lost so many ships. It has cost them dearly. They will not forget."

Harlowe agreed. "Wiz thinks he knows where we're going."

"Yes. Unikala will follow you, but at a safe distance until he has the advantage. He will not make the same mistake twice."

"Probably not."

Quay turned away and drifted toward the window, her face filled with worry. "It is not so simple."

"He said something was stolen from him. Was it you he was looking for?" Harlowe asked.

Her gaze turned from the nebula back to him. "I am promised to him."

Harlowe's eyes shot open, almost laughing at the absurdity. "No way."

"My father has promised my hand in exchange for privileges with the Consortium."

"Rights of Passage?" Harlowe asked, trying to understand.

Quay nodded.

"But why would one of his ships try to kill you?"

"That was not their intent. I was running away. They were trying to stop me from my escape."

Harlowe took her in his arms. He had heard enough. "No more running."

Quay was surprised by Harlowe's statement. "You have no fear of the Consortium?"

Harlowe switched back to a reassuring smile. Her hair looked as though it might have grown another inch since he first kissed her on Number 2. "You've never met General William Tecumsa Gunn. He frightens me. The Consortium and the Fhaal are toads compared to him."

"He sounds like a Peacemaker?"

"If that is a bad dude, he was. In spades."

"He was more powerful than Unikala?"

Harlowe laughed. "The General could part an ocean with a single look." His face sobered again as his hands held hers. "I wish you could have met him."

"He was a part of you?"

A deep respect for the old soldier would always remain in Harlowe's heart. "A part of us all. Without him we would not be here looking at such wonders," he said, staring at the end of the nebula drifting by. They were moving very fast. "He used to sit in this big old, overstuffed chair every day and watch the sun go down while his recruits ran rimmers. He said it was what he and Mary loved the most, to watch a beautiful sunset together."

"Mary?"

"His wife. Other men killed her."

Quay came closer and put her arms around him. It was much easier this time. She seemed to sense that he wanted her near him.

"Please, touch my lips with yours," she said to him.

It was a good minute before they parted.

"Do all Peacemakers act this way?" she asked.

His forehead wrinkled. "That's the second time you called me a Peacemaker. Why?"

"Because I know now that is who you are. You are the Peacemakers of our ancient legends. My search has ended. I have found you."

Harlowe had never heard of the term before, except perhaps in an old B-western on late night TV. "I think you're mixing us up with someone else. These Peacemakers, who are they?"

Her head tilted slightly as she smiled and began her tale.

"Many, many thousands of passings ago, before Omini Prime, before Tomar, before the Consortium and the Fhaal, great warriors called Peacemakers traveled between the stars. It was said they came from the old worlds near the galactic core where travel to other stars was common long before our forefathers walked upon our planets. As time went on, the inner worlds began to reach out. They discovered young civilizations that were not as wise in the ways of the cosmos as the Old Worlds. They often used their technology to conquer the less powerful. And so it began. Peace in the galaxy turned to massive destruction and domination. The lust for power and to build new empires spread like a rabid disease. No longer could civilized worlds live and trade and prosper in harmony together. Even the old worlds became infected, forced to build vast arsenals to defend their existence.

"Then a group of them, twelve in all, took it upon themselves to rid the galaxy of this madness of death. They didn't care about the petty reasons for acquisition and the use of force. They simply wanted the madness to end. So the twelve built a force so powerful it would become the ultimate force of the galaxy, and they called themselves the Peacemakers. The task of building the Peacemakers was given to one being. His name was Kron. He was given absolute authority and endless resources. It was not an easy task to find the best soldiers, the best leaders and minds in the galaxy, to help him. He did it with sheer force of will. The word spread that he needed the good and the great to build an ultimate force to save the galaxy from the madness, and they came. They came by any means of transport available. They came from the galactic core to the distant ends of the known galaxy to join his force of Peacemakers. Like all things new they made mistakes in the beginning, but they learned quickly. After a thousand years the old world's dream, the twelve, was completed. Peace and harmony in the galaxy were restored. Empires everywhere feared the ultimate force and bowed to the sight of a single Peacemaker ship. For a hundred thousand passings, the peace was kept this way. No world, no empire ever risked confrontation with the Peacemakers for fear of being destroyed themselves."

Harlowe's eyes lit up with fascination. It took Quay over an hour to complete her story as she told him all she knew of the Peacemakers legend she had heard about since she was a little girl. Harlowe was captivated. He listened to every word. When she had finished, he asked her, "So what happened to them? If they were so powerful, where did they go? Why aren't they here to protect you and other travelers from the Consortium?"

Quay looked down with sadness. "Because many believed that such a powerful force caused more problems than they solved. They were told to disband because there were no more wars to fight. They thought the peace would last forever without the Gamadin, but they were wrong. Peace is never forever. It must always be watched and cared for."

Gamadin! Harlowe was stunned. *She called them Gamadin!* He looked around the room, at the bulkheads, the thick dura-steel beams, the glow of warm light from the ceiling, the window of impenetrable glass while he listened to the faint hum of *Millawanda's* boundless energy propelling them billions of miles per second across the last wispy fragments of the nebula. His eyes fell upon the furniture, the floor of rich, dark blue carpet, his clothes, and the emblem on the sleeve of his shirt... the emblem of the starburst that was Gamadin. Was he really a galactic soldier from a distant past? All that was here around him, inside of him, and next to him—could it be that they were the culmination of an old-world technology that had been part of this ultimate force of Peacemakers that had flown between the stars over a hundred thousand years ago?

Were Peacemakers and Gamadin one and the same?

"Millie," Harlowe called out. A holographic screen materialized nearby and waited patiently for his query. Mrs. M had said Gamadin were the only ones who could save Neeja from the Fhaal. Had she really meant Peacemakers? He had to know. "Translate the word *Gamadin* from Neejian to Quay's home language on Tomar."

"*Peacemaker*" read the screen.

Harlowe sat down, his mind delirious.

Gamadin were Peacemakers?

Their role of Gamadin had just taken on new meaning. The California coast was as far away from the galactic core as anyone could imagine. Yet here he was, Harlowe Pylott, an eighteen-year-old Lakewood High surfer kid turned starship captain of a really bad police force that went around the galaxy, saving planets from the bad guys. He had to have known that all along, but when someone else said it, it took on a whole new significance.

How sick is that, Dog?

"This Kron you mentioned," Harlowe said. "He sounds a lot like General Gunn. They could have been soulmates."

Quay spoke to Millie and asked her to bring up the portrait of Kron from her memory banks. An instant later the picture of a tough old soldier in a grey uniform appeared on the screen. "This is Kron," she said.

Harlowe's mouth fell in his lap as the image of the gruff old soldier stared him right in the face. The head was wrapped in cloth much like a Bedouin tribal leader, but his large, aquiline nose, his thin, slitty eyes, and his ruddy hard face were clearly those of someone very close to him... General William Tecumsa Gunn.

Ain't it a small galaxy...?

Part II

Omini Prime

That whenever any form of government becomes destructive to these ends, it is the right of the people to alter or to abolish it...
— Thomas Jefferson
The Declaration of Independence

30

Gibb

It took two more weeks for *Millawanda* to travel the interstellar distances to the Omini Prime binary star system. The fourth planet out was called Omin, but no one called it by that name. It was known all over the quadrant simply as Gibb, named after the oldest and mightiest intergalactic city in the quadrant, and it had no rivals.

In that time, too, the tiger cubs were given their new names, Molly and Rhud. Molly's name came from Riverstone's dog back on Earth, and Rhud was named after Simon's old orange cat he'd had growing up. Not exactly the perfect names for snow-white cats, but Simon said his old orange cat was the baddest cat walking and of course, no one ever messed with Riverstone's Rottweiler! So the names stuck.

The cats had doubled their size in that time and had become as much a part of the crew as anyone else.

Riverstone and Simon acknowledged that their detour to Gibb, away from Earth, could have been worse. They could have run into another Consortium mothership or someone else who wanted the prize they had on board. Maybe they were lucky, but what really sealed the deal was the unconfirmed rumor going around the ship that Quay had a beautiful, younger sister who was unattached. It was said Ian and Harlowe had started the rumor but neither confessed to anything. Riverstone and Simon, being easy marks for a hot date, suddenly found their sea legs. They figured a few hundred light-years of traveling the vast distances of space for a chance to test the waters with a hot babe the caliber of Quay was worth the risk. After all, wouldn't Captain Julian Starr and his loyal second-in-command, Mr. Riverstone, help a damsel in distress like Quay and her hot sister? In a heartbeat they would! They were both "all-in." They shook hands, agreeing that whoever lost became the chauffeur on the first date. With sly grins of over-confidence, the deal was struck and to the victor went the spoils.

The journey itself had been routine. At this point in their short careers, traveling between the stars seemed less worrisome than anyone had imagined. Still, thoughts of home were never far away. After delivering Quay to Gibb and spending a few days among the natives, they would be back on the road and home again.

The thought of visiting a true alien city sent chills up their spines, especially Ian. He was eager to walk on streets that Quay said, and Millie confirmed, had been laid out and constructed before humans walked upright on the Earth.

That's killer!

As for Harlowe, he could have waited a lifetime to arrive at Gibb. Riverstone had seen the foreboding look on both their faces as they came closer to the ancient city. Monday was the only one who seemed to have no expectations about their destination. He kept himself busy working out with Quincy, doing laps in the pool or pulling double shifts on the bridge. Monday seemed to be the human extension of the ship. Harlowe's First Mate was *Millawanda's* number-one fan and caretaker. Anywhere Harlowe ordered him to go, he would go with no questions asked. The ship was his baby, his reason for being. It was as simple as that.

"Receiving transmission from Gibb central, Mr. Riverstone," Ian announced over the com. "They want us to slow down before entering their star system."

Riverstone received the pitch back from the robob catcher and replied, "Aye, Wiz. Better let Harlowe know."

"Already done," Ian replied. "Squid and Rerun have been notified, too."

"Very well. Give me ten, Wiz."

From a distance it takes the speed of light to travel in one hour, the Gamadin ship decelerated out of hyperlight travel and slowed to more maneuverable sub-light approach into Gibbian space. Quay had explained that all vessels wishing to land at Gibb had to stay within a well-defined path as they entered the system because of the crowded nature of Gibbian air space. On the ship's sensors, Ian had already picked up hundreds of spaceships converging on the planet from all the different sectors of the quadrant. Gibb, it seems, was the oldest and most important trading center in this section of the quadrant. Its base was well located strategically for weary interstellar travelers and traders. For that reason, Quay had also warned them that Gibb had the deserved distinction of having the most corrupt and dangerous gathering of beings the quadrant had to offer. She assured them, though, that the times she had been there, she had encountered no trouble. If they kept to themselves and minded their own business, they would have no difficulty enjoying the city. Everyone understood this. Driving through parts of Los Angeles was much the same way. The last thing anyone wanted was trouble. Harlowe had given explicit orders that anyone who stepped out of line would have to walk all the way home from Gibb. Nothing more needed to be said. Everybody got the point.

Ian displayed a three-dimensional holo of Gibb's geographical features. The planet was the fourth planet in a binary star system of twelve planets. It was slightly smaller than Earth, with a near surface gravity of .91 that of Earth. Gibb took approximately 681 days, shy by a week of Mars, to revolve around an average yellow star of Omini Prime, while its white dwarf companion, Omini Beta, drifted benignly in a circular orbit one light-day out from the primary. A day on Gibb was 25.71 hours long. Gibb resembled Earth in other ways as well. Like Earth, its climate varied according to the latitude, so it had deserts, long mountain ranges, and rainy tropical forests. However, Gibb's oceans were small, making up only two-fifths of the planet's surface. The three major continents made up the rest of the landmass. The largest continent by far was an enormous plateau twice the size of North America. It was so immense that when the Gamadin ship made her way past the first of Gibb's three moons, the geological formation could be seen clearly through the main observation window without the aid of any visual devices. The Gibbian space center was located in the northeast quadrant of that plateau.

The space center was not a large airport like LAX or Kennedy; it was massive on a galactic scale, covering an area larger than the state of Texas. Some of its runways were a hundred miles long, with parking stalls large enough to accommodate enormous cargo transports fifty times the size of the Gamadin ship. For even large ships unable to land on the planet's surface, colossal docking facilities hovered in stationary orbit a thousand miles above the planet's surface. From there, shuttles would transfer travelers and cargo to the surface.

"Captain on the bridge!" Monday announced as Harlowe entered the control room from his cabin dressed in the crisp, dark blue-and-gold trimmed uniform of the day. Only slightly behind him was Quay, regal and beautiful as ever in a stunning royal-blue 54th century jumpsuit. Back in the 1940s on Earth, men would have called her a "knockout." Regardless of the time period, Quay was "hot" on a scale that was off the charts.

Riverstone tried to relinquish the center chair to Harlowe, but Harlowe laid a calm hand on his shoulder. "As you were, Mr. Riverstone. You're doing fine."

"Aye, Captain. Steady as she goes, Mr. Platter," Riverstone ordered, not at all bothered by the responsibility.

"Aye, steady as she goes, sir," Monday acknowledged from his chair at the helm.

"Watch the portside. That's a big one," Riverstone added confidently, watching the long cargo ship pull under them off to the left.

"Aye. I have her, Mr. Riverstone," Ian replied.

Everyone but Quay watched in awe at all the spaceships leaving and entering Gibbian space on such a grand scale. *Millawanda* appeared like a shuttlecraft as they drifted by the giant cargo ships docked beside their stationary orbital bays. Riverstone let out a long whistle of relief after they sliced between two more freighters without a scratch. It was all so grand, complex, and overwhelming. The resources it took to build such galactic structures were mind-boggling.

"It must have taken thousands of years to create," Ian said to Quay, at the same time never taking his eyes off the giant window and overhead readouts that Millie was updating constantly in real time.

"Yes, many thousands of passings," Quay acknowledged.

Seeing Harlowe there with Quay, Riverstone envied his longtime friend. Some people never find soulmates, but Harlowe seemed to have a knack for meeting his, even hundreds of light-years from home. Would he ever find his soulmate? Riverstone wondered. He sighed. The future looked grim. His heart often felt as though it were lost somewhere in a deep subterranean cave.

Then to Quay, Harlowe asked, "What is that circular symbol? There's a ton of ships with it," pointing at a large cargo ship drifting by. "They don't appear to be Consortium."

Quay looked on with pride. "No. They are my father's. Gibb is one of his largest accounts."

That stirred the pot.

"Whoa!" Simon cried out, swinging around in his chair and matching everyone else's shocked disbelief. He didn't care now if Quay's sister looked like a blown tire! "Your dad owns all those ships?" he asked her.

"Keep your eye on the screen, Mr. Bolt," Riverstone quickly ordered.

"Yes, they belong to the Tomar Corporation," she replied.

Simon returned to his screens, his face blanching with incredulity. Not even his scriptwriters could imagine such wealth! "Makes Bill Gates look like a welfare case," he uttered to Ian, sitting nearby.

"Must keep him busy," Ian added, exhaling some astonishment of his own as the largest vessel yet came into view. It was Tomarian as well. Its cargo bay had enough room to swallow *Millawanda* a hundred times over.

"Mother is always scolding him to slow down. He had planned to relinquish power to my brother, Turfan," she replied, her face turning worrisome. "But now the Consortium alliance with the Fhaal has made such a transition impossible. He's had much to think about. I worry about him. He has not been himself for many cycles."

Harlowe's face reflected her concern. "Maybe we can help."

Three sets of shoulders suddenly slumped at once.

She turned to him, their eyes meeting, speaking to each other silently. "I wish that were so. But as brave as you are, you are but one ship against an empire."

Harlowe winked a glint of confidence. He wanted to take her in his arms but duty controlled his conduct. The bridge was a sacred place of honor and protocol. He would not violate its purity for a weakness of the heart. "We'll convince them," he said to her.

* * *

Final clearance was granted and the Gamadin ship was instructed to land at Area 17 on the outskirts of the city. Quay informed them it was a prime location, yet she wondered aloud why they had not been given clearance to land on her father's private docking facilities within the city. "I will tell my father of this insult upon our arrival," she told them, looking annoyed. "That is the least I can do for your kindness of bringing me this great distance."

"Is your father's office nearby?" Harlowe asked.

"We must walk the streets of the city. It will take some time," she informed them.

"Perfect. My crew is anxious to see Gibb. We will enjoy being tourists," Harlowe said. He then asked: "Has your family done business here long?"

"Yes, for over a thousand passings. My family has had a long and prosperous association with Gibb," she replied. To everyone in the room, she announced, "On behalf of my family and my planet, Tomar, I invite you and your crew, Captain, to be our honored guests while you are here on Gibb," she said to the Gamadin crew.

Without hesitation, Harlowe thanked her for everyone and accepted the invitation.

* * *

As they drifted down to their landing site, Gibb, which had been visible from a hundred thousand miles away, grew spectacularly larger than life the closer they came, expanding almost exponentially before their eyes. They had seen large cities before with fifty-story buildings in downtown L.A., and pictures of larger hundred-story skyscrapers in Chicago and New York. The structures on Gibb, however, would have dwarfed the Sears and Hancock towers in Chicago a hundred times over. The city was larger than the state of Rhode Island. A city founded, according to the sensors, nearly a hundred thousand years ago!

Millawanda appeared like a small coffee plate against any one of the immense, mile-high Gibbian superstructures. The sight was nothing short of mind-boggling.

"That's sooooo sick, dudes!" Simon whistled out loud.

Harlowe marveled over the ancient buildings as if they were glassy, incoming waves. "Sweet!" he gasped.

Monday followed next. "I bet we could put her down on that balcony over there, Captain," he remarked, pointing at a large patio area the size of ten football fields three thousand feet above the streets.

"Why did they build them so big?" Ian asked Quay. His eyes looked as though they were about to pop out of his head.

"There are many merchants and traders that come to Gibb. It is the center of our quadrant, Omini Prime. They need much room to conduct their affairs," Quay explained.

"What do they trade?" Monday asked.

"Everything," Quay replied with frankness, as though she knew there was much more to talk about but too little time. "There are no constraints of trade on Gibb."

"Even people?" Ian wondered, not really expecting an answer.

"Yes, all living things have value, Ian, even people. An activity that is quite profitable for my father," she added. "Do they trade in beings on your planet?" she asked.

Riverstone frowned. "Some places, but it's mostly outlawed now."

"My father says this will happen someday in the quadrant," she replied.

"I hope so," Riverstone injected, his face twisted with revulsion.

"He is a good man. You will meet him soon."

"Yeah, that would be cool," Simon replied, almost giddy at the prospect of meeting the man behind such inconceivable wealth.

A few minutes later, *Millawanda* eased gently down on the large open area designated as Area 17. After 323 light-years, two weeks, four days, and seven hours of traveling through interstellar space from Barnard's #2 planet, they had finally and safely arrived on their second living world outside of their own planet Earth.

Riverstone sighed, relieved that he had guided *Millawanda* safely through rush-hour traffic and parked her with no damage to her flawless surface. He stood up to a round of applause for a job well done. After he took a deep bow, Jewels handed him a blue shake as if the robob servant had read his mind. Riverstone gratefully accepted the drink. "Thanks, dude."

"Grab what you need on the way down," Harlowe ordered.

Quay had already left the bridge and gone to her cabin below to gather her things. "From what Quay says, we have some hoofing to do, and we don't want to be out there after dark." Then to everyone he said, "Out of your uni's and into your civvies, stat! Pack your Gama-belts and meet back at the center blinker in twenty. Any questions?"

Simon raised his hand. "We packin', Skipper?"

"To the hilt, Rerun," Harlowe replied. "Extra ammo clips, too."

"You sound like you're expecting trouble, Captain," Ian said.

Riverstone replied for Harlowe. "From the way Quay described the streets here, if you're not packin', you're walking dead."

Harlowe looked around the bridge with paternal regard. Not since their thousand-mile trek across Mars had he been away from *Millawanda* for more than a few hours. "Okay, Mr. Platter, you have the bridge. Take good care of her while we're gone."

Monday returned a confident wink. "Millie's in good hands, Captain."

Harlowe was about to leave when he nearly tripped on a robob cylinder in his path. He bent down and picked it up. "Jewels?" Harlowe inquired.

Monday laughed. "Never leave home without him, Captain."

"Thanks, Mr. Platter, I won't."

31

E.P.

SIMON AND IAN powered down Millie's console. The telltale background hum of energy faded until there was only the quiet of the crew moving about and making small conversation amongst themselves. Regardless of their individual feelings, they each knew this was going to be one tourist stop they would never forget. Everyone but Monday went to their rooms and changed into their standard off-world clothes of Nikes, Levi's, and warm long-sleeved shirts. Sensors indicated a brisk 56° F on the streets below and much colder at night, so Simon designed dark blue Gamadin jackets for everyone but Quay, who wore her jumpsuit with a matching velvet cape. Simon complimented her on how gorgeous she looked, followed immediately by Riverstone saying she would be stunning wearing a potato sack.

As arranged, they all met at the center hatchway inside the main foyer. Before stepping on the blinker, Harlowe silently surveyed his crew's Gama-belts, making sure everyone was packing the proper hardware. They were ready. Ian took things a step further and handed out tiny communicators that fit discreetly inside their ears, along with the SIBA medallions around their necks. "Standard precaution," Ian remarked, "in case we get separated." He gave Quay her own SIBA medallion. She had been instructed on its use during the trip from #2.

Harlowe bent down to the cubs as he placed the communicator in his left ear. "You two will have to stay here," he said, petting their white satin manes. He was amazed at their fifty-pound weight gain and the foot of growth they had achieved over the last week alone. They were now over a hundred fifty pounds each and four feet long without their tails. Soon, Harlowe figured, they'd need an entire storage room for their cat box. He was just glad he didn't have to clean it.

"Oh, no. They want to go, too," Quay noted, putting her arms around Rhud's neck.

Harlowe looked around for help. The idea of putting up with two playful cubs on their first outing into an unknown alien city seemed like an unnecessary risk to him. Riverstone, Ian, and Simon all looked away with *I'm-not-getting-into-the-middle-of-this* grins. He was getting no help from his crew. Harlowe gritted his teeth ready to stand his ground, but Quay's large, dark eyes spoke volumes. He had already lost the argument with no grounds for appeal.

"Hold on," Riverstone said, and ran off to the nearby utility room. A minute later he was back, holding a sturdy dura-wire Y-shaped leash in his hand. "Try this."

Harlowe nodded his approval but wasn't about to take the leash. "Good. You're in charge," he said to Riverstone, and walked away.

Riverstone tried to hand the leash off to Simon, but he wasn't biting. He quickly stepped on the blinker and winked out of existence the same moment Harlowe grabbed Quay's hand and disappeared. Before Riverstone could confront Ian, Ian waved and blinked away.

Riverstone vented a hot string of *never-agains* as he looped the ends of the leash around the cubs' necks, resigned to the fact that he was their designated keeper.

* * *

Down at the perimeter edge, as they stepped away from the ground-level blinker, they were greeted with an onslaught of beings wanting to hawk their wares or beg for a handout. Poverty, it seems, on the outskirts of the massive city was as vast as its architecture. Fortunately, the shimmering wall kept them from being mauled the instant they stepped off the plate.

At first Harlowe wasn't sure how he was going to handle the situation. They just wanted to get by without being mobbed. Quay then began reading the crowd the riot act in a kind of street language the universal translators only garbled back in bits and pieces. The crowd parted slightly, enough to walk by. When Riverstone joined them with the cats, Rhud let out a snarly growl and everyone scattered. This gave them more than enough room to start walking anywhere they pleased.

One problem solved, another appeared. Immediately stepping through the barrier, the suffocating stench of Gibb hit them like a fist in the nose. This was not at all what they expected their first alien city to be like! Los Angeles smog was a breath of mountain air compared to Gibb. The air reeked as though they had stepped into a sewer that had never been cleaned. The incredible amounts of brown smoke and dust only added to the misery.

The ground wasn't much better. Simon took two steps past the barrier and found a pile of something nasty. He coughed, covering his mouth, trying to draw in a breath that didn't reek. He scraped the bottom of his Nike thoroughly, disgusted with further exploration of Gibb. He'd had enough. He tried turning back to the ship, but Harlowe kept him moving forward. "Don't even think about it, Rerun."

Ian made a dash for the barrier, but Harlowe grabbed him by the back of his jacket. "Where do you think you're going, Mr. Wizzixs?"

"Squid needs my help with the sensor array."

Harlowe nodded toward Quay, who was ahead leading the way with Rerun, Riverstone, and the cats. "If we get to talking about astrophysics, I'll need you around to make me look bright." He then twisted him around and they both marched quickly to keep up with the others.

According to Millie's surveillance of the city, they had a good ten miles of narrow, winding streets and high-rise blocks of cubicle housing made of mud and stone to go through. Quay said this area and the creatures that lived in it were called "Horritan." Only when they had passed through this squalor would they come to the colossal superstructures of the main city where, even from ten miles away, the housing towered over them as though they were tiny insects in a world of giants.

Incredibly, Quay found her way through the Horritan streets without a GPS, leading them down dusty back alleys so narrow they had to duck under laundry flapping in the breeze that was stretched across their paths. Harlowe doubted if even Millie could help them find their way out if they got lost in the endless maze of streets.

The small entourage did their best to keep to themselves, ignoring pestering beggars and hustling peddlers and the many others who looked like they would slit the group's throats the moment they weren't looking. For the most part, the Gamadin were much taller, stronger, and more heavily armed than any Horritan they saw. During the daylight, Harlowe felt as comfortable as one could while walking through a city of cutthroats. The city at night would be another matter, so they hurried at a fast pace through the miles of Horritan shanties, the extraordinary noise of grinding stone and clanking metal, and the working-class poor stoking their fires and peddling their wares that seemed to cover every square inch of street-level ground.

As they passed one of the vendors, an incredibly foul odor turned them toward a rafter of strange, fleshy hunks of meat that moved on ends of sharp corroded hooks. The smelly liquid from the moving hunks dripped into a dirty, ancient gutter. Behind the counter, a heavyset being, with a dark, chiseled face as ugly as any evil Marvel comic-book character, took something alive from a cage and laid it on a bloody butcher block. It looked like a miniature horse with tiny hooves, a soft blue coat, and sweet, cow-like eyes that pleaded for mercy. It whinnied briefly before the butcher cut off its head with a large, bloodstained cleaver.

Riverstone turned away, swallowing hard to keep from losing his lunch. Another large being, a head taller than Riverstone, bullied by and flipped a large token toward the vendor. The vendor snapped it out of the air as if he had eyes in the back of his head. The hungry customer stabbed a hunk of moving flesh from the rack with his own knife and swallowed the entire morsel whole. Riverstone had never seen anything so disgusting in his life. His idea of a fast-food stand had just been redefined back to the Stone Age.

The being pushed his way past Riverstone and the cats. His surly body, reeking with stench, disappeared into the throngs. As the being wiped his blood-soaked mouth with his sleeve, several more large, dark beings broke away from the hordes and headed toward the counter. Riverstone pulled the cats away, wanting desperately to put some distance between them and the vendor.

They continued walking past the many peddlers, merchants, and traders shouting their pitches for anything and everything they had of value. There were no rules or regulations here in the Horritan filth. Gibb had no laws except for that of survival and worth.

Not one vendor seemed to have anything of value for them until they came upon one particular vendor who was a dead ringer for someone they all thought had disappeared before they were born.

"Elvis, my man," Simon said, taking the vendor's hand. "You look well, bro. So how's it shakin', E.P.? These are your new digs, huh?" Simon glanced over the filth and wooden shanties. "Movin' on up, I see."

Of course the vendor didn't have a clue as to what Simon was talking about. "You mistake me for someone else," the vendor told him. With his thick, dark hair combed high and slick straight back, the vendor looked so much like the King it was scary. To make matters even more bizarre, he was peddling a musical instrument that resembled an Earthly guitar. However, when the vendor played the instrument, it sounded melodically more like a harp than the twang of a guitar.

"Do you play?" the vendor asked Simon, offering him one of the instruments to try.

Simon smiled graciously, taking the instrument from the vendor. Harlowe and Riverstone exchanged glances of disbelief as they stared at the vendor's coal-black hair, easy smile, and low southern drawl that made their skin crawl with *déjà vu*.

Simon readjusted the strings, tuning them to suit his needs. That done, he proceeded to play a short medley of "Jailhouse Rock," "Blue Suede Shoes," "Hound Dog," "Little Sister," and "It's Now or Never" that practically brought tears to Quay's eyes. By the time Simon was finished with his little recital, he had a sizable crowd of fans gathered around him, clapping and bouncing around with the beat, crying out for more. Simon took a graceful bow and thanked them. He hadn't had so much attention since his last movie premiere. He was about to give the crowd an encore when a hard look from Harlowe told him to cut his singing career short. Simon gave his apologies and handed the guitar back to Elvis. They were in a hurry.

Elvis stared at Simon like he was an idol. "I will never forget you. Did you compose them?" he asked Simon.

Simon smiled. "No, but I dated his great-granddaughter."

"He was a great musician?" the vendor asked.

Simon tried to return the guitar. "Dude, he was the King of Rock. The greatest!"

Elvis would not accept the guitar's return. "Please, you play so beautifully. I want you to have it."

Simon gratefully accepted the gift. "Thanks, bro," he said; then they continued on up the street of vendors.

Ian caught up to Simon and asked, "You really dated Elvis Presley's great-granddaughter, Rerun?" He was genuinely impressed.

Simon was still admiring his new treasure and answered as if it were an everyday thing for a movie star of his stature. "We were both on the rebound."

Harlowe leaned over to Riverstone. "If Rerun sings like that to Quay's sister, you'll be hauling him around in a rickshaw, pard."

Riverstone sighed. He knew Harlowe was right. Simon had a voice that could make a doe swoon. "Maybe he'll catch a cold," Riverstone quipped.

Harlowe laughed and moved ahead to catch up with Quay. That gave Simon a chance to ask Ian a question he'd wanted to ask for months. "How does the Skipper do it?" Simon asked, nodding at Harlowe and Quay, walking together up ahead.

Ian grunted. "He doesn't lose."

Simon added an observation. "A million light-years from Earth and he finds a woman on a deserted planet. It isn't fair, I tell ya! So far all I've seen of the babes around here are ones with bugs crawling out of their hair. Can't get much worse, Wiz."

Ian agreed, wishing he was back at the ship, tinkering around one of the utility rooms.

Simon turned his guitar over, and on the backside of the instrument were the vendor's initials. They weren't exactly clear, but one didn't have to stretch his imagination too far to see the inscribed letters written in a stylish hand, "EP."

Simon pointed at the letters for Ian to see. "Now that's rad, dude."

* * *

"These are so beautiful," Quay remarked, coming to a table of fine jewelry. "You made them?" she asked an old, hunched-over woman a third their height.

Riverstone smiled at Harlowe. In silence, they marveled at how small, pretty things that sparkled attracted women everywhere, no matter what part of the galaxy they came from.

Surprisingly, Quay picked out the least sparkly piece of jewelry on the table. It was a braided copper ring with a small heart-shaped design in the middle. "Yes, this one," she said, holding it up for Harlowe to see.

The old woman looked up with a toothless smile. "That is such a common ring for someone as beautiful as you, my lady."

Quay shook her head. "No. I want this one." She put a coin in her palm. Where she had gotten the coin, Harlowe hadn't a clue. He had never seen one like it before, and wondered if she had stopped off at a nearby ATM when he wasn't looking. She obviously didn't have one on her when he brought her aboard the ship. The only explanation could be that she'd had Millie make her a few before they left the ship. "Is this enough?" she asked.

The toothless old woman tasted the coin with a long wet tongue. "Yes. Most adequate, my lady."

Quay turned back to Harlowe, her eyes full of warmth. "This is for us, my Captain."

Harlowe and Quay let the other three Gamadin go on ahead as they lagged behind for a private moment together.

"Do you like it?" Quay asked Harlowe, holding him close.

Harlowe looked at the interwoven strands that formed around side-by-side heart-shaped designs in the setting. "Yeah, sure. It's cool," he told her. Quay took the ring and amazingly, it separated into two parts.

"It is a custom on Tomar," she explained, her dark eyes looking up at his as Harlowe caught Simon and Riverstone stealing glimpses back, smiling and rolling their eyes skyward, "that we give a ring to the one who gives us meaning to our life." Quay kissed Harlowe gently on the lips. "Matthew is right. We are one."

Harlowe turned a sharp eye toward Riverstone. "He told you that?"

Quay kissed him again. "He did," she said, and slipped one-half of the ring on her finger. She took Harlowe's hand and put the ring over the fingertip of his left ring finger. It would never fit. As she pushed the ring on, Harlowe's eyes widened with surprise as it expanded easily to accommodate his thick ring finger.

"Does that mean you're going steady, Doggy?" Riverstone asked from a safe distance away.

Harlowe turned without missing a beat. "It means you're sleeping in the cat box tonight, Mr. Riverstone, if you say another word."

Harlowe took Quay in his arms and properly thanked her for the gift while the crew walked on, giving them their moment.

Minutes later, they quickly caught up with their small entourage. They went along for another twenty minutes before they turned the corner and proceeded down a dark, dimly lit alley off the main avenue. It was deserted and obviously a risky place to be at any time of day, but according to Quay, it would shorten the trek by half. They were all-in. Any way to shorten their stay on Gibb was worth the risk.

Soon after that, Quay led them across the boundary of the Horritan masses into the dark underworld of Gibb itself.

32

Netherworld

Two thousand feet above the city streets, intra-city shuttles raced between the towering structures, shuttling hurried passengers to their destinations while beings far below appeared like specks of dust on the dark, crowded streets.

"What keeps this all from being one big traffic collision?" Ian asked, nearly tripping over one of the cubs. He gawked straight up at all the comings and goings of the never-ending air traffic above the mile-high skyscrapers.

Quay guided Harlowe away from a large hole in the side of the street that he almost fell into. "The Overseer of Path," she answered Ian. She gestured toward a large golden ball on top of the tallest structure in the city. "It controls all movement in and out of Gibb."

Harlowe stared into the black crevice that had nearly swallowed him whole. He caught a brief glimpse of a wide, fast-moving underground river of filth and sewage. The smell was not quite the same as that of the Horritan city, but it reeked on the same high level.

Only a trickle of light from Omini Prime found its way to the lowliest bowels of Gibb. Quay informed them that the dull yellow streetlights were always on, night or day. Knowing that did nothing to alleviate the sudden depressive chill that crawled up the Gamadin crew's spines the moment they passed from the light of day to the shadowy darkness of Gibb's netherworld. An ominous foreboding of danger was on everyone's minds, regardless of Quay's thoughtful spin. At street level it seemed the welcome mat on Gibb had been swept way eons ago.

As dirty and smelly as the Horritan city had been, at least it had been bright with light. Here at the base of the superstructures, light was scarce. The dark, dreary city smelled appallingly bad, like an ancient catacomb of the dead. No getting around it, a bad stink seemed to be a prerequisite for cityhood on Gibb. The stench lingered within the heavy dampness and body aromas of the crowded street before them. Quay explained that this was a better day than usual. "A recent rain may have swept the streets of the foulest layers," she told them as they ventured out into the throngs of beings that strolled along the massive streets. Beings from all over the quadrant hurried along like White Rabbits, late for an appointment, while others meandered slowly on a deliberate path to their destination. There seemed to be no in-between. While some beings were tall, very tall, a few were almost toy-like. There were dark-skinned beings, light-skinned beings, and all shades of beings in between. A small group that brushed past them gave the cubs a wide berth. They had an odd cranberry-colored skin with yellow-colored paint marking their humanoid faces, like Indians on the warpath. Still other beings appeared indistinguishable between male and female. Creatures with spiky colored hair and body piercings through their noses and ears made the crew feel almost like they were home. Nevertheless, as odd as the streetwalkers appeared, the Gamadin welcomed the observation that most of the beings they saw did indeed seem quite human.

They walked along, threading their way through the flow of pedestrians to the other side of the two-hundred-foot-wide boulevard. They were on a pedestrians-only avenue, while a thousand feet above their heads, the ancient transport system they had seen earlier at the edge of the Horritan city was busily clanking along in one direction while another transport was noisily returning in the opposite direction. There were many transports moving above them. Some were incredibly large and multi-decked. They stopped for only a moment at their stops, picking up and depositing passengers at different levels before darting away on their railless tracks.

Harlowe touched the butt of his pistol, surprised by the number of beings carrying weapons. Many beings were as armed as they were. Those that weren't had heavily-armed bodyguards who were.

"Where are the police?" Riverstone asked.

"Protection is one's own responsibility on Gibb. It is the more efficient way," Quay replied.

"That's cool," Riverstone quipped.

"And justice?" Simon asked.

"It is what you buy," Quay answered coldly.

As the others were watching the crowd, Ian strolled over to an ancient mile-high structure and touched the stone. The ancient cornerpiece was covered with a slimy, colorless fungus. Here and there tiny rivulets of water flowed between the ancient cracks and collected in the time-worn gutters at their feet. He stared at his fingers and smelled the age. His face winced with revulsion. He was glad he'd had the foresight to bring an antiseptic wipe to clean his hands.

Harlowe zipped up his outer jacket tighter as he brought Quay closer to his side. "Stay alert," he said to the group as he eyed the heavy traffic of beings walking in both directions.

The cubs swayed fearlessly ahead, clearing the way. They seemed unaffected by the dreariness. Their eyes glowed soft blue, penetrating the darkness like light-gathering opticals that vacuumed in stray photons. To them, Riverstone figured, Gibb was probably civil compared to the land of giants and merciless death they encountered on #2.

He took a firmer grip on their leash, relieved that they were so obedient. He figured they were quite capable of ripping his arm off if they wanted to. They were only a third the size of what they would ultimately become, if Harlowe's description of their mother was anywhere close.

Quay motioned for everyone to keep moving. It wasn't wise to stop for long in this part of the city.

They hadn't gone far when Harlowe, Riverstone, and Simon stopped sharply and went for their pistols. Together they zeroed in on a grossly overweight being across the street, bartering with a street vendor. The grotesque being had a head of hair that resembled something close to wet seaweed. His skin was mottled and clammy white, as if he was wearing heavy stage makeup to hide his moonscape face. What startled them to action was that the fat being had two ugly beasts his bodyguards held in check with thick, heavy chains. The beasts were unmistakable. They were the same nightmarish black beasts none of them would ever forget. Without a doubt they were the same disgusting creatures that had chased them in the box canyon in Utah and nearly eaten them alive. If it hadn't been for Mowgi, they would have been alien pet food that night on the mesa.

"No!" Quay shouted, grabbing Harlowe's and Simon's pistols, urging their restraint. "Not here," she cautioned. "He's a Lagan trader. We must not make trouble with him. We've come this far."

"Those pets of his," Harlowe asked, ready to put a plas round between their eyes at the slightest provocation. "What are they?"

"A grogan. You know of the beast?" she asked. "They are extremely rare."

Simon's face twisted with devilish memories as Harlowe answered. "We've sucked face with them before," he replied, not holding back his hate.

"Come. Let us leave then, Captain," Quay urged, pushing him forward. "We must not linger. We must make it to my father's building, where we will be safe."

They didn't take their eyes off the Lagan and his two grogans until Quay led them down a back alleyway that she said was the short route to her father's office building.

Not far into their new direction, they quickly discovered the fat being's entourage was following them. This time the grogans were not held back by their restraints. They were freely roaming in front of the small entourage, completely without discipline. Like the one that had attacked them on Earth, their heads resembled a gargoyle with a long black snout of razor-sharp teeth from beneath snarling lips. The grogans' sole purpose was obvious: to protect their master while meandering through the dark, ghoulish back streets of Gibb.

Riverstone did his best to keep the cubs focus on the alley ahead while putting distance between them and the fat Lagan's entourage. But the grogans saw the cubs as Happy Meals, and charged. No one from the Lagan's group did anything to restrain the animals. Judging from the hideous smiles on their faces, they didn't care what happened to the cubs.

Riverstone had no way to protect them. His hands were occupied with keeping them from breaking loose. It didn't matter; the grogans were lightning-fast and covered the short distance in an amazing burst of speed.

33

Kicking Booty

QUAY HELD HARLOWE'S hand in check. His sidearms were unnecessary. The cubs were fearless. Molly and Rhud faced their attackers with blinding speed, slamming the savage beasts backward onto the pavement. Molly grabbed the first grogan by its neck and crushed it as if she were eating a hard biscuit Harlowe had tossed her. The sound of bones cracking under the pressure tore through the air. Molly then picked up the lifeless carcass and smashed the pathetic mass against the stone wall like it was worthless rubbish. The second grogan was more fortunate. It howled in excruciating pain as Rhud clamped his jaws around its throat, waiting for Harlowe's okay to put an end to its miserable life. Dark blood splattered onto Rhud's white fur as his jaws sank deeper. Then Harlowe snapped his fingers before the grogan suffocated from a crushed windpipe.

"Okay, Rhud. Let him go," Harlowe ordered.

The Lagan and his four henchmen stood in stunned outrage. Simon and Riverstone quickly drew their pistols as two in the group went for their weapons. With the wicked Gamadin barrels leveled at their faces before they could blink, the two showed a small amount of good sense, easing their hands away from their holsters.

Rhud obediently released the beast without another word from Harlowe. As quickly as they had turned hostile, Molly and Rhud were purring full throttle, brushing up against Quay and Harlowe's legs. Riverstone breathed a large sigh as he gathered their leashes.

The Lagan stood, shaking and stroking his seaweed hair behind his bodyguards. "What kind of magic do your pets possess?" he asked, his round, greasy face poking out from between his two bodyguards' shoulders. "My grogans have never been beaten," he told them.

Harlowe checked the cubs for injuries. They appeared unharmed. "No magic, toad. They just don't like being hassled."

"Sell them to me. I will be generous," the fat official demanded, as his guards helped the injured grogan rise.

"They are not for sale at any price," Harlowe sneered, guiding their group away from the scene. As they moved away, Simon and Ian walked backwards, covering their backs.

They had not gone far when the fat Lagan called out, "I will get what I want, you cowardly slops. You will see." His high-pitched, raspy voice echoed off the wet, dank stone of the alley.

Harlowe put a comforting arm around Quay's shoulder as they walked. She was shaking from the aftereffects of the altercation.

Riverstone, however, was in high spirits. "Did you see how the cats kicked booty? Man, I couldn't believe it. The General would have been proud." He reached down and patted them both on their backs. "You two were bad!"

Harlowe looked at Quay, his right eyebrow rising slightly. "How did you know?"

"Their mother," she said simply.

Harlowe recalled how the cubs' mother had almost killed Rex back on #2. The battle could have gone either way. She was that tough.

Harlowe took a quick glance back down the alley. The Lagan had waddled out from behind his guards and shot his injured pet through the head. Harlowe turned back, his skin crawling with disgust, wishing the fat alien had taken a plas round through his head.

"My father hates all Lagans," Quay commented with distaste. "They are known for their corrupt and dangerous ways. This one I have never seen before, but he appears particularly treacherous. We must hurry to my father's building. There is no telling what revenge he plots. Come, the Tomar Building is not far now."

Harlowe and Riverstone exchanged somber glances as Simon and Ian rejoined them, keeping their weapons drawn in case more trouble followed them.

* * *

After what seemed like another mile, they came to a large, open park with wide, grassy areas and trees that were like everything else on Gibb . . . gigantic! A single tree's shadow covered acres. Even the smallest treetops were twice as tall as the sequoias back on Earth. Thankfully, except for the shadows beneath the canopies, the sun finally made its way to the ground, brightening their way. It was a welcome relief to feel the warm rays on their faces instead of the cold mustiness of ancient stone.

As they walked along, beautiful bright red, white, and yellow flowers as tall as a man swayed in the slight breeze through the park. Their fragrant scent was a welcome surprise after what they had endured most of the day.

"There," Quay announced, pointing to the far end of the park. Two miles away was the most magnificent, emerald-green structure any of them had ever seen. The building rose over a mile into the sky, poking through a thin layer of white clouds. It was unlike any colossal structure they had seen so far on Gibb, or anyplace else, including Earth. "My father's office. The Tomar Building," she told them.

34

Tomar Building

THE GAMADIN CREW felt like Dorothy, the Scarecrow, the Cowardly Lion, and the Tin Man when they saw the Emerald City in the *Wizard of Oz* for the very first time.

"The Tomar Building is where my father resides when he is here on Gibb," she explained, so nonchalantly that she could have been talking about a piece of common furniture. Aside from its two-thousand-foot towers, the main superstructure of the building was over a mile high and as wide as two Manhattan city blocks combined. Unlike the other tall skyscrapers of the city, the Tomar Building was alone, surrounded by nothing but a great park of dense jungle and open meadows. At various locations around the building were six giant landing platforms, jutting out from the sides of the building, where shuttlecraft from all parts of the quadrant were coming and going as they engaged in commercial activities with Quay's father. Near the top of the structure was a smaller platform where Quay indicated her father would land his private space yacht if he were here.

Unlike the many ancient, weather-worn superstructures on Gibb, Quay's father's building was modern and new, and as green as a precious African emerald. It was constructed of giant beams of bronze metal, not old stone and mortar. The platforms were trimmed in a dull gold, along with many of the support beams that held together

217

the massive sheets of green-faceted glass. At the very bottom was a grand stairway that led up to the main entry level of the building.

Everyone stopped cold in their tracks and stared at Quay. "No way your father owns all of this!" they all gasped in amazement.

Quay stood puzzled, returning their looks of confusion. "Yes, of course. He uses the building to conduct his business here on Gibb. Should this be wrong?" she asked them.

Harlowe laughed at how she was misinterpreting their awe.

"Please, tell me what it is that is inappropriate. I can assure you my father is an honest trader with one of the oldest and most respected enterprises in the quadrant," she said defensively.

Harlowe came to her side. "Quay, nothing is wrong at all."

"Then why do you laugh? You are dissatisfied," she said, almost in tears.

"We are not laughing at you, Quay. We're stunned by your father's building." He spread his arms out fully. "Wow! We didn't realize your father was so...so..." Harlowe had trouble locating the words that adequately conveyed his feelings.

"Freaking rich, girl!" Simon said, helping Harlowe out.

"Aye," Harlowe countered.

"I bet God comes to your father for a loan," Riverstone said to Quay.

"No doubt," Ian added.

She still didn't get the truth behind the digs. "I must apologize. This is one of my father's lesser buildings. On Tomar his palace office is much more appropriate, I assure you. Judging by your ship, I can understand how disappointed you must be about our facility on Gibb."

Harlowe held her shoulders and looked into her gorgeous, dark eyes that would melt Titan methane crystals in an instant. "It's the coolest building we've ever seen, Quay. We laugh because it's way more than we expected."

Her face went from disappointment to pride. "Come then. Let me show you more. My father is eager meet you."

"He's here on Gibb? I thought you said he lived on Tomar," Harlowe said, suddenly becoming nervous at the prospect of meeting her father.

Quay pointed at a gleaming craft drifting down between the clouds. "I was mistaken. He is here now." The bright silver ship, worthy of any fabulously rich merchant who owned a godlike mile-high building on Gibb, slowly came to a gentle descent onto the private landing bay Quay had pointed to earlier. "Come. We must hurry! He will want to hear how you rescued me from the Consortium devils."

* * *

With a hurried pace, they covered the two-mile distance across the park in short order. Close-up, the magnificent structure was not as new as it appeared from a distance. The stone stairs leading up to the giant, three-story-high bronze doors were worn as though they had been used for centuries. Ian's com readings proved their suspicions right. The building was well over twelve centuries old. It was old by their standards but practically new for Gibb, and probably the reason it was built on the outer periphery of the city and not within the city itself.

Guards at the entrance tried to stop them from entering the building with the cats. Once Quay informed them of who she was, they were quickly escorted into the Great Hall with Molly and Rhud rambling alongside, wary of a new kind of jungle.

Inside, the crowded main floor seemed to cover acres. On the walls were magnificent ancient paintings of distant settings from all parts of the quadrant. Continuing forward, they passed beneath a hundred-foot-tall archway and moved out into the Great Hall itself, where traders and business patrons from all parts of the quadrant bustled about, negotiating their wares and services. High on the distant wall were gigantic billboards displaying the trade schedules for the quadrant. The translators inside their heads could not decipher the written figures on the billboards, but Quay understood the universal trader's language that was used throughout the quadrant.

Situated in the different sections of the Great Hall were diplomatic agencies that engaged in the selling of Consortium Rights of Passage for the thousands of vessels that traveled across the quadrant's trade routes. The Consortium rule within the quadrant was absolute. Interstellar travel across the quadrant without the proper transport permits was forbidden. Ships that were caught without travel documents were immediately confiscated, their cargo taken with no right of appeal. Consortium permission was costly, sometimes requiring thirty percent of the cargo's value for a one-way passage across a single sector. In less than two passings, Rights of Passage fees had increased two hundred percent, if one could purchase the rights at all. This was why Quay had brought them to Gibb. She wanted Harlowe to be legal.

Harlowe had his own opinion. "We don't need a hall pass to travel anywhere, Quay."

Quay didn't understand what a "hall pass" was, but she got the meaning. "The Consortium will stop you the moment you leave Gibb if you travel without a Rights of Passage."

"They will lose a lot more ships if they try that," Harlowe said, confidently.

"As strong and as powerful as I know you are, my brave Captain, you cannot fight the Fhaal and the Consortium alone. Why provoke such trouble when I can obtain the Passage here?"

Harlowe saw himself treading water on this one, and sinking fast. He wanted to tell her not to worry. They could take care of themselves. But when he saw the worry in her eyes, his dad's quote about arguing with a woman came to mind. "Most arguments with a woman," his dad would say, "are at best exercises in futility, son. It is better to ride the wave into shore than battle with a tsunami."

Harlowe graciously accepted the unbeatable outcome and said, "Yes, dear," agreeing to the hall pass.

While Quay was rewarding Harlowe with a big hug, Ian took the opportunity to play tourist with the Great Hall's twelve-hundred-year-old stone columns and walls for a backdrop. Who would believe this massive structure back home? Simon, of course, was never camera-shy and always struck the perfect pose with Riverstone and the cats. The four made the perfect Kodak moment.

Quay found what she was looking for. "I must go to the Pulgarian agency over there," she said, pointing to the busiest section of the Great Hall. "They will also inform my father of my arrival." Harlowe started to go with her, but she held him back. "No, I must go alone. I must follow protocol, even here."

Harlowe didn't like that. "One of us should go with you." He wasn't losing this one. "Take Molly then," he insisted, looking for a small victory.

Quay nodded her willingness to take one of the cubs with her. Riverstone separated one of the restraints and handed it to her. She kissed Harlowe for his wise compromise and threw him a small glint of *don't-worry-I'll-be-okay* before she walked away and disappeared into the crowd, leaving Harlowe looking like an abandoned puppy dog.

Watching her walk away, Harlowe breathed a sigh of heartache. He hadn't realized until this moment that saying goodbye to her would be this tough. Over and over in his mind he tried to think of a way to take her with him. As she had told him in their many conversations during the journey across the quadrant, Gibb was where they must part.

You are without a doubt the bravest of all warriors. I will miss you dearly, you know that, but one day after Tomar and Neeja are free and the Fhaal are defeated, we shall have our time together. I see it clearly. It is written in the stars that our paths must separate. You do understand, don't you? The Fhaal must be stopped. The freedom of Tomar and Neeja will depend on us. The Quadrant's independence is more powerful than we are, my courageous Captain from the stars.

He closed his eyes, feeling the hollow ache in his gut. He remembered someone else very dear to him telling him a similar story of freedom and the importance of the greater good for all. His memories of Lu came flooding back. She was never very far away, even now. Like Lu, sadly, Quay was right. Freedom from the Fhaal, or any tyranny, was much more important than either of them.... *We mutually pledge to each other our lives, our fortunes and our sacred honor,* he recited to himself. It was the final line of the Declaration of Independence that he recited to himself during the times his mission and trust called for him to use the power he was given.

Riverstone put a caring hand on Harlowe's shoulder. "She'll be okay, Dog. Molly won't let anything happen to her. You know that."

Harlowe kept his eyes in Quay's direction. He made a half-hearted attempt at a grin, but failed miserably.

Quay was gone only a few moments when Molly's loud snarl echoed across the floor.

35

Anor Ran

RHUD NEARLY RIPPED Riverstone's arm off as the white cub tore through the stunned crowd of onlookers. The Gamadin bolted right behind him, charging through the gap created by the powerful cub. When they arrived at the scene, Quay had Molly in a headlock, struggling to keep her from tearing a squad of a dozen armed security personnel apart. A security officer had his weapon pointed at Molly and was about to fire, when Rhud leaped. The crowd went wild as Rhud slammed him to the floor. Before the cub crushed the officer's skull, Harlowe jumped between them all and blew three pistols away from the other guards who were about to fire their weapons. Other guards tried to ambush Harlowe when he turned to check on Quay. Simon and Ian had their Captain's back, shooting half a dozen weapons away in a blink with precise shots. On the other side of the crowd, Riverstone coolly placed his pistol at the back of two black-helmeted heads who had snuck up from behind, and said, "Drop them, dudes," to the surprised guards. He nodded toward the floor, and the guards obediently dropped their pistols, the metal clanking on the ancient stone.

Knowing that his crew had the situation under control, Harlowe patted the white cat on the side of his mane and said, "Let him go, Rhud." Like he had done earlier in the dark alley with the grogan, Rhud released the officer's head and grudgingly backed away, his steel-blue eyes ready to pounce the moment the officer made any threatening advances.

Harlowe shot a quick glance to Quay and Molly, making sure they were okay. "I let you out of my sight for one second and you stop the world."

"Speaking to the Lady Quay in such a disrespectful manner is death," the officer on the floor scowled at Harlowe.

Harlowe stepped on the officer with his size-nineteen Nike, squashing his face against the floor. "Don't worry about her, toad, worry about the cat. I haven't fed him yet, bro." He then turned to Quay and asked, "What happened?"

Quay was about to answer when a hundred black-uniformed security guards stormed into the Great Hall, forcefully pushing the crowd aside and surrounding them all. The Gamadin squared off, ready for confrontation, when the troops opened up like the parting of the Red Sea. In the middle of the great divide, a tall and slender middle-aged man with coal-black hair and round dark eyes like Quay's, olive skin, and handsome features marched regally into the large inner circle like he owned the place.

"My father. Anor Ran. He is the Tomar-Rex, the master of all that surrounds us and beyond," Quay informed Harlowe before greeting her father. She was about to add a respectable bow when another imposing figure joined them in the circle. "Unikala..." she gasped.

Harlowe pulled Quay protectively behind him and faced Unikala, his pistol ready as the two cats recoiled and hissed, poised to attack. Harlowe didn't care how many weapons were trained on him. Unikala would be the first to die.

"Please...Please..." Anor Ran said with a casual gesture of his hand. "Put away your weapons. No one is in danger here." He indicated with his convincing eyes to the dozens of armed security forces around them to lower their weapons. Any further resistance was an insane man's choice.

The guards obediently followed the Tomar-Rex's orders and lowered their weapons. Harlowe slowly lowered his pistol and motioned to his crew that it was all right for them to do the same. He touched Molly on the back of her mane. "It's okay, girl." There was no other choice.

"I am happy to see you, Daughter," Anor Ran said, greeting her with a warm fatherly embrace.

"No thanks to Unikala," Quay sneered.

"The Pulgarians were evading a Consortium bureau ship, Anor," Unikala said in his defense. "They had no Rights of Passage. Their orders were to confiscate the vessel and retrieve the Lady Quay, whom we were led to believe was taken against her will."

"That is false, Father! I was not abduct—" Quay tried to say before the Tomar-Rex raised his hand and cut her off.

"This is hardly the place to discuss our private matters, Quay," Anor Ran said with finality. He then turned to Harlowe and asked, "And you are?"

Harlowe wondered if should extend a hand of greeting, but Quay's father appeared to know little of Earthly etiquette. Why should he? Harlowe was the being from another world, not Anor Ran. Sizing the man up in that instant, Harlowe saw a man of extreme wealth and power. Judging by the cool confidence in Anor Ran's large, dark eyes, Harlowe guessed he was in the presence of the Big Dude who controlled it all.

Harlowe was comfortable with power. Anor Ran did not intimidate him. He had known Harry and Sook Mars, a couple as powerful as any monarchy or heads of state on Earth. He had survived a

year under the iron fist of General Theodore Tecumsa Gunn. He
had dealt with the President of the United States and brought the
administration to its knees while handing a corrupt government back
to the people. He was well tested when it came to powerful beings.
Except for the women in his life, Lu, Quay, and his mother, there
were no other beings in the galaxy who could make him shake. He
was, after all, a Gamadin. Gamadin, as the General so often drilled
into their heads, were afraid of no one. *You are without a doubt the
toughest, most lethal weapons in the galaxy!*

Harlowe withheld his hand and allowed Anor Ran to set the tone
of the greeting.

"Captain Harlowe Pylott, sir. My pleasure."

Anor Ran was surprised. "I've heard a great deal about you. You
are much younger than I imagined."

"That's cool. I was thinking the same of you, sir," Harlowe replied
with a cautious smile. He did not bow, kneel, or give any indication
that he was anything but an equal to Anor Ran. He stood tall and
comfortable, his eyes clear and confident as he turned to the other
Gamadin, their sidearms still drawn in a defensive, circle-the-wagons
position around their Captain. They reholstered their weapons as
Harlowe introduced them. "This is my crew. My second-in-command,
First Officer Matthew Riverstone; Science Officer Ian Wizzixs; and
First Mate Simon Bolt." The step up in rank to First Mate did not
go unnoticed by Simon. They clicked heels together and saluted
the Tomar-Rex, who shook their hands and looked into their eyes
one by one.

Molly growled her displeasure. Harlowe looked down at her bright
blue eyes with an apologetic smile. Harlowe had forgotten the cats
in his introductions. "Oh, yes. This is my security team, Molly and
Rhud."

Molly growled again, acknowledging her place among the crew. Rhud, for his part, didn't seem to care one way or the other. He simply lay on the floor licking his forepaws, appearing relaxed and unconcerned as though nothing in the world bothered him. He started to go for his private parts, but Riverstone gave him a gentle kick in the rump to cool it. "Not now, Rhud," he grunted out the side of his mouth.

"They are exquisite animals," Anor Ran said, eyeing the cubs with great admiration.

"Quay found them," Harlowe informed him.

The Tomar-Rex took a brief moment to study the cats, watching their movements, their mannerisms, and the way they glanced at Quay but stared at Harlowe for direction. "Yes, they do adore her, but you are their master." Harlowe found the observation interesting, whether her father was making a simple comment or whether there was something much more meaningful in his remark. He reminded himself that a man of such wealth and power did not control all that he had by making idle conversation to placate anyone.

Finished with the introductions, Anor Ran stretched out his hand, parting the sea of security guards. He led their small party from the circle toward one of many massive columns in the middle of the Great Hall. "Let us go to my private chambers, where you may enjoy some of our famous Tomarian hospitality. I am sure you are weary from your journey."

Harlowe thought briefly. Getting to know the big guy in the quadrant was a plus, and spending more time with Quay was a two-fer. "We're down with that, sir," he said, graciously accepting the invitation. Simon and Riverstone were ecstatic. They had their minds set on meeting Quay's unattached sister. The plotting for a shot at the grand prize had already begun the moment they heard about her. As for Ian, as long as he had his camera and a com to study the ancient structures, he was a happy camper. So with no objections, everyone was all-in, even the cubs, who were happy as long as Quay and Harlowe were with them.

As they moved along, Quay took her father's right arm and matched his casual stride. Flanking both sides of the entourage were Molly and Rhud, lumbering along like they owned every square foot of floor they stepped on. No one doubted their self-anointed right either, giving them a wide berth. Behind them in the second tier of the official delegation were Unikala, Riverstone, and Simon, along with a number of well-armed security guards. Ian was almost last, enjoying the architecture and taking readings on everything but the tile grout.

Unikala wasn't thrilled at all about being relegated to the second tier. Riverstone and Simon wasted no time giving the Consortium high official some old-fashioned, earthly tomfoolery as if they were old business acquaintances. "Hey, Uni," Riverstone began, "in the market for some new attack fighters?"

Not to be outdone, Simon wondered who his tailor was and if he could get an emerald studded belt just like his to add to his collection. "By the way, Uni, do you know of any hot spots where the babes hang out? I say, it's been a long trip, old sport, and wow, would you get a load of those clodhoppers, bro!" Simon laughed, pointing at Unikala's oversized black boots.

Riverstone's eyes widened. "Dude, a friend of ours named Rex would be envious of those toes, huh, brah?"

Simon stared in amazement. "He would rip them right off your feet, pal."

Unikala never grunted or glanced their way once. That didn't stop Riverstone and Simon from trying. They kept up the digs until

Harlowe had heard enough, and turned around with a *knock-it-off* glare for them to cool it.

"The Captain saved my life more than once, Father," Quay added, careful for the moment not to betray their closeness.

"You will be handsomely rewarded, I assure you, Captain," Anor Ran said. "I thought we had lost her. Her mother will be equally as grateful as I am."

"Thank you, sir. No reward is necessary. We would have done the same for anyone who needed our assistance," Harlowe replied.

"My travels are quite extensive throughout the quadrant, Captain. I must confess I have never seen uniforms like yours. Where is your home, Captain?" Anor Ran asked.

"We are not from this quadrant," Harlowe informed him.

"Near Amerloi, perhaps?"

"A great distance from here, sir," is all Harlowe would give him. Anor Ran nodded his understanding, for he was savvy enough to realize by Harlowe's reply he would get no further information about his home world.

"I have seen your markings before, I believe. Are you traders?"

"That's right, sir. We travel for trade," Harlowe replied.

Anor Ran nodded. "I see." Harlowe doubted he believed him. It didn't matter. He was sticking to his story. Anor Ran then asked, "Have you traveled far?"

"We have."

"Perhaps you will spend some time here on Gibb and enjoy our hospitality," Anor Ran offered.

A not-so-subtle glance from Quay brought a positive response from Harlowe. "My crew would enjoy the time off." His answer brought a happy smile to her face.

The entourage arrived at a massive column where magnificent gilded doors, twenty feet high, opened up to an equally wide platform. It was large enough for their entire entourage to stand comfortably. Without a word from Anor Ran, only the first tier was allowed to enter the lift, along with a sizable squad of armed bodyguards. Considering the number of guards that traveled with Quay's father, Harlowe was unsure whether they were guests or prisoners. Sometimes the line between the two seemed difficult to determine.

The ride up the platform was rapid. Judging from the pressure on his legs and the levels flashing by, Harlowe figured they must have traveled a few thousand feet straight up in less than a minute. When they stepped off the platform, the Tomar-Rex made his apologizes. He had an important business matter to take care of first and would join them later at the evening meal. In the meantime, Harlowe and his crew were free to enjoy Tomarian hospitality.

Anor Ran then left the living arrangements in the capable hands of his daughter. The moment her father disappeared down a vast hallway taking the guards with him, Quay whisked off Harlowe to a nearby private balcony, where she kissed him long and passionately. After catching his breath, Harlowe nearly lost it looking out across to the great city of mile-high superstructures. He quickly realized he might have been off by a few thousand feet in his estimate on how far up Anor Ran's private chambers were above the Gibbian park.

Harlowe gasped in awe. "Sweet!"

The view was breathtaking. Here, above all the darkness of the lower world, basking under the bright orange star of Omini Prime, Gibb was once again a gloriously old city, full of massive architecture and ancient avenues. From here one could clearly see the Overseer of Path and its golden ball that guided the ships from all over the quadrant to a safe landing on Gibbian landing platforms. Harlowe tried in vain to locate his ship, but Gibb was too large and congested and too far away for him to see anything beyond the city. He wondered affectionately if *Millawanda* ever felt loneliness without her crew to dote over.

Suddenly Harlowe's communicator went off. Monday was calling in. "It's Squid," he said to Quay with a sigh. "I have to take it." Tapping behind his ear he asked, "What's up, Mr. Platter? Are the clickers behaving?"

Monday answered almost immediately. "Quiet as ghosts, Captain. They're on a union break. How 'bout you?"

"Some excitement along the way, but things are cool now. We're at Quay's father's place. We'll be staying over a few nights."

"Roger that, Captain. Have Rerun and Jester found any quail to hunt?" Monday asked.

"No quail, but they're checking on hunting licenses as we speak."

Monday laughed. "Aye, sir. Understood."

"Can you handle the vamps all by your lonesome?"

"We're like old drinking buddies, sir."

"Cool. Carry on, Mr. Platter. I'll check in regularly as planned."

"Aye, Captain."

"Captain out."

Riverstone's excited voice interrupted. Harlowe beckoned him to the balcony, where Riverstone saw from the looks on their faces that he was invading their privacy. "Sorry, Captain."

"What's up?"

His face lit up. "It's the biggest thing I've ever seen, Dog."

"Slow down. What is?"

"The pool! I swear it's like a small sea in there. Ya gotta check it out, Dog. All it needs is a few waves and we're in paradise." Riverstone's face suddenly became worried. "Oh no, Rerun! I gotta get back, Captain. He's already found a couple of babes to show us around. Man, this place is hoppin' with them." Riverstone displayed two thumbs up. "And no worms, brah."

Harlowe looked at Quay, pleading to be released. She laughed, pushing him toward the corridor. "Go on, my Captain. I must see my mother or she will call her personal bodyguards to find me."

Harlowe kissed her quickly on the cheek. "Meet us at the pool," he said as he ran off with Riverstone like a couple of schoolkids to find the indoor sea.

36

The Bargain

Anor Ran sat at his desk, reading an ancient document with deep interest. On a small holo-screen to his right was the image of the golden saucer his daughter had arrived in that morning. A side window in the corner of the screen zoomed in on the symbol just below its sweeping, top-level windows. Another holo-screen next to the first had images of the young soldiers his daughter had arrived with. In particular, he was more interested in the symbols they wore on their uniforms than in the young soldiers themselves.

"Anor Ran!" an angry voice boomed from outside his office chambers.

Anor Ran quickly tapped an activator at the edge of his desk, and both holo-screens disappeared in a blink.

"You promised her to me, Anor Ran!" Unikala roared up at the monitor as he stomped like an angry grogan into the Tomar-Rex's outer offices. From inside his small private office, Anor Ran stared with contempt at Unikala's image on the overhead screen above his doorway. For a man of such wealth, one might expect a lavish office of rich cloth and bejeweled wood, carved stone, and sculptures imported from the far reaches of the quadrant, but that was not the case with the great Tomar-Rex's personal office. It was small and basic. In the center of the office was an uncluttered desk of stone imported from his home world of Tomar. Placed at both ends of the desk were two comfortable chairs for clients or staff to sit during those rare meetings.

Anor Ran cherished his privacy. He enjoyed the solitude of his office and holographic scenes of his home world and family. A single round window looked out over the city and the park. It provided the room's only natural light. On the wall to his left, three other screens displayed views of the docking area where his sleek private vessel was parked. The second screen displayed the giant pool and its lush jungle, while the third displayed the long hall outside his office where his staff worked round-the-clock to keep his vast empire running smoothly. If he desired, with a spoken word, he could change the screens to one of a thousand other views inside the giant building or outside in the nearby park. At the moment, he had a strong desire to change the one with Unikala back to his wife, Sharlon, walking toward the pool with his daughter Quay.

The Tomar-Rex's personal guards moved to cut off the Consortium Commissar's entry.

"Let him pass," Anor Ran said, waving him in. Before Unikala entered his office, Anor Ran covered the document he had on his desk with unimportant papers. After Unikala entered, he dismissed his guards and went to a wooden cabinet, removing an old bottle. "Please, take a chair, Commissar. I have some Tomarian brandy I know you will enjoy. It is of excellent vintage."

Unikala refused and remained standing in front of Anor Ran's desk. "Our agreement, Tomar-Rex. I want it kept," the Commissar demanded.

Anor Ran returned the bottle to the cabinet without pouring a glass. It would be a shame to waste the noble spirit on one with such an indiscriminate palate who could no more distinguish a Tomarian brandy from a Naruckian ale. "The agreement still stands. I gave my blessing to the union of my daughter. Our bargain is honored."

"She has obviously forgotten her obligation. This Captain of hers has twisted her mind."

Anor Ran let out a small chuckle. "Come now, Commissar. Quay will not be easily swayed by anyone. I know. She is my daughter."

"She has been corrupted, I tell you," Unikala insisted.

Anor Ran saw no problem. "He will leave shortly. Then you will have her, and that will be the end of her brief affair."

Unikala stepped forward, resting his hands on his sidearms. "It is not so simple, Anor Ran. The Consortium lost many vessels in the pursuit of your daughter. We wish compensation for the loss of thirty-one attack fighters and a frigate. My battlecruiser has also sustained considerable damage. The Consortium must be reimbursed for the losses," Unikala demanded.

Anor Ran turned his head cynically. "Well, Commissar, that is a tragedy, but how can the Tomar Corporation be responsible for your losses? Quay was in transit to Tock-hyba. You were given the co-ordinates and her course. As you know, her ship had no proper Rights of Passage to travel along the sector. All you had to do was apprehend her vessel. Such a simple mission for a fleet like yours, is it not? What happened?"

Unikala was almost too embarrassed to explain. "It was this Captain Pylott. He interfered."

The Tomar-Rex laughed at the absurdity. "Interfered with a Consortium battlecruiser and its squadrons of attack fighters? How is that possible?"

Unikala lowered his head almost shamefully.

"Did they not have a Rights of Passage, either, Commissar?" Anor Ran asked.

Unikala silently replied with a negative turn of the head.

"You had the authority, did you not?"

"These demons do not respect authority," Unikala stated.

Anor Ran leaned forward on his desk of foot-thick stone. His forehead furled in befuddlement. "I don't understand. Quay contends they are but simple traders."

"They are not simple traders, Tomar-Rex," Unikala argued. "They are demons."

Anor Ran pointed at the screen displaying the giant indoor pool surrounded by a lush Tomarian jungle of native trees and waterfalls. He zoomed in on the three humans frolicking in the water, splashing each other, dunking heads and diving off the rocks next to the main waterfall. "Have you seen them? They are boys. They play like children. Surely they cannot be the evil demons you describe who are capable of destroying so many Consortium ships. What really happened, Unikala? Before I can justify paying you for your losses, I must know how you lost your ships. I must have details, Commissar."

Unikala wasn't laughing. If he were human, one would have seen the red embarrassment in his face. Instead, his face turned shades of a sullied green and yellow. "They may act undisciplined, but I assure you, Tomar-Rex, they are more than they seem. Their ship is more powerful than you could imagine."

Anor Ran quickly lost his mirth. "Mercenaries for the Fhaal, perhaps?"

"No. They act alone."

"How can you be sure?"

"They are not from this quadrant. There is no record of their ship anywhere in the archives."

Anor Ran had already discovered that much, and a great deal more. He wanted to know, however, how much the Commissar knew. "Do you know of their origin?" Anor Ran asked.

Unikala did not.

Anor Ran then moved from around his desk and walked over to a wall-sized star chart with all the known stars systems of the quadrant on display, along with the Tomarian trade routes in between. The map covered vast distances. "They came from somewhere. Where did your ships first confront this Captain?"

Unikala pointed at the lower left portion of the map. "There. In the Cerealian sector along the frontier."

The Tomar-Rex studied the area carefully. The sector was beyond the quandrant boundary and nearly off his star chart. "Yes, indeed. That is a great distance away, Commissar. You chased my daughter to the frontier and this is where you lost your fighters?"

"And a frigate," Unikala added. "My battlecruiser will take months to return to Gibb. I ordered the Oggian battle group to pick me up and bring me here."

"Your fortress at Og is a little short-handed then?" Anor Ran wondered.

"Hardly, Tomar. A Fhaal battlestar has arrived and is waiting for their shipments of thermo-grym crystals. Og is well-protected."

"And Sar? How is His Excellency these days?"

"Losing patience for his thermo-grym deliveries," Unikala replied with a harsh undertone.

Anor Ran's eyes narrowed as he faced the Consortium Commissar. "There was a shipment scheduled for delivery before the last cycle."

"It never arrived. It seems your daughter may have diverted it. She was taking it to Tock-hyba as payment for her asylum."

"Resourceful."

"A family trait, perhaps?"

Anor Ran was not offended. "I understand why the theft was never reported. Very well, inform Sar I will have a replacement shipment diverted for his battlestar before the end of this cycle."

For the first time since coming into the room, Unikala grinned evilly. "The Roshmar shipment?"

"Where else? It is en route. I trust you can handle the details, Commissar? Like a safe escort to Og, perhaps? We must not keep His Excellency waiting."

"The Viceroy will not take the news too kindly," Unikala pointed out. "Roshmar is fast approaching its cold cycle. Cinnebar will not survive without thermo-grym."

Anor Ran's concentration was still on the map. He cared little about the consequences of a diverted shipment of thermo-grym when it came to placating the supreme commander of the Fhaal invasion forces at Og. "Regrettable but necessary, I'm afraid."

Unikala turned to the wall-sized star map of the Omni quadrant, changing the direction of their conversation. "Do you recall the reports of a Fhaal battle squadron being destroyed beyond the frontier a passing ago?" Unikala asked.

Anor Ran had read the secret documents of the Fhaal defeat. He had paid a sizable ransom to obtain the information and knew the reports to be true.

"The reports were unverified if I recall, Commissar."

Unikala had intelligence resources of his own. "Possible, Anor Ran, but if they are true, this Captain may be responsible," Unikala speculated. "His ship appears to have traveled from that section of the frontier."

"They were unverified reports, Commissar, nothing reliable," Anor Ran pointed out.

"Of course, if this was the ship that destroyed the battle group and the Fhaal knew this was here at Gibb, what then?"

Anor Ran remained in deep thought as though Unikala was no longer in the room. He stepped slowly behind his desk, and leaned forward. "I would consider what you divulge to the Fhaal Commander, Unikala. The price you seek may cost the Consortium more than it bargained for."

"We must know more about this ship, Tomar-Rex. With Quay at my side, the Consortium and Tomar would be in a position to profit immensely from the Fhaal invasion."

"Then what of the Consortium, Commissar? A plot against the Supreme Council, perhaps?"

Unikala's face turned dirty green again, as if he had been caught with his hand in the cookie jar. "Perhaps no more a plot than the gathering of the Burgesses here tonight."

Anor Ran always played his cards close to his chest. "They are a small and powerless group, Commissar. What fear do you have of them? You are more than welcome to attend our social gathering, if you wish."

"I have a busy schedule, Anor Ran. Perhaps another time."

Anor Ran bowed his head in mock respect. "As you wish, Commissar."

"Can I tell His Excellency Sar the final shipments of thermo-grym will arrive from Erati by the end of the cycle?" Unikala asked.

Anor Ran forced a smile. He didn't even try hiding his contempt for Unikala. He raised two fingers. "Two cycles, Commissar. Delivery will be made no sooner."

"Sar has already threatened to seize Erati and take whatever he needs," Unikala warned. "Why test his patience further?"

"Or what, Commissar? As the Consortium has discovered, extracting and producing thermo-grym is a process unfit for self-serving regimes. When their stardrives have exhausted what they take from Erati, who will produce their precious yellow crystal then? The Consortium, perhaps? Sar is no fool, Unikala. He knows Tomar is his only source of pure thermo-grym for his stardrives for a thousand parsecs." Anor Ran scoffed. "Don't be fooled by His Excellency's petty posturing. The Tomar Corporation is their only source of continuous fuel. They must come to us to feed their battle fleets or remain idle as they have done for so many passings for lack of fuel." Anor Ran leaned forward. He was not a man who frightened easily. "Two cycles, Commissar!" he said sternly. "Sar will wait for Erati's fuel, or his fleets will be nothing but impudent hulks drifting in space. Even a Consortium frigate could destroy them then."

Unikala thought greedily. He liked the idea of an impudent Fhaal battle fleet. "Sar does seem hurried."

Anor Ran returned his gaze to the star map. "Yes, and for what purpose? I believe our impatient Fhaal commander has discovered our little quadrant a bit distasteful to his liking."

"What of Quay and this young Captain, Tomar-Rex? Do I have your permission to take what is rightfully mine?"

"Is it worth thirty-one more attack fighters, a frigate, and a crippled battlecruiser, Commissar?"

Unikala mused slyly. "A bargain, perhaps?"

"And the Captain's ship?"

"You may have it, but on one condition. The Captain's head is mine."

Anor Ran agreed. "Our business has concluded, then. Quay is yours. The ship is Tomar's."

Unikala left the office with an arrogant strut, satisfied that he had bested the great Tomar-Rex at his own game.

Anor Ran shut the door on the lingering bad odor before he returned to the secret document on his desk. In it he saw his triumph over the Consortium and the Fhaal, and how it would come to fruition. If the ancient scriptures were correct and the golden disk was indeed the ship of the "old ones," Tomar and the Burgesses would control the Consortium . . . and the Fhaal.

Smiling with the deep satisfaction that he was on the verge of complete victory within the next two cycles, his gaze returned to the screen with his daughter. She had done well, he mused gluttonously, seeking his third triumph.

The death of the boy Captain . . . tonight!

37

Sharlon

RIVERSTONE'S DESCRIPTION OF the gargantuan pool as an indoor sea was no exaggeration. It was so large that Harlowe felt Millie could bellyflop in the deep end and be lost forever. Ian's measurements were less inflated—his com readout was a bit more than five acres. The lush jungle island in the middle of the pool covered an acre by itself. The gentle sloping shoreline was made of salmon-colored sand and contrasted beautifully with the clear green water that reflected the jade stone from the bottom of the pool.

Harlowe and Riverstone had been doing forward and reverse 360 tucks off the hundred-foot cliff into the lagoon when they spied the two goddesses entering the pool area.

"Whoa, dude!" Riverstone marveled, nearly losing his footing from the cliff's edge. "That's Quay's sister?"

Harlowe caught his first officer by the arm and pulled him back from the brink. "She's a babe all right," he admitted.

Riverstone had found heaven. Quay's sister was even more beautiful than he imagined. "Who else could it be?"

Fearing Simon would hone in on his action, Riverstone searched the pool for the movie star's whereabouts. Luck was with him. Simon was occupied with a couple of locals on the other side of the rock island. The lush tropical trees, rock waterfalls, and tall palms surrounding the island blocked his line of sight. Riverstone would have to move quickly, though. This doe was too hot to go unnoticed by Simon's radar for very long.

Wasting no time, Harlowe and Riverstone dove off the side of the cliff together. They slid gracefully into a deep, clear pool and broke the surface like playful dolphins. Together they raced across the three hundred yards, knifing through the water with their powerful strokes, each trying to best the other in record time. At the halfway point, Riverstone pulled out in front, but only by a stroke. With a hundred left to go, Harlowe was even. Riverstone took back the lead with twenty yards left to go when Harlowe grabbed his ankle and crawled over the top of him to the finish line. On any other day, Riverstone would have bolted out of the water with thoughts of a punishing revenge, but up close, Quay's sister stopped all aggression. As the two goddesses stood regally at poolside, arm-in-arm, the two Gamadin climbed out of the pool dripping wet, gawking like goofy dimwits at the two visions like schoolboys stumbling over their first crush.

Quay broke the spell by making the introductions. "This is Sharlon, my mother."

Harlowe nearly fell over backwards into the pool, while Riverstone plotted.

Unlike Simon, who had no moral dilemmas about running off with another man's wife, Riverstone did. Only one time in his life had he ever thought about adultery and that was with Leucadia's mother, Mrs. M. The chance of Mrs. M ever leaving Harry was about as large as the Pope marrying Miss America. Still, that didn't keep Riverstone from fantasizing over the possibility of stealing Mrs. M from Harry, for she was at the time the most beautiful "older" woman he had ever known and the first real love of his life. When she was slain by the Dakadudes that night in Las Vegas, he figured he would never love any woman as much again...until now. Now stealing another man's wife suddenly crossed his mind for the second time in his life. Committing adultery with Sharlon seemed quite doable, and visions of whisking her away to some remote part of the galaxy were not so preposterous after all!

Quay's mother wore a soft green dress that floated in the shallow breeze around the pool. When Riverstone's lungs began pumping air again, his mind kicked in. It was obvious where Quay had inherited her stunning beauty. Sharlon was not quite as tall as Quay, six-foot-three tops. Up close and personal, however, that was her only trait that was second to her daughter's. In all other aspects Sharlon was Quay's equal, even though she was her mother. To Riverstone, this was not a competition. How could one distinguish one beautiful rose from another? It was the same here. Quay's hair had grown another few inches since leaving #2, and it now covered her large, sculptured ears. Sharlon's hair was the length of Quay's before the attack on her ship. It was long and dark and glistened under the bright artificial lights that hung down from the ceiling in great glass chandeliers. Her skin was tanned and young. She carried herself like Quay, gracefully proud and confident, leaving little doubt in Riverstone's mind that Sharlon was the queen of the Tomarian empire and an equal partner of Anor Ran, the Tomar-Rex, the king of his planet. The only thing that set mother and daughter apart were Sharlon's radiant green eyes.

Harlowe and Riverstone quickly traded surprised glances. Quay, after knowing them these many weeks, also picked up on their silent communication.

Sharlon held out her hand to Harlowe, who received it warmly. "I'm honored, ma'am."

"You must be the brave Captain Quay has told me so much about," Sharlon said, her eyes bright as jewels.

"Captain Harlowe Pylott at your service, ma'am," Harlowe replied, graciously bowing.

"You both swim well. Do you come from a water world?" Sharlon asked, her insightful eyes studying them as if peering into their souls.

"Yes, ma'am, we love the water," Harlowe replied.

"You would like Tomar, then. It also has much water to enjoy." She smiled, gracefully stepping to the water's edge. "I hope our little pool is adequate for your needs."

"No doubt. We've never seen a pool like this, ma'am," Harlowe replied, smiling approvingly, his eyes never far from Quay as he spoke.

This did not go unnoticed by Sharlon as she turned to Riverstone and asked, "And this handsome young man is?"

Riverstone tried to shake his hand dry before he took hers and stuttered embarrassingly, "Sorry, ma'am."

"Your hand is fine," Sharlon told him, her smile understanding. She took his sopping-wet hand without a second thought and held it warmly. Her touch was so soft and gentle; it felt as if he were holding something holy. Now he knew what an angel's hand felt like.

"First Officer Matthew Riverstone, ma'am." He bowed, following Harlowe's lead, and sighed regrettably when she released his hand.

Sharlon turned back to Harlowe. "Quay has told me so much about you and your crew, Captain." She hesitated, catching herself as though choosing her words very carefully.

"You have a very exceptional daughter, ma'am," Harlowe said.

"She has told me you saved her life more than once."

Harlowe glanced at Quay. "We saved each other. She's a good shot," he added.

Sharlon smiled graciously, as though knowing every detail of their relationship together. "I see; a mutual bond."

Harlowe didn't know how to respond to the comment and kept silent.

"Quay says your fish ta . . . ta . . ."

"Taco, mother. It is called a fish taco," Quay corrected.

"Yes. Taco. She tells me it is a delicacy beyond belief," Sharlon said.

Harlowe smiled. "You should visit us on Taco Tuesday."

"And a Doer dog," Sharlon tried to say.

"Dodger Dog, ma'am," Riverstone said. "Very famous from where we come from."

"Where is home, Matthew?" Sharlon asked casually.

"Uh, why, we're from —," Riverstone tried to say before Harlowe cut him off.

"We're not from this quadrant, ma'am," Harlowe replied.

A slight change in the glow of her green eyes allowed Harlowe a glimpse of Sharlon's objective. He had seen that look many times before in Lu when she was after something he wished to keep secret.

Sharlon then extended the Gamadin crew an invitation. "I would be pleased if you would join us tonight for a taste of our Tomarian food," she said. "I hope you will find it as tasty as a . . . a . . . fish taco, perhaps."

Riverstone's face had "all-in" written all over it. Harlowe accepted. "We'd love to, ma'am."

They continued walking along the water's edge when Sharlon spotted the white tigers across the lagoon. Rhud was sleeping on his back with legs up, exposed to the world. Molly was much more dignified as she sat vigilantly, watching the small group from her soft, grassy patch nearby along the shoreline.

"Your animals are exquisite, Captain. They seem to like our little natatorium," Sharlon said.

"It reminds them of their home," Harlowe replied.

"And that is..."

Harlowe returned a friendly wink. He would not be trapped. "Not of this quadrant," Harlowe and Sharlon said together.

"Yes, Captain, I am beginning to understand. You wish to keep your home's location confidential."

"It is best, Sharlon."

"Why do you look at me so, Captain?" Sharlon asked straightforwardly. "Have we met before?"

Harlowe didn't realize his gawking was obvious. "No, ma'am. We've never met, but a very close friend of mine had eyes like yours."

"My mother is not Tomarian," Quay said for her mother. "She is from a planet called Neeja."

Sharlon picked up on Harlowe's sudden look of surprise. "You know of my planet?" she asked him.

"Yes, ma'am."

"Was your friend from Neeja, Captain?" Sharlon asked.

"No, ma'am. Her mother was."

"Do you know her name, Captain?"

"Her name was Sook."

Sharlon looked away, toward the waterfall and the island.

"Did you know my friend?" Harlowe asked Sharlon.

Sharlon nodded. "I knew of her. She was an elite Triadian soldier of Neeja."

The idea that Mrs. M had a military background was no surprise. Harlowe recalled how lethal Mrs. M became the instant the Daks attacked the beach house that night in Newport.

Sharlon went on to say that her father was an archeologist working in the ancient catacombs of Amerloi, where he found a manuscript in the ruins of Hitt that told of a group of enforcers who kept the peace throughout the galaxy.

"The Peacemakers," Harlowe said.

"Yes. You have heard of them?" Sharlon asked.

"Quay said they were protectors of the peace."

"The Fhaal were about to destroy our beautiful planet when my father believed he had found a way to save Neeja. He felt the only hope for Neeja was the Peacemakers, but someone inside the Consortium Supreme Council betrayed Neeja before the Peacemakers were found. When the Fhaal attack forces struck Amerloi, my father had only enough time to tell one soldier of his findings before he was killed. That soldier was a Triadian." Her bright green eyes briefly lost their glow before she finished. "That was so many passings ago. It appears the Triadian you call Sook never found my father's Peacemakers."

Harlowe traded "all-in" glances with Riverstone. "Maybe we can help, ma'am," Harlowe told her.

Sharlon's expression suddenly changed from futility to almost a laugh. "You have the guile of a Peacemaker, Captain, I will give you that. The Peacemakers no longer exist. They live only in the stories of the ancients. My father's dreams of finding the saviors of Neeja are like Amerloi, gone with the winds of time." A deep sadness fell over her as she turned and started to walk away.

Quay rushed to her side. "Mother..."

Sharlon turned to Quay, taking her hands. "Quay, my daughter," she began, "the Peacemakers were mighty warriors. Their power was great and vast, but Omini Prime must fight the Fhaal on their own." She looked over to Harlowe. "I am sorry, Captain. I truly do not mean any disrespect. I am Neejian. There is no going back. Our saviors will never come. My father's effort was noble, but alas, he found nothing. Nothing! Because the great and powerful Peacemakers are gone." Now she had lost her laughter, turning almost angry with her loss. "Now we must do as Anor Ran believes he must do. We must strike a bargain with the Fhaal before it is too late."

Sharlon turned back to Harlowe. "The game is lost, Captain. The grogan devil is upon us. The quadrant's only hope is to survive amongst its conquerors."

Harlowe raised his chin high. "I don't believe in losing, ma'am."

"Then you will die," Sharlon said coldly. She excused herself, leaving them at poolside.

* * *

"That went well," Riverstone quipped.

"Swimmingly," Harlowe added.

Quay's eyes brimmed with tears for her mother.

"What now?" Riverstone asked, watching his new heartthrob disappear through a lavish archway.

"What's to talk about? The mission hasn't changed. We free Neeja," Harlowe replied simply, his word of honor still firmly intact.

Quay looked at Harlowe with futility. "My great and wonderful Captain, you have but one ship against a mighty empire and no Rights of Passage to go anywhere in the quadrant. You are lost."

Harlowe grinned at Riverstone. "Only one empire. That puts the odds in our favor."

Quay stared at Harlowe as if he had too much water sloshing around in his brain. "Are you not listening to what I'm saying, Harlowe? Surely, you do not mean such silliness?"

Riverstone laughed. "Oh, he does, Quay. He means every word."

"Such talk is suicide."

Harlowe's focus turned back to the island in the center of the pool. For him, there was more concern over Simon's whereabouts than evil empires. "Has anyone seen Rerun lately?" he asked Riverstone, searching the island where he was last seen.

Riverstone pointed to the far side of the island where the cubs were still lounging on the grass. "Last time I saw him he was wooing the locals with his Hollywood stories."

"Rerun is with my sister, Sizzle," Quay stated.

Harlowe stopped mid-breath and stared at Quay. "Sizzle? Your sister's name is Sizzle?"

"Yes, that is her name. Is something wrong?" Quay asked innocently.

Harlowe quickly tapped his ear communicator and called for Simon to respond. After several tries it was obvious the movie star had gone dark.

Ian replied over the com link, "I saw him swimming pretty fast, Dog, toward the far balcony." Standing on a tall rock near the cubs, Ian was tiny in the distance, but they could see him pointing in the direction Simon had taken.

"Maybe he's bringing her back," Riverstone said.

Harlowe knew better. "You've seen Quay and now her mother. Her name is Sizzle. What do you think she looks like? Would you bring her back?"

Riverstone stared at Quay. "Rerun's history."

Harlowe groaned, with his eyes fixated on the far balcony. "Sweet…"

38

Sizzle

"HOLD ON, SIZZLE," Simon said to Quay's younger sister. They were both standing at the edge of a wide outdoor balcony off the indoor sea. Simon had activated his SIBA, deploying the exo-suit's wispy-thin gossamer wings from under his arms. Once Sizzle had wrapped her arms around Simon's waist as if she were a passenger on the back of a motorcycle, they prepared to leap off the balcony and glide down to the park for a stroll through the lush forest a mile below.

"You'll have to stop kissing me long enough to strap you on, girl," Simon told her.

"Must you wear that mask?" sked, referring to the SIBA bugeyes covering his face. "I can't see your handsome blue eyes."

As eager as Simon was to leap off the balcony with Quay's drop-dead beautiful sister before Riverstone and Harlowe found them, he didn't want to lose her during their flight or crash into the Tomar Building trying to keep her steady on his back. That would be embarrassing, he thought, chuckling inside.

Except for her radiant green eyes and high cheekbones, Sizzle was Quay's near-physical twin. She was tall like Quay, well over six feet in height, and slender like an Italian model with long black hair, not straight like Quay's, but wavy in long gentle ripples that flowed softly down past her waist. Her olive skin was smooth. Simon doubted she had ever experienced a zit in her life. Her beauty was heart-stopping,

251

and he constantly felt as if had to wipe the drool from the side of his mouth when he talked to her.

As if a genie had granted all three of his wishes at once, his female radar had zeroed in on her the moment she stepped out onto the pool deck. Not two minutes earlier, he had watched Riverstone and Harlowe swim across the lagoon to meet Quay and her sister. Bummed that he had missed out again, he climbed to the top of the rock cliffs to lick his wounds when lo and behold, the new Mrs. Bolt came wandering into the pool from the opposite doorway. He didn't know Quay had more than one sister, nor did he care. An unattached twelve walking free in a land of tens required his immediate attention. With Riverstone and Harlowe occupied with their own Catch of the Day, Simon's opportunity was his alone. In a you-snooze-you-lose move, he dove off the high indoor cliff and while still in midair, activated the medallion that hung down around his neck. In a blink, the SIBA swallowed his body like Rex would eat a goat. Just before he struck water, his gossamer wings filled with air and he was skimming across the water, making a beeline toward his Tomarian goal. He swooped up over the pool edge and landed gently in front of the Grecian goddess, deactivating his skin just before touching down.

"Do you always introduce yourself so boldly?" the twelve had asked him.

"I do," he told her. He bowed, then took her hand and kissed it.

"You must be the brave soldier who saved my sister's life," she stated with confidence.

Simon wondered what sister she was referring to. Knowing only one, he made a stab in the dark that she was another sibling. "Quay?"

"She is my only sister," the twelve replied.

That was a shock. *Who was the other twelve across the pool, then? Did it matter?*

Simon's mouth had inexplicably turned dry while his tongue tripped over his normally smooth delivery. Talking to hot babes of this caliber required a rock-steady coolness that months of isolation had dulled. He was rusty. He had slipped up with Quay. He had let Harlowe beat him to the starting line. Not so here! He had finished first and intended to make the most of it. "That would be me," he replied, with no regard for fact. He then asked, "I was hoping to find a guide to show me around. Are you the one?"

He remembered how amorously her bright green eyes had looked the moment he dropped out of the sky and put on his first moves. For the longest moment she studied him curiously without saying a word. He wondered if he had blown it again. He was about to say something stupid like "Take me to your leader," when she saved him from further embarrassment. She took his hand and said with a warm smile, "You have found your guide."

All he could think of at the time was, *Ya gotta love this family...*

"Are you afraid?" Simon asked Sizzle, who was now firmly attached to his back.

"Should I be?" she asked, and then wondered what name he was called.

"Call me Reru—uh, I mean, call me Captain Starr," Simon said boldly.

She squeezed him closer, ready for launch. "Then let us fly away together, Captain Starr."

Looking east into the Omini Prime setting sun, they pushed off from the balcony like two mating dragonflies caught in the evening trades, gliding high in the air, first plunging down, extending their wings, then soaring playfully upward as the bright orange star slowly went down on the horizon. They dove through fluffy purple-and-orange-colored clouds as what remained of the sun shone through.

Its radiance was electrifying as it shot brilliant green, deep red, and yellowy orange spears of fading light through the colossal buildings of the city. The brisk and constant winds never faded, keeping them aloft while the SIBA's filament wings vibrated a steady treble hum. Simon faced them into the wind for altitude, and then they drifted silently in a quiet leeward direction. They were beautiful together as one, while three thousand feet below the giant overgrowth of the Gibbian park glowered grim and monstrous, steeped in the pitched blackness of night.

39

Turfan

Not far from the Tomarian office building, in one of the darkest regions of the Gibbian park, Unikala and Turfan, Quay's older brother and apparent heir to her father's commercial empire, walked side by side under the black canopy of the trees. It was a good place to talk privately. Except for bodyguards stationed around the perimeter, they were alone and well beyond any listening devices around the Tomarian Building.

Turfan was tall and strong like his father, with handsome, dark features and his mother's radiant green eyes. He wore the dark purple Tomarian uniform of the elite officer corps of the company. At his side, his weapon rested low and comfortable on his hip. His skill with a pistol was legendary. Turfan and Unikala often sparred with each other during their target sessions in the private range located just above the family living chambers. They had a mutual respect for each other's ability and often goaded each other on who might win an actual gunfight. Though neither dared try the other, it was almost a given that one day, as predictably as Omini Prime rising in the west each morning across the Gibbian mesa, the contest between them would finally be settled.

"Tell me, Unikala, about these strangers my sister has brought to my father's house," Turfan began as they moved along the hidden pathway.

Unikala breathed a heavy sigh. "I'm afraid I know very little, Turfan. They are a mystery."

"My father says they are quite young and undisciplined, hardly a crew that could command a ship that would cripple a Consortium mothership and her escort ships."

"Their youth is deceiving," grunted Unikala, the anger in his voice expressing his need for revenge. His sinister silvery eyes glared at the Tomarian heir, wondering how he had gotten such sensitive information. "The Tomarian Corporation will repay the Consortium in full for their loss, my friend."

"My father agreed to that?"

"We have an agreement or there will be consequences," Unikala warned.

"Do not mistake my father for a fool, Unikala. He has eyes and ears in the deepest bureaus of the Consortium, just as you have your eyes in ours. He knew before your arrival at Gibb that you had lost many ships to this stranger. It seems you were most fortunate to have escaped alive."

"The young Captain will not survive our next encounter," Unikala stated with determination. He then asked Turfan, "Has your father's spies discovered their origin? There may be more."

They continued walking again. "No. He seems as mystified by them as you. He sent a team of his best investigators to their ship parked just beyond the Horritan city and was unable to penetrate their shields. They found little. Like you, my father wonders who they are and why they are here. Were you able to probe their systems at all during the attack?"

"The evil grogans deflected our probes. We had to rely on secondary systems to make it back to Omini Prime."

Turfan's eyes became slits of death. "This is worrisome. These strangers must be eliminated. They could interfere with our plans. Have you contacted Sar?"

"Yes, Sar is aware of the situation. He wants the strangers stopped here at Gibb before they cause more trouble."

"My father departs for Roshmar after the banquet. We will take care of the strangers then."

"Sar will be informed of your swift action, Turfan," Unikala said.

Turfan looked at Unikala with a probing eye. "That Fhaal snake knows something about these strangers he is not telling us."

"Sar only cares about their ship and its destruction. Destroy the ship and Sar assures me he will give us what we ask for. Tomarian trading ships will have free passage throughout the quadrant after Omini Prime falls. This will include all Fhaal territories between Omini Prime to Po-Hara and a hundred parsecs out, including the Cerealean sector."

Turfan thought deeply. For someone who had just been given the richest trading routes in the quadrant, he was suspicious. Not even his father had achieved such access without Rights of Passage. "That is very generous of the Commander for the elimination of a single ship," he pointed out. "I have little trust in this Fhaal commander, Unikala. You would be wise to distrust his motives. My father always says if a deal is too good, there is a catch. We must know what the catch is and why Sar fears the strangers' ship. "

"We don't have a choice, Turfan. If we fail to destroy the ship, Sar will destroy us when the Fhaal invasion forces arrive."

"Understand, Unikala, there is no place in a Fhaal world for us unless we create one. They care not for commerce, only dominance over all that we possess. The Fhaal need the thermo-grym crystals from Erati. We must have patience, old friend. Their fleets are still cycles away. If we destroy the ship without knowing why, we could lose our advantage."

Unikala held his chin in thought. "Yes, I understand, Turfan. Of course, you are right."

"Have you seen Quay and reconciled with her?"

"I will handle her after tonight," Unikala grumbled.

"Eliminate the strangers quickly, then."

"Yes, after this Captain has disappeared, I will have her," Unikala said, his face beaming like one who had made a lopsided deal. "Anor Ran has agreed."

Turfan laughed, slapping Unikala on the back. "My father cannot give something he never had, old friend."

"She is his daughter. She must obey him," Unikala insisted.

Turfan continued to laugh. "Ah, if it were only that easy. You chased her across the quadrant, and still she eludes you."

"This Captain will pay the ultimate price for his interference, I assure you, Turfan."

"Take heart, Unikala, for many passings now my father has tried to control both my sisters' activities, but they are like my mother. No one, not even my father, could control her. I am afraid, Unikala, if you want my sister you will have to take her forcefully, for she will not willingly go with you if she has not the mind." Turfan turned Unikala around and they headed back toward the office building. "Come. Let us enjoy a good meal together. Sitting with the Burgesses will be great fun. We may even learn more about the honored guests my sister has brought so graciously to our door. Who knows, we may yet discover who they really are and why our dear friends the Fhaal are so concerned with them." As an aside, Turfan added, "Have you seen their sidearms, dear friend? Most unusual, wouldn't you say? I would like one for my collection. I wonder if they can use them or are they simply for pretense. I intend to challenge the Captain. Shall we see what he is made of, my dear Commissar?"

Unikala grinned slyly, knowing the outcome. The idea had merit, but the duel would never come to that. He had other plans in mind.

40

Eavesdropping

"Oh, Captain Starr..." Sizzle whispered, nuzzling close to Simon without his SIBA. For the past half-hour they'd been hiding behind a clump of thick bushes off the walking path. As much fun as flying around the Gibbian evening sky was, things got a little too dangerous when Sizzle tried to pry open his SIBA in midair to kiss his neck. In a situation like that, Simon made the only prudent maneuver he could think of; he dropped like a stone to the ground. The problem was, they hadn't been alone for more than a few minutes when their small isolated clearing in the dark suddenly became Grand Central Station in New York.

Simon watched Unikala and the strikingly handsome uniformed humanoid leave the clearing. "Who is the tall toad?" Simon asked, feeling a tinge of jealousy. He had waited too long to be with this heavenly doe. He didn't need any competition.

"My brother, Turfan," Sizzle replied. "He is responsible for my father's elite personal guard."

"They were talking about us, weren't they?" Simon asked.

"Yes."

Simon sighed. He had to warn Harlowe.

Sizzle's bright eyes suddenly refocused. Quickly, she straightened up and tied her long, wavy hair behind her head. She was all business now, counter-plotting, her mind already working on a plan to help

Simon warn his crew of the pending danger. "Yes, we must hurry," she told him, as if a moment ago was a distant memory. She took his hand. "Come, there is a hidden path back to the Tomar Building."

"You don't seemed surprised at all by this," Simon said.

Sizzle's eyes saddened. "My mother has known of my father's subversions for many passings. It is something we live with. One day maybe this will change. I fear for you and your crew, Captain Starr. I do not understand why Unikala and my father are so fearful of you. What have you done?"

Simon finished snapping on his Gama-belt and adjusting his sidearm. "When we found your sister, we had to damage a few of Unikala's ships. He got a little rad about that."

Sizzle didn't understand. "Your fleet of ships confronted the Consortium?"

There was no time to explain how one ship had destroyed the Consortium fleet. Besides, commanding a fleet of ships was a lot more plausible than one. It stepped him up another notch in his captain's position. Simon left out the details and replied, "It's complicated, Sizzle. Come on, I gotta make a call to the Cap—, I mean my First Mate Pylott."

He took her by the hand and started to lead her out of the under-brush when she yanked him back.

"No, they are searching the grounds," she said, pointing to a half-dozen heavily armed guards coming their way with scanning devices. "My brother is very thorough. His guards have sensors scanning the area where he and Unikala have been. If you activate your device too early, it will betray us."

"Hold still," he told her, pulling her down with him and sur-rounding her with his arms and legs. He then touched the medallion around his neck. When his 54th century SIBA deployed, it spun its stealth qualities around them both, encapsulating them inside its protective cocoon.

The guards came within a few feet of them with their instruments, but they detected nothing. Simon waited for the guards to finish their scans and leave the clearing before he deactivated his SIBA.

They rose together and stepped out of the bushes onto the pathway. Simon took her in his arms, looked down at her intelligent, deep green eyes, and kissed her. "One for the road," he winked. At that moment, a Tomarian guard came back to the clearing as if he had forgotten something.

The guard stopped, reacting in disbelief that anyone was in the clearing.

All Simon could think of was protecting Sizzle. In the distant past he would have thought of only himself and fled the clearing. No one was worth his life, not even a gorgeous doe. His life had changed. He was Gamadin now. It didn't matter whether or not she was a lovely goddess with brains or whether she thought he was a good guy or an ugly gomer. If anyone needed his help, he was there to give it. With no thought of his own safety, he launched himself at the Tomarian guard. Before the guard could draw his weapon, Simon was on him, collapsing the guard with a single kick to the head.

"Run, Captain Starr!" Sizzle shouted.

Not far behind the first guard was the rest of his platoon. They saw the other guard on the ground and reacted. They were Tomarian's elite guards, but even six were no match for a Gamadin-trained soldier.

Simon charged, surprising the squad with a vicious attack. With impossibly fast fists he snapped necks, broke faces, spattering noses, and crushed thoraxes, while spinal cords cracked from powerful kicks. Before they understood what kind of power had struck them, every guard was down and scattered around the small clearing.

Sizzle's mouth hung open in awe as she stared in shock at the fallen guards, some still twitching, but all very quiet.

When Simon returned to make sure she was okay, he saw the stunned look in her eyes. "What's wrong?" he asked her.

She was speechless for a long moment, her eyes fixed on the bodies. "You beat them."

"Yeah, I had no choice."

"Yes, but you... They were my father's finest guards and you overtook them so effortlessly." Sizzle might have thought Simon was a playful toy at first, but now her eyes studied him with a whole new respect. "Who are you?"

"Captain Starr, remember?"

"No one fights that way. Are you a cyborg?" She was serious.

Simon was caught off guard by the question. He wiped the blood from his face where a branch had scraped him when he charged the first guard. He took her in his arms and looked in her deep green eyes. "I'm no cyborg, Sizzle." He pointed at his cheek. "See, I bleed. I'm as human as the next guy. If he had shot me, trust me, I would have felt it." He looked around for a way out. "So where's this path back to your dad's place? I've got to tell Harlowe."

Sizzle grabbed his hand before he could move for his communicator. "No. Turfan's sensors are everywhere."

Simon didn't argue the point. Sizzle knew what she was talking about. The cocoon trick worked only if they were stationary. They had to move fast before another platoon came looking for the other security guards.

"Which way?" Simon asked, looking around in the darkness. Still stunned, she nodded, pointing in the direction. He grabbed her by the hand and started running. Once out of the clearing, they found another path leading back to the Tomar Building. They took one step and heard a loud pop, jolting them to renewed readiness. A brilliant orange flash of light exploded out of the night before either of them could react.

41

Spearmint

WHILE HE WAITED for the call to summon them to dinner, Harlowe stepped outside in the fresh air to the great balcony outside their room, leaving Riverstone behind to finish primping. *Worse than a woman*, Harlowe thought. He scratched Rhud behind the ear as the growing cub lay at the doorway, grooming his pure white fur. Molly was with Quay. Anor Ran's security guards might be all over the floor protecting the family, but an uneasiness gnawed at Harlowe. He didn't know why. It had been one of those days. After watching how the cubs had handled the grogan beasts in the alley he'd thought he could relax a little, knowing they were up to the task.

The Gibbian city lights were breathtaking. The giant ball of the Overseer of Path shone high above all the other giant structures, guiding ships into port from places Harlowe had only thought about in his dreams. The great skyscrapers surrounding the Overseer of Path were even more majestic at night. At this height, a mile above the great park, the sounds of the jungle made a strangely soothing cacophony of screeching birds, squawking animals, and fiddling insects. The air was cool and sweet, with only a small taste of Horritan odor invading the tranquility of a perfect night. He could understand why Anor Ran had built his private quarters so high. From here, far above the Gibbian corruption, his family's private quarters were a sanctuary of serenity and peace.

Yet *Millawanda* lay hidden from view behind the walls of the city, and Harlowe worried maybe more than he should have about her safety. *She's a big girl, toad. She survived thousands of years without you; a little longer won't hurt.* Except for the trek across Mars that nearly killed them all when the General dropped them off at the edge of Schiaparelli Crater, this was the longest time he had ever been separated from his ship. The separation made him uncomfortable and anxious. He felt like a doting father worried about his daughter being out too late on a Friday night.

"We're cool here, Captain," Monday reported during his last check-in moments ago. "Quincy is beating me in chess and the toads are still trying to find a way through the barrier." Monday giggled. "No problem. I sent a few clickers out to keep them honest."

Harlowe laughed silently, musing over the clickers making scrap metal out of Unikala's equipment.

Still, as upbeat as Monday sounded during his report, Harlowe's gut told him otherwise. Unikala wasn't stupid. He was jealous of his relationship with Quay. It didn't take Dr. Laura to tell him the Consortium Commissar was plotting something against the Gamadin for nuking his battlecruiser. He felt like a turkey in the middle of hunting season with five shotguns pointed at his head and no place to hide. The fortunate discovery of Quay's mother being Neejian made staying for dinner a must. A few hours of socializing to gather information about her planet was well worth the risk.

If your opponent is of choleric temper, seek to irritate him; so says Sun Tzu.

Rhud suddenly stopped his grooming and jumped to immediate readiness. Harlowe sensed the tension as two massive doors from another section of the balcony opened with a loud clank. Four

Tomarian guards double-timed through the doorway, securing the area. Anor Ran appeared momentarily, meandering casually between his guards, out onto the large stone deck. He was dressed in a smart red silk smock, very plain but rich in style, with a golden belt filled with no doubt the rarest of jewels. His trousers were a darker red. His sandals were gold-laced and adorned with a single, 500-carat green stone in the center of each buckle.

Rhud stood ready in the middle of the deck, blocking Anor Ran's path. The guards didn't know quite how to handle the white beast. Before things got out of hand, Anor Ran, with a wave of his hand, dismissed his guard and stepped around the cub.

"Nice duds," Harlowe said to Anor Ran, as he strode up next to him on the balcony.

"Your pet goes where he pleases," Anor Ran commented coolly on the cub.

"A free spirit," Harlowe replied.

"My guards might have hurt him."

"I doubt it."

Anor Ran grinned at Harlowe's confidence. "Have I come at a bad time?"

"It's your place," Harlowe replied and pulled out a stick of gum.

"What is that called?" Anor Ran asked, eyeing Harlowe's gum with interest.

"Spearmint," Harlowe replied, putting the stick in his mouth. "Want one?"

Anor Ran didn't see where Harlowe kept his supply. He saw only one stick.

Harlowe saw the dilemma and called to the slightly open doorway to his room. "Jewels, a spearmint for Anor Ran, if you please."

A moment later, Anor Ran's eyes widened as Harlowe's robotic servant came clickity-clacking out from the room with a stick of gum in its pincers.

"I was unaware you had brought servants," Anor Ran said, taking a piece of gum from Jewels.

Harlowe smiled. "Never leave home without them."

Jewels turned and dutifully left the balcony.

With the first bite, Anor Ran was unexpectedly surprised by the superb taste. "Remarkable. One of your trade products?"

"You'll love our double-doubles."

He held up the uneaten portion of the stick. "Perhaps you can sell a quantity to me."

"I'll have a batch brought over. On us." After a gracious thank you and more small talk, Harlowe asked, "What brings you to the balcony, Anor, the view?"

"Do you know of the Fhaal?" Anor Ran asked Harlowe.

After thinking a moment, Harlowe offered, "Is that a basketball team?"

"A mighty empire of tyrannical beings."

Harlowe shrugged. "Sound like Daks."

"They intend to overthrow our quadrant."

"That can't be good for business," Harlowe stated.

"Yes. For many it will be the end."

"And for you?" Harlowe asked.

"I will survive."

Harlowe smiled wryly. "You sound like a dude who lands on his feet."

"Your ship. I would like to purchase it," Anor Ran said, then added, "I will include Quay with the bargain."

"Didn't you try that one with Uni?"

"The Commissar will never have Quay."

"With or without my ship, I have Quay. That is no bargain," Harlowe replied coolly.

"In this quadrant I have the final say on Quay's disposition."

"I am not from your quadrant."

"All who pass through the Omini Prime are subject to its laws."

Harlowe blew a bubble with his gum, admiring the city lights. "They're bad laws. People should be free to travel where they wish without fear of Consortium authority. The Quadrant would prosper more with freedom rather than restraint, Anor."

"You sound like a Burgess," Anor Ran said.

"If they stand for freedom, I'm all-in."

"They are meeting here tonight."

"Cool." Harlowe then asked, cutting to the chase, "My ship is long past her warranty, Anor. What makes her so valuable to you? You have everything." Harlowe nodded toward Anor Ran's lavish personal spacecraft. "My ship is not much compared to what I see you flying around the quadrant in."

Anor Ran remained coy. "I have my reasons, Captain. I have made a fair offer. Do you accept?"

"You have made no offer at all," Harlowe countered.

It was Anor Ran who broke first. "Come, come, Captain. I can make you wealthy beyond your dreams, your crew included."

"Would you trade Erati for my ship?" Harlowe asked, out of the blue.

Anor Ran and Harlowe locked eyes, testing each other's resolve. It seemed Harlowe had hit one out of the ballpark with the Tomar-Rex. "What do you know of Erati, Captain? Quay?"

"Too late. Offer withdrawn. I was trying to see how far you would go. It seems you have your limits, too. Like Erati, my ship is not for sale at any price."

"I offer protection."

Harlowe turned his focus back to the city lights and stated confidently, "I have protection."

"Your arrogance may make it difficult to leave Gibb, even with my daughter," Anor Ran warned, seemingly helpless to stop any external threat to Harlowe and his ship.

Harlowe closed his eyes, enjoying the sweet aromas of the night air. "The evening was moving along so nicely, too."

A Tomarian servant stopped at the doorway and announced that dinner was ready.

"Heed my warning, Captain. I will have your ship before the next cycle is complete," Anor Ran, his words thick with malice.

Harlowe blew a bubble that covered half his face before it popped. "Shall we chat with the Burgesses, Anor? I believe our conversation is done here."

42

No Jo-Li Ran

TURFAN HAD NEVER seen his father so angry. Anor Ran stomped into the great hallway from the balcony seething mad after leaving the visitors' chambers. "I should kill them now."

Turfan bowed. He would carry out the order while the guests slept.

"Tell me of your progress," Anor Ran demanded.

"A thousand pardons, father, but there has been no breach of the ship's barriers," Turfan replied.

"I grow weary of excuses, Turfan. We must have access within the cycle or we will not be in any position to stop the Fhaal advance."

"Agreed, Father, but this barrier is mystical. Their energy field has power beyond what our scientists can break. The ancient documents must hold its secrets."

Anor Ran turned his head, his large, dark eyes wild with frustration. "The old ones were careful, Turfan. I have read the scrolls of Hitt thoroughly. They divulge nothing of the Peacemaker ship, except their warning that the fearsome Gamadin of the galactic core will cleanse the stars and there will be peace. That we cannot have."

"Surely you don't believe these young humanoids could be Gamadin, father?" Turfan questioned. "Their actions speak for themselves."

Anor Ran saw the whimsical mistrust in his son's eyes, and agreed. "Yes, I have watched them play. They are juvenile. However, I have

271

seen the reports, as have you. Their power signature is unknown. A single ship destroyed the Consortium battlegroup in the Cerealean sector and damaged the Commissar's mothership. The facts cannot be dismissed, Turfan. What power is capable of such distruction? Not even the Fhaal possess such a weapon. This Captain may seem youthful and inexperienced, but we must act prudently. He is either fortunate as a trulac or a very shrewd imposter. I for one will assume the latter until proven otherwise."

Turfan brought his hand to his sidearm that hung low on his hip. "May I have your permission to test this imposter, father? Perhaps I will expose his deceit openly."

Anor Ran answered with a sly grin. "Quay says he is the fastest she has ever seen."

"She exaggerates. I'm afraid her fondness for this Captain has clouded her judgment."

Anor Ran nodded his approval of his son's plan as they continued down the corridor. "Yes, by all means, make your challenge. Killing the young Captain may make Unikala forget his losses."

Turfan crossed his right arm in front of his chest, saluting his father before departing. "By your leave, father."

Anor Ran had a more pressing matter to settle before he was dismissed. "And what of your meeting with Unikala, Turfan? Has the Commissar made his bargain with you also?"

Turfan tried to feign innocence. "Father?"

"It is quite clear why the Fhaal advance on Omini Prime was halted and why they need our power crystals. They have exhausted their resources searching for this Gamadin ship they believe will destroy them. How much did Unikala offer you, Turfan?"

Turfan stuttered, unsure of his answer. He then bowed his head in disgrace. It seemed his father knew every detail of his collaboration with the Consortium Commissar. Anor Ran then answered for his son. "A high position in the Consortium High Council, no doubt. Just where do your loyalties lie, my son?"

Turfan had a response, but Anor Ran still would not let him speak. He lifted his open hand to save his son from a pathetic reply. "Do not speak my son, for the words you utter will only betray you more. I would then have to end your life here before your duel with the young Captain." Anor Ran lifted Turfan by his chin, wishing he had half the inner strength of his younger siblings, or but a fingernail of the young captain's courage. His heart was heavy that he had to eliminate the captain and his crew. They would have made fine additions to the House of Ran. During his many relations over the passings, he had learned that those with such virtuous convictions were the most difficult to control, for they could not be bought or manipulated at any price. However, they had weaknesses. Anor Ran has dealt with high moralistic beings before. In nearly every case, their weaknesses centered around three basic principles: the beings who serve them, their families, and their idealistic goals. This Captain was no different. He had the same limitations. They merely had to be identified. His crew, Anor Ran's daughter Quay, and his ship were what defined this Captain. Control them and he controlled the Captain and through him, the prize he wished for most of all—the Gamadin ship.

Anor Ran said, "Ah, I nearly forgot. The Captain's crewman you have captured tonight with Sizzle. Have you killed him?"

Turfan's eyes glowed with surprise. His father always knew too much. "No, Father. He is alive."

Anor Ran was relieved his son had not gone too far. "Do not harm him, Turfan. He is more valuable to me alive."

"Yes, Father."

"Unikala will use Sizzle as security. His plots are so predictable. I will deal with our ambitious commissar in due course. For now, let him believe his vision of an imperial Consortium is close at hand."

"Yes, Father, as you wish," Turfan replied, bowing.

Anor Ran turned away, his guards flanking him on both sides, leaving his son to brood on his future. He had taken only a few steps when he turned back to Turfan. "Regrettably, your mother and Quay have planned a banquet with the Burgesses in the Captain's honor. No doubt Sharlon enjoys the company of these young officers," an observation Anor Ran found puzzling. "I will allow her to go with her flirtations." He touched his chest. "Even the Tomar-Rex must make sacrifices for the good of freedom," he laughed. He then glanced at Turfan's sidearm. "Then afterwards," he shrugged unemotionally, "you may have your trial."

Turfan returned the smile. He was delighted with the task to match his pistol against the pretenders. He bowed from the waist proudly. "I am honored by your charge, Father."

"Remember, allow your mother her moment."

Turfan bowed with an evil smirk. "I will, Father."

Anor Ran then dismissed his son with a distasteful wave of his hand. His shame-filled eyes followed Turfan down the long arched corridor and into the elevator with his bodyguards. It was not his proudest moment. Anor Ran felt that his failing as a father was never more evident. His son was flawed and weak. There was no Jo-Li Ran that ran through his son veins. The ancestor, who a thousand generations ago began the Tomarian enterprise, had no male heir. Turfan was pathetic and devoid of character. Sadly, his son would never become a Ran.

When the doors of the lift closed on Turfan, it was only then that Anor Ran spoke. "You heard?"

From behind a hidden panel, Sharlon stepped forward. "Release the Captain's crewman and Sizzle, Anor," she demanded.

Anor Ran turned. He could not face his wife directly, for she was not weak like her son. Jo-Li Ran ran through her in rivers, as it did in Quay. "In time," he said coolly.

"They are of no use to you."

"They will not be harmed, I promise you."

"You will never capture the Captain's ship."

"You believe this is my goal?"

"I have known you for many cycles, Anor. I know it is. I see you plotting even as we speak."

Anor Ran's silence meant he believed the capture of the vessel was within his grasp.

"You will not defeat the Gamadin, Anor."

Anor Ran looked at Sharlon. "You believe they are the ancient ones?"

"I believe what Quay has seen with her own eyes. Unikala's losses were no illusion. "

"No, they were not," Anor Ran admitted.

"The old ones made certain their power lived on. Though they are but boys, her power may live within them. By all that is holy, Anor, if the ancient scriptures my father discovered at Hitt are true and these boys are indeed Gamadin, then they will cleanse the stars for all."

"And free Neeja, a dream I would give you, Sharlon, if it was within my power."

"The Captain makes no secret of his plan to free my planet."

Anor Ran expressed his disbelief. "A noble cause, but hardly possible. The young Captain would have to destroy the entire Fhaal invasion armada to free Neeja. Even a Tomar alliance with the

Consortium would not accomplish such a foolhardy endeavor. It is self-destruction."

Sharlon stared at Anor Ran with tenderness. "I fear for you, Anor. If the Gamadin resides within them, all will be crushed; even you, Anor."

"Unless there are more, this young Captain will fail. He is but one ship against an empire and the Omini quadrant."

"Quay speaks of freedom for the quadrant."

"It is a dangerous course she plots."

"The Burgesses will stand with her," Sharlon stated defiantly.

"They are all fools." Anor Ran felt self-preservation was the only way.

"She is Jo-Li Ran."

Anor Ran sighed. Yes she was, of that he had no doubt.

"Anor, you must listen. Alliances with the Consortium and the Fhaal will not save Tomar. We must stand together to fight the oppression that has invaded our quadrant. With the Gamadin, there is hope. Fight with Quay and this young Captain. Let Sizzle and the crewman go, and join with the Burgesses and Quay in their quest for freedom."

Anor Ran took Sharlon in his arms, looking her in the eye. "I will give you my answer tonight." He then released her and together they began walking toward the dining hall. "It has been many cycles since we have enjoyed a meal together. Let us enjoy a peaceful gathering with the company of Quay's young Captain, his officers, and our dear Burgess friends."

41

Burgesses

DINNER WITH THE Anor Ran family and invited guests was a formal occasion. Harlowe, Ian, and Riverstone were given dark green togas with gold and jeweled clasps to wear for the occasion. The clothes were a little tricky to put on. They needed help from Quay and Sharlon, draping the long ends over the shoulder first before they emerged from their rooms looking like regular members of the Tomarian upper crust.

After seeing so many movies like *Indiana Jones and the Temple of Doom* where the main course was monkey brains and stuffed giant beetles, they were more than a little anxious about what they might find at the dinner table. Riverstone thought about faking a stomach-ache and sitting out the dinner, but when Quay informed him he would be sitting next to her mom, monkey brains seemed like a Cold Stone triple-scoop cone dipped in chocolate. The menu may have lacked double-doubles and cookie-dough shakes, but to their pleasant surprise, there were many familiar-looking foods;: crusty breads, corn, various odd-colored vegetables, and a copious assortment of meats. The meat dishes were covered with rich fruit glazes and yellow sauces, which may have been a plus considering what they had seen earlier that day. Quay assured them that none of the meats were the small horses from the Gibbian market.

It was the custom to sit cross-legged at the long, low table. It reminded them of the Japanese back on Earth who ate their meals in the same fashion. All the guests were seated around the table with Anor Ran and Sharlon at the head. Sitting next to Sharlon was a very happy Riverstone. Ian was next, while Quay and Harlowe were seated to the right of Anor Ran. There were four empty places. Two next to Harlowe were for Simon and Sizzle when they showed up. At the far end, Sharlon had reserved a place for her son Turfan, whom Harlowe had yet to meet. The other guests were the Burgesses who had come from all parts of the quadrant to be here tonight.

When Riverstone took the first sip from his glass, the look of surprise on his face prompted Anor Ran to ask him, "Do you find the drink offensive, First Officer? Would you like something else? Perhaps something a bit more gentle."

Riverstone went with the flow by taking another long drink before he replied. "No, this will do fine. Nice taste but a little weak. On our planet we usually have our cola a little sweeter."

"You have this drink from where you come from?" Anor Ran asked, intrigued.

"Yes. It is very popular."

Anor Ran was surprised. "It is a rare beverage on Tomar. Only a very few have ever tasted it."

Riverstone lifted his glass and the servant obediently refilled it. "If you put it in a bottle and sell it six at a time, trust me, brah, you'll make a fortune overnight."

"Has anyone seen Mr. Bolt?" Harlowe asked, interrupting the flow of conversation. "He should be here."

"He is with Sizzle, Captain," Sharlon replied. "I'm sure they are fine." Her golden robe was studded with the finest jewels, befitting royalty.

"Yes, ma'am, but I like my crew together when we dine. He has not checked in with me in several hours."

"Would you like for me to send a few of my personal guards to find him, Captain?" Anor Ran asked.

Harlowe caught a hidden tell in Anor Ran's glance. *The dude knows more than he is letting on.* After their conversation on the balcony, he wasn't surprised. He figured their chances of having to fight their way out of the building were pretty good.

With a slight nod, Rhud came to Harlowe's side. Harlowe then whispered instructions in the cat's ear before he said to his host, "No worries, Anor Ran. My cats will find your daughter and my officer and bring them back to the table."

Anor Ran's eyes followed the cubs out the massive bronze doors of the dining hall. "They are remarkable pets, Captain. Would you consider selling them?" he asked.

"They are not for sale, Father," Quay quickly countered.

"Everything is for sale, daughter, even the Captain's beautiful cats. Am I correct, sir?"

Harlowe forced a smile. "I don't own them. You would have to ask them, Anor."

After a hearty laugh, Sharlon clapped her hands. "Well said, Captain." Then to Anor Ran she said, "See, my husband, not everything has a price."

Anor Ran forced a defensive smile. "Of course, my lovely wife is quite correct. My apologies, Captain, if I offended you and your pets."

"We have a saying where we come from, Anor Ran. 'No harm, no foul,'" Harlowe replied.

Anor Ran laughed, and so did his guests. "A worthy quote, Captain."

"And where is your home, Captain?" a Burgess guest asked from across the table.

Harlowe politely replied, "A fair distance, sir."

"Your Rights of Passage must have cost you plenty?" another Burgess asked.

"Not a dime," Harlowe shot back.

"Dime?"

"A form of exchange, sir."

"You paid nothing for your Rights of Passage, Captain?" a third female Burgess asked. She was dressed in a plain yellow jumpsuit. She seemed much older than the other Burgesses around the table.

"We are free travelers, ma'am. We travel where we please."

"Without fear of the Consortium?" the female Burgess asked.

"Without fear of anyone."

"The Fhaal?" someone at the far end of the table asked.

"Especially the Fhaal," Harlowe countered, poised with self-confidence.

The table began clapping. "We don't know how long you will live, young Captain, but we admire your audacity."

"Is there no place in the quadrant where one is free to travel the stars in peace?" Ian asked.

"If you have Rights of Passage you can," a Burgess joked. He was the only one who laughed.

The next Burgess who spoke was a large man. On Earth they would call him rotund, maybe even fat. "It is the price we pay for security."

"The Fhaal is knocking at your doorstep," Harlowe pointed out. "What security is that?"

"This is why we are here, to discuss what we should do," said the second Burgess. "What is your suggestion, young sir?"

Quay leaned forward to join the discussion, but Anor Ran thought it unwise. "Quay, do not join in the debate."

"It is the quadrant's debate, Father." She turned back to the table and stated, "We must rebel against the Consortium!"

"No, Quay, not here!" Anor Ran pleaded.

"What are you talking about, Quay?" the older Burgess lady asked.

"The Consortium is planning an alliance with the Fhaal. Together they plan to rule the quandrant, sucking our resources dry."

The older woman saw no harm in the pact. "The Commissar has promised otherwise. He states the sacrifices to the Fhaal will return great wealth to our enterprises. The Fhaal Empire is vast and mighty. Should we not at least hear them out?"

The Burgesses turned to Anor Ran. "Is that true, Tomar-Rex? The Consortium plans an alliance with the Fhaal?"

Anor Ran was caught off guard. He wasn't expecting the dinner to go down such a treasonous road. "The Consortium is in negotiations with the Fhaal for a treaty between the Empire and Omini Prime."

"And whose interest does the Consortium bargain for, his own High Council or the Quadrant, Anor Ran?"

"The Quadrant, of course," Anor Ran replied.

"Not true!" Quay argued, rising behind Harlowe, making herself visible to everyone. "Commissar Unikala has already agreed to increase all tariffs into Gibb. Rights of Passage will double for every travel route. The levies will not end there. I can assure you that many more are planned unless we stop them now."

Everyone stood up. "Gibb will cease to exist!" a Burgess cried, rising from his place. "Only Tomar has the power and the resources to stand against the Consortium," another said.

"But not against the Fhaal," Anor Ran countered. "The Empire is too vast to challenge alone."

The elderly woman agreed. "The Burgesses must temper their thoughts against the Consortium. The Fhaal Empire has been at our door for many passings. They have respected our treaty. This we cannot deny. What would you have the Consortium do? I detest the Fhaal, as you do. The Consortium is our representative. They have protected our trade routes, our commerce, and our worlds. Let them continue to do their task."

The rotund Burgess turned to Harlowe. "What do you say, young Captain?"

Harlowe rose from his place at the table, scanning the determined faces. This was not a time for diplomacy or pleasant-sounding platitudes. The Burgesses had the courage; they just needed someone to show them the way. "You are right to be skeptical. Those who speak of sacrifice do not have your interests in mind. They want control over your offerings. They want control over you and your freedom. I have fought the Consortium. I have fought the Fhaal. Neither is trustworthy. They want to be your masters. If you allow this union, you will become the servants and they will be your masters."

"What you speak of is treason against the Consortium," the old lady stated.

"What I speak of is freedom," Harlowe responded.

"You call yourself simple traders. What gives you the authority to dictate anything to us?"

Quay tossed a green crystalline cube onto the center of the table. She clapped her hands twice and a projection of an ancient document materialized above the table. It was the same document Riverstone had projected above the beach party campfire on #2.

"This is my Captain's authority. Read it! Read every word as I have. Within this document is the authority for freedom for everyone in the galaxy... Quay leaped onto the table and pointed at the passage... *when a long train of abuses and usurpations, pursuing invariably the same object evinces a design to reduce them under absolute despotism, it is their right, it is their duty, to throw off such government, and to provide new guards for their future security.*

"How can we rebel against anyone? We have no power to fight them," someone said from the table.

Harlowe replied without hesitating. "I will help. My ship and my crew will give all that we have to secure your freedom from the Consortium."

"You are but one ship against an empire. How can you stop anyone?" the Burgess lady asked.

Quay stepped in front of Harlowe. "Because they are Gamadin!" she announced.

44

The Promise

THE CHILLING CRY of a wild predator brought all life within the Gibbian park to a standstill. For a long moment nothing moved or breathed until the terror passed. A hard, blunt poker jabbed Simon in the back, shoving him along. This was no time for man or beast to be in the park, even with protection.

The Tomarian guards took no chances with the stranger who had just disabled five of their men. They had stripped him bare and taken his medallion. All he had on was his briefs and a black sack over his head. His hands were tied behind his back. He could see nothing. He had no idea how long he had been unconscious or where he was. His only concern right now was telling Harlowe he was headed into a trap. The Tomarians and the Consortium wanted *Millawanda*, and they would pull out all the stops to get her.

A second beastly cry shook the forest, but from another direction. This cry was closer, as though it had found the scent of its prey.

Simon had no feel for direction on a planet where even the sun came up on the wrong side. He remembered the orange flash and wondered feverishly where they had taken Sizzle. He wondered, too, if they knew who she was. A voice cried out in his head. *Of course they do, you stupid toad! Someone as important as Anor Ran's daughter would be a valuable prize against her father.* He was uncertain as to what they would do with him. *A worthless sack of dooey* was all he could think of when it came to himself.

As he marched along, the numbing effects of the stunner were nearly gone. He prayed Sizzle was unharmed as well and found it strange how that feeling about her wouldn't go away. When it came to babes, this was not his norm. For someone whom he'd met only a few hours before, she had changed his life. Except for his mates and Lu, he had never felt so selfless toward another human being.

You're all whacked up, bro. Stay focused or you will *be a sack of dooey.*

He would endure a thousand deaths across the Martian wastelands to get her back safely in his arms again.

If she were alive . . .

Simon quickly stuffed the delirious downer to a black hole in his brain. *Think positive, Puke! You're Gamadin, not a gomer. Think like one.* I'll find you, babe, if it takes forever, he promised Sizzle. *That's better, Gamadin! Stay cool. Everyone depends on you now, Captain Starr.* He then shut his eyes, forcing his mind clear of any lingering doubts.

With his mind uncluttered, Simon thought of how he would deal with his captors. Taking out the first two guards nearest him was a no-brainer. The third and fourth ones behind him were just as doable. Even with his head covered, he knew exactly where they were at any given moment. The other guards were too far away and too spread out for him to try anything provocative just yet. The guards appeared well trained. If he made even the slightest deviation from his normal gait, he got a painful jab in the back.

He sighed, thinking back to Sizzle. In his heart there would always be a place for Leucadia Mars. She had been his dream a long time ago. She always was and would be his first true love. Right then and there, his hands shackled and walking with a sack over his head, he promised Sizzle if somehow they ended up together, he would never look at another woman again. Not even Lu. He squeezed his eyes shut again. *I promise, I promise, I promise!* Could he make the transition? Did he have it within himself to stay honest with Sizzle forever? One soulmate? One being? One single babe for life? He nodded without hesitation. The vow was struck!

I PROMISE!

More loud cries shocked the night again, only this time the growls were in stereo as if the beasts were calling to each other, plotting, stalking their prey with evil craftiness. Being held hostage by a bunch of Tomarian thugs was one thing; being eaten by a wild beast on a planet so many hundreds of light-years from Earth had an even more unsettling effect. Out of habit, he reached for his medallion. It was still gone, along with his Gama-belt. Even with his formidable Gamadin strength, he couldn't break free of his restraints.

In his darkest moments, the General's commanding voice stayed with him. Simon had hated him back on Mars, but now he saw why. The General had taught him to be patient and think. There was always a way out of the toughest problem. *When your moment comes, be ready, Gamadin!*

The screams grew louder and closer, as goosebumps raced up the back of his spine in waves. When push came to shove, there was no doubt he was the sacrificial lamb, fresh meat for the beasts to feed upon while the Tomarian scum ran away.

Suddenly, mass destruction broke loose, bringing chaos and death everywhere.

Shots exploded from discharging weapons. Guards screamed in terror as a deadly force pounced, breaking bones and ripping limbs from bodies.

Simon sought escape, but where would he go? The beasts were everywhere, with no place to hide. There was nothing he could do but wait for Death to find him.

45

Test of the Gamadin

"Do I hear treason spoken against the Consortium at my father's table?" the voice of Turfan asked, interrupting the talk of rebellion. He walked into the dining hall, chinup with arrogance, paying his respects to Anor Ran and Sharlon before greeting the Burgesses at the table with a respectful nod.

"You missed a spirited debate, Commander," Anor Ran said to Turfan.

"I apologize for my tardiness, Tomar-Rex, and to your honored guests. I had important matters of a lost battlecruiser and attack ships to discuss with the Consortium High Council," Turfan replied, looking directly at Harlowe.

Anor Ran said, motioning her off the table, "Please, Quay, let us resume our festive dinner with our Burgess guests." Quay remained defiant. Her call for rebellion had only just begun.

Turfan turned to Harlowe. "You must be the young Captain Pylott. I have heard of you and your tiny ship."

Harlowe nodded, keeping his thoughts and opinions to himself. Riverstone, however, couldn't resist. "We're a messy lot, sir. A 'tiny' ship is easier to keep clean than the beastly hulks we've run across lately."

The Burgesses chuckled, embarrassing Turfan at his attempt to belittle the honored guests.

Turfan looked around the table. "Where is Sizzle, father? She never misses a meal."

Anor Ran pointed to the two empty places at the table. "She is entertaining one of the Captain's crewmen."

Turfan lent a sly smile toward Anor Ran when he said, "They must be an inexperienced crew."

Harlowe knew how the game was played, but Riverstone was a master. "So how many ships did Unikala lose, Commander?" he asked.

"Do you always allow your officers to speak for you?"

"Only when they're right," Harlowe replied pointedly.

Riverstone kept up the attack. "Were they expensive, Turfy?"

"Turfan," the Commander corrected. He then replied, "Very," in a heated tone of contempt. Turfan had lost his sense of humor. Losing face in any game, verbal or otherwise, required an immediate response. Locking eyes with Riverstone but directing his words at Harlowe, he added, "I would be careful of words, Captain, especially from a pompous subordinate."

"When you insult my ship and those who serve her, look me in the eye when you say it, Commander. I will not allow my ship nor my crew, who serve me well, to be tarnished behind their backs by anyone."

Anor Ran remained seated and did nothing to stop the pending confrontation. Quay looked at her mother, hoping she would find some way to stop what would end tragically. However, like her husband, Sharlon appeared curious to find out how their guests would stand up against her son. Turfan glanced at his father and received the go-ahead nod of approval. "I see the sidearm at your side. Are you as good with it as you are with your tongue?" Turfan challenged, standing to confront Harlowe.

Knowing she would get no support from either parent, Quay tried to intervene but Harlowe stopped her with a cautious hand. He stepped to the side, away from her, slowly moving his hands from his weapons, not wishing for a fight. With hands open he said, "I do not wish to fight you here at your parents' table, Turfan." He then turned to Anor Ran and Sharlon. "Forgive me, sir. You have been most gracious hosts, but I believe it is time for us to leave." Ian and Riverstone then left their places and waited for Harlowe at the end of the table.

"Where will you go from here, Captain?" Sharlon asked.

Riverstone felt his heart sink over their sudden departure. He hoped he had made some kind of impression on her. He would never know now. He reminded himself that she was still a married woman, unavailable, and way, way beyond his pay grade.

"To Neeja, ma'am," Harlowe told Sharlon.

"That is Fhaal-occupied territory," a Burgess said. "To travel there is suicide."

Harlowe spoke confidently. "We have a good ship and a good crew. If we are attacked, it is the Fhaal who will suffer, sir." He then bowed slightly, as did Riverstone and Ian. Before leaving the table, Harlowe bent down and kissed Quay on the side of the cheek, whispering, "Duck."

Harlowe moved along the table. He joined Riverstone and Ian. They made their way toward a tall doorway at the far end of the giant dining hall. Quay slid to one side with a caution for Turfan.

"Be advised, brother. I have seen your skill with a pistol. You have no peers, but I have seen the Captain with my own eyes. If you insist on carrying out this senseless confrontation, you will surely die."

"He is leaving as a coward," Turfan said.

"He left because to stay and kill you would bring dishonor to our family." Turfan scoffed at the thought. "He is above your pettiness, brother."

Her eyes traveled to her mother and father, making her thoughts clear and unambiguous. "Did you not hear me? The Captain *is* Gamadin. Make no mistake, Father, Turfan is a mere child against this warrior from the ancient past." Quay surveyed the table. No one was listening. If the Burgesses were going to rebel, and follow a boy who believed himself to be Gamadin, then they needed to know the power of this young captain. Her warning had fallen upon deaf ears.

Turfan's face went rigid. Like Quay, he had heard the ancient tales of the Gamadin since childhood. These imposters were no warriors from an ancient past. He was willing to stake his life on it. He laughed like someone who is trying to conceal his weakness. Harlowe and his officers were still walking away.

The imposters were near the giant door when Turfan called out, "Little boys!" He stood with his hands at his side, touching the polished, jewel-studded handles, ready to draw and kill the young captain in the back if he didn't turn and confront him before walking out the door. "Are you really that good?"

As Harlowe had cautioned her, Quay jumped from the table. She knew what was coming. Turfan arrogantly blinked at her sudden movement. In that instant, Harlowe whirled, drawing his weapon from under his toga, discharging lethal plasma bullets with such ferocity that before Turfan's mind could connect one synapse to make his hand pull his own weapon, searing bolts of hot blue plasma had already cut through his holster, severing both pistols from his hips. At that moment, more bolts drilled through Turfan's pistols, turning them into molten lumps of useless metal before dropping on the stone floor.

Harlowe wasn't finished. Before class was dismissed, the Gamadin Captain sliced through Turfan's shoulder emblems, tearing away pieces of his exquisitely tailored uniform. As quickly as the lesson began, it was over. In that time frame so immeasurably small, before the beat of a heart had completed a single pulse, within that blink, Turfan felt for himself the swift, incalculable power of the Gamadin!

And so had the Burgesses, Sharlon, and Anor Ran...

46

Assault on Tomar

"Nᴵᴄᴇ ᴛᴏᴜᴄʜ ᴡɪᴛʜ the holster, Dog," Riverstone commented to Harlowe as they strode down the vast hallway toward the elevator.

"I saw that in an old western once," Ian said.

"Did you see her old man's face?" Riverstone asked.

"Everyone was shocked," Ian commented.

Riverstone went on: "Dog, Anor only cared about you. He didn't give a whit about his toad-faced son."

Harlowe's thoughts had moved on. He had more pressing things to occupy his mind than recent history. The safety of his crew and *Millawanda* turned somersaults in his stomach. Simon was missing, and they had to find him before returning to the ship.

"Ya think we'll be asked back?" Riverstone asked sarcastically. "I'm going to miss that pool."

Harlowe grabbed his com. "Forget the pool. Where's Rerun?"

"Aye, the cats should have found him by now," Ian replied, meaning that if the cats had been sent to find him, it was way past time for Simon to check in with his com.

Harlowe made the call. After several attempts, it was clear Simon wasn't answering. The cold stare in Harlowe's eyes meant only one thing: Simon was in trouble. He may have left the pool without permission, but not even Simon would go this long without checking in, even if the doe was a twelve.

Riverstone rushed to Simon's defense. "Rerun would have answered, Dog, if he could."

Harlowe's lips went thin with concern. "Aye." Next, he contacted Monday back at the ship. "Mr. Platter, has Mr. Bolt checked in?"

Monday answered almost immediately. "Negative, Captain."

"You keeping the neighborhood safe?" Harlowe asked.

"It's getting more intense, Captain. It's like they're pulling out all the stops. I told them no more partying at the door, and then I fried their weapons. They left after that. Watch yourself coming back, Captain, they've stationed a few hundred guards around the perimeter. Let me know when you're coming through so I can put them to bed."

"Very well, Mr. Platter. Prepare Millie for takeoff. Put your resources on locating Mr. Bolt. We'll be slamming out of town in a hurry."

"Sounds like trouble, Captain?" Monday asked.

"Aye, things are heading south in a hurry, Mr. Platter. Keep me informed about any changes coming our way."

"Understood, Captain."

"So we're just leaving?" Riverstone wondered. "You're going to take off without Quay?"

Once into the corridor, they threw off their Tomarian togas revealing their Levi's, T-shirts, and Nikes under their garments.

"Not a lot of choices, Mr. Riverstone," Harlowe replied, adjusting his Gama-belt.

"You make it sound like she's a lost cause," Riverstone countered.

Harlowe's intense blue eyes met Riverstone's. His tone was clear and uncompromising. "Look, I don't like it either, but Millie, Rerun, and Neeja are one, two, three. There isn't any four, Mr. Riverstone, until they are safe." He checked one sidearm, then the other, snapping a fully charged magazine in each. The round indicators went bright blue.

Riverstone eyed the concern on Harlowe's face as he made his own weapons check. "I guess we're back on the clock, huh, Captain?"

"We were never off."

Harlowe's communicator sounded. "Go ahead, Mr. Platter."

"Not sure if it means anything, Captain, but a dozen attack fighters just launched from one of those Consortium battlecruisers in orbit above the city. They're making a beeline for the Tomar Building."

At that moment the sound of plas discharges echoed down the great hall. The Gamadin drew their weapons and waited. A football field away, a barrage of plas rounds blazed across the intersection. A half moment later Quay broke into view, coming around a distant corner.

Harlowe and Riverstone ran flat out to meet her. Harlowe shouted to Quay, "HIT THE FLOOR!" as a dozen guards charged into the corridor with guns blazing.

Harlowe and Riverstone cut down every Tomarian guard that came around the corner while Ian covered their backs from the opposite end.

While Harlowe ran to Quay, Riverstone's deadly shots didn't miss. Bodies kept piling up, as Riverstone kept the rest of the guards pinned against the far corner.

"My father's guards are everywhere!" she cried out above the crack of plas fire.

Suddenly out of nowhere a loud explosion rocked the building.

"What was that?" Riverstone shouted.

"Consortium attack ships!" Harlowe shouted back, lifting Quay off the floor. They retreated back down the corridor, at the same time nuking more guards who poked their faces out into the hallway.

"That was fast," Ian stated, continuing to cover their retreat down the hallway as he steadied himself against the wall from the sudden jolt.

"You want me to bring Millie to you, Captain?" Monday asked.

"No, Squid, stay put," Harlowe replied, running behind Quay to protect her from the plas rounds. "We need to find Rerun and the cats first. Millie is your only concern. Anyone threatens her, take appropriate action."

"Aye, Captain."

Harlowe turned to Quay. "Where's your mother?"

Quay closed her eyes. The expression on her face told the story. Riverstone stopped firing as his heart sank.

Harlowe slammed a forearm shiver into Riverstone's back. "Mourn later."

Riverstone blinked out of his trance. "Aye." He then quickly deposed of two guards charging from a doorway.

The four came to another intersection. Harlowe snapped fresh magazines into both weapons. "Which way?" he asked Quay.

Quay didn't hesitate. She pointed down the corridor to the right. The four charged down the long hallway, leaping over the dead bodies until they rounded a corner, and surprised another squad of Tomarian troops.

Quay was right. The guards were everywhere, coming out of walls, doorways, and shadowy nooks. Harlowe and Riverstone cut them down before they knew what hit them, as they had done to the first group. Quay continued to be amazed at how swiftly the Gamadin mowed down every guard who tried to stop them. Every so often she would glance at them as if they were an aberration. One moment they could be so friendly and carefree, almost childlike in the fairy tale way they played and toyed with each other. Then, in an instant, they altered their state of being and became deadly warriors.

As they ran, Ian's com picked up troop transports landing on Anor Ran's private landing platform, disgorging hundreds of grey uniforms onto the platform. They would be inside in a matter of moments. If they didn't find a way out of the building now, they would be trapped!

"Better step it up a notch, Dog," Riverstone cried out as they listened to a wild exchange of gunfire coming from the far end of the giant corridor. It sounded as though Anor Ran and his guards were firing back to defend themselves against the Consortium onslaught. Harlowe didn't need Ian's com to envision the night sky with a dozen more transports coming in, landing on the ground and at the other platforms around the Tomar building. It was a full-on assault, one Unikala didn't intend to lose, Harlowe figured. He needed a plan soon. He was flying blind.

"Which way is the elevator?" Riverstone asked Quay.

"No time for elevators," Harlowe barked. "They could be blocked."

Harlowe and Riverstone exchanged glances as they looked back toward their room. "Let's do it!" they said in unison.

"Take Quay back through the room, Wiz," Harlowe instructed and then pointed at the medallion around Quay's neck. "Get her suited up. We'll be leaving in a hurry."

"We winging it, Captain?" Ian asked.

Before Harlowe could answer, a blast grenade blew open an entire wall behind them at the far end of another corridor. The atackers were coming at them from different directions. A split second later, Consortium soldiers were pouring through the gaping hole.

"Go, go, go!" Harlowe cried out, pushing Ian and Quay. He didn't have time to cover Quay and Ian back to the room. Riverstone had already started to charge the surprised soldiers at the other end of the corridor with both guns blazing. Harlowe was barely a nose behind him. Together their weapons sounded like runaway submachine guns, spewing sizzling bolts of blue plas through black helmets and body armor. It was a bloodbath. Harlowe had replaced two mags by the time the last Consortium soldiers hit the floor. His Gama-belt was empty. Riverstone was in no better shape. He had completely discharged both pistols, continuing to pull his trigger with nothing coming out of the barrel. Harlowe laid an arm across his chest, pulling down his twitching arms. "It's okay, Matt. We got 'em."

Riverstone shut his eyes. All he could think of was blasting at more guards for what they had done to Sharlon. He stepped back from his rage for a moment before reaching for another twenty-round mag and coming up empty.

Nearly weaponless, they bolted through the bullet-riddled doorway of their room with only a moment to spare, just before the next assault wave of Consortium troops blew into the corridor. They had bought only a little time. The explosions continued far down another great hallway as large numbers of troops charged their way through the massive security doors of the building. Soon the clamor of body armor and heavy weapons would be coming their way. They had two choices left: fly or die.

47

All Hung Up

QUAY AND IAN were already in their SIBAs staring at the night with their big, round bugeyes when Harlowe and Riverstone came charging back into the room, with plas fire chasing them the whole way.

"Why didn't you take off?" Harlowe cried out.

Ian pointed at the roaring fire on the balcony. "Look!"

Harlowe gritted his teeth as he struck his medallion and yelled, "Jewels!" The robob servant came flying out of the flames, leaped, and collapsed back to a cylinder. Harlowe snatched it from the air and stuffed the loyal servant into his Gama-belt. Behind them, plas rounds were riddling the doorway, clearing the way for the final assault into the room. He grabbed Quay and headed through the wall of fire, darting between fallen beams and broken stone columns. Riverstone and Ian were right behind them. The raging fire had already engulfed the outside of the building. Their SIBAs protected them against the inferno as they leaped out over the side of the balcony railing without looking where they were falling. Harlowe nearly slammed into a hovering troopship two stories down. Once past the ship, he deployed his wings and began soaring freely three thousand feet above the park. It was pitch black below him, but he could see as if it were daylight with his bugeyes. Stabilized and flying true, he glanced behind him to check on Quay's progress.

She was gone.

Fearing the worst, Harlowe circled back and found Quay. She was hung up on a hovering attack ship's delta fins, which he had almost hit himself coming out of the flames from the balcony. Unfortunately, Quay lacked Gamadin skills. Her reflexes were quick, better than those of most humanoids, but not Gamadin-quick. That shortcoming had cost her. If she couldn't release herself from the end of the wing before the ship took off again, or if the ship's crew spotted her, she was a casualty. All the ship had to do was make a sudden movement in any direction and she was toast. Even with her SIBA, without inertial dampeners to protect her from the extreme G-force of sudden acceleration she would die, and inside the SIBA her body would turn to mush.

Harlowe glided back toward the attack ship and made his way toward her. He told her through their coms to stay put and if the crew inside even twitched, "Blast them with your pistol." The problem was, she didn't have any plas rounds. "It's empty, Harlowe."

Sweet! That complicates things!

Harlowe ordered Riverstone and Ian to continue away from the burning Tomar Building. There was nothing they could do to help, and they were already too low in the sky to do any good. "If we get separated, we'll meet up at the park entrance." After that, it would be back to the streets of Gibb, then weave their way through the Horritan city and back to the ship.

As flight-worthy as their wings were, they were not meant for flying like birds. The suits were meant for gliding. Birds can go up and down. Humans with wings are limited. If they want to go up, they need a strong updraft to assist them. Unless Harlowe found a stiff wind, going up would be next to impossible, even for a Gamadin. The Gibbian night was windless. He was a good five hundred feet below Quay and right now, he had no way of reaching her on his own no matter how hard he tried.

Unless…

He quickly glanced at his pistol. He had seven rounds left. He would have to retract his wings, but his idea was doable. The instant he withdrew his wings, he began dropping like a stone. Quickly and in one smooth action, as he had trained for so many times back at the Mons, he pulled out his pistol, attached the spool of dura-wire to a piton head at the end of the barrel, and fired.

Whizzz!

PING!

A bright spark glanced off the hull of the attack fighter. A Gamadin piton could sink into the hardest rock, but penetrating the blast-hardened frame of a Consortium attack fighter was a no-go.

Now what?

Harlowe re-deployed his SIBA wings and found himself another five hundred feet lower than when he started.

There's always a way, soldier! Gunn's voice nagged at him as his wings filled again, gathering enough speed to stay aloft.

Harlowe studied his options, canvassing anything available to him. If there was another attack ship anywhere he could get his hands on, he would break in and steal it. He saw nothing close. The ships were all either too high or racing around the building, moving way too fast for him to catch. Even if he could catch one, how would he get inside? To them, he was just a fly on the window.

"Harlowe, where are you?" Quay asked over the com.

"I'm down here, Quay. I'm trying to get to you."

"They are moving away from the fire to protect their ship from the falling debris. Once they have all their troops cleared of the building, they will take off."

"I'm coming!" Harlowe called up to her.

"Hurry, Harlowe!"

He almost said "Yes, dear" but bit his tongue as he thought about what Quay had said. *They are moving away from the fire...*

That was the answer. *Fire!* He had been staring at it all along. The fire from the building was at full rage. The troopships were evacuating their soldiers before they got fried. They had done their job and now they were burning rubber to escape before they got caught in the flames. If he could get near the fire without getting too close to the burning building, he could ride the superheated updrafts to Quay before the ship took off.

He didn't need to speculate as to whether his plan would work. It was his only option. The moment he turned toward the burning building, his wings began to fill with hot air. In no time he was making his way high and higher. Two zigs and a zag and he was above her, making a beeline for the hovering ship still protecting the retreating troops.

"Harlowe!" Quay cried out.

She sounded worried. "Problem, girlfriend?" Harlowe asked quickly.

"I think they saw me."

"I'm almost there."

"Yes, they see me," Quay told him calmly.

Whap! He made it, and clung to the wing like a gnat. He quickly grabbed her leg, trying to free it from the wedge she was stuck in. With one hard yank and the proper leverage, he pulled her free. They shoved off from the ship with Quay holding on to Harlowe until she was able to deploy her wings on her own. In the short time they were on #2, Quay had experienced the SIBA and knew its properties, *except* for the wings. On #2 she never had the opportunity to experience the gossamer extensions of her arms, but as Harlowe learned the first time he fell from the side of the Mons escarpment, SIBAs were forgiving. Harlowe had to teach her on the fly. As she spread her wings, Harlowe steadied her yaw and pitch with a couple of taps on her wings from above. Soon she was flying on her own as if she had been born to it. Together they drifted away from the building and over the giant park, looking like a couple of lost geese heading south, trying to find their way in the night. Harlowe contacted Riverstone and Ian to let them know he and Quay would be at the rendezvous in a few moments. He was about to sign off when Quay pointed frantically behind them.

"Problem, Dog?" Riverstone asked.

"Yeah, that Consortium transport is about to run us down!"

48

Good Friends

THE SILENCE THAT followed the slaughter was chilling. Simon felt as if he were the only thing alive left in the forest. He struggled to take a breath of fresh air but the smelly, blood-splattered rag that covered his head was suffocating. His hands were still tied behind his back. The fact that he was lying flat on the wet, dewy grass was no help. A guard had slammed into him, fleeing the wrath that had savaged the squad. For reasons unknown to Simon, he had been spared. He should have been the first entré, but hey, he wasn't complaining. He was alive! Unless he removed the stinking bag over his head, though, it wouldn't be long before he was sprouting angel wings!

Then something powerful broke branches as it rambled through the underbrush. The cracking sounds were coming his way. It wasn't like before, though. The sound was unhurried and slow. Beyond that, somewhere far off, loud explosions boomed at the far end of the park. He remembered how the explosions began just as his captors started marching him through the forest. Simon didn't have to guess whether Harlowe and his mates were in the thick of it. He knew!

He scooted along the ground, going crazy as he struggled to slip out of the sack. The Captain needed his help, but until he removed the bloody rag from his face, he was a useless puke.

A low growl suddenly stopped his efforts. A sixth sense told him to stay calm. If it was the beast returning, it just might leave him alone again if he stayed quiet as a post.

The throat snarl came closer and closer until it was only a few feet away. Suddenly it morphed into a purr, reminding him of his day-old Aston Martin idling at a stoplight. With his nerves shot, mouth dry as dust, and unable to breathe, he could take it no more. Beast or no beast, the bag had to go or he would kill himself and save the predator the trouble.

In a *why-didn't-I-think-of-this-sooner* move, Simon bent in half and grabbed the end of the bag with his bare feet, yanking the bag from his head with ease. His first lungful of air was heaven. After feeling the bliss, he opened his eyes and found himself face-to-face with two glowing blue dots. He nearly wet his pants before he realized the radiant eyes were friendly.

"Geez, Molly, you scared me to death," he said to the white cat. He rolled over and lifted himself up to his knees. From his new elevation, waves of stunned disbelief shot up his spine. Broken and very dead bodies were spread out all over the trail. He gulped another fresh breath of air before gasping, "That's sick..."

His sixth sense had been right. Death was everywhere around him. Not one soldier had been spared. Rhud was off to the side, licking his forepaws like it was just another day in the jungle. Both cubs completely ignored the loud reports that lit up the night with bright flashes of fire coming from the Tomar Building.

Simon watched the Consortium attack fighters dive down upon the massive superstructure with their powerful beams of searing orange and green plasma bolts. Debris from the burning building was raining down on the park. In the midst of the confusion, a small vessel scooted out from the side of the building away from the onslaught and headed for deep space. Several attack fighters broke off their assault on the Tomar Building to pursue the fleeing craft. Simon wondered if Harlowe and Riverstone were aboard. A pang of guilt swept over him as he thought about sneaking off with Sizzle. It didn't take a gomer to realize he was in deep trouble, because Harlowe had sent the cubs to fetch him. He should have been up there helping his mates. Just when he was about to ram his head against a tree, three tiny specks in the night sky saved him from a serious migraine.

Are you kidding me?

He watched them glide away from the burning building like a flock of birds. They could only be Gamadin, he thought, as he breathed a sigh of relief. He tried to get their attention by jumping up and down, waving his arms at the sky. "Right on, bros!" he called up to them. "I'm down here!"

The specks were too high and now they were well past him, moving away from his field of vision behind the black canopy of trees.

Simon figured his mates were headed back to the ship. That was a no-brainer. For him, it wouldn't be so easy. He didn't have wings and neither did the cats. They would have to make it back to the ship on foot. That was the least of his problems. Finding his way out of the park and back through the winding streets of Gibb and the Horritan filth was another matter. He didn't have his SIBA or his com to show him the way back. He would do better with the stinking sack over his head, he scolded himself.

Molly then growled at Rhud, as if being told to get off his duff and move out. Simon was down with that idea. She wanted to return to the ship as much as he did. If the cubs had found him in the middle of the Gibbian park, they could find anything. They didn't need 54th century gadgets, only a nod from him to go.

Simon laid his face on Molly's glistening fur. Her coat was so pure it reflected the orange-green-yellow light of the burning Tomarian superstructure. "You da best, babe," he told her. Molly growled appreciatively. He then turned around and held out his still-bound wrists. "A little help, Molly, if you please." He shut his eyes, hoping she wouldn't miss. Like a skilled robob, she sliced through the heavy cord like she was cutting through sewing thread. He rubbed his wrists back to life and thanked her with another hug.

Finally free, his thoughts went immediately to Sizzle and how he could save her. If he left the park without her, he might never find her again. They might take her off-world; then where would he be? He took one step toward that goal of heroism and stopped abruptly in his tracks. His heart sank. For a brief moment, he thought he was Captain Julian Starr and he would find all the weapons he needed along the way to rescue his damsel in distress. *This isn't a stupid movie set, toad,* he scolded himself. *What do you think you were going to do? Swing from a vine and whisk her away from the bad guys in your shorts?*

Simon examined himself. He was covered with splattered blood, dirt, and wet grass. He smelled worse than a dead skunk. All he had on was his baggy shorts that hung on his hips like they were about to fall off. *Go after her with what? Your looks? Get back to the ship, stupid. Get back to your shipmates. They'll help you get her back. They're Gamadin. The most powerful dudes in the galaxy, right?*

He touched Molly's soft white mane with a affectionate pat. "Okay girl, let's go. Back to Millie." It was his only choice. He had to leave the park and hoped Sizzle would still be on Gibb when he returned. Without help from the Gamadin he was helpless, and so was Sizzle.

Molly growled, found her location, and moved off through the thick underbrush in a single powerful leap, surprising Simon by the direction she took. If it was left to him, he would have gone the other way. Rhud followed right behind Molly. The waist-high, two-hundred-pound cubs made it look effortless. Simon did his best to keep up but with bare feet and shorts, he occasionally had to call out for the cubs to slow down.

49

City Streets

Harlow, Riverstone, Ian, and Quay landed in a small clearing on the far side of the park. It was in sharp contrast to the first time they had been there earlier in the day. The park was dark and deserted. The darkness that surrounded them seemed as dangerous as any lawless city on Earth. The moldy, ancient buildings of Gibb had replaced the sweet odor of flowers and trees. The lofty Overseer of Path still loomed high above their heads, guiding travelers from the distant stars to one of its countless parking facilities around the city. The huge blasts that rocked the city had no effect on the giant ball performing its duties. Even in famine, flood, and war, commerce thrived on Gibb.

They reduced their SIBAs back to medallions so they could easily blend into the hordes on the streets ahead of them. Quay had warned them that Consortium soldiers would be looking for them all over the city. Blending in with the crowds was their best protection while they made their way back to the ship.

After confirming that everyone was together, Quay pointed the way out of the park. Harlowe was the only one with any plas rounds left . . . six. Riverstone and Ian were empty and Quay had no pistol at all, having dropped her weapon during flight. With one working pistol and six rounds, they headed out of the park. A couple of times they saw shadows moving in the dark, but no one threatened as

Quay led them from one jungle to the next through the city streets of Gibb.

Moving quickly along the stone pavement, Riverstone asked, "What are we going to do about Rerun?"

"He knows what to do," Harlowe replied flatly. "If the cubs found him alive, they'll lead him back to the ship."

"We should have heard from him by now," Riverstone pointed out.

"Not if he's dodging bullets."

"Roger that. Ya think he got out of the building in time?" Riverstone wondered.

"He was with the doe, remember?" Ian replied.

"Yeah, he was gone way before dinner," Riverstone concluded.

"When we return to the ship, you and I will load up and find Rerun," Harlowe said.

"Aye, Captain. I wonder how Squid and the clickers are holding up?"

Harlowe only grunted. The idea that there was a war going on when he was so far away from his ship didn't sit well with him.

* * *

They arrived at a main avenue, where they recognized the wide street they had walked through the first time. It had been only a few hours ago, but it seemed like an eternity had passed since then. Neither the Gibbian night nor the Tomar Building fire slowed the traders, peddlers, and foot traffic from the wheeling and dealing along the ancient streets. They trekked their way through the heart of Gibb with little trouble, pushing through the crowds and back alleys until they arrived at the edge of the Horritan slums, where its horrible stench greeted them like a hungry beast ready to swallow them whole. If walking through the twisted back alleys and dirt-filled streets in daylight was dangerous, walking through them at night was suicide. Everyone looked as evil as Death itself waiting for them with open arms.

Harlowe checked his pistol. Six rounds. That was it. A belt full of fresh ammo clips would have made him feel a whole lot better. Two white cats that saw in the dark like bugeyes... *freakin' awesome!*

Shortly after they crossed the boundary into the Horritan shanty-town, five shadows emerged from the darkness. The shadows were all dressed in grubby uniforms and holding weapons of various sizes and shapes. Obviously they were more of a gang of cutthroats than a disciplined squad of Consortium soldiers. Riverstone thought he recognized the one in the middle as the being who had bulldozed into him at the butcher's stall, eating the little horse raw.

Harlowe stepped in front of Quay, joining Riverstone, and said to the five, "Let us pass," in a stonecold tone.

The point of a weapon twitched slightly. It was the last synapse the shadow's brain made before Harlowe put a plas round through his left eye. In the next second, four more bodies hit the pavement, joining the first. Harlowe glanced at his power indicator. The blue light was barely glowing. He had one round left... maybe.

"Everyone okay?" Harlowe asked, pivoting around, searching the darkness for more shadows.

"Good to go here, Dog," Riverstone replied.

Quay moved quickly to grab a loose weapon from the bodies on the ground. Even if it was a piece of junk, it was better than nothing.

Harlowe sidestepped an open sewer in the road and managed to catch a glimpse of the river of filth flowing a hundred feet below. "Hurry, there could be more of them," he said to Quay in a low whisper.

Riverstone was moving to help Quay collect the weapons when a clear metallic sound stopped them both. From the blackness, a brilliant flash of orange light exploded in Riverstone's face. The bolt was so fast his Gamadin-trained reflexes couldn't avoid it. Harlowe twisted around and watched Riverstone drop like a dead weight, his entire body engulfed in a lingering orange light. At that same moment, Harlowe dove for the pavement, firing his last round at the darkness. Quay picked up a weapon and fired. Another orange blast went wild. That gave Quay enough time to run for Harlowe with a loaded weapon. Facedown in the slimy vileness of the street gutter, Harlowe grabbed his medallion with his free hand. A paralyzing bolt grazed his shoulder, stunning half his body with its energy. Rolling toward the sewer, he tried eluding the next orange bolt fired at him. The last thing his mind registered was Quay screaming his name, as she reached out for his hand before he slid off the edge of the sewer gap and into the waiting oblivion.

50

Counting Prizes

R<small>A-LOC KICKED ASIDE</small> the two dead bodies of his bodyguards who had the misfortune of stopping the plas rounds that had his name on it. "At last, Perto," the Lagan trader said, congratulating himself to his head servant as he waddled his fat little body out from behind the barricade. "I have my prizes." On his way to inspect his trophies, Ra-Loc carefully stepped over the other five dead gunners he had hired earlier in the day. He was relieved that he'd had the foresight to hire them instead of using up his own personal bodyguards. He heard rumors that these humans were fast, but by the heavens, he never believed their power was supernatural. Next time he would ask for triple the reward in koorants for humans and stand his ground. He felt fortunate to be alive and thought rather whimsically on the brighter side that the humans had saved him a goodly sum of money. While Perto and he were assessing the prizes, he had his other servants retrieve the koorants that he had already paid to the now dead assassins. After all, he thought, a contract is a contract, and the hired guns had not kept their bargain.

Surveying his collection of precious bounty, Ra-Loc was taking no chances. Perto kept his loaded pistol trained on his prisoners just in case the stunners did not live up to their specifications. He kicked one in the side, then the female. He grinned approvingly. No one moved. Indeed, the stunner's paralyzing shock had worked as

313

advertised. Yes, all of the humans had been effectively incapacitated. The stunners had been well worth the extra koorants. As he looked around, he wondered where his white beauties had disappeared. He wanted their pets above all else. He howled, speaking obscenities in four different Omini Prime dialects, slurred together as one. His prizes would fetch a great sum, but his beauties were beyond value. Where were they? His sources told him they were with the humans, within the great Tomar-Rex's private quarters.

"Drak!" Ra-Loc cried out. His beauties had to be here somewhere.

Alas, after searching the area with special sensors, his beauties were nowhere to be seen. They had vanished. The animals were worth far less than the girl and the special bonus the human called "Pylott" would fetch. Nevertheless, they gave him a sense of power and he wanted them dearly, even more than his prizes.

"Master," Perto said, "we are two humans short."

Ra-Loc had been so consumed about losing his beauties he had nearly forgotten about his prizes. He quickly counted the bodies and agreed with Perto, "There should be four humans and the girl."

Perto, large and lumbering with a head twice the size of the humans, recounted the bodies and looked up the street to where the last human had been shot. He pointed with the end of his stunner at the wide gap in the gutter where the last human fell. "He was there, Master. I saw him go down. His body glowed. You saw it, Master, he was there. As for the other . . . there were only three. That is all anybody saw. There were no other humans, Master."

Ra-Loc looked into the shadows, seeing his profits dwindle further from what he had expected. He didn't have the courage to venture out on his own, so he sent three of his servants ahead of him while he stepped cautiously behind them in search at the missing human.

When they came to the place Perto pointed to, no other human was in the gutter. Perto looked around and shrugged. "He should be here, Master."

Ra-Loc pulled a light from his belt and trained it around the alleyway, without success. "Well then, he must be here. I don't understand. If he was shot, he should be here. That is only logical, Perto."

Perto pointed the light at a large slit in the pavement where a drain flowed into the street's sewage ducts. "Perhaps he fell in there, Master," his servant suggested.

Ra-Loc bent over and beamed his light into the slit. Deep below the surface, a swift-moving current was carrying all that was disgusting and rank from the city sewers to someplace unknown. If the human had fallen in there, he figured, he would no longer be alive. If he was dead, well, he was worthless to him. Humans had value only if they were alive, Unikala had warned him.

Ra-Loc waved his hand in disgust. "It is done. We have the girl and the one called Pylott and his officer. We will make an impressive profit. Not as much as I wanted, but a good profit, Perto."

"Yes, Master," Perto replied, then added, "we must hurry. Unikala should not be kept waiting."

Ra-Loc laughed. "Drak him, Perto! Let the Commander wait. We have his prizes. Unikala will wait for as long as it takes, and he will pay dearly for them." The Lagan trader continued his greedy sneer as he watched his servants lay the two bodies in the antigrav cart. With the two most precious humans captured, his days of licking the gutter as an ill-bred Lagan trader were over. He would be very powerful and famous after this night. His peers would revere his accomplishments. He would rank above them, while clients would seek him out and offer him the most lucrative contracts. Wealth would be beyond his dreams. Still, a sad emptiness hung over his triumph. He would have traded it all away for his white beauties. *Yes, Ra-Loc, you are rich. Soon you can afford that planet in the Tular system you always wanted and buy more precious animals.*

Ra-Loc's face suddenly twisted with rage. *I WANT MY BEAUTIES!*

"Please, Master," Perto urged. "There are bounty hunters like ourselves in search of the humans. There will be problems if we don't hurry. We must move quickly back to our ship, Master. I will contact the Commissar to rendezvous with us."

Ra-Loc stared unhappily down the alley, still hoping his white beauties were somewhere in the shadows. Sadly, he saw nothing. No more humans and no more white beauties. "Yes, yes. Very well, Perto. We should go."

He wiped the greasy sweat from his cord-like hair that draped past his shoulders and shrieked wildly with loathing, "Draaaak!"

51

Cold Feet

AFTER LEAVING THE park with only a few scratches, Simon and the cubs were quickly consumed by the crowds of pedestrians and peddlers again. The scene reminded him of Las Vegas, where no one ever slept. It would have been wonderful to stop and pick up something to wear if he had money or something to offer in trade. Even if he had one, no one on Gibb had ever heard of a platinum card.

He glanced down at the cubs' furry paws, wishing for a pair of Uggs like theirs. More than a few peddlers, shopkeepers, and pedestrians along the way had offered him a king's ransom for his magnificent beasts. He paid them no attention and kept walking on his cold stumps for feet. He was in such a sorry state! He laughed as he added a few twists of his own to an old Master Card commercial he remembered. Nike workout sweats he desperately needed...one hundred dollars, Mesphisto walking shoes...three hundred dollars. Two really narly white tigers escorting you back to your spaceship through the horse's-hind-end of an alien city...*priceless!*

With his focus on one thing and one thing only—making it back to his ship and his mates—Simon gritted away the pain, the cold, and the hunger, knowing that whatever he was suffering was nothing like what he had endured back on Mars. He knew in the back of his mind that he should be thanking the General for preparing him for this moment of hardship. He saluted his ghost. That was the best he could do for now.

With the cubs flanking him on each side for protection, he plowed his way through the throngs unimpeded. When he arrived at an intersection, he stared down one way, then the next. Each direction looked the same. The dark and crowded stone avenues were unwholesome everywhere he looked. Nothing looked familiar except for the masses of moving beings. The cubs were never hesitant. They *knew* the way. His confidence in himself may have wavered, but he never doubted them. He trembled inside, knowing if he had been alone he would have spent a lifetime aimlessly wandering the streets.

He put out his hand. "Lead on, girlfriend," he said to Her Highness in a voice etched with pain and thirst. Without the slightest hesitation, Molly strolled her way gracefully forward down the avenue, parting a sea of pedestrians as she went.

* * *

Hours later, Omini Prime was bright and sweltering as Simon and the cubs broke out of the darkness of tall superstructures and into the light of the Horritan slums. They had traveled throughout the Gibbian night without sleep. Thankfully, the added heat warmed his feet to where they felt attached to his body again. The stench, however, hit him as if he had stepped into a cesspool.

It took a moment for his eyes to stop watering and his nose to adjust to the new environment. After adjusting to the vile stench, he moved with the cats onto the soft Horritan dirt alleys. A short distance into the slums, Rhud stopped abruptly and began to bob and weave, growling and meowing almost frantically. Simon couldn't figure out why the cub was so disturbed. He had never seen him act that way. Then Molly chimed in, sniffing the ground where Rhud had started his frenzied hysteria. They were both howling in pain.

"What's the matter?" Simon asked them.

He looked around, trying to search for clues as to what got them so agitated. Rhud cried louder. "All right, I believe you," Simon told them. "Something happened here, didn't it?"

Molly growled. That was a yes.

Simon studied the ground, holding his nose. If there was something important here, his limited senses couldn't make it out. He moved along a stone gutter and arrived at an open sewer in the street. He carefully stepped aside to avoid falling through the gap.

An incredible foulness exploded out of the opening, taking his breath away. He turned and gulped a less sour breath before looking down. It was like peering into an inkwell. The gurgling flow of a river in the putrid depths led him to wonder: if someone did fall into the abyss, how would the person survive?

He turned to Molly and looked into her bright blue eyes. "There's nothing we can do here, girl. We have to get back to the ship first, where I can get my Gama-gear and come back." He grabbed her mane and led her on. Reluctantly she agreed.

Rhud pawed at something in the dirt next to the gap. Simon picked it up and right away he knew that it was the ring Quay bought from the old, toothless lady and had given to Harlowe. A great wave of dread shot up his backbone. Neither Quay nor Harlowe would ever give up their rings, not for all of her father's wealth.

Simon closed his fist around the ring. They would have to pry his cold, dead fingers apart with a plas-cannon before he would give up its contents. He glanced at the cubs, his lips quivering with fear, and pointed the way. "Hurry!"

The cubs took off through the alleys, leading the charge. Simon kept up, jumping and leaping, forgetting away his pain, straining muscles beyond their limits to keep up as he ran, knocking over peddlers buckets, splashing mud and sewage, racing past Elvis and the old, toothless lady with her table of simple trinkets. Through the twisted slums of smoke and noise and the masses of life in their cesspool of existence, the three of them leaped and ran. He was frightened as never before in his life. He had a package so dear and so priceless to deliver that no bullet, no Horritan thug, no Consortium elite guard could stop him from completing his mission.

Bursting out of the alley, Simon and the cubs found themselves in the middle of a small plaza, where they suddenly stopped and looked up, gawking in amazement. There she was. *Millawanda*. His golden Gamadin ship was only a stone's throw away, parked silently, undamaged and alone, serenely peaceful and beautiful in the mid-morning light. Her wheat-colored surface was unblemished, pure, yet restrained and powerful as She hung over the mass of Horritan shanties like some divine goddess guarding her flock.

Simon was so enthralled with his vision he hadn't noticed the four Consortium soldiers standing at the opposite end of the plaza, gorging themselves on tiny blue horses. Alone, ragged and filthy, he blended in with the hordes. They might not have paid him any mind except for the cats. They were twin beacons of light pointing right at him. They drew attention in any crowd.

Simon was helpless. He had no cover and no weapon to protect himself or the cubs. He was also tired and thirsty. He hadn't eaten or slept in two days. He was a worthless puke, he thought, as he stood embarrassed at his stupidity for not thinking the Consortium would be thick as flies around the ship. They spotted him the instant the cubs leaped out into the plaza, but if he was surprised at the guards' presence, the guards were even more surprised at what Simon brought with him. They dropped their food and went for their weapons.

The cubs' speed was swift and lethal. In that split second of surprised hesitation, the white cats were upon them, tearing into their flesh and ripping them apart before they could react. All Simon could do was stand by and watch, his mouth agape in total amazement as he watched the two cubs mercilessly take the guards with such deadly force that it made him shudder. Still stunned, he swallowed hard and pulled them away from the scene before more soldiers were alarmed.

Simon had no plan once he left the plaza except to stay away from any roving squad of Consortium troops. He knew more soldiers would be after them soon. Molly and Rhud couldn't kill them all. There was little time. The only plan left was making a beeline for the ship.

After relieving a twitching guard's hand of his weapon, he poked his head around a dilapidated shack at the far end of the plaza. What he saw made his heart leap into overdrive. A full battalion of heavily armed troops was positioned all around the perimeter of the ship. He had not expected so many! He looked down at the cubs, who were eager to rumble.

"Don't even think about it," he told them.

It was a good two hundred yards to the perimeter rim. Between them and the ship were hundreds of troops, along with large grey-and-black guard dogs with steel-trap jaws and thick necks. Nothing the cubs couldn't handle, but there were dozens of beasts chained to posts all around the sensitive science equipment.

Rhud growled impatiently, unafraid of anything.

Looking past the sentry dogs, he saw the soft blue light of the shields still holding and no one inside the barrier. That was a good sign. Next to the perimeter were steel-grey cutting devices and plas cannons spread out next to the barrier. Obviously they had little luck in breaching it, he thought. He let out a small chuckle. *If they only knew*... It was like trying to open Fort Knox with a can opener.

Directly in his path to the barrier were dozens of guards and half again as many science types working on the barrier with their devices. A small group of scientists moved a large plas-cannon into point-blank range of the barrier. While they were making their final adjustments to the cannon, an officer ordered his guards away from the barrier for a hundred yards in each direction. They also untied the dogs and took them away from the area for their safey. The dozens of guards double-timed away from their stations and took positions behind portable shields placed at various locations to protect them from the residual blast effects. As he watched, an idea struck him. If he timed it right... maybe. He and the cats wouldn't get a second chance. He couldn't afford to wait until it was dark. High noon would have to do.

Suddenly a loud shrill blasted over the entire section of the city as dozens of soldiers began running toward the street entrance into the city that led directly back to the plaza.

The Consortium had found the bodies. It wouldn't be long before the dogs found him here if he didn't do something quick.

Then the dogs caught sight of the cubs and any plan he had went down the toilet. A soldier leveled his weapon at Molly, but Simon blasted the soldier between the eyes with a clean shot. With their cover blown, Simon acted in desperation, leaping onto Rhud's back. He grabbed the cub's mane and hung on. Bolts of plas-fire caught up with him, whizzing past his head. He ducked and bobbed from side to side, trying to make himself as small a target as possible while riding the cub's back. The cubs ran like silver bullets. They were too fast for anyone to fix a bead on. Twenty yards from the barrier, a plas round caught Simon in the shoulder, knocking him off his ride. The past two days of physical abuse had cost him that slight edge. Lying facedown in the dirt, another plas round found its mark, cutting his legs out from under him as he tried to get up. He tumbled over, his forward momentum taking him within a few yards of the blue wall. He got up again just as another shot caught him in the back. He went down hard, doing a face-plant into the dirt. His nose bleeding and broken, he reached out, grabbing for anything that could drag him the last few feet through the barrier. He was only half a body length from the shimming edge when the world around him exploded, ringing his clock. He could almost touch the blue wispy light as he lunged for the wall with all that was left inside of him. Another stinging shot struck his side, then another, and another. His back arched up, reeling in pain. He cried out violently, thrusting his body at the barrier. Exploding grit and dirt were so heavy he couldn't breathe. Then he saw the blue shimmer in front of his face. He was almost in! *I'm so close,* he thought. *Push, Rerun, push!* he screamed at himself. Just when he thought one more leap would do it, a hand reached out and grabbed him.

52

Cold Grey Cell

THE DULL, HEAVY sound of clanking metal woke Ian from unconsciousness. It was like someone had just closed a vault door. He carefully twisted around to a sitting position, holding his throbbing head. Bewildered and disoriented, he tried to gather his wits and understand his situation. The last thing he remembered was hustling back to the ship through the Horritan back alley. Harlowe was ahead of them, with Quay in the middle. Riverstone was guarding their backside when a bright flash burst in front of his face. He closed his eyes and exhaled a long breath. That was it. That was all he could remember. Everything else beyond the orange flash was a blank.

So where am I?

He opened his eyes and saw Riverstone. Harlowe and Quay were nowhere in the room. He took a quick look around and discovered they were in a small cubicle cell. Its walls were grey steel. There was one door and a small porthole of a window opposite the door. That was it. There wasn't even a pot to go to the bathroom.

He nudged Riverstone. "Wake up, Matt," he mumbled low in his ear. He, too, grudgingly came to life.

While Riverstone groaned back to consciousness, Ian tried to stand by pushing against the side of the wall. He had his sights on the porthole. He wondered why they had been brought here and not left for dead in the alley. Where was this place? Where were Harlowe and Quay? Were they close by? Who was responsible? He had a million questions and not one answer.

Finally reaching his goal, he saw nothing but bright, hazy stars of hyperlight space outside the porthole. There was nothing solid like a planet or moon in any direction, and he wondered where they were headed—Another question with no answer.

He looked back at Riverstone, who was sitting up and holding his aching head.

Ian bent down and helped him sit against the grey metal wall of their cell. Then he explained what he had already discovered about their captivity.

"Where's Dog?" Riverstone asked.

"They're not here," Ian replied.

Riverstone held his head as if trying to slow its spinning. "How long were we out?"

Ian shrugged. "I don't know. You know as much as I do."

With a loud clank, the door unlatched. Ian thought briefly about launching himself at whoever was coming in, but Riverstone put a cautious hand on his arm. "Not yet."

Ian nodded reluctantly. Riverstone was right. Whoever put them here in the first place got them here without resistance. They could do it again. Besides, no one was in good enough shape to put up any kind of an assault.

"Ha, ha, ha," came a sick laugh through the door. Ian and Riverstone exchanged glances. They both remembered the laugh but didn't place the face until the fat being entered the cell behind another large being holding a pistol. "Ah, now you are awake, Pylott," the fat alien said, staring right at Riverstone between heavy strands of thick wet hair. "That is your name, Pylott, right, human?"

Riverstone was about to deny the claim when Ian's sharp elbow struck him in the side reminding him to hold his tongue.

"Yeah. That's right. I'm Pylott. What of it, greaseball?" Riverstone acknowledged, pointing at himself.

The being's chubby cheeks glistened in the dull light of the cell. "I am Ra-Loc. Your host." He punctuated his reply with a greasy laugh.

"What do you want with us, Ra-toad?" Riverstone asked with great disdain.

Ra-Loc's repulsive face explained, "Wealth, Pylott. For you I will receive a great ransom."

Riverstone chuckled. "You're going to split it with us, fifty-fifty right?"

"You will both make me very rich. The female..."

Riverstone rose, and as he did, Ra-Loc's oversized guard stuck the muzzle of a pistol against his head. "The girl. Where is she?"

"Easy, Perto," Ra-Loc said. "We do not want to harm the merchandise before it is delivered."

"So where's the girl, toad? If you've harmed her—" Riverstone tried to say.

Ra-Loc's face sneered with indifference. "Oh, her. The girl. Yes, lovely creature. She has been well taken care of," he said, glancing at Perto, who laughed morbidly, mocking his master.

"The other human who was with us. What happened to him?" Ian asked.

Ra-Loc sobered, sighing. "I'm afraid he was far too much trouble. We had to kill him."

Ian launched himself at Ra-Loc's throat. "Why, you..."

Before his fingers reached their mark, Perto fired his stunner, stopping Ian before he could do harm to his master. Riverstone caught

Ian before he struck the floor. In doing that, he didn't see the boot that struck the side of his face.

53

Simon's Duty

SIMON SAT UP in bed and gazed at the heavy drops of rain pounding the skylight of his room, wondering if he was alive or dead. While the storm raged outside, his room was eerily quiet. The grey cloudy day reflected off of his pale, unshaven face. His bloodshot eyes revealed the battle he had fought to survive through the night. Clickers, he thought. They had pulled him through the barrier before he was gonzo. It was the only explanation as to why he was still alive.

He tossed back the covers and jumped out of bed, charging naked for the closet. This wasn't time for R&R. He had to tell Harlowe about Quay's sister and how she was taken by the Consortium, and about Turfan and Unikala and their plans. He had to tell Harlowe all the things he had learned so he could get Sizzle back.

After a quick shower and shave, he jumped into a fresh uniform and was out the door, his insides aching with dread. He didn't know where to begin. He needed clarity and help from his mates to find his love again. *What would Captain Starr do?* In the past, he had always turned to the make-believe movie Captain to help himself through his problems, relying on his Hollywood strength to rescue him from the Dakadudes of his mind. Captain Starr would have found a way to get Sizzle back, and all inside 120 minutes, too!

Dude! You're Gamadin, he reminded himself. *You're tougher than Captain Starr, and much more capable. You're part of a team that is*

328

real and the best there ever was, Rerun! Hurry! Find your mates and the Skipper, because they're the best. With him and your mates at your side, you'll get her back.

Hurry, Rerun, hurry!

He ran up the corridor as if the General were behind him, kicking his backside. He didn't stop until he stepped on the blinker up to the control room. He couldn't remember when or who first coined the term "blinker" for the pad that scrambled their molecules and rematerialized them on another pad inside the control room, all in a "blink" of the eye, but that's what everyone was calling them now. In that blink of an eye, he was topside, stepping onto the bridge, staring out through the giant curved windows at the rain that was coming down in sheets. The control room, however, was unusually quiet. One of the cubs was on the portside couch stretched out, sleeping on its back with its legs sprawled. Had to be Rhud, he thought. Molly was too dignified to sleep that way. Where Molly was at the moment, only Millie knew. The ship was so large one could hide for a lifetime if one wanted. Then the center chair turned around and Simon saw the first friendly face he'd seen in days.

"Platter! Where's the Captain?" Simon cried out, stopping at the center of the room. Before Monday could answer, Simon cried out again. "Is he in his cabin?" He ran to Harlowe's door in a panic and slammed the activator to open the door. Looking inside, he saw no one. "Platter, where's the Captain? I need to talk to him. Where is he?"

Monday met Simon in the middle of the room, grabbing him by the shoulders to settle him down. "He was looking for you."

"I lost him," Simon shouted back. "Where is he?"

"He's not here."

"Where is he? I saw him flying across the park. He's got to be here by now. Did you see the fire?"

"I saw it."

"The Consortium launched an attack on it last night."

"That was two nights ago, Mr. Bolt," Monday informed him.

Simon's jaw dropped. "Two nights?"

"Yeah, you were out all day today and last night."

"Why didn't you wake me?"

"I'm all alone up here. I've been pretty busy protecting the ship."

"So where are the Captain and Riverstone?" He looked around the control room frantically. "Where's Wiz? They were ahead of me."

Monday was confused. "They never made it."

Simon looked at Monday as if he wasn't talking sense. "What? They didn't make it? They had to! I saw them. They were headed back to the ship. I saw them, Platter!"

"I know you did. They were almost here but they never made it," Monday explained. "I sent clickers after them, but they were too late. By the time they arrived, they were gone."

"Gone? Gone where?"

He stepped over to the control console and brought up one of the holographic screens. "I don't know. They were in the alley here," he pointed. "Then suddenly, their locators when dark. I lost them."

Simon stared down at the screen, feeling his world collapse around him. Sizzle was one thing, losing her was devastating, but losing the Captain and his mates was unthinkable. At that moment he turned away disgusted at this turn of events, Molly materialized on the control deck and sat there looking at him, with her eyes confident and blue in the grey light as though she was waiting for him to make the call.

Think, Rerun, where could the Captain be?

He walked over and knelt down next to her, hoping to absorb a part of her strength. *Look farther than your nose, toadface!* Her bright blue eyes stared back, worriedly hoping for direction from him.

"I wish I had an answer, girl. I'm sorry," he told her.

He then turned to Rhud, who had awakened and moved off the couch. His white fur reflected the dullness of the sky and the nearby lights from the control console as he stared longingly through the massive window, waiting for Harlowe or Quay to appear.

At this moment, Simon felt that everybody's lives depended on him for their survival. He had the Ship. He had Platter, too. He understood well the decisions he made from here on out might affect whether his mates would live or die. The idea that they might already be dead had never crossed his mind. They were all alive and he would find them, if it took an eternity to do it!

The question then was where to start. With each journey there is that first step. *Don't fret over whether a decision is right or wrong. MAKE THE DECISION, RERUN!*

His first thought was to return to the street where the cubs had found their last scent, but how would he get there? He was still surrounded by hundreds of Consortium guards who were still trying to break through the barrier. He couldn't walk beyond the barrier without getting shot at again. The thought of Consortium scientists penetrating the barrier had occurred to him, but that was hardly probable. There was only one answer. He had to leave the safety of the ship.

The rain subsided somewhat, and through a break in the clouds he saw the Overseers of Path's golden ball. In the overpowering skyline, the ball dominated even the largest superstructures of Gibb. Quay had said many times it was the center of Gibb. In all the chaos it was the only thing that had order and harmony in the ancient city. From it they had been able to fly safely through crowded space from a billion miles out.

As he stared at the golden ball, a thought came to him.

Take them out… his mind echoed, again and again.

Yeah, take them out. You can do it. You have the power. Millie can do it. Take them all out.

He rose calmly from his chair and looked out. The ball had the answer. Control. The control was here with *Millawanda*. He just had to use it. He looked at Platter, his sad, worried eyes turning hopeful. He touched his former bodyguard's shoulder. "I know you outrank me, Mr. Platter, but I believe I have an idea on where to look for the Captain."

Rank between Gamadin had no meaning when it came to doing the right thing. Monday was listening.

Simon recounted his story: meeting Sizzle, their short romance in the park, overhearing Unikala and Turfan plotting against the Tomar-Rex, then his capture and escape, and finally finding Quay's ring on the street. "The ring?" His face suddenly went fraught with worry. "The ring! I lost it. I had the ring with me."

Monday pulled out the delicate band from his pocket. "This one?"

Simon sighed. "Oh man, yes, that's it! Where did you find it?"

"It was clutched in your hand. The clickers nearly cut off your fingers to pry them loose."

"The Captain will make you an officer for that," Simon replied, looking at it with relief that he hadn't lost it. He handed it back to Monday. "Put it in a safe place. I don't want to lose it."

"Tell me your plan," Monday said.

"I'm going back to the alley. We're going to find the Captain, and that's a good place to start."

"What about the Consortium? We're surrounded."

"What were your orders?"

"The Captain said take them out if they cause any trouble."

Simon headed for the blinker. "Then do it." He disappeared to the lower level, with Molly and Rhud blinking right behind him.

Simon made a pit stop by the storage room off the center rampway to pick up another SIBA and grab a fully loaded Gama-belt and pistol with plenty of rounds. Then he took off down the ramp with the cubs loping beside him. At the perimeter, a party of high Consortium officials was waiting for him. They didn't appear to be having a good day. Simon, however, didn't care about their problems. He had bigger ones of his own. "Leave the area immediately or I will make sure you do!" he demanded before any of them opened their mouths.

Simon was shaking in his boots. He had never been a commander in real life before. He kept reminding himself he was in the role of his life and he had to play an Oscar-winning performance to make it all work. He was Gamadin and Captain Julian Starr rolled into one.

As he figured, no one took him seriously. Simon raised his hand up and snapped his fingers. "Time's up, pukes!" A half-second later, a powerful surge of blue light burst forth from the rim of the ship. For a mile in every direction outside Millie's protective shield, every living thing collapsed to the ground in a hyper-unconscious state.

Simon stared approvingly at the mass of Consortium bodies. "Toads." He then stepped past the barrier with the cubs at his side and headed through the stun zone and back to where he had found the ring and the scent of his mates.

54

Black Log

WEARING HIS SIBA, Simon returned with the cubs to the site in little time. While the cubs raced along on the ground, he used his limb-enhanced suit to leap across the crowded rooftops of the Horritan shanties. At first they debated about which direction the scent led. Rhud wanted to go one way and Molly had her nose stuck down a sewer drain. It didn't seem probable that anyone had dropped through the sewer gap, yet Molly was persistant. Simon peered down into the dark gap with his bugeyes and saw nothing but a massive river of black sewage flowing to only who knew where.

Simon opted for Rhud's conclusion.

They followed the scent down a crowded Horritan street until the scent turned into a back alley, which took them to another busy street. It seemed like forever, but eventually they came to a wide-open zone where smaller ships landed and unloaded their cargo. The cubs sprinted out into a vacant parking bay and stopped. Simon soon caught up with the cubs. They were pacing back and forth, searching for the ship that was no longer there.

"They were here, weren't they?" Simon asked.

Both cubs howled loudly their affirmative reply.

Simon scanned the area with his com and found nothing. He then asked a couple of beggars if they knew anything about the ship that was previously docked here. No one answered him. Traders took care of themselves. They would not give him an answer. He looked up at the grey sky, the rain pouring down again. He knelt beside the cubs and hugged their sad, wet faces. "Another dead end, huh? There's nothing more we can do here. We should go back," he told them. "Maybe we missed something." He guided them away from the parking pad after making a mental note of its location.

By the time they had returned to the alley where they first picked up the scent, Omini Prime had gone down, and it was pitch black on the Horritan streets. Simon checked in with Monday, but there was nothing new to report. He was about to call it a night when Molly once again had her nose poked down the sewer opening in the street.

Simon tried to push her away. "Molly, you're making me sick. Get out of there, girlfriend!"

She wouldn't budge. On the third try to pull her away, she almost took a hunk out of Simon's arm with a swipe of her paw.

Simon turned to Rhud for help but he sauntered over to Molly and stuck his nose into the same crack.

Monday, who had been listening the whole time, reminded Simon of how acute the cubs' sense of smell was, even in the driving rain. As he had in the park, he bent down beside her and said, "Go for it, girl. Find whatever it is you're looking for."

A short cat grunt and Molly bolted through the Horritan narrow streets, only this time in a totally different direction. With his bugeyes, Simon was able to follow the cubs' body signatures comfortably behind them through the crowded, smoke-filled streets.

Miles later, according to the readouts inside his bugeyes, the cubs were far outside the Horritan streets and following a wide sewer channel that opened into a mile-wide toxic river filled with all the filth and waste that Gibbian skyscrapers and Horritan hovels could dump out. When Simon got the first whiff of it he fell to his knees, reeling from the overpowering stench. It wasn't until he switched on the internal breathing filters of his SIBA that he was able to walk upright again. He winced when he thought about the cubs ahead of him and what they must be going through. They had no masks or SIBAs covering their noses.

After two more miles along the toxic river, the cubs disappeared over a steep embankment. Simon quickly caught up to them and saw them licking the top of a long, black, log-like object on the side of the noxious bank. He wondered again what they were doing licking a disease-infested log. Disgusted, he leaped down the side of the bank, fearing the worst as he slipped and slid into the black goo up to his hips. His black, repugnant hands pushed against the muck, helping him keep his balance as he rushed to push the cubs away from the vile object. *How crazy was that?* The smell must have wrecked their brains, he figured, as he yanked them away from the log. "Stop that! What are you thinking?" he screamed at them, but they wouldn't stop. They fought him off and returned to the log the instant he let go. Angrily he grabbed Rhud around the neck and started to yank him back, when the log moved...

55

Where's Pylott?

RIVERSTONE AWOKE FROM a dreamless sleep when he felt the pitch of the engines change. It was the familiar sound of a ship coming out of the faint purr of hyperspace and into the low, throbbing hum of subspace. Ian was already awake and staring out the porthole.

"Now what?" Riverstone asked groggily.

"We've got company," Ian answered, as though their predicament had just taken another leg down.

Riverstone climbed to his feet and joined Ian at the porthole as a massive battlecruiser drifted to a stop alongside Ra-Loc's ship.

"That's Consortium," Ian stated.

Riverstone agreed. "A big one, too, like the one we took out at #2."

A small shuttlecraft appeared from the side of the giant cruiser and pull up to Ra-Loc's ship.

"I don't like the feeling I'm getting," Ian said, watching the shuttle line up its connecting hatchway with small bursts of maneuvering thrusters. It attached itself to the ship with a loud clank.

"Dittos," Riverstone replied.

It wasn't long until their cell door opened and a tall, dark shadow stood in the doorway. After they had destroyed half his attack ships and his own battlecruiser, Ian didn't think Unikala had come to pay them a social call.

Unikala's face instantly narrowed. "Where's Pylott?" he demanded angrily.

The Gamadin traded confused looks. "Who?" Riverstone asked as though he had never heard of the name before. "Does he play for the Dodgers?"

"Pylott! Where is he?" Unikala demanded again.

"Oh, him. He had a previous engagement," Ian replied.

"He didn't like the party's host," Riverstone added.

Ra-Loc poked his fat face into the doorway and pointed to Riverstone. "There. He's the one. That's Pylott."

"Ra-Loc, you degenerate fool," Unikala blared. "That is his second-in-command. Neither human is Pylott, you grogan pile of waste!"

"I...I don't understand. It must be. He said—"

Unikala slapped Ra-Loc hard across the face. Two of Ra-Loc's guards tried to protect their master, but Unikala shot them down dead before they could take a step. The two prisoners stared in disbelief at the guiltless killing.

"I will destroy your vessel for leading me to these imposters," Unikala said, seething with rage. He grabbed Ra-Loc by his collar and lifted his fat body off the deck with one hand before sticking the muzzle of his pistol into Ra-Loc's face.

The Lagan trader's stubby legs wiggled in the air as he struggled desperately to save his miserable life. "Commissar, I beg you! I have the girl," he whined. "Surely she is worth a commissar's ransom!"

Unikala was shocked. "You have the girl?"

"Yes, yes, Commissar. I believe she means a great deal to this Pylott. I have seen this." Ra-Loc saw his way out when Unikala's pale face lit up like a spring morning. It didn't take a grogan's brain to see that Unikala was more interested in the girl than the human called Pylott.

"Keep her, oh powerful one," Ra-Loc went on, grasping at a last, desperate attempt to save himself. "Keep her and you will have the one you seek. He will come to you."

The heat from Unikala's face drained. "Ra-Loc, you may have just saved your pathetic life," he said, breathing disgust through the cord-like hair covering his face. He tossed Ra-Loc's body against the bulkhead, and nodded approvingly as he stared down at the Lagan trader, flat in the doorway of the cell. "You will find Pylott for me and tell him I have the female at the Consortium acropolis on Og. I'll be there waiting for him." Unikala's crazed eyes glowed as if they could tear Ra-Loc's soul out of his body. The Commissar pressed his heavy black boot across Ra-Loc's layered neck. "If you don't find Pylott and lead him to me before the next cycle of Omini Prime is complete, I will find you myself and kill you, and then bury you inside the pit of grogan waste from which you came."

Ra-Loc's eyes bulged like they would pop out of their sockets. "Yes, yes, Commissar," he gurgled. "Whatever you want, I will do. You can rely on that. I will tell him. I will see that Pylott knows where you have taken the girl."

"Take me to her now," Unikala demanded, kicking the Lagan to his feet. "Quickly!"

"Yes, yes!" Ra-Loc cried, leading him down the corridor. Perto locked the cell behind him and followed his master at a safe distance, along with the rest of Unikala's entourage.

Three doors down, Ra-Loc waited frantically for Perto to open the cell door. Inside the chamber, the female was unconscious against the wall.

"If you have harmed her . . ." Unikala seethed, going to her on the floor.

"No, no, Commissar, I assure you, she is quite well! It was necessary to drug her to keep her from injuring herself," Ra-Loc explained.

Satisfied that Ra-Loc was telling the truth, Unikala waved for his Consortium guards to take the girl back to his ship.

"What of the imposters, Commissar?" Ra-Loc asked timidly, bowing as Unikala passed him with his guards transporting the girl to his battlecruiser.

"Kill them!" Unikala ordered without thought. He then leaned closer to Ra-Loc's greasy face. "Do not fail to bring Pylott to Og, Ra-Loc."

Ra-Loc kneeled lower and lower until his face touched the floor. "Yes, yes, Commissar! Rest assured, I will deliver Pylott to you."

Unikala suddenly lost it. He lifted Ra-Loc, slamming his face against the bulkhead. Dark blood spurted everywhere. Ra-Loc's feet kicked as he screamed at the top of his lungs. Unikala wasn't done. He kicked the Lagan repeatedly with his boot, then spat on his face. "See that you do."

* * *

Even after Unikala's shuttle detached itself from the Lagan freighter, Ra-Loc's cries of pain still echoed throughout the ship. As terrible as his master looked wearing all that blood on his face and chest, Perto knew Ra-Loc was fortunate to be alive. He called for more guards to transport Ra-Loc's quivering mass to the ship's infirmary. Then he lumbered back down the corridor and made his way back to the impostors' cell. He looked at them through the small portal in the door. Unikala had ordered them killed. Perto knew they were trouble. They were not normal creatures. There was something about them that frightened him even more than Unikala did. If it were up to him, he would toss them out into the cold of space and leave the

Omini quadrant forever. But he had his master to think of first…and himself. He pulled his weapon from his belt. If he didn't carry out the Commissar's orders, he and his master would both be dead.

56

Unikala's Dreams

UNIKALA STEPPED OUT of the airlock and into the corridor of his Consortium battlecruiser. His first officer and several subordinates were standing at the side, waiting to receive their commands. Behind Unikala, two other guards brought the girl from the airlock. "Og, Captain. Best speed." The first officer and his subordinates saluted and snappily left to carry out their instructions. Unikala then faced the soldiers guarding Quay. "Take her to a holding cell."

"Yes, Commissar," the guard replied sharply.

"You will not get away with this, Unikala!" She looked deep into his red eyes. He did not intimidate her. She was above him and he knew it. "My father made you Commissar of the Consortium fleet. Now you repay him by kidnapping his daughter."

Unikala smiled shrewdly. "Daughters," he corrected. He nodded to a subordinate, who switched on a nearby wall panel. The screen energized and Quay saw Sizzle slumped unconscious in the corner of a holding cell, her hair ravaged, her clothes filthy.

Quay couldn't believe her eyes. She turned and faced Unikala, her eyes cold and vengeful. "You will pay for this, Unikala! You are a coward of the lowest order, and I will see you destroyed."

Unikala laughed. "Hardly, my dear Quay. I will have you and your father's enterprise by the end of this cycle." He dismissed them with a wave of his hand. "Take her away."

342

Consumed by pride for his coup and the thought of destroying the mighty house of Tomar, he continued watching the guards drag Quay to the lower levels of the ship to join her sister. His silver teeth glistened with arrogance. Yes, he had won. His beautiful prize was returned to him. Now he would concentrate his resources on Pylott. Once he exterminated Pylott, he will have the powerful ship. He knew what that meant: that one ship had the power to control the quadrant and far beyond. He thought of the ancient parchment his troops had stolen from the great and mighty Tomar-Rex's office. The ancient document he now possessed read: *For it is written that the coming madness will awaken the fearsome Gamadin of the galactic core. The wrath of the Gamadin will be felt throughout the stars and lo, while some people trembled in despair still more rejoiced; for the wrath of the Gamadin cleansed the stars for all; and there was peace...*

He mused confidently. The peace would come later. Once he had it all, it would be *HIS* peace. The Fhaal had searched many passings for the Gamadin ship. It was his now. He knew where it was and how to get it. The mothership was coming to him, and all he needed to do was allow his trap to work. The Fhaal would grant him sole possession of the quadrant. They would bow before him, just as Ra-Loc had done. The Gamadin captain was the key. The scriptures didn't lie. Destroying him would transfer the power to him. He laughed out loud as he walked to his quarters. The Consortium's rule over Omini Prime and quadrant would be complete. Tomar was doomed. The Tomar-Rex's vast trading empire would be his as well. His planet, and the magnificent rose-colored palace of stone at the edge of a vast sea, was all his for the taking. He laughed again. The Consortium was no servant of the Fhaal, he mused. They would be *his* vassals by the end of the next cycle.

Unikala stopped at a side portal to take in the vast expanse of a billion stars. His evil face reflected off the glass with a giddy air of success etched permanently into the lines of his arrogant grin. His gaze didn't stop at the quadrant's boundary; it extended far beyond the quadrant's frontiers.

57

Pinned Down

SIMON COULDN'T BELIEVE his eyes. He brushed away the vile muck from the log and found Harlowe covered with all that was rank and toxic from the black river of ooze. Of all the places on the planet, the sewage spillway was the last place he would have thought to look for anyone. Not even 54th century equipment could have tracked him here. But the cats? *Wow, the cats knew!* He stared at them in awe. Never again would he doubt their ability. In his eyes they had redefined Gamadin.

With one great heave, he pulled the log from the muck and carried it up the embankment away from the contamination. "Mr. Platter, come in!" he yelled into his com as he frantically began pushing away the heavy sections of sticky goo from Harlowe's face and neck. I found him, Squid! I found Dog!" he kept repeating.

Monday wanted to know only one thing: "Tell me the Captain's alive, Mr. Bolt!" The strain in his voice was unmistakable.

"He's hanging on. His SIBA kept him alive. You've got to lock on to me."

"I've got you."

"Bring Millie quick! I don't know how long he can last."

"Roger that, Mr. Bolt, on my way. Platter out."

Then to Harlowe he said:

"Captain! Can you hear me? Talk to me, Dog. Come on, talk to me."

Harlowe couldn't hear him. He lay there, still as a corpse.

Molly and Rhud started licking the sides of Harlowe's arms and shoulders in their effort to help. Simon pushed them away. "No, no. Stay back. It's poison," he told them. "You can't help him by doing that. You'll only make yourselves sick." He jumped over Harlowe's body in front of Molly's snout. She wasn't taking no for an answer. "Stop it, Molly. Get away. Didn't you hear me? He's covered with all kinds of bad things." He pushed her away again. "Now move away, Molly. I've got to handle this now. Be a good girl. Please."

She growled her frustration but didn't force herself again. Something else had her attention.

It was Consortium troops. Hundreds of them! They were coming out of the bushes a quarter mile away and making their way to them along the riverbank. The swampy muck would slow them down somewhat, but not for long.

"Squid, the neighborhood's starting to go south with bad guys," Simon said, his tone urgent. He pulled out a hypo from his med kit and injected the blue fluid into the side of Harlowe's chest. When it was empty, he tossed it and drew his pistol. For anyone but a Gamadin, the Consortium troops would be out of range. Simon started plucking off those in the front first, but he wouldn't get them all. There were too many. He would run out of plasrounds before he could make a dent in their numbers. He just needed to slow them enough for Millie to arrive.

Plas bolts began screaming back, whizzing over his head. He slid Harlowe back down the embankment enough so they had some cover in case a stray shot got lucky.

"Mr. Platter. Did you hear me? We're pinned down here," Simon repeated.

"I heard you, Mr. Bolt," Monday replied calmly. "I've got my hands full. Attack ships are coming out of the woodwork," he commented wryly.

"Nuke them if you have to, Mr. Platter!" Simon shouted back, continuing to pluck off Consortium heads coming his way.

"Aye, Mr. Bolt!"

Simon looked around frantically. Where were the cats? They had disappeared.

He lifted his head above the bank to get a glimpse. A string of four-letter expletives almost left his mouth the instant he saw the cubs racing across the swamp like they were on solid ground, headed straight for the mass of oncoming troops. The crack of plas rounds split the air like machine guns gone berserk. Everywhere was mayhem.

Simon watched in awe as twisted bodies scattered across the swamp. Heads were torn from necks like paper dolls, spinning like tops in the air, while arms and legs yanked from their sockets soared outward over the killing field. The troops didn't know how to react to the killing machines. They were overwhelmed. Many ran away, only to be cut down in retreat. Others stood their ground but shot wildly, missing the fast-moving targets by yards. Still, Simon knew that unless the Ship arrived in time, not even the cubs could take out every Consortium trooper. There were just too many.

Simon reloaded and tried to cover the cubs against the troops that were zeroing in on them. How long he could keep it up, he didn't know. Then one of the cubs got hit in the hindquarter. His bugeyes zoomed in. It was Rhud. The cat twisted sideways, turning over in the muck. Simon shot at a trooper who tried to take a second shot. Molly, seeing what had happened to Rhud, leaped thirty feet into the air and came down on the five soldiers heading straight at the fallen cat. She mauled them to pieces before they could take a shot. A squad of six more came charging up from her backside. She didn't see them. Simon got the first two out in front but ran out of rounds before he could finish the job. He ejected the spent cartridge and tried to reload just as a storm of plas fire ambushed him from the side, forcing his head back down below the bank. They were out-flanking him, coming up from both sides of the spillway. Soon he would be sandwiched between two battalions of troops.

Simon finished snapping in a fresh mag when he saw a familiar cylinder protruding out of the goo nearby. "Nikto!" Simon yelled. "Nikto!" In an instant Jewels sprang to life, joining the fray. The robob servant fished Harlowe's second pistol out of the mud and popped a fresh mag Simon gave him into the chamber. After that it was all Jewels. The robob leaped over the bank and headed for the cats. With Simon as backup and Jewels leading the charge, Rhud found his legs again and was shredding the soldiers who were now after Molly.

Simon searched the sky. "PLATTER, WHERE ARE YOU?"

At that moment the heavens went dark. Three hundred feet above his head, a golden disk drifted silently overhead and covered the entire sky. An instant later, what seemed like a zillion bolts of light struck out from the perimeter rim of the saucer.

Then all was quiet, as if all life on the battlefield had suddenly winked out of existence. Not a single plas round whizzed across the marshes or barking command was heard anywhere. The only sound that remained was the gurgling of the toxic goo that lapped against the black sides of the spillway.

58

My Captain

QUAY RAN TO SIZZLE'S slumped body, praying she was still alive. She lifted her head. Sizzle's face was swollen and purple. She had been beaten severely, but she was alive. Her large, raven eyes suddenly went cold and penetrating. *You will pay for this, Unikala! The Gamadin will find you. You cannot hide from their justice!*

Quay gently began to dab at her sister's face and arms with a small rag she'd found nearby. She worried about her condition. Sizzle had not moved or spoken a single word in the short time Quay was beside her. She kept wiping, praying for a miracle as she drew another deep breath of hope for her Captain. Had he survived? If he had, where was he now? Did Unikala have him, too?

She looked around at the wall of cold metal. If he was nearby, how could she help him?

Suddenly, she felt a change in the Consortium's ship. She carefully laid Sizzle to one side and stood up to peer out the cell portal. What she saw froze her in place, and at the same time, answered many of her questions. The Consortium battlecruiser drifted up alongside a massive starship, appearing like a small shuttlecraft floating against its giant superstructure. It was the Fhaal, she knew. She recognized its circular markings. She trembled again. It took her breath away, seeing its size. She had never seen anything so monstrously evil in her life.

How could any fleet in the quadrant fight such power, she wondered? How would she and her Captain save the quadrant now?

Distraught with despair, Quay slid back to the floor next to Sizzle. She could think of nothing to do to improve her condition. There were no choices for her and no way out. A great exhaustion fell over her. She could barely keep her head up. Her arms felt heavy as she cradled Sizzle close to her and stroked her sister's long, wavy hair. Despair and loneliness overwhelmed her, while she wished Harlowe was holding her in his arms. Quay's fingers touched the Gamadin necklace around her neck. The medallion gave her some comfort that her Captain was there with her. Her mind replayed reaching out for him in those last moments in the Horritan gutter before he fell through the crack and disappeared from sight. She promised herself that the last touch of his hand and the loss of the ring would not be their final moment together. It was easy to doubt, yet she fought against the evil spell that kept them separated. She clutched her medallion tighter. It gave her hope. Her chin fell against her chest. She needed sleep. After she rested she would think more clearly. Now she was weak and broken. *You must rest now, Quay.* Her body slid gently to one side against her sister's shoulder. Just before she joined her in a fretful sleep, her last conscious thought repeated over and over.

I will find a way, my Captain…

59

Trio Drobnosi

WHEN SIMON STEPPED off the blinker onto the bridge, the first person he saw was Platter sitting in the center chair, like an ever-vigilant sentinel watching for any sign of danger.

"Permission to relieve you, Mr. Platter," Simon announced, as he strode into the heart of the powerful Gamadin ship. He was dressed in the uniform of the day: dark blue tunic, long sleeves, and beltless matching pants with thin gold trim around the cuffs and waist. His black, calf-high boots were polished and his pants creased, with not a thread or cuff out of place. He was ready for duty. As he looked around the bridge, it was miserably still and quiet. The ever-vigilant lights and screens of the ship's console were waiting for his inspection. As he moved to the front, his insides shook with dread. Outside, through the massive observation windows, the rain he and the cubs had run through to find Harlowe had become a hurricane-force storm. The wind was snapping trees and whipping up the spillway water into great, black waves across the mile-wide drainage channel. The rain kept pounding the windows as lightening exploded all around them. No storm on the planet could harm *Millawanda*, he knew. Her shields were on. Not even the sound of the thunderous rumbles could penetrate the wispy blue veil that protected them. It was like watching an IMAX movie in silence.

Millawanda had not moved since Monday brought her here two days ago. She was too large for one person to command. She needed its crew to make her alive and beautiful again. He closed his eyes and prayed a little for the strength he would need to endure until Harlowe was stronge enough to resume command. He should have been up and around by now, Simon thought. Was he all right? He hadn't checked with Millie today, but last night his readouts were questionable.

Monday waved him forward. "Permission granted, Mr. Bolt. Come ahead."

"Any word from the Captain?" Simon asked.

Monday looked down, his face tired and drawn. "He'll make it."

"What does Millie say?"

"That he'll live."

Simon breathed a long sigh of relief. "I thought he was..."

"The Captain's tough. It'll take a lot more than toxic waste to kill him."

Simon agreed. There was no one in the universe as unkillable as Captain Harlowe Pylott. Then he asked Monday, "How about Rhud?"

"Filling up the cat box."

Simon nodded approvingly. He then asked if Monday had heard anything from Riverstone or Wizzixs.

"Nothing. Millie's summation is they were transported off Gibb. She's picked up no bio signs from either of them anywhere on the planet."

"Quay?"

"The same. She's nowhere on the planet."

"I guess I don't need to ask you about her sister."

"They're all gone, Mr. Bolt, I'm sorry."

Simon wanted to sob. For a brief moment of weakness he wanted to collapse on the floor and cry his eyes out for failing his mates and for Quay and Sizzle, but he couldn't do it. Blame and self-pity were from another life. He had a job to do and a duty greater than himself to think about before he would let himself turn back into what he had been before becoming a Gamadin. He reached down inside of himself to summon up all that he had for them—for all of them. *No D.O.R.s here, Gamadin!,* Gunn's voice echoed from the past. "Yes, sir!"

Monday stared at Simon, confused. "Mr. Bolt?"

Simon pulled himself together, holding his god-awful pain in check for when he was alone. "Nothing, Mr. Platter. It's okay."

They acknowledged each other as old friends, mates who knew there was no retreat. Then Simon asked, "When's the last time you slept?"

Monday stared, red-eyed, as if he were close to passing out on the floor. "Days," he replied.

Simon pried him out of the center chair. "Come on, Squid, you're done here. Get some sleep."

Monday pointed to the starboard observation couch. "I could sleep next to Rhud."

"Negative. Go, Squid. I've got it covered. I'll let you know if there's a problem," Simon assured him.

"I'll have a clicker put a blinker in my room," Monday said.

"Cool. Now get out of here."

Monday didn't need a whole lot of convincing. He thanked Simon a couple of times, almost leaning against the bulkhead next to the blinker before he winked down to the lower level. Simon called a couple of clickers to follow Monday to his room in case he passed out along the way.

Alone now, Simon checked the console first to get himself up to speed on their situation. The last two days had been pretty quiet. No attack fighters had made any attempts to destroy *Millawanda* since Platter had wiped out three of their squadrons. He figured the Consortium would think twice before losing another five hundred troops and twenty-seven attack ships.

Then the soft, sad sound of a violin brought his attention to the port side of the control room. The music was coming from Harlowe's quarters. As the music played on, Simon felt the tears falling from his eyes and a lump in his throat he couldn't swallow. Every note, every measure was bowed with such *con amore* and pain that the *Trio Drobnosi*, Opus 75a by Antonin Dvorak, sounded as though the violin was crying along with him. Simon lingered there near the doorway until the *Trio Drobnosi* was completed. Only then did he step up to the arched doorway, standing stick-straight at attention, click his heels, and wipe his eyes clear before he pressed the call actuator and announced, "First Mate, Simon Bolt, reporting for duty, Captain," in a confident, soldierly voice.

60

Pep Talk

HARLOWE HEARD THE precise notes of Simon's call and his announcement that he was reporting for duty. Even if his First Mate had said nothing, he would have known it was Simon. Everyone on the ship had a call sign taken from a classical piece of music. When they pressed the actuator at the side of the door the notes played, announcing the caller. Simon's notes were taken from Mozart's *Variations on "Ah vous dirais-je, Maman"* (better known as "Twinkle, Twinkle Little Star"), while Harlowe's was Beethoven's *Fifth*.

Harlowe laid his Stradivarius across his lap as he sat on the floor, using the observation couch for a back support. He gazed out at the storm as if he were counting every drop that splattered the window. He didn't want to answer just yet. Lying dutifully nearby were Molly and Rhud. They'd followed him like shadows from the moment the robobs carried him out of med unit and to his quarters.

He stroked Molly's soft white fur, in awe of how fast they were growing. He had no idea how large they would eventually become. If their mother was any indication, they had another six feet and several hundred more pounds to go. They had also earned their place as respected members of the crew.

With his bowstring, he touched the tops of their heads like a king bestowing knighthood to a brave warrior. "As Captain of the *Millawanda*, I hereby grant Molly and you, Rhud, all rights and privileges of true Gamadin." He half-expected some jubilant reaction, but Molly only yawned and lay back sleepily against Rhud, who continued to lick his paws and wash his face.

"Pukes," Harlowe sneered at his ungrateful inductees. He then carefully sat his Stradivarius in its old leather case, latched the case, and handed it to Jewels, his loyal robob servant standing nearby. Jewels dutifully took the Strad and clickity-clacked away to another room, leaving Harlowe to himself.

A second call reminded him that Simon was still waiting at the door. He would have to wait. All Harlowe had on were the boxer shorts he wore when he left the med room. He didn't need to see himself in a mirror to know he was a haggard mess. His eyes were tired and swollen. He hadn't bothered to shower or dress since waking up hours ago.

I should have seen the trap, he kept telling himself over and over in relentless self-incrimination. *I should have known better than to have us all in one place!* He cursed his youth and inexperience for not knowing how better to protect his crew and his ship. He poured the last blue drop from the bottle and slammed the shot home. "Another bottle of *Blue Stuff*, Jewels!" he cried out in his half-crazed stupor.

The pain. He needed something for the pain. *They caught me with my pants down. I should have seen it coming! We're at war here. Everywhere we're at war. Know that, toad! Never assume anything. We're in a far- off place where the rules haven't changed.* He gazed at his favorite books along the front of his desk. There they were, all lined up with their priceless life lessons speaking to him: Hannibal, Hornblower, Machiavelli, Patton, and Sun Tzu, all rich with cunning, plotting, and deception. Their instructions were clear and precise. He had read them all many, many times. Even then, he had ignored their lessons. *The blame lies with you, Captain Toad!* His head lowered as he wiped more dribble from his nose and spittle from his chin and tried to clear his eyes. *They would be safe with us now if I had remembered my training!*

He heard movement again at his door. He lay his glass down and stood, nearly tripping over Molly's outstretched legs. "Sorry, girl," he groaned. He caught himself against the observation window and looked outward. The storm appeared to be breaking up. In the far distance the only thing he could see of Gibb was the golden ball of the Overseer of Path peeking over fluffy white clouds. He remembered how Quay had described the way the Overseer of Path controlled all movement on Gibb.

"DOG!" a gut-hard, bullhorn voice bellowed. "Get your sorry hind-end together!"

Harlowe's eyes flew open. He knew that voice and went stick-straight to attention. His eyes didn't see anyone. He didn't have to. The voice was clear enough. "YESSIR, GENERAL, SIR!" he cried out as if he were a green recruit again.

"Those Gamadin of mine can't wait forever for you to get your pukey act together, Dog."

"Yes, sir!"

"They need your help."

"Yes, sir!"

"Now what are you going to do about it?"

"I...I'm going to find them, Sir!"

"What are you going to do, Dog?" the voice shouted again in his ear for clarity.

"I am going to find my crew and kick booty, sir!"

"Are you a Gamadin?"

"Yes, sir!"

"Then start acting like it, soldier. Did I train you to give up?"

"No, sir!"

"Did I throw you off that cliff on Mars and make you march a thousand klicks for you to cry in your blue water?"

"No sir!"

"Then clean yourself up, soldier, and nuke those toad-faced dorks!"

"YESSIR!"

He snapped his right hand to his forehead and waited for the voice to acknowledge his salute. A long silence went by before he realized no counter-salute was coming. He looked from side to side and saw no General Gunn standing next to him. Molly and Rhud looked at him, tilting their heads slightly at an angle, wondering what had shaken his tree. He continued searching his quarters, finding no one else in the room but the cubs. Harlowe rolled his shoulders forward, trying to restore at least a little presence of mind. The General may have lacked the physical presence, but his spirit was alive and well. He was right, too. This was no time to feel sorry for himself. The past was behind him. No one else could lead them to his friends and crewmen. He felt for the ring Quay had given him. He closed his eyes in despair. It was gone, like her. He promised her, wherever she was in the galaxy, he would never let her down. He would find her, too.

Harlowe struck the call button but didn't open the door. "Mr. Bolt, give me thirty."

"Aye, Captain, thirty," Simon's voice replied. From the snappy reply, Harlowe could feel the relief in his first mate's voice that he had finally answered his call.

"Do you have a report for me?" Harlowe asked.

"Affirmative, Captain."

"Put it on my desk. I'll read it when I come out."

"Aye, sir."

Harlowe then strode off toward his bedroom to take a sorely needed cold shower. On his way to his room, he stopped between the cubs and stroked the nape on Rhud's mane. As he did so, he found something black and sticky.

He blinked his eyes clear, rubbing the substance between his fingers. "What is it, Rhud?" he asked him. He had never seen it before. It wasn't from Rhud, he knew that much. It reeked with a vile odor that instantly twisted his face with revulsion. He would never forget that vile stench if he lived a thousand years. It was the dried blood of a grogan. He remembered the first time he'd smelled the nauseating black beasts back on Earth, when he and Riverstone were nearly eaten by two of them on the high desert plateau of Utah. The thought of how close they came to literally losing their heads made him shiver. He held his hand as far away as he could and started for his bedroom to wash the foulness from his hands before he hurled all over the floor.

The door slid open. As he walked through, he stopped in mid-stride with a thought. It was a long shot, but it was the only one he had. He found a tissue and wiped the goo from his fingers as he called for his servant. Harlowe didn't need to know if Jewels was there or not. He wasn't even surprised that Jewels materialized so fast. He expected it. That robob always popped out of nowhere when called. Harlowe handed the tissue to Jewels and ordered his servant, "Take this to Millie. Tell her I want a full analysis of that pukey stuff by the time I get out of the shower." The robob nodded and carefully handled the tissue with his mechanical fingers. Harlowe then grabbed a quick shower.

61

No Day for Surfing

FROM THE COMMAND chair, Simon stared at the wind-driven rain smashing against the forward windows of the bridge. For him, life couldn't be more unjust. Though he trembled over the loss of Sizzle, he was even more concerned with the fate of his Gamadin mates, Ian and Riverstone. Where were they? Were they alive or captive somewhere? Did the Captain know? Was there something more he could do for them than sit here?

"Any change, Mr. Bolt?" Monday asked, stepping off the blinker. He was early for his shift. Judging from the big Gamadin's humorless manner, the deliberate stride in his step, his wide unblinking eyes, his right-to-the-point question, the same fears for his missing shipmates had also led him to a sleepless night.

"No change, Mr. Platter," Simon replied.

With their fellow Gamadin out there, somewhere, they needed direction. They were warm and safe inside a powerful ship while time was wasting. Neither knew how bad the situation was, because no one had heard from either Ian or Riverstone for over two days. Harlowe was the only one who might have the answers.

As if he heard their call, the door swished back and Harlowe emerged from his quarters. Simon and Monday stood to attention and announced together, "Captain on the bridge!"

Harlowe strode into the room with a spring in his step. He was dressed to the nines in his dark blue uniform of the day. He saluted the two Gamadin before he moved to the front of the bridge and checked the readouts and the upper screen.

With his hands behind his back, Harlowe stared out at the foul weather. "Not a good day for surfing," he said.

"Not a good day at all, Skipper," Monday replied.

Though Harlowe remained standing at the side of the three command chairs, Simon gladly relinquished the center and took his place at the weapons station.

Following behind Harlowe, the cubs sprang for their favorite places to hang. Molly's place, as always, was beside Harlowe. She would lie near his center command chair and wait patiently for his arrival. Rhud then took his place at the sunrise side of the observation couch. He liked to gaze out the window like a happy dog going for a car ride in the country. The only thing missing was the wind in his face.

"Looks like we'll be on the clock for a while, gentlemen," Harlowe informed everyone as he strutted to his command chair.

"Aye, Skipper, on the clock. Glad to see you back," Simon confirmed.

Harlowe wasted no time with further pleasantries. "I read your report, Mr. Bolt. Excellent! Unikala...well, we knew he was a scumbag. But Turfan...I figured him for a toad, but I didn't figure him for a loon. What was he thinking?" Harlowe mused before he went on. "A vast trading empire and a planet all his own, and he's sucking face with the Consortium."

"Yes, sir," Monday said.

"Someone has our crew," Harlowe said in a flat, even tone.

"What happened, Captain?" Monday asked.

Harlowe turned angry. "They hit us coming back to the ship. They got Quay, too."

Simon stared out at the tempest, contrite. "I take full responsibility for what I did, Skipper. I should have been with you when it all happened. I deserve whatever punishment you give me. I was thinking only of myself. I'm sorry."

Harlowe turned to his First Mate. His eyes were clear, blue, and unshakable, but there was no hint of malice in them. On the contrary, they seemed understanding and benevolent. He pursed his lips with a slight grin. "Aye, Mr. Bolt, you screwed up royally, but this is one time your indiscretion may be cool."

"Sir?" Simon questioned, confused at Harlowe's lack of anger toward him.

"From the way you described Quay's sister, she tried to save you."

Simon's eyes went round with pride. "She's a keeper like Quay and Lu, Skipper. You should have seen her take on those dudes when they attacked us."

"No more gooey apologies, Gamadin. Under the circumstances I would have done the same. She tried to help you, huh?"

"Aye, sir."

"She risked her life for you?"

"Aye, sir."

"What more can you ask from anyone, especially a man-up woman with guts. We'll get her back for you, Mr. Bolt."

Simon perked up. "That would be awesome, Skipper, but what about Riverstone and Wiz?"

The confident look in Harlowe's eyes left no doubt. "We'll get them back, too, if we have to search every star system in the quadrant."

Simon forced a smile. "Yes, sir." Then he reached into a hidden pocket in the front of his uniform. "I think this is yours, Skipper. I found it in the alley."

Simon placed the ring in Harlowe's hand. It seemed like an eternity ago when Quay had given it to him.

He wrinkled his nose as he wiped a small wetness from the side of his eye. He didn't have to say thanks. One could see in his eyes what the ring meant to him. He looked at it for a moment before he squeezed it like he would never let it go again.

"So what will we do now, Captain?" Simon asked, hopeful that his captain had an answer.

Harlowe's eyes were on fire. "The Fhaal and the Consortium don't know it yet, but we're putting them out of business."

Simon's eyes widened in disbelief. Harlowe had often pushed them way beyond what they thought was possible. Taking down a powerful empire and a suppressive government at the same time was off the charts! "Both, Skipper?" Simon asked.

Harlowe eyed the golden Overseer of Path with fascination as he replied. "Both," he reiterated. Harlowe asked Simon if he remembered the number of the landing pad where the cats lost the scent.

Simon would never forget the number in a million years. "Pad 05-27!"

"We start there."

At that moment, Jewels stepped up to Harlowe and handed him a small piece of paper. Harlowe eyed it briefly before he said, "Millie, jailbreak that slimy Overseer of Path. See what you can dig up for Pad 05-27."

Millawanda's holo-screen materialized above the console in front of the observation window. The screen listed the ships that had been parked in that space for the last seven days. There was only one, and the ship was registered to a Lagan trader by the name of Ra-Loc. They had the trader's name and his vessel. Now it made sense.

"Give me the transit info for that Lagan vessel."

No information available, read the screen.

Harlowe remained cool. "Ra-Loc isn't stupid. A toad like him would hide his tracks everywhere he went." He looked up at the screen. "Alright, check the Path to see if it knows about a Lagan trader by the name of Ra-Loc."

The screen blinked. *No information available.*

Harlowe's teeth gritted. "Nothing, huh?"

The screen didn't change.

Harlowe stared coldly at the golden ball. "Why don't you know? You're supposed to know everything." A cloud drifted in front of the Overseer of Path as if it were trying to hide itself from Harlowe's wrath.

"Come back here, toad!"

Harlowe looked as though he were about to shoot the Overseer off its perch. One could see he was in an ocean of pain. His crew, however, knew he wasn't quitting, he was merely reloading. He looked around the room, seeing the powerful lights along the back wall and the forward console, and observed, "We have all this power, gentlemen. There's got to be an answer somewhere. What do you say we find it?"

Molly rubbed up against his pant leg, wanting to help, while Rhud waited patiently for a sign.

"Aye, Captain, something Holmes would find for a clue," Simon stated.

Harlowe stood up and looked over the Gibbian skyline. "A wisp of ash, Mr. Bolt, anything to give us direction."

The discussion then centered on returning to the city and retracing their steps. It would set them back for days, but there seemed to be no other choice. They couldn't leave Gibb without knowing where to go first.

Just as the clouds over Gibb broke, allowing Omini Prime to beat down on the city, Harlowe saw the piece of paper Jewels had given him lying on the carpet. It had been on his lap. He reached down and read it, but like before, it made as much sense to him now as it did then. Harlowe almost wadded it up to toss away for good when he asked, "What is this, Millie?" holding the paper to the screen.

The control console in front of him suddenly came alive. Lights switched on as a series of colorful three-dimensional graphs projecting up from the console. The three Gamadin stared at the screens in the hope that they were looking at their wisp of ash. Simon wished he had spent more time paying closer attention to Ian's explanations of graphic interpretations. Alongside the brightly colored graphs was a rather detailed description that only confused him more.

"Please simplify, Millie," Harlowe ordered.

He made the request two more times until the computer's analysis finally got down to their level of understanding.

The sample is associated with a species commonly known as a "grogan," the screen read. The holographic display then brought up an image of a hideous dog-like beast with long, horrible teeth and a massive, black head.

"Harlowe, you dummy!" he murmured under his breath. It was the little bit of luck he needed to show them the way.

Harlowe sat up in his center chair. "There can't be too many places where something that ugly exists," he commented to Monday and Simon. He returned to the screen and asked, "Where can I find a grogan, Millie?"

Harlowe's luck held. According to the computer grogans were indeed rare. The grotesque black beasts were known to exist only in one part of the galaxy, on a planet called Naruck, 333.04 light-years away from Gibb.

"Our wisp of ash, Skipper?" Monday asked.

Harlowe gave his First Mate a reassuring wink before answering. "I believe it is, Mr. Platter," he replied.

This time the distance across the quadrant was of no issue to either Simon or Monday. "May I suggest best speed, Captain?" Monday asked.

Harlowe sat comfortably at the edge of his chair, his face confident and focused. He looked over the console, eyeing *Millawanda's* readouts carefully. She was ready for whatever was asked of her. "Any slower and Rerun and I will be outside pushing, Mr. Platter."

Monday grinned. "Aye, Captain."

To Simon he added, "Jump into Wiz's chair, Mr. Bolt, and give us a course heading for Naruck. Best speed."

Simon leaped out of his seat as if he were wearing gravs. "Aye-aye, Skipper!"

Without Riverstone and Wiz, they would be shorthanded. Millwanda would be difficult to run, but not impossible. Shifts would be continuous. Two Gamadin would always be on the bridge while the third rested. During the two weeks it would take for them to travel the distance to Naruck, they would adjust the autopilot controls to make operations easier. The task would be difficult, but when they were done, the Ship would run as smoothly as one could expect from half a crew. They would make it work.

As soon as the Ship cleared Gibbian space, Harlowe gave Platter permission to enter hyperlight...best speed.

The shimmer of stars changed to a brilliant white as they entered the world of hyperlight travel. With *Millawanda* on her proper course, Harlowe left the control room to Simon and Monday and headed directly for his bedroom. A robob medic was standing by Jewels, who was catching the flying pieces of Harlowe's uniform. Without a stitch of clothing, Harlowe slipped into bed. He never saw the robob administer the sedative. The last thought he had before his mind crashed into a deep, dreamless sleep was the promise he'd made: one week, ten weeks, ten years. He would not give up. He would find Riverstone, Wiz, and Quay...and Sizzle, too. Find them all alive and nuke those who were responsible, even if he had to search beneath every rock in the universe to do it!

62

Erati

"IF THESE THRALLS are as worthless as the last ones you brought here, Ra-Loc," the Erati mining foreman warned, "I will personally find your impotent lump of grogan dung and bring you back here to finish the work I lost from the last time you swindled me."

Ra-Loc tried to hide his nervousness behind a pathetically weak smirk. "No, no! They are of the finest stock, I assure you. Look at them, Gant. They are powerfully built and young. I venture to say you have nothing like them anywhere in the depths of Erati. They will last many more work periods than the norm, you'll see."

In the dim light of the underground rock room, Riverstone and Wizzixs were slumped together on the cold, stone floor with their hands and legs manacled in heavy irons. Perto and two Erati security guards stood behind them, keeping them from falling on their faces. Clumps of hair were missing from Ian's scalp, while dark contusions and red welts marred Riverstone's face, neck, and arms. They had the look of shore-leave swabbies who had been in a barroom brawl and lost. In their semiconscious state, their eyelids hung lethargically half-open, while their eyes appeared vacant. Their minds were an incoherent, semiconscious mess. Ra-Loc wanted no trouble from the humans when he removed them from their cell. Since the rendezvous with Unikala eight days earlier, he had kept them sedated with enough drugs to keep them only half-alive until their arrival on the mining planet of

Erati. The Lagan had hoped to sell what was left of his prizes to Gant, the Erati mining foreman, to recoup some of his losses. It was Perto's idea. Ra-Loc, his nose heavily bandaged from Unikala's bite, found the idea wonderfully acceptable. It dulled the pain somewhat to know that all of his efforts were not a total loss, in spite of the much reduced return from what he had originally expected. His dreams of buying his own planet and retiring with all his magnificent wealth had suddenly turned to dust. At this moment, his only worry was the hope that he could salvage enough from the humans to escape before Unikala discovered he had fled the quadrant without finding Pylott.

"They had better last as long as you say, Lagan," Gant replied, his deep voice filled with snarling contempt at Ra-Loc's smelly presence.

Four other security guards stood beside the Erati foreman. All of them looked as though they had spent their entire lives in the mines. They were all thick and bulky, with heavy muscular frames. Their features were rugged and unkempt. Their bodies reeked of unclean, unhygienic habits. Their pocked skins were colorless and white behind crusted, dark beards, while their large black eyes glared evilly in the low subterranean light. To look at them made one crave the brightness of life above ground.

"Here," Gant said, pushing a small pile of tokens toward Ra-Loc. "Take your money."

Ra-Loc stared at the sum with dismay. It was far less than he had expected. "That is not our agreed-upon price," Ra-Loc protested.

"I have subtracted the loss I suffered from the last degenerate slimes you brought me," the foreman explained.

Ra-Loc was about to object further when Gant leaned over his desk and said slowly, leaving no doubt as to the consequences: "Ra-Loc, if you find the terms disagreeable, you and your grogan scum," eyeing Perto, "can join them."

Ra-Loc hastily changed his attitude, "Oh, no! You are more than fair, Gant. You are quite right to subtract what you deem appropriate." Ra-Loc dropped the tokens in a small pouch and began backpedaling out the doorway. "Sorry I can't stay to discuss more Consortium commerce, gentlemen," he said, bowing slightly to Gant and his men, "but I must be on my way. Thank you and...uh...," he glanced at new the Erati residents, "happy digging, slops. Ha, ha, ha..."

Ra-Loc waddled out the door, his low, sick laugh reverberating off the dark stone walls of the underground complex like something out of a nightmare.

Gant hacked up an undulating wad of dark spit in the direction of Ra-Loc's departure, his yellowed teeth displaying the same advanced stages of rot and decay as those of the others in the room. "What I wouldn't give to get that fat grogan pile of waste in the mines for one work period," he said, continuing to stare at the exit. The guards who relieved Perto proceeded to examine their new thralls, probing them each like a side of beef.

"Take them to the holding cell and get them prepared," Gant ordered, returning to the business at hand. "Tell Dagger his new inductees are waiting for him."

"Yes, Gant," the guard barked, pushing the two humans out of the rock doorway into a long, dimly lit hall. Inside the corridor, he kicked Riverstone's backside to hurry their progress. "Come along. We have to get you ready for your new position in our little paradise."

After a short walk, they stopped in front of a heavy metal door. The guard unbolted the iron latch, opened the door, and shoved them through the metal doorway. Riverstone's face thumped against the backside of the cell. He hardly felt a thing. "Don't get too comfortable in there, thralls," the guard warned as he watched Riverstone curl into a ball on the wet stone floor. "This is only temporary until

Dagger retrieves you." The guard's ghoulish laughter echoed repulsively as he slammed the door shut, cutting off what little light there was from the corridor.

The drugs that had helped to temper their terrible treatment were starting to wear off. The stench of rodent droppings and puke hung in the air like a heavy gas. The only available light was what filtered through a small crack beneath the cell door. A shallow pool of slime on the floor soaked into their clothes. It was a rank mixture of leftover waste and death from previous residents of the cell. Ian started to retch. What little he had left in his stomach dribbled out the side of his mouth and added to the pool of filth next to Riverstone, who managed to turn around and sit on the cold, wet floor. Ian gagged and hurled again. Riverstone pulled Ian's face out of the dirty pool and tried to comfort him.

"Hang in there, Wiz," Riverstone said, holding him close to keep him warm. His own tongue swelled from thirst, but he dared not touch the foul moisture with any part of his mouth. He swallowed back his own urge to puke, thinking it would be better to die of thirst than to drink the devil's own urine.

As Riverstone fought against the drugs that fogged his mind, he understood all too well that their predicament was grave and right now, out of their control. It was like nothing they had ever faced before. How would Harlowe find them here, he wondered, wherever "here" was? For a brief moment he thought if he could release his hands he might end his life, but he knew he could never do that. He thought back to the time on Mars when they first met General Gunn. He had survived then and he would survive now. More importantly, his Gamadin mates were still out there, looking for them. They would find a way. They had to. What other hope did they have?

* * *

After an indeterminable amount of time passed, the sound of heavy footsteps stopped outside the cell door, waking them up. Gruff voices exchanged solicitations and laughter before the thick, heavy bolt clanked back with a loud jolt. The metal door opened, flooding the cell with light. Riverstone squinted, squeezing his eyes hard against the sudden brightness. Standing in the doorway, a large, ominous shadow loomed,

"I am Dagger," the shadow announced in an angry voice. "Now get up off your lazy chirts or you'll be late for your first work period."

Dagger's large, powerful hands lifted them bodily out of the cell and threw them both down the corridor. "We must prepare you before you start."

Riverstone's face was sickly white as he tried to rise to his feet against the rock wall of the corridor. The problem was, his hands were still tied and it was impossible for him to maintain his balance. His face was the only buffer he had to keep from falling. Dagger lifted him again and pushed him forward, bouncing him off the sides of the rock. He fell again but Ian was there, lifting him with his foot while balancing on the other foot. Riverstone climbed and moved along just ahead of Ian before Dagger struck again. A short time later they arrived at an open room, where another guard waited for them. The guard unshackled their wrists and ordered them to strip off their clothes. A small disk dropped out of Riverstone's pocket. The guard saw it and picked it up off the dirt floor.

"What is this?" he asked, toying with the disk.

Riverstone tried to focus. "A slug," he replied with a hoarse grunt.

The guard tried to bite it. When he broke a tooth, he threw it on the ground and crushed it into the dirt.

After they finished disrobing, they were given workers' uniforms. The garments were dirty, brown, and old, made of something like burlap. Dagger explained that the previous thralls, who were no longer alive, wore them.

"Where are we?" Ian asked as he tied the drawstrings of his over-sized pants around his waist.

From out of nowhere, a blinding punch to the face sent Ian to the floor. "You do not talk unless you are told to, thrall!" yelled Dagger.

Ian lay in deep pain, his face twisted on the floor from the blow. Riverstone, risking the same consequence, rushed to Ian's side. He tried to help him up but Ian resisted briefly, digging in the dirt with one hand while his other hand held his jaw that had been nearly torn off his face. Ian was deceptive enough that he doubted anyone saw him pick up Riverstone's disk from the floor.

"This one obviously has not been enlightened," the other guard said. "Tell them, Dagger."

Dagger rested his hand on his whip that hung on his wide leather belt. "Erati, slime, is a mining planet. You are now the proud citizens of the Erati work force." Dagger leaned forward, and with a slower, menacing tone, explained further, spraying his putrid, sour breath into Riverstone's face, "That means if you ever speak again without being told, you will get a strong taste of my whip."

Riverstone nodded as he helped Ian to stand. He was coughing and spitting blood out of his mouth. Riverstone wondered if he was acting more than he was letting on. The General had trained them well for this kind of torture. They were tough but Ian, nevertheless, understood only too well that if they were to make it out of Erati alive, they would have to go along for the present until they under-stood exactly what their situation was. *Know your enemies better than your friends,* the General always said. Once they understood their state, then and only then could they plan their escape from Erati. Riverstone promised himself that if he ever made it out alive, he'd find Ra-Loc and wrap his hands around his greasy neck and squeeze the life out of his puky body until he was dead as stone.

After they were properly clothed, Dagger led them down another corridor and attached a set of heavy iron braces around their ankles and waists. Now, according to Dagger, they were ready for transport to their level, where they would begin enjoying all the amenities Erati had to offer.

Dagger held up his whip. "Step out of line, human, and you will feel this." He then grabbed them by the backs of their belts and threw them like sacks of garbage down the long mine tunnel, whipping them twice across the back so they would get a taste of what it meant to disobey Dagger.

The next place they came to was a vast, bottomless open shaft. Dagger poked Ian in the back with the butt of his whip as they all walked onto a circular platform that had the capacity to carry more than a hundred slaves like themselves. When Riverstone peered over the side of the platform, he saw nothing below him. The shaft seemed to drop down forever. When Dagger saw the surprised look on Riverstone's face, he began laughing loudly. Then he pulled a lever that released the platform like a lead weight. As many times as he had leaped off the high cliffs of the Mons, this descent was bothersome. He reached for the nearest handrail and hung on tight. Ian, on the other hand, simply kept his vacant gaze downward toward the floor as if he were still in a delirious fog.

Down, down they went.

The descent felt endless. The farther they dropped into the planet, the higher the temperature inside the shaft rose. Riverstone was

unable to judge the distance they had traveled, but it was considerable. During the drop, they passed what must have been hundreds
of levels of the mine. In the little time he had to look, each level
appeared to be huge and vast. By the time they began to slow down,
the hot, thick air made breathing difficult.

Finally, the platform came to a halt at the opening of a great,
horizontal shaft.

Dagger lowered a side ramp off the platform to the edge of the
shaft, and then motioned them off the platform. "This way, thralls,"
he ordered, pointing the end of his coiled whip toward a vast open
tunnel cut deep into the solid rock.

Riverstone grabbed one last glimpse of the void beneath the platform
before he stepped away. The shaft they had been traveling down for
over an hour still had no end. Lights from countless other horizontal
tunnels still glowed from below, seeming to extend forever, down into
the depths of nothingness. He looked up. It was as equally endless
upward. The vastness in each direction seemed infinite. How old was
this mine? As old as Gibb? Surely not, he thought, but to have created
such a network of tunnels out of solid rock was unimaginable.

Riverstone tried to cast the thought from his mind. He just wanted
to escape.

Then a ghastly nightmare came to life before their eyes.

Just past the opening of the great shaft, they saw the multitudes of
thralls inside the cavern pounding endlessly at the rock. The heavy
constant sound of pounding was everywhere. It was not the sound
of one or two hammers, or even a dozen sledgehammers striking
the hard stone, but thousands upon thousands of hammers striking
the solid mass of rock at once. Riverstone's most dreaded fear had
come to life, and this was only one shaft out of thousands they had
passed on the way down.

Oh, my gawd! Riverstone cried out in his head, *I've been here before!*

Dagger pushed Riverstone off the platform and out onto the dirt. He then turned his attention to Ian, who seemed to be looking over the side of the platform in a curious way. It was as if he was contemplating the unthinkable.

Dagger stepped back onto the platform, his hate-filled eyes concerned that Ian was too close to the edge of the platform. He raised his whip like a club and went after his new thrall, who had no idea of what was coming his way.

"Ian!" Riverstone called out.

Dagger came at Ian as though he was worried about losing his new thrall to the depths of the shaft. Riverstone lunged forward in a heroic effort to get to Dagger before Ian was bludgeoned. But he stumbled, falling to the ground, tangled in his manacled chains at the edge of the platform. Dagger swung, coming down with a smashing blow. Somehow, Ian must have seen it coming. He ducked backwards just as the metal end of the whip struck the guardrail, sending fragments of wood in all directions. His momentum out of control, Ian moved hastily to dodge the blow and fell backwards over the rail. Riverstone caught Ian's look of futility just before he disappeared into the abyss.

"WIZ!" Riverstone cried out. There was nothing he could do but watch his lifelong friend and Gamadin brother disappear into the bottomless shaft, gone forever.

63

Naruck

I<small>T HAD BEEN</small> nine days since *Millawanda* left Gibb and the Omini Prime star system. The crew had never felt their ship so empty, so silent, so devoid of human life. In that time, their emotions had gone through many upheavals. Without *all* of their shipmates to banter and mingle with, *Millawanda* had lost part of her soul. She wasn't whole. The spirit and moral compass that made her powerful seemed lost. She lacked that human essence that gave her life.

For Harlowe, getting through the first week was the toughest of all. Eating, working, and playing without his lifelong friends was, at times, almost too difficult to bear. When he first walked into Quay's room that night after leaving Gibb, the blue dress she had worn that first day on the beach when he blew his nose at her feet was draped over a chair. He almost lost it then. He gathered the dress in his arms and held it close to him. When he touched her pillow, she was there, too. Her fragrance lingered everywhere in the room, touching his soul. After only a few moments, he had to walk out. As with his friends, it was too hard to bear the thought that she was gone.

Though the pain was still inside of him, his mind found the strength to go on. The General had instilled in them all that they were Gamadin. *Act like it,* his baritone voice would shout. On the fifth day of their journey to Naruck, Harlowe had summoned Monday and Simon to his quarters and told them in no uncertain terms that

377

the suffering was over. "Yeah, this sucks," he'd said to what was left of his loyal crew, "but this isn't who we are. We can't help our mates if we're broken. What we do from now on, we do together. Instead of separate duty schedules, we will have overlapping schedules. We manage the ship together. We will eat at the same time, play at the same time, and sleep at the same time whenever possible. We will share this burden of ours together, and together we will come through it and find our mates. We'll get them all back, every last one of them... That is a promise I will honor until I die."

A tear welled up as Simon fought to control himself. It was as if the burden of Atlas had been taken from his shoulders. "Thanks, Dog." Jewels came clickity-clacking into the room and sat three blue shakes down on the table. For the first time in days they smiled, clicked their cups, and drank.

The vow was now complete.

* * *

Four days after their vow, a musical chime from the intercom brought Harlowe into the here and now.

"Approaching Naruck, Captain," Simon announced. Harlowe laid his Stradivarius in its case and went directly to the control room. When he arrived, the dark grey planet of Naruck filled the front and starboard-side observation window. It looked as unholy and macabre as the grotesque grogans he was searching for.

Monday put *Millawanda* into a standard orbit a thousand miles above the surface of the planet. It was the fourth planet in a system of seven. Its primary was a single, main-sequence, orange K-class star, with a surface temperature of 3820 K. Naruck, itself, was a rugged Q-class planet. Its many mountain ranges rippled side-by-side, giving it the wrinkled appearance of advanced age. Sensors warned that the atmosphere, though breathable, had a dangerously high level of radioactivity toxicity associated with it. Millie recommended wearing SIBAs to protect anyone from over-exposure.

"How long can the cats hang?" Harlowe inquired.

Rhud's head came up under Harlowe's hand as he sat at his center command chair. Both cats had grown another foot since leaving Gibb. Their high-pitched whines had been replaced by adolescent growls that became deeper and throatier as they continued toward adulthood, when they would be twice as large and three times heavier.

Twelve hours, thirty-one minutes, was the screen's precise reply.

Harlowe patted Rhud on the head. "All right, you can go but you can't spend the night." Rhud growled his approval. Harlowe then ordered Simon to find the main control center. "Tell the toadheads who we are, Mr. Bolt."

Several minutes later a being from the surface appeared on the screen. Harlowe's description of a toadhead had not been too far off. If grogans were loathsome and ugly, these so-called intelligent life-forms did not deviate from the norm. The thugs he had aced on Gibb were gorgeous compared to the twisted, pockmarked face he was speaking to now. The being on the screen looked male, but it was only a wild guess. The being had large, heavy eyebrows that cast dark shadows over his sunken eyes. His ears were big and hairy, while his face was cratered with crusted scabs. Harlowe had a difficult time comparing him with anyone he knew, except for maybe Freddie Krueger in the movies. Its clothes appeared medieval. A thick leather breastplate coverd a heavy wool undergarment that appeared to need a week's soaking in chlorine bleach. This seemed to be the dress code on Naruck.

"State your name and purpose," the ugly-faced man ordered with a cantankerous undertone.

Harlowe's first impression of Naruck left a lot to be desired.

"My name is Captain Harlowe Pylott," Harlowe answered evenly. "I am looking for a beast called a grogan."

The face grunted. "What do you want with a grogan?"

"Sir, I personally could care less for one. I am here in search of a Lagan trader who calls himself Ra-Loc. Perhaps you know him?" Harlowe asked.

The eroded face turned away as if Harlowe were an irritating pest. "There is no Ra-Loc here! Go back to where you came from."

Harlowe, however, quickly lost his patience with the bureaucratic gibberish. "Listen, toad, I didn't come this far to play around with—"

The screen suddenly went blank.

Harlowe turned to Monday. "I was being nice, too."

Simon shrugged. "Maybe something was lost in the translation."

Seconds later Millie's sensors picked up several missile launchings from the surface. The missiles were nuclear and were on a direct intercept course toward the saucer. In order to protect the population on the surface from any fallout from the missiles, Harlowe allowed the projectiles to rise a hundred miles above the surface before Simon vaporized them to subatomic dust. To command a little more respect for the Gamadin ship, Monday located every missile launch facility on the planet, which Simon quickly eliminated from their 1,000-mile-high orbit with blue bolts of high-energy plasma.

Landing coordinates appeared on the screen not long after that.

"I think they found religion, Captain," Monday remarked.

"Proceed, Mr. Bolt," Harlowe said, his face displaying the disgust of having to put up with such needless behavior. "Watch out for surprises on the way down, Mr. Platter," he added warily.

"Aye, Skipper."

As they descended into a heavy brown haze, Harlowe had a feeling this was going to be a place where bad dreams lurked. The wait was short. The moment the ship was close enough for a visual of the surface, they saw the reason why Millie's sensors picked up so much radiation.

Rubble—nuclear rubble, left over from an atomic holocaust. The city below, with its heaps of building rubble and its treeless and barren streets, was all that remained of a once-thriving metropolis. According to the sensor readouts it had all been blown to bits centuries ago. No wonder the beings of Naruck appeared so revolting. They were all warmed-over remnants of a nuclear past. Nature was a thousand centuries from fixing what had been so brutally destroyed on this planet.

They landed *Millawanda* in a wide clearing that was surrounded by high mounds of ancient remains. From the appearance of some buildings, attempts had been made over time to reconstruct parts of the city. For whatever reason, their endeavors had been nothing more than failed ambitions. There was nothing structurally sound anywhere in the city.

An eerie mist drifted around the base of the piles, absorbing the orange sun's rays that filtered their way through the layers of fog. Apparently, bright sunny days on Naruck no longer existed. Harlowe stared out, his eyes saddened. He'd had the same sick feeling back on Mars when they came upon the City of the Dead. He couldn't understand what drove civilizations to commit suicide like this on a planet-wide scale.

"What a sucky place this is," Simon commented as they all gazed in disbelief through the windows over all of the destruction.

Harlowe agreed. He took in a deep breath of revulsion before turning to the cats. "Molly, Rhud, it's showtime," he called. The cats leaped to the blinker and disappeared to the lower decks. They didn't need to be asked twice. "You have the bridge, gentlemen. You know what to do if we run into trouble. Don't hesitate. We're not here to make friends."

"Aye, Captain," Monday replied.

64

Prigg

HARLOWE STEPPED DOWN the center ramp with the cats and deployed his SIBA. The very sight of Naruck was depressing. The less time spent on this planet, the better. He felt his sidearms and tested their ease of draw. A glance down at the tiny blue light on each weapon indicated both were fully loaded. He then gave the cats the go-ahead. After being cooped up on the ship for two weeks, they were eager to stretch their legs. The ship was large and its corridors long, but being confined in a ship as large as *Millawanda* was not the same as the freedom of the open air, regardless of its purity. Even Harlowe felt the freedom of the wide-open planet's surface.

When they stepped through the Ship's blue force field, the smell of Naruck's air slapped them all in the face. The air was incredibly foul. It was like a public urinal that had never been cleaned. Harlowe activated the SIBA air filter. Molly and Rhud weren't as well equipped. They dropped to the ground and covered their noses with their paws, groaning.

Harlowe felt their pain and wished he could have made them a breathing device like his. After a few moments of agony, they surprisingly appeared ready to continue. He checked them over, thinking maybe it would have been better to leave them behind. To his surprise, they managed to compensate for the foulness. Their eyes cleared and they were breathing easily again. His only explanation as to how they were able to withstand the stench was that they were simply sucking it up.

Satisfied that the cats were unharmed, Harlowe motioned them forward. He wasn't sure which direction to take. It didn't matter, since a small party of six heavily armed soldiers was coming his way to greet him. He couldn't tell if their rifles and sidearms were conventional weapons or not. He clicked the safeties off both pistols, figuring Millie would make up for any shortcomings, big time.

The greeting party was made up of beings of different sizes and shapes. The one in the lead was without a doubt the ugliest of all. Harlowe wondered if grotesqueness was a prerequisite for leadership on Naruck. His eyes were so misplaced on his face that Harlowe wondered how he could see straight at all. One eye was an inch above the other, while his nose looked like it had been slammed into a door.

Without even a casual salutation, the leader waved for Harlowe to follow him.

The group marched along several blocks, with three soldiers in front and three in back. Harlowe had to be particularly careful where he stepped so as not to break or twist an ankle along the way. The cats simply traveled naturally.

After twenty minutes of fast marching, they arrived at what was once a large cathedral-like structure. It appeared to be the only building in the city that was halfway stable. It reminded Harlowe of an ancient gothic church back on Earth, except that its once-tall bell towers were gone and the flying buttresses that had supported its roof were in need of major structural repair. None of the arched window openings or rosettes had glass. Like the great wheel window above the central portal, they were all blown out of their mullions long ago. The once-beautiful stone carvings in the niches either had been worn away by time or destroyed by the same nuclear blast that devasted the city centuries before. Everywhere the massive stone shells that remained were black with wet muck and grime. And this was a *good* building on Naruck!

Harlowe hesitated a moment at the bottom of the stone steps, thinking any loud noise could bring the structure down on top of his head. His escort motioned for him to keep up. Harlowe swallowed hard and promised himself he wouldn't think about its structural integrity as they climbed up the front of the stone stairway and strode cautiously into the nave of the building.

Once inside, the echo of his escort's heavy boots against the stone pillars mixed with the low sound of mumbling voices. They continued toward the entrance of a great hall, where a large crowd of Naruckian elites was awaiting his arrival. Upon seeing Harlowe and the cats, the crowd silenced immediately and parted, dispersing to both sides of the great hall and giving Harlowe plenty of space. What Harlowe took to be their leader or king was sitting on a throne at the far end of the hall. The monarch looked every bit as ugly and deformed as anyone he had met thus far. Harlowe also saw immediately that he had come to the right place, for flanking the king on both sides were six black, evil-looking grogans. These beasts were much larger than either of Ra-Loc's pets, and they looked twice as loathsome. The moment Harlowe entered the hall with the cats, the grogans went into a howling, blood thirsty rage, made even louder by the cavernous stone walls of the cathedral. Their jaws snapped wildly as their grizzly black chests lunged against the knuckle-thick chains that held them back.

Molly and Rhud, however, seemed hardly affected by the attention. They sauntered into the room by Harlowe's side as if they were on a Sunday stroll in the park with no one around to bother them. Harlowe silently wanted to borrow some of their courage as he strolled through the hostile crowd.

The king struck the hilt of his sword on the stone floor. His keepers then rushed to control his pets while he readied himself to address the unwanted guest. Discipline here seemed to work here as it had with the ancient Vikings of Earth: only the mighty survived to rule.

"What do you want, alien?" the low, gruff voice of the king demanded.

Harlowe released a snap at the top of his head and pulled down his skin mask, exposing just his head. The crowd was startled at first, thinking his SIBA skin was the real him. The stench was worse than he had thought. It took every ounce of Gamadin discipline to fight off his urge to puke his guts out at the foot of the king's throne. After a brief moment of self-control, Harlowe replied, "Your Lordship, my name is Captain Harlowe Pylott."

Harlowe was a toad out of water when it came to the proper etiquette of addressing world leaders as Quay did. He wished she were here to help him. Instead, he borrowed what salutations he did know from the movies he had seen on Earth.

"I've come a great distance in search of a being called Ra-Loc. He is a Lagan trader who also enjoys the company of grogans." Harlowe turned to the king's keep. "Since grogans are rare and unique to Naruck, I thought you could assist my search. He has taken items of great value from me and I want them returned, Sire."

Harlowe finished politely, even bowing slightly at the head, showing his respect.

The king didn't answer right away. He seemed preoccupied with tossing a live rodent the size of a raccoon to his pets to fight over. After watching with giddy amusement while his grogans tore the rodent apart, he turned back to Harlowe and said, "There is no Lagan trader named Ra-Loc here. You have wasted your time, alien. Go away."

"Your Lordship," Harlowe persisted, taking a step forward. The sound of metal clanking against metal echoed throughout the hall as cocked weapons were aimed at him. Molly and Rhud crouched, taking defensive positions, ready to pounce upon any aggressive movement toward Harlowe.

With hands out, Harlowe figured he might have acted a little too hastily. He stepped back slowly, patting the cats. "Molly, Rhud. Sit," he said, trying to ease the moment.

The king's marbled features twisted evilly. A slight tilt of his sword motioned for his soldiers to back off. "It is good your animals are so well-behaved. I should warn you that my grogans have not feasted today, and it is sometimes difficult to control them. You should leave now before it is too late."

Harlowe heard the mumblings of the crowd. He knew he was being insulted. It didn't matter. He was here for information, not to prove his prowess. "Thank you, Your Lordship, but—"

Harlowe stopped as a slight nod from the king to one of the keepers released two of the grogans. The speed of the beasts raised the hairs on Harlowe's neck. In the split of a heartbeat the beasts crossed the short twenty paces and were upon the cats. Instinctively, Harlowe was about to go for his guns. He could have shot the beasts before they made it halfway to the cats, but he didn't. He remembered what they'd done to Ra-Loc's grogans back on Gibb, and what Quay said before the attack. She'd touched his arm, telling him the cats would be all right. They were only cubs then. They were twice that size now and much stronger.

Harlowe let the cats go.

The swiftness of the cats' counterattack was ruthless. The king's pets were not from a planet of dinosaurs. Rhud greeted the first beast with a single swipe of his paw, breaking its neck while it was still in midair. It landed ten feet away, spinning like a top at the foot of the guards who had led him into the hall. The first grogan was lifeless as the stone floor.

Molly wasn't as merciful. She met her assailant head on, stopping its forward charge as if she were an immovable stone wall. She grabbed the grogan's neck with her jaws and tore out its throat before it knew what had happened. With her right paw she slapped the beast to the floor and gripped the back of its skull with her open jaws. The room reverberated from the echoes of bone crushing as the beast's head burst, spreading bits of brain and dark blood onto the awestruck onlookers. Not wishing to deal with the carcass any longer, she picked the grogan up bodily and tossed it unceremoniously at the feet of the king.

The entire exchange was over in moments.

Harlowe was proudly amazed. He'd never had any doubt about the outcome but shook in awe at the thought of what they would be like, fully grown. *That's sick!*

Harlowe remained calm, as if it were an everyday occurrence for his cats to eat grogans for lunch. Out of the corner of his eye he saw two guards draw their pistols on the cats. Before they could clear their holsters, Harlowe shot their weapons away from their grips.

Harlowe held his pistols steady as the crowd backed toward the wall. He saw no more challenges and rapidly replaced one of his pistols back in its holster. Now he saw a renewed respect in the king's horrified face. In a world ruled by brutality, he had struck terror in the mind of every Naruckian in the room, and he knew it.

"Ra-Loc!" Harlowe called out, directing his anger at the king, pointing the barrel of his pistol at the king's face. "Where is he, Your Highness?" Harlowe mocked.

The king sat up as if he had been stuck with a cattle prod. He looked around for support from his guards and subjects. But after what they had just witnessed, no one came forth to assist the monarch. The king was alone.

"Yes, yes, Ra-Loc," the king blurted, his deformed eyes nervously watching the cats licking themselves clean of grogan tissue and blood on the floor next to Harlowe. "The Lagan . . . It has been many passings since his return."

"Find someone who knows him before my pets feast on the rest of your pathetic beasts," Harlowe ordered, devoid of patience.

The king's head nodded nervously, acknowledging the request. "Prigg!" he called out, looking around the great hall. "Where is Prigg?"

"Yes, Sire," echoed a timid little voice from the crowd. A small, unassertive Naruckian stepped out from behind the crowd. He stood barely four feet tall. He had the distorted facial features of everyone else on Naruck, but with one distinction. He had large, chameleon-like eyes that seemed to stare in two different directions at once. "I am at your service, Sire."

"Prigg will know," the king assured Harlowe. "He has had many dealings with this Lagan trader, Ra-Loc."

Harlowe gave the king the go-ahead to proceed.

His Highness turned to the bowing subject. "Tell our guest what you know of Ra-Loc, Prigg. If you forget anything, I will feed you to his animals."

Prigg's eyes were unable to focus as he stared at the two cats preening their white coats. "Ye-yes, sir. I will answer truthfully."

"Good," the king said. Then to Harlowe, he said, "He will answer your questions, Pylott."

Harlowe walked over to the little Naruckian and kneeled down to his level. "What do you know of Ra-Loc, Prigg?" Harlowe saw the fear of Molly and Rhud in his wayward eyes and added, "Don't be afraid, Prigg. They won't hurt you."

After what he had just observed, Prigg had his doubts. He had one eye on the cats while the other eye drifted reluctantly to Harlowe. "There is little to know of the Lagan, Your Majesty. He appears only when it is time to acquire items that he needs. His stays are never long."

Harlowe could certainly understand that. A day on Naruck seemed an eternity.

"It is known that after he leaves Naruck the Lagan always goes to Palcor," Prigg quickly added.

"Palcor? Where is this place?" Harlowe asked.

"Only three light passings from Naruck, Your Majesty," Prigg replied. "His habit was always to travel to Palcor after Naruck. I know this much."

Harlowe could see the little Naruckian searching his mind. "Is there anything else you can tell me, Prigg? Anything at all?"

Prigg addressed Harlowe with both eyes steady. "He never talked much about himself, Your Majesty, only business. It was strictly business with Ra-Loc."

Harlowe felt certain Prigg was telling the truth. Unlike the others, this little Naruckian was different. He was kind and respectful to everyone. All things considered, with the threat of death hanging over him, a very brave little dude, he thought.

"Thank you, Prigg," Harlowe said, adding a reassuring smile, "I appreciate your help."

"You scathing little Trodad!" the king hollered. "You have nothing more to add than he goes to Palcor?"

Prigg's whole body visibly shook. "Yes, Sire. That is all I know of Ra-Loc."

Harlowe felt compassion for the little guy. He knew that Prigg had told him all that he knew. If the Overseer of Path on Gibb had nothing on Ra-Loc, how could he expect much more from a frightened little subject from this godforsaken planet?

"Guards! Take this piece of grogan dung and use him for feed," the king ordered.

Harlowe acted quickly and raised his hand. "No! You will not kill this being. I need his services."

"Services?" the king questioned, surprised. "What services could this Trodian afterthought provide?"

"I need him as a guide," Harlowe said, thinking fast. He was unaware of where his compassion for the little guy was taking him. "Once I arrive at Palcor I will need someone to guide me to the other merchants who may have dealt with Ra-Loc in the past. Having Prigg with me will speed up my search considerably." As he spoke to save the king's little subject, he realized that it might not be such a bad idea after all. Prigg could be quite helpful. As a merchant of the quadrant, the Naruckian would be much more informed about the trading habits of the Lagan than he. Without knowing it, he had just stumbled onto a lucky break in his quest.

Harlowe knelt down again to Prigg and looked into the small, deeply deformed face. "What do you know of Palcor, Prigg? Could you help me find Ra-Loc there?"

Prigg's eyes darted interchangeably between the cats and Harlowe before one eye focused back on the Gamadin. Harlowe was starting to find it a little difficult to keep his own eyes from crossing.

"Oh, I am quite familiar with Palcor, Your Majesty," Prigg began. "My business has taken me there often. I have traveled quite extensively throughout the quadrant and a hundred passings beyond." Prigg's head bowed slightly. "As for finding the Lagan, I must admit to Your Majesty, I doubt if he can be found if he does not want to be found."

Harlowe nodded. "I understand, but I need your help, Prigg. Please consider accompanying me to Palcor. I will make it well worth your while." Harlowe felt sure he had found someone he could trust who would aid the Gamadin quest.

Prigg's right eye drifted to the king. "It is not for me to decide, Your Majesty."

"Yes it is," Harlowe quickly retorted. "You have the right to say yes or no." Prigg's other eye went back to the cats. "Don't worry about the cats. They are harmless if unprovoked."

Prigg wasn't convinced. Harlowe figured Prigg had never been free to choose his own destiny. However, Harlowe also knew that if the little Naruckian stayed, his fate would surely be as grogan fodder. "If my Lord..."

"His Lordship won't refuse," Harlowe said confidently. "He'll let you go or I'll nuke what remains of his kingdom for good."

With a wry grimace, Harlowe stood up and faced the king. "Your Lordship, I will take Prigg with me to Palcor. With your permission, of course."

The king grunted his disappointment that he would not have fresh meat for his grogans, but then, not wishing to upset the alien who had just destroyed every missile base on the planet and two of his finest grogans, replied, "Yes, yes, by all means, go. I have little use for this subject. You may take him."

Harlowe forced a smile. "Thank you, Your Lordship, you are most generous," he replied, nodding slightly. "Good day."

Harlowe walked out of the great hall with his new guide. The cats lingered for few moments longer until Harlowe and Prigg were safely past the nave and walking down the front steps. Before leaving the great hall, Rhud turned to the crowd and let out a loud, blood-chilling roar that froze anyone who might have entertained any thoughts of following them.

The cats caught up with Harlowe and Prigg just as they turned down the last street before they reached the ship.

"Your Majesty?" Prigg asked.

Harlowe found it uncomfortable being called "Your Majesty" and explained to Prigg that he was not royalty and would much prefer to be addressed by his name, Captain Pylott. "Now what is it you wanted?" he asked, thinking he had made his point about the name issue quite clear and understandable.

Prigg had to run to keep up with Harlowe's impatient stride to leave Naruck. "Please, Your Majesty," Prigg said a moment later. It appeared Harlowe's name request had fallen on deaf ears. The little Naruckian was too frightened to take such liberties with a being who had just intimidated the life out of his own king. "If it is not too much to ask, I would dearly love to say farewell to my family before I go."

Harlowe stopped abruptly. He was somewhat surprised by the fact this diminutive being with his heavily deformed features would have a family! He felt ashamed that he had not asked Prigg from the beginning if he had any personal business to take care of before he left on the voyage to Palcor.

Prigg pointed with his slightly bent middle finger. He had only three on the right hand, four on the left. "They live around the corner from here. May I, Your Majesty?"

Harlowe stared at Prigg with a deeper respect. He found it heartwarming that love hadn't completely died on Naruck. He was even a little envious that this gentle being was able to say goodbye to someone he loved. His own someone was still out there, somewhere, waiting for him. He drew in a breath of foul air, trying to hide his pain. "Of course. Take as long as you need, Prigg."

"Thank you, Your Majesty. I won't be long. My wife is quite understanding and used to my leaving on a moment's notice," Prigg replied, bouncing joyfully up the street ahead of Harlowe and the cats. "Thank you, thank you, Your Majesty!" he repeated.

* * *

Prigg's entire family met him in the middle of the street as they rounded the corner. His arms, as short as they were, surrounded all eight of his jumping children while his devoted wife looked on with pride. Harlowe felt a slight stinging in his nose as the mist in his eyes became heavier and his throat tightened. When the children saw the cats, they were a little frightened at first. Then one daring little girl, the smallest of the group, came up and started petting Molly, completely unafraid. Everyone except Harlowe held their breath. Molly's large white head began rubbing affectionately against the little girl's shoulder. After that, all eyes relaxed, and soon the other kids were taking their turns playfully caressing and cuddling the cats as if they were their own. A proud Prigg informed Harlowe that tomorrow his children would be celebrated by the other kids throughout the city because they had bravely touched the mighty beasts that had killed the king's grogans... and lived!

After everyone had their turn with the cats, they all began walking slowly toward the clearing where the saucer was parked. Two of the children rode on the back of Rhud while the brave little girl who was first to touch Molly was on her back. The rest of the children playfully ran alongside, each with a small hand on their beautiful white coats. Prigg carried his youngest child in his arms. When they all came to the ship, he kissed the child in his arms and gave him to his wife. Then he said his goodbye to each child individually as if each was the most important one in his life, which they all were. Finally, Prigg put his small arms around his wife, giving her a big hug and a kiss. They touched noses and foreheads for a long, heartfelt moment before saying their last goodbyes. Harlowe turned away in tears, knowing that he was an inch away from losing it. After the goodbyes were over, Molly and Rhud bounded up the ramp, followed closely by Harlowe and his new guide, Prigg. At the top of the ramp, Harlowe and Prigg looked back as all nine little Naruckians waved goodbye.

"Are you sure you don't need more time?" Harlowe asked.

"No, Your Majesty," Prigg replied, happily satisfied. "They understand how I must leave at once if we are to have any luck in finding the Lagan trader."

Harlowe put his hand on Prigg's shoulder, envying Prigg's family that had the kind of love and beauty one could only hope to have in a dream. "Your family is wonderful, Prigg."

They stepped away from the ramp as it closed.

"Thank you, Your Majesty. I will miss them dearly."

Harlowe knew the feeling well. How long had it been since he saw his family? Almost two years, he reckoned. Since leaving Mars, he had lost touch with them completely. Not a single word could he send to them over the Internet or any other communication device. He took a lungful of heartache with him as they went from the center foyer of the ship to the corridor on their way to the bridge. Harlowe tried again to explain how he would rather be called "Captain" instead of "Your Majesty," but quickly discovered it was easier to sell cosmetics to Naruckian women. The look in Prigg's wayward eyes told him his efforts were futile; his respectful manner was simply part of the little dude he could never change.

65

His Excellency

UNIKALA AND THREE of his best bodyguards strode out of the airlock and into the mighty Fhaal starship. Their pace was easy and confident as if they were walking on a cloud of conquest. Unikala was expecting His Excellency, Commander Sar, to be waiting for him at the dock with a welcoming cadre of his finest guards, saluting him like a conquering hero. Instead, as he stepped into the docking bay, there was no welcoming party to meet him except for one nondescript soldier of obvious low rank. Though he had never met the Fhaal Commander, he was certain his reputation had preceded him, and why not? In less than a cycle he had solidified his hold on the quadrant by destroying the Tomarian trading empire and soon, with his powerful Gamadin ship, he alone would rule over the quadrant. He was a power to be reckoned with, not one reduced to the lowest of ranks.

His escort of one impatiently waved Unikala and his small entourage forward. Unikala protested, but to no avail. The escort was only following orders. If he wanted to meet with the Imperial Commander, Unikala had to go with him or leave. The choice was his.

For the time being, Unikala put his anger aside and allowed the escort to lead him and his guards through a doorway and down a long, dimly lit corridor. Unikala felt more like a servant than an equal as they made their way to the end of the passageway. This was a mistake, he thought. Sar had to know who he was! Hadn't Sar been told that he, Unikala, was responsible for the Fhaal invasion forces overtaking the quadrant without resistance? Hadn't he spent many passings dealing with the Fhaal to make this day possible? Surely this Fhaal Commander was aware of his recent accomplishments.

When they reached where Unikala presumed Sar's quarters were located, the escort motioned for Unikala and his guards to stand in front of a wide, heavy metal doorway. The escort then left the Consortium contingent alone in the waiting area.

As far as Unikala could see, which was a considerable distance, no one was moving about the corridors of the starship. He found it extremely odd in a ship of this size not to see a single crewman carrying out routine duties. The residual low hum from the depths of the star-class ship was pervasive. It made waiting all the more uneasy.

The moments turned into minutes and then nearly into an hour before anything happened. Unikala was about to pound on the door when a heavy clank unlocked a thick metal bar. The door creaked slowly open.

The room behind the door was darker than the corridor. Unikala's pride would not allow him to be seen as weak or angered by his treatment. Upon entering the room, he kept his head high. He would not let this Fhaal Commander intimidate him. With a slight wave of his shiny, pale hand, he motioned for his three guards to wait at the doorway while he spoke with Commander Sar. A slight glint from his eye told them to stay alert and be ready for any threatening move by the Fhaal. Sar would have to do much more than make him wait to shake his nerve, he thought.

Unikala strode directly to the middle of the room. It took a little time for his eyes to adjust as he searched the sizable area for any occupants. He saw no one.

"I am here, Sar. Unikala of the Consortium," he finally announced as he squinted, looking for life forms in the darkness.

Suddenly, out of the pitch darkness, a bolt of white light struck each of his guards, blasting fist-sized holes cleanly through their armored chestplates. Unikala was aghast. He tried to go for his weapon when a fourth bolt struck him in the chest. To his amazement, the blast did not penetrate his uniform. Instead, the bolt stunned his body, paralyzing his extremities. His legs buckled beneath him and he fell to his knees, gasping desperately for a breath of air. It seemed like an eternity before he could force enough air into his lungs to breathe. When he was finally able to open his eyes, a giant shadow was standing over him.

"You dare enter my chamber without proper respect," the scowling, deep voice echoed inside the chamber, "and call my name as though you are an equal."

Unikala struggled for enough breath to speak. "I apologize a thousand times over, Your Excellency," he stammered, kinking his head up at the massive shadow.

"Do not look at me unless I give you permission, thogg," Sar's voice roared.

Unikala shook. He felt death would be upon him at any moment. "Please forgive me, Your Excellency. I am your servant," he groveled, his voice broken and hoarse as he kept his eyes level with the Commander's giant black boots.

He heard the click of a weapon and then something hard against his temple. "You worthless thogg," the voice boomed.

"Yes, Imperial Commander Sar. I am as you describe, a worthless thogg. I will never be disrespectful again. Please. I assure you. A thousand apologies. I bring you great news, Your Excellency. Great news!"

"You have the Gamadin ship you promised? That is the only news I wish to hear."

"Nearly, Your Excellency," Unikala pleaded. "It is within my grasp. I have destroyed the Tomarian leader. Their fleets are at this moment under Consortium control. Without them you will have no resistance when you enter the quadrant, Imperial Commander." Unikala's head pressed against the metal floor. It would go no farther.

"That is news to me, Unikala," Anor Ran said, emerging from the dark shadows of the room. "Are you privy to information I am not aware of, my esteemed Commissar?"

Unikala gasped. The last being in the quadrant he'd expected to see in Sar's chamber was the Tomar-Rex, Anor Ran. "I have been betrayed, Imperial Commander. I beg for your mercy."

"What should we do with this worthless thogg, Anor Ran?" Sar asked, hovering over Unikala. A short moment later, two black grogans came forward, restrained by their handlers. The beasts panted hungrily and fought to break their thick chains. "Should I allow my pets to gorge themselves on his pathetic carcass?"

Unikala scraped his face along the floor as he tried to put distance between himself and grogans. "The Gamadin is within my grasp, Imperial Commander."

Sar stepped over to one of Unikala's fallen guards and tossed the body to his beasts as easily as one would toss a child's toy. The grogans caught the lifeless form in their maws and quickly tore it to shreds.

Unikala heard Sar's deep inhale. "None of your petty offerings have given meaning to the great Fhaal Empire, Unikala. You say you destroyed the Tomar-Rex and yet, here he stands. Why should I believe you now?"

"Yes, Your Excellency, I understand. My worthiness has yet to be proven," Unikala replied. He then proceeded to explain his plot of luring the Gamadin into a trap using Anor Ran's daughters as bait. The only part he left out was the part that he would keep the Gamadin ship himself for his own protection.

A massive hand grabbed his chest and lifted him off the ground like a rag doll. He stared into Sar's horrifying face. He wanted to evacuate all his waste pouches in his suit. The Imperial Commander's six red eyes, each as large as his fist, stared at Unikala as if Sar were about to rip the worthless thogg's head off with his large snout of long, razored teeth. "Is this true, Anor Ran? Has this grogan waste captured a Gamadin prize?"

Anor Ran smiled. "Yes, he has, Sar." The less-than-respectful salutation Anor Ran used with the Fhaal Imperial Commander did not go unnoticed by Unikala. What power did Anor Ran have over the Fhaal? "In the form of my own daughters," he replied.

Sar laughed. "How creative, Anor Ran. A subversive scheme with your own family."

"A small price for the welfare of the empire, Commander," Anor Ran replied.

Sar held Unikala several feet above the black, metal floor and inquired of Anor Ran, "Then you believe such fiction?"

Anor Ran stood calmly and replied, "I believe it is a plan with merit, Sar. The Gamadin Captain is weak and inexperienced. Half of his crew is missing. He travels the quadrant in a desperate search to find them. I would allow the Commissar's plan to play out for the moment. We can always kill him later."

With his other arm, Sar picked up the second Consortium body and tossed it to his pets. "You wish to join your guards, thogg?" he asked Unikala.

"No, Imperial Commander."

Suddenly, Sar bit off Unikala's left forearm and swallowed it whole. "You taste like grogan waste, thogg." Unikala couldn't believe his own eyes. His left forearm was gone, bitten off clean below the middle joint. Still in shock, he struggled for breath, trying to speak as his dark green blood splattered on the floor.

"As Anor Ran suggests, I will allow you to live for the moment," Sar growled. He then tossed Unikala out the door and into the corridor, where two escorts were waiting. Finally, Sar reached down and tossed the remaining guard to his grogans, giving Unikala one last warning. "Fail me, thogg, and I will have your head for a feeding bowl."

The Fhaal escorts dragged Unikala back to the docking bay and tossed his bleeding body through the airlock to the surprise of his stunned crew. The giant starship detached itself from the Consortium cruiser and drifted away. Minutes later it went into hyperspace and was gone.

66

The Medallion

QUAY KNEW HER sister was dying. During the past few hours, Sizzle's condition had deteriorated. Her breathing was weak and shallow. She needed something beyond the stale water and the meager bits of food Unikala's guards tossed them through their cell door. Sizzle needed medicine and a physician or she wouldn't make it to the next feeding cycle. The few times she had regained consciousness, Sizzle seemed aware that Quay was with her. She was never awake long enough to mumble anything beyond a single word or two. Quay continued to hold her sister in her arms. If she was going to die, she did not want her alone in those final moments.

Sizzle moved in her arms, moaning, fighting the discomfort of her injuries. Quay helped turn her so as to give her comfort, the way they had for each other when they were little girls feeling sick or hurt or sad. Quay touched the golden chain around her neck and the Gamadin medallion Harlowe had given her. She smiled slightly, like a person who shares a bond so personal that only two people in the universe know its secret. She brought it around and lay it gently on the small of her neck. Then a light went off in her head. *The medallion was like a Swiss Army knife,* he had told her. When she still looked puzzled, he explained that it meant that the little disk contained many useful tools. *When you wear it, it gives you added strength to run great distances without tiring. At night it lets you see into the darkest corners. It keeps you warm in deep space and hides you when you don't want to be seen. It does so many things, I'm still discovering what it does, Quay. The SIBA even fixes you when you're sick...*

Quay held the medallion, remembering his words. *The SIBA even fixes you when you're sick...* Yes, yes, that was what her Captain told her! She was certain of it. They had been eating those crispy things on Taco Tuesday. They were so good, but she had poured too much of the red sauce over the green stringy vegetables and ate too many of the tacos. Before the dinner was over her stomach was on fire. She remembered how Harlowe laughed. At the time, she didn't think it was funny. He then touched her medallion. When the outer skin covered her body, he told her to wait and soon she would feel normal again. It was the most amazing thing! Almost instantly her stomach calmed and her head cleared of any discomfort. He tapped her above her breastplate again and the SIBA retracted back into its medallion shape like magic. Then he explained that one of the SIBA's functions was to keep the Gamadin warrior healthy under high battle stress or injuries. The skin did this by constantly regulating and testing the body for any physical change. *If it sees trouble, it adjusts your temperature or injects you with fluids to make you well again. I don't know how the thing works exactly. It just does. If you want to know more, ask Wiz. That's why I keep the disk with me at all times,* Harlowe explained.

Tears flowed down the sides of her olive-colored cheeks as she remembered his deep, confident voice, unafraid, positive, and reassuring. He had a way of speaking with words she had never heard before in all her travels throughout the quadrant. He was so different and reckless at times, but never deceptive. Her soldier from the distant past offered only the truth.

She breathed deeply, praying for her Captain, his crew, and Sizzle. She pressed the medallion around her sister's neck. Like magic, the SIBA molecules spread over her body like a protective coating of super dura fabric. How the skin fit inside a disk so small was inconceivable. In Harlowe's own words she remembered him saying, *Don't try to figure it out, Quay. We don't know how it works, either. It just does and that's all you have to think about. Let it do its magic and you'll be cool.*

Her Captain was right. If it saved her sister's life, what difference did it make how it worked? She just needed a miracle, with no questions asked.

67

Palcor

"WOW!" SIMON CRIED out.

Palcor was breathtaking. As *Millawanda* entered Palcorian tracking space, Harlowe, Monday, and Simon sat mesmerized, gawking at the immense emerald-green superstructures hanging brilliantly against a black field of tiny white diamonds. From two million miles out, weary travelers to Palcor could easily see the twinkling lights of its friendly welcoming beacons. Prigg explained that it was known as the jewel of the interstellar trade routes.

Palcor sat alone in the vastness of space, totally independent of any star or planet around it. It owed its life to no one. It was not nearly as old as Gibb, but it was old nevertheless, with an age spanning eons of time. It was as large as the Earth's moon in mass and as wide as Mars when measured at its most distant ends. It reminded Harlowe of a complicated green snowflake, the way its largest modules connected to each other by giant translucent tubes. The colossal shafts served a dual purpose: to keep the floating megalopolis together and to allow transport between the different structures. Though manufactured, Palcor had all the features of any planet except for changing weather. Weather on Palcor was constant and almost nonexistent. It never rained or snowed and was never too hot or dry. Palcor had never seen a cloudy day, a beautiful sunset, or a glorious morning. It had its own artificial gravity, water, and food supplies. The large center module, nearly three times the size of any other module, was the main hub of Palcor's structure. From there, the hundreds of sub-structures of smaller sub-cities and agri-modules radiated out in interconnecting lines, dedicated mostly to the regeneration of Palcor's energy, resources, and air supply.

The journey to Palcor had taken two days longer than planned. Prigg had said earlier that Palcor was "only three light passings" from Naruck. However, he had not meant it in terms of Earth light-years. A passing on Naruck, he explained, was the equivalent of what amounted to five Earth years. Instead of three light-years away, it was fifteen. That was not a great deal of difference to a 54th century ship of the stars. But for Harlowe, who was eager to find the rest of his crew, Quay, and Sizzle, it aggravated his emotional state to the point where he had to take it out on Quincy, his android sparring partner, five times a day instead of two.

"Do you wish landing instructions?" a sexy woman's voice asked over the ship's open com. The voice came from the equally gorgeous face of the female operator on the overhead screen. This welcoming face was a far cry from the Naruckian greeters. "Whoa, Skipper, whatta babe!" Simon blurted out from his chair. Finally, they had found a place where they didn't need to shower the moment they stepped beyond the force field. They were all weary of grogans, ancient cities, and smelly, radioactive planets. "It's about time we put down on a 'real' space city," Simon added.

Harlowe agreed. "A Captain Starr kinda place, huh, Mr. Bolt?"

"Aye," Simon replied, cocking his head to the side, suddenly a little disappointed.

Harlowe noticed a familiar circular trademark behind the woman operator. "That's a Tomarian symbol isn't it? What's going on, Prigg?"

Prigg's expression was one of obvious knowledge. "Tomar owns Palcor, Your Majesty. It's common knowledge."

"Small quadrant, Captain," Monday quipped.

Harlowe mused over the new revelation. "Growing smaller every day, Mr. Platter." He returned to the operator and stated that he needed landing instructions for his vessel. After the usual why-are-you-heres, they were graciously given their landing coordinates. Because of Millie's size and shape, they had to put down on one of Palcor's back parking modules that was wide enough to accommodate her.

Harlowe turned to Prigg, who had one eye on the overhead and one eye on him, and said, "I hope the ground transport is acceptable."

Prigg assured Harlowe it was. "Yes, Your Majesty. Palcor is very accommodating."

They put down a short time later at Parking Platform 27, a circular module twenty miles in diameter. As large as the parking structure was, the large Ship fit like a glove in the space provided. Monday had only a few yards to work with as he squeezed *Millawanda* between a couple of small transports.

After systems shutdown, Harlowe stretched out of his command chair and said, "Let's see what Palcor has to offer, gentlemen." He didn't want to waste a moment to begin their search for Ra-Loc.

"Shutdown complete, Skipper," Monday announced.

Prigg added, "We've been cleared to enter the city as well, Your Majesty."

"Any bad guys out there wanting to rumble, Mr. Bolt?" Harlowe asked.

Simon lifted his head up from the com screen. "None that Millie can find, Skipper. Seems pretty quiet."

"All right, Mr. Platter, you're with me on the first round." Harlowe was well aware that Monday hadn't been off the ship in weeks, so when Simon began to protest staying behind, Harlowe said, "Your turn to hang, Mr. Bolt. Mr. Platter needs to stretch his legs. He's coming with Prigg and me. You're staying. No arguments."

Simon slumped back into his chair, mumbling a string of nonsense as Monday appreciably replied, "Thanks, Captain. I could use it."

* * *

Everyone met at the center foyer. The robob servants were handing out Gama-belts to Harlowe and Monday while the giant hatchway opened and the rampway deployed. The cats led the way, leaping in great strides down the ramp, followed by Harlowe, Monday, and Prigg. As they stepped down the incline, Monday asked Prigg if he came to Palcor often.

"Oh, yes, Mr. Platter. I travel to Palcor often in my line of business. It is a wonderful place."

Harlowe and Simon traded lighthearted glances; neither had been able to break Prigg of his habit of calling Harlowe "Your Majesty," Simon "Mr. Bolt," and Monday "Mr. Platter." They tried many times in their off-duty hours to explain that it was okay to address them by their first names or even their call names.

"When we're off the clock, Prigg, you can call me Simon or Rerun. Everyone else does."

"Yes, Mr. Bolt" was Prigg's courteous reply every time Simon tried to explain things to the little Naruckian. No amount of persuading or explaining could change what he thought was right and proper, so the Gamadin crew let sleeping dogs lie and accepted the inevitable. Harlowe was "Your Majesty" and Simon and Monday were "Mr. Bolt" and "Mr. Platter." End of story.

Everyone had quickly discovered that Prigg was no third leg. In the short amount of time he had been on board, they found him quite knowledgeable about travel around the quadrant. A lucky find, Harlowe thought, patting himself on the back more than once for his decision to bring the Naruckian along.

Though *Millawanda* could fly with a crew of three, it took many more to run the ship at her highest level of efficiency. Learning to pilot the saucer had taken the five of them many months. If Consortium ships or roving bands of space marauders had attacked them, there was no telling how they might have fared. *Millawanda* had superior speed, power, and maneuvering capabilities, but Harlowe knew they could still be in a world of hurt with a skeleton crew jumping from station to station while working sixteen-hour shifts. Prigg's contribution relieved some of the stress. As helpful as he was, however, the lost mates were irreplaceable. Prigg was who he was . . . a fine addition to the crew, not a substitute.

Simon accompanied Harlowe, Platter, and Prigg as far as the bottom of the ramp while Molly and Rhud were already frolicking about, playing tag, and stretching their legs under the massive hull of the ship. "You have the keys to the car, Mr. Bolt," Harlowe said. "Don't dent the fenders or you'll be cleaning the cat box for a month."

"Ouch, Skipper," Simon replied, wrinkling his nose at the thought. "I'll have the clickers give her a good polish while you're gone."

Harlowe looked up at the undersides, noticing the blemishes the vast distances had imposed on her once beautiful golden luster. "Good idea, Rerun. Give her a nice bubble bath and a pedicure. She deserves it."

"I'll treat her like a movie star, Captain."

Harlowe was about to turn away when he noticed Prigg's drifting eyes trying to zero in on his waist.

"What's the matter, Prigg?" Harlowe asked, sensing the scrutiny as though he had his fly unzipped.

Prigg pointed to Harlowe's sidearms. "Pardon me, Your Majesty, but weapons are not allowed on Palcor."

Harlowe put his hands on his hips and stared defiantly out at the city. "Well, we'll see about that." There were too many times in the recent past when his life and others' had depended on his sidearms. He wasn't going anywhere without them.

"No one is allowed to carry any kind of projectile weapon on Palcor, Your Majesty. One misplaced discharge, whether intentional or not, could puncture the superstructure of the city. That is why they are forbidden."

Harlowe bent down at Prigg, trying his best to look eye to eye with him. The problem was which eye was looking at him? It was nearly an impossible task. His own eyes felt like they were tripping over themselves. "No one else has weapons either?"

"No, Your Majesty, they are forbidden," Prigg repeated, his focus split, one eye up, one to the side.

Harlowe decided looking at a narrow spot between his eyes was the most comfortable. "You're sure?"

"Yes, Your Majesty. I can assure you. They are forbidden."

Harlowe didn't like the idea at all. "That sucks," he stated, but he understood the intent of the law. It was a law that made sense. Like a lighted match to a scarecrow, one break in the pressurized skin of Palcor could cause a lot of damage.

"All right," Harlowe breathed reluctantly, "if that's the way it is, then I'll leave them behind." He unbuckled his weapons belt and

handed it to a waiting robob who'd popped out of nowhere, antici-
pating its service. Besides, he thought, Molly and Rhud would be
with them, and they were better than any light weapon.

"You look naked, Skipper," Simon joked.

It wasn't a laughing matter to Harlowe. "I feel it, too," he admitted, and walked away in an uneasy mood.

Harlowe called the cats to his side on their way to the lift that would
transport them to the central module. They made him feel secure as he
marveled at Palcor's amazing modular structures. It was an awe-inspiring
example of what intelligent life could do if cool minds were put to work.
Palcor's beauty was grand. He wished he could have shared it with Quay
and the rest of his crew. Their absence marred the grandness. All the
Palcors in the universe wouldn't distract him from his quest.

At the lift, Harlowe stepped onto the platform and motioned for
Molly and Rhud to follow. "Come along, puddy cats. Up you go."

A monotoned voice came from a small screen on the lift control
panel. "Lower forms of life are not allowed inside the city. They
must be confined to specified quarantine sectors or taken to one of
the agri-modules," the voice said.

Harlowe bent down to the screen, his lips curling back. "Lower
forms of life!" he shouted. "Listen here, puke, they are not lower
forms of life! They are light-years ahead of every toad-faced being
I've encountered in this quadrant!!"

"Lower forms of life are not allowed inside the inner city," the
voice repeated, unfazed by Harlowe's outburst. The voice proceeded
to explain to Harlowe where he could board his pets during his stay
on Palcor.

Harlowe was steamed. "That really fries my…" He wanted to put
a fist through the screen.

Monday tried a more practical approach. "We won't be gone that long, Captain. We've come a long way not to check this place out. We'll be all right. We'll have Prigg with us. He knows the place like the back of his hand. Right, Prigg?"

"Yes, Mr. Platter. I know the city quite well," Prigg replied.

"See, Your Majes—" Monday laughed. "Oh no, the little dude's got me doing it, too, Captain."

Harlowe saw no humor in the joke. "You start calling me that and I'll jam one of those module connectors down your throat, Squid."

"Aye, Captain."

Prigg pointed out as diplomatically as he knew how that the lift would not move until Molly and Rhud were off. After cooling his jets, Harlowe patted both cats gently on the sides and told them he had no choice but to leave them behind. Molly growled her disapproval. "I know, girl, but my hands are tied. The Palcor toads won't let you in." He looked at Rhud pathetically and led them off the lift where they sat, dejected, as if they were the most abused animals in the galaxy.

* * *

To say that Harlowe was bummed that Molly and Rhud had to stay behind was an understatement. Now he really was naked. While they were being whisked away in one of the thousands of inter-module transports that crisscrossed the vast Palcorian complex, Harlowe apologized for his earlier outburst. "Finding that fat Ra-Loc toad has gotten me so mad I can't see straight." Harlowe glanced down at Prigg, whose eyes were moving around in several different directions at once. Harlowe split a gut. "Prigg, you're a good guy to have around."

Harlowe hadn't laughed since Gibb, and it felt good. It broke the tension he had felt since leaving Naruck. Prigg, of course, was oblivious as to why His Majesty was in such good spirits, but he wasn't about to say anything that would take away from the moment.

68

Og

THE THICK, HUMID sky over the Consortium's black rock fortress on the planet Og was filled with a haze of grey volcanic dust and sulphuric odors from an eruption two hundred miles away. For Quay, the small patch of dimness that was visible through a high, small opening of her dungeon was a misery beyond pity. She was cold and hungry. She had not slept in days. There was no stellar cloud full of stars, no far-off nebula, no constellation with an ancient past to give her hope. The dim light that lay beyond the thick metal bars was far less wondrous than the bright light she had shared with her Gamadin warrior on the small planet they simply called #2 those many weeks ago. The stars above Og were tarnished. They had no sorcerer's magic to make them bright, no playful sounds of an ocean, or feel of a warm, gentle breeze whispering a loving song in her ear. It was as if a callous thief had stolen all the magical things her Gamadin Captain had shared with her.

Unikala's fortress was made of unclean stone that teemed with alien vermin living in the cracks and crevices of its lightless walls. Outside, the dark silhouette of heavily armed, monolithic turrets and sawtoothed battlements surrounded her prison keep. Along the stone ramparts, faceless guards moved slowly day and night, keeping a watchful eye on their only prisoners, while miles away three attack fighters—parts of the Consortium air forces on Og—floated

414

down to a nearby landing area to join the squadrons already parked on the mesa. The orange glow of their hyperdrives contrasted bright against the dark backdrop of the inhospitable planet. The fortress was a security outpost for Consortium activities on the outer frontier of the quadrant. Before they transported from orbit to the planet's surface, Quay counted ten more Consortium battlecruisers in orbit above the planet next to Unikala's flagship. Others were undoubtedly drifting in orbit beyond her narrow view. Each battlecruiser came with scores of attack fighters. She estimated there were over twelve hundred fighters, and those were the ones she could see. In spite of the odds stacked against Harlowe, Quay feared her Captain would try to rescue her. It would be hopeless folly, even for a Gamadin. There had to be a way to save Tomar and her Gamadin Captain.

Why come to Og, she wondered? The fortress was obsolete, with little or no strategic value to anyone. Why didn't Unkala go to Tomar itself and force her father's hand to surrender? Was he afraid of her father's alliances with Tock-hyba and Phellon? Maybe. They would be powerful together. Tock-hyba had been reluctant in the past to break its treaties for fear of losing Consortium protection. Phellon, however, was naive and spineless, she sneered. Phellon had been immune to the inner conflicts of the quadrant because, out there at the edge of the quadrant, it was isolated from the other worlds by the great distance from Omini Prime. In the past it had always allowed the inner worlds to struggle among themselves while Phellon waited and watched safely from a distance for the cosmic dust to settle so it could extend its hand to the victor. That was the past. Now that the Fhaal had entered the quadrant, no world was safe. Distance to the Fhaal was meaningless. That was why the Consortium had made its pact with the evil that had already conquered a third of the quadrant. They did it to survive!

If Quay could know all this, and know that the Fhaal were already in the quadrant, Unikala had to know it as well, she mused deeply. The Commissar did not rise to the top of his Consortium government by acting unreasonably. Unikala had many vile attributes, but stupidity was not one of them. He was ambitious, self-serving, perceptive, calculating, and a master of tactics as well. Why would Unikala bring her and Sizzle and all his resources to a world that made no strategic sense?

Quay kept staring through her only window at the pitiless sky as a tarnished yellow cloud drifted by her prison window. The cloud was unusual. It was wide and flat. If she stared hard enough, she could almost believe if it turned on its edge it would be round like her Captain's ship. She smiled faintly. The golden cloud seemed to bring warmth to her den of darkness. The tarnished cloud let her pretend her Captain had arrived to take her away in his beautiful golden ship. She cradled the medallion around her neck, holding the thought of him closer to her side.

Suddenly her breathing stopped. Of course, she knew why! She had known it all along! She closed her eyes tight as the aching pain of truth came rushing back and tore through her insides as if a plas round had exploded. Her Gamadin Captain! Unikala knew her Captain would risk everything to find her, no matter where she was in the universe or how many ships surrounded her. *Nuke 'em!* she heard her Captain say, *Nuke them all! I don't care if they have a million attack fighters and battle cruisers lined up and pointed at us! I will nuke the toads to subatomic dust, Quay!*

She shook her head back and forth, almost laughing at the absurdity of how simply her Gamadin, her soldier from the distant past, saw the universe. His world was black and white with little to no grey. He attacked injustice like a charging Tomarian bull. Someday there will be an obstacle too impossible to overcome, she'd argued with him once. *You think so, huh? Well, that's gomer speak, Quay!* he barked back at her. There were no obstacles in his universe. *There are only obstacles for timid and insecure maggots with no lives. Gamadin eat obstacles for breakfast, lunch, and dinner. We do the impossible and then we move on to the next impossibility. We're unstoppable, Quay. Know that, we are the impossible,* he said that night as they ate what they called animal-style double-double In-N-Outs in the forward observation room of his ship. The fearlessness in his dark blue eyes made her a believer. She had never felt so safe as then, that night before their arrival on Gibb. When he kissed her, she knew that her Gamadin Captain would remain by her side forever.

She closed her eyes, musing over her Captain's odd combination of loyal crewmen. Observing them, it was difficult to believe they were warriors at all. At times they seemed so undisciplined and immature. They lacked the kind of military preparedness necessary to resist any kind of organized force like the Consortium. They appeared to disagree on practically everything. In the beginning she thought they were enemies somehow thrown together by fate. She quickly realized, however, during what they called their "off-the-clock" hours, that it was their nature to be hostile toward one another. She had to learn to accept their odd behaviors, their unruly language, and their lack of the militarism so common to her people. Especially Harlowe. He would constantly remind her to "read between the lines." He would laugh and half-teasingly say things, she often thought. *Back home they call it man-speak.* Then he would smile after that, explaining that more often than not the meanings of their statements did not represent the actual way they saw the world. *Watch what we do, not what we say, Quay. See behind our eyes. That's where you'll find the real truth with us Earthlings,* he told her. *We really are a sorry lot at times. I would really rather be surfing a glassy wave than out here tooling around the galaxy, being a toad, searching for the meaning of life. What the hey, girl, aren't we all searching for something?*

Tears flowed down the side of her cheeks as she sadly watched the golden cloud move from her line of sight. *Oh, Captain,* she thought, *I know you are brave and fearless, but do not be foolish! Og will take your brave Gamadin life!*

She breathed a heavy sigh, borrowing his strength. *Do not worry, my brave Gamadin Captain. I will do the impossible for you. I will find a way to escape. I will find you again amongst the stars and save you from coming to Og for me.*

Her plea would fall on deaf ears, she knew, for he would come. There was no doubt in her mind that no empire, no Consortium ship in the galaxy, would stop him.

Not only was her prison fortress surrounded by Consortium forces, it was also located atop a 14,000-foot mesa surrounded by impossibly sheer cliffs. The only way on or off the mesa was by air transport. She became frantic. The thought of escape became a desperate motivation. She had to inform Sizzle of her conclusions.

The Gamadin suit had worked a miracle on Sizzle. The SIBA, as Harlowe called it, saved her sister's life. Within hours after she had activated the suit and Sizzle awakened, they were holding each other for an eternity. That was when Sizzle told Quay of the time when she and Rerun had overheard Turfan betray them and their father to Unikala in the Gibbian park.

"It is up to us, Sister," Sizzle told her. "Now that we know the Fhaal have joined with Unikala to take over of the quadrant, we must find a way to warn the Gamadin of their plot."

Quay agreed. They planned an escape at the first opportunity, but Quay hadn't figured on Unikala splitting them up the moment they entered the fortress. She would not leave her sister behind to be beaten again by Unikala's troops. Quay had not seen her sister since coming to Og. She prayed no more harm would come to her. She had to act fast. Time would serve neither her sister, her father, nor the quadrant well. Somehow she and Sizzle had to find a way off the planet together. It was up to them. Unless she could escape and warn the quadrant of the Fhaal, they were all doomed.

Unless...

Unless the ancient stories were true...

69

Ela

RIVERSTONE STOOD IN silent shock where Ian had fallen from the platform. *Why did he do that? That wasn't like Wiz to do something that stupid,* he kept telling himself over and over. *We suffered more than that back on Mars. Why did he do it?*

A powerful hand came from out of nowhere, jolting Riverstone away from the platform rail. "Get away from there, thrall!" Dagger yelled. He spat a wad of thick, dark goo at the shaft before he picked Riverstone up by the back of his iron belt and threw him like a bale of hay down the long mine tunnel as he went on with his tirade. "I will not lose another to the depths."

The constant pounding of heavy rock hammers thundered in his ears as they drudged their way along the shaft. It wasn't long before they came to a vast maw in the earth, where Riverstone saw for the first time his most dreaded fear come to life: thousands of toiling slaves beating the unforgiving rock of Erati.

"Dude…" Riverstone gasped, feeling his blood trickling down the side of his cheek from Dagger's recent blow.

Dagger kept shoving Riverstone forward until they were deep inside the vast cavern. "You will start over there," Dagger ordered, thrusting a heavy hammer into Riverstone's hands. "You are my responsibility now. Since one was lost, you must do the work of two. Do a good job and I will spare you this." Dagger raised the butt of his whip as if he were going to strike him again, but Riverstone didn't flinch. He was coming out of his drug-induced stupor. Maybe there was a little surprise in Dagger's eyes that Riverstone failed to cower. Whatever the reason, Dagger did not follow through with his threat. Had he struck, Riverstone would have defended himself and easily killed the miner. However, he was in no condition yet to escape. He had surveyed his situation coming in. There were too many guards like Dagger in the area. Had he overpowered this bully, then what? Where would he go? How many other guards would he have to slay to survive the miles and miles to the top of the mine? Riverstone knew nothing about Erati's system of control. Finally, and most importantly, what would he do for food and rest along the way? All these questions and more had to be answered before he could make a successful escape. He was miles beneath the surface. He needed time to figure out his condition before he tried anything. What were the words that Harlowe quoted from Sun Tzu—*the Earth comprises distances, great and small; danger and security; open ground and narrow passes; the chances of life and death.* He needed time to devise his plan and to understand the distances that would give him the chance to escape the depths of Erati. As much as he wanted to be rid of the low-life scum, he stuffed his anger and obediently shuffled off in the direction that Dagger had pointed.

"I will be back shortly to check on your progress, thrall. Do not disappoint me or you will understand what it means when Dagger becomes angered." He smiled cunningly before he strode off to check the rest of his miners.

To quell his anger and clear his head, Riverstone gripped his hammer as if it were Dagger's throat and began striking the rock, imagining the miner's head beneath every impact. "Do not despair," an unseen presence uttered after Dagger left the area. The voice sounded kind and warm, but Riverstone could not see which digger was speaking to him. He thought he was hearing things, so he resumed his pounding. He did not really believe in angels, but the voice sounded like one. "I will help you," the voice said again.

This time he knew someone was talking to him.

Riverstone caught a guard walking down the work line and quickly returned to hitting the rock. Once the guard passed, he searched again for the source of the soft voice.

"I am here, New One." Riverstone kept searching. "Here," the voice called out. "Over here." This time he spotted the source. Three bodies to his right, ten yards away, a slender form covered with dirt turned its face toward his. The light was dim, but he thought he was looking at a female. She sounded like one, anyway. She was small and thin, almost frail-looking; maybe a foot shorter than Quay, he thought. Her filthy hair was coal black, knotted, and matted to her head. Whether the hair itself was dark like Quay's or sandy like Harlowe's, he couldn't tell. The dust covered too much of her to get an accurate idea of what she or her hair really looked like. Even in the dim light of the cavern, her eyes were kind, like an angel's. That much he could see clearly. She would need a good scrubbing before he could make any further judgments about her appearance.

"Who are you?" Riverstone whispered.

"Ela," she replied carefully. The others around them pretended to give them no mind. They did not want a taste of a guard's whip for talking in the line.

Riverstone continued to pound away, ignoring the possible consequences. "How long do we work?"

Ela answered simply, "Until the end."

It was hardly the reply he was looking for, but then there were no clock-watchers or union breaks. They were all nonexistent on Erati. The mining slaves worked until they were told to stop.

Riverstone was stunned to see that Ela's hammer was as big as his. He had only started, and already his arm ached from the hammer's weight. Ela, on the other hand, kept wielding hers almost effortlessly. "Will they feed us?" he asked. He was so hungry after coming out of his drug-induced stupor he could have eaten the rock if he had some ketchup.

"Yes, you will get nourishment then," Ela replied cautiously.

Food was music to Riverstone's ears. He had forgotten the last time he had eaten. He was about to ask Ela another question when she cut him off. "Do not talk any more, New One. Wait until the rest period."

Riverstone nodded but was not deceptive enough to avoid the long leathery whip that cut across his neck and shoulders. He twisted his back upward and saw Dagger's cruel eyes staring down at him. He had come out of nowhere. "Get to work, thrall!" he growled. "No one talks on my line. Only digging."

Riverstone fought against snapping Dagger's neck again. He gripped his hammer and struck the rock, slowly at first, and then, harder, transferring his pain to the stone.

Pound. Pound. Pound.

After the first hour, his hands became numb. After the second hour, they bled from blisters and cuts. He wondered how long he could hold out. Would he even make it through to the end of his first work period?

* * *

Hours later a loud whistle blew. Riverstone was so exhausted, he did not hear the high-pitched scream of the horn. A slave next to him nudged him in the side to stop hammering. All the workers lay their tools down where they worked and stood up waiting in single file, ready for the order to march. After kneeling for such a long time, Riverstone found that standing was difficult. He hadn't felt this miserable in a long time, not since his first days on Mars. His Gamadin training was paying off. The General was right. His hard work around the rimmers would someday save his life. He knew he was alive because of it. His mind began to wander. He thought he would never again object to mowing his parent's lawn or running twenty rimmers without a smile. It was all he could do to crawl up the side of a mine cart. His knees wobbled a bit, but they held steady. He felt thankful every moment for General Gunn's preparations.

Walking, however, was another matter. When the order was given to march, his legs gave out, and he stumbled and fell. He tried to get up, and fell again. It was no use. He was too weak to walk. Ra-Loc's drugs and malnutrition had sucked him dry of any reserves. He thought he would stay right where he was until the next work period, but then someone came up from behind and lifted him to his feet.

It was the little angel, Ela.

At first, Riverstone was concerned that Dagger or one of the other guards would whip her for helping him. "You mustn't, Ela. They will hurt you," he said, faltering badly.

"No, New One. During rest period, we are allowed. Only during work period is contact forbidden," Ela explained.

Riverstone was grateful, but he had guessed wrong about her height. Ela was much shorter than Quay. Her frail looks were also deceptive. She was incredibly strong. He could feel her lifting his six-foot-nine-inch frame practically off the ground as she helped him along. He did nothing to stop her. He couldn't. Where had she found the strength? She had worked as long as he. He wanted to get another look at her face, but he was too tired to concentrate on such superficial curiosities. Instead, he closed his weary eyes and allowed himself to be taken to wherever they were going.

During the rest period, the laborers dispersed themselves throughout the levels in the different abandoned shafts around the main cavern. When they came to her section of the shaft, Ela eased Riverstone carefully to the ground, propping him up against the side of the cavern wall. She made him more comfortable by placing sand from the floor around the small of his back for support. It was not a soft, 54th-century chair from his ship, but it was equally as restful. Light in the abandoned tunnels where the laborers made their sanctuaries came from a few scattered dim lanterns that hung from the ceiling. Ela's eyes, like those of the Erati guards, were large and used to the low light levels.

Next, Ela retrieved a small metal container from a nearby cache and stuck it under a narrow outcropping of rock. After a moment, she brought the container back, placed her hand inside, and then brought her thin, calloused fingers to Riverstone's parched lips.

Riverstone grabbed her hands and started licking her palms and fingers for all the moisture he could find. "Slowly, New One, you must not drink all at once." She helped ration his sips as he fought back the urge to gulp the contents of the container down in a single swallow. After he had drained the container, he handed it back and asked for more. This time he couldn't wait. He quickly chugged the water, spilling large amounts of it down the sides of his face and neck.

Ela made several trips to the crevice before he had drunk enough. Riverstone was only able to breathe a sigh of thanks before he passed out in her arms.

Cleansed the stars for all...

THE LOUD CLANK of a heavy bolt slid back. The door to Quay's iron chamber opened and flooded the cell with light, hurting her eyes. She did not have to see to know who it was. She could smell his vulgar odor of smoke and drink as her eyes continued to stare out the far window. "What do you want, Unikala?" Her tattered rag of a dress covered her leather-bound feet. A small light from outside her window illuminated the heavy lines of imprisonment across her body, but even that could not mar her beauty. "Something worthy of your minuscule intellect, no doubt."

Unikala's silver eyes stared down at Quay as he curiously hid his left arm behind his back. He was surprised by her words and her tone. She acted as if she had no fear. The veins in the side of his neck bulged as he spoke. "We can end this suffering now if you will consent to our union."

"Suffering? What makes you think I suffer when it is you who will die a thousand deaths within the cycle? Soon you will know what suffering means to kidnap the daughters of Anor Ran."

Unikala laughed at the absurdity.

"Why have the Fhaal joined with the Consortium, Commissar? What did you promise them for such an alliance?" She spoke to him as though his own words or queries were too trite to bother with a reply. This vexed him even more.

"I could force you."

"It must be something very valuable or they would have killed you by now." She looked into his steely eyes, searching for the answer. Unikala did not try to hide the amused glint of haughty superiority shown by people who believe that they are superior because they are keeping a dark deep secret. "They would have killed you unless…" She thought for a moment, trying to imagine what he could possibly have in his possession that the Fhaal might want. She decided to play with his arrogant ego. "Unless I have underestimated your worth, Commissar."

"Join me and I will give you the quadrant and beyond, Quay."

Quay laughed out loud at this farce. "Such confidence, Unikala! You would need vast power to keep an empire like the Fhaal at bay. What is this hidden exponent, Commissar? Do you wish to share such information or keep it to your pitiful self?"

"Let's just say that I have prepared for this moment, my lady."

She tried to peer around his body to see behind his back. "What are you hiding from me, Unikala? A prize worthy of the queen of an empire?" she mocked.

Unikala suddenly lost his confident spirit. "Do not come near me!"

"Then I have not underestimated you. You are weak and pitiful. You cannot even show me what you have hidden from my view. You are a coward of the first order, Unikala. It is obvious."

Unikala became enraged. He thrust his amputated stump in front of her face. "Is this what you want to see, my lady? Your sister has made a remarkable recovery, and obviously once again is well enough to amuse my guards."

The look on Quay's face betrayed her. Unikala knew he had found her weakness. "I gave an arm for this power. So know this, Quay, I will do all that is necessary to obtain and keep it. When I have it, I will have control of the Fhaal and you will come willingly, or I will devour your precious Tomar and all that is dear to you."

Quay swallowed hard. She needed something to lean on, something to keep her upright before she collapsed on the stone floor. She struggled to keep herself from falling as she defied him again. "No one has that much power, Commissar! The Fhaal will feast on the rest of you before they will submit to anyone's control."

An evil smirk crossed over Unikala's thin lips as he raised his stub in front of her eyes. "They have taken their last taste, I assure you. The Gamadin ship will see to that."

Quay stared at him, like someone does who just heard something so outlandish that it just might be true, especially since she had witnessed the power of the ancients herself with her own eyes. She forced a smirk to keep the bizarre nature of the tale alive. "To believe that one ship could possess such power to destroy an empire such as the Fhaal is pure illusion. I am surprised at you, Unikala, a Commissar of your stature falling for an old child's fable." She giggled, covering her mouth with her soiled hands. Her bogus grin grew deeper. "I have been with these soldiers. I have seen them close up and witnessed their power. They are hardly worth the trouble, Commissar. They are just ancient tales, nothing more."

A guard handed him an old scroll tied together with a piece of tattered leather. "The scrolls of Amerloi do not lie, my lady." He untied the strip around the middle and read aloud. "For it is written that the coming madness will awaken the fearsome Gamadin of the galactic core. The wrath of the Gamadin will be felt throughout the stars and lo, while some people trembled in despair still more rejoiced; for the wrath of the Gamadin cleansed the stars for all; and there was peace..." He looked up at her, regaining his overconfident glow. "Now you see why you will be at my side when I have the ship of the Gamadin. I, Unikala, will have the power of the ancients, and the Fhaal will destroy Tomar just like they destroyed your mother's beautiful Neeja."

"The Gamadin are no fools. They will never fall for such a trap," Quay countered.

Unikala played with his severed stump, coming closer to her face, "I have made sure that they will. Even a fool knows this young Gamadin of yours is brash and overconfident. He will come because he wants you. When he does, I will have my vengeance, you, and my empire..."

Quay stared at Unikala coldly. *Play your hand to the end.* This was something she had learned from her young Gamadin captain. She leaned back casually and relaxed, displaying no fear as she spoke. As she did, she perceived a minute tell in Unikala's eyes. Small as it was, she let him take her fearlessness fully before she spoke. She had been taught well. "In my Captain's own words, I will say this: I will lead the Burgesses against the Consortium. Rights of Passage will be history. The quadrant's inhabitants will be free to travel the stars forever!" Her eyes focused like narrow beams of burning light. "The reign of the Consortium government has come to an end. Your missing arm is only the beginning of your loss. Heed the scrolls before you. The warning is for you, Unikala... 'the wrath of the Gamadin cleansed the stars for all,' it says. It does not say except for Unikala and his Consortium. It says for all. As strong as you think you are, even your precious alliance cannot defeat the power of the Old Ones. Their power comes from the heart of the galactic core itself."

Unikala laughed, his eyes peering down to her, glowing brighter in the darkened room. "Then I have you, my dear Quay. My equalizer. Your mighty warrior will not interfere if he knows you may be harmed, will he?"

Try as she could, Quay could not hide her innermost feelings. Her eyes betrayed her. She had not learned the "poker face" technique as well as her Captain had taught her.

Unikala's hideous laughter rumbled before he added, "Your ultimate warrior will not stand in our way. If by chance we do meet again, he will taste the might of the Consortium. He is like your precious Tomar...doomed." He then turned and left the dark chamber, his malignant laughter echoing off the stone walls of the fortress.

Quay slumped to the floor, disoriented. If her Captain were here, she would have the strength to fight the Consortium and the Fhaal. Together they were a force against all the enemies of the quadrant. Was this a distant dream? She would have to escape Og if Tomar and the Gamadin were to survive. She crawled up the side of the wall and peered out the window. Beyond the walls, Consortium attack ships and their slow blinking running lights stood ready to defend the fortress. The low hum of their hyperdrives reverberated over the mesa, waiting for the Gamadin ship to come looking for her.

She slipped back down to the stone floor and back into her darkness. She had to think of the possibilities, not the obstacles. She had to think of a way out.

She removed the small medallion from her hair, hoping it would give her an answer. Even in the darkness the pendant's luster fought against the gloom. She had to stay strong and mentally alert if she was to carry out her plan.

71

Varmit Face

PRIGG PROVED AGAIN that he was a godsend. He saved them many hours of searching by leading them directly to the five-star accommodations right off of Palcor's main thoroughfare. As in Gibb, beings of all varieties and shapes scurried about in the crowded street, doing their business. The hotel was ideally located near the social gathering places where traders and travelers alike congregated. It was an excellent place to begin their search, according to Prigg. Looking around the immediate vicinity, Harlowe's first impression was a positive one.

"You da man, Prigg," Harlowe said appreciatively, patting the belt-high little dude on his blotchy head of hair.

"Thank you, Your Majesty," Prigg replied proudly, his eyes darting in different directions.

Harlowe tossed a small bag of what Prigg called koorants at Monday. As it turned out, koorants were a heavy metal currency that Millie had analyzed as no more than gold. She could make it by the ton if necessary. Harlowe wanted only enough to carry comfortably for a couple of days of high living. He wanted to look the part of a wealthy trader, not a schmuck from south central L.A. "Check us in, Mr. Platter, while Prigg here gives me the nickel tour."

"Aye, Captain. Do we need a view?"

"Make it first cabin, Squid; I want to see the whole city from here."

"Understood, Skipper," Monday replied, stepping through the entry.

After Monday left to register, Prigg said to Harlowe, "I am afraid that getting information about Ra-Loc may be difficult, Your Majesty."

"Why is that, Prigg?" Harlowe asked, moving off toward the plaza across the street.

"It is simply that way, Your Majesty. Traders are very secretive. It is an unwritten way of life for them, I'm afraid. For many, their pasts are confidential for fear of reprisal."

Harlowe understood. It was one of those universal truths, "honor among thieves," that was prevalent everywhere in the universe. It didn't take long for Harlowe to discover that Prigg was right and the adage was in force on Palcor as well. They weren't going to get anywhere asking about Lagan traders. The beings they met had no interest in being friendly. They cared only about their next transaction or where they had to be during the next cycle. The whereabouts of another trader was of no concern to them, not even for a sizable bribe. Harlowe decided to regroup and returned to the hotel to find Monday.

Their room was clean and furnished in a comfortable Palcorian green with a panoramic view of the city, fifty stories up. Harlowe thought he had seen every type of bed made until he tried out the antigrav one in his room. When he pressed the button, a low-intensity light filled a rectangular-shaped area two feet off the floor. Prigg explained that if the shape was undesirable, one could mold it the way one wanted by stretching the edges. Easily accommodating resting spaces was necessary because of the many different requirements of the alien visitors to the city.

Harlowe hesitated, wondering if it was safe to sit down. He felt as if he would fall right through the low-intensity light.

"Please, Your Majesty, it is quite harmless," Prigg said, sitting himself down on the edge of the beam. Amazingly, he did not fall through. "You see, it is very comfortable," and leaned back with hands behind his head.

Harlowe hesitantly lowered himself onto the field. "Not bad." He bounced up and down a couple of times, testing its stability. "That's so sick...," he added as he looked over at Prigg, who was about ready to nod off.

"Prigg," Harlowe snapped, nudging his little assistant away from the bed. "This one's mine. You're not sleeping with me." Prigg's eyes darted off in their usual comical positions, searching for equilibrium. "Get your own bed."

"Of course, Your Majesty," Prigg replied, scooting himself off the edge of the beam. "I'm in the next room," he pointed with his portside eye.

Harlowe kicked his shoes off and lay back, stretching his legs. "Close the door when you go."

They got four hours of rest. Then, for the next three Earth days (Palcor had no day-night cycles), they wandered throughout the city, hanging out at the many gathering places they thought would attract someone like Ra-Loc. These were not places where you would take a date, but if you wanted to hire a hit man or a greedy Lagan trader, these were places to search. This seemed more promising than milling about the plaza. The beings they met in these places more often than not had many of the same seedy human characteristics as Ra-Loc. To no one's surprise, they had no trouble finding beings who knew Ra-Loc. His reputation was quite well known. Without exception, every being they met had nothing positive to say about the

Lagan trader. It seemed Ra-Loc had no redeeming qualities. Leads on Ra-Loc's whereabouts, however, were not forthcoming. Traders knew who he was, but as in the plaza, no one offered Harlowe any information on the Lagan's location, especially since many of them wanted to kill him themselves first. Ra-Loc, as Harlowe had already discovered, was a marked man, one who always covered his tracks well. He came and went and never stayed around long enough for anyone to trace his movements or activities. By the end of the third day, Harlowe became discouraged and expressed his intention to move on to another city-module.

"We're getting nowhere, Prigg," Harlowe said, shaking his head. It had been a long day of false hopes and dead ends. Harlowe was about to pack it in when a varmit-faced being motioned for them to cross the street and come to him.

Harlowe shrugged, glancing at Monday for a second opinion.

Monday returned a *what-do-we-have-to-lose* shrug of his own and said, "It's a trap, Dog."

Harlowe's mouth twisted with a no-doubt smirk. "Yeah, if we're lucky."

* * *

"Are you Harlowe Pylott?" the sinister being no taller than Prigg asked as they walked up to him.

Harlowe had a question of his own. "Who wants to know?"

"I have information for Harlowe Pylott only."

Harlowe felt his stomach gnaw. "Yeah, I'm Pylott. You know about a fat toad named Ra-Loc?"

Varmit Face motioned. "I know him. Follow me."

Harlowe caught Prigg's worried, wayward eyes. "Yeah, we know, Prigg. Stay alive," he cautioned as he strode off, following their lead.

Prigg's eyes froze. He had every intention of staying alive, but following this sleazy creature was no way to find the Lagan trader. Reluctantly, with his large eyes searching independently every shadowy nook and crevice along the street at once, he fell into step behind Harlowe.

The three of them followed the contact for several blocks down the busy Palcor avenue until the creature turned down a narrow, deserted alleyway. It reminded Harlowe of the back alley on Gibb where they'd first met Ra-Loc and his grogan. He stopped at the entrance and watched the figure continue on, motioning for them to keep up. It was times like these that Harlowe wished he had Molly and Rhud, or one chinneroth named Mowgi, tagging along for backup.

"Stay here, Prigg. That worm is going to try and nuke us when we walk in there and we don't want you in the way," Harlowe explained.

Prigg didn't have to be asked twice. "Yes, Your Majesty. I'll wait here," the little Naruckian agreed, extremely relieved.

With that, Harlowe and Monday spread themselves apart and cautiously went forward into the dark alley. When they arrived at the point where he'd last seen the contact, Varmit Face was gone, mysteriously vanishing somewhere in the shadows. They looked around in the low light. All was eerily silent. It wasn't long before they were joined by a dozen large figures who surrounded them both and blocked their way back out of the alley.

"Harlowe Pylott?" a hollow voice asked.

"Where's Ra-Loc?" Harlowe countered.

"He's not your concern," another voice responded.

"He's my only concern, worm. Where is he?" Harlowe inquired angrily as Monday cringed. Harlowe always had a way of making himself clear. "I want to know where that fat toad is right now."

"Enough talk, Pylott, you're coming with us," the first voice demanded.

Harlowe didn't budge. "Where's Ra-Loc, puke?"

The shadows started tightening their circle around Harlowe and Monday. The one who had been talking sprang at Harlowe at the same moment three others tried to take out Monday. A tiny gasp of fright came back from the street. The Gamadin were ready. Harlowe's opened hand struck the voice across the bridge of the nose, sending parts of his skull back into his brain while breaking his neck backwards. The three coming after Monday found similar fates. His assailants' lives twitched a moment longer as the heel of Monday's foot caved in a chest. A straight arm snapped the neck of the second, and the third's jaw broke from a lethal shot to the face. Harlowe elminated two more with little effort, sending their ribs through their hearts and lungs before the rest of the assailants fled the alley. Monday had one more in his grip, and was about to take his head for a 360-degree spin when Harlowe cried out, "No, Squid!"

Monday stopped.

"I need one alive," Harlowe said as he walked over to Monday. "He can't help us if he's dead."

Monday released his captive. Harlowe then lifted the semiconscious body in the air and slammed the pestilence against the wall. He was about to get his answers when an orange bolt flashed out of nowhere. Monday went down like a fallen stone.

"Squid!" Harlowe dropped the assailant and rushed to Monday's aid. He couldn't tell if he was alive or dead. He didn't see any plas wounds anywhere.

"He's alive," a cool voice said.

Harlowe turned to the voice and two more dark silhouettes emerged from the cracks, stepping over bodies as they walked.

"You are the best I've ever seen, Pylott," a tall, slender figure said.

Harlowe didn't reply as he waited for the new arrivals to come closer. This new being had more poise than the previous group of assailants. He was more guarded than the others, too, but more importantly, the dude had a weapon pointed right at Harlowe's gut.

"I've heard you are also fast with a pistol," the tall figure continued. "Killing five, or was it closer to eight, Murrins while they still had their weapons on you. Impressive. That's mighty fast, Pylott, yes, mighty fast," he emphasized.

"Hand me a pistol, toad, and you can see for yourself," Harlowe countered calmly.

The new arrival continued his slow gait around Harlowe, assessing him at a respectful distance. He would not make the same mistake the others made before him. "I think not," the tall figure replied. He motioned with the point of his weapon for Harlowe to step back. "I would do as I say. I've seen how fast you are but I don't think even you are faster than my stunner. Now move," he ordered sternly.

Harlowe followed instructions and stepped back, recognizing the second being as the Varmit Face who'd led him into the alley. He also had a stunner and never took his eyes off Harlowe while the tall figure checked the bodies.

"They were my best employees," the tall figure said, making a smacking noise with his lip, "and you killed them like they were amateurs." There seemed to be no malice in his tone, only respect for Harlowe's ability. He checked the last body Harlowe had pinned to the wall and was surprised to find him alive. "He lives?"

"Information," Harlowe replied, straightforward. He felt there was little reason to be coy about anything, especially with this street-wise being.

The tall figure faced Harlowe again, still at a secure distance. "Makes sense."

"Do you know Ra-Loc?" Harlowe asked.

"I know the Lagan," the figure replied sourly.

"Good. Then tell me where he is and I'll let you live," Harlowe said.

The figure snickered. "Ra-Loc's whereabouts is unimportant. It's you I want."

"Me? Why? I don't know you," Harlowe stated.

"You have a very high price on your head, Pylott, and I mean to collect it," the tall figure replied coolly.

Harlowe let out a small laugh. "You don't say? Since when did I become a rock star?"

"Since someone put a hundred million koorants on your head."

Harlowe was genuinely surprised, wondering what he had done to deserve such a sizable bounty. "Imagine that."

The tall figure was through chatting and motioned with his stunner to proceed down the alley.

Harlowe stayed put, daring the tall figure to come closer.

Click into black!

72

Escape

It was the middle of the night on Og, dark, cold, and smelling of moldy stone walls. Quay lay quietly on her bed of rags, pretending to sleep until her guards made their last round of inspections before morning. For the last three nights until dawn, she had activated her medallion and practiced crawling and scaling the walls inside her cell with her SIBA. She felt comfortable and refreshed after each outing, as the Gamadin suit immediately began replenishing the bodily nourishment she needed to maintain her strength. The vile food and water the guards gave her went untouched. When they weren't looking, she tossed it out her window to make them think she was eating. She did not want the guards to become suspicious of her nightly forays. Soon she felt she could venture out to find her sister. Sizzle couldn't be too far away, she thought. Tonight she planned to leave her cell and locate her sister's cell. Once she made contact, they would work together and plan their escape.

She waited another long hour before she made any attempt to move.

The night was dark everywhere on the moonless planet. It was the perfect setting for anyone wishing to slither along the fortress wall without being seen.

She touched the face of her Gamadin medallion. Instantly, as it had the previous nights, the impervious fibrous fabric engulfed her.

439

Now she could see clearly in the darkest night as though she were under the midday suns of Omini Prime. Almost instantly she felt the suit's regenerative resources kick in. Her cold, stiff joints became warm and flexible. She took a long breath of filtered air as her body felt the flow of energy from the life-sustaining fluids pulsing through her veins.

After confirming that all was well with her suit, she removed a small device from the side of her utility belt. She cradled the small device with care as though it was as dear to her as the ring she had given Harlowe back on Gibb.

What is it? she had asked Harlowe the first time he had shown it to her back on #2.

A 54th-century Swiss Army knife, he grinned, holding it up for her to examine.

Quay remembered looking at him as if he were making fun of her again. He took the tarnished gold-colored device and opened it up, showing her all the miniature features inside.

Harlowe eyed the device the way guys do when they're showing off one of their favorite tools. He pointed at the many tiny devices inside the small case. *That's a knife. That's a drill. From the end of the drill you can make a torch. Watch!* He pressed a tiny button on the side and a small blue light shot out from the end of the drill's tip. *Pretty sick, huh? Then if you twist this around and pull this out like this,* he said, extending a clip of the pendant into a six-inch bar, *and attach the other end, the disk, to something solid. You've got a rope!* Harlowe smiled back, satisfied. *Don't let its thinness fool ya. This is rad. The thread is tough as bat doo-doo,* he told her.

Finally, he placed the pendant at her feet, showing her the coolest part of the gizmo. He nudged her over the pendant and instructed, *put your hands at your side and step on it.*

Quay hesitated. *I don't want to harm your gift.*

You won't hurt it. It's bulletproof.

Bulletproof?

Just step on it, Quay, you can't hurt it!

She did. At that instant, a strange, wispy veil surrounded her entire body and swallowed her up. She blinked once and opened her eyes. Incredibly, the jumpsuit she was wearing was replaced by a malleable, thin outer covering.

What is it? she asked, touching her arms.

A SIBA. You're a real Gamadin lady in this, girl. It keeps you warm and protects you from hostile environments. It's the coolest thing in 54th century tech, trust me. It even allows you to see in the darkest night. Look, he said touching his side with his hand, *when you do this you sprout wings. Now you can glide like a bird in the thinnest atmosphere. Cool, huh?*

At the time Harlowe was explaining the suit to her, she was more thrilled by the fact that it was a gift from her Captain than in it's being something useful. That it might save her life one day didn't cross her mind. Before he finished with the lesson, they were kissing. She forgot almost everything he had told her, until now. Fortunately she had a good memory. With a little practice from the previous nights, she felt reassured she could break out of the foot-thick stone walls and the two-inch diameter, case-hardened metal bars that blocked her way to the outside world.

Remembering her Captain's lessons, she took the device between her fingers and snapped the diminutive torch nozzle into place. She pressed the sides of the device exactly as he'd showed her, and a small, needle-thin line of blue light appeared. She then pointed the end of the nozzle at the heavy chain around her ankle and squeezed. The chain split in two as easily as Tomarian pudding being cut by a warm knife.

She stared for a moment in awe. It was almost too simple! Gathering confidence, she looked up at the high window in the wall, and with her dura-metal claws, easily crawled up the side of the stone wall to the window and looked out. Miles off to the horizon, lit up by their landing platforms, a squadron of Consortium attack fighters rested silently with their engines off. If she and Sizzle could get past the fortress walls to one of the ships, they had a chance to escape the planet. They would try to stop her. Once she was in the cockpit, she was certain she could fight her way back from the frontier and warn her Captain.

After cutting her way through the bars, Quay soundlessly pulled herself through the window and clung to the side of the massive keep wall like an insect. Outside, a thirty-knot wind was whistling past, doing what it could to blow her off the side of the wall. Her claws held fast, however. When she looked down, she almost lost it when she saw the angular spiked rocks jutting up from the ground five hundred feet below her. A few yards away, the rock spears fell away to a sheer 14,000-foot dropoff. She wondered briefly what she had gotten herself into and decided the best way to cope with her anxiety was simply not to look down. If they had to make the descent, she wondered whether the line would be long enough. She glanced at her small device and smiled. *Wishful thinking,* she told herself. *Of course not, silly!* If they could make it to one of the Consortium ships, the length of the line would hardly matter.

She was glad she had spent the time in her cell to become proficient with her SIBA. Crawling up and down the stone embattlements was effortless. She leaped back to the window and pulled herself through to look around. On both sides of her cell were more windows like hers. Since she had no idea where her sister was located, she had no choice but to check every window until she found Sizzle. If it took a hundred nights of searching, she would not leave the fortress or the planet without her.

A loose stone broke away and dropped to the ground. An alert guard trotted along the rampart and stared directly at her through a shoulder-wide merlon while she hung defenseless out in the open. Strangely, the guard pointed his weapon down the wall but didn't shoot. Quay waited anxiously for the guard to see her and blast her from the side of the wall, but nothing happened. One merlon after another, he looked between the gaps before he finally grunted satisfaction that nothing was amiss and returned to his post.

Quay let out a huge sigh, wondering why the guard had completely missed her. Was she invisible to the guard? She stared down at her hands and arms, and discovered another Swiss Army quality of the SIBA—stealth.

Taking no chances that she might not be as fortunate a second time, she hurried along the outside wall tower of the central keep, like a curious spider, peering into each window as she went along. It was almost daylight when she was ready to give up her search for the night. Crawling along the lowest level of the castle to avoid the changing of the guard, she found her. Quay didn't believe it was possible that Sizzle's cell chamber could be more disease-ridden than hers. Sizzle was shackled to heavy irons against the wall, seemingly oblivious of the rodents biting at her feet and ankles. She was bruised and bloody like before. Unikala had been good on his threat. Quay wanted to cry, search out Unikala, and kill him instantly wherever he was in the keep. *Such wickedness! How could someone be so evil and live? It's not right!*

Fighting to keep her cool, she gathered her wits and in an instant, cut through the bars, slid through, and made her way to her sister's side. Inside the chamber, she sliced through the horde of rats with her torch, her claws, and her feet. The rats tried in vain to fight back, but they couldn't break through the tough fibers of her suit. Once Quay had wiped out the rats, she sliced through Sizzle's manacles and laid her on the floor.

"Your medallion? Where is it, Sizzle?" Quay asked, searching the cell with her enhanced vision. Sizzle tried to fight her off. She thought Quay was another guard slapping her. Quay grabbed her flailing arms and held her down as she spoke to her in slow, comforting words. "It is okay, Sizzle. It is me, Quay." Sizzle was too weak to put up much of a struggle. When she opened her eyes, the struggle began anew with even more energy. Quay grabbed her sister bodily and held her close, continuing her comforting words until Sizzle decompressed in her arms, too exhausted to resist.

Quay, seeing the problem, pulled the top of her SIBA down from around her head. "Sizzle, it is me, Quay. I am here for you."

"Quay?" Sizzle murmured weakly as she focused on Quay's warm eyes. She was barely able to stay conscious and drifted in and out of lucidity.

"Where is your medallion? Do you have your necklace?" she asked again.

Fighting to stay conscious, Sizzle lifted her finger, and with great effort pointed at the heavy cell door.

Quay thought she understood. "The guard has your medallion? Is that right, Sizzle?"

All Sizzle had the strength for was a slight nod.

Her plan was not going smoothly. If she and Sizzle stood any chance of escape, she needed Sizzle's medallion.

Quay laid Sizzle back down on the floor to find the guard with the medallion when the sound of heavy footsteps and laughter came toward the heavy door. From the sound of their voices, the guards were drinking and coming back for another late night of fun beating up her sister, a girl of privilege.

The bolt of the heavy door slid back with a loud clank.

73

The Line

"NEW ONE," THE angelic voice called.

The voice sounded to Riverstone like it was far away. He wanted nothing to do with anyone. He ignored the voice and remained motionless, hoping whoever it was would go away and leave him alone.

"New One. It's time."

Riverstone had plenty of sleep left in him. During his exhaustive sleep he had convinced himself that his arrival on Erati was a bad dream. When he opened his eyes, he would see his bedroom on the ship with Molly and Rhud putting their noses in his face, trying to wake him.

"New One, wake up. It is time for work period to begin," the frail voice persisted. The voice had moved closer and someone was touching him, shaking him awake.

"Go away," Riverstone growled. "Let me sleep."

"You must awaken. Work period is near and we must be at our stations or Dagger will punish us," the voice warned.

Riverstone's eyes flew open. "Dagger" was the word that shocked him back to reality. He reached up and felt the heavy iron braces around his ankles. It was not a bad dream after all. It was a horrible nightmare, and he was still in it!

Riverstone stared at Ela's frightened face. "You are real."

Ela had no clue as to what Riverstone was talking about. Her worry was immediate and she didn't have time to explain. She pulled him to his feet and urged him forward down the mine shaft.

Riverstone had only enough time to scoop a couple of fast gulps of water before they dashed down the dark cavern tunnel to the line. If they did not make it to the line before the whistle, Dagger would make sure he paid the consequences. Ela would be punished too because she had helped him.

He ran faster. He couldn't let that happen. He ran on, forgetting the pain in his muscles. *No, it wasn't her fault, Dagger! Don't punish her for something that wasn't her fault!*

There was no one left sleeping in the mine shafts as Ela and Riverstone ran through the empty cave toward their places on the stonecutters' line. The corridors were empty. Not a soul was left anywhere in the outer caverns. There was no excuse good enough for being tardy, not even for second, unless you were dead.

As they ran along, Ela handed Riverstone morsels of food. "Eat, New One. It is all that I have."

Riverstone had no time to thank her. All he could do was stuff whatever food she had given him in his mouth and swallow. The substance was uncertain, while its smell was even less appealing. It made no difference to him at this point. He stuffed the slimy mass down his throat without thinking. It was nourishment, and that was all that mattered. He was still chewing when he found his place on the line and the whistle blew.

Dagger hovered over Riverstone as he picked up his hammer and started hitting the stone. "You were fortunate this time, thrall," Dagger yelled in his ear above the relentless pounding.

Riverstone kept his eyes forward. He did not want to give Dagger any excuse to strike him. He struck the rock with his hammer like a good slave, attending only to the work. It was not in Dagger's nature, however, to allow his line to think Riverstone had gotten by unnoticed, and he struck the side of Riverstone's face with the butt of his whip.

The muscles in Riverstone's jaws knotted, feeling the urge to kill his tormentor in a heartbeat, but eliminating Dagger was not the answer. There were too many other Daggers waiting to take his place. He knew what he had to do was survive. He had to recover, lay low, and get his strength back until he could take control of the situation. He had to be ready for that moment when he *could* escape. When he was ready, once he knew where he was and what he was up against, once he knew his enemy, he would then deal with the situation. *Restrain yourself, Gamadin,* he heard the General's voice caution him. *Don't let your enemy's pleasure keep you from focusing on what you need to do.*

Escape!

Thinking of the future enabled him to survive. Riverstone obediently picked up his hammer and began pounding away at the stone like an obedient thrall. Dagger grunted approvingly. He had made his point. His hulking shadow plodded off down the line, looking for someone else to feed upon. Riverstone wondered how many more "next times" it would take before Dagger would push him too far.

74

Break Out

QUAY HAD ALREADY climbed to the stone ceiling by the time the three drunken guards entered the cell. She left Sizzle lying on the floor. She didn't have time move her out of harm's way. Had she done that, she would have lost the element of surprise. Seeing Sizzle lying on the floor unshackled among the hordes of dead rats stopped the three drunkards cold in their tracks. That moment of hesitation allowed Quay to drop from her perch and slam the three to the ground. Two were knocked out instantly when she smashed their faces against the stone floor. The third bounced off the sidewall momentarily stunned. He had expected to torture the daughter of Tomar-Rex; what he got instead was darkness when Quay delievered an upward kick to the jaw. He collapsed and didn't move, his head bent to the side in an unnatural pose of death.

As the guard fell, there was the clank of ringing metal hitting the stone floor. A bright yellow disk had fallen from his pocket and rolled out onto the floor. It was the medallion.

Quay quickly scooped it up and placed it under Sizzle, activating the SIBA. Within moments, her sister's body was engulfed by the Gamadin device.

There was no time to check whether the suit was working. Heavy footsteps were charging toward the cell, having heard the commotion. There would be more to follow, many more, she knew. If they were to survive, she had to fight them all. It was the only course open to her, and Sizzle was in no shape yet to move on her own. She was alone.

Outside the door, she found a weapon left on a nearby bench. Obviously, the drunkards had not figured on Sizzle giving them any trouble. Before anyone arrived, Quay shot out the overhead lights. Around the corner, a half-dozen other guards came to a sudden stop inside the darkened corridor. They couldn't see her but she could see them, clear as day. She owned the darkness. As they charged into the outer security chamber, she plucked them off in rapid succession, dropping them all before they knew what hit them.

She heard more guards coming, but they were far off. The sound of the plas shots had awakened the garrison. A heavy door on the level above her swung open. She stole an extra moment to snatch a fresh weapon from a fallen guard and ran back to Sizzle. Beams of light were already filtering their way down into the outer chambers. They wouldn't have much time. "We must move, Sizzle," she urged as she lifted her from behind and stood her on her feet.

As miraculous as the SIBA was at reviving a near-dead Gamadin, the suit needed time to work its magic on a common being. "Quay..." Sizzle mumbled faintly. "Is it you?"

"Yes, I am here, Sizzle. You have a suit around you. You will be better, but we must go. The guards are coming. Can you walk?"

She nodded feebly. "I will try."

Quay tried to guide Sizzle toward the window, but the guards were already in the outer chamber. They would be in the cell in seconds. The moment the guards broke into the cell, it would be over for them.

Quay remembered the earlier incident of the guard looking down at her from the top of the wall. She quickly pulled Sizzle to the side and whispered into her ear, "Be quiet as a chee, Sizzle. The suit will hide us, but we must be still. Do you understand?"

Before Sizzle could answer, the guards entered the cell. Beams of light struck out like knives through the darkness as Quay and Sizzle stayed flat against the wall. At first the beams waved frantically, searching for anything that moved. A frightened guard shot a rat as it scampered to find its hole. Another guard kicked other dead ones out of the way on the floor with disgust. "Where did she go?" a guard shouted angrily. "She couldn't have gotten past us!" another said. A beam of light focused on the upper window of the chamber. "There!" he shouted. "The bars have been cut! Look, Captain, she has escaped through the window." Then a beam went around the room again, ever so slowly, passing them by as if they were part of the wall. "Incompetent dogs!" the captain shouted, staring down at the broken bodies. "Unikala will have our heads for this." He turned his beam back to the door. "Sound the alarm! She can't be far."

The guards then double-timed it out of the chamber, their beams of light dancing through the darkness as they left.

"Come, Sizzle, we must hurry," Quay said, holding her sister so she wouldn't fall.

"Quay, the Consortium battlecruisers are all here. What is going on? Why have they gathered here on Og?" Sizzle wondered in a sudden panic.

"I know. I have seen them. They are waiting for the Gamadin to come and save us, but it is a trap."

"Rerun!" Sizzle cried out, the fear of losing her Gamadin soldier evident in her voice.

Quay held her close, comforting her. "We must find a way to warn them."

Sizzle turned to Quay. She was feeling stronger. The SIBA was working overtime. "You have a plan, Quay?" she asked, hopeful.

"A slim one. Attack fighters are close by. We must try and take one."

"Their range is short. We couldn't possibly make it to Tomar in a fighter," Sizzle pointed out.

"Patol is not far, well within range of a Consortium attack fighter."

Quay did not have to see behind her sister's bugeyes to know she was worried about her Gamadin soldier. "Do you think they are still alive?" Sizzle asked.

Quay cradled Sizzle's head in both her hands. "It will take more than the Consortium to kill our Gamadin warriors, my sister."

Strength was returning to Sizzle's body as they embraced. "I know you're right, Quay, I have seen their power."

"As have I, sister."

The sound of a blaring siren turned Quay toward the door. "We must hurry then and find our way off this forsaken planet so we can warn the Gamadin of Unikala's treachery with the Fhaal."

Sizzle's first few steps were shaky, but as she kept walking, her strength improved with each stride. By the time they made it to the outer chambers of the dungeon, Sizzle knew she could run if she had to. On the way out of the chamber, Sizzle grabbed a weapon for herself. More sounds of heavy boots and barking orders intermixed with the continuous blare of the sirens as they made their way toward the outside walls of the keep. Along the way, Quay didn't have time to give Sizzle instructions on how to use her SIBA, instead using short phrases like, "Be still and they won't see you," and "Use your claws to grip the stone." It was "learn-as-you-go" and "hope-for-the-best." If they stayed hidden and avoided the searching guards, they had a chance of making it past the outer walls to the landing pads where the attack ships were kept. Speed was as essential as stealth. Instead of moving along the walkways and footpaths of the fortress on a direct route to the ships, they kept to the darkest crevices of the battlements, avoiding the guards who were looking for two women on the ground.

From their place on the wall they could view their objective clearly. The blunt noses of the Consortium ground ships were not far from the outer walls of the fortress. The main gate, however, was packed with guards searching the grounds with heat detectors. The SIBAs protected them from anyone looking at them, but Quay was unsure if the suits hid them from probing sensors as well. She didn't want to find out. "We have to go around, Sizzle," Quay said to her sister. "We can't get through this way. We must find another way."

Sizzle understood the problem and inched her way above a parapet to get a better view of the fortress layout. When she poked her head inside the merlon, a guard came from out of nowhere and stared at her, eyeball-to-eyeball. At first the guard's expression was amazement at seeing another head poking up on the wrong side of the stone gap. His face quickly changed to panic when he suddenly realized he was looking straight at an inhuman form with large, bulging eyes. He pointed his weapon at the bug's face and was about to pull the trigger, when the thing reached across the merlon and pulled him through the gap and over the side. The scream of the falling guard alerted everyone within earshot. Quay joined Sizzle on the wall-walk and they ran. Several more guards met them along the way, but all were caught by surprise by the appearance of two inhuman beings. Everyone was searching for tall and beautiful Tomarian women; no one was expecting stealthy invaders who moved invisibly through the night like shadowy wraiths. Quay and Sizzle quickly disposed of the two guards, yanking them over the walls like they had the others.

When the beams of light and heat detectors flooded the battlements, Quay and Sizzle jumped off the wall-walk to an adjacent tower and clung to the stone sides. They raced along the circular walls, avoiding windows and catwalks until they came to the far side of the tower. From there, they jumped to another wall and discovered to their dismay that they were now close to the main keep where they first began. "This way," Quay called out above the plasfire around the fortress. Every guard was firing willy-nilly at anything that moved. She knew where she was. If they could get to the backside of the keep, there was another way out. Making it to the Consortium ships this way was suicide. They had no chance of getting past the outer wall and the landing pads without being detected. As her Gamadin Captain would say, it was time for "Plan B."

By now, the Consortium guards understood what they were looking for—not defenseless women but deadly ghosts that clung to walls. On the opposite side of the compound, wispy green beams of light were scanning the same walls they had just crawled across. Gone were the focused beams of white searchlights. Once they were located with the green beams of light, the batteries of auto plasguns would lock onto their body signatures and that would be the end of the ghosts.

"Follow me," Quay urged. She grabbed the end of a stone outcropping and leaped twenty feet in the air, sticking to the back corner of the main keep. Below she saw the stone spears. If Sizzle missed, she would fall and impale herself on the rocks hundreds of feet below. "Do it now!" Quay yelled at her. As she did, a green beam of light found her. A hot bolt shot out of somewhere across the other side of the compound. But Sizzle was quick. An instant before the plas-bolt struck her, she leaped the chasm. As the bolt of green fire exploded on the opposite wall, Quay grabbed her by the arm, bringing her in. After that, they scampered around the corner just before another bolt nearly found them, bursting huge chunks of the keep away from the stone wall.

"Where are we going?" Sizzle yelled as they moved along.

"To our only chance," Quay replied.

Sizzle let out a small laugh. "We have a chance?"

"Always," Quay replied. She turned around and glanced back at the keep. Unikala was on the roof, looking down at them with his disfigured arm waving frantically, shouting commands at the frazzled guards. She turned back to Sizzle the moment they jumped up onto a parapet and looked down. Sizzle gasped and hung on to Quay, staring at the fourteen-thousand-foot drop off and trusting that her sister knew what she was doing.

Before Sizzle had a chance to think, Quay grabbed her hand and jumped.

75

Lormagan

THERE WERE TWO dozen giant agri-modules in the Palcor system, each nearly the size of the island of Kauai back on Earth. Plants gave Palcor its air, food, and water. Without them, the food supply and atmospheric gases would need constant replenishment from external sources. Three-quarters of the agri-modules were used for food production while the remaining six, like the one where Harlowe had been taken, were unattended and allowed to grow into a dense, untouched jungle. Unlike the city-modules, the agri-modules had day and night cycles, because the plants could not survive without periods of alternating days and nights.

Upon awakening, Harlowe's first conscious thought was of the throbbing pain inside his head. "I feel like a toad," he groaned. That was the second time in a month he had been hit with a stunner and it was making him mad. Beyond the pain, he heard the sounds of birds singing nearby and some wild animal calling to its mate. He tried to move his arms and legs, but felt the resistance the manacles gave his wrists and ankles. Finally, after a long moment of self-inflicted suffering, he opened his eyes and discovered he was chained to a large tree trunk. Dim, ambient light filtered down through the thick jungle canopy above him. Whether it was the morning side or twilight side of the agri-module's cycle, he could only guess. More relevant to his situation were the two very attentive guards staring at him a few feet

456

away, their stunners pointed right at his face. Looking farther, flexing his muscles to bring the circulation back to his limbs, he saw a small hut with a dim light glowing through the window. He remembered the alley, the tall thin figure, and the brief conversation he had with him before he was zapped. They, whoever they were, wanted him. They were willing to pay big bucks to get him, too. Why? He could understand why they wanted Quay. Her father would give a planet to have her back. But him? Why would anyone want him on Palcor? He had been here only a short time, not nearly enough time to cause any trouble, he figured.

Harlowe stared at his two watchdogs and asked them if he was allowed one phone call. The two said nothing. Harlowe hadn't really expected an answer, but it gave him a way to pass the time while his mind tried to calculate a way out of this mess. The jungle was so thick, and he had no clue as to where he was.

Turning to his right, he saw Monday chained to another tree trunk. His chin was resting against his chest and he was snoring loud enough to keep any wild beasts from entering the camp.

"Squid!" Harlowe called over to Monday. "Wake up. You're killing me." His head was about to explode, but Monday wouldn't wake up.

After several more angry shouts, one of the guards stepped over to Monday, obviously tired of hearing Harlowe's whining, and struck his side with the muzzle of his stunner. That did the trick. Harlowe was eternally grateful. "Thanks, butthead. You did the jungle a great service."

Stepping back to his place, the guard said to the other, "Get Lormagan. Tell him his prizes have awakened."

The second guard went inside the hut and returned with the tall, familiar figure he had met in the alley. Harlowe recognized the lanky shape the instant he stepped out of the hut.

"Ah, you are with us now, Pylott," Lormagan said. His voice was cheery and upbeat. His face had a friendly smile. His nose, legs, arms, and fingers were all extraordinarily long. He had short black hair, bright green eyes, and dark skin. He stood a head taller than Harlowe's six-foot-nine height, yet he probably weighed no more than half Harlowe's weight. Lormagan was quite thin. His clothing was like the rest of his motley band: leather-like breeches, loose brown shirt open at the neck with lace eyelets down the middle to keep it together. His feet had tight-fitting, sock-like shoes. His walk was as unhurried as his unassuming demeanor. He didn't appear to be trying to prove he was better than those around him. He seemed simple and straightforward, honest even. Under different circumstances, Harlowe thought he could have liked Lormagan. "How are you feeling?"

"I could use a chocolate shake," Harlowe said, his face looking like he had pulled an all-nighter.

Lormagan ignored his request and said, "We just received word that they have landed and soon I will be a hundred million koorants richer." Lormagan's tone had the sweet sound of success attached to it, and his face glowed with self-congratulatory pride.

Harlowe smiled back, not wishing to rain on Lormagan's parade . . . just yet. "You da man, Lory."

"Are you always this arrogant and rude?" Lormagan asked.

"You just shot me with your stunner and I'm stuck to a tree. How do you expect me to feel?"

Lormagan smiled. "Bravo, Pylott, you have a point. Life as a prize does have its downside, it seems."

Since Lormagan and he seemed to be hitting it off, Harlowe decided to take advantage of his captor's overconfidence and outward friendliness by asking a few questions. "So who's paying the big bucks?"

Lormagan crossed his arms in front of him, keeping a respectable distance away. "You really don't know, do you?"

"I haven't a clue," Harlowe conceded with a yawn, acting the part.

"Why, someone from the Tomar High Command, of course."

"Tomar?" Harlowe shot back.

"You look shocked."

"I am." He was, too. "I was trying to help them."

Now it was Lormagan's turn to be surprised. "You? Help Tomar? Why? They need no one's help."

"Why do you say that?"

"Because Anor Ran is too cunning. He is a decendant of Jo-Li Ran, the quadrant's greatest man of trade and commercial exchange."

"I know the type."

"Are you new to the quadrant, Pylott? You sound like it."

"I'm a quick study."

Lormagan's face twisted with confusion over Harlowe's use of earthly slang. "The Consortium would never attack Tomar. They are allies, not enemies. Their relationship is symbiotic. Their mutual interests give power to the other. To cut one arm off would cut the other's arm."

"Maybe the right arm figures he can get along just fine without the left. You need to Google the recent news flashes from Gibb. The Consortium tried to kill Anor Ran and his family last month. Made a big mess of his building."

"I heard about the raid."

"Yeah, well, a Consortium commander by the name of Unikala and Anor's toadfaced son—"

"Toadface? Tomar-Rex's son is Turfan."

Harlowe grinned with a chuckle. "Grogan waste. He's a gomer."

Lormagan laughed. "Ah, I get it. A jest. Yes, he is grogan waste. What did you call him?"

"A gomer."

"Gomer. I like the sound of the word." He repeated the word several more times until he got the correct sound that he wanted. Then he said, "I like you, Pylott. You make me laugh. Too bad there is such a large price for you. We would have a good drink together."

Harlowe kept trying to make sense out of everything as he continued the interrogation of Lormagan and returned the compliment. "Yeah, I like you, too, beanstalk. You're a real slap-on-the-back kinda guy."

"They say your ship destroyed a Consortium battlecruiser. Is that true?"

Harlowe smiled. "We got lucky."

Lormagan was stunned. "I find that impossible to believe."

"Does a dude named Unikala ring a bell?"

Lormagan's face went slack. "You're running with some pretty bad company, Pylott..." Lormagan's voice trailed as though he had just thought of something. "Yes. I remember now. There was word of late that a space battle had taken place about that time. It was thought to be space gossip, but it was said that a single ship destroyed a fleet of Consortium attack ships. Was that you?"

"Release me, Lory, before I have to end our beautiful friendship."

There was a mixture of fear and renewed respect on Lormagan's face as he stepped back. "You're Gamadin?"

"Maybe."

"They were only legend."

Harlowe said nothing. It looked as though whatever Lormagan knew of the Gamadin was enough to shock him more than words could say.

Lormagan let out a low whistle. "If I had known that, I would have tripled my premium." He whistled again, jumping up and down like a man holding a winning million-dollar lottery ticket. "It all makes sense now. The way you killed my best guards so easily. Only a Gamadin could kill with such ferocity. Yes, it makes sense now."

"So you'll let me go," Harlowe suggested lightheartedly.

Lormagan laughed. "I admit, Pylott, if I had known who you were at first, I would have had second thoughts about capturing you. But," he smiled, his grin now twice the self-satisfied width it was a few moments ago, "since you're here, I might as well make the best of the situation; like a billion golden koorants will do, for starters." Lormagan looked away, shaking his head. "Trying to pull one over on old Lormagan, huh? Well, we'll see about that!"

"There's an old saying where I come from," Harlowe informed Lormagan.

"And it is?"

Harlowe glanced over to Monday with a wry smile. "Tell him, Mr. Platter."

"Pigs get slaughtered, dude," Monday replied, his face also looking haggard.

Lormagan paid no attention to Harlowe's cheap advice. The tall bounty hunter suddenly focused on Harlowe like a gun sight. "Your ship, Gamadin?"

"My ship?"

"Yes, your ship. That is what Tomar is paying me for. Your ship. It's not you they're after. It's your ship. If indeed you are the one who destroyed the Consortium fleet, I can see why Anor Ran wants the possession so badly. A ship that can destroy so many Consortium ships is very valuable indeed." His eye went round with revelation. "So that is it! The Fhaal have joined the Consortium to take over the quadrant—"

Harlowe perked up. "The Fhaal?"

"Yes, the Fhaal. Have you heard of them?" Lormagan asked.

Harlowe nodded. "I have."

"Then you know they are unstoppable. They began eating away at the quadrant many passings ago. Little by little they have swallowed up systems until now it is said that within the next cycle of Omini Prime, they will dominate the entire quadrant. The pieces of the puzzle have been revealed."

Not to Harlowe—he saw things only in black and white. "Enlighten me, Lory, you lost me."

Lormagan took his time to answer, shaking his head with incredulity. If Harlowe could have reached him, he would have kicked him in the face to get his answer.

Lormagan said, "The Tomar-Rex is indeed Jo-Li Ran."

He chuckled, trying to restrain his logistical breakthrough. "He's paying for protection, not only from the Consortium...but the Fhaal. As strange as this may seem, your ship, Gamadin, is the centerpiece between the three powers."

Lormagan turned, walking in a thoughtful circle when another idea struck him. "A bidding war, perhaps?" He laughed greedily, unable to control his growing lust for power and money. "With Lormagan as broker. Yes, that's it. What will they bid for a ship of legend? One billion? Do I hear two? How about its infamous Captain for added value? How about ten billion koorants, gentlemen, for the chance to own the ship that will change the balance of power of the entire quadrant?"

"So that's what been going on all along! It's my ship. All these toads want my ship so they can become king of the hill, huh?" Harlowe realized aloud.

"That doesn't make sense, Captain," Monday stated flat out.

"I agree. These idiots see us as empire destroyers. If we're around they can expand their business." Harlowe tried to get Lormagan's attention focused on another subject while he was still flying high and picking out his new planet to call home.

"Have you heard anything from the Consortium about a female named Quay?"

"Anor Ran's daughter?"

"The same," Harlowe replied.

Lormagan thought briefly. He shook his head negatively, his thoughts preoccupied with counting his future wealth. "Quay, huh?"

"Turfan's sister."

Lormagan smiled knowingly. "Ah, yes, her beauty is legendary. I have also seen her sister. Many stories are spoken of her as well. Are they as beautiful as they say?"

Harlowe nodded. "Incredibly hot." Then he asked, becoming short. "Do you know if she is being held somewhere?"

"I know nothing of Quay," Lormagan replied, "nor do I care."

"What do you know about a fat toad named Ra-Loc?" Harlowe asked eagerly.

"Ra-Loc?" Lormagan echoed, his face showing obvious distaste. "You asked me that before."

"I'm still asking. Do you know where he is?"

It appeared Lormagan hated him as much as Harlowe did. "Ra-Loc. Yes, he truly is a gomer." He liked that word. "If I ever find him, he will repay his debt to me."

Harlowe cut Lormagan off. "Where is he?" He didn't feel like listening to anyone else's problems with Ra-Loc. His was quite enough.

"Nowhere." Just mentioning the Lagan's name wiped the greedy grin off Lormagan's face. "He lives nowhere. Ra-Loc cannot afford to stay long in any one place for fear of losing his wretched hide to one of his creditors."

"Do you know where he was last seen?"

Lormagan thought a moment. "The Crimoors maybe ... or Athela ..." He shook his head. "I don't know, Pylott. Ra-Loc is too sly. He never stays in one place long enough for anyone to find him."

One of Lormagan's guards stepped up and offered up a rumor. "I heard recently, Lormagan, that Ra-Loc was seen on Roshmar?" the guard volunteered.

Harlowe's eyes lit up. "Roshmar? Where is this place?"

"A deserted planet far away from Palcor. I don't know why he would be there unless he plans to travel to ..." Lormagan hesitated when he heard movement outside the clearing.

"Unless what, Lormagan? Tell me," Harlowe urged.

"Why do you worry, Pylott? Knowing Ra-Loc's whereabouts will be of little use to you now. You will excuse me. I hear my clients coming."

The crimson uniforms of Tomarian soldiers broke through the underbrush and into the clearing. Lormagan turned to greet them. They were all heavily armed with plas weapons. Undoubtedly no one had informed them of the rules against carrying weapons into Palcor.

"Welcome, friends," Lormagan said with outstretched arms. "You have come for the Gamadin? Yes."

The officer-in-charge strode forward of his advance squad with a deadly serious presence in his manner. The instant Lormagan said "Gamadin," the officer's eyes blinked as though he had not expected Lormagan to know what he had captured.

Lormagan didn't miss the officer's hesitation, either.

The officer waved his black-gloved hand for his troops to relieve Lormagan of his prisoner.

"Hold on, friend," Lormagan said, placing a cool hand on the officer's shoulder. "There's been a slight change. The merchandise stays put until we work out an agreement. This is no ordinary—"

The officer unholstered his pistol. Without a second thought, he shot Lormagan through the heart. He was dead before he hit the ground. The officer's troops then followed his lead and ruthlessly gunned down the rest of Lormagan's men where they stood. After that, the officer gave the all-clear signal to another soldier outside the clearing. A moment later Turfan stepped out of the jungle, brushing off his uniform of jungle foliage as he and a small escort marched into the clearing. After what Harlowe had just learned from Lormagan, he was beginning to feel he knew only a small fraction of Anor Ran's vast holdings. He owned entire planets, and Harlowe realized he had to think on a whole new level in order to grasp what was really happening.

"Turfan, you toad," Harlowe began, before Anor's son could speak. "Why doesn't it surprise me that I'm seeing your sorry face here?"

Turfan grabbed one of his escort's rifle-like weapons and slammed the butt end into Harlowe's gut for his impudence. Monday's face cringed. That had to hurt, but Harlowe saw it coming. The blow barely registered in his eyes. Turfan drove the butt again across Harlowe's face, drawing blood from a large gash across his jaw. Harlowe spat a wad of red at Turfan's feet. "Everyone's trying to stay on my bad side this morning." He turned back to Turfan. "You do that again, and I'll have to kill you this time. I don't care if you are Quay's brother."

Turfan was visibly shaken, like a spoiled child denied his reward. "Shut up, Gamadin! Enough of your insolent talk or I will kill you where you stand," Turfan cried angrily.

Harlowe spit red again and laughed in Turfan's face, challenging his manhood. "You're not going to kill me. You're a coward." Turfan flipped the rifle around and pointed it at Harlowe's face. "Pull that trigger and your old man will have your head on a platter. Kill me and the ship is history, puke."

Turfan hesitated, trying to peer deep into Harlowe's soul, looking for weakness. *Was he telling the truth or was he lying?* Turfan had obviously never played Texas hold 'em. Harlowe didn't flinch. His eyes were cold. Impenetrable. Backing down in the face of Death was not his style. Turfan, on the other hand, feared Death. For someone like Harlowe, exposing his fraud was easy. Turfan began to shake in his boots. His face went slack. Both Harlowe and Monday could see Turfan's troops sensing his spineless character. Boxed into a corner, unable to pull the trigger on Harlowe, who was still chained to a tree, Turfan did the only thing his cowardice would allow him.

He shot Monday.

76

Their Special Place

THE SCREECHING HIGH-PITCHED whistle ended the work period. Riverstone pried his fingers apart and let the hammer drop on the crushed rock and yellow crystals. Both his hands dripped from bleeding blisters. When the whistle blew this time, even the wall couldn't help as he struggled to his feet. There was no doubt in his mind that without Ela's help he would have died an unceremonious death before the last work period even began. Still, he felt triumph. He had survived his second round with Dagger and pounding stone. The next time he would do better, he challenged himself. His mind was thinking clearly, now that his body had sufficiently dissipated Ra-Loc's drugs in his system. Even so, without a SIBA or *Millawanda's* medical facilities, his body was weak. His Gamadin training was the only thing now that was keeping him alive. Once again, the General's harsh demands and constantly pushing them beyond their limits had proven their worth.

Ela tended to his cuts and sores and gave him food from the cart. The food was her ration, not his. Only those who were able to fend for themselves could get food from the cart. And anyone who didwas were allowed only one portion. Those were the rules. Anyone who tried to get more would be killed. Water, on the other hand, was plentiful. Underground streams flowed everywhere. Survival was possible if one knew the rules.

The food was barely edible. Riverstone closed his eyes. He was afraid if he saw the slimy mass he wouldn't eat it. He had to eat or he would cease to function. He didn't fear ingesting something harmful. Millie's innoculations had seen to that, but his immunities wouldn't help him to regenerate if he didn't eat. Escape was everything. It would be possible only if he could function both mentally and physically. He had to eat.

"Has anyone ever escaped from this hole, Ela?" Riverstone asked, as they sat next to each other along a dark abandoned tunnel away from the main digging chamber.

Ela looked at Riverstone as if he were slightly touched. "Oh, no, New One. No one has ever escaped. You must not think of such things."

"I will die here if I don't find a way out," he told her.

Her worried eyes fell upon his. "There is no escape, New One. Please, do not try. I do not want you to die." Her large, dark eyes looked as though she was about to cry.

Her answer was not surprising. The descent into the mines was considerable. Impossible, perhaps, for a normal human or a slave to think about escape, but not for a Gamadin, he thought confidently. If he didn't try, he would surely die; that much he did know. "Don't worry, Ela. I will not attempt any escape today."

Ela's tilted her head back, a little confused. "Day? What is day, New One?"

Riverstone smiled at her cuteness. "You don't know what 'day' is?" Ela shook her head negatively. "Day is day," he continued. "When the sun's out and there are no stars. It's day, like a million torches all lit up at once. You can see everything—the trees, the mountains, and the waves breaking along a long white beach."

He went on describing the world aboveground. It wasn't long before he realized for the first time that Ela had never seen a tree, a mountain, or a long white beach. Her life had always been belowground. Descriptions of life above ground were beyond her ability to visualize.

Through her crusted, dirty face, a fairness peeked out beneath the grime. He had an idea. "Come here a second, Ela." She moved over obligingly. He took the end of his shirt and wet it from a nearby cup of water. He then said to her, "Stick your chin out." As he began to wipe the dirt from her face, he asked her if she had ever washed her face before. She had never heard of the term.

"I thought so."

Riverstone continued to scrub the layers of Erati dust from her face. She seemed to like the attention and didn't mind at all the way Riverstone had to dig in with the knotted-up end of his shirt to get the deeper pores of her skin clean.

"My name is not New One, Ela," he continued. "Everyone calls me Riverstone."

Ela frowned, trying to concentrate. She wanted to get his name right. "Ri...Ri...er," she tried pronouncing with great difficulty, but sighed in frustration.

"Close. Ri-ver-stone," he corrected slowly. No matter how he tried to teach her, she could not pronounce his last name. It always came out, "Rieee-something," Finally, after a couple of awkward tries, he gave up.

Ela asked: "You have no other name?"

Riverstone thought for a moment. He had many names, several of which his mates called him whenever they were off the clock. However, he didn't feel they were worthy of Ela's innocence. "My mother calls me 'Matthew,'" he finally said.

"Maaatheew," she replied. She found his first name much easier to say.

Riverstone grinned with accomplishment. "I think we have a winner."

"That is proper? Maaathew?"

"Close enough, Ela."

After several rinses, he completed the task enough to lean back and admire his work. He was amazed at the transformation. He had gotten more than he had imagined. In the dim light was the pleasant, kind face of a surprisingly beautiful girl. Her eyes were large and sad, her mouth thin, uplifted, and small. Her turnedup nose countered any unhappiness her eyes may have displayed. Looking down, he found the rest of her equally as lovely. Her neck was smooth, slender, and graceful. Though her clothes were rags and unflattering, they could not hide her tall, lean form underneath. Riverstone grinned ear-to-ear.

In his eyes, Ela was a ten!

"You're gorgeous, Ela," Riverstone complimented, unable to take his eyes away from her. "The guys would be jealous," he beamed

"What is 'gorgeous,' Matthew?" she asked.

"You, Ela. You are gorgeous." Ela was still having difficulty with the concept of what outstanding beauty meant to a young man from Earth, so he simply explained that a gorgeous person was somebody pleasant to look at, inside and out.

She bent her head down. "I...I gor...gorgeee..." It was another difficult word for her to say. If the light had been brighter, he was sure he'd see a face flushed with a rosy color.

Riverstone pushed back a lock of her crusty hair. "Yes, Ela, you are very gorgeous."

Ela giggled. She smiled easily, and he envied her for that. He wondered how anyone could laugh, living in a place with so much cruelty and death around her. He began to cry a little and wiped a tear or two from his eyes. To take his mind away from the hopelessness, he asked, "Ela, where do you come from?"

Another puzzled look clouded her face. "Ela is from here, Matthew."

"No, Ela, I meant where did you come from before you were brought here to the mines?"

Ela thought for a moment, her confused expression even more pronounced. "Ela always from here. Not come from anywhere. Always here."

Riverstone found that difficult to believe. How could anyone be from deep inside the Erati mines? "You mean you've never been anywhere but here? You were born here?"

"Yes, Matthew, I was born here."

Riverstone's eyes widened, amazed. No wonder she didn't know what a day was. If she had never seen a star or a bright, warm sun, how would she know?

"Then you have never been to the world above or seen anything but this cavern?" he asked her.

Her face displayed no emotion. "Others who have been brought here have spoken of such a place, but I have never seen the world above, the sun of a million torches, or the stars that you speak of, Matthew."

Riverstone was stricken with sadness that anyone could live an entire life without ever spending one day aboveground. "Is it as wonderful as they say, Matthew?" she asked.

Riverstone nodded, his thoughts numb from the concept. "Oh, yes. It is a wonderful place, Ela," he replied almost mechanically. The idea that someone as noble as Ela had never seen a star was more than sad. It was cruel, beyond all that he knew. He turned to her and held her by the shoulders as he looked into her kind eyes and promised, "Someday I will show you how wonderful the world is above us. We will leave Erati together, Ela. I promise you on my life that will happen. You will see a heaven full of stars and a sun that warms you and shines bright on everything wonderful around you."

"Stars, Matthew?" Ela wondered.

He looked up as though his eyes could see through a hundred miles of solid rock. "Oh, the stars, Ela! I will show you how bright and twinkly they are, I promise! You will not believe them otherwise." He breathed in a long sigh of longing for the outside world. "There's nothing more wonderful than lying on a beach in the warm sand, listening to a gentle ocean with the salt air blowing across your face. Above you, high in a deep blue sky are white fluffy clouds drifting free, just hanging there, waiting to be touched. I'll show you clouds, too, Ela. One day I will show you the world above and all its beauty."

"Oh, Matthew! Will you really show me a cloud floating in your wonderful sky of stars?"

"Yes, Ela, I promise. I promise we will do it together. I will show you a cloud and the stars and much, much more. It will only be the beginning for us."

Riverstone promised himself, never again would he take another cloud for granted, or a sunset, or a clear blue ocean. How sad it was that there were beings that spent their entire lives underground and had never seen a glassy wave roll into shore or a glimmering aspen tree's leaves in the wind!

A cold shiver suddenly knifed through his back and exploded at the base of his skull. Could it be that for the rest of his life, day in and day out, he would pound the stone, never leaving this black hole of a planet, never seeing the light of day or the stars at night or his home, uncountable light-years away?

Never! That was unthinkable!

Riverstone wrapped his trembling arms around Ela, wishing he had her strength of survival. He was about to kiss her when two large silhouettes blocked their light coming from a small single torch down the tunnel. They were not guards. They wore the same dirt-encrusted clothes as the rest of the slaves.

"What do you want?" Riverstone asked, releasing Ela, looking up at the shadows.

"Ela, come," a deep voice commanded. They were both grotesquely ugly and smelled equally bad. "You have been away too long. You will come with us," they demanded.

Ela edged closer to Riverstone. She was frightened. She obviously wanted no part of their demands. "I belong to no one, Vog," she countered sternly. "Go away."

"You will come or I will take you," Vog insisted.

The other reached down to grab Ela, but Riverstone's hand stopped him cold. He then stood up and took the wrist with him. "Ela doesn't want to go with you, toad, so take a hike, ugly." Riverstone's eyes glared hot. He wasn't in the mood.

Vog spat as he reached out for Ela, only to be stopped again by Riverstone. "I said she does not want to go with you."

Both intruders were a good hundred pounds heavier and a foot taller than Riverstone, a fact that did not deter his resolve to protect her.

Vog grunted his disdain and tried to push Riverstone aside with his powerful arm, but Riverstone didn't move. With Gamadin-trained swiftness, a hard open fist caught Vog across the bridge of the nose. Another shot across the temple, and Vog fell to the ground like a fallen tree. He didn't move.

Seeing Vog's fate, the other charged Riverstone from behind, trying to catch him off guard. The other's forward motion suddenly stopped as if he'd struck a solid rock wall. Riverstone's foot had struck the frontal lobe of the other's head and didn't stop. Before he hit the ground, he was also dead.

Ela leaped into Riverstone' arms. She held him, trembling with fear. When she could breathe again she stared back down at the bodies. "But how, Matthew? No one has ever defeated Vog, and you did it so easily."

He brought her close again, their hearts thundering between them. "It's a very long story, Ela. Someone insisted I learn."

"Will this someone come for you?" she asked.

Riverstone kissed her on the forehead and then held her close again. "Yes, they will come for me one day," he told her calmly, and wondered silently to himself if he would ever see Harlowe and his mates again.

77

Confession

HARLOWE'S RAGE FRIGHTENED every creature in the agri-module as he screamed at Turfan's cowardly act. As Monday bled down his chest, his chains were the only support keeping him up as he slumped toward the ground. Harlowe yanked on his own chains with every fiber in his body, trying to break free to help his crewman. Turfan was a dead man. He would strangle Anor Ran's son with his bare hands for shooting Monday.

"I'll kill you, toad! So help me, if it's the last thing I ever do, I'll kill you! There's no place in this universe you can hide. Understand that. No mercy, coward! After I kill you, all that will be left of you is grogan food and that will be your legacy for all eternity, butthead! You're dead. Know that! Your last breath is near."

Turfan had at last found Harlowe's weakness. His men.

* * *

Nervously, Turfan stepped back. He didn't take Harlowe's threat lightly. If he'd had the guts, he would have killed Harlowe while he was still chained to the tree, but the Captain was right. His father would kill him if he harmed him without bringing back the Gamadin ship. Losing the ancient ship was the only reason he kept Pylott alive. Once the prize was secured, he would kill Pylott and throw his body into the fires of Omini Prime, he told himself.

Turfan then motioned with the end of the rifle for the officer to unshackle Harlowe. Turfan's shakes intensified, watching them break him loose from the tree. He stepped back farther, putting a wall of his escort guards in front of him, each with a weapon pointed at the Captain's head in case he made any kind of threatening move. While this was all going on, the Captain uttered not a single word. His death stare totally locked on Turfan was enough.

A soldier was just about to cut Harlowe's last manacle from around the tree when a loud cry shattered the dead quiet of the jungle. The cry was so chilling that the soldier who was cutting the shackles hesitated. Another cry from the opposite side of the clearing shook the jungle. It was equally intense and chilling, only this one was much closer. The soldiers readied their weapons and took defensive positions around Turfan, searching the jungle in every direction for whatever was coming their way.

Turfan ordered the soldier to quickly finish his task. As he was about to cut through the last chain, a wild beast roared from the jungle thicket behind him. From the opposite side of the clearing, something powerful was coming their way. Tree branches cracked as the underbrush split loudly.

Harlowe's eyes brightened. The chilling roars of the beasts were familiar.

Suddenly, two snow-colored tigers broke out of the underbrush like apparitions and attacked the horrified soldiers so ferociously that no one could react in time to train his weapon on the speeding cats.

The soldiers never knew what hit them. Some were dead in an instant while others lay about in broken, twisted configurations. The soldier who had been working to cut Harlowe free never finished his task. Harlowe crushed his windpipe with an open hand to his neck.

He then picked up the soldier's torch and cut himself free. The officer who had killed Lormagan tried to shoot Molly. His first shot went wild, while his second shot never left its chamber. Harlowe snatched a dead soldier's pistol from his belt and got the officer before he could fire another round.

With his soldiers and escort slaughtered all around him, his clean, expensive uniform splattered with blood from his own men, and Rhud about to end his cowardly life, Turfan fell back against the tree, his pants wet with fear. "No, Rhud," Harlowe yelled. The growling white cat reluctantly obeyed, his jaws full of six-inch incisors brushing against Turfan's horrified face.

At the same moment, a tiny, exhausted voice called out from between two tall ferns. "Your Majesty!"

"Prigg! Over here," Harlowe waved, rushing to Monday's aid with the torch. He would have been happier to see the little Naruckian if Monday were still alive. In all the excitement, he hadn't stopped to figure out how Molly and Rhud had found him in the first place. Now he knew.

Prigg's eyes went ballistic when he saw the carnage on the ground. "Oh, Your Majesty, Tomarian soldiers?" Then an eye saw Monday. "Mr. Platter...oh, my, Your Majesty." Prigg's face froze. "Is he...?"

Harlowe checked the side of Monday's neck. His eyes shut briefly. "No, he's still alive." He turned to Prigg. "Do you have your communicator?"

Prigg reached inside a pocket and handed Harlowe the small device. "Yes, Your Majesty."

Harlowe activated the com and said, "Mr. Bolt?"

Simon answered almost instantly. "Aye, Captain. We were getting a little worried about you—"

"Cut the pleasantries, Mr. Bolt," Harlowe shot back. "I need med clickers down here stat. Platter's been shot bad and I'm not going to lose him."

"I sent four to trail Prigg and the cats just in case, Skipper. They should be there," Simon replied.

Leaping over ferns and popping out from the jungle underbrush with Gamadin medical kits, the clicker med team sprang into action.

"Good man, Mr. Bolt; you may have just saved Squid's life. How's my ship?"

"Not a scratch, Captain. Had a few altercations earlier, but they're drifting with the stars now. Palcor got a little rad when I was firing plasbolts near their modules."

Harlowe glanced over the dead Tomarians still clinging to their weapons. It seems Palcor allowed weapons inside their city after all—if you had the right connections, that is. "If they give you any more problems, Mr. Bolt, tell them I'll slice up this city for scrap. Captain out." Harlowe didn't wait for a reply. He shut off the device and handed it back to Prigg while the med clickers crawled all over Monday, performing their healing miracles on the spot. They ripped apart his uniform and began cutting through flesh in an effort to save his life.

Knowing he could do nothing more for Monday, Harlowe turned his attention to Turfan. Rhud sat facing the Tomarian heir, his large, blue eyes unblinking, as though he hoped Turfan would make a foolish move to escape. Turfan stayed put.

Harlowe walked over to the giant tiger and placed a hand around Rhud's white mane, patting him for a job well done.

"Don't kill me," Turfan begged.

"Say your prayers," Harlowe said cold-heartedly as he backed away to allow Rhud room.

"My father will shower you with great riches!"

"I doubt it."

Turfan looked fearfully back and forth between Harlowe and Rhud.

"Don't worry about him. Worry about me. I'm the dude who's going to kill you if you don't answer my questions."

Turfan's eyes welled up. His jaw trembled, weighing the fear of an immediate death over the fear of certain death if he told Harlowe what he wanted. "I can't tell you anything!"

"Not an option."

With blinding precision, Rhud's paw ripped a section of Turfan's uniform from his chest. Turfan stared, horrified, at the open wounds in his chest as his blood flowed freely down the front of his tunic. If his bladder had anything left, it was now flowing in rivers.

"He'll peel you back like an onion if that's what you want," Harlowe informed him.

That was all Turfan needed to hear. "I'll talk."

"Who was behind the abductions on Gibb?" Harlowe wanted to know.

Turfan appeared genuinely surprised. "Abductions?"

"Quay. Two of my crew. The Consortium? Were they behind it? You know, don't you?" Harlowe insisted.

Turfan's face remained dumbfounded. "Quay was with you?"

"She was until a fat toad named Ra-Loc ambushed us on Gibb."

"Both my sisters are missing?"

"And two of my crew," Harlowe added.

"If they're not with you—"

Harlowe motioned for Rhud to come closer as Molly looked on.

Turfan looked small and frail, crying alongside the white cat. "No. I swear. I don't know who took my sisters or your crew. It was not my father. He wouldn't kill them. I would know."

"But he'd use them for bait, wouldn't he?" Turfan clammed up. Harlowe grabbed him by the neck and lifted him off the ground. "Wouldn't he? He'd use them for bait."

Choking, his face beet-red from the loss of air, Turfan answered, admitting reluctantly, "Yes, he would do that, but he wouldn't kill them, I swear." Turfan hesitated. "Unless..."

Harlowe saw the truth in Turfan's face and finished the thought for him. "Unless he uses them to get my ship."

Turfan's head drooped, knowing he was a dead man.

Harlowe backed off, letting Turfan's feet touch the ground. He wanted in the worst way to let Rhud finish the job of tearing Turfan to shreds. Instead, he stuffed his hate by straightening Turfan's shredded tunic over his wounds.

"Listen up," Harlowe began, "tell your father that after I find his daughters and clean up this rat-infested quadrant, I'm coming after him with my ship. The same one that is going to wipe out the Consortium fleet."

Turfan's eyes went wide with surprise. "You're not going to kill me?"

Harlowe picked up Turfan's hat off the ground and placed it on his head. "You are a fortunate dude today, Turfan." He then twisted around, eyeing the carnage. "There's no one left alive to tell your father anything...except you." He leaned into Turfan's face, pressing the shreds of bloody uniform against his chest. "If I find out that you're lying to me about anything or Anor Ran is behind my missing crew and your sisters' kidnapping, and if they've been harmed in any way, and if my crewman you shot doesn't survive, I will come after you. There will be no mercy. I will burn your planet to the ground. You want an empire? I'll send you to an empire in heaven.

Are we clear?" Turfan shook, nodding rapidly. "Tell Anor what I have told you today. Word for word. Tell him Harlowe Pylott and his Gamadin are still alive with the most powerful ship in the galaxy. Let him know we're coming after him when we finish cleaning up his mess. Got that, puke?"

Turfan trembled, his mouth gasping for breath he couldn't find. Harlowe didn't care if he understood or not. He'd said what he needed to say and released the gutless heir to faint in his own muddy urine at the base of the tree. Harlowe spat a disgusting red wad that stuck to the side of Turfan's unconscious face before he turned away, angry at himself for allowing him to live. He couldn't answer why, exactly. Maybe it was Quay, he thought. Maybe he didn't have the courage to face those heart-stopping dark eyes and tell her he had killed her own brother. He had to admit it. As worthless as Turfan was, he didn't have it in him to pull the trigger. He rolled his eyes skyward, shaking his head. It was one of those "love me, love my family" kinda moments, he concluded.

After leaving Turfan, Harlowe and Rhud met up with Prigg and Molly back at the clearing. Prigg, shaking uncontrollably, held a device in his hand he had found on one of the dead officers in the Tomar raiding party. "Your Majesty. This is a Fhaal locator. If they have made an alliance with Tomar…" He was too horrified to fin- ish his statement.

Harlowe watched with concern as the spindly clickers carted Monday back to the ship. He then took the locator, glanced at it briefly, and said, "A pox on all their houses, Prigg. We'll deal with them when the time comes. Right now, I don't care about anybody except my crew."

"Yes, Your Majesty."

Harlowe slid the Fhaal locator in his pocket and grabbed the com from Prigg one more time. "Bring all systems to full power, Mr. Bolt. We're leaving Palcor the moment everyone's back onboard."

"Aye, Skipper. Destination?"

The giant cats disappeared into the underbrush, leading the way out of the clearing while Prigg hustled alongside the fast-stepping Harlowe, who was anxious to return to the ship. Now he had a lead.

"Have Millie put us on a course for Roshmar, Mr. Bolt. Best speed."

"Aye, Skipper, best speed," Simon acknowledged.

Before leaving the clearing, the giant circular Tomarian marquee caught Harlowe's eye. What Prigg had pointed out upon their arrival at Palcor jogged his memory. The words "Why, Tomar owns Palcor, Your Majesty" were still fresh in his mind.

"Mr. Bolt?"

"Yes, Skipper."

"Put Millie on jailbreaking every bit of information she can from the Tomarian computer banks," Harlowe ordered.

"Got a plan, Skipper?" Simon asked.

Harlowe had a gnawing itch he couldn't scratch. "Just do it. Captain out." Yes, he needed a plan. *Victorious warriors win first, and then go to war,* he recalled from his readings of Sun Tzu, *while defeated warriors go to war first and then seek to win…*

Yet, there was something about the big picture he wasn't grasping. It began with knowledge. He was floundering in a sea of ignorance and knew it. He was a rookie in a game of seasoned pros. They had the edge because it was their turf. Before the next hand was dealt, he had to know more about the players in the game. The Tomarian server was a good place to start. He couldn't count on being lucky every time he went to bat because his enemies, whoever they were, were out to kill him with every hand. They needed only to be lucky once.

Along the way, Harlowe stepped past Lormagan's body, his mouth and eyes frozen open in his final expression of surprise. Harlowe grimaced, leaving the dead bounty hunter one last thought. *Pigs get slaughtered, Lory...*

He turned and left the clearing to catch up with his crew.

78

Roshmar

ROSHMAR WAS A desert planet of hot sand and small oceans on the far side of the quadrant. It took ten days for *Millawanda* to make the journey. Harlowe spent the first thirty-six hours camped outside the med room, where Monday battled for his life. He didn't sleep once, making sure that everything was done to save his First Mate's life. By all accounts, Harlowe and Simon figured that even Millie was sweating bullets to keep the big guy alive.

Monday pulled through the worst of it by the third day and began getting used to his new mechanical heart. Unlike Wizzixs, who found 54th-century body replacements disturbing, Monday was grateful just to be among the living. He would have preferred a thumpity-thump-thump model. The steady hum of a dura-motor heart pumping his blood took some getting used to, even if it was an upgrade from his old one. Monday was up and around in four days, humming along like new. He would have been back in two if Harlowe had allowed him. "*Nada*, Squid. You're off the clock, dude," Harlowe said, pointing to the bridge blinker. "Go read a book. Take up knitting. I don't care. I don't want to see you on the bridge for another two days. Captain's orders."

Though Monday felt fit and was ready for duty, Harlowe didn't care if he could run a three-minute mile with a fifty-pound pack; the bridge was off limits. Knowing it would be easier to convert the

Pope to Islam than to butt heads with Harlowe, Monday followed orders. He returned to his room and read a book.

On day nine, while everyone, including Monday, was at their stations, *Millawanda* dropped out of hyperspace and drifted into communications range with the planet. Harlowe put the order to Prigg to contact the highest-ranking entity there. He wasted no time. He was going straight to the top of the food chain. It took some doing, but after taking out three missile batteries around the city, Harlowe got a face-to-face meeting with the authoritarian figure he'd ordered on the holo-screen. The middle-aged humanoid looked arrogant and elitist in his heavily decorated military uniform. He wore a black-billed hat with gold braiding around a bright red and crimson brim. Dark sunglasses covered his three-chin face. Harlowe didn't need an introduction to know that this being was a stupid toad. The instant the official opened his mouth, Harlowe knew his presumption was correct. The authoritarian general, or whatever rank he claimed, looked off to one side with a conceited, why-was-I-disturbed, attitude.

"I am His Excellency, the Lord High Maha of Roshmar," he began in a very highbrow voice. "For what purpose are you destroying our defenses?" he asked Harlowe.

Harlowe got a cautionary glance from Monday to keep his cool. The long search for Ra-Loc was trying his patience, especially with pompous toads in authority. As much as he would have liked to stuff the Maha's medals down his throat, Harlowe displayed his best diplomatic face and smiled graciously for His Excellency, the Lord High Maha.

"I am Captain Pylott. I'm in search of a Lagan trader by the name of Ra-Loc. I have reason to believe he is here on Roshmar. My business with him is urgent, Lord Maha. Do you know his location?"

Harlowe asked politely. He stole a quick glance back to Monday and Simon for their approval of his diplomatic form.

Both gave Harlowe a *you-did-good, Captain* thumbs-up.

The Maha's face suddenly changed to one of deep concern. "The Lagan has left Roshmar. Now leave us."

Suddenly, the bridge went quiet. Monday shut his eyes. *So much for diplomacy!* They had been a little premature on the congrats. Prigg's eyes darted in three different directions before they ended up 180 degrees polar opposites, knowing the peace was short-lived. Simon was the only one who was pleased. He smiled at the screen, his fingers itching to nuke the Roshmar official where he stood. "I've got him in my sights, Skipper."

"Cool your jets, Mr. Bolt," Harlowe cautioned, as much as he wanted to dust the toad himself.

He sat up a little taller and said straight out, "My ship is going nowhere until I get the information about the Lagan."

"Ra-Loc is an outlaw of Roshmar—"

"Good. Then we'll look for him together," Harlowe said, cutting off Maha. Any more talk with this pigheaded toad would give him a migraine.

Harlowe glanced at Monday for an overview of what the sensors had shown in the way of planetary defenses. Monday returned a pathetic smirk, shaking his head. He wasn't impressed.

After the screen went blank, Harlowe turned to Prigg. "He's lucky we're the good guys. Coordinates locked in?"

"Yes, Your Majesty, coordinates on screen," Prigg announced.

"Good. How's the weather down there, Mr. Platter. SIBAs?"

"No, sir," Monday replied, checking his readouts on the console. "Conditions well within tolerable levels. Temperatures are warm. Like Vegas in early summer. Hot and dry, Captain."

Harlowe pointed to the large grassy park where a river flowed through the center of the city. "Put Millie over there, Mr. Platter," thinking the cats would love the wide-open grass to stretch themselves on after their long journey.

"Aye, Captain," Monday confirmed.

* * *

As *Millawanda* drifted slowly down through the upper atmosphere and over the vast deserts, they saw a few large bodies of water. All were quite small compared to Earth's great oceans. More like shallow seas, Harlowe thought. Green patches of life followed the edges of the shorelines and contributory rivers, while back in the interior near the tall ranges of mountains, patches of dark green forests hovered in the higher slopes. If Roshmar had been any closer to its primary, these green patches, as well as its oceans, would have evaporated eons ago, he thought.

The capital of Roshmar was Cinnebar. The city was near one of the forested areas in the higher-latitude regions of the planet, at the very edge of a vast desert. A wide, meandering river ran through the middle of the city and connected the city with the ocean a thousand miles away. It was a strategic location. In the ancient past, anyone wanting to conquer Cinnebar would have to traverse a vast. desolate desert to reach the citadel. Now, the desert barriers of the past are useless against the weapons of modern space warfare.

The site Harlowe picked out was not a normal landing pad. It was a large grassy knoll just east of the city. *Millawanda*'s sensors showed a large number of missile launching pads hidden in underground bunkers surrounding the park.

"This gomer doesn't know what a bad day he's going to have if he even twitches a nose hair in a hostile manner," Harlowe mused out loud.

Monday slowly brought the saucer over the park and hovered a thousand feet above the grassy knoll, waiting for Harlowe's final okay to descend. "On your toes, Mr. Bolt."

"Aye, Skipper, I'm a ballerina dancing across the stage," Simon joked. He then winked at Prigg in the next chair. "No worries, little buddy."

When Harlowe gave the go-ahead, Monday gracefully deployed the 350-foot, curved landing pods and softly touched the Ship down on top of the grass near the river. Harlowe changed into a dark blue Gamadin uniform with a knee-length cape. (Simon had added this touch of coolness.) Before stepping on the blinker, he checked his pistols to make sure they were fully charged. He stepped onto the blinker with Molly and Rhud, and the three blinked only a few yards away from the ship's perimeter edge.

Make no mistake about it, Harlowe was here to do business—it was clear from his gait, his tall, focused demeanor, and the cats, a half-ton each of white, porcelain destructive power. Molly and Rhud leapt away the instant they materialized, poised and ready, their keen, bright eyes searching like intense blue sensor probes across the open knoll for any hint of danger.

Harlowe wasted no time striding alone past the barrier as if he owned the planet. First impressions were important. Except for the cats, he had ordered his crew to stay behind. In case things went south in a hurry, he wanted all available hands and eyeballs on any problem that came their way.

The Maha, with a sizeable entourage, was waiting to greet him at the edge of the park. What caught his attention more than his Excellency was a tallm flaxen blonde standing in back of the group. Dressed in a bedouin wrap of fine natural linen that shielded her from the sun, she appeared the only humble being among the crowd.

She was also the only woman. Huddled close to the Maha, and spread throughout the group, were many heavily armed guards with weapons, cocked and ready, pointed at him and the cats.

After been cooped up for over a week, the cats found the open space energizing. Rhud bolted out in a sharp spurt of speed, celebrating his freedom with a loud roar of delight. His sudden outburst frightened the jittery guards. Several guards lowered their weapons on Rhud as if they were about to shoot. Without breaking stride and from a hundred yards away, Harlowe drew both pistols and fired before the guards could pull their triggers, shooting every weapon clean from the security guards' hands. At that same moment, the batteries surrounding the knoll opened up on the saucer as if it was their plan to do so all along. *Millawanda* absorbed the discharges as if they were little more than small irritants. Harlowe tapped his com and spoke to Simon. "Nuke 'em, Mr. Bolt."

Simon's delighted voice replied, "My pleasure, Skipper!"

A moment later, powerful bolts of blue light struck out from the saucer's perimeter and reduced the entire surrounding battery emplacements to molten piles of metal.

Harlowe continued on, never breaking stride as he strutted straight up to the Maha. Two security guards tried to intercept him, but they were quickly slapped to the ground like misbehaved children.

"See here—" the Maha tried to protest before Harlowe administered his special form of diplomacy. He nailed the Maha across the jaw, sending His Excellency to la-la land.

Harlowe stepped over the Maha's unconscious body and addressed the crowd of officials. "Anyone else want to shoot my pets?"

Everyone but the woman shook from the Gamadin's query.

Harlowe was impressed. He dismissed the others with a wave of his hand as he politely asked the woman to stay.

No one had to be asked twice. Harlowe's upper lip curled with contempt as he watched the cowards stumble and fall over each other as they ran for the nearest shelter. After the crowd had dispersed, he turned back to the woman. They were the only two beings left on the knoll.

The woman was lovely, the type men back on Earth would write bad checks to impress. His smile was gracious. She was tall, perhaps a little over six feet. Her blond hair was wavy, falling down past her shoulders. Her skin had a pink cast, as if she had been exposed to the sun that day. Her eyes were dark blue, almost black, round, and intelligent. She stood regal and confident. If Harlowe intimidated her at all, she didn't show it.

"And you are?" he asked her.

"Ruloma," she replied. She bowed her head slightly, then met his stare, smiling as though genuinely pleased to meet him and added, "I am the Minister of Trade on Roshmar. How may I help you, Captain Pylott?"

She was direct and to the point. He found her manner refreshing. Not only that, she smelled sweet and flowery as if she had just stepped out of a tropical shower. All of this was making it difficult for him to concentrate. "Thank you, Ruloma," he said, and apologized to her for the rough introduction. Whether she was too tactful to offend the Gamadin or understood all too well his anger, she made no comment. She let him speak.

"I come to Roshmar in search of a Lagan trader named Ra-Loc. I was told he passed this way recently. Do you know him?"

Her eyebrows rose slightly. "Yes, I know him well," Ruloma replied, "but I'm afraid he has already left Roshmar. The Lagan has committed many grave offenses. I doubt if he will ever return. His life is worthless here."

He swallowed the sour taste in his mouth. "Yes. He is not worth much to me either, except that I must find him. He knows the where-abouts of my friends," he explained, and asked if she had information on where Ra-Loc might have gone after he left Roshmar.

"No, Captain," Ruloma replied, "but others who have dealt with Ra-Loc would know. I have several traders in mind. If you will allow me some time, I will search out these individuals for you."

Harlowe thanked her and appreciated any help she could give him. Molly strolled beside her, looking for affection, as Rhud lazily rolled over on his back in the tall cool grass nearby. "It has been a long journey for them," Harlowe said, looking up at the sun, feeling the warm yellow rays on his face. "For me too."

"Your animals are beautiful. I have seen none like them before." She reached out and petted Molly with the same apparent fearless-ness she had displayed with him.

Harlowe smiled like a proud father, when suddenly loud sirens blared from within the city walls. There seemed to be no apparent rea-son for the outburst until Monday interrupted their conversation.

"Millie has a lock on a dozen missiles launched from the second planet, Captain. We've been following them for a while, Captain. They're definitely nukes, Captain. Waiting for your orders, sir," Monday said, calmly.

"Friends of yours?" he asked Ruloma.

For the first time, Harlowe saw actual fear in Ruloma's eyes. Her eyes darted back and forth, searching for a place to hide. "It's Tnoir. We have been at war with them for many passings," she explained. "Their spies have already informed their high command we are defenseless. Cinnebar will be destroyed." She turned to Harlowe. "You must leave Roshmar before it is too late, Captain. Hurry, save yourself and your beautiful creatures."

Behind them, the Maha's guards had already taken him away and disappeared from the knoll, presumably for the nearest shelter. "Hold on," Harlowe said, calmly. He was still in communication with Monday. Before Harlowe could make his call back to the ship, Monday was on the line.

"They'll be knocking on our door in twelve minutes, Captain. Do you want me to slam them?" Monday asked.

"Aye, Mr. Platter. Take them out," Harlowe ordered coolly.

"Aye, Captain," Monday replied.

Harlowe gave Ruloma a wink of confidence. "We'll handle it, Ruloma."

A split second later, a series of long blue bolts streaked toward the heavens from the thin perimeter edge of the saucer. One hundred thousand miles distant, twelve interplanetary missiles vaporized harmlessly in deep space, lighting up the bright afternoon sky like an exploding star gone nova.

Ruloma looked at Harlowe, amazed.

Harlowe closed his eyes, feeling the warmth of the sun again, appearing to have not a care in the world. He took in a deep breath of fresh desert air and said, "We're cool now. Cinnebar is safe."

A few seconds later, the sirens of Cinnebar sounded the all-clear.

"Who are you?" Ruloma asked, as she stared with renewed respect at Harlowe.

"Simple traders," Harlowe replied.

Ruloma wasn't buying Harlowe's shallow explanation. She scoffed. "Please, do not play me for a fool, Captain. One who possesses such power is not a simple seeker of Lagan traders. You are much more than space-faring merchants. Merchants do not wear uniforms like yours or fire weapons from the hip with godlike skill. Again, I ask you, Captain, who are you?"

Harlowe had made a mistake, however unintentional. He was trying to be simple when instead he should have been up-front and truthful. "If I would have said we are Gamadin, would you have believed me?"

Ruloma almost laughed. "You are so young. You don't look like an ancient crag."

Harlowe was amused by the comment, however unintended the humor. "True. You might say we've taken over the payments." He pointed to *Millawanda*. "She may have a few miles on her, but she's still a hot babe."

Ruloma blinked at the absurdity. From the extreme doubt expressed in her eyes, Harlowe had gone from a straightforward lie to outright deceit. In either case, Harlowe had two strikes against him. If he was going to get anywhere with Ruloma, he had to convince her that his requests were noble or he was going down with a big K in the hit column. "If you wish my assistance, Captain, you must be more open about your intent," she replied bluntly.

"How much do you know about the Gamadin?"

"Our ancient history has spoken of their mythic power." She looked skyward as if searching her memory, and said, "For the wrath of the Gamadin cleansed the stars for all..." Her intelligent dark eyes turned to Harlowe, wanting to know, "Is this the reason you have come to Roshmar, to cleanse the stars for all? Have you come here to destroy us, Captain? Because we are at war with Tnoir?"

They walked to a small rise that overlooked the meandering river. Over the mellow sounds of the gurgling, running water along the shoreline, Harlowe replied, "We're the good guys, Ruloma. Gamadin use their power to protect, not to destroy," he explained.

"You are so young. Are you a god, Captain? For only gods have such power."

Now it was Harlowe's turn to laugh. "Oh no, I assure you, I am no god, Ruloma. If you cut me, I bleed. Ask my sparring partner, Quincy."

Ruloma didn't know what Quincy had to do with Harlowe's godliness, but she seemed willing to listen to the young captain.

Harlowe turned back to the grassy knoll, where *Millawanda* was quiet now. The silent blue light around her perimeter glowed softly, pulsing like a heart at rest. It was all that remained of her sudden fury. "Allow the Gamadin to bring peace to Roshmar, Ruloma."

Ruloma's face expressed her doubt that peace would come to Roshmar. "Roshmar has not known peace for many passings. Even with such power, Tnoir's defenses are formidable. Your beautiful ship and you will be killed."

Harlowe smiled confidently, leading her away from the river view, toward the saucer. "We should get started. We have much work to do. While your people are searching the planet for leads on the toadhead Ra-Loc, you can tell me of your war with Tnoir." They took the long way along the river's edge. "Come with me to my ship. We will travel to Tnoir and find a solution."

"Tnoir will not bargain," Ruloma warned.

Hawlowe recalled an old movie about gangsters he'd enjoyed with Riverstone when they were kids. "I will make them an offer they can't refuse," he told her.

Solving the problems of two warring worlds would delay his search for Ra-Loc, but saving billions of lives was more important. Making peace was part of a Gamadin's job. It came with the uniform. It was what being Gamadin was all about. He could no more neglect his duty to save a planet from destruction than he could stop breathing. He also knew that his Gamadin mates and Quay would have wanted it that way.

Ruloma had trouble comprehending what kind of offer Harlowe would give Tnoir that would be irrefutable, since Roshmar had been at war with the inner planet for generations. But to bring peace to Roshmar, Ruloma said she would travel with the young man from the stars. "Let us die together, then, Captain."

Her smile was disarming. He took a deep breath, thinking he should have been a monk. He wanted more time in the sun and a swim in the river, but duty called.

They walked an hour longer along the river's edge, enjoying the flowers along the banks and the wide-open sky above their heads. While they discussed the interplanetary differences between Roshmar and Tnoir, it gave the cats more time to play. When the sun had nearly set with an incredible red glow at their backs, he guided her back toward the ship. Nearby, just inside the perimeter boundary, a blinker was left on the grass. After brief introductions of his crew, *Millawanda* lifted off on a sub-light journey toward the inner planet of Tnoir.

79

His Netherworld Goddess

RIVERSTONE BROKE A yellow crystal from the rock. He eyed it quietly. "Thermo-grym," he whispered, remembering what Quay had called it that night around the campfire on #2. It had never appeared to him to be worth much. It was not like gold or silver. It was a simple yellow crystal like the ones he had seen many times in his science classes back home, yet its power, according to Millie's analysis, was enormous. It powered starships and planets from one end of the quadrant to the other, and Erati was full of it. Whoever controlled Erati controlled the quadrant. For a brief moment he wondered if there was a way to make a bomb or a hand grenade to assist his escape aboveground. What had Ian said? *You would need to refine a ton of crystal first with induced nuclear distillers for every gram of thermo-grym.*

Riverstone didn't know how much explosive power was in a gram of thermo-grym, but he did know induced nuclear distillers were in short supply a hundred miles underground on Erati.

He tossed the crystal aside and sighed, turning his attention to Ela as she gathered fresh water from the pool. It took several rest periods, but he had created the pool by damming the small, subterranean stream that flowed continuously from the rocks. Now every day he saw how beautiful she really was under the layers of caked-on dust. Her skin glistened softly and unsoiled in the dim tunnel light. She was his goddess of the netherworld.

They made their own private home together in one of the abandoned tunnels, away from the other diggers. At the edge of the pond they had a soft bed of pulverized rock dust. In the rock, they had carved out caches for the food they gathered from vegetation that grew without light and the meat from the abundant rodents that Riverstone killed with his rifle arm. Word had spread quickly how he had defeated Vog so handily. This made life better for him and Ela among the other diggers. They were left alone, and no one ventured into their private area of the tunnel for fear of tasting Riverstone's wrath. As long as Riverstone's output continued at the high level he had set for himself, even Dagger kept his distance and allowed them their peace. Ela was the cornerstone of his survival. He owed all of his success in the underground tomb, his crypt with no sun, no stars, no sky full of fluffy white clouds or sandy beaches, no Harlowe, and none of his mates, to her. She was his anchor. It broke his heart watching her every work period, toiling away at the eternal rock. How could he take her from Erati? Alone, he felt confident he could make it to the surface. With her, it was a risk he wasn't prepared to take. Not yet, anyway. If he escaped without her, the rats in the mine would descend upon her. Now that she was clean and visible to all eyes, he saw how others, even Dagger, looked at her. Riverstone would not risk such a fate for her. He waited, planned, and began to teach her things she would need to survive the trek to the surface. If they had any chance of escape together, she had to learn how to defend herself and climb rocks without a rope.

Erati sucked by anyone's standards. Here, without day or night, one lost all concept of time. Riverstone figured, and it was only a guess on his part, that it had been over a month since he last saw Ian and much longer since he saw Harlowe and his mates. He shook inside. The pain of losing his lifelong friend was constantly with him whenever he relived that helpless moment watching Ian fall into the bottomless shaft. At times his guilt was so great that he wished he had fallen instead of Ian. At his lowest moments Ela was there, keeping his thoughts of an inglorious end at bay. With Ela by his side, his life had meaning and hope. His total existence centered around that day in the future when he would give her that greatest gift of all . . . the life of the world aboveground, the feel of the sun's warm touch on her shoulders, the sight of a drifting cloud in a deep blue sky, a starry night of glittering stars, a fresh breeze on her face, and the roar of an ocean wave rumbling up a sandy shore where they stood together. As beautiful and loving as Ela was, he wondered how much longer he could hold out. As a surface dweller, how long could he live without life aboveground? Still, with Ela, he made it through each work period and was thankful that his mind still served him, that he was alive, that there was food in his stomach and a warm bed with someone he loved lying next to him. These were all victories, small triumphs over the misery of his tomb. If he remembered all that, then together they could survive long enough for Harlowe to find them . . . if he could.

Harlowe doesn't lose, he kept reminding himself. He would find a way.

Whenever his netherworld goddess returned from their subterranean pond all lovely and clean, his greatest triumph came toward him. He had never loved anyone so completely. If he had to choose between life aboveground without Ela or the darkest dungeon with her, it was no contest. A life without her was no life at all. Of this, he was certain . . .

80

Making Peace

MILLAWANDA'S SENSORS INDICATED that Tnoir's physical makeup was far more Earth-like than Roshmar. It had milder temperatures and vast oceans. Its size, its blue color, its swirling white clouds in each hemisphere, were all similar to Earth's. Harlowe, Monday, and Simon traded heartfelt sighs of home as they realized just how much they missed their own world.

"You think they might have In-N-Outs, Skipper?" Simon asked, trying to lighten the mood on the bridge.

Harlowe tried to force a grin as he stared at the blue planet with Ruloma sitting in the chair to his right. The best he could do was an unemotional nod. Until his pards were safe and sitting with him on the bridge, his thoughts of double-doubles and beaches with waves were meaningless. Until they were found, he was a monk giving all of his worldly possessions away. If he never surfed another wave or never tasted another animal-style fry, so be it. If he never kissed another girl again, that was the price he was willing to pay. His friends were his mission, their lives his only quest. Nothing else mattered, not even his own life.

During the sub-light trip to Tnoir, Ruloma detailed the dispute between them. The most recent escalation of the war came during the last cycle, when the price of thermo-grym crystals rose to a point that Roshmar could no longer afford to pay the premium the consortium extracted.

"You were tapped out, huh?" Harlowe asked.

"If what you're saying is we no longer had the koorants to pay Erati, that is correct. We are not a wealthy planet like Tnoir, Captain," Ruloma replied. "We had no choice but to intercept the Erati supply ships or face planet-wide energy shortages during the next cold cycle. Millions of my people would have perished. Our planet depends on the thermo-grym crystals for their survival. Out of desperation, we took Tnoir's shipment to avoid planetary death."

Harlowe found the problem baffling. "You mean Tnoir doesn't produce the thermo-grym crystal, either?"

"No. It is mined on a distant planet called Erati and transported to our system," Ruloma explained. "Tnoir and Roshmar are only two of Erati's hundreds of customers in this section of the quadrant who must rely on thermo-grym for survival."

"Produce your own energy, Ruloma," Harlowe pointed out logically. "Cut out Erati altogether."

Her eyes suddenly lost their passion. "Thermo-grym crystals do not exist on Roshmar, Captain."

"Try something else. You've got a ton of solar energy. Use that!"

"Our primary is erratic. Its output is never constant. When Roshmar is close to the primary, our supply of energy is plentiful. Then its orbit swings out on its elliptical path and the primary's output is insufficient. In the past, we overproduced energy during the warm cycle and stored it in great underground rock chambers which we used to resupply Roshmar's needs when the cold cycle came. During our severe cold cycles, our primary's thermo output is insufficient. Our chambers would run out of thermo heat before the warm cycle returns, and many thousands would perish. Death during the cold cycle was always common until the Consortium offered a better solution. They would supply Roshmar with all the thermo-grym we needed to heat our homes and cities at a cost that we could not duplicate, even during the hottest cycle. Roshmar quickly grew prosperous from our new source of energy. Over time our planet halted its storage production. It made no sense to put valuable resources to work for something that was no longer necessary."

"Don't tell me. Let me guess," Harlowe said, eyeing the cookie-dough shake on the table. "Not long after you stopped producing light energy, you let your solar equipment deteriorate. Soon after that, Erati prices began to rise."

Ruloma was stunned at Harlowe's understanding. "For one so young, you seem skilled in the ways of the Consortium. Have you had dealings with Erati also?"

Harlowe nodded pathetically, expressing his opinion. "Once they have you sucked in, they squeeze you until your life is theirs." Harlowe then asked, "How long would it take to bring your light energy collectors back on line?"

Ruloma's face went long with gloom. "It would take at least three passings to make the transition back to light energy production. But before that could happen, many millions would perish from the cold during the next cycle. Our planet has already turned and will soon become cold."

"Tnoir can't like this either," Harlowe pointed out, seeing a possible ally. Misery does love company, he thought.

"Tnoir is much wealthier than Roshmar, and their winters are not as extreme. They will pay the premium to ensure their people a warm cycle to avoid rebellion."

Harlowe understood that fundamental law of human nature as he returned to the table and picked up his shake. Once you've tasted a cookie dough shake, it's hard to go back to vanilla. Harlowe then said after a sip, "Maybe I should be talking to the owners of Erati instead Tnoir. That would set the neighborhood straight again."

"The Consortium sets the prices. There is no concession. Not even Tomar can renegotiate the contract," Ruloma explained.

Harlowe almost choked on a cookie-dough chunk. "Tomar? What do they have to do with Erati?" Harlowe asked.

Ruloma was surprised at Harlowe's ignorance. "Why, the Tomar Corporation owns Erati and all the crystal production in the quadrant."

Harlowe sucked his shake dry and called for Jewels to bring another round of cookie-dough shakes, plus two glasses of Blue Stuff for chasers. "Is there anything that toad doesn't own?" Harlowe glanced at Ruloma's surprised stare at his sudden outburst.

"Who is toad?" Ruloma asked.

"Anor Ran. He's got his hand in everything," Harlowe explained.

Ruloma was finding it difficult to follow the young captain's line of thought. "Do you know the great Anor Ran?"

Harlowe skipped the shake and went right to the Blue Stuff from Jewels, whose timing couldn't have been better. He was dry. "I know him." He lifted his ring finger and showed Ruloma the simple band. "His daughter and I are friends."

Ruloma was impressed. "His daughter belongs to you?"

Harlowe tried to laugh. It came out a little stunted. "Hardly. Quay belongs to no one. Not even her father controls her."

"I can see her in your eyes. She is your heart."

Harlowe turned toward the large observation window and the ever-growing size of Tnoir, his mind far away on another distant blue planet, wishing Leucadia were here to assist with his diplomatic skills.

Ruloma went on: "It is said she is very beautiful."

Harlowe nodded, only partially listening. "Oh yeah, she's hot, all right."

Ruloma looked away. "She is the reason you came to Roshmar," she stated, partially turning back.

"One of the reasons," Harlowe admitted. "Her sister and two of my crew were taken by the Lagan toad I told you about."

"Now I understand why it is so important you find her," Ruloma said.

Harlowe was about to order another glass of blue stuff when Monday wanted his attention. "Captain, a whole slew of missiles have launched from the planet's surface."

Harlowe saw the worry in Ruloma's eyes before he turned to Simon at his weapons station and ordered, "Nuke 'em, Mr. Bolt."

"Aye, Skipper."

Next, he faced Prigg with another command. "Contact the head dude, Mr. Prigg—"

"Her name is Xiomara," Ruloma interrupted.

Harlowe looked at her with surprise. "Do it, Mr. Prigg. Tell the head babe I want to have a chat with her."

81

Black Gold

FIVE DAYS LATER, Harlowe and Ruloma stood together on the palace balcony where the Lord High Maha of Roshmar once lived. Simon and Monday stood at attention off to the side dressed, like Harlowe, in formal Gamadin cobalt-blue uniforms. When they returned from Tnoir, Harlowe had done a little arm-twisting among the powers that be. His Excellency was out and Ruloma was in.

Ruloma was reluctant at first. She did not like the idea of becoming a Lord High anything. The title sounded too far above the people she cared so much about. "Be their president, then," Harlowe suggested. "I think President Ruloma has a nice ring to it. You'll be great. In four passings, if they like what you're doing, they can vote you in for another term."

"Our people have never heard of such a system," she replied, intrigued by the idea. "How would we know how to run this new government?" she asked.

Harlowe had a rolled-up document in his hand made of parchment and handed it to her. "My gift to you and your people," he said, as he looked out over the millions who had gathered in the open square and up and down both sides of the Cinnebar River. They came from all walks of life and from all parts of the planet to say goodbye to the mighty Gamadin who brought peace not only to their world, but to Tnoir.

Ruloma took the scroll gratefully, her eyes a mixture of tears of joy and sadness that Harlowe was leaving. She wanted him to stay longer to ensure the organization of Roshmar's new government went smoothly.

"It's a guide. It's worked for my people for over two hundred passings. It will work for Roshmar...guaranteed," he said, with a wink of confident pride in his eyes.

An aide walked up to her and opened a hand-carved, bejeweled box. Ruloma removed a platinum-colored medallion with a 500-carat-if-it-was-an-ounce, red stone as its centerpiece. "And for you, Captain Harlowe Pylott, giver of peace, savior of my people, the gift of Synon," Ruloma said as she placed the medallion of peace over his head and gently allowed the weight of the bejeweled symbol to settle on his chest. It was Roshmar's highest award, given by the supreme goddess of Roshmar herself, she told him. "You are a god equal to all other gods, Harlowe Pylott. You will forever be worshiped from this day forward by all the people of Roshmar."

Harlowe's face turned several shades of red as Simon and Monday rolled their eyes skyward. He tried to disguise his embarrassment at such a high honor. He looked at the medallion, gawking at the largest red jewel he had ever seen. He thanked Ruloma and waved to the people. The roar that followed made his knees weak. He felt humbled. He would never forget this moment for the rest of his life.

"I haven't brought back the crystals yet," he told her.

It was Ruloma's turned to smile confidently. "You will, Captain. I have witnessed the Gamadin might and have never seen Xiomara as frightened as when Molly and Rhud introduced themselves."

"They do make an impression."

Ruloma went on. "Your ship is without peer. How could anyone deny a Gamadin anything? Before the cold cycle begins, Roshmar will have its thermo-grym. As you say…" She thought briefly. "You can take that to the bank, dude."

Simon and Monday could barely control themselves.

Before Harlowe answered Ruloma, he crossed a "zip it" hard glance their way. Then Monday handed Harlowe a small glass container of black liquid.

"Another gift?" Ruloma asked, puzzled by the vial.

Harlowe held it up to the sunlight. "Mr. Platter and Mr. Bolt over there," he said, nodding toward them as they gave her a snappy salute, "have been checking out your planet. Beneath the sand our sensors found this." He turned it around in his hand, eyeing it with satisfaction.

"What is it?" she asked.

Harlowe handed it to her assistant. "We call it black gold on our planet. Texas tea. With that you won't need Tomar's crystals after this coming cold cycle. In time, together with the sun, you'll have plenty of energy to make Roshmar very prosperous, Madame President."

"This is energy for my people?"

"In spades, Ruloma. You have an ocean of it down there," he said pointing to the ground.

A tall, dark-haired man came from nowhere and took the container of black liquid from the assistant's hand. "I have seen this resource once before. What are its heating properties per sec-loon?" The tall figure was none other than Anor Ran.

Upon seeing, Anor Ran, Ruloma knelt to one knee, bowing in deep respect. The rich and powerful Tomar-Rex had never visited Roshmar before. "Great Anor Ran, Roshmar welcomes you. How may we serve you?" she said to him, her face still looking down at the stone floor of the palace.

Not many things surprised Harlowe lately. Prigg had earlier announced that a Tomarian starship was parked in orbit above Roshmar, so Harlowe expected Anor Ran's appearance. Harlowe, however, acted with surprise, as if Anor had popped out of thin air. "What rock did you crawl out from under, Anor?"

Anor kept studying the black gold. "I just arrived."

Harlowe and his crew were the only ones not on their knees bowing. "What, no entourage to guard you?" He helped Ruloma off the stone floor. "Stand, Ruloma. You're the President of Roshmar. You bow to no one, least of all this dirtball."

Ruloma was shocked by the obvious scorn Harlowe had for the Tomar-Rex. She was even more taken aback that Anor Ran allowed the disdain to continue without consequence. Then again, a cycle ago she had never met a Gamadin.

Anor Ran released the top of the container and stuck his finger in the dark liquid. "I didn't want them killed," he replied in response to Harlowe's question about having no entourage.

Harlowe snickered at the Tomar-Rex's common sense. "Smart." He then shot a quick glance over his shoulder. "Did that worthless son of yours relay my message?"

"That's why I'm here," Anor Ran replied, standing tall and arrogant as if he owned Roshmar, and Harlowe never doubted that he probably did. The Tomar-Rex then asked Harlowe to walk with him, making the request sound dangerously close to an order. He handed the black liquid back to his assistant just before he and Harlowe stepped away from Ruloma and the others and walked alone across the open veranda.

Harlowe had a shopping list of concerns about Anor Ran. Distrust was at the top.

They strolled across the pink-colored stone to its end, neither of them seeming to be in a hurry. At the corner of the balcony, Anor

Ran stood at the stone guardrail, gazing over the crowds in the plaza. "They worship you."

"They love freedom," Harlowe replied. He glared at Anor Ran with cold eyes. "You were screwing them over. You had them hooked on the crystals to survive."

"The price was fair. For many passings no one complained. Why now?"

"You've raised their premium to a point where they must starve to pay for it. That's hardly fair."

Anor Ran looked surprised. "I did not sanction such a price increase. For over a hundred passings this has been so," Anor Ran explained.

"Better check your books, Anor. Prices have risen over five huncred percent in the last three passings."

"You know this?"

"I've seen the invoices."

"The Consortium has altered the contracts then. That is the only explanation."

"You and Unikala *are* in it together, butthead. I know about your mining gig at Erati, and what it costs to produce a single 'ut' of crystal." Harlowe smiled. "Now, I'm all for free enterprise and making a profit. I come from a country that thrives on profit, but you have a captive audience toad. That's not a free market."

"If what you say is true—"

"It is true."

"All right. If what you say is true, I will see that the price is rolled back to the previous levels."

"You'll do better than that. You'll have a shipment of crystals brought here, Anor, and to Tnoir, too, before the next cold cycle, with enough to get them through the next five cold cycles, and you'll do it for free. That should cover the overcharges."

"How do you expect me to stay in business if I'm giving out the product at a loss?"

"At no cost, Gomer," Harlowe stressed.

"Impossible."

"I'll put Erati out of business and I'll start with Tomar if you don't."

"Is that a threat?"

Harlowe's eyes didn't flinch. "Big time."

Anor Ran scoffed at the threat, then tried to play the guilt trip. "You would destroy Quay's home. I've seen how you look at my daughter, Captain. I find your threat wanting."

"If she knew you were sucking face with the Fhaal, what would she say then?" Harlowe caught the sudden dread that flashed across Anor Ran's face. "Why, I would almost bet that both Quay and Sharlon would light the match that would burn you at the stake."

"You play the game well, Captain."

"Like you, I play to win, Anor. Losing is not an option," Harlowe stated.

"How about we—" Anor Ran tried to say before Harlowe cut him off.

"No compromises, toad."

Anor Ran remained expressionless, as though the threat didn't faze him. His focus drifted to the golden disk miles away, parked on the grassy knoll, surrounded by the thousands of worshipers. It was clearly evident in his gaze that the yearning to possess Her was on his mind more than any discussion of thermo-grym production. Even at this distance, her sleekness and beauty was extraordinary. "She is a beautiful ship, Captain," he said.

Harlowe understood his desire and aimed to put it in perspective. "You'll find it easier to walk back to Tomar than to acquire my ship."

Anor Ran turned to Harlowe. "Everybody has a price, Captain. What is yours?"

Harlowe's eyes did not retreat. "You're right. I do."

Anor Ran was no fool. He knew Harlowe's price was more than wealth. "And that would be?"

"Freedom for Neeja. Can you arrange that, Anor?"

Though Harlowe's price was irrational, Anor Ran found it intriguing. "A planet for a ship, Captain? Such out-of-the-way property."

"Not to the Fhaal."

"The Empire would have to be persuaded to abandon their prime outpost in the quadrant. I am afraid even I have no power for such a transaction."

"That is my price."

"What is the price for your crewmen, Captain?" The Tomar-Rex pointed to the distant rooftops. "My assassins are stationed everywhere, Captain. With a nod, one of your crewmen will be killed unless I have that ship. A second nod will kill the second. A third and Ruloma will die, and so on. The choice is yours. The ship or your men."

Harlowe remained silent, placing his hands on the balcony rail, unamused by the Hobson's choice.

Anor Ran grinned with conceit. "I play to win, Captain," he said, repeating Harlowe's earlier words.

* * *

Hidden in the shadows, a thousand yards away, a Tomarian assassin kept his keen eyes focused on the Tomar-Rex, waiting for the signal to shoot the blue-uniformed Gamadin. There were others like him in position , sighting in on their targets. He prayed his round would fly straight and true. He had the smaller, dark-haired one in his sights. It was a clear shot. All he needed was the signal and the glory of the kill would be his.

Click.

Something behind him moved.

* * *

"Do you value your men, Anor?" Harlowe finally asked, unshaken by the Anor Ran's threat to execute his crew standing at ease, conversing with the delegates on the balcony as if their lives were secure.

Anor Ran replied wryly. "My men understand their duty, Captain. Their lives are expendable. You are different. I have studied you. Your men are sacred to you. You would die before you would see one of them killed. Admirable, but I'm afraid a weakness that will be your undoing. The ship will be mine or they will die. What will it be, Captain? Your ship or your men?"

Harlowe faced Anor Ran, cool and impassive. "You are quite right, Anor, my men are my strength. That is why I take all precautions to protect them. They will not die today or any other day by your assassins."

Harlowe removed a baton-shaped object from under his coat and tossed it onto the deck. The tarnished gold-colored object rang like fine dura-steel as it rolled along the stone and stopped in the middle of the deck. "Nor will they be pawns to your stupid plots."

Anor glanced at the object. "What is this, Captain? Something that will change the game?"

"I never leave home without them," Harlowe replied, and pointed to a distant rooftop across the plaza. "Watch carefully, Anor. You will soon learn how the game is played." A moment later, dark-clothed beings were falling from the rooftops and balconies like black rain, as if someone was tossing them over the side of their hidden niches.

Anor Ran watched in silent disbelief as every assassin plummeted to his death. "Your expendables have now sprouted wings."

Anor Ran suddenly lost his cool, his face red with the heat of anger. Before Anor Ran uttered another word, Harlowe spoke to an unseen crewman. "Nuke 'em, Prigg."

Within seconds, blue bolts of razor-thin light shot up from the saucer's edge, crisscrossing the heavens, lighting up the sky in a high orbital thunderstorm.

Anor Ran looked around, knowing he had lost control of the state of affairs and all that was going on around him. "What happened? What did you do?"

Harlowe turned back to the group and called out to Monday, "Mr. Platter. Toss me a nugget, if you please."

Monday reached into a pouch on his utility belt and removed a small, baseball-sized object. From a little over a hundred feet away, the First Mate tossed a strike over to Harlowe, who caught it easily with one hand. He then turned to Anor Ran and said, "He used to pitch for the Yankees." Harlowe lied, but who would know? Harlowe held the golden ball up for Anor Ran to see. "We call them nuggets. We don't actually know what their technical term is. Wiz would know, but then I digress. The ship you came in was eighty-sixed. Bummer, too. It was a cool ride. Oh, and the fleet that came with you, it's also dead in the water. Their stardrives were vaporized."

"Impossible!" Anor Ran shot back.

"Call your people," Harlowe suggested.

Anor did, but no one answered his call. His communicator was completely dead, as if his fleet didn't exist. The look on his face told the ultimate story. He had found religion.

"There's a few dozen of these in orbit around Roshmar and Tnoir," Harlowe continued. "They'll protect the planets once we leave the star system. The black stuff you found so intriguing?" Anor Ran nodded. "Within three passings, your crystals will be history for these planets. Tnoir and Roshmar have oceans of the stuff. There's new competition in town. The locals are back in charge."

Harlowe grabbed Anor Ran by the tunic and lifted him in the air, his feet fluttering, searching for solid ground.

"So you want to mess with me, dude? Go ahead. Sleep well." He motioned toward Molly and Rhud. "My cats own the night. You have no idea what I can do to you, and I haven't even warmed up. I may be a young skull full of mush in your eyes, but when you screw with my crew, I become your worst nightmare. Tomar, your beautiful planet, will be subatomic dust when I'm finished. Are we clear, Anor? ARE WE CLEAR?" Harlowe shouted, spraying his face purposely with spittle, his eyes about to bulge from their sockets. He was hot. "I will rip your head off and stuff it down your throat. There's not a rock you can hide under in this whole galaxy where I won't find you."

Anor Ran's face was red with anger as he tried to speak. "Perfectly clear, Captain..." he replied, his voice raspy and barely understandable.

Harlowe breathed a heavy sigh. "I wish I could toss you over the side like your expendables." He let him down gently and straightened the Anor Ran's tunic as he said, "but I need you to tell me where Quay and the rest of my crew are."

Anor Ran took a moment to breathe again. "I don't know where they are."

"Molly," Harlowe called to Her Highness, lying in the shade of a nearby column. Rhud was laid out flat, snoozing two columns down from her. It was his way of fighting the heat and political hobknobbing. "Do you believe him?" Harlowe asked as she came lumbering up. Molly snarled. He turned back to Anor Ran, his temper becoming short again. "She doesn't believe you. Would you rather talk to her or me?"

Molly opened her mouth and roared, silencing everyone on the veranda. Anor Ran froze. His fear of being eaten alive was quite real. "I don't know where your crew was taken, Captain. That is the truth," he said quickly.

"But you know where Quay is?" Harlowe countered quickly.

With a careful eye on Molly, Anor Ran's words were genuine. "Yes, Unikala is cunning but has few options." He looked drawn and worn-down. Harlowe thought in his early years Anor Ran would have put up more of a struggle. Whatever his age was, life had suddenly caught up with him. "She was taken to Og."

"Og?"

"Unikala's fortress. She is there. I am certain of it."

"And Sizzle?"

"Why do you care about her?"

"I care about your whole family, Anor, even that suckwad son of yours."

"You have learned a great deal since meeting my daughter."

"Yes, more than I bargained for. I know how you allowed the attack on your office building to fake out the Burgesses. I know how you allowed Turfan to believe he would become the next Tomar-Rex by sucking face with Unikala while he believed he had an in with the Fhaal. Sweet. Kill two birds with their lust for power while you've negotiated with the Fhaal to supply their ships."

Anor Ran concurred. "Everyone needs thermo-grym."

"Always an angle, huh, Anor?"

"Survival, Captain."

"Well, this time you ran out of Jo-Li Ran. The well went dry. But why risk your family? They could have been killed during the attack."

Anor Ran closed his eyes with regret. "The Fhaal killed many billions of Sharlon's people when they captured Neeja."

"They will pay," Harlowe affirmed sternly.

"If Sharlon knew I was associated with the Fhaal..." He turned away, unable to look Harlowe in the eye. "She would leave me. I could not bear to see her eyes and the hatred in them."

Harlowe stood there, slowly shaking his head in disgust as he looked down at how pathetic and small Anor Ran suddenly became with the revelation.

"No one will defeat the Fhaal, not even you and your magnificent ship, Captain."

"Then why come after me? I'm the guy who rescued your daughter, remember?"

"And lost her again."

Harlowe had run into that one. Anor Ran was right. He had lost her, possibly forever. "If the defeat of the Fhaal is a hopeless cause, why not let me seal my own fate?"

"If the stories of the ancients are true, Captain, to possess the ultimate power in the quadrant, perhaps the galaxy..." He looked out across the city to the open space where the golden ship was parked, almost laughing at the absurdity. "Well, if they are true, then no price is too high, is it?" He turned, squinting from the bright sun. "Sharlon has told me many times how her planet, Neeja, had found the ancient scriptures of the Gamadin at Amerloi, a very ancient world on the frontier. They believed that if they found the Gamadin, they could save them from the Fhaal invasion."

"Did they?" Harlowe knew the answer.

"No. They did not. They tell of a young Triadian soldier who escaped the excavations at Hitt just before the Fhaal captured the ancient city. Many believe the Triadian never found the Gamadin mothership." He looked into Harlowe's soul for truth. "Do you believe he was killed, Captain?"

"She," Harlowe corrected. "The Triadian was a she—my girlfriend's mother, who was murdered by the Fhaal. They will be going down when I am finished with them."

If Anor Ran was surprised that Harlowe may have known of the Triadian's mission, he didn't show it. Instead, he was quite frank with his assessment. "The Fhaal are unstoppable, Captain. Once they have their thermo-grym, they will overrun the quadrant. There is nothing else to be done except make our deals with—"

"The devil, Anor?" Harlowe interrupted.

"Yes, with the devil, Captain."

Harlowe looked out over the sea of faces, hearing their shouts of joy, calling to him, their champion. "I can't let them down, Anor. I can't let Gibb down, Tomar, Quay, or Sharlon. Neeja will be rid of the Fhaal when I'm done. That is the promise I made to the Triadian soldier you spoke of, and I *will* keep it. The Gamadin will rid the quadrant of corrupt governments and invincible empires. Omini Prime will once again know the taste of freedom. That is my promise."

"Admirable, my young Captain, but I'm afraid the fate of the quadrant has already begun. A thousand ships like yours will not stop the future," Anor Ran told him.

Harlowe grinned as he reached down and helped the tired Tomarian leader to his feet. "Perhaps, but I still have a few surprises, Anor. Can you delay the thermo-grym shipments to Neeja?"

"I could for a short while."

Harlowe led the dejected Anor Ran along the pink stone veranda, back to the group. "That's the spirit." The cats, however, stuck to the shade as much as possible.

"Why?" Anor Ran asked of the Neeja shipments.

Harlowe's mind had shifted into hyperdrive. "A plot you would enjoy, Anor."

"Unikala is expecting you to come after Quay. It is your ship he's after."

"Millie is everybody's favorite."

"Do not underestimate Unikala. He is no fool."

Harlowe agreed. "I don't underestimate anyone. Not even you to delay those shipments."

Anor Ran's eyes smiled at the young Gamadin's ambitious plan. His optimism was infectious. "Understood, Captain. I will do what you ask. You can count on that." He then asked, "Where will you go next?"

"To find a Lagan greaseball called Ra-Loc."

"Lagans have a reputation for their elusiveness."

"Ruloma has discovered he was headed for Sebas," Harlowe replied.

"It is a short journey from Roshmar. I will send word to our office there to hold this Lagan for your arrival."

"It has been weeks since he left Roshmar. He probably only stopped to fill his tank."

"My resources are vast, Captain. We will find him together," Anor Ran assured Harlowe.

Harlowe patted the Tomar-Rex on the back. "Perhaps you're not such a suckwad after all."

"Maybe one day you'll come to Tomar as a friend."

Harlowe laid a heavy hand on the Tomar's shoulder. "Don't press your luck, Anor. We're a long ways from sharing a tray of animal fries."

"Perhaps some day."

"When we've cleaned up the garbage."

"Agreed, Captain. Until then, may the fortune of Jo-Li Ran be with you."

"I need all I can get."

They shook hands. Then Harlowe called the ship. *Millawanda* gently lifted off from the grassy knoll and drifted quietly over the plaza, stopping within inches of the palace balcony. Her great circular hull cast a massive shadow, blocking out the primary, five hundred feet above the multitudes of well-wishers. The cats couldn't wait. They'd had enough of Roshmar's heat for a lifetime. Before the ship's perimeter was close enough to step on, Her Highness first, then Rhud, leaped the thirty-foot closing gap from the balcony edge. They made it seem effortless as they touched down on the topside blinker that transported them instantly to the cool environment of the bridge. Monday and Simon were not quite so bold. They waited for the ship to stop before stepping off the veranda and winking up. Harlowe was the last to leave.

"For all my planet, I thank you," Ruloma told him as the other dignitaries, including Xiomara from Tnoir, showed their gratitude. When all the goodbyes were said, Ruloma and Harlowe were left alone on the balcony.

"Your information has been received, Ruloma. I will find my friends now," Harlowe said, holding her hands. Her blue eyes revealed her thoughts. She wanted him to stay forever.

"Will you ever return to Roshmar?" Ruloma asked, with a heavy sadness in her heart.

"One day." He felt terrible inside. She deserved better. There were moments he had almost let her love overtake him when they were tired and worn-out from the long hours of negotiation with Tnoir. He had resisted, and he told her why. He could love no one until he had found his friends. They were his life, his reason for being.

She looked at his simple ring. "I envy her that she has you from across the stars," Ruloma commented, holding his large, powerful hand.

Harlowe twisted the ring as he tried to swallow the lump in his throat. "You are amazing." He wanted to tell her something more worldly, such as that maybe they would meet again someday, or how, if he had met her first, things might have been different. They were words the old Harlowe from Earth might have said. Words like "we'll do lunch when I swing back this way again." He was Gamadin and a gentleman now. He had the General's moral eyes staring at him over her left shoulder, while his dad glared at him over her right. That was no way to treat a lady, they would say.

His eyes drifted skyward. "I will miss the pink skies of Roshmar and the long walks we had along the cool waters of the Cinnebar."

"I will miss your double-doubles and Taco Tuesdays," she said with a gracious smile.

He sighed. *Man, she wasn't making it easy!*

She squeezed his hand one last time.

He pulled back, not quite letting go. He would rather have suffered another stunner than to say, "I have to go."

"Goodbye, my Gamadin Captain, savior of worlds."

"Goodbye, Ruloma."

With a heavy sigh, he let go of her hand, turned, and moved toward the golden disk. He looked back one last time at her deep blue eyes, full of tears. He tried to touch her again but the ship had drifted too far. *Millawanda* was pulling away. He waved goodbye to a roaring crowd, saluted her crisply, snapping his heels, then stepped onto the blinker and flew away.

82

Standing Tall

RULOMA AND ANOR Ran watched the great golden ship as it drifted slowly through the pink, fluffy clouds, its giant shadow touching the thousands of worshipers who waved enthusiastically from the plaza, the grassy knoll, and the banks of the meandering river. Ruloma clutched the gift the Captain had given her: a muted golden cylinder.

"This will protect you," he had told her. "Many changes will be taking place. Some you can control, some you can't. Those who have power will be reluctant to give it up. They will try to stop you." He handed her the cylinder. "Friday will guard you against those who wish you harm."

"Friday?" she questioned. "It has a name?" recalling the Captain's own mechanical servant, Jewels, and the many times it appeared during the trip to Tnoir. She watched in amazement as the robotic servant popped to life from its cylindrical form.

The Captain smiled. "Yes, Friday knows a lot of cool stuff. You can count of him twenty-four–seven. He never sleeps."

She didn't quite understand what he meant. Friday seemed like an odd name to call a servant. But after working side-by-side with the Captain over the weeks, his unusual articulations and mannerisms were amusingly refreshing. She doubted she would ever again meet a group of beings quite like the Captain and his crew. During what they fondly called their "off-the-clock" time, they would do the most unusual things. Inside their ship was something they called the "rec room," where they often congregated. There they swam in a large pool or played a game call "V-ball." Even their mechanical servants participated. They struck a ball the size of someone's head over a thin intertwined rope. Many times they became so angry at each other when the round object came close to a boundary line that she thought they were going to hurt each other in a battle. But a war never broke out. Their shouts and angry fits would end as soon as one of the servants threw the ball up and hit it again. All very peculiar, she thought.

* * *

Anor Ran's powerful glance of authority let it be known he was still in charge after the Gamadin left Roshmar space. All on the balcony understood that he wished to be alone with Ruloma. When all had departed, he spoke. "It has been a long time, my Ruloma."

Ruloma kept her eyes on the direction the golden ship had flown before it winked from the sky and was gone. Only then did she answer the Tomar-Rex. "A long time for everyone, Anor Ran."

He stepped closer to her, his dark eyes displaying a history they had shared. He reached out as if wanting to touch her. She stopped him, guiding his hand away forcefully.

"The Captain made an impression on you, I see," Anor Ran said.

"An impression on everyone." She drifted away cautiously, holding her gift close, keeping the distance between them constant and measured.

Her coolness disturbed him. He was not accustomed to disloyalty. "The bargain was, you were to keep him here for another cycle. Has the beautiful Ruloma lost her allure?"

"Perhaps, but the Anor Ran's own family has made more of an impression than I, I'm afraid."

"Quay?"

Ruloma nodded. "I could not sever their bond." She saw futility in his eyes. "I see she is not one you have control of either, Anor Ran."

"I still control you, Ruloma." He looked at the hot sun, feeling the heat, adding "and this miserable planet."

Her eyes brightened with confidence. "No more, Anor. What we had in the past has ended. There is nothing more between us."

He leaned into her space. "It is over when I decree it is over, or Roshmar will not survive the next cold cycle. Have you forgotten it is I who supplies Roshmar with its precious thermo-grym?"

She glanced skyward. "I have not forgotten."

"Your Captain will not save you this time, Ruloma." He laughed arrogantly.

Her face was unafraid. "Not even the great Anor Ran can defy this Gamadin Captain," she replied with confidence. "You are powerless. Roshmar's deliveries will be met, I assure you. You would rather sleep with a grogan than lose your empire."

"You dare belittle me?"

"I don't have to. You have belittled yourself. I saw with my own eyes how this Captain reduced your authority to an impudent chee. He destroyed your ship in a wink. He has left you here on Roshmar with only the clothes you wear. Tut, tut, tut. What are you going to do now?"

Anor Ran's face went wild. "I will kill you!" He pulled from his boot a small weapon and would have killed her in cold blood, but in the instant between the threat and its execution, the cylinder cradled in Ruloma's hands came to life. Before Anor Ran could fire his weapon, the stickly form grabbed him by the arms and slammed him hard onto the stone deck of the balcony.

Anor Ran's eyes spun from the sudden change of direction. The triangular head of the mechanical stickman touched his nose, its glowing blue rim pulsating as if it could bring an instant end to the life of the richest being in the quadrant.

Ruloma had other plans. "Thank you, Friday." The speed of her dutiful new servant had surprised even her. "It appears my Captain is still with us, Anor Ran."

"Impressive." Anor Ran tried to break Friday's hold. No matter how hard he fought, he could not dislodge the dura-steel hands from around his neck. He was pinned as if he were nailed to the stone. "Is this necessary?"

"The shipment, Anor Ran?" Ruloma inquired. "It will be delivered before the end of the next cycle. Is that correct?"

Ruloma stood above him and waited for Anor Ran's reply. She was about to run out of patience when Anor Ran finally relented. "Yes, Madame President. Delivery will be made as bargained by your Gamadin Captain."

"Then your business on Roshmar is done," Ruloma said dismissively. To the mechanical servant she directed, "Release him, Friday, and escort the Tomar-Rex from the palace grounds."

"I would love to depart this unholy planet, but as you know, I have no transport to leave Roshmar. I will need a ship to take me back to Palcor," he said. It was more like a demand.

"Tut-tut, Anor! If my memory serves me, you always have an escape vehicle hidden somewhere. Summon it and be off with you." Ruloma then turned to join the rest of the dignitaries inside the palace ballroom.

"It is not meant for interstellar distances beyond a quarter cycle," Anor Ran called after her.

Ruloma turned her back on the Tomar-Rex. "In the words of our young Gamadin Captain... 'That ain't my problem.'"

Ruloma was almost to the door when Anor Ran added, "It will not make any difference, Madame. The Gamadin will not survive the cycle." He began to laugh. "Og will be his doom."

Ruloma hesitated briefly as if she was about to counter his statement. But she didn't. She kept walking through the doorway and disappeared among the dignitaries. Her new servant, Friday, clickity-clacked behind Anor Ran, lifting him bodily off the stone deck. The Tomar-Rex flailed his arms and legs and shouted Tomarian obscenities as Friday showed him the back door.

83

Run or Die

FIVE HEAVILY ARMED guards walked down the line of thralls toward Dagger. The guard leader in front was thick and dark, his face beastly, ashen, and pockmarked. His lieutenants were no less loathsome and a full head taller than Dagger. The security team looked more like a pack of wild animals on the prowl than guards hired to protect the levels from disobedient thralls. Walking between the working diggers, they brutally kicked the slow movers out of their path like rubbish. The leader stopped and looked down at Dagger. From what Riverstone could overhear while pretending not to was that they were searching for a band of rebels that had revolted on the lower levels and killed many guards.

Dagger spit a vile mass on the bare back of the nearest digger. "There are no insurgents on my level," he stated flatly, assuring the guards.

"Two work periods ago we discovered their secret tunnels. We managed to kill all but their leader. He is called The Gama. We believe he has escaped to this level."

"I have seen no Gama, officer. If he comes here," Dagger scoffed, holding his whip for all to see, "it will be the end of him. No one gets by Dagger. If he comes to my level, I will cut off his head and place it on an iron spike for all those to see."

The officer approved of Dagger's crusty manner. "I believe you will, Dagger. Your reputation is duly earned." His eyes traced down the line of diggers. "They dig well."

"I see to that. Check the production quotas. Dagger's line has exceeded work orders by nearly twenty-two percent for the last fifty work periods." Dagger spat another black wad. "A record, officer."

"We are to remain here until further orders." The officer's eyes fell on Ela. "In the meantime, my guards will need the use of your quarters for the rest period."

Dagger pointed at his small, wretched dwelling cut out of solid rock. "Take what you need."

The guard leader added, "We will also need entertainment. The wait may be long," he said, casting his lustful eyes upon Ela. "We will take her."

Dagger hesitated. It was no coincidence that his record production output had coincided with new thrall's arrival. The guard leader saw the reluctance in Dagger's face and quickly removed a bag of koorants from his thick belt. "Is this enough?"

Dagger smiled evilly. He would have taken much less. "Agreed." He nodded at Ela. "You have an eye for good stock." Dagger stopped him momentarily. "Go easy on her, friend. My production line depends on her."

The lead officer motioned for his subordinate guard to take possession of their purchase. "As you wish."

Dagger nodded, his crooked teeth filled with dark decay and rot. "Enjoy!"

A guard reached down and tried to lift Ela from the line. "No!" Riverstone cried out. The officer and the guard were momentarily stunned that a digger had such audacity and contempt for authority. The officer pulled his weapon and was about to shoot Riverstone, when Riverstone skillfully kicked the weapon from the officer's hand as if it were a toy, then slapped him back against a line of thralls. The guard holding Ela froze. Rebellion was rare, but when it happened, thralls always revolted in packs. They never resisted alone for obvious reasons. They were too undisciplined and unskilled at self-defense. Thalls knew only one thing, pounding their hammers against the rock. Corrective action against a thrall was swift and brutal, usually ending in death, with their mutilated bodies put on display the way Dagger had described earlier. It made a lasting impression.

Dagger knew he must act quickly or suffer the consequences of a reprimand for one of his thralls stepping out of line in front of the guards. Even with this minor insurrection, he would lose face among his peers. When Dagger came up behind Riverstone with the butt end of his whip, he had death in his eyes. Riverstone, Gamadin-trained, saw the blindside coming. Dagger didn't know what hit him. He tumbled backwards into a rock pile, out cold. Seeing how swiftly the officer and Dagger had been dispatched, the guard tried to use Ela as a shield. His idea was short-lived. Ela kneed him between the legs, doubling him over. Another time, another place far from a hundred miles underground, Riverstone would have given a "Way to go, Ela!" followed by a high-five and a kiss, but not now. Now there was no time. Like it or not, they were committed to escaping from Erati. They had to act or die.

A third and fourth guard came at Riverstone and Ela with heavy bars. Riverstone grabbed Ela and pulled her out of the way just as a bar was about to crack her head open. For now, Ela was more of a problem than an asset. The guards were too strong for her to handle. Sparks exploded in the guard's face when the bar missed and struck a small crystal in the rock. With the guard momentarily blinded, Riverstone grabbed the rod and smashed it into the guard's face, breaking open his skull. Wheeling around, he parried the fourth guard's bar and nailed him too. The guard who had held Ela was coming out of his pain and preparing to swing a stone hammer across Riverstone's skull. With blinding speed, Riverstone grabbed the hammer and landed a swift kick to the guard's head, dropping him to the ground.

"Stop, thrall, or I will kill her!" a voice cried out.

Riverstone turned, still holding the bar in his hand, and faced the voice. The officer whom he had stunned earlier had a weapon at Ela's head, cocked and ready to fire if Riverstone didn't yield.

"Harm her and you're dead, puke," Riverstone said coldly.

"Drop the bar, thrall!" The officer's eyes darted from side to side, looking at what was left of his men at his feet. His huge hands had Ela by the neck. He would have easily broken it if she hadn't been the only reason he was still alive.

Riverstone knew that the instant he let go of the bar, he and Ela were dead. He needed a break. Any tiny hesitation in the officer's concentration would be enough. If he was wrong by only a fraction, the officer's finger could twitch enough to set off the weapon.

Then it happened. Dagger moved.

With only his gun to protect him, and being the lone survivor among the hordes of thralls, the frightened officer took his eyes off Riverstone for a split second to regard Dagger. It was the break Riverstone needed. He fired the bar at the lead guard's head. The missile struck home, jolting the officer backward. The weapon fired, but it was a harmless shot in the air. Ela went down, still held fast by the officer's twitching hand.

Riverstone ran to her side and yanked her free from the loathsome grip. There was no time to make plans. They had to reach the deserted, outer abandoned mine shafts before the fallen guards were discovered. All Riverstone could think of was flight. He grabbed Ela's hand and they ran. There was no coming back, no justice in the underground tomb of Erati. They had to escape or they would both die.

84

New Course

PRIGG'S WAYWARD EYES stared at the star chart on the main overhead screen. They had missed Ra-Loc at Sebas by three weeks, and at a small planet called Aberna by eighteen days! After that, it was twenty more light-years' travel to Asku, and they were still no closer to the Lagan than when they had left Roshmar.

The simple reality was, the sly Lagan trader had eluded them. Whether Ra-Loc was two weeks or two days away, Harlowe was clueless. Anor Ran had warned him weeks ago that the Fhaal were pressing him to complete his shipments. He had run out of excuses to give the Fhaal High Command. A communication from the High Commander Sar himself confirmed that the Fhaal would raze Tomar if the shipments were not delivered to Neeja before the end of the cycle. Harlowe was running short of time. He had five days left to wrap things up or Anor Ran would be forced to deliver the thermo-grym shipments to Sar.

Ra-Loc was leading them through distant star systems, even for Prigg. He had only heard about them in conversations with other traders. He had never ventured this far out of the quadrant. Some planets were entirely unknown to him. As Prigg studied the star chart, Harlowe noticed the little Naruckian's wayward eyes moving about more abnormally than usual.

"You okay, Prigg?" Harlowe asked. He was anxious to get to Linot, the next planet in their search.

"Yes, Your Majesty," Prigg muttered in a low voice, as if anything louder might disturb his concentration.

"Problem?" Simon asked, looking over the console for any miscalculations. "We're about a day and half from Linot, Prigg."

Prigg's bidirectional eyes continued scanning. "Yes, Mr. Bolt. You are quite correct." Suddenly both eyes locked. Someone who had never seen Prigg's eyes function might have believed the coordination was unusual. But to the Gamadin crew, who had worked with the little Naruckian every day for the past few months, it meant a great deal. Prigg had reached a decision he was about to share with the bridge. "I have discovered a pattern I did not see previously, Your Majesty."

The three Gamadin glanced up at the screen with their mouths half-open, searching for anything that made sense.

As Prigg's hands deftly glided over the controls in front of him, the screen converted to a large macro view of the quadrant frontier. Gibb was to the far left of the screen. Naruck was almost off the overhead but close to Palcor, which hung slightly below and to the right of Naruck. Roshmar was close to Sebas. Directly to the right were Aberna and Amerloi near the edge of the screen. The blinking blue dot was the Ship moving away from Asku. Linot was not on the screen yet, but a small blue arrow pointed in its direction.

"Forgetting Naruck and Palcor, Your Majesty," Prigg said, continuing, "you will notice the Lagan has not reversed course once since leaving Palcor." Prigg drew a blue line connecting the star systems they had traveled in the quadrant. "It appears Ra-Loc's journey is nearly a straight line after Roshmar, making many stops in the process. We know he is in a hurry, but his pattern suggests otherwise. He makes many stops. Why?"

Harlowe expelled a small jet of hot air. "That's easy. Ra-Loc is a creature of habit. The scumbag can't pass up a chance to screw someone over at every planet he passes. For him, they're new marks ready for the plucking."

Prigg agreed with Harlowe. He then went on, explaining that he did not believe Ra-Loc knew they were tailing him. "It is possible the Lagan believes the Consortium will not reach him on the frontier."

Simon added his comment. "He's become careless."

"I believe he is, Mr. Bolt, as you say, careless. Under normal circumstances the Lagan would have taken better care to conceal his direction of travel. His actions, however, lead me to believe his side trips may not have been as successful as he hoped since there are so many. His resources appear low and he is forced to take a more direct approach toward his self-serving exile," Prigg explained, highlighting one area of the screen. "You will notice the area I have marked. It is a vast star desert called Cartooga-Thaat. There is only one star cluster before the boundary, the Nual Cluster. In that system there are seventeen stars of various magnitudes and densities. But only one system in the cluster has a planetary body capable of supporting life for one such as the Lagan. The planet is called Patol. If I were a Lagan who wanted to disappear, Patol would be the place I would choose, Your Majesty. There is not a habitable planet for another hundred light-passings from there. Unless he turns back to the quadrant, Patol is his next destination. I am sure of it. He will stop there, Your Majesty."

Harlowe studied Prigg's theory on the overhead. If he was right, a lot of time would be saved. And with *Millawanda's* superior speed, there was a better-than-even chance he could overtake the Lagan before the fat toad arrived. If Prigg was wrong...another six months, maybe a year. They could even lose him for good. It was a big galaxy.

"Patol, huh?"

"Yes, Your Majesty."

Harlowe looked over at Monday and Simon. They were both all-in.

Harlowe leaned back in his chair, thirsting for a thick cookie-dough shake. "Patol it is, Mr. Bolt. Lay in the course change."

"Aye, Skipper."

"Mr. Platter, when you have the coordinates, all-ahead full. We're going to beat that rat barf there before he has a chance to smell the air."

"Aye, Captain," Monday replied.

85

No Way Out

THEY HAD BEEN lucky so far. But from here on out, Riverstone knew their chances were next to nothing unless they could find a way off their level. Up or down, it didn't matter. If they couldn't find their way to another level, they were toad waste. They could elude Dagger and the other Erati guards for only so many work periods before they would eventually catch up. They had to find a way out fast.

After the skirmish with the guards, Riverstone and Ela ran back to their hovel by the pond and gathered all the food and water they could carry and still be nimble enough to keep ahead of the search parties coming after them. Before the work period was over, the shafts were indeed flooded with guards carrying real weapons, not thick metal bars. The Erati higher-ups were wasting no time. The order was out: kill on sight. No mercy. Eliminate the rebellious thralls and do it swiftly, before the insurrection spreads.

Growing up in the mines, however, had its advantages. Ela knew the tunnels better than the security forces. They managed to stay just ahead of the search parties, but even an eternal optimist would have understood the guards were systematically closing the gap between them. Even with her knowledge, their search for a path up to the higher levels was fruitless. There seemed to be no way out of the ancient and vast tunnels. Ela confirmed as much over and over during their rest periods. "No one has ever found a way out, Matthew," she told him. "We are here, and this is where we must stay."

After running for miles and miles in the twisting dark underground tomb, Riverstone finally understood the futility. They were trapped.

Unless...

"Ela," Riverstone said, looking into her dark eyes that peered like those of a nocturnal animal into the lightless tunnels. "We must make it to the main shaft."

"The vertical," as she called it, "will be heavily guarded, Matthew," she warned him.

"We have to chance it, Ela."

"How, Matthew? I know of no tunnels to lead us there."

Riverstone had a plan. "We can climb." Ela's small nose turned upward, frightened. "My mates and I did it all the time at the Mons. I know you don't understand, but..." He took her in his arms and held her, kissing her once before he finished his explanation. "Do you trust me?" She nodded. "You must follow me and do exactly as I tell you, no matter what," She nodded again. Ela was "all-in."

"Good. We'll be okay. We can do it. We need some rope and a hammer. They're lying around everywhere. Chisels, too. We'll make carabiners to tie our rope to so we won't fall. You'll see. I'll show you." He went to the wall of the shaft and climbed like a human insect to the top. "See?" he called down to her. "It's cool. You'll be great." He dropped back to the ground and held her in his arms. "When we get to the main shaft, we can climb out of here. It's a long way, many, many miles, but we will make it, Ela. We will make it."

Ela clapped her hands with joy. "Yes, my Matthew. We will make—"

Clang!

Something metallic suddenly clanked on the ground somewhere down the shaft behind them. Fearing the worst, Riverstone grabbed Ela's hand and began running in the opposite direction.

BOOM!!

The percussion device exploded, ripping Ela's hand away from Riverstone as they both blew back against the far wall and dropped like stone-cold rocks to the ground.

86

Patol

"AH, PERTO. AT long last, Patol," Ra-Loc sighed, his heavy, inflated jowls rippling as they expelled his putrid air. He gazed out of his observation window and stared happily at the towering mosques of the city. Ra-Loc would have preferred a planet with lush foliage and thick, humid air, but he was tired of traveling and low on capital. A Lagan in his position had little choice but to settle for an out-of-the-way planet until he could recapitalize and think about the future.

Ra-Loc went giddy with self-congratulation at finding a peaceful planet where he could relax. Peering out, he spied an open parking bay in the center of the city. "Set the ship down there, Perto," he pointed hurriedly, "before someone else takes it."

"The docking fees will be quite high there, sire," Perto pointed out.

"Yes. I don't care." Ra-Loc waved his hand impatiently. "That is where I want to be."

Perto shrugged. "Yes, sire." What did he care? It wasn't his money.

* * *

A short time later Perto came to his master's quarters with the news. "As you ordered, Ra-Loc, we have acquired excellent accommodations in the center of town."

537

"You had no trouble?" Ra-Loc asked. There was a hint of surprise in his tone.

Perto shook his head. "No, sire, none whatsoever. The docking fees were quite in line, I might add. No gratuity was required. The authorities on Patol are very cooperative."

Ra-Loc changed into fresh silk-like clothes that hung on him like a Persian tent. His eyes narrowed as he looked out his window at the other ships nearby. "Really, Perto, nothing extra for this bay?" he asked skeptically.

"No, sire."

"Hmmm. Most unusual." He was indeed surprised but waved his hand, unworried. "You did well, Perto. I should not be concerned with such providence on Patol. I saw a gathering place not far from here. It's a short walk. Yes, you did quite well, Perto."

All the same, Ra-Loc had not survived this many passings in his line of business by letting down his guard completely. When he saw that the beings on the street were carrying weapons, his paranoia returned. He was sure no one knew him there but a little precaution was always prudent, he reminded himself. "Have my grogans and two more guards than usual accompany us, Perto. I am not familiar with Patol. It is wise to be well-protected."

"Yes sire," Perto replied.

"With fully charged plas-pistols, not stunners, you understand," Ra-Loc ordered. He turned away from the window. "Yes, that should be enough for this pathetic little city. Hurry, Perto!" Ra-Loc added. He was thirsty.

With his armed escorts as his side, Ra-Loc led his entourage and two pet grogans down the narrow, dusty streets of Patol. The beings of Patol appeared to be unfamiliar with grogans and stared fearfully at the two beasts, giving the entourage a wide berth as they walked down the clapboard walkways.

Patol's mosque towers spread throughout the city were the highlight of its charm. The colorful blue religious points were a stark contrast to the dirt streets and adobe buildings. The planet was home to fewer than two thousand nondescript beings. "Patol" was the name of the spaceport. The planet's name was actually Xaller. But everyone, including many star charts, simply called it Patol because the city was the center of all known trade activity on Xaller. Nowhere else on the planet would anyone come to trade and do business. The rest of Xaller was desert and uninhabitable. Xaller did not rotate on its axis. It always faced its primary. Patol itself was located within a small strip of temperate land between the boundaries of night and day. It was the only place on the planet where life *could* survive. As a city of commerce, it was unimportant, but because it was the last space terminal before the great star desert of Cartooga-Thaat, it had value. No one ventured farther than Patol unless they were prepared to risk the emptiness beyond.

When Ra-Loc and his entourage entered the gathering place he had seen from his ship, he found it disgustingly unappealing. His stay on Patol would be short, he concluded, protecting his nose and mouth with a long, silky cloth. Other than being crowded, there was nothing unusual about the establishment. He had been in many barrooms like it throughout the quadrant. It had a large smoke-filled room with many tables of chance surrounded by beings playing cards and drinking their way toward oblivion. Like Ra-Loc, many of the debauched beings looked as if they were running from some nefarious past.

Ra-Loc felt many odious eyes stare at him as he entered the establishment. He was relieved that he'd had the forethought to bring along extra protection.

"There are no places for us to sit, Ra-Loc," one of Ra-Loc's gruff-voiced hired guns pointed out.

Ra-Loc smiled, guiding his grogans toward a large, circular table where a group of six gamblers sat. "Excuse me. Can anyone play?" he asked the table.

A player wearing an unusual set of clothes, dark glasses, and a blue-billed hat with the symbol "LA" along the brim got up and offered Ra-Loc his chair. "It's all yours, mate," the player said.

"Let's see your money, fatso," another hard voice said from across the table opposite the first player.

Ra-Loc glared at the being who spoke so rudely. He had a muscular build and a white shirt with a blue inscription across the chest. If Ra-Loc had understood the language, it would have read: *Dodgers*. The large, muscular being was quite young and wore the same blue hat and dark glasses as the first player. The being's unshaven face was hidden in shadow. In his hands he had a deck of cards that he shuffled in front of him like a professional player, cutting the cards with one hand.

Impressive...

Ra-Loc snapped his fingers and Perto tossed a pouch in front of him. Ra-Loc opened the pouch and spread the gems for all to see. His gluttonous grin widened. "Is that satisfactory?" Ra-Loc asked, taking the empty chair while Perto and the others spread themselves around the room. "Are we here to play or quibble?" he added.

The rest of the table moved away, leaving only the two players with the blue hats at the table. It seemed the pot was suddenly too rich for the other players.

"If you would be so kind as to show me your stake, friends, before we play," Ra-Loc said.

One of the beings put his palms up, indicating that he was putting his hand inside his coat pocket. Ra-Loc's henchmen eased back as the being retrieved a stone from his pocket and tossed it in the middle of the table.

Ra-Loc's eyes went wide with fascination. The stone was brilliant, projecting a blue radiance like no gem he had ever seen before.

"Good enough?" the being asked, his tone actually mocking Ra-Loc's wager. "That's for the both of us," he added, nodding toward the other blue-capped player.

"Yes. Yes, indeed," Ra-Loc replied, his eyes instantly turning bright with greed. He had to have that stone at all cost. "Where did you get it?"

"None of your business, fatso," the player opposite the dealer said.

The being started to deal the cards.

"New deck," Ra-Loc demanded.

The dealer snapped his fingers and a four-foot-tall mechanical stick-like waiter, classily dressed in black and white coat and tie, clickity-clacked up to the table and tossed several unopened decks on the table.

"Pick one, toad," the dealer said.

Ra-Loc pointed to the middle deck. The dealer picked up the deck and tore open the wrapper, shuffling the cards, all in one easy motion.

"Me and my friends came to enjoy your lovely city," Ra-Loc commented, trying to make conversation as he studied the dealer's traits. "We were hoping to rest a little and—"

"We don't like greaseballs with smelly pets. Cards?"

Ra-Loc looked at his cards. It was an excellent hand. "I'll play these," he uttered, forcing a nervous smile.

"You have a good hand, huh?" The dealer tossed out an even larger blue stone. "Would you care to increase the wager, puke?"

Ra-Loc stared at his cards. There was only one hand capable of beating his. He watched the dealer put his discards to the side, keeping one. The chances of him drawing the four cards he needed to beat Ra-Loc were next to impossible.

Ra-Loc nodded to Perto. His servant bent down, putting a second pouch in front of him. "Master, this is all we have." Ra-Loc showed Perto his cards. "Yes," he said approvingly, and stepped back out of the way.

"The wager is matched," Ra-Loc said, and pushed the second pouch of gems out into the center of the table, adding his wager to the pot. Ra-Loc then turned up his cards for all those to see. "I believe this fortune is mine."

Ra-Loc started to gather in the blue stones when a short wooden stick stopped him. "Not so fast, Lagan." The dealer spread his hand across the table. "You lost." It was the only hand that could have beat him, and the dealer had done it with a four-card draw. Ra-Loc knew he had been cheated. It was the only answer. No one could have beaten him like that honestly.

"Impossible!" Ra-Loc whined.

"You calling me a cheater, dude?"

Ra-Loc waved a self-confident hand at his henchmen. "My friends say you are not so honest."

The being took a casual sip of his blue drink as Ra-Loc gathered in his fortune. "You may not get another chance to finish your drink if you doubt them," Ra-Loc growled as his hired guns gathered beside him, backing up his threat with force.

The dealer remained unmoved as Ra-Loc eyed the blue stones. "Yes, they are enchanting. You have more? I will make you a generous offer. More of these for your life, perhaps," he chuckled menacingly. He then brought his grogans to his side. As that happened, there came a low, deep growl from beneath the table next to the dealer. Ra-Loc knew the growl was not one of his grogans rumblings. Both of his black pets started to snap at something under the table. They were both extremely agitated. Their keepers could hardly control their chains, as they tried to get at whatever was under the table. Perto shuffled around the table and glimpsed the large white form that was bothering his pets.

The dealer coolly took another sip from his drink. "Take one step away from the table slimeball and you're dead."

Ra-Loc was beside himself. He had not planned on this! He had come to Patol for a nice, relaxing escape from his problems with the Consortium Commissar, Unikala. Now, to his chagrin, he has to deal with a problem he did not expect in such an inhospitable world. He was tired. He didn't want problems. He just wanted a comfortable chair and a drink. He would even go so far as to pay the cheat a few koorants if he would just accept the fact that he had gotten caught! Normally, Ra-Loc would not have given much thought to killing a cheat. It was quite appropriate, but hardly a way to begin his stay. He glanced at Perto. He had his face to save in front of his men as well. What choice did he have? The being had insulted him in front of everyone. He sighed heavily, resigned that he might as well kill him and be done with it.

Ra-Loc gave the sign for the henchman to release his grogans. In a heartbeat they disappeared under the table and attacked the shadowy form. The table rose up slightly as the scuffling erupted. As if a door had slammed in their faces, the bloodthirsty growls of his grogans were abruptly silenced. A moment later, a headless grogan was tossed out from under the table like worthless garbage. Another muffled crunch sounded and the other grogan's twitching form followed the first, landing heavily at Ra-Loc's feet next to his other pet. Its head was crushed, its neck broken backwards across its shoulders. It was as lifeless as the first grogan.

A deathly hush fell over the room as everyone's mouths, except for the blue hats', hung agape in shock.

The dealer shook his head slowly. "Having a bad hair day, huh, Ra-Loc?" he said, as the massive head of a white, blue-eyed tiger poked out from under the table. "Remember Rhud, puke? You've met him before. He was a little smaller then, but you get the idea. A back alley on Gibb ring a bell?"

Harlowe removed his hat.

Ra-Loc slumped back, trying to hide behind his henchmen. "You..."

"Yes, me." Harlowe nodded toward the other blue hat.

Simon removed his hat as well. "I came along to watch, fatso."

"Very resourceful, human," Ra-Loc commented to Harlowe.

"Your stench was not hard to follow," Harlowe countered.

Ra-Loc motioned to his hired guns. Perto stepped back. He had been there and saw the humans dispatch the hired guns Ra-Loc had with him that night on Gibb. He knew what to expect. Before the four bodyguards could touch their sidearms, they were riddled with fiery blue bolts of plasma. They lay on the floor next to the headless grogans, adding to the pile of carnage.

Harlowe looked at Perto as if to say *leave us or die*. Perto needed no further nudging. He backed out the door and ran down the street to his ship. Ra-Loc tried to waddle his way out, too, but another white cat stepped coolly in front of the swinging doors, blocking his exit.

There were months of pent-up rage inside Harlowe. He wanted to end Ra-Loc's miserable life at that very moment, but he needed answers only a live Ra-Loc could give him.

"I have questions, Ra-Loc," Harlowe began. The Lagan's round, bulbous face poured waterfalls of sweat. "If you even think about giving me a wrong answer, Molly here will make grogan waste out of your stupid head. Are we communicating, fatso?" Ra-Loc shook. Yes, he did understand. "Good. Two girls and two of my crew are missing. What have you done with them?"

Ra-Loc shook his head. "I didn't do..."

Harlowe was pressed for time. He nodded to Simon. In a blink, Simon blew away Ra-Loc's ear.

Ra-Loc's face turned green as he howled in pain. "Stop, stop! I will tell you anything you want to know!"

Harlowe's lips were thin with impatience, fighting off the urge to personally finish what Simon had started. "Molly, show Ra-Loc how much you've grown this last year." The big cat moved toward the Lagan, backing him up against the far wall as he held the side of his green-bloodied face. She then crawled up the side of the wall, stretching her forepaws ten feet above Ra-Loc's shaking body. Ra-Loc could feel Molly's hot breath on his face. "What do you think she'll do to you if I tell her you're the one who took her mother from her?"

Ra-Loc started to cry, begging Harlowe not to kill him.

Harlowe snapped his fingers and Molly slumped back down on the floor, backing off slightly.

"Tell me where they are...NOW, PUKE!"

Ra-Loc couldn't control his composure. He curled up into a sobbing ball on the floor, wailing his guts out. Harlowe yanked the Lagan up from his fetal pose. "Where are they?" he continued to shout. Then, slightly calmer, he went on, "Tell me or so help me, Molly will shred your greasy hide clear across Patol. Where are they?"

Ra-Loc tried to faint, but Harlowe wouldn't let him. He lifted the Lagan bodily in the air again and slammed him against the wall.

"You're not passing out on me, toad! TELL ME WHERE THEY ARE!"

"The males..." Ra-Loc gasped. "Erati..."

"Erati?" Harlowe had heard the name before. It was where the crystal came from that was so important to Roshmar's survival, he remembered. "The mining planet?"

Ra-Loc nodded, his feet dangling, trying desperately to find the floor. "Yes... That is where they are."

Harlowe shook him again with Simon looking on, eager to blast the Lagan with a hot round between the eyes. "The females. Where are they? Are they there, too?"

"I know of only one female."

"Where is she? Is her name Quay?" Harlowe demanded.

"I don't know."

"Molly!"

"Yes, yes! That is she! Anor Ran's daughter. Unikala has her. She must be at Og. Yes, yes, that is where he took her!"

Simon leaned in over Harlowe's shoulder. "What color hair did this female have?"

Harlowe squeezed until Ra-Loc was about to burst like a giant zit.

"Unikala. He has her," Ra-Loc kept repeating. "Night. Her hair was..."

He never finished his sentence. The Lagan fainted in Harlowe's hands. He tried to shake Ra-Loc back to conscienceness, but his efforts were ineffective. He let him drop to the floor. Simon reached down to feel his vital signs, finally pulling back an eyelid. No life remained in the Lagan body.

"He's dead, Skipper," Simon concluded after the brief examination.

Harlowe nodded and turned to the gathering place's owner. "Keep the stones." The owner thanked him with a silent nod. Harlowe and his entourage walked through the astonished crowd and out the door. Tears filled his eyes as he went from a loping jog to a full-blown sprint back to the waiting rover and *Millawanda*. The pain inside him cried out, *Time is running out!* His friends needed him more than ever.

Molly and Rhud galloped alongside him, while Simon kept pace a half step behind. Quincy was there, waiting for them in the granny wagon. When everybody was secure, the android slammed the accelerator forward. He didn't need to be told to hurry. As they raced across the desert to the hidden gully where they had parked *Millawanda* out of sight from Ra-Loc's ship, Monday reported that Millie was at full power, ready for immediate departure. Moments after they stepped on the blinkers and reappeared in the control room, the saucer broke atmosphere and throttled into hyperspace, on a course for the planet Erati at flank speed.

87

The Gama

RIVERSTONE FOUGHT HIS way back from an incessant horror of fire and pain to find Ela. Someone touched him, making him jerk away in a frightened spasm. He didn't care about the pain; he cared only about Ela. A gentle hand caught him and held him firm until his trembling stopped, soothing his fear of losing her. "Ela?" Riverstone whispered in a throaty rasp. His mouth was dry, his body numb. He could feel no sensation other than the gentle warmth of someone wiping his face and forehead.

"It's okay, Matt," a voice replied.

"Ela...Ela..."

The last thing he remembered was Ela holding his hand as they ran. She was with him until they heard something click against the rocks. He had her. Then—

"Ela!" Riverstone cried out. "Don't take her away from me, please! Ela, come back!"

He tried to reach out for her, but the pain!

"Sit back, Matt," the voice told him. "You're hurt. Don't move. You have to rest."

"Ela."

"Sit back, pard, you have to rest."

Riverstone's lips formed around a word from his past. He vaguely remembered a name. It seemed so long ago that he had heard it. It was a different lifetime, he recalled, in a place very far away from Erati.

"Swallow this," the voice said to him. A helping hand slid under his head and lifted him up. Rough fingers put a small capsule in his mouth, then gave him a sip of cool water. Almost immediately his pain began to ease.

"Is it working?" the voice asked.

Riverstone nodded. He forced his eyes open slightly to look at the humanoid form hovering over him. The form turned away briefly and rummaged through different items in a sack. A small flame from a makeshift lamp was the only source of light. He gazed at the rock formation inside the small crevice, but he didn't recognize his surroundings. There were many tunnels, of course. He and Ela had searched out many in their desperate flight to escape the guards, but this was not a shaft they had seen. This one was different from all the others. It was smaller and quiet, and the pounding hammers of the thralls were a great distance away.

The humanoid returned to him after he had found what he was looking for. "Try eating this."

Riverstone accepted the morsel of food. It tasted like dried crusty bread. "Who are you?" he asked skeptically. He trusted no one except Ela.

The form gave Riverstone more food and water before he brought the lamp from the small rock ledge and shone the light in front of his face. The dark hair and dirty beard were covered with dust, but the blue eyes were kind and familiar. His own eyes began to fill with tears. Slowly, he reached up with his shaking hands to make sure the form was no ghostly dream. His arms were weak and trembling as he grabbed the rag of a shirt and held his rescuer as if he would never let go. "Wiz..." he said in hoarse disbelief. Ian was the last person in the universe he'd expected to see.

Ian smiled. It was a smile that did not come easy. There seemed to be great suffering behind the creases of his mouth and eyes.

"I thought you'd died," Riverstone said, his eyes shut, squeezing the tears away so he could see again.

"The old Gunn trick, remember?" Ian said. "When the toad wasn't looking I tied a line to the side of the platform. I knew it was my only chance. The line was too thin for him to see. I faked still being drugged. I was hoping you saw what I was doing and would follow me. I must have dropped a thousand feet before I stopped and bounced and swung to the side of the shaft, where I found an abandoned level. No one saw me. I lived there, survived, and found food and water. It was my worst nightmare, pard, never seeing the sun, never knowing if it was day or night. Never knowing if you were okay. I thought I was going to die." Ian wiped his nose, then his eyes, with the back of his hand before continuing. "I wanted to end it then but Gunn wouldn't let me. His face—The Dude wouldn't let me die, Matt. He wouldn't."

Ian turned away, wiping his eyes again. "Then the others found me. They were renegade slaves like me. We started raiding the upper levels at first. We got good. We really disrupted the goonies before they finally found our stronghold and killed many of my friends. I don't know how. I think we were sold out." He sighed with a heavy sadness as though resigned to his fate. "It doesn't matter now. It's happened and now I'm here."

"How did you escape the slaughter?" Riverstone asked.

Ian stared at the light, his eyes unblinking and distant as though the grief and his soul were one. "Gunn was right. The training paid off. I felt something was wrong. The moment before the goonies hit us, I got everyone out of the shaft. They had us surrounded and we lost a lot of good people. The only reason I was able to escape was, well, I don't think they ever expected to run into a Gamadin in the mines of Erati. I don't know how many I bonked. A mess of them, I guess. Everyone separated. We knew there would be more the next time, with more weapons, more explosives, and more death. I escaped through the back tunnels. My SIBA kept me alive. I owned the dark. I dusted so many of the toads they simply gave up and sealed the level, leaving me alone. I was doing okay until I ran out of power."

"How..." Riverstone tried to ask, letting go, his strength sapped, looking Ian in his eyes, still wondering if it was really him.

Ian knew the question. "I searched level by level until I found you."

Riverstone looked down at his broken and mutilated legs. Below both knees were bandages and splints made of old rags and iron.

"Your legs were crushed from the rocks that fell on you. If I had gotten there sooner..." Ian lamented, the ache in his voice showing the heavy guilt he felt about finding him too late to do anything about his brutal injuries.

Riverstone pulled him closer and spoke slowly, his voice cracking and hoarse under the stress of staying conscious. "You were right on time, pard." Riverstone let out a small chuckle for no apparent reason. "Harlowe. Ya think he's okay?"

Their eyes met. Sure he was. "You know Dog."

Riverstone nodded feebly. "Yeah..." He knew Dog. After a long moment he added, "He's looking for us, you know."

Ian's eyes drifted with a crazy glint as he stared off into the darkness, unblinking. "And he'll find us, too."

Riverstone felt the same confidence. "Erati's toast when he does."

Ian sighed. "Harlowe is hurting as much as we are."

Riverstone closed his eyes, knowing Harlowe's pain. A flood of terror suddenly rose inside him. The drug that Ian had given him allowed him to recall more terrible things, lifting the euphoria that had blocked his thoughts of Ela.

"Oh my god, Ela!" Riverstone rolled over, trying to get up. He fell face down in the dirt. All he could do was crawl like an injured animal.

"What are you doing?" Ian asked, fighting with Riverstone to keep him still.

"Let me go, Wiz! Ela! If Dagger finds her, he'll kill her," Riverstone cried. He was shaking now, visibly trembling with fear not for himself, but for her.

Ian took hold of Riverstone's shoulders and forced him back down. "The girl who was with you?"

Riverstone buried his head in Ian's shoulder, sobbing, biting his ragged shirt to keep himself from falling from a cliff of despair. "Ela…my…Wiz. You gotta…" Riverstone's faraway stare of horror was enough for Ian to understand Ela was someone he had to find. "Oh, God, please, Dagger, don't take her from me!" Mercifully, the drug finally took hold and Riverstone slumped into a drug-induced sleep in Ian's arms.

* * *

Ian covered Riverstone with more old rags to keep him from losing any more body heat. After making him as comfortable as he could,

Ian decided to clear up some of the loose ends. He placed the tin of water beside Riverstone along with what was left of the dried bread. If Riverstone's girl was still out there, she was in the deepest pit of death imaginable. His words echoed in his mind. *Ela...you gotta...* Ian didn't need to hear the whole sentence to know the thought. Riverstone's girl had to be found.

"Ela?" Riverstone mumbled from a delirious subconscious dream.

"Don't worry, I'll find her before you wake, pard." He was sure no one knew about the place hidden in the rocks.

"Dagger..." Riverstone wheezed, coming out of his sobbing semi-conscious state briefly before dropping back into a dreamless void.

Ian pulled the rocks away from the entrance of the small crack that led into the concealed shaft. "I'll take care of him," he said, and then crawled through the small hole and resealed the entrance. He would find Ela and would not return until he did. Finding Riverstone's girl was, as Harlowe would say, the right thing to do. The girl of a Gamadin was special. She was like family, one of their own. His mission was simple: to find his pard's girl and bring her back to him.

As Ian took off down the shaft, he wasn't sure what he was up against. If the goonies were anything like the guards on the other levels, he would have little trouble. Between rest periods he would mingle with the slaves and ask questions about Matthew's woman. That was the name he went by, Riverstone had told him. Ian had his doubts about Ela's survival at the hands of the guards. He had seen too many times the brutal savagery the guards of Erati could show a slave. It was not pretty. If she was alive, he would slither into the goons' compound and find her. With the Gamadin abilities that had allowed him to survive these many months in the inescapable depths of Erati, he would take her from under their noses. If they tried to stop him, he would dust them too, like the others.

* * *

During the next rest period, Ian stepped from the shadows and joined a line of diggers slouching back to rest on the piles of broken rock. Not surprisingly, no one wanted to tell him anything. He was not from their level. They did not know him. They would not risk the wrath of Dagger to tell him anything. *No one called Matthew is here*, they said. *Go away. Leave us alone,* they told him. Then he met an old woman. Her eyes appeared much younger, but Erati had a way of aging any being prematurely. She had heard he was asking questions about Matthew, and told Ian how the one called Matthew had saved her once from the sickness. She was saddened to learn of his death. Of course, Ian could not tell if the old woman was telling the truth. He doubted she was. If the goonies got wind that she was talking to him, they would surely kill her and then begin searching the abandoned shafts for him until they found him.

Ian's thoughts suddenly froze. As confident as he was in Harlowe and *Millawanda's* powerful sensors, he knew from experience that Millie's probes would never find them a hundred miles below the surface of the planet.

Ian shook, expelling all the negativity from his brain. If the tiniest hope prevailed, Harlowe Pylott, his lifelong friend, his Captain, would rather suffer a thousand deaths than give up finding his pards.

As he'd feared, the old woman said the goons had taken Ela to their compound. It was that way, she told him, near the vertical shafts, where it was cooler.

The old woman waved for Ian to follow her. "I will show you the way," she told him.

Ian looked around the tunnel. If there was ever a trap in the works, this was it. His keen eyes saw no one other than the resting bodies of slaves. He saw little to trust in the old woman, but she was the only source of information he had. Although her eyes appeared sincere, why would she risk her life when the others didn't? *To survive,* he answered, already feeling the outcome.

Cautiously he motioned for her to go on. He would follow. Like a predator in the dark, he watched the shadows and kept his keen eye on a path of escape in case he was suddenly discovered or, worse, betrayed.

As they stepped over the resting slaves, the old woman recalled hearing screams from the guard compound during the quiet of the last rest period, but that was all she knew. She was sorry that she could add nothing more.

Ian was about to thank her when several large black shadows appeared before him. He turned as more shadows moved quickly to cut off any escape back into the mine.

He was trapped.

The middle shadow tossed the old woman a morsel of food. She speared it from the air like a ravenous vulture, stuffing it into her mouth, cackling like a twisted psychopath as she scampered away back into the depths of the mine, disappearing among the sleeping thralls.

An evil voice rumbled. He turned and watched a bestial figure slog toward him. It was a lifetime ago, but he would never forget Dagger's bloodthirsty laugh.

88

Access Denied

HARLOWE STOOD IN front of his chair, staring at the image of the Erati mining supervisor on the overhead screen. "My name is Pylott. I have traveled a great distance in search of friends who were brought to this planet against their will."

The supervisor was hardly sympathetic. "A search is out of the question, Pylott. Our labor force is too vast for an individual pursuit. Leave us."

"I have at my disposal instruments that can find the individuals I seek," Harlowe countered quickly. "None of your resources or time will be required. I respectfully ask for permission to carry out my search."

The supervisor looked away. His manner was almost jokingly indifferent. "The company strictly forbids any unauthorized personnel from entering the mines. I am sure you understand. Security reasons."

"I have authorization from the Tomar-Rex himself," Harlowe shot back, holding up a signed document for the supervisor to see. "I am not leaving here without my friends."

"I suggest you leave the Erati system or be subject to our defenses."

Harlowe stepped closer to the screen. "Listen, toad, if you do not allow me to enter your mines, I will enter anyway, with or without your permission. Do you— "

The screen went blank.

Harlowe turned to his crew. "On your toes, gentlemen. We've worn out our welcome." They didn't have long to wait for the supervisor's promise of action to come true.

"Your Majesty," Prigg said, his wayward eyes displaying their worry.

"Sensors have picked up the launch of several attack ships," Monday said.

Harlowe leaned over toward Simon. "We don't have time to play, Mr. Bolt."

"Nuke 'em, Captain?" Simon asked.

Harlowe sat back in his chair as Prigg displayed on the screen the ten attack ships that were charging up at the Ship from the surface of the planet. "Aye. Nuke 'em."

"Aye, Skipper."

The Erati ships were faster than Harlowe anticipated, but then, a rich mining planet would have the best attack ships their koorants could buy. At a stationary position orbit, ten thousand miles above the planet's surface, the Gamadin ship fired ten blue bolts of high-energy plasma before the oncoming attack ships broke atmosphere. On the screen, the first wave of Erati's best was turned to subatomic dust before the mining supervisor's eyes.

Harlowe wasn't finished. To teach them whom they were dealing with, Millie vaporized all 110 attack ships in the fleet while they still sat on their landing pads. Moments later, he wiped out all the missile batteries aboveground. In just under fifteen minutes, the entire Erati defense system was completely obliterated by the lone Gamadin ship. After that, Harlowe did not ask for permission to land. The Erati supervisor whom he had spoken to earlier reappeared on the overhead screen. His smug, self-absorbed attitude had transformed to stark fear at facing the new bully on the block.

"You've made your point, Pylott. We will negotiate—"

Harlowe cut him off. "No deals, puke. You had your chance. My bodyguards and I will be the only ones who will leave the ship. If I do not return, my crew has orders to put Erati out of business forever. Is that clear? The planet will be history," he said sternly.

"You will be given safe passage. You can be assured of this," the supervisor replied, and the screen was blank again.

Harlowe uttered coldly to his crew, "We may have to nuke this dude before we're through."

* * *

As *Millawanda* came around to the night side of the planet, she drifted down through dense clouds toward the surface. There was nothing to see through the windows, but the sensors told a different story.

Prigg's eyes steadied on the readout. "Your Majesty, high-power surges detect additional defenses energizing below the surface. I would advise caution."

"Thank you, Prigg," Harlowe replied calmly, before turning to Simon. "They just don't get it. Do your thing, Mr. Bolt. Take them out," he added, tired of the game-playing.

Simon lined up the plotted marks on the screen. A second later, simultaneous bursts of blue streaks struck out at all twelve points. The cleanup was complete. All defense batteries above and below ground were blobs of molten white-hot metal dripping down the sides of their massive turrets.

"All clear, Your Majesty," Prigg announced from his sensor console.

Monday guided the Ship down, spreading the curving, spindly pods gently onto the paved surface in front of the main surface operations compound. Harlowe released his chair restraints and stood, looking out at the pithead of the mine—a tall, dark, fog-shrouded building that housed the offices and the elevator shaft. Harlowe was taken aback by the overhead screen display of the mine shaft that went down hundreds of miles into the planet's crust. Simon and Monday had never seen Harlowe as cold and angry as when he looked out at the black and dreary surface of the mine facilities. "Heaven help this place if they're not okay." Then he called out an order. "Millie, transfer all of Riverstone's and Wiz's bio-stats into my hand com, if you please." The Ship's sensors were sensitive enough to locate a blue-speckled tick with hemorrhoids ten thousand miles high in orbit, but probing beneath a hundred miles of solid rock was another matter. They were limited to only a few short miles for precision readouts. They had to go down into the mine tunnels themselves to get the precise data they needed to locate any specific body.

Harlowe called Molly and Rhud and headed for the ramp.

"Captain!" Simon bolted out of his chair and went after Harlowe before he disappeared to the lower deck. "I want to go along, Skipper." Harlowe was about to object, but Simon held his ground. "Please, Captain, I want to help find Wiz and Jester."

Simon's long face appealed so earnestly, Harlowe couldn't refuse. He glanced at Monday for approval. Monday nodded, *let him go.* He and Prigg could handle things here. "Aye. Get your things stat, Mr. Bolt," Harlowe reponded, going for the blinker.

* * *

Harlowe and Simon gathered the additional supplies the two of them would need on the trip down into the mines. Just before they stepped onto the blinker that would transport them from the utility room to the perimeter edge of the ship, Harlowe issued last-minute orders to Monday and Prigg. "When we start down the shaft, we'll probably lose contact with you pretty fast. So if we're not back in a reasonable amount of time, start making a little noise up here, gentlemen."

"Understood, Captain," Monday responded.

"Yes, Your Majesty," Prigg added, moving into Simon's weapons chair.

Harlowe waited for Simon and the cats to blink before he added one more thing that had been gnawing at his mind. "I don't want to seem like a sore loser, Mr. Platter, but if we don't come back, I want you to nuke this pile of energy rock. The Fhaal will get nothing from this mine...ever!"

"Roger that, Captain! Understood," Monday retorted matter-of-factly.

89

Brutal World

THE ENTRANCE TO the main pithead of the mine was large enough for Harlowe's small entourage to walk through side-by-side. Once inside the doorway, they were "greeted" by two characters who redefined a Dakadude. They were the ugliest beings Harlowe had ever seen. The thick, smelly guards led them down a narrow rock corridor to a large underground room just below the surface. There were six more Erati guards inside the room, and all except for the mine foreman behind the desk had their weapons pointed at Harlowe as he stepped into the room.

"Are you the toadhead in charge?" Harlowe asked the surly-looking foreman. The stench from the guards was foul. Their nauseating odors were suffocating. Besides their repulsive white faces, bad teeth, and twisted noses and eyes, the guards were covered with layers of black dust. Harlowe wondered if they had ever bathed in their pathetic lives.

"I was told you were looking for someone, Pylott," the foreman said.

"That's right, I am." The foreman's eyes opened wide when Molly and Rhud lumbered into the room and let out low, throaty growls as they moved alongside Harlowe. Their powerful gait and take-no-prisoners presence sent chills up Harlowe's spine. He could only imagine what it did to the Erati staff. He was mighty glad they were on his side. Simon followed the cats out of the corridor.

561

"I've been ordered to open our operations up for your pleasure," the foreman said, nodding toward the direction of the elevator shaft. "Go ahead. Search," he finished with a low, chilly snicker.

Harlowe disregarded the remarks and demanded the foreman show him personally the way to the lower levels.

"Find them yourself," the foreman replied, his guards raising their weapons.

Harlowe saw no reason to waste any more time trying to convince the foreman this was no social call. "Mr. Bolt, if you please." As quick as it takes the human eye to blink, six Erati guards slammed backwards against the wall and dropped to the ground, still holding their weapons.

Simon snappily returned his pistols to his holster as the foreman's shocked eyes looked over the bodies on the floor.

Harlowe folded his arms in front of him. "Lead the way, puke." It was not a request.

The foreman jumped from behind the desk and led Harlowe and his entourage straight to the elevator platform. After opening the gate, the foreman stepped onto the platform and went to the lighted control panel. "How far do you want to go?" he asked. His crooked fingers pressed the power panel, sending a roaring surge of energy into the giant winding gears above them.

"You tell me," Harlowe said, following the foreman onto the platform. Molly and Rhud looked down into the bottomless shaft as Simon boarded ahead of them. The cats had second thoughts, but nervously leaped onto the platform when Simon told them it was all right.

"It depends where they are needed," the foreman replied. "The levels are uncountable. I process too many thralls to remember individuals." The foreman spat over the side. "They're all the same to me."

"Not to me, toad," Harlowe shot back angrily. "Remember that. Your sorry life depends on it."

Harlowe pulled out his com and switched the blue indicator light to "on." He studied the preliminary readouts and believed the foreman was telling the truth as he studied the screen. There was no telling how many thousands of slave diggers Erati had processed over the past months. He pitied all of them but for the moment, he cared only about two. "Then go. I'll tell you when to stop." Next he turned to Simon and ordered, "One wrong move, Mr. Bolt. Nuke 'em."

Simon grinned, eyeing the foreman as if he were his next meal. "A pleasure, Skipper."

The foreman nervously threw the large switch lever and down, down, down they plummeted into the rock depths of Erati. A mile every thirty-seven seconds. On the outside Harlowe maintained his cool and confident demeanor, but on the inside he was a storm of worry, foreboding, and fear that he may have been too late to help his friends. He hadn't realized just how extensive the mine was until they were over an hour into the descent with no sign of slowing down or finding the bottom of the shaft. As Harlowe kept one eye on the pulsing blue readouts, Molly and Rhud continued to pace back and forth, growling with displeasure at the depths of darkness and gloom. Every so often Simon would look down over the edge of the platform.

After the second hour, they were still traveling at the same rate of descent as when they started. The endless vertical shaft connected to a countless number of lighted horizontal caverns was all that anyone ever saw.

"Even if your friends are alive, you will never find them, Pylott," the foreman uttered heartlessly, hissing with contempt.

Harlowe stared back with an equal amount of disgust. He found himself wishing the foreman would give Simon an excuse to end his pathetic life. "You'd better hope I do."

They were well into the third hour when a tiny beep came from the com. "Hold it!" Harlowe yelled out in surprise. The foreman slowed the platform to a full stop. The com light was now a steady signal but very dim. They had made contact with something, but they had passed the level. "Go back," Harlowe ordered.

The foreman hesitated. Harlowe glanced at Simon. In a blur, Simon blew off the foreman's ear. "You heard the Captain. Go back!" Simon demanded.

"Slowly," Harlowe added.

Holding the bloody side of his face, the foreman touched the panel and they began to rise. They passed a number of horizontal levels before the com light started to glow bright again. It got brighter and brighter until Harlowe found the level with the brightest readout.

"Hold it!" Harlowe cried out.

The foreman followed instructions, stopping at the level.

Harlowe stood in place tapping the side of his com, aghast at the readouts, believing the screen was wrong. He looked up, the sound of pounding wracking his ears. What he saw horrified him. When they were descending into the mine, they were traveling too fast to see what lay inside the horizontal levels. Now that they had stopped, the vast numbers of slave diggers toiling their pitiful lives away at the endless rock were clearly visible even under the dim, artificial lights of the cavern. The com had not malfunctioned. There were not hundreds but thousands of poor souls pounding the rock. Tears blurred his eyes as he stared at the foreman with a renewed hatred. It was the most evil display of suffering he had ever seen. It was a Hell not even the Devil would have tolerated.

Molly and Rhud leaped over the platform gate before it was open, relieved that they had finally stopped. The foreman must have figured he had an opportunity to take advantage of Harlowe's shock. From the side of the control panel, the foreman found an iron bar. Harlowe had only time to deflect the blow with his com. It saved his life, but the price was the loss of the com. The deflection knocked the com over the side of the platform and into the bottomless void. He dove to try and save it, but it was a useless effort. The device was gone.

The foreman scurried to his feet for another try. But before he could bring the heavy rod down, a solid fist knocked him over the side of the platform. Like the com, the foreman disappeared into the inky darkness of the shaft, his dying scream fading with him.

"Thanks, Mr. Bolt," Harlowe said.

Simon looked down the mine shaft and spat. A fitting obituary.

Harlowe turned his attention back to the hordes of slaves, his focus already back on his search as he stared out at the sea of toiling souls. Without the com, where would he begin? How would he find his mates in the mass of misery?

Harlowe and Simon stepped off the platform and joined Molly and Rhud at the threshold of the vast open level. The air was heavy and hot, filled with the repugnant stench of the digging slaves. The thought of trying to find anyone without the com's sensors was disheartening. Harlowe looked back toward the shaft as if there might be a way to retrieve the device. It was wishful thinking and wasted thought. They would have to go back. There was no other way. The search was impossible without the sensor device. He took a deep sigh of defeat, resigned to the idea of returning to the surface. He guided Rhud toward the platform with a small pat. He was about to call for Molly to come and saw her sniffing the ground like she had found a familiar scent. Harlowe's face brightened with astonishment as he traded hope with Simon.

"You don't think…" Simon tried to say, as stunned as Harlowe at the cat's pulse-quickening dance.

"What is it girl? Have you found them?" Simon asked Molly, her bright eyes pleading for him to release her.

She growled once, took a short walk in a circle to make sure of her bearings, and then bolted off into the vast underground level that was large enough for *Millawanda* to land in with plenty of room to spare. It was all Harlowe and Simon could do to keep up with the giant cat. They were afraid they would lose her in the low light.

They ran harder.

Several times during the chase, Molly stopped to sniff the ground. This allowed them a moment to catch up, but it was only a brief stop. She continued on, darting ahead as she leaped easily over ore carts and working slaves.

More than once Harlowe stumbled over diggers and nearly lost his footing. Simon took out a whole line of thralls when he made a misstep. A half dozen times guards, who didn't know about their open invitation to search the mines, tried to stop them. Neither Harlowe nor Simon found it necessary to stop and chat about their reasons for being in the mine. A stinging plasshot on a dead run was explanation enough. Not one slave cared about anything. Even the cats, as large and ferocious as they were, caused few meaningful reactions amongst the thralls. It was as if nothing was important to them except the mining of the rock.

The incredible suffering Harlowe saw made his eyes sting. If they were alive, his mates must have already suffered unbelievable evil. Whatever they had endured to this point was unimaginable. If he stopped to think of this for a moment, his feelings would overwhelm him. He couldn't stop. Not now. He would never stop until he found them.

After over a mile, Harlowe and Simon caught up with Rhud. He was waiting for them. Molly had already gone in another direction. It was a small opening off the main tunnel. They activated their SIBAs so their bugeyes would allow them to see into the pitch-blackness of the lightless tunnels. The cats saw easily. Their SIBAs were switched on at birth. They owned the darkness.

Harlowe held onto Rhud's mane as they went into the offshoot tunnel. The smell of waste was even fouler than the smell he experienced coming in. As on Naruck, he pitied the cats, which did not have breathing filters to guard themselves from the heavy stench.

A short time later he heard Molly's faint growl. She had found something.

Harlowe hesitated. His neck hairs stood up. He shook, taking in a deep breath, and then he walked on. Simon stayed two steps behind, covering their backside. He saw the faint glow of a candle. Molly was sniffing at a lump of rags. He told himself it couldn't be anyone he knew. The being hadn't the physical shape of a human being. There was barely anything left of its body. It was the skin and bones of a person who had been starved and tortured.

Oh, my gawd! No!

Harlowe reluctantly moved to the being's side and lifted the rags from around its face. "Oh no, oh, no, oh, no, no, no..." It *was* Ian!

Harlowe couldn't control himself as the tears flowed down the side of his face. His hands and body shook, believing he was too late. He kneeled beside Ian and ever so carefully picked his frail form up in his arms, holding him, trying to comfort what spark of life was left inside him.

Harlowe brought his face up to his. He felt the tiny wisp of breath. Ian was still alive! His skin was cold and clammy, but Harlowe could still hear the faint hum of his heart.

He glanced upward. *Thank you!*

Hastily, Harlowe stripped what was left of Ian's rags. He placed a medallion on Ian's bruised and broken body and activated the special medical emergency SIBA. The 54th-century fabric quickly engulfed his body and immediately began pumping it with life-sustaining fluids.

The med SIBA did not have bugeyes like the normal soldier's gear. It had openings at the eyes and mouth. The nose was covered, forcing the energized oxygen to flow into his lungs.

Ian's lips moved. "Riverstone?"

Harlowe took a small water tube and put it on Ian's lips with his fingers.

"No, it's me, Wiz. Dog," he said, fighting his composure. "It's all right. I'm here, pard. I found you. I've come to take you home, Wiz."

Ian's lips moved, trying to gather the strength to speak. "Dog?"

"Yeah, it's me. I'm here, Wiz," Harlowe replied, his voice breaking as he spoke.

"Matt said you would come," Ian uttered. His breathing was labored but not as faint as before. The drugs would stabilize him, but Harlowe had to get him back to the ship for the robobs to do their magic.

"Riverstone? Where is he?" Harlowe asked. "Is he alive?"

Ian nodded, trying to answer. "Aye..." He lifted a finger, pointing weakly off into the distance.

Harlowe looked around. He couldn't see anything but filth and excrement. "Where, Wiz? Where's Riverstone?"

"Shaft," Ian replied weakly. "Hidden." He raised his head slightly and pointed past where Simon was guarding their backs.

Harlowe trembled with fear. *Please, let him be alive...* He picked Ian up and handed his broken, meager form over to Simon. With painfully red eyes he said, "Take him back to the platform."

"You going after Jester, Skipper?" Simon asked.

Harlowe nodded. He had no stomach for conversation. He went to Rhud and put an arm around his mane. "Go with Simon, Rhud. Protect." Rhud growled. The cat understood his responsibility. He then turned to Her Highness and pointed down the vile tunnel. "Find Riverstone, Molly."

And they ran.

They ran as though every second meant the difference between life and death. They ran back through the hordes of slaves. Nothing on heaven or Erati would stop Molly. Harlowe kept pace. Like a running back sprinting through the broken field to the goal line, he leapt over slaves, rock piles, and overturned carts, never letting Molly out of his sight. More guards tried to stop them. They had been alerted to the intrusion of the unauthorized beings and knew the reward would be great for their capture. But Harlowe and Molly stopped for no one.

They ran for miles, never stopping. Soon they were in the inky darkness well inside the abandoned mine shaft. Now and then, Molly stopped to sniff the ground before she charged ahead. Harlowe never saw Her Highness hesitate and wonder if the scent was clear. She was always certain. How far must they go to find Riverstone? Would he be alive? Remembering the way Ian looked, would he even know his best friend in the universe when he saw him?

He glanced skyward again. *Please, make it soon!*

For a brief moment, Harlowe lost sight of Molly. She disappeared after coming to an intersection of three abandoned shafts. Which way? He tried to guess. He couldn't. They were all equally right or wrong. A low growl brought his attention straight ahead. He hustled forward and found Molly scratching away at a pile of rocks in the shaft wall. He could see she had already made a small opening in the wall. He rushed to her side and began pulling away the stones hiding a small opening. When it was large enough for him, he dove through, leaving Molly behind. There was no room for her. No time to dig an opening large enough for a ten-foot, thousand-pound cat to squeeze through.

It didn't matter.

"Matt!" Harlowe called out in a fearful panic.

A pile of rags was hidden behind the opening a few feet away in a hollowed-out niche of the wall. Quickly, he pulled back the rags around the body and stared in horror. What he saw, his mind was not prepared to see. The once physically fit specimen of a young man was no more. The skin hung on his bones like an afterthought. His face was unrecognizable. He was more like an animal in a backstreet alley, waiting for death to take his malnourished and tortured form to a better place. His skin was bruised and broken, with mottled open cuts and sores that couldn't heal, while its color was blanched white under the crusted dirt that covered his entire body. How had he survived? What he had suffered was beyond anything one could imagine anyone surviving. He tried not to choke up on the welling knot in his throat as he worked on what was left of Riverstone's feeble remains.

The body moved. He was alive!

He's alive!

"Ela..." Riverstone breathed. The sound was barely audible, but Harlowe's well-tuned SIBA had picked up the word clearly.

"It's me, Matt. It's Dog," Harlowe told him, stripping him as he had done with Ian and activating the enviro-bag around his body. "I'm here, pard. I'm here," he said, reassuring his friend. His hands had never really stopped shaking as he raced to save Riverstone from taking his last breath in his arms.

No! I'll never let that happen! Never! Never! NEVER!

"Ela..." Harlowe thought he heard him say.

Riverstone's lips moved while his mind wandered deliriously behind the mask of the med SIBA. What he was saying didn't make sense. "Ela," Riverstone kept repeating over and over.

"What is Ela, Matt?" Harlowe asked as he positioned his body to slide back out through the opening of the niche.

Riverstone forced his lips to move. "Doggy?"

"Yeah, pard, it's me."

"What kept you?"

Harlowe cradled him closer in his arms as Riverstone coughed. He sounded like death had already come knocking. "Babes. You found babes, didn't you?"

"Yeah, lots of them. All tens."

"Ya see..." and then Riverstone's mouth stopped moving.

Nervously, Harlowe gave Riverstone another injection. "You're not going to die on me, Gamadin! You got that? You're not!" Harlowe kept busy, fumbling to get Riverstone out of the small tunnel. "We've got a lot of things to do yet, First Officer. So don't get lazy on me, Mr. Riverstone, or I'll kick your backside right here! Do you read me, Gamadin?"

Harlowe crawled out first and pulled Riverstone through. He didn't know if Riverstone heard him or not. It didn't matter. He figured the sound of his voice was comforting. Molly was so excited, she was nearly making a pest of herself wanting to lick Riverstone on the side of his face inside the enviro-bag. Harlowe had to push her back. "Let him breathe, Molly."

Riverstone pawed feebly at Harlowe through the enviro-bag's small window. "Ela... Must find her, Dog..."

Time was crucial. They had to start back to the Ship now. Both Ian's and Riverstone's lives depended on every second saved returning to the ship's infirmary. Harlowe lifted Riverstone's frail body in his arms and began trotting back toward the main work area, where Simon was waiting with Ian and Rhud.

"What are you saying, pard? Who is Ela, Matt?"

"My girl... Dog... my girl..." His head was moving back and forth, trying to force his mind to work long enough to explain what he meant. He coughed. "Dagger. Find Dagger. He knows."

Harlowe didn't know if he would have the time to figure out what Riverstone was trying to tell him. Nothing he was saying made any sense. He sent Molly ahead in case there were those who wanted to dust them along the way. Ela was someone close to him, he'd figured that much, and obviously someone as important to him as Lu and Quay were to him, but who or what was Dagger?

With every stride back to the platform, tears continued to blur Harlowe's eyes and his rage returned. When he emerged out of the passage, a large, vile form was waiting for him, along with a number of beastly guards.

"Where are you taking my digger?" the one at the head of the pack asked. They were all heavily armed.

"Get out of my way, pukes!" Harlowe ordered.

"Dagger," Riverstone kept mumbling. "His voice. Dagger."

"You're Dagger?" Harlowe asked.

Dagger grunted. "That's me. Now put down my digger—"

At that moment Molly came out of the shadows and into the dim light. Her Highness opened her giant maw of knife-like teeth and expelled a blood-chilling roar that reverberated across the entire cavern. The Erati guards cowered back. They had never seen a beast so frightening, nor had they ever seen a beast from the world where light ruled the heavens.

The guards dropped their weapons and ran for their lives, including Dagger.

Before Dagger could take two steps, Harlowe shot his legs out from under him.

"I wasn't done talking to you, worm," Harlowe said, stepping up to Dagger, his pistol pointed at his head while still carrying Riverstone in his arms.

Dagger turned over on his back, his face contorted with pain and fear, moaning as he grabbed his bloodied legs.

Riverstone turned his head sideways and said just loud enough for Dagger to hear. "These are my pards, Dagger."

Molly opened her mouth inches from Dagger's face, showing off her six-inch incisors. Dagger nodded, terrified.

"She'll swallow your head whole if you don't tell me the truth." Dagger nodded rapidly again. "Where is Ela?" Harlowe demanded.

Dagger's yellow eyes shuffled back and forth as if he knew the answer would mean instant death.

Harlowe kicked him in the face. Not a lethal blow, but hard enough to splatter his nose flat. He then picked up a thumb-sized yellow crystal from the ground and inserted it into Dagger's crooked mouth. Calmly he said, "Tell me or I'll ignite this where you lay."

Dagger tried to push Harlowe's hand away. Choking, unable to speak, he pointed to an opening on the other side of the tunnel not far away from the main elevator shaft.

"Touch that crystal and you're dead," Harlowe warned as he strode off with Riverstone toward the opening where Dagger had pointed. Molly loped alongside as they made it past the working thralls and broken ore carts. Harlowe set Riverstone down at the side of the entrance. He didn't want to chance Riverstone being hit by stray fire. When Harlowe heard a low growl from inside, he knew he was in the right place.

Harlowe unholstered both pistols and entered, his bug eyes illuminating the darkness. After seeing Riverstone and Ian, he didn't know what he would find. The idea that they had done something like that to his crew was too painful to think about. Someone would pay big time.

He pushed back thoughts of vengeance so he could continue on. Inside were rooms not even pigs would stomach. Harlowe figured it was the guards' quarters. He felt like adding to the filth by hurling his guts out, but he swallowed hard to keep himself in check. He stepped into another room and found the remains of a mauled guard. He let out a sigh of relief. It wasn't a woman.

He walked on, turned one more corner, and saw Molly's tail. The sounds she made were as if she was moaning in pain. Harlowe stopped breathing as he stepped into the room. He feared for the worst, and found it. Lying still as death in the filth of the dirt floor was a spindly form of a tortured female. He jumped to her side and carefully turned her over. Her face was brutally beaten, and she was covered with deep, bleeding cuts and large contusions. She had obviously been tortured but somehow, like Riverstone and Ian, she was still alive. He wondered what kind of woman could survive such an ordeal. *No wonder Riverstone couldn't leave her behind!*

She was man-up!

Harlowe wrapped her in another enviro-suit. Then he picked her up and ran back to the entrance where he had left Riverstone. There was no time to waste. He could lose them all if he didn't get them back to the ship in time.

Harlowe laid Ela next to Riverstone so he could see that she was with him now. The moment they touched each other, they began to stir, as though they wanted to share what little life they had left between them. It was heartbreaking. They barely had the strength to move; yet Riverstone moved his fingers over to her hand and laid them next to hers through the layers of the bag. He didn't have the strength to hold it there for long. He just lay there, next to her. Without opening their eyes they knew they were close to each other.

From the interior of the tunnel, Harlowe heard a groan. When he finished securing Ela to Rhud's back, he looked to find the source of the sound. It was Dagger trying to sit up in the dirt, far off in the distance. He was looking their way, about to take the crystal from his mouth. His expression was wicked, as if he was proud of the suffering he had caused. Harlowe's teeth clenched as the muscles in his jaws rippled tight. He'd had all that he could take. From over a hundred yards away, he was about to fire his weapon and end Dagger's wretched life forever, but he held up at the last moment. This was not his life to take. Instead, he stepped to Riverstone's side and undid the enviro-suit enough to place the pistol in his pard's hand. On his own, Riverstone could neither hold a weapon nor fire it if his life depended on it. With Harlowe's help, Riverstone's hand lifted up and fired. Dagger would never harm another being again.

90

Forever Changed

THE JOURNEY UP the mine shaft had been uneventful. With the hundreds of clickers protecting their way, no Erati security forces could get within visual range of the retreating Gamadin. Riverstone, Ian, and the girl were now safely aboard and in the Ship's infirmary. Harlowe could do nothing more to help them. Their survival was in the hands of Millie, the clickers, and the Almighty. From the doorway, Harlowe watched three teams of robobs work feverishly to save their lives. Colorful wall graph displayed extremely weak life signs in every patient. Their outlook was grim. Even Millie said little, giving him the impression that even she had her doubts. What updates he did receive were brief. No prognosis or chances of success was forthcoming. As good and miraculous as the 54th-century healers were, they were not gods.

After making sure that everything that could be done was done, Harlowe ordered Monday to set a course away from Erati at light speed. Their destination? He didn't know or care as long as it was far away from the planet. Throughout the night and the following day, the Gamadin crew had little sleep. In the control room, as the bright white stars of hyperlight drifted slowly by, they watched the infirmary readouts on the bridge screens, waiting on edge for the moment when any change in their outcome, good or bad, came. What could they do but wait it out and hope for the best? By the end of the third day, Ian was responding to treatment. Ela and Riverstone were another matter. They seemed to be stuck in a divine tug-of-war between life and death.

Keep fighting, pards, keep fighting, Harlowe silently pleaded to them both. *Don't give up! I need you, Matt. Please, don't give up!*

When Harlowe finally left the routine chores of running the Ship to his crew and wandered back to his cabin. Jewels had already laid out his violin on the table next to his cabin's observation couch. Outside, as the pink and green cloud of a starlit nebula drifted by, he wondered, *if one died, could the other survive?* After all the suffering Riverstone and Ela had gone through, their lives might just depend on the survival of each other to make it.

Harlowe remembered when his grandparents passed away some years ago. They had been together for seventy-two years. Even at ninety-one, his grandparents were towers of strength and health. Harlowe was certain that one of the national morning shows would be announcing their hundredth birthdays. Then Grandma fell and broke her hip. Within days of the accident she caught pneumonia. A week later she died. His grandfather followed his lifelong love a month later. Their towers had crumbled right before his eyes. The doctors had no answer, but those who knew them did. Grandpa had died of a broken heart.

He reached for his violin and reflected. Even though the Erati system was a mere speck of light in the starscape of a hundred billion stars, his thoughts of the mining planet filled the observation window. His hatred of the mining planet was so strong that he never saw the awesome nebula. He would never forget what he saw deep inside its shafts of brutality. The insane cruelty and inhumanity would remain with him forever.

And he had experienced only one day on Erati.

What had the months done to Ian and Riverstone? The unimaginable pain and suffering they must have experienced was beyond his comprehension. He remembered an ancient saying back on Earth that "those who strive for great deeds must also suffer greatly." They had all suffered beyond greatly. He had seen it in their faces. Erati had changed *all* of their lives beyond what their Gamadin training had prepared them for. The General could never have envisioned such brutality. Could they ever laugh again? Tell jokes? Swim an ocean, ride a glassy wave, or leap from a cliff in the same way again? Would life ever be normal again? He shivered. His bow slid across the strings, sounding like fingernails scratching across a blackboard.

The answer was all too clear. Neither he nor his friends would ever be kids again.

"Pardon me, Captain," Monday's voice called to him over the com. He had been trying to get Harlowe's attention for a couple of minutes.

Harlowe blinked after a long hesitation. "Yes, Mr. Platter."

"We are coming upon a star system, sir. At our present course and speed, it will be days before we reach another habitable star system. We should try and stop there, Captain."

Harlowe leaned back against the cushy blue couch, his mind distant and unfocused. He didn't care. Just land. "Habitation?" he asked, almost mechanically

"Nothing significant, although life-forms are indicated. Seems to be an extremely young planet, sir. We will have to come closer for a more thorough reading."

"Atmosphere?"

"Breathable with mild temperatures, Captain."

Harlowe reached for a glass of blue stuff. "Good to go, Mr. Platter." He lifted his glass and stared curiously at its blue color with the nebula's muted light behind it. He lay back and set the half-filled glass on his chest. He fell asleep in that position with his violin at his side, like an old friend. Both cats stretched out on the floor below the window, doing the same.

They landed three hours later. Immediately, an army of stickmen began cleaning the outside of the ship. After the long journey, she needed a scrubbing to make her bright and beautiful again. While the clickers were busy giving *Millawanda* her bath, other robobs were setting up the outside chairs, tables, and sports equipment like they always did when the Gamadin crew was off the clock for an extended period of time.

91

Catching Up

THE DAYS WENT by at a snail's pace on the unnamed planet. It was now a waiting game. Monday had put *Millawanda* down on a long, white sandy beach. Unlike #2, the landscape behind them was flat and nearly devoid of life except for a few mounds of grass where small rodent-like animals scurried about from one hill to the next. There were no tall palms that dropped coconuts as large as basketballs or squawking birds jumping from tree to tree in a thick, dark jungle. No T-rex's, either. No large beasts of prey for clickers to guard against while the crew rested and recuperated. It was a Precambrian world that was just beginning its geologic and evolutionary epochs. As the sensors had indicated, temperatures were pleasantly mild and humid. A quiet green sky held a few wispy, pink clouds. The sea was warm with small but rideable waves. Their sound washing up against the long, flat shore helped break the overriding silence of the planet. In the far distance, a line of volcanos spewed plumes of hot ash into the atmosphere. This did not bother them. They were too far away, and the slight prevailing winds carried their smoky clouds well away from their isolated landing place. At night, they could hear the rumbling explosions of the volcanoes like distant thunder and watch the bright red cauldrons light up the night with fiery rivers of white-hot rock flowing out the sides of their tall funnels. In another time, the Gamadin would have been jaw-dropping spectators, awed by the sight. Until their mates could be with them again, however, no light in the galaxy could brighten their day.

Harlowe, Monday, and Simon passed the time by swimming in the ocean or watching the sand crabs dart in and out of the shallow shore break looking for food. No one knew how Prigg occupied his off-the-clock hours. Water frightened him, especially the waves, even when the smallest ones rolled up on the beach.

Harlowe's swims were short, unlike those on #2. No one cared much about surfing, even though the waves were glassy most of the time. Before the wind came up in the afternoon, one could ride a good distance, from the point all the way into the shore. The sensors found no harmful life-forms on the land or in the water. There was no need for vigilant robobs to guard against predators. Microbes, crabs, and shellfish were the dominant inhabitants on this unknown planet. As long as their mates were fighting for their lives, though, being off the clock had lost its appeal. There were several nights when they nodded off and spent the entire night on the sand. At the end of one of those nights, when one of the double suns was peeking above a fresh pink horizon on the wide, private ocean, Harlowe was awakened from a troubled sleep by a tap on the shoulder.

It was Ian.

With the aid of Molly and Rhud, he'd walked out from the ship to where Harlowe and Simon were sleeping on the beach. Monday was with him, walking alongside, making sure he didn't stumble or pass out along the way.

For a moment Harlowe didn't move. He couldn't. The realization and joy of seeing his friend standing in front of him, alive, froze him in place. Ian and death had been close enough to play cards. To see him alive and standing over him in light blue, silk pajamas felt like nothing less than a miracle! The pajamas hung on him as if they were ten sizes too large. His face was shaved clean of every whisker and his hair was freshly cut, but he was still grossly thin and pale behind the dark glasses that protected his eyes from the rising sun. The robobs had fixed his body, but Harlowe wondered, as he stared in silent amazement, could they fix his soul?

Harlowe stood and put his arms around Ian, holding him and not wanting to let go. Simon awoke, hearing the goings-on, and froze. "Dude..." he gasped, barely able to talk. From one day to the next, one moment to the next, no one had known whether he would live or die. The medical readouts told them many things, but no one could be sure of the final outcome until now.

After a long embrace, Ian looked up at the morning sun, feeling the rays against his pasty white face. "You have no idea how sweet that feels," he said, weak and shallow, but to everyone there it was a symphony.

Ian staggered a little, his legs obviously feeling the strain of the walk. Harlowe steadied him, easing him down carefully onto a towel in the sand. He snapped his fingers at a robob, and the stickman quickly retrieved a beach chair for Ian to sit comfortably on. Ian swallowed hard, as though fighting back nausea. He nodded a thank-you. There wasn't a dry eye among them. The emotion hit Harlowe particularly hard. A stinging pain behind his nose came with the tears that flowed down the sides of his cheeks in a steady downpour. His lips trembled as he searched for words. For a long time no one spoke. What was there to say? They were all happy to be together again and in each other's company.

Molly and Rhud, not fully understanding the ways of humans but feeling their sense of well-being, wandered a short distance away and lazily lay down in the warm sand and watched.

"There were times...I never thought," Ian swallowed, then went on with difficulty, "I'd see you again."

Harlowe wiped his runny nose. He understood all too well that same doubt.

Ian's sunken eyes found Harlowe's. "Matt?" he asked, his eyes pleading for hope. "Tell me he's okay, Dog."

Harlowe looked down. The truth at this moment needed a little dressing up to be decent. "He's hanging in there, Wiz." He kept it simple.

Ian gave a small nod. He knew Riverstone was grave. He had been so near death when he found him. Who knows how he had survived for so long under Dagger's whip? "Quay...she was with us."

"Quay?" Harlowe replied anxiously.

"She was with us on Ra-Loc's ship. Then Unikala took her. I don't know where to, Dog. I'm sorry."

Harlowe swallowed hard. "We think we know where she is, Wiz," he told him.

Ian's eyes brightened. "That's good news, Dog."

Simon then asked, "Do you remember Sizzle, Wiz?"

Ian tried to remember, but her name didn't seem to connect. "Quay's..." Ian began.

Simon finished the sentence for him. "Quay's sister."

"Back on Gibb?" Ian wondered. It was like a distant time, another place far in the past.

"Yeah, on Gibb," Simon replied, seeing hope.

It took a moment for Ian to connect the dots. "She was with you. Hot babe..."

"Yeah, very hot. We were separated. Unikala's guards took her. Was she with Unikala when he came for Quay?"

Ian shrugged, his eyelids droopy, fighting to remember. "I don't know. We never went aboard Unikala's ship."

Dejected, Simon thanked Ian before he rose and started to leave their little circle.

"I wish we knew more," Ian told him, seeing his pain.

Simon thanked him again before he wandered down the beach to be by himself. At times his head was low, and at other times he was looking far off toward a distant volcano. Rhud followed him at a comfortable distance, as if he knew Simon needed his space but at the same time was always watching over him.

"Where are we?" Ian asked, looking up at the sky.

Harlowe shrugged. "About nine hundred light-years from home."

Ian let out a small laugh, keeping the funny thought to himself. Harlowe looked at him puzzled, waiting for Ian to come clean. Ian said, "I wonder who the Dodgers are playing tonight?"

Monday laughed with him. "The Padres."

"Yeah. The Padres..."

"A four-game sweep, too."

"No doubt."

Harlowe then told him how he had found them, starting with the grogan blood in Molly's fur that led them to Naruck and Prigg. Harlowe didn't leave out any details. He told him how Anor Ran had put a bounty on him because he wanted Millie's power to help fight the Consortium and the Fhaal in his scheme for sole control of the quadrant. He told him of Roshmar and Tnoir and Ruloma and how he'd saved their worlds from destruction. He told him, too, about the energy crystals mined at Erati, how they were the center of power, how Anor Ran and the Consortium had conspired to enslave the planets with the Erati crystals, and how the Fhaal needed the power source to conquer those remaining sectors of the quadrant that were not already under its domination. Finally, he told him the story of Ra-Loc, and how Molly had scared the fat Lagan to death on Patol before Simon could finish him off for eternity.

Ian saw the hidden concern in Harlowe's eyes. "It's Quay, isn't it? You're going after her next?"

"Yeah," Harlowe acknowledged, staring far out to sea. "We're going to make some noise."

Ian nodded. "I wish you could have seen her stand up to Unikala. She told him and his whole Consortium where to stick it. She's something else, Dog. A keeper like Lu was."

Harlowe's head bent down, biting his lower lip. "They're alike that way."

Monday saw the change in Harlowe's eyes. "You have in mind where we're going next, Captain?"

Harlowe wiped his nose. "Og, a planet Anor told me about."

"It could be a trap, Captain."

"That's a given."

"If he's harmed them?"

Harlowe stared across the calm, featureless sea. "No mercy."

Monday looked at Ian. Then he looked back toward their golden ship, all nice and shiny after her bath, and the nearly half-mile distance to the center rampway. He might have discussed the merits of taking on the entire Consortium and Tomar empires single-handedly, but not today, when Harlowe was so certain of the path they were following next.

Ian's head tilted to one side as if he was falling asleep. "He's a little tired, Captain," Monday said. Harlowe was about to pick Ian up when Monday offered, "It would be an honor to carry Wiz back, Captain."

Harlowe accepted the gesture. "Sure, Squid. Wiz would like that."

They had gone twenty steps when Ian awoke and complained about how hungry he was. "Cooking still good?" he asked weakly, with Monday holding Ian in his arms.

"The best in town," Harlowe replied, stepping up beside Monday and Ian.

"I could go for some animal double-doubles myself," Monday said, adding, "How 'bout you, Wiz?"

Ian struggled to smile. "Something small if you don't mind, Squid."

"Sure, Wiz. Whatever you want," Monday replied.

Within a few short moments, Quincy drove up in the wheelless rover. A robob with a dress and long blond hair bounced out from the shotgun side of the car with a trayful of burgers, shakes, and fries. Harlowe pored over the selections, picked out a small cheeseburger with grilled onions, and handed it to Monday to give to Ian. Harlowe grabbed an animal double-double for himself, then he lay a bag of fries, a double-double, and a shake on the beach towel. "We'll leave this for Rerun."

After their satisfying meal sitting in the grannywagon, Quincy flew them back to the center rampway, where they were greeted by someone no one had expected to see for days, if at all.

Riverstone.

He was sitting at the bottom of the rampway with his feet in the sand, staring down, his eyes unblinking, distant, and unfocused. He wasn't moving. He was completely still, as though alone in a far-off land. No one believed he had even seen them drive up.

92

More Beautiful than a Cloud

WHEN ELA AWOKE, she let out a loud, chilling scream. She tried to thrash her arms about and push away her attackers. She wanted her Matthew. They kept coming, hurting her badly, slapping her and hitting her again and again. The pain...the terrible pain!

Then something touched her softly on the side of her body. It calmed her. Though her eyes were still closed, she believed she was safe. The warm, gentle touch held her hand and caressed her face and arms. No one else felt like Matthew. Sensing the pain was gone, she was able to open her eyes and looked down at herself. She was dressed in strange blue clothes. She smelled the collar of her shirt and smiled. It smelled like Matthew. She had not dreamed of his presence after all.

She searched her surroundings in the low light, keeping very still. She was too scared to do otherwise. Her eyes could see well in the dimness. There were many strange things she had never seen before: colorful lights, odd shapes, and lines that moved with no purpose. Something near her moved. It was not real either. It made a soft clicking sound and touched her gently. Its purpose seemed harmless but her mind could comprehend none of it. She had never seen this part of the mine before. Where had Dagger taken her? What would he do to her now? She didn't know what she was supposed to do.

A swishing sound turned her eyes toward two dark silhouettes entering the room. Overcome by fear, she began to tremble. She reached for something to kill herself and discovered that she was bound to the table. She would not go through such hurt again.

A hand reached out and touched her softly to steady her. "Ela," a voice called to her. The tone was like her Matthew calling to her. "Ela," she heard again as a gentle warmth came to her side and kissed her face. The moment she felt his touch, she knew her Matthew was next to her. Her fear eased and she was okay now. He released her hands and she was free to hold him close, laying her face in the crook of his arm. "You're awake," he said to her.

"Where are we, Matthew?" Ela asked weakly.

"Safe, my darling. On my ship," Riverstone answered.

"Is it the one you always spoke of?"

"Yes."

"That flew between the stars?"

"Yes, yes, Ela. That one."

"Harlowe came like you always said he would."

"Yes, he came."

"I am so happy for you."

Riverstone brought her closer and covered her with small kisses. "And for you, Ela. Erati is no more. Never again will you have to dig or hammer or be a slave to anyone. I've taken you away from there forever."

Ela looked around. "Are these the stars you spoke of, Matthew?"

"No. We are inside. We must go to another place to see them." Riverstone paused, his eyes teary with happiness. "I love you, Ela. I am so happy you are awake."

Ela pulled Riverstone closer to her and kissed him on the lips. "And I you." She looked into his eyes. "If we cannot to be together for much longer, Matthew, I will always have happiness in my heart because I know you are well and safe with your friends."

"No, Ela, please don't talk that way. You are safe here. My ship will make you better. We will be together forever now."

* * *

The next day, still weak and frail, Riverstone found Harlowe back out on the beach. It was near sunset, that time between light and dark when all is quiet and peaceful. Riverstone was riding on top of Molly. "I need help, Dog. Ela would like to see the clouds."

Harlowe jumped up. "Sure, Matt."

"She has never seen a cloud before, Harlowe."

Harlowe understood. The look of urgency in Riverstone's face was clear. Harlowe knew from talking with Ian that Ela's medical readouts were grim. Riverstone had obviously seen it too, and like the injured tiger cub, knew there was nothing more Millie could do for her.

Quincy arrived in the grannywagon not long after that and whisked the two of them back to the Ship. Once inside the med room, Riverstone introduced Harlowe to Ela and explained to her that this was the pard whom he'd spoken of so many times that would one day come for him.

Ela smiled at the two of them. "You are together now."

Riverstone brushed a small strand of hair away from her eyes. "Yes, Ela. Together."

"I can see the happiness in you. I am happy too."

"Harlowe is going to help me take you outside. It will be okay." He didn't want to frighten her ever again.

Ela nodded. That was the most she could do.

Harlowe then lifted Ela gently from her table-bed, and with the aid of a couple of sturdy robobs for Riverstone, they met up with Quincy, who was waiting for them at the top of the rampway in the grannywagon. The big android drove them back to the beach, where the unnamed suns were ending their day with a spectacular show of red and orange, with streaks of green and deep purplish hues. Small waves slapped the shore, while a soft warm wind put the finishing touch on this Sorcerer's serenity.

Harlowe made them comfortable with pillows, water, and snacks. Then, feeling like a third leg, he left them alone, except for the cylinder he stuck in the sand in the event it was needed. Side by side, Riverstone and Ela looked out at the breaking waves and drifting clouds, while the suns were setting and the stars were just showing themselves overhead.

"It is even more beautiful than I could have imagined, my heart," Ela began. She tilted her head back, dazzled by every point of light in the heavens. "And those are the stars you spoke of, Matthew?"

Riverstone's eyes saw only her. He didn't have to look to see what Ela was talking about. "Yes, they are the stars..."

Her eyes filled with wonder at the tiny splinters of light. "And those. They are the clouds?" She was straining.

He kissed her softly on the cheek. "Yes."

"Is there anything more beautiful, Matthew?"

"You, Ela. You are more beautiful than a cloud."

Ela smiled with happiness. She touched the tears falling from the corners of his eyes. "Be strong, my darling. No one will ever take our love away from us. You know this. You will always be with me...always. Dog, Wiz, Squid, and Rerun. They need your help now, my Matthew. Do not let this moment of our parting take you away from them. Promise me you will be okay."

He found it hard to equal her strength and look into her eyes. His mouth stuttered and shook, trembling with fear. "I promise…"

"Did I remember to say I love you?" Then she closed her eyes and rested against his shoulder.

Riverstone wept uncontrollably, holding Ela, rocking her back and forth, calling her name over and over, to come back to him.

But she was gone to a world that would never hurt her again.

93

Saying Goodbye

THE FOLLOWING DAY, Harlowe picked out a grassy hill for Ela not far from the Ship. It had a panoramic view of the sea. Riverstone was too distraught to think of such things. They had a small ceremony. Simon and Harlowe played their flute and violin rendition of the Beatles' songs "Here Comes the Sun," followed by "P.S. I Love You." After that, everyone left Riverstone to be alone with Ela.

For three days he lay next to her grave, opening his shirt, touching the sand that was now her. Harlowe did not disturb Matt's grief, but he would not let his longtime friend lapse into a coma or succumb to any other harm. A nearby clicker periodically injected Riverstone with a vial of blue fluid. Molly and Rhud were also there and never left the hill for a moment. At night they kept him warm and protected him from any creatures that might find him easy prey. When the rains came, Harlowe stood over him with an umbrella. He doubted if Riverstone knew or cared what was being done to protect him.

Near the end of the third day, Harlowe felt a nudge on his shoulder. He had been sleeping at the foot of the mound, waiting for Riverstone to come around. When he looked up, Riverstone was standing over him. "She told me to leave and let her sleep," his frail voice said. He looked back at the mound. A simple cross marked her grave. He wiped his nose. His eyes shifted from side to side, his mind tormented and lost. "I promised her I would help." He turned back and gazed at the ship. "It's time to leave, Dog. It's time to find Quay and free Neeja."

Riverstone didn't wait for Harlowe's reply. He simply walked on toward the ship with Molly at his side to give him support. His gait was weak and feeble, but at the same time he strode with a determined resolve to carry on. At that moment, Harlowe thought he was looking at the bravest man he had ever known. He stood at attention and saluted him until Riverstone had blinked away into the ship.

* * *

In her honor and for her memory, Harlowe announced before liftoff that the unknown planet would henceforth be named "Ela." "To a courageous and loving woman," he said, standing at the side of his control chair.

Riverstone nodded in appreciation from his old chair, to Harlowe's right. As *Millawanda* rose slowly into the heavens, Riverstone went to the starboard-side observation window and kept the grassy mound in view for as long as he was able. He followed the long curve of the window, watching her mound drift out of sight, pressing his face against the window to the end for one last glimpse.

Harlowe kept the planet Ela in sight for another hour before going to hyperlight.

94

Harlowe's Dilemma

AT THE START of their journey away from Erati, Harlowe had first given orders for a speedy course to Naruck. He wanted to return Prigg to his home planet. It was Harlowe's decision, not Prigg's. Prigg wanted to stay until his job was complete. "You have not recovered Quay and Sizzle, Your Majesty. That was my promise to you, that I would remain your servant until you found them all."

Harlowe was in the workout room, doing a few rounds with Quincy at Level Four when Prigg confronted Harlowe on the subject.

"No, Prigg," Harlowe said flatly, his eyes never leaving the mannikin as they circled each other. "I'm taking you back and that's final."

Quincy jumped, his right leg thrust outward, and aimed for Harlowe's face. Harlowe parried the blow with a forearm thrust and slammed the android to the padded floor with a loud wallop. Harlowe followed that with a hammering fist to the heart that would have killed any human alive. Quincy's beady red eye lights blinked twice and then went out. At the same moment, a programmed response that had been downloaded into the android's memory during their days on Mars sighed, "Ahhh, ya got me, toad..."

Prigg threw Harlowe a towel. Sweat was pouring off of him in sheets. He lumbered over to Prigg and knelt down beside him, his chest heaving in and out like overworked bellows. "Please try to understand, Prigg. It pains me to take you home. I'm going to miss

594

you really bad, little buddy," he said, looking at him eye-to-eye. "No one could ask for a better co-pilot or a more loyal servant than you." He wiped his face. It stopped the beads of sweat only briefly. "It's too dangerous. You did your part. Without you my crew would still be lost. I couldn't have done it without you." Harlowe tried to keep his own eyes from crossing as he looked at Prigg's dejected face. "Oh man, your family. How could I look all those little Priggs in the eye if something happened to you? No! I'm not going to tell them their father is—well, you know. I'm not going to do it. So don't try to talk me out of it, Prigg. My mind is made up. That's final."

"But Your Majesty—" Prigg tried to say.

"No buts, Prigg. I've set course for Naruck and that's all there is to it."

"I will lose face. My king will feed me to his grogans."

Harlowe looked at Prigg. His mother used to try that tactic...the guilt-trip thing. She was a master at making him feel an inch tall for something he had made up his mind to do that she didn't want him to do. Prigg had obviously studied from the same playbook. They were hundreds of light-years from Earth and Harlowe could have sworn that Prigg had been talking to Tinker. Well, he wasn't falling for it.

"I just told you," Harlowe said again, "that you did everything I wanted, that no one could ask for more from you. We got my friends back. I can go on without you now."

"I will be killed."

"No, you won't. The king knows what I would do to him if he harmed you."

"After you are gone, he will kill me, Your Majesty. That is certain."

"That's not going to happen."

"Oh, it most certainly will happen, Your Majesty. I will be fed to the grogans after you leave. That is certain."

"I'll tell him we found everyone. He'll never know."

"If my sire asks me, I must tell him."

"He'll never know unless you tell him, Prigg." He glanced at the cats lying against the wall and waved at them. "They can't talk either. So what's the big deal?"

"I must tell him, Your Majesty. It would be dishonorable for me to tell my king anything but the truth."

Harlowe stared at Prigg. How anyone could see out of those eyes was beyond him. "You would, huh?"

"Yes, Your Majesty, it is my duty."

Harlowe's eyes narrowed. He felt himself sinking fast. He almost said, "Yes, dear." Instead he asked with all sincerity, "Have you ever met my mother?"

Prigg's maligned face twisted, confused. "Your Majesty?"

"Grogan meal, huh?"

"Yes, Your Majesty."

Harlowe stood up straight, cracking his back and letting out a large sigh of exasperation in resignation to the idea he was on the losing end of the discussion. "I'm not going to win this one, am I?"

Prigg's face twisted again. But before he could say anything more, Harlowe had started for the door, saying, "All right. You're in, but if you die on me, you little toad, I'll personally feed what's left of you to the king's grogans myself."

Prigg's wayward eyes came to an abrupt halt.

95

Back on the Clock

FOR OVER A week, no one was allowed in Riverstone's room, not even a clicker. Harlowe tried on several occasions to communicate with his First Officer, but he never answered the com. It tore Harlowe's guts out to watch his best friend deteriorate before his eyes. If they were going to confront the combined forces of the Fhaal, the Consortium, and most likely the Tomar Corporation, he would need Riverstone to be whole again. Harlowe was tired of waiting for his First Officer's Zen moment. Too many lives were at stake. As Captain, it was his duty to keep his crew in top condition, mentally and physically. He had to face Riverstone directly and snap him out of his depression. Otherwise, the rescue of Quay and Sizzle would be in jeopardy, along with the most critical mission of all: taking back Neeja from the Fhaal. Everything they had fought for, searched for, and sacrificed for was coming down to this final mission. By now Harlowe figured Anor Ran had delivered the thermo-grym crystals to the Fhaal. All the parties involved would be at full battle strength and gathering their forces for their respective slice of the quadrant. It was up to the Gamadin to stop them. Without Riverstone at his side, he had only half a crew, and he knew it. He had tried the hands-off approach, hoping things might work themselves out on their own. They hadn't. Riverstone's sense of duty had not returned. It was now time for Captain Harlowe Pylott to act. Maybe his call to duty hadn't worked, but he had one hold card left in his hand that he had put off using until now. He felt bad that it was necessary, but Riverstone had left him no choice.

Time was up!

Harlowe stood in front of Riverstone's door, ringing the doorbell, Beethoven's Fifth resonating loud and clear. When his First Officer didn't answer, Harlowe knew what he had to do. He turned to the massive android standing next to him, buttoning down the shirt pocket on its desert camouflage uniform, adjusting the two stars on its lapel, and straightening the beret on its hairless head. "All right Quince, do your thing."

Quincy's tiny blue dots immediately began to morph into steely hardened eyes that were so evil Harlowe gasped at their piercing death. When the aquiline nose and sprouting hairs of a military haircut were complete, Harlowe stuck a piece of spearmint in the newly formed mouth to add a final touch to General Theodore Tecumsa Gunn's rebirth.

Harlowe touched Riverstone's door activator, overriding the locking controls. The door slid open with a swish, revealing the black hole inside the room.

"Where is the slimy puke?" the General asked.

Harlowe saluted with a crisp snap of his hand, then pointed. "He's in there, General, SIR!"

Part III

...and Promises to Keep

All warfare is based on deception...
  – Sun Tzu, *The Art of War*

96

Permission Granted

AFTER THE NINE-DAY voyage to the far side of the quadrant, Harlowe and his crew were eager to assault the Consortium fortress at Og. Visions of the horrific misery Quay and Sizzle had to be suffering in the wake of what had happened to Ela, Riverstone, and Ian haunted all of them every waking moment. The time was now to go all-in.

During the voyage, Riverstone and Ian made remarkable recoveries. In less time than Harlowe figured it would take for Riverstone's soldier-to-soldier chat with the General to work, Riverstone blinked onto the bridge and stated with authority, "Permission to return to duty, Captain." Standing firmly at attention while waiting for his Captain's consent, Riverstone stared at the ceiling like he had just spoken to his Maker. He was tall and rigid and suited up in his fresh blue uniform of the day. His face was washed and clean-shaven and his hair cut short and trimmed close to the ears, just as Gunn would have demanded. The day after Millie left Ela, Riverstone and Ian could have been mistaken for clickers walking through the corridors. However, with a steady diet, exercise, and medical support, they were rapidly regenerating their spindly bodies. They were still far from their normal weight, but in a few short weeks they would be fitting into their old clothes again. That was on the outside. Their faces revealed another story. Deep lines remained etched on their faces, portraying a past that would never be erased, even with time.

Everyone on the bridge stopped what they were doing at that moment and rose from their chairs. Simon started the clapping. It was slow at first, and then Monday added his hands. Ian and Harlowe followed, and Prigg finally joined in after he understood what it all meant. The clapping continued for a long while before Harlowe led the salute and said, "Permission granted, Gamadin." He pointed to the control chair to his immediate right. "I believe this place is yours, Mr. Riverstone."

Riverstone walked stiffly to his chair. He was still weak and infirm. He carefully sat himself down to Harlowe's right, on the side where he had always been even while they grew up together. "Thank you, Captain," he said, and nodded his appreciation to everyone. His eyes were red and brimmed with pride. "You're da best, brahs."

97

Shipzilla

EVEN FROM A distance, the crew could see that Og was fortified like nothing they had ever come up against in their short Gamadin careers. Getting through the planet's defenses without being destroyed first would be next to impossible, even with a bulletproof plan. Harlowe asked Prigg what he thought of the situation. Having some knowledge of this section of the quadrant and of Consortium defenses, his response was something akin to: *Are you crazy? It's suicide. All Consortium outposts are heavily armed. Trying to slip through their sensors without bringing the full weight of their fleets down upon you before reaching Og is nothing less than brainsick stupid!* As always, Prigg told them this in his kinder, diplomatic way.

Everyone reluctantly agreed. It was a no-win situation, that is, until they stumbled across a giant spaceship headed to the same Brittilian Star Cluster as the planet Og.

"It has Consortium markings, Your Majesty," Prigg confirmed.

"That's a plus," Simon countered. He was in the "so-what" side of the conversation.

"They had to have spotted us by now," Riverstone said.

"No, Mr. Riverstone, it is a space freighter," Prigg replied quite confidently, "it has only limited sensor capabilities to keep it from ramming into space debris or floating asteroids."

603

"There doesn't appear to be anyone on board," Ian added, staring at his sensor screens.

One of Prigg's eyes looked at his console while the other studied the long-range view of the massive freighter on the screen. "The ship is robotic. It has a preset course that will take its cargo to the particular outpost requesting supplies without any sentient beings aboard."

Harlowe sat back in his chair, looking positive. "Sick."

"It's bigger than a Fhaal battle cruiser," Riverstone commented, looking at a close-up on the overhead screen.

"Not quite, but close," Ian countered.

Simon pointed up at the overhead. "Look at that storage hold. We could play frisbee with Millie in there," he commented jokingly.

"Yeah, with room to spare," Ian added as he continued his sweeps of the giant ship's interior.

Harlowe told Monday to change course and match the speed of the slower-moving freighter. "We've been wracking our brains trying to figure out a way into Og. This could be our ticket to ride, gentlemen."

"Shipzilla isn't going to let us change its course just because we're cool dudes," Riverstone pointed out.

Harlowe grinned. He liked the name.

He had a plan. He turned to Prigg for advice on the Consortium freighter. Prigg's eyes went ballistic.

"What's with him?" Riverstone asked.

"Oh, that's normal," Simon explained. "He gets that way every time he freaks out about the Skipper's plans."

"I'm down with that. How long does this take?"

"I saw him that way for two days when Harlowe went after Tnoir's entire planetary missile system."

Fortunately this time, it was only a few minutes before Prigg's eyes settled back to normal. "All right, Prigg," Harlowe began after the short wait, "what do you know about the freighter? Is it boardable? Can we change its direction?"

Ian turned to Harlowe. "If we board it, I can change its course," he said confidently.

Harlowe motioned for Prigg to answer his questions.

"I have never known such an act to be accomplished. It is a Consortium ship, Your Majesty."

"Understood, Mr. Prigg," Harlowe said, maintaining his patience. "Forget that it's Consortium. I want to know if we can board her."

"I am quite certain there are precautions against such undertakings, Your Majesty."

Harlowe was tired of the discussion. He stood, arching his back in a big yawning stretch. "All right. We just do it, then," and that was that.

* * *

With Prigg's guidance, Monday maneuvered *Millawanda* alongside the giant freighter. The Ship appeared like a small dinner plate against the massive black hull. During the approach, Ian kept a close eye on the sensor arrays for any troubling changes the Consortium freighter made while Harlowe, Riverstone, and Simon suited up in their SIBAs with full Gama-belts. After stopping by the utility room for some added supplies, they blinked topside to the perimeter edge. Together they jumped across a few yards of open space to the freighter's tarnished, space-beaten hull. Sensors indicated there was no atmosphere or heat supply inside the freighter. They would have to remain in their SIBAs the whole time unless they found a way to turn on the environmental controls.

Prigg didn't know about that, either.

With their grippers, they clung to the side of the dark metallic hull like flies. Acting like magnets, the grippers worn on their hands, knees, and feet stuck to any surface, regardless of its molecular properties.

"Don't look down," Harlowe commented through the com at the entrance hatch.

Riverstone glanced around in several directions. "Which way is down?"

"It's all down," Simon concluded.

While Harlowe and Riverstone studied the entry hatch for a way in, Simon located a touch pad of lighted buttons nearby. They made a couple of half-hearted attempts to figure out the right combination, all without success. Harlowe's patience was thin. He pulled out a plasma cutter and fired at the hatch. Sparks flew in all directions, but the results were what counted. As soon as the hatch came ajar they placed an expander inside the small opening and forced the hatch the rest of the way open.

Once inside, they returned the door to its original position. Strangely, the airlock automatically began to pressurize. Simon grunted expletives to express his displeasure over the freighter's welcome mat. When they walked through the second door, lights snapped on, sending everyone's neck hairs straight.

"Mr. Wizzixs, are you sure there are no life-forms onboard?" Harlowe asked.

"None registering, Captain," Ian replied.

Harlowe glanced over to Riverstone and Simon. "I've got a gut ache."

"Prigg just picked up some movement he can't explain, Captain," Monday said, cutting in.

"That's rad," Riverstone commented, removing his pistol from his Gama-belt. To Harlowe he said, motioning with his pistol, "You go first. You're the Captain."

"Thanks," Harlowe said as he cautiously stepped out into a long corridor. The black metal bulkheads of the hallway seemed endless. Harlowe made it to the first turn, and then Simon followed. Riverstone guarded their backs. They turned left and followed the schematic the sensors made of the ship's interior displayed inside their bugeyes. It might not have been the proper path to take to the main control room, but it was the most logical. A Garmin road guide would have come in handy.

After several more corridors and three more turns, they came to a wide opening. Harlowe bent over the guardrail and looked down. It was the freighter's vast cargo hold. "Whoa!" they all gasped.

"Look at all that stuff!" Riverstone whistled. There was a wealth of supplies: giant generators, heavy equipment, plasma cannons, fifty-story cranes, building materials, beams for construction with massive crates, and thousands of metal containers of who-knows-what. Right below them, taking up most of the space was a single item that was painful for everyone to see.

Erati thermo-grym crystals.

Stacks and stacks of containers were filled with the glowing yellow crystals. Riverstone seethed as he thought about the number of lives it had taken to produce that much crystal. Harlowe lay a comforting hand on his First Officer's shoulder. "Don't worry, pard. The Consortium's not getting a single rock."

Riverstone fought for control as he glared at the shipment with disgust. "Whatever we do to get rid of it, I want to pull the trigger."

Harlowe agreed. "You've got it."

"Not much room for us here, Skipper," Simon observed.

"We'll have to do a little unpacking," Harlowe said. He didn't seem too concerned about the magnitude of the unpacking or how they would accomplish it. He motioned for Riverstone to follow him.

"Stay here, Mr. Bolt. Keep an eye on things while Mr. Riverstone and I check out Shipzilla's control room."

Riverstone continued to watch their backs while Harlowe followed the schematic inside his helmet. At the next intersection, Riverstone pointed. "Looks like we take this corridor here. It dead-ends fifty yards ahead, then we head right."

"Right," Harlowe acknowledged, checking his pistol.

"Worried? We haven't seen a soul."

"Yeah, about that thing Prigg said moved," Harlowe replied, entering the corridor. Then to Prigg back in the ship he asked, "Any more movement, Prigg?"

"Yes, Your Majesty," Prigg replied, his usual high-pitched voice raising a few octaves when he started stressing out. "But it stopped when you turned into the corridor you're walking in now."

Riverstone rechecked his weapon's power gauge. "That's comforting."

When they arrived at the end of the corridor, they stopped to reassess their next move. The control room wasn't far. Two more turns and they were there.

"How's it look from your end, Mr. Bolt?" Harlowe inquired.

"Quiet as a monk's tomb, Skipper," Simon replied.

"Nothing unusual happening, Mr. Platter?" Harlowe asked.

"Cool here, Captain," Monday replied.

"Mr. Wizzixs?"

"Spooky, Captain," Ian replied.

Harlowe and Riverstone traded glances before Riverstone asked: "What's spooky mean?"

"Spooky is spooky. I don't like the quiet, is all," Ian replied.

Harlowe waved his pistol for Riverstone to go first this time. "Your turn."

With Riverstone as point man, they turned the corner slowly and quiet. Sensors had shown nothing alive anywhere on the ship, but instincts told them otherwise. They had seen too many Freddy Krueger movies to believe something unalive wasn't laying in wait for them at the next turn.

When they made the last turn to the control room, the sound of metal rubbing against metal stopped them in their tracks.

"Did you hear that?" Harlowe whispered.

Riverstone nodded.

Harlowe tapped Riverstone on the arm, and then pointed at himself, indicating Riverstone was to cover him as he went forward.

Riverstone grabbed Harlowe's suit. "Careful."

Harlowe held his pistol out front in an arms-locked position as he edged along the corridor wall toward the control room entrance. It wasn't long before it was time to poke his head into the dimly lit room. If someone or something were waiting for him, he would soon find out. There were no more places to go after this.

Ever so carefully, Harlowe edged himself around the corner. Next time, he thought, he was going to have the forethought to pack along a clicker for this kind of work.

This is nuts!

He stopped. Suddenly, sticking his head out didn't seem like a bright idea. He had visions of getting blasted by another stunner. Man, how he hated stunners! If he was going to be shot at, he preferred a good old plas round than a brilliant flash of orange light.

He turned back to Riverstone, who was motioning him to get on with it. Harlowe waved him off and removed a flashlight from his Gama-belt. He held it up for Riverstone to see. Riverstone didn't care. He waved him on again. *Just do it, Dog!* Harlowe tossed the light out past the corner of the turn. The instant he did, three rapid shots blazed out of the darkness. He looked down at his flashlight lying on the metal floor, riddled with smoking holes.

Harlowe glared back at Riverstone, who shooed him forward again. Harlowe took his second pistol out and turned back to the blind corner. Without wasting much time to think about a plan, he crouched low and sprang out into the control room with both pistols blasting hot blue plas bolts in the direction of his unseen assailant. Two more bolts streaked past his head during the brief exchange. Whoever was on the other side was fast, almost inhumanly so! Harlowe kept firing, emptying half a clip before he heard something heavy and metallic crash to the floor with the sound of someone pushing over a twelfth-century suit of armor.

Riverstone advanced cautiously and asked, "Sounded like a vamp in the kitchen?"

Harlowe held up his hand to keep Riverstone from venturing closer until he was sure.

"Did you get it, Dog?" Ian's voice asked in a whisper.

"Sounded like it," Monday replied.

"Maybe there's more," Riverstone commented.

If Harlowe hadn't been wearing his SIBA, Riverstone would have seen his sour-faced smile.

"It's still your turn," Riverstone said, nudging Harlowe forward.

Harlowe grunted displeasure as he raised himself off the metal floor and entered the room. There was no movement coming from the darkness. His night-vision bugeyes saw nothing inside the lightless control room except for the blinking lights of the freighter's console working on full auto. Then he saw it" a huge robot full of sizzling holes, lying in a heap on the floor.

Riverstone came into the control room as Harlowe bent down to examine the robot. The robot's right hand held a light pistol. He removed it and handed it to Riverstone. "No wonder the sensors didn't show any life-forms."

Riverstone's bugeyes scanned the large room. "Let's hope he's solo."

Harlowe was worried. "Did you get that, Wiz?"

"Aye, Captain. Prigg's already working on it," Ian replied.

"Protect your backside, Mr. Bolt," Harlowe warned, believing there was more to come.

"Will do, Skipper," Simon replied.

Then Ian broke in with more info. "We got 'em, Captain! Onscreen. Looks like there's a nest of them and they're buzzing your way!"

Tiny blue dots flashed on the interior schematic of the freighter, pointing out where the mechanical guardians were located throughout the ship. There were dozens stationed all around the Consortium freighter. It was as if they had disturbed a nest of bees.

Suddenly they heard the loud shots of plas rounds from down the corridor.

"They're thick as flies down here, Captain!" Simon shouted in his com.

"We'll be all day taking these out," Riverstone complained.

"They have to have a shutoff," Ian said. "Give me a shot of the room. I'll see if I can't locate it for you."

Harlowe followed Ian's suggestion. The control panels were simple. Once Harlowe's bugeyes had scanned the control panels, it took only a few moments for Ian to find what they were looking for. Ian gave Harlowe the location of the robot switch. Two clicks later, the freighter's guardians were effectively immobilized.

"What's your status, Mr. Bolt?" Harlowe asked.

"That stopped them, Captain. Thanks!" Simon replied, quite relieved.

"Nice work, gentlemen," Harlowe said, praising his crew. Meanwhile, his mind was already focusing on the controls of the monster freighter. "Now let's empty this tub."

Harlowe opened the rear cargo doors and told Ian to take Millie two miles to the rear of Shipzilla. "Call me when you're there," he told Monday. It took twenty minutes for the giant door to open. Once that was accomplished, Millie was waiting exactly where Harlowe had instructed.

"Put the tractor beam on wide and pull everything out," Harlowe instructed.

"Everything, Captain?" Monday's voice asked.

"Gut it!" Harlowe confirmed.

"Aye, Captain," came the reply.

While the cleaning chores were being done, Harlowe and Riverstone turned their full attention to the control panel. With Prigg's guidance, it didn't take long for them to find the controls for changing course. "This is the main drive, right?" Harlowe asked Prigg over the com.

"Correct, Your Majesty," Prigg's small voice said in Harlowe's ear. "To the right is the power consumption grid. Left is velocity. Above is guidance."

"Piece of cake," Riverstone commented.

"Yeah, it seems Shipzilla was only meant for one thing, taking stuff from one outpost to the next. Nothing trick about that," Harlowe said and pointed to another set of indicators on a small side panel. "What's this, Prigg?"

"That appears to be environmental control, Your Majesty."

"Nice. Maybe we can get a little heat in here," Harlowe said, turning to Riverstone.

"See if there's a hot tub, Skipper," Simon suggested.

Harlowe stared at Riverstone, wondering if Simon ever stopped thinking about the pleasures in life. He wasn't in the mood for jokes.

It appeared the freighter was going to work out perfectly for their purposes. Thirty minutes later, Shipzilla's hold was cleared and Monday slid *Millawanda* into her new parking space inside the hold. Harlowe and Riverstone returned to the overlook where Simon was standing, watching over the whole operation. Together they watched the massive outer doors close gently behind Millie. Harlowe looked down at his beautiful ship, her satin skin radiating a rich, golden complexion.

Sighing with pride, Harlowe uttered, "She's so hot."

Riverstone nodded, his eyes equally wide, full of awe. "She's a keeper, all right."

They waved at Ian, Monday, and Prigg on the bridge through Millie's large wraparound windows. Ian waved back, but Prigg and Monday seemed to be too focused on their jobs to stop for such behavior.

"I don't think he sees us," Riverstone observed with a slight grin. "His eyes must be bouncing around like pinballs about now."

"Yeah, the thought of taking on the Consortium fleet at Og doesn't sit well with him," Harlowe said.

If they could have seen each other's eyes, they would have shared the thought that their next stop would not sit well with anyone else, either.

98

Plans Gone Bad

"ENTERING THE OG star system in twenty minutes, Your Majesty," Prigg's voice resonated over the com.

Sitting at the controls of the massive freighter, Harlowe leaned forward and spoke into his com unit. "Understood, Mr. Prigg." If they had been traveling in their own Gamadin ship, they would have made it to Og days ago. Shipzilla traveled much slower. It took over a week to cover the relatively short ten-light-year distance, a small trade-off considering the benefits their disguise had given them. Several Consortium battlecruisers had already passed them on their way into the Britillian Cluster without giving them a single thought. Three days earlier, a complete battle group of fifty ships skipped by them and no one bothered to stop or check the giant freighter for stowaways.

"Steady as she goes, Mr. Bolt," Harlowe said. "Let's keep her in hyperlight for as long as we can."

Simon made a few minor course adjustments to the guidance controls before he replied, "Not too much longer, Skipper, or they'll wonder why we're coming in so fast."

"Good point, Mr. Bolt. Decelerate at your discretion." Harlowe set aside his bowstring. Playing music or going rounds with Quincy was his way of coping with the long, at-a-snail's-pace voyage and his thoughts about Quay—her condition and whether she was alive or dead or something in between. The closer they came to Og, the more his stomach twisted in knots. He had not seen her in over six months. What would she look like? How had she survived her imprisonment? Was she well? Had it been as horrifying as Riverstone and Ian's experience? What kind of girl would she be when he found her? Would she be Quay, or someone he didn't know? If he found her, and he *would* find her, would she still love him? So many questions, none of them answerable until he saw her again.

He closed his eyes, fighting hard to concentrate on the current problems in spite of the distraction she caused. She was close. He could feel her. His vision of being with her again was solid. He would not let one negative thought deter him from believing she was okay.

"Better tell Squid to get Molly and Rhud inside," Riverstone advised.

Harlowe made the call to Monday and was told they were already inside the ship. He sat back in the makeshift beach chair they had brought from the ship when they discovered the Consortium freighter had no places for humans to sit. He gazed out at the unusually large and orange Oggian sun.

"I love those cats," Harlowe commented.

"I remember when Quay first found them," Riverstone said.

Harlowe smiled slightly, reflecting back to #2 when he was nearly eaten by the T-Rex.

"If the Consortium hadn't attacked, you would have let them go," he pointed out.

Harlowe nodded in agreement. "Yeah, she would have left me there if I did."

Riverstone snorted. "No doubt, and fed you to Rex's kids for dessert."

Harlowe forced a slight grin. As close to death as he had come that day, Riverstone was right. She would have saved the cats first.

"Nice to know where you are in the pecking order," he sighed as he drifted back to one moment, hundreds of light-years from their present position.

They were standing together at the bottom of the rampway, and he had just kissed her for the first time. He closed his eyes and remembered the fresh smell of her hair and the sweet taste of her lips. *Man, it was so beautiful that sorcerer's night!* He heard her laugh and turned his head, thinking it was really she. It was all a head game. What he heard was the computer making an adjustment from the lighted bulkhead of the freighter's tiny bridge. He kept looking anyway. Maybe he was wrong. His nose burned again. He didn't want Riverstone to see the mist in his eyes. How many times had he reached out for her in his dreams and found no one there, just the way he still did at times with Lu? Sometimes he would go for days without thinking of Lu, but she always returned. It was spooky. After all this time, she was still with him. Would he ever let her go? Would anyone, really, ever take her place?

A bright yellow light on the console bleeped on, rushing Harlowe back to the present.

"Slowing Shipzilla down, Skipper," Simon announced. As soon as they left hyperlight, their console was taken over by the Og Central Control.

"Are we riding it out?" Riverstone asked, somewhat alarmed.

"Have to," Harlowe replied. "If we try to override, they'll know something's up."

Riverstone agreed but then countered with a cautionary footnote. "This isn't a simple outpost, Dog." He pointed to all the battlecruisers and ships of war parked in their respective stationary orbits around the planet. "They're expecting something."

"Yeah, us."

"How do you know?"

"It's a given. Anor Ran knows it. Unikala had this in mind the whole time. That's why he brought Quay here."

"You've known all along this is a trap?" Riverstone asked, sitting up in disbelief.

"We'll get Quay and her sister out of there first, before we go in with guns blazing."

"That's not a plan."

"It's the only one I have."

Riverstone eyed the massive Consortium fleet with worry. "It's suicide, Dog."

"Yeah? Well, has that ever stopped us before? The U.S. Government, the Consortium, the Fhaal? Does it matter? When hasn't it been suicide? That was always part of the plan."

Riverstone kept staring at the buildup of warships. Part of the plan or not, this much firepower was way over the top, even for Harlowe.

Harlowe gave him a confident wink. "Millie will take care of them."

"It's a war zone out there, Harlowe! They're going to be at full security alert."

"I know."

"Which means if this freighter isn't expected, they're going to be mighty suspicious."

"Yeah, that's a problem," Harlowe admitted off-the-cuff, as if unconcerned.

Riverstone groaned as if Harlowe had gone daft. In the old days he would have fired back something along the order of *who are you trying to kid, Pylott? You've never had a plan in your life! It's always been "just do it." Devise and improvise as we go along. The only plan that you've ever gone by is called chaos. So don't make me laugh with this 'plan' garbage!*

Instead, an insight from Erati gave him depth and vision. Riverstone said, "You've thought this one through, haven't you?"

Harlowe kept his eyes on the Consortium fleet. "I'm all-in, pard." He then drifted over to one of the two small viewing ports and looked out. Outside, the freighter was passing one of the five outer moons of the planet. They were only a couple hundred thousand miles from the surface. The planet's geographical features were clearly visible to the unaided eye. None of the bodies of water would be considered an ocean by Earth's standards. The few that were visible were no larger than any of the North American Great Lakes. The planet itself was only slightly smaller than Earth, with large polar regions that extended well below the fifteenth parallel of each hemisphere. It looked cold and foreboding, especially since a great deal of the planet's surface appeared to be made up of wrinkled, black jagged mountain ranges that looked like something out of a Bram Stoker novel. It had a breathable oxygen-nitrogen atmosphere. Its days were much longer then Earth's—thirty-seven hours and some change.

"Unikala's throwing in all his chips on this one," Harlowe commented, genuinely amazed at all the firepower the Consortium had mustered for their arrival.

Riverstone elbowed Simon in the side and nodded toward Prigg on the com screen, his eyes roving in different directions. "Look at those eyes move, will ya! He's giving me a headache." Prigg and Ian were on the Gamadin bridge, keeping an eye on the sensors from there.

Simon snickered. "That's his really worried look, but I've never seen his eyes jump around that fast before." He leaned over and tapped the com screen display. "Hey, you okay down there, little buddy?" he asked Prigg.

Removing a small pair of binos from his utility belt, Harlowe focused in on the battlecruisers. His face turned intense as he scanned the heart of the Consortium battle group. Their size and numbers were humbling. He counted six battlecruisers and row after row of support transports, frigates, and other ships of war. Harlowe wondered how anyone could counter such a force without an equally equipped force. This was the mightiest armada he had ever seen. That is, until he switched the magnifiers inside his binos to high. From beyond a far moon, coming out of the shadows was a starship, the likes of which dwarfed all that he had ever seen before. Not long after that, two more gargantuan vessels appeared out of the shadows, following the first starship.

"Fhaal..." Prigg emitted in a low, fearful gasp from the com.

Harlowe handed the binos to Riverstone. "Right you are, Mr. Prigg. The three ships coming out from beyond the Consortium fleet are Fhaal Class One starships."

Riverstone looked over at Harlowe with a sardonic grin. "Part of the plan, Captain?"

Harlowe returned a similar grin, but with a little added glint in his eye. "I've got them right where I want them, Mr. Riverstone. An old general once said, 'Don't wrestle with pigs. You get dirty and they enjoy it.' Well, what's a little dirt among enemies, right, Rerun?"

Simon was looking a little nervous himself. "Right, Skipper."

"You knew the Fhaal were coming to the party, too, didn't you, Captain?" Riverstone asked, looking for the signs of deception in Harlowe's manner.

"That was the plan," Harlowe said confidently.

Simon glanced at Riverstone for a little support. "This could be tougher than we thought."

Riverstone's eyes rolled to the heavens. "It usually is," he murmured.

"Are you sure they're Fhaal, Captain?" Simon asked.

Riverstone kept looking through the binos as Harlowe replied, "I recognize their emblems. They're the same toads who screwed with us back on Earth when we had nothing left to shoot at them but Jester's rifle. They're Fhaal, all right." He then added, "Question is, where is Señor Ran? He's late for the party."

"After what you did to him on Roshmar, Skipper, you're still expecting him to be here?" Simon asked.

"He wouldn't miss a chance at the brass ring, Rerun," Harlowe assured his First Mate. Suddenly, his face lit up and he pointed to the opposite side of the planet from all the military activity. "There he is! Fashionably late as usual. Must be a Tomarian trait," he said, nodding toward the fleet of starclass warships still entering Oggian space. They were as massive and powerful as any ship out there, including the Fhaal.

"Where did he get those?" Simon asked.

"It seems that Anor has been on a shopping spree since Roshmar," Harlowe said.

"I figured they were all enemies. You'd think they would be blasting each other to pieces by now, Skipper," Simon said.

Harlowe didn't reply to Simon's statement. He kept his focus on the fleets like someone who's got the best hand at the poker table.

"You don't seem surprised," Riverstone said to Harlowe.

"At everyone protecting their interests? No. That doesn't surprise me. What's the old saying? 'The enemy of my enemy is my friend.' You're looking at lot a of backslapping friends out there, gentlemen. A good old kumbaya."

Simon eyes darted back and forth like they were about to join Prigg's in a race for confusion. "I don't get it. You're saying this was all an elaborate plan for us?"

"That's right, Rerun," Riverstone replied.

"But why?"

Harlowe saw Ian on the screen, looking as though he had some sort of explanation but needed a little push to get it out. "Mr. Wizzixs, you look like you've given it some thought."

"Some, Captain," Ian replied, staring into the screen. "I was thinking back a few years, when Avitia and his Locos tried to take over Lakewood. They started small at first. They tried to get the small gangs to come in and do the dirty work, remember? That didn't work. He found out you and Riverstone were the ones getting in their way. So Avitia thought he could do it himself. That didn't work, either."

"Is there a point to this, Wiz, or we just reliving the past?" Harlowe asked, as he continued studying the combined fleets.

"Well, sir, I think if we listen to the past, we can assess the future," Ian continued thoughtfully. "I'll give you odds that the Fhaal toadface that Riverstone and Monday saw in Vegas is behind all of this, and I'll bet a tray of double-doubles he's in one of those ships out there. Like Sullivan, he's tried several times to kill you and can't seem to figure out how to do it. He keeps coming up short."

Ian went on. He was on a roll, and Harlowe seemed to be enjoying Ian's account. Maybe it was all a stretch, but it was a good way to pass the time while they were making their way toward the planet. "So like Avitia, he's gathered all his forces and is just waiting for us to step into the trap, only this time he figures he's got enough firepower to do the job."

Harlowe turned away from the window, his eyes unblinking, fixed on the possibility that maybe Ian was on to something. "So you think Lizardface has set us up, too."

"I think he knows you'll come after Quay, Harlowe, just like Avitia took Leucadia because he knew you'd be after her in a heartbeat.

Once you enter the trap, he'll let the other players put down their hand first."

"If they have better hands than he does?" Simon asked.

"Lizardface will kill them in a heartbeat," was Ian's cold reply.

Harlowe began to slowly nod in agreement. "You're saying I'm a very predictable guy, Mr. Wizzixs?"

"Very," was Ian's short reply.

Simon had been quietly listening from the sidelines, and hadn't asked any questions until now. "So what's the payoff, Skipper?" He looked at Riverstone's blank face. "Everything has a payoff, right? In every movie I made, there was always a payoff at the end. The bad guy was motivated by something—the girl, the power, or both. The only thing that stood in his way was I, Captain Starr." Simon grinned. "So what's Lizardface want?"

Riverstone grunted. "To kill us all."

"Kill us all?" Simon questioned, surprised.

Riverstone explained. "Yeah, kill us all. He's got no choice. The dude's feelings were hurt when a couple of Lakewood toads dusted his attack fleet last year. He's got a score to settle, and it's personal. If he takes us out, he gets Millie, the quadrant, and his revenge. He gets it all, including his pride."

Simon saw the script writing itself before his eyes. "Yeah, that's his payoff. Kill us."

Riverstone was more specific. "Kill the Gamadin," he corrected.

Harlowe's looked as if his mind were a thousand light-years from Shipzilla. He hadn't moved or spoken the last part of the conversation.

Harlowe blinked. "Jester's right. It's not only Millie they want, they want us...the Gamadin," he whispered, almost inaudibly. He repeated it louder for everyone. "They want us all dead because we're the only ones who can stop their vision of a Fhaal galaxy that goes beyond the quadrant, and that includes Earth, gentlemen."

"Now that makes a lot of sense," Simon stated sarcastically. He pointed out the window at the fleet of starclass battleships. "With ships like that, why would he want a salad plate like ours?" He glanced down at the com screen. "What? We're about five percent of their mass. Isn't that right, Wiz?"

"Less," Ian added over the com.

"See? Less," Simon echoed, as his eyes focused intently on Harlowe. "How do we stand a chance against them?"

Harlowe turned to the middle overhead screen, where an overhead shot displayed the Ship, all golden and round, parked silently in the vast cargo hold, waiting like a coiled spider ready to leap on its prey. "Everyone is afraid of Millie, our government, the former President and his pinheads, the Consortium, Lizardface, and Quay's father. They all fear Millie, and rightfully so. She's a man-up lady."

"That's not an answer, Skipper," Simon commented, disappointed.

"It will have to do for now, Rerun," Harlowe said.

"What about Quay and Sizzle?" Simon asked.

"The plan hasn't changed, Mr. Bolt. We're going to find Quay and Sizzle. We're going to get them both back alive—and we're going to beat these toads." Harlowe promised this with such finality that everyone knew they were going ahead with their plans, regardless of the odds against them.

Simon liked what he heard. "Aye, sir." He was all-in. If Harlowe was going through the gauntlet of Death to get his girl, he was going right along with him.

Riverstone swallowed hard as he looked out across the gathering Fhaal and Consortium fleets, and now the addition of the Tomarian fleet. The ends of his mouth slowly turned up in a wry sort of way.

"Ya think we can find a nice beach after this?" he asked, staring into Harlowe's cold steel eyes.

The glint in Harlowe's eyes was confident and unshakable. "A glassy tube in a warm, salty ocean? I'll arrange it."

"So when we get the ladies back, I'm going to hold you to that promise," Riverstone said.

Harlowe pulled away and straightened his uniform. It was almost as if he was brooding over his answer. During his moment of formulation, his deep blue eyes remained focused on the gathering fleets. Riverstone shuddered. He had seen that look only a few times in all the years he had known Harlowe. It was the look of Death. Harlowe turned his chair and stood up. His face was stone cold, unemotional and pitiless, as though all the warmth inside him had suddenly been struck dry from his veins. Then he said, "No mercy, gentlemen. None!"

The silence in the control room was chilling. Riverstone nodded. He understood. This was the end. There was no fence sitting. No going anywhere but forward, into Death's own backyard. The fight would end here. There would be no battles to fight over after this, no more planets to save, no more places to go. Og was the end of the line. Death would be the only victor from this moment on. This was the option forced upon them.

Simon's face went slack. He sensed the finality and shivered.

A sudden jolt shook the giant ship, cutting off any more conversation between them. It was as if something had grabbed Shipzilla from behind and wouldn't let go. The slowdown was so sudden and abrupt, the inertial force slammed everyone in the control hard against the bulkhead. The inertia dampeners on the freighter were minimal. They were only meant to keep the robots from destruction, not human stowaways. Inside *Millawanda*, Ian, Monday, and

Prigg felt only a slight tug on their control chairs, just enough of a jolt for them to know something wasn't right.

"What was that?" Riverstone asked, as Harlowe helped him to stand.

Harlowe looked out the porthole. "I think permission to land has been denied."

Riverstone joined Harlowe as they watched a couple of attack fighters launched from nearby battlecruiser bays.

"I think they're coming, Skipper," Simon pointed out as he righted his chair and climbed back into his seat at the console.

Harlowe watched their afterburners kick in. "Time to evacuate, everyone!"

"Aye, Captain," Ian announced. "Three birds on a direct intercept course."

"Understood, Wiz," Harlowe replied coolly. "We're on our way home."

"Any plans, Captain?" Riverstone asked as he concentrated on the fast attack ships streaking toward them. They would be in firing position in less than a minute. "We should hurry."

Harlowe turned around to Simon. "We need to override the controls again, Mr. Bolt."

Simon's hands flew across the controls. It didn't take a lot. "Override complete, Skipper. Ready for new course, Captain."

Riverstone kept his focus out the starboard view port. "Uh-oh," he said in a low, worrisome tone.

"Captain!" Ian's voice boomed over the com. "Sensors indicate attack ships powering weapons, ready to fire."

"Turn Shipzilla toward the planet, Mr. Bolt," Harlowe ordered calmly. He turned to his First Officer next. "Quit gawking, Mr.

Riverstone. Make yourself useful. Help Mr. Bolt get those forward shields to full power," he demanded, pointing.

Riverstone quickly went to the shield station and began following Harlowe's command. "They'll only take one hit." The panel of lights lit up, indicating the protective barrier was activated.

"Understood, Mr. Riverstone."

"They've launched torpedoes, Captain!" Ian called out. "Impact three seconds. Two. One..."

The three on the freighter's bridge braced themselves. As expected, the impact completely obliterated the weak shields on the first salvo. Fire and smoke followed immediately. If they didn't leave the control and get back to the Ship before the next burst of plasfire, they would die when the energy bolts struck Shipzilla.

"Go now, you two! That's an order!" Harlowe barked, as he pulled Simon out of his beach chair and pushed him toward the exit hatchway. He then made a few last-second adjustments to the control console.

"It's useless, Captain, the ship can't take another hit!" Riverstone shouted above the explosions against the massive hull.

"Take off, I said! I'll be right behind you," Harlowe shouted back, shrugging off Riverstone's grip. "Just one more thing..."

Simon grabbed Riverstone's arm. Reluctantly they bolted through the open hatchway and headed down the corridor at light speed. Harlowe made one last twist to a knob and then he, too, was out of the hatch, running full tilt toward the massive cargo bay where Millie was parked.

"The disguise, gentlemen," Harlowe shouted as they ran. "The plan was okay," he continued in spurts. "It just needed a little tweak from the bad guys."

Explosions inside the giant freighter rocked them inside the corridor, knocking Simon to the floor. Riverstone helped him to his feet and they continued running, with Harlowe a half-step behind.

As they ran, they could hear Ian's voice shouting over the com inside their SIBAs.

"They've powered up again," Ian relayed from sensor console inside the Ship. "This one's going to break us apart, Captain. Where are you?"

When they got to the stairway that led to the hold, it had been blown away into twisted parts. The only thing left for them to do was jump.

"Almost there, Wiz!" Harlowe called back as they hit the metal floor hard and rolled forward, dispersing the energy of the fall like acrobats. They didn't waste time checking for injuries. They ended up tangled together, knocking into each other, tumbling over and over onto their backs and sides.

Riverstone felt his ankle twist, but it wasn't broken. His new 54th-century leg implants were too tough to break.

"Three seconds to impact," Ian's voice called out. They were almost to the catwalk above the Ship. To survive, they had to be on the other side of the barrier, inside *Milliwanda* itself.

"Two, one."

Harlowe and Riverstone grabbed Simon by the back of his SIBA and leaped.

"IMPACT!"

99

Call to Battle

FROM BEHIND HIS command port, Sar watched with satisfied eyes as the brilliant fireball streaked across the Oggian sky toward the planet's surface.

"The vessel is breaking up, Commander," his First Leader reported. "It has penetrated the atmosphere and is disintegrating."

"Excellent. Do we have a report on the cause of the security breach?"

"Consortium officials suspect a system malfunction, Commander."

"Vessel origin?"

"A Class-Three, intra-system freighter, inbound from the Erati mines, Commander."

"A crystalline power ship?" Sar scowled.

"Yes, Commander. Self-operating."

Sar's evil yellow eyes glared angrily at the bridge. "That shipment was critical, First Leader!" Sar roared. "How could that occur with so many redundancy overrides?"

The First Leader looked at his notes. "I have no answer, Commander, unless it was sabotaged."

Sar looked off into the distance. *Even they would not be so bold!* He turned quickly to his subordinates. "Send a ship down to the surface. We must consider all possibilities, even the most doubtful ones. I want to know why that Erati freighter broke security."

"I will launch a survey mission immediately, Commander."

"Warn the Consortium pigs and the Tomarian dogs that if they come close to the wreckage, they will be killed," Sar added scornfully. He wanted no mistakes, and trusted no one.

The freighter struck the night side of the planet on a vast uninhabited plain. The blast was so brilliant, it lit up the planet like the high noon sun. Seconds later, shock waves from the explosion reached Sar's battle cruiser, rocking the massive Imperial starship but causing no damage.

Sar watched the billowing mushroom. "Were mass readings taken of the vessel before it was shot down?" he asked.

The First Leader turned toward a console of graphic information. A minor blimp darted away from burning mass. The anomaly registered so small on the First Leader's sensors, he passed it off as an irregular reflection caused by the aftershocks. "Yes, Commander. Standard procedure in case enemy vessels—"

"I am aware of standard procedure, First Leader," Sar interrupted. "Give me the data."

The First Leader turned on a switch along a wall console and listened for a brief message. He then reported nervously. "Commander Sar, mass readings indicate the freighter was carrying something of unusually high density. It is not known what the source was. Data reveal an unknown mass signature pattern that does not fit the crystalline nature of the cargo."

"Speculation?"

"Unknown, Commander. Until the crash site is searched, we have no recommendations at this time," the First Leader replied.

Sar turned his attention back to the planet, recalling the Gamadin mothership that had destroyed his flagship and every ship in the battle group nearly a passing ago. The power his flagship had measured before the Gamadin blasted his ship was immeasurable. He was fortunate to have escaped alive in the shuttle. Paradon, the Great One, had been right. *The security of the Empire is at stake, Commander. The risk is too great to disregard... We have to have it for ourselves. With it, our need for thermo-grym will be no more... If this mission fails and the Gamadin ship escapes, the Fhaal are doomed.*

To his amazement, the Fhaal High Command had treated him like a hero when he and a few other survivors were finally rescued along the frontier. When he asked why he had not lost face and suffered a sizable reduction in rank, Paradon's answer was simple: *Because you have felt the power of the ancients. Failure, Commander, is often the greatest teacher.*

Sar was determined not to fail again. He would lead his battle group to victory and capture the most prestigious prize in the history of the Empire. The Gamadin mothership would be the Empire's before the end of the cycle.

"First Leader!" Sar called out. "Bring up the mass meter readings of the vessels that attacked my fleet on the frontier." He knew there was only one vessel that had the power signature of the ancients. He was fortunate to have escaped to tell about the battle with the mothership. He laughed inside. The High Command had even rewarded him with its highest accolades for his valor and cunning, for returning to the planet alive and with what was left of his crew.

The First Leader's eyes followed the readouts. "All mass indicators normal, Commander. Except for one." His eyes widened. "There is a match. The vessel that attacked our glorious battle group was made of the same high-density alloys. There is definitely a signature duplication, Commander."

"Power density?" Sar asked.

The First Leader stared at the screen in disbelief. "This has to be a mistake, Commander! These figures are off the scale, Sire."

Sar stared coldly at his officer. He didn't need to ask any more questions.

"I will have the answer, Com—" the First Leader began to say.

"No!" Sar shouted. The First Leader had never seen his Commander so emotionally enraged over something so trivial. "All fleet ships to highest alert! All pilots to their attack ships. Order all battlecruisers to full battle readiness!"

The First Officer nodded and followed Sar's orders. Alarms blared loudly as the mighty battlecruiser came immediately to full battle alert. The colossal parabolic dishes along the backside of the command ship swung into action, searching the planet's surface and the vastness of space for anything that moved with such a powerful mass signature.

100

A Place to Hide

WITH SHIELDS AT full power, *Millawanda* broke out of the fire just before impact, rising like a Phoenix and racing forward like a whisper in the wind, skimming silently at treetop level toward the distant mountain range. The after-effects of the explosion would give them a limited amount of time to leave the crash site without sensors detecting their escape, but they had to act fast. They had to find a hiding place before their window of opportunity closed.

With Harlowe, Riverstone, and Simon pulling themselves together from their latest near-death experience, Ian was at the controls, flying the Ship toward a nearby range of mountains that Prigg put on the screen. They covered the three-hundred-mile distance in less than thirty minutes, maintaining a speed well under the sound barrier so as not to tip off anyone scanning the planet's surface of the unnatural object leaving the crash site.

The mountainous pinnacles of black basalt shielded them from prying sensors. Harlowe maneuvered deftly between the steep mountain valleys of jagged rock cliffs while Simon searched for a suitable place to hide a 1,500-foot-wide salad plate. It wasn't long before he found exactly what they needed: a wide niche under a massive granite overhang, three miles above an impossibly steep ravine. Far beneath their perch, an angry river was a tiny thread of quicksilver powering its way through the black rock gorge below.

Harlowe took his time to slowly sandwich Her Highness without a scratch between the overhang and the ledge. There were only inches to spare.

"We'll need a crowbar to get us out of here," Riverstone commented as he looked up at the jagged rock overhang above the outer windows.

Harlowe said little. There was too much crowding his mind to make comeback remarks about his sleight-of-hand parking. "Shut down everything, Mr. Platter. I don't want a light bulb left on to give us away."

"Aye, Captain."

Simon, Monday, and Riverstone then turned off all unnecessary systems, except for Millie herself. She could never be turned off completely, of course, but a trickle of shielded, undetectable power was all She required.

101

Another Plan

"THAT'S THE PLAN then," Harlowe said. They all sat around the large table in Harlowe's cabin. The entire crew was clean and rested, enjoying a gourmet dinner of double-double cheeseburgers with grilled onions, thick tomato slices, pickles and guacamole, tacos, chunky salsa, and chips on the side with tall blue ice-cream shakes. It was a banquet fit for a king.

"Jester, Rerun, and I will take one of the rovers to within a hundred miles of the escarpment. We'll travel the rest of the way on foot, hopefully avoiding any patrols we come into contact with. If we're successful at that point, we'll climb the escarpment here," he said, pointing to a holographic model of the fortress at the cliff edge. "Quay has to be in one of these two towers, here or here. The com should have her bio signs figured out by the time we reach the outer walls. The fortress is set up for a space invasion, not a small force of three climbing up from below. We can be in and out of there with Quay and Sizzle before Toadface even knows they're gone."

Harlowe looked around the table at the half-eaten burgers, bowls of corn chips and wavy potato chips, and guac. Ian's distasteful frown caught his eye. "Problem, Wiz?"

"You make it sound so easy, Captain," Ian said. "You know they'll have that place tricked out with a ton of sensor probes to guard her with things we can't even imagine."

Harlowe met Ian's rational stare. "You're right, Wiz. But we've got a few tricks of our own. With you, Squid, and Prigg backing us up, I feel pretty confident we can be in and out before they know they're gone. We won't be able to talk to you directly for obvious security reasons, but when the signal does come, you'll know what to do."

Riverstone chuckled. "Yeah, and come fast, too, 'cause we'll be hip-deep in doo-doo by then, brah."

Harlowe's lip curled as he ignored the offhand remark. "Once we blink back into the ship, I want all available power to the shields," he said, looking directly at Monday and Prigg.

"Aye, Captain," Monday responded.

Prigg's eyes darted, one down, one to the side, then zeroed in and focused. "Aye, Your Majesty."

Harlowe continued: "Every ship in the neighborhood is going to be after us. As much fire power as we saw coming in, I don't have to tell you what to expect." He then gazed around the table at the impassive faces, looking for more objections. "Any questions?"

For a long moment there was silence as everyone looked at each other. Finally, Riverstone shared his objection. "Why don't we drive around the back side and drop us off? We don't have to climb a twenty-thousand-foot cliff that way."

Harlowe shifted the holograph of the fortress around so that the long flat side of the mesa came into view. "They've got two airstrips here and here, protected on both sides by plas-cannons in twelve different emplacements," he said, pointing out the cannon positions. "If we come up this way in the rover, we're target practice for these guys for fifty miles out without a twig for cover. We'd look like Clint Eastwood riding in one of those spaghetti westerns across the Great Plains with no cigar."

"Yeah, but that cliff's four miles straight up. Eagles don't fly that high, Doggy."

"We did it plenty of times on Mars," Harlowe countered.

"Sure, but we had power clamps and winches to make things easier. Why can't we take them along?"

"Because they'd set off detectors. That's why we're leaving the rover behind, remember?"

Riverstone thought about other equipment they could take that might help but wouldn't need power to work. Harlowe had obviously thought it out more fully than he and come up with the most practical list of 54th-century tools for the assault, except for one. "Okay, but we take the piton guns, right?"

Harlowe started to object, rethought, and agreed to the added tool to the list. "Do it." His attention shifted to Ian, whose face was heavy with disappointment. Harlowe knew that look. He wanted to go along. Harlowe eased over next to Ian and said, "It'll work, Wiz. We talked about it last night. I know it's not a perfect plan, but what is?"

Ian's solemn features nodded the intellectual approval that his gut was unwilling to give. He picked up a tall, half-full glass of Blue Stuff and said, "It's suicide." Then he chugged the remainder of the glass.

Harlowe took him aside for a little pep talk. "You're still the smartest of all of us. If something happens to us, you've got to get Millie away from here. Fast. You know what would happen if any of these toads got hold of 54th-century technology. There would be no stopping any one of the slimeballs from taking over the quadrant and who knows what else!"

"I know, I know."

"If you were me, who would you have backing you up?"

Ian looked at Riverstone, whose eyebrows lifted twice with *You're wasting your breath. It's a done deal.* After a long moment, he returned to Harlowe with a slight shrug. "You're right. I'll stay. You three go ahead and get your buns shot off."

The three exchanged looks as though they might have just been scammed.

* * *

It was pitch black outside. The sun had set hours ago. At the cliff ledge, Quincy kept the grannywagon steady in the gale-force updrafts that scraped the mountain, while Harlowe made some last-minute checks of their equipment. Riverstone and Simon made sure the dura-rope tiedowns were snug and tight.

"Come on, Jester!" Harlowe shouted above the howling winds. "Get it done!"

Riverstone put one last cinch on a strap before he jumped into the rover and gave Harlowe the thumbs-up. Ian was standing to the side like a worried mother when Monday came running down the ramp in full combat gear, carrying his plas-rifle and an extra ammo sack. Harlowe couldn't believe his eyes. Neither could Simon and Riverstone.

"Permission to come along, Captain!" Monday shouted over the high winds, standing tall and rigid with his weapon at his side.

"Squid, you know you hate heights. This will be like the Valles, big time!" Harlowe shouted back, referring to the vertical, four-mile-high cliffs they'd scaled inside the Martian Grand Canyon, Valles Marineris.

"I know, sir, that's why I have to go! I've got to do it, Captain! I've got to get past it. You know I've gotta do it!"

Harlowe turned to Riverstone and Simon for help. Simon wasn't so sure, but Riverstone was all-in. "Let him go, Dog!" Riverstone shouted back. "We'll need him!"

Monday was determined. He stood there, battle-ready, weapon at his side, Gama-belt packed to the hilt, SIBA fully charged. How could Harlowe say no to this elite soldier? He waved him in. "OORAH, SQUID!"

Monday's face glowed like that of a giddy kid given permission to go camping with his big brother. "AYE, AYE, CAPTAIN!"

Riverstone leaned over and gave Monday a hand. "Make one hesitation at ten thousand feet, brah, and I'll cut your safety line myself." The look in Riverstone's eyes let Monday know he meant it, too.

Monday saluted. "Understood, Mr. Riverstone."

Harlowe returned one last high-five to Ian before motioning for Quincy to take off. The android eased the rover over the edge of the cliff and floated down to the base of the gorge within a few feet of the misty river. It was as if they had settled into an overcast day back at 42nd Street. Quincy put the throttle to the floor, jerking their heads back from the acceleration, and followed the river's course where it broke out of the mist and flowed away from the mountains onto a vast forested plain. They would have made better time if they had cut across the great desert to the south, but the forest offered more cover from probing sensors and air patrols.

They had to cover slightly less than two thousand miles to the Consortium fortress. Much of the trip took them through dense growth, but there were many open spaces and one more mountain range between there and the prearranged stopping point. Had they been able to go flat out, they could have easily covered the distance in a few hours. But the path they had chosen kept them from reaching the grannywagon's 400-mph cruising speed for most of the trip.

There were places where simply getting to fifty was a struggle. But with Quincy's white-knuckle driving and some seat-of-the-pants blind luck, they made it to the dropoff point fifty miles from the base of the escarpment just before sunup. As they'd planned, they unloaded their equipment and rechecked that their SIBAs were fully charged. After everything checked out okay, Harlowe tapped Quincy on the shoulder and sent the android and the grannywagon back to the ship.

Harlowe adjusted his bugeyes to full magnification. He tilted his head up at the 20,000-foot escarpment wall that towered above the four of them. Even from fifty miles away, the rock face was formidable. He remembered the cliffs of Olympus Mons. This escarpment was taller, and in the stronger gravity, much more challenging to climb. There would be danger at every step.

"I wonder if they saw us coming?" Riverstone inquired casually.

As Harlowe checked the settings on his wrist-nav, Simon answered the question. "Why worry about what's coming from down here?"

Riverstone ramped up his bugeyes, scanning the impossible wall in the far distance. The bright orange sun was breaking across the plains behind them. It was the largest star they had ever seen. It would be another two hours before it rose completely. Harlowe motioned that it was time for them to stop gawking. Harlowe led the way, with Simon a half step behind. Riverstone and Monday matched strides behind them as they all bolted off into the forest. They arrived at the base of the escarpment wall at high noon. The massive sun took up much of the sky.

"Break out the com," Harlowe ordered, breathing hard from the run.

Riverstone detached the device from his Gama-belt. They could use it to take sensor readings on anything from the escarpment wall to Harlowe's toe jam, if they asked it.

Each of them familiarized himself with the task ahead, kinking
their heads up and studying the vertical ridge that lay before them.
Meanwhile, Harlowe pointed the com up and digested the readouts.
He already knew the fortress was built along the cliff edge and that
they were directly beneath it, four miles below. What he didn't know
was the present condition of the escarpment itself. Before they began
the climb, they had to pick the most efficient way up and do it right
the first time. There was no time for experimental or alternate routes.
The com's assessment of the escarpment was crucial. His decision,
based on his interpretation of the data, could mean the success or
failure of the mission.

While Harlowe studied the readouts, the others swept across the
rock face searching for anything, as unlikely as it seemed, that the com
might have discarded as unimportant. At the end of the visual pass,
Riverstone caught something odd that had nothing to do with the
escarpment. It was a leafy vine growing outward from a tree's massive
canopy like a wayward hair, upward at a wild angle toward the cliff.

"Do you see that?" Riverstone asked, pointing at the odd
growth.

Simon looked in the direction Riverstone indicated. "See
what?"

"That vine. How does it climb that way without breaking?"

"It seems to be crawling along a line or something, Captain,"
Monday said, refocusing his bugeyes.

Before Harlowe could order anyone to check it out, Simon volunteered. "I'll do it, Skipper," and leaped to the nearby branch,
following the vine to its end. Because they were "dark," for security
reasons, they had to wait for Simon to return.

"Dura-line, Skipper," Simon reported, walking back.

"Ours?" Riverstone asked, finding it more than a coincidence.

"Aye," Simon confirmed.

Harlowe looked around. "Any ideas?"

"None that I like," Riverstone replied.

"Any ideas, anybody?" Harlowe asked.

"Quay?" Monday suggested as if it were a given.

"She has a SIBA," Harlowe replied.

"I gave Sizzle one, too," Simon added.

Everyone looked at Simon as though he'd committed a sin. "What? We took a little flight off the balcony. What was wrong with that?"

Harlowe quelled the bickering. "I need ideas, not arguments. Thoughts?"

"What's the com say? Anyone besides us out there in the forest?" Riverstone offered.

Harlowe checked the readouts for life-forms. "Nothing but a small ocean a hundred miles away in that direction," he indicated, pointing fifty degrees away from where they had come.

"They could have made it here but were caught again," Monday speculated.

"Or they might have made it," Simon believed.

"Or they could have—" Riverstone tried to add before Harlowe cut him off.

"No, we're going up," Harlowe decided. "We're going up because the com still says they're up there. There's nothing indicating otherwise, Mr. Bolt."

"Aye, Skipper."

"You're the point, Rerun. Scoot yourself up along that line on the left," Harlowe ordered.

Simon took two steps and sprang twenty feet straight up the side of the cliff and stuck to the rock face, making it look effortless. After testing his claws, he waved to everyone to follow him. If all went according to plan, they would reach the fortress before the end of the short Oggian day. Even with a couple of rest periods, for the most part it was a straight climb to the top. At various prearranged intervals, they attached themselves to the face of the rock like spiders and took short catnaps. They ate and drank along the way. Unlike the time on Mars when the General left them with only a day's supply of food and water at the edge of the Schiaparelli crater, a thousand miles from the Mons, they had stuffed nutrient packs and fully charged energy packs. They could last for weeks if they had to.

When Harlowe reached the hundred-foot level, he looked back at Riverstone with a thumbs-up. Riverstone turned to Monday. "Age before beauty, Squid."

Monday didn't hesitate. He sprang to the first vertical slab and stuck like he was defying gravity by kneading his claws into the black rock of the cliff wall. As if gravity were nonexistent, he quickly caught up with Harlowe. Riverstone was right on his tail. Thereafter, everyone moved as if they were one. On Mars they'd had plenty of practice climbing up the sheer rock faces of the Mons and the Valles, but Mars's gravity was half that of Og's. The force would make a difference later in the climb. For now, their Gama-gravs were working flawlessly and all was going smoothly. Their only safety device was the line between them. If one fell, the others could easily be ripped away from the wall if his claws weren't set in the rock. According to the com sensors, the mild winds rising from the warm forest floor at the low levels would add problems the farther up they went. By the time they hit the 15,000-foot level, the winds would be near hurricane-force. As if fatigue and high winds were not enough, there were always the inevitable "unknown factors" they hadn't planned for. Those kinds of problems were inescapable.

The first three thousand feet of the climb went quickly. It had been over a year since they had done any serious climbing, so it took the first thousand or so feet to get back into the groove. Because the ascent was going so easily and no one was tired, Harlowe skipped the first rest period. When they passed through the next three thousand feet, Riverstone needed a break. He had made a remarkable recovery since Erati. Still, after his months underground, he wasn't quite up to speed yet. A complete physical recovery would take longer than a few weeks. Harlowe understood this and as much as he wanted to press on, Riverstone's condition was more important. He needed a rest.

Harlowe spotted a small niche ahead and let everyone know they would pause there for a brief period.

Riverstone placed a tired hand on Harlowe's shoulder, thanking him for the relief. "You're a saint."

When they reached the niche, they secured themselves to the side of the rock with piton grippers and hung comfortably like human hammocks between the walls of the niche. Riverstone didn't know whether he was more hungry than tired or more tired than hungry. After five seconds in a horizontal position, the question was moot. He was out cold, sleeping like a baby. Eating would come later.

Harlowe, on the other hand, didn't rest. He used the downtime to prep for the next segment of the climb. The com readouts displayed a more difficult climb ahead. After his study was complete, he reattached the com to his belt and tried to relax for the remainder of the break.

* * *

CRACK!

The Gamadin practically jumped out of their SIBAs when they were abruptly awakened by an exploding thunderclap, followed suddenly by a drenching downpour.

"I was getting such a good tan, too," Simon yawned, detaching himself from the rock face.

Their SIBAs kept them warm and dry regardless of the outside weather, but the driving rain added problems to the climb. Rivers of falling water were cascading all around them and channeling around and through the niches and fault lines they planned to use on their ascent. Instead of fighting the falling rivers and taking unnecessary risks, they took refuge under a nearby ledge and let the tempest run its course.

An hour later, the storm drifted off. Three of Og's moons had poked their bright faces above the horizon in the cloudless night. The crew wasted no time moving out. The storm had put them behind schedule. They progressed nicely, making up some of the time on the next two thousand feet until they arrived at a large vertical slice in the side of the escarpment. They scampered to a wide, flat ledge at the mouth and peered into the black void. It appeared to go back an incredible distance. Even with their bugeyes at full power, no one could see where it ended.

"What's the com say?" Riverstone asked, gazing into the cavern.

"A couple of things," Harlowe stated. His tone reflected the fascinating readouts he was observing on his com. "This slice goes back for miles."

Riverstone leaned over Harlowe's shoulder to take a gander for himself. "Wow! It does...it does...it does..." he said, his elevated voice echoing off the cavern walls.

Harlowe quickly covered Riverstone's mouth with his hand. "That's the second thing. There are life-forms all over the place in there."

"What kind of life-forms?" Simon asked, peering into the void.

Harlowe shook his head. "Not sure, but they're out there, and lots of them."

"How big?" Monday wondered.

"About four feet and moving about." Harlowe looked up. "I think they're flying."

Riverstone grabbed hold of his stomach. "Narly!"

Leaning back at arm's length, Harlowe kinked his head up. "We've got a ways to go. If we follow the rim, we can avoid getting anyone upset in there."

As Harlowe spoke, another storm struck with a vengeance. Thunder, lightning, and rain drove them farther back into the void.

"This could last all night, Dog," Riverstone pointed out.

Harlowe didn't care. He was determined to make it to the top of the escarpment before daybreak. He reassessed his com readouts before pointing. "That way."

Up they went. With brilliant charges of lightning dancing around the rim of the cavern, they continued on, looking like long-legged insects crawling up a black slab of slick, polished granite with only a single strand of dura-web between them.

They made good time until they reached within five hundred feet from the top of the opening. From three hundred feet inside the cavern, they could see that the rain was still coming down in sheets, but the thunder and lightning had dissipated considerably. The waterfalls had lessened. The moons and stars were out, clear and visible again. Hopefully the storm had moved on. That was the good news.

The bad news was another problem completely unrelated to the storm. As they began making their way out of the cavern, they came to a crevasse that was too wide to leap across. They had two choices: go back down a thousand feet or so and find another way out, or throw a line across the distance and pull themselves to the other side with their pulleys. Once there, it appeared the way to the top was a snap.

Harlowe stared across the two-hundred-foot gap. "Do you see anywhere I can snag a grapple?"

Riverstone leaned out over the ledge to give Harlowe some advice and accidentally dislodged a fist-sized rock. Monday grabbed his arm to keep him from losing his balance as the rock disappeared into the blackness below. An entire minute passed before the distant echo of clanking rock returned to them. They traded glances, knowing each other's thoughts.

"Careful," Harlowe cautioned.

Riverstone continued his search for a place to attach the grapple. "It's slick over there, brah."

Harlowe removed a device from his Gama-belt. "We'll use the fine-adjustment tool, then."

"That will wake the neighborhood, Captain," Monday warned as he watched Harlowe attach a wickedly lethal tip to the muzzle of his pistol.

"My call, Squid."

The piton attachment was an arrowhead projectile made of super-tough dura-metal at the end of a wire line. When it impacted, it sank into the rock and welded itself to whatever it struck. The explosion the arrowhead made upon impact would be loud.

Harlowe took careful aim and fired. An instant later, just as they knew it would, the blast sent a thunderous shock wave back through the cavern. It was so loud Simon nearly lost his footing from the report.

"That will wake up their ancestors!" Riverstone shouted above the echoes.

"It was a little louder than I thought," Harlowe confessed as he returned the piton pistol to his belt.

Monday finished the dura-line bridge by pounding another piton into the rock ledge at their feet while Harlowe pulled the line taut, readying it for crossing. When he finished cinching it, Harlowe turned to Riverstone. "You first."

Riverstone stared at the thin line, a little hesitant. "It's been a while."

Harlowe gave him a small shove. "Like riding a bike. Just do it."

"Don't worry, Mr. Riverstone, I'll be right behind you," Monday added for comfort, much in the same way Riverstone had helped him the many times on Mars they'd had to fly across the Valles with their SIBA wings.

Riverstone removed a small pulley from his Gama-belt and attached it to the line with a reassuring click. Like he had done countless times on Mars, he swung down and hung easily in the air. With a little forward thrust of his hips, he scurried right along to the opposite edge.

"How was it?" Harlowe called to Riverstone in a hushed voice so as to not add to the noise he had already made.

Riverstone swung himself up and perched himself on a small ledge. "Like riding a bike!" he called back in an equally hushed voice.

As Simon was attaching his pulley to the line, Riverstone heard an odd sound coming from the ink-black bowels of the cavern.

"Did you hear that?" Riverstone asked, just loud enough for everyone to hear.

Harlowe stopped what he was doing briefly to listen.

The sound was very noticeable and growing louder.

"That?" Harlowe said, pushing Simon off onto the line. Once there, Simon moved quickly across the gap.

Riverstone removed the com from his utility belt. His teeth clenched upon seeing the readouts. "Hundreds of things are flying this way. Move it, Dog!"

Monday was having trouble attaching his pulley. "Hurry, Squid!"

"It won't snap into place, Captain!" Monday grunted.

Harlowe bent down and snapped the pulley into place with one quick finger twist. He then strung out Monday's connector on his utility belt and pushed him off the side of the ledge. In the early days back on Mars, Monday would have freaked out, too scared to move an inch. Months of training had gotten him past his frozen state of inaction. He was still scared, but not dysfunctional. He thrust his hips out, all three hundred pounds of solid muscle swinging from side to side, as he rushed toward the far end of the line, where Simon was already getting a helping hand up from Riverstone.

Harlowe didn't wait for Monday to make it across. He clamped his pulley into place and swung himself down and out over the void. "How far are they?" he cried out, pushing away from the ledge with his foot.

"DUDE!" Riverstone cried out, pulling his own pistol as he traveled along the thread. The creature's black hairy body was four to five feet long, with evil red eyes and long, gaping teeth that hung out of its snapping, saliva-dripping mouth. Riverstone didn't have time to reply. In one quick motion he reattached his com and drew his sidearm, firing bright blue shots of plasma into the darkness at objects no human eye could see without 54th-century assistance.

One shot, one kill. The first creature Riverstone wasted crashed on the ledge where Harlowe had just shoved off. When it fell over the side from its momentum, Harlowe saw what it was: a giant bat!

102

The Horde

HOLDING ON WITH one arm, Harlowe fired backward at the incoming hordes with the other. One after another, the bats dove down upon his position like kamikaze pilots trying to dislodge him from his hold on the line. Even with Simon adding to the plasfire with Riverstone, they could do little to help Harlowe. They had their hands full keeping themselves alive while covering Monday, who was almost to the other side. The hordes were attacking him, trying to knock him from the line, too.

"Hurry, Dog!" Riverstone yelled. No one was interested in being discreet. His light pistol blazed like a strobe in the night. He was already on his third clip of plas rounds. There didn't seem to be any end to the bats.

Wave upon wave of the giant bats, three and four at a time, slammed into the wall, dead, their heads riddled with plas-holes, then fell into the void, continuing their blood-chilling, high-pitched, frenzied screams until they disappeared forever into the nothingness.

How long could they keep it up?

Suddenly, out of nowhere, the situation took a turn for the worse. Riverstone and Simon were lifting Monday from the line when a lone bat separated itself from the hordes. Harlowe blasted the beast several times, blowing its body in two, but thanks to its momentum, the upper half with the gaping mouth of razored teeth cut the line.

Harlowe fell.

Riverstone watched helplessly as Harlowe dropped like the fist-sized stone earlier and disappeared into the black void.

"DOGGGGGG!" Riverstone yelled at the top of his lungs. There was no time to see where Harlowe landed, if he had at all. He was gone. There was no time to search, either. The swarm of giant bats continued their unrelenting assault on their position. They had to keep blasting away or they would end up like Harlowe.

"DOG!" Riverstone called out again as two more plas-riddled bats dropped from the air. One struck the wall beside him while another fell between Simon and Monday. Monday kicked it away and hammered at another, crushing its skull with the butt of his pistol.

Out of the corner of his eye, Riverstone caught a glimpse of the line twitching, suddenly going rigid, moving up and down as if something was coming up the line. Like a rising ghost, Harlowe emerged from the void, reaching out hand-over-hand as he climbed up the thread like a scampering spider.

"COVER ME!" he shouted from below.

The quick wave of relief that washed over the Gamadin put an added burst of energy into everyone's shooting. "WE GOT YA, DOG!" Riverstone cried out.

In a moment, they were all side-by-side again, pistols blazing like out-of-control plascannons. As rapidly as their fingers could pull their triggers, they fired and replaced ammo clips. Still the hordes kept coming, now six and eight at a time diving from all directions. Somehow they managed to repel the onslaught. They saw dozens of dead bats lying and twitching in heaps across the opposite ledge. That was small compared to the uncountable hundreds that had fallen into the void below.

As the hours passed, fewer and fewer of the giants continued the attack. It was as if they were finally running low on bodies.

They resumed their climb. Harlowe gave an exhausted Riverstone a hand up the cliff side. "Try to climb, Matt. I'll cover you," he said, his lungs trying to suck in enough air for his own needs.

Riverstone nodded weakly, then fired over Harlowe's shoulder at a single bat trying to attack Monday.

Harlowe downed two more before saying, "Try for the next ledge. Rerun, stay with Jester," knowing Riverstone still wasn't his total self yet.

"Aye, Skipper."

With Simon's help, Riverstone made it to the next outcropping. When he reached the ledge, he turned to Harlowe with a thumbs-up okay. Monday went next, then Harlowe joined them. The routine worked and they finally reached the top of the cavern. For another few hundred feet, the bats stayed with them, but only in single sorties. Fighting the bats was manageable now even in their condition. When they emerged from the opening, an enormous moon was overhead. A much smaller moon was lower on the horizon. The other two moons were gone. Too much light, Harlowe thought. They might as well have been in broad daylight. He took out his com and checked the colossal moon's position. They were in luck. Its orbit was tight around Og. In two hours, according to the readouts, it would be down the backside away from the escarpment face.

They felt as if they had just passed through one of those moments, and their luck had turned around. The bats, too, had stopped their attacks. The two hours before the giant moon drifted behind the fortress gave them time to park themselves for a much-needed rest. At the first place of refuge, they attached themselves to the rock and hung like insects on a wall and then fell into an exhaustive sleep for hours longer than they had planned.

103

Overslept

THE CAWING OF a bird-of-prey as it drifted by lazily on escarpment updrafts jolted Harlowe from an exhaustive sleep. He stared at the time chronometer inside his bug-eye screen in shocked disbelief. It was only two hours before sunrise. *NO!* Harlowe's mind cried out. How could he have slept that long? He checked the horizon. The immense Oggian sun would be showing itself within the hour and they still had a couple of thousand feet to go. Four-letter outbursts began spewing as he detached his anchor from the rock. "Everyone wake up!" he shouted, slapping the sides of the others' SIBAs. "We overslept!"

Riverstone groaned, twisting around to a more comfortable position, their situation not totally registered in his mind. The gravity of the problem bolted him upright, as if someone had slapped him across the backside with a wet towel. "Overslept?"

"That's right. The sun will be coming up in an hour," Harlowe explained. If they didn't finish the next two thousand feet to the top, they'd be out in broad daylight. They had to move fast or lose the night and the element of surprise.

Simon and Monday gathered themselves with equal alacrity. No one needed further convincing.

In no time at all the Gamadin were climbing upward again, feeding on nutrient tubes as they climbed. Twice large cracks inside the escarpment reminded them of what they had been through earlier. They took com readings of the depths and found them devoid of bats.

Harlowe looked at Riverstone, cocking his head in bewilderment. Riverstone pointed toward the vast forest miles below. "They're feeding, but they'll be back soon."

Relieved that the bats were seemingly occupied, another problem hit them as they passed the 19,000-foot line.

Wind.

A slight breeze from the heat rising off the forest floor had always been with them from the beginning. As they gained height, so did the wind's velocity. Now that the storms had finished for the night, the thermodynamics of the escarpment were getting weird. With the clear air came a sudden temperature drop. The warm air from below was causing a push-and-shove match with the cold from the top, creating turbulence where they met. The crew was caught right in the middle. The only escape, they knew, was to get over the crest of the escarpment edge and out of harm's way as soon as possible.

"Find a fault line and follow it," Riverstone yelled over the howling winds. "It might help!"

Harlowe secured himself to a rock to free his hands, then slipped the com from his utility belt. He studied the readouts and soon found a fault line a couple hundred feet above and to the right.

Harlowe pointed in the direction they needed to take and led them in a sideways crawl to the new fault line.

It was a tricky crossing. A couple of times one or another of them would almost lose footing, but the effort was worth it. As Riverstone had figured, once they were inside the fault line, the winds dissipated considerably. As before, they made good progress until the fault line ended. Harlowe located another line. When they emerged out of the first, they discovered the wind had increased to hurricane force.

"This is nuts!" Riverstone shouted after he was nearly blown away from the ledge when he tried to hang on to a crevice. Only a secure hold with his claws prevented him from being ripped away from the cliff.

Riverstone was about to try again when Harlowe pulled him back down into the line. "Hold it," he said, staring at the bright blue screen of his com readouts. He pointed with his claw at a thin line across the screen. "Look there. It looks like a..." Harlowe tapped the screen to be sure the device was working properly. Of course, 54th-century technology always worked properly. It was never wrong. "...a trail?" He wasn't exactly sure, but then it did appear to be some kind of path.

Riverstone peered over his shoulder. "You mean that trail's been there the whole time and you didn't see it?" His voice screamed from the frustration of having battled everything that they had along the way—rain, lightning, bats, wind, and plain exhaustive misery—to get to where they were. They could have just taken a trail that led to their destination instead.

Harlowe looked at Riverstone with a helpless shrug. Riverstone didn't need to see Harlowe's face to know there was an embarrassed grin behind the bugeyes of his suit.

"You dumb..." Riverstone was so bent out of shape he couldn't find the words to express his true feelings. He let out some steam before he asked, "How do we get there, Hawkeye?"

Harlowe pointed.

Without waiting for Harlowe this time, Riverstone struck out on his own, head down, against the wind. He reached out with his claw for what he thought was a solid rock ledge. The outcropping disintegrated in his hand. The problem was, it wasn't rock. It was black ice. When he grabbed it with his powerful claws, it exploded like shattered glass in his hand. His claws snapped at a ledge that wasn't there. The wind yanked him backward. In a blink he was dropping like a heavy stone away from the cliff.

Harlowe didn't see the mishap. He was too busy trying to figure out how he had missed the trail when the force of Riverstone's weight suddenly yanked him from his perch.

Down they went.

Then Simon. He had been clinging to the rock, but wasn't paying attention to Harlowe and Riverstone's discussion because he couldn't hear what they were talking about.

It was all up to Monday. He was the only one to have the slightest chance of saving them. However, their sudden misfortune momentarily disoriented him. He wasn't able to find a hold to stop their downward plunge, either. Sparks from his claws shot out from his dura-metal talons as he tried desperately to locate a hold on the hard, slick surface. Then the cliff fell away and they were all in an unstoppable free fall.

There was no time to think. In a desperate move, Harlowe reached down to his Gama-belt and found the piton gun. He didn't know which way was up, down, right, or left, or even if he was pointed at the cliff when he pulled the trigger. His sense of orientation was purely from instinct. If he couldn't hit a 20,000-foot cliff wall ten feet from his face, then he deserved to meet his maker!

The loud crack of the piton head exploded. Then the jolt of the line screamed as it stretched to the limits with the weight of the four Gamadin, swinging in gale-force winds 18,000 feet above the forest floor.

"Next time I'm coming with someone who knows what they're doing!" Riverstone shouted from below while he swung like a pendulum from Harlowe's belt.

"Next time?" Harlowe yelled back. "There isn't going to be a next time, you clumsy jerk, because I'm not going anywhere with a gomer like you anymore!"

"Gomer?"

"You heard me, puke!

"YEAH! Any captain with common sense would have had a plan. That would have included knowing about the trail, Doggy!"

"I've got a plan!" Harlowe fired back. He and Riverstone were close enough to shout above the winds, but Simon and Monday were fifty feet below, still swinging out of control.

"You've never had a plan in your life except the one that always gets us in trouble up to our eyebrows!"

"As soon as we get out of this, I'll show you the plan!" Harlowe shot back angrily, eyes blazing hot behind his bugeyes.

"Do that! While you're at it, swing me over to the ledge. I'm tired of hanging around down here like a dingleberry!"

Harlowe took hold of the line and with a couple of well placed heaves, shoved Riverstone and the others to the escarpment wall. Riverstone's claws let out a sharp ringing click as they firmly latched themselves to the solid rock face of the escarpment. After that, Harlowe swung himself to the ledge and started climbing upward again. Twenty minutes later they passed the broken ledge where they'd originally lost it. Not long after that, they found themselves on the trail Harlowe had located with the com. The trail had been carved out of the escarpment wall uncountable lifetimes ago by a long-forgotten civilization. The ancient path went for only a few thousand feet of ascent before it terminated abruptly under a long overhang a hundred feet from the top of the escarpment. From what they could determine, the path had been cut this way for the purpose of protecting those who lived above it. The path ended here because of the nearly impassable angled ledge that jutted outward from the cliff wall and blocked any ascent to the top of the mesa.

"They must have had a trick way to get past this," Riverstone said, looking around.

Harlowe held up the com. "Yeah, it doesn't even show up on this."

Riverstone took the com from Harlowe to see for himself. After the recent events, he was beginning to question Harlowe's ability to read any com screen properly. "You're right," he said, shocked by the revelation. Harlowe took the com back. "That doesn't mean it doesn't exist," Riverstone added. "It could be hidden someplace back down the trail. No one builds a trail this far up the wall and stops with only a few hundred feet to go."

Harlowe put the com back on his belt, then leaped up to the underside of the rock ledge. His claws stuck firmly to the surface. "Doesn't matter. We don't have time to look for it." From his upside-down position, he moved outward like a fly and disappeared around the edge.

Riverstone groaned before he pushed Simon and Monday ahead. He wished he could wiggle his nose and be at the top. He swore to himself all the way as he followed the others over the top of the fallen rock.

He got his wish. Partly. As they figured, the path did continue once they got around the obstruction. The rest of the way was a piece of cake. Soon they found themselves directly under one of a number of large parabolic dishes that pointed upward toward the heavens, protecting the fortress from the skyward enemies of the Consortium. Here on the ground, they were safe. The Consortium had no one to fear from below.

It was different once they reached the ledge of the escarpment wall on top of the mesa. It was dead calm. The stars were bright and beautiful. The biggest moon was nearly gone. Only one small moon was left, keeping watch on the night for the others. Overhead, in high orbits over Og, what appeared to be large bright stars were actually the giant star-class battle cruisers of the combined forces of the Consortium, Tomar, and the Fhaal, at least 37 of them. Those were the ones they could see. Undoubtedly there were more, swarming around the battle cruisers like bees around a hive, dozens of tiny pinhead points of light.

"Attack fighters," Harlowe surmised casually. A hundred times that number would not divert his thoughts away from Quay, or his original goal—freeing Neeja for Mrs. M.

He turned his head from the heavens and concentrated on the stone walls of the fortress. At any other time, like they did so many times on Mars, they would have congratulated themselves for conquering another galactic giant of nature, but not now. Their accomplishment was already far behind them. The escarpment was only one part of the puzzle that stood in the way of Quay's rescue. In fact, it may have been the easiest obstacle but the escarpment and its challenges had come at a price. It expended every ounce of energy they had. Even Harlowe's unwavering desire to find Quay and release her from the Consortium was blunted by the impossible fatigue they felt deep in their bones. They needed more rest before moving on. The Oggian dawn was another hour away. They wanted to be inside the walls by now under the cover of darkness, but plans always have a way of changing on the fly. Thirty minutes of sleep would be all the rest they would get. They hunkered down next to the base of the parabolic dish to allow their SIBAs to recharge their bodies while the fortress loomed dark as pitch against the heavens.

104

The Fortress

THE PRE-DAWN WIND that blew across Harlowe's face mirrored the cold chill he felt in his veins. He had not slept at all during the rest period. He would not rest as he studied the fortress walls from their location at the base of the ground dish a mile away. The deep orange edge of the Oggian dawn was spreading along the distant horizon. It was obvious that they were wasting time sitting around any longer. Riverstone stood and held out his hand. "Let's do it, Dog."

Harlowe took the offered hand and stood. When Simon and Monday joined them, they all clicked their claw-knuckles together, affirming their readiness. There was no small talk, no jokes, no lighthearted bantering as they made their way with deadly stealth to the ancient walls of the Draculean fortress. All their training, their hard work, their chronic intimacies with Death, were coalescing here at the wall that stood before them, five hundred feet high.

Harlowe felt the unholy darkness of the wall's existence. He turned and nudged Riverstone. Five miles away on the mesa plateau, they saw battle-ready attack ships, dark and cold, lined up five abreast and three rows deep, prepared for takeoff at any given moment.

Harlowe breathed deeply. As he predicted, the plateau was too well guarded with parabolic dish cannons and attack fighters for them to have fought their way in from above without jeopardizing Quay and Sizzle. He'd made the right choice of stealth and cunning from below.

Harlowe looked up at the battlements and the dim globes lighting the walkway behind the ramparts. He saw only two guards along the entire quarter-mile stretch of the five-sided, irregularly shaped fortress. The fact that there were only two guards surprised him. It was only a skeleton crew. As he thought about it, Prigg's words came back to him: the Consortium did not take prisoners. They were too cumbersome to care for unless they had value.

Riverstone stared at all the gathered forces of the three empires, shaking his head. "You know..." he began, "I sure hope the cavalry arrives in time."

"I thought *we* were the cavalry," Simon replied.

Riverstone scratched his head, facing Harlowe. "We're the cavalry?"

Harlowe agreed casually. "That's the plan."

"You keep talking about a plan. How can you be so confident?"

"It's my nature."

"I don't get it," Riverstone said.

"Stay cool. It's all coming together," Harlowe assured everyone.

"These toadheads know you're coming after her, don't they?" Riverstone asked.

Harlowe glanced skyward, admiring the armada. "Yep," he replied, without skipping a beat.

Riverstone recalled Unikala's outrage when he'd discovered that Riverstone wasn't Harlowe. "You should have seen Unikala's eyes. I thought they would blow a fuse any second."

As he went on, Harlowe kept his focus straight ahead, calm, expressionless, and seemingly unaffected by Riverstone's description.

"He's fast, too, Dog. I've seen him kill his own dudes. He's good, Dog, real good with a pistol. I think he's better than you." Riverstone wasn't kidding.

Harlowe lifted the com and turned on the screen. "Maybe."

Simon stepped up. "I'll second that, Skipper. When they had me back at Gibb, that was all those toads could talk about, how fast Uni was. They said there were even rumors that the Fhaal Commander Sar is faster than all of them put together."

"Don't worry. We get the babes and then off the planet into hyperlight. No gunfights, Mr. Bolt. Not today."

Riverstone peered over his shoulder. "Is she there?" he asked, wondering whether the com had picked up Quay's bio-signature. Like fingerprints or retina scans, a being's bio-signature was unique to that being. No one else in the galaxy had the same exact signature. If Quay or Sizzle was anywhere within a five-mile radius, the com would pinpoint her exact position inside the fortress.

It took a few moments, but after a couple of minor adjustments, Harlowe breathed in a sigh of relief. "Yeah," he replied, tapping the screen. "That's her. The readouts match her perfectly."

"Oh, yeah? Let me see," Riverstone stated, his tone reflecting doubt. After a careful study, he added, "It's not an exact match."

Riverstone felt Harlowe's eyes burning at him through his bugeyes. Nevertheless, the readouts didn't quite jibe. Whether or not there were serious enough variances to make the readout invalid, he wasn't expert enough to know. They needed Wiz for that. Since he wasn't with them, they had to go with what they had, which was Harlowe. The bio information the com had was months old. His own bio-scans had not changed at all in the time he was gone, and his body had been through a lot of upheaval. Harlowe's and Ian's were unchanged as well, but Quay was not born on Earth, he reminded himself. She was different. Maybe it was possible a minor change in her bio-scan was common.

"There are a couple of discrepancies, Dog," Riverstone pointed out.

"It's her," Harlowe insisted.

"If Wiz were here, he would confirm it."

"He's not here." For Harlowe, the subject was closed.

"You're right. I guess it's her," Riverstone finally agreed. There was no turning back. "How 'bout this one? Is that Sizzle?"

"That's my thinking," Harlowe replied.

"Maybe they'll have them wrapped and ready for shipping, too."

"Don't count on it."

Riverstone didn't. No one did. Everything seemed almost too quiet. The still, chilly air was full of ozone from the night's storms. Nothing moved or creaked along the walls of the fortress either. It was more not to like. Way too quiet.

"I've been in too many movies like this," Simon said. "It's too easy."

Monday looked over Harlowe's shoulder. "See anyone else around, Captain?"

"Nada," Harlowe replied.

Riverstone gazed up the fortress wall. "Let's make some noise."

Faster than any earthly commando squad, they leaped up the side of the fortress wall, practically invisible to any sentient beings.

They made it look effortless. At the top, they leaped between the merlons and onto the rampart. After neutralizing the two guards with soundless duradarts, they separated. Riverstone and Simon went left. They would go for Sizzle. Harlowe and Monday took off in the other direction, seeking out Quay. When they had the girls, they would meet back here at the top of the rampart. The idea then was to launch themselves off the escarpment using their gossamer SIBA wings, drift down to their waiting Ship below, hovering at about the 5,000-foot level, land topside, strike a blinker, and off they would go to hyperlight, without ever looking back.

Harlowe and Monday leaped across the fifty-foot-wide outer ward to the top of the guard barracks. Crawling silently over the roof to the other side, they jumped down into an inner courtyard. After that, they made a quick dash between two unoccupied stone buildings, climbed over another stone wall, and jumped into another inner ward. Here they saw the massive fortress keep clearly. It was dark and formidable, a good fifty times the size of any castle on Earth. Atop its four corner towers were more parabolic dishes. Unlike the large outer dishes, these constantly moved, up and down, side to side, sniffing the air like dogs for game. The bright lights inside the stone structure also confirmed that Consortium business never slept.

Harlowe checked the com to ensure they wouldn't be crossing some hidden sensor wire. The way appeared clear.

The building they wanted was to the right of the keep. It was a small, converted guardhouse next to the heavily guarded fortress.

Harlowe crossed the yard. Monday followed. He was halfway across when the door of the guardhouse opened and two soldiers stepped out. Monday stopped in his tracks. He had no cover except the camouflage of his SIBA.

He stayed motionless for a moment until he understood that the soldiers were coming his way. A bright flash struck the two soldiers, collapsing them in midstride.

Monday bolted the rest of the way across the openness and thanked Harlowe with a nod. Harlowe then turned nervously, appearing hesitant to look inside the building where Quay was being held. Over the top of the rampart, the faint pink light of the Oggian sun was coming over the wall.

Monday made a sign with his hands, asking where the door was.

Harlowe pointed that it was on the other side of the keep.

She's there, he kept telling himself. *She's all right.*

They walked around the building and stood at the front of a thick metal door. The tiny yellow and green lights meant it was a code-lock entry. It would not open on its own unless they had the sequential code…or blew it apart.

For the longest moment Harlowe stared at the entrance, reluctant to open the door and look inside. *She's there,* he kept telling himself. *The com never lies! She's there! There is no other place in the quadrant for her to be except in this building at this moment.*

"Go on, Captain," Monday said calmly. He wasn't about to interfere. It was Harlowe's call. He was there for support. "She'll be okay."

Harlowe took a deep breath as he pulled out one of his pistols. He clicked the power setting to full and fired. The blast knocked the door partially away from its jamb. Harlowe stepped forward and with one swift kick, broke the hinges away from their slots. The door crashed heavily to the floor like a dead soldier shot in the head. Before the smoked cleared, Harlowe was through the entry and into the room.

He saw nothing at first. Then something moved in the far corner of the room. It wasn't human.

105

Duped

THE ROBOTIC SNARE moved slowly to one side of the room, hesitated, then turned again, drifting silently on its antigrav cushion back to where it started, then back again in its endless loop. On top of its spherical domed head, a tiny white light pulsed its broadcast of Quay's near-exact bio-signature. As Riverstone feared, they had been duped!

Harlowe closed his eyes briefly before he nuked the device with a plas round through its single blinking eye. He turned and walked back out the door. He appeared unfazed by the scores of Consortium soldiers in the courtyard forming a great semi-circle in front of them. Along the high ramparts of the inner compound, another two hundred rifle muzzles pointed at them from above.

Harlowe wondered why no one made any advances toward them.

Monday rolled his shoulders forward, waiting for the first shot to be fired. "What are they waiting for?" he asked, resigned to their predicament.

Their questions were quickly answered when the line of soldiers on the ground separated, allowing two uniformed officers through. Unikala and Turfan came strutting toward them like a pair of arrogant roosters. Riverstone and Simon came out of the nowhere, drawing their weapons. "This is for Elaaaaa!" Riverstone cried out.

The one-armed Unikala was faster. Much faster. Riverstone flew backwards, jolted by the hot bolt that hit his chest. Simon took one in the gut, doubled over, and dropped. Harlowe gasped as he turned to catch Riverstone's falling body. He was cut short as another bolt from Turfan cracked, catching Harlowe in the right shoulder, sending him twisting to the ground in fiery pain next to Riverstone and Simon.

Monday was about to add his two cents' worth when Harlowe called for him to stand down. "No, Squid!" he shouted before he committed suicide. "It's too late."

Unikala raised his hand to his troops. "No! Do not shoot. That Gamadin is mine," his booming voice commanded.

Harlowe went to Riverstone. His friend's breathing was shallow, his eyes unfocused, searching for control as Harlowe found a suit patch from his utility belt to cover the wound.

"I told you. He's fast, Dog," Riverstone said in short, wheezy breaths. "Faster than you." There was little blood. One virtuous effect of a plas-bolt wound was that it was relatively bloodless. It cooked the flesh, searing the ends of capillaries and veins as it burned through the body like a white-hot poker.

Harlowe nodded in silence, removing his bug-eyed mask. His stare was distant. The muscles in his jaws rippled beneath his skin as he gritted against the stinging pain in his bloody shoulder and stared at the ugly duo.

"They said you would come for her," Unikala said, thrusting his stump at Harlowe's face.

"Where is Quay?" Harlowe demanded, his voice the temperature of blue ice.

"You're the best I've ever seen, Gamadin," Unikala continued. "A worthy opponent."

There was rage behind Harlowe's eyes. They did not blink, move, or quiver, as if he were possessed. Words have no place where death is the only subject.

Unikala stepped forward arrogantly. "The ship, Gamadin. I want the ship."

"Where is Quay?" Harlowe repeated angrily. He wanted what he came for.

Unikala laughed hauntingly. "In the end I will have everything."

"Except my ship. Where is she?"

Turfan stepped beside Unikala. "My sister is dead, Gamadin, trying to escape the fortress." His inhuman laugh bellowed venomously. "A stupid mistake, I'm afraid." He shrugged, uncaring. "The mothership, Gamadin. Where is she?"

"What about Sizzle?" Simon gutted out, his face twisted in agony. "Where is she?"

Turfan looked down, pitiless. "They both are gone, Gamadin, a valiant effort, all for love. How touching!"

"You really are one screwed-up puke, Turfan!" Harlowe growled, wishing he had ended his life on Palcor when he had the chance.

"You should be silenced now for your insolence, Gamadin," Turfan cried out boldly, reaching for his weapon as if he were going to draw on Harlowe. Harlowe waited. However, Turfan, always the coward, lacked the courage to test his skill against the warrior from the ancient past, even wounded.

"The mothership, Gamadin. Where is she?" Unikala demanded again.

"Bite me, puke!" Harlowe snapped.

"That-a-way, Harlowe," Riverstone wheezed, his teeth gritting against the pain, "make them feel like you have the upper hand."

"Guards!" Unikala called out. "Focus all weapons on the young Captain's crew," he commanded, crossing his arms in front of him, staring at Harlowe with his cold threat. The clicking and scraping of metal against the stone merlons quickly echoed around the inner ward as the guards carried out Unikala's orders with instant precision. Like two savage heavyweights meeting at the center of the ring before the fight, neither blinked nor backed away. Each had only the desire to take down the other.

Before another word was spoken, a familiar low hum changed the air. Drifting down in the cloudless morning sky was a shuttlecraft Harlowe had seen a lifetime ago in the red desert canyon lands of southern Utah.

It was the Fhaal.

106

No Mercy

Sar, all eight feet ten inches of scaly hulk, thick lizard head, and yellow bulbous eyes, stormed down the rampway, his large sidearms low and menacing at his side. He was flanked by a contingent of his elite guards, all as scaly and ugly as he was. Their massive weight pounded the heavy black metal grate like thunder as they stomped down the rampway onto the inner courtyard. Their presence was so overwhelming it made all others inside the courtyard seem small and pathetic. There was no doubt in anyone's mind that they ruled and that what they had come to claim was theirs and theirs alone.

Riverstone eked out from between his clenched teeth, "Anyone we know?"

Harlowe laid Riverstone back down, his eyes never leaving the growing group of dignitaries. "Old Lizard Head," he replied.

"Him again," Riverstone grinned, pathetically. "Did he bring his pets?"

"I'll ask," Harlowe quipped.

Quite unexpectedly, Harlowe watched in disbelief as the giant reptilian Fhaal Commander, without missing a step, drew his sidearm and blasted both Unikala and Turfan into blood-chilling fragments. Unikala's silver-eyed head bounced off the nearby inner courtyard wall and came to rest in a muddy quagmire. Turfan's body was cut in half, his lower portion left standing as his head and torso disappeared inside the guardhouse doorway. After that, all hell broke loose. The Consortium troops were as shocked as the Gamadin. Their short span of traumatized hesitation was all the Commander's elite guards needed to open up on the Consortium guards inside the inner courtyard and outer ramparts.

It was a slaughter. The Consortium guards got off a few useless bursts before they were cut to pieces like defenseless green troops against a crack team of professional soldiers. By the time the Fhaal stopped shooting, no one was left alive except the Gamadin.

"Gamadin!" Sar called out as he stomped his way pompously to the inner courtyard. He kicked Turfan's lower body out of his way like a child's ball. It landed with a splat in the same muddy pit as Unikala's head. "The ship! Where is she?"

Harlowe stood. He seemed unhurried as he faced the monstrous Fhaal Commander. High in the morning sky, brilliant lights flashed as incredible explosions rocked the upper atmosphere of the planet. Harlowe knew what they were. The Fhaal were making the slaughter of its rivals complete by destroying the Consortium and Tomarian fleets.

Harlowe surveyed the death surrounding him. Buzzing insects had already begun the feast. This was the fate of all those who defied the Fhaal Empire. Neeja had already been eaten. Omni Prime was the next Happy Meal. Would Earth be dessert? His promise to Sook was more than a commitment to her. It was an obligation to himself, his family, his planet, his crew, and to freedom-loving beings everywhere. The feeding would end now!

He turned to the Fhaal Commander, his eyes hardened with a duty to complete his mission. "Welcome to the party, Sar."

"Where is the Gamadin ship?" Sar persisted.

Harlowe casually scanned the horizon. "She's around."

"Bring me *Millawanda*!" Sar demanded.

As though Sar's command were the magical phrase that launched a spell, a powerful throbbing hum broke through the morning air. It was difficult to tell from which direction the deep, haunting sound was coming. Automatic sensor alarms screamed as the golden disk rose over the fortress walls like a giant sun. In that same moment, parabolic dishes swiveled in an almost panicked way to zero in on the saucer. The beautifully sleek and polished disk moved forward like a goddess descending upon her misbehaved subjects. Before the parabolic dishes could focus their high-energy beams, blue bolts of intense plasma blew them from their turrets. The squadrons of attack fighters parked on the mesa scrambled to protect the fortress. Before they could lift off, two wide bursts of blue light flashed bright and hot from the Ship's perimeter rim and vaporized the squadrons.

The golden disk continued her advance. She was unstoppable.

Fhaal squadrons broke their orbital formations and hurtled down from the sky, spitting yellow plas-bolts at the slow-moving disk. For a short time the golden disk appeared powerless to fight back. The attack ships were relentless. Millie's shields glowed bright blue, absorbing the intense bursts like an iridescent sponge. Before the fighters could fire another fusillade, the Gamadin mothership from an ancient past awakened with infinitely more powerful bursts of her own. The sudden flashes from her perimeter knifed up at the heavens, engulfing the lines of attack ships. Sar and his elite guard watched helplessly as the Fhaal attack ships burned inside the blue envelope of destruction, their molecular ashes falling over the dark forests of Og.

The power of a thousand suns continued, unrelenting.

With every Fhaal ship blown clear from the heavens, *Millawanda* trained her powerful heat on the pride of the Fhaal battle group, Sar's Imperial Starship, high in orbit above the planet. With one short burst of blue fire, the starship was gone like its attack squadrons. Fhaal cruisers, some as far away as the most distant moon, lit up as the Fhaal battle group exploded like a hundred stars going nova across the Oggian sky.

The battle was over before it had even begun. In mere moments, the Fhaal armada had been obliterated from existence.

The golden ship silently drifted over the wide-open inner courtyard and stopped. It did nothing after that. It remained eerily still above the fortress, waiting for her final command to end it all. On the ground, an unnerving hush shrouded the courtyard like death, halting all movement as if time itself had stopped between the seconds. Harlowe stood with his hands at his side, his wound insignificant, both sidearms fully charged, waiting for the Fhaal Commander to make his move. A wisp of wind blew coldly from nowhere. No one moved, twitched, or breathed. Not even Sar's elite guards dared shift or move or blink lest they provoke a defensive backlash. The great Oggian sun seemed to halt its morning rise skyward in fear of retaliation from the Gamadin mothership.

Sar's yellow eyes twitched. Before His Excellency could unholster his weapon, Harlowe drew with invisible speed, blowing away Sar's arm clean from his body, pistol and all. Forgetting his shoulder, focusing all his anger and pain through his pistols, exploding bolts riddled Fhaal soldiers as if they were standing targets in a circus arcade. Gone! Everywhere gone!

No mercy.

Sar, his body shaking from the blasts, was already gone, unable to fall from the onslaught. In the next instant, his elite guards were tumbling backwards from the force of Harlowe's discharges. Gone! Their plas-riddled bodies slamming against the shuttle's black hull, dropping in piles to the ground, then still, never moving again. Ever!

No mercy.

His weapons depleted of energy, Harlowe's trigger fingers kept clicking off rounds as though he had an endless supply of ammo. Already dead, the armless Commander collapsed to his knees. His scaly mass teetered momentarily, then what was left of his carcass crashed forward, his body a mass of shredded meat and his clothes smoking from the rounds that had cut through them to cook the ugly toad underneath. Very, very gone!

No mercy.

Monday grabbed Harlowe's gun hand. "It's over, Captain. There's no one left." He reached his thick arms around Harlowe, bringing him closer, locking him in a tight body hold until his spasms stopped. "It's over, Captain. It's really over."

The silence was total.

No mercy.

107

All for Freedom

A LARGE DISK section disengaged from the underbelly of the saucer and floated down, touching the ground a few feet from the Gamadin. An instant later, Ian, the cats, and four med clickers winked into existence and stepped off the oversized blinker. Even Harlowe gawked with surprise. It was the largest blinker he had ever seen

Ian returned a tired smile. "Figured we needed a larger size, Captain." He looked around at all the carnage before he asked, "We done here?"

"Finished," Harlowe said wearily, about to drop.

Monday relieved Harlowe of his pistols and handed them to a robob. Other clickers were busily working with Riverstone and Simon, tending to their injuries with medical probing devices before placing them on antigrav stretchers to transport them back to a med room in the ship. Both cats lumbered up to Harlowe and began rubbing their bodies against his tired body, nearly pushing him over with their joy at seeing him alive and well.

Harlowe scratched and petted both cats—Rhud behind the ears, his favorite spot, and Molly along her beautiful white mane. "You did good, Wiz," he said, exhausted.

"I had a lot of good help, Captain," Ian said, looking at the saucer, full of pride. Turning back to Harlowe, he added, "You planned this, didn't you?"

Harlowe humbly smiled up as *Millawanda* as if she were a goddess. "You were so awesome today, girl," he said to her before answering Ian, "More like a fortunate turn of events."

Ian needed more clarity. "It was a trap?"

Harlowe saw the confusion on Ian's face and explained in more detail. "After the shootout on Gibb, I discovered Anor Ran had joined the race to capture Millie. He had been trying to put the Consortium out of business because they were squeezing his crystal business. If he had Millie, the Consortium would be toast overnight. Problem was, Quay messed it up for him when she wouldn't go along with his plot. His once-loyal daughter had changed sides."

"Because of you."

"No, something bigger than me. Something bigger than all of us. Bigger than the Gamadin."

Ian stopped mid-stride and stared at Harlowe. "What could be bigger than the Gamadin?"

"Freedom, pard. After she read the Declaration that night at the campfire, she went nuclear. She wanted freedom for every planet in the quandrant. She was all-in for freedom. She wanted to single-handedly eradicate the Rights of Passage, the Consortium, and the Fhaal, all by herself."

Ian laughed. "I remember the look on her face. She would have done it without us, too."

"No doubt. She turned red, white, and blue right before our eyes."

"That's sick!"

They stepped into the nearest med room with the stretchers. The moment they did, brilliant three-dimentional graphics switched on, announcing the arrival of the new patients.

"Yeah, it was all Riverstone's fault, too," Harlowe joked as he brought his wounded friend to a med table. "Don't tell him he jump-started the entire Omini Prime quandrant on its way to revolution. He'll be wanting his face on a one-koorant bill."

Riverstone sneered at Harlowe from his stretcher. He had been listening the whole time.

A robob medic touched Riverstone with a blue strobe. His eyes turned heavy. "Father of the Quadrant has a nice ring to it..." he murmured with a grin before he drifted off into la-la land. Neither Harlowe nor Ian saw that one coming.

A clicker transferred Riverstone to a med table. Riverstone and Simon were both out cold. As the robobs began stripping them naked, two more robobs treated Harlowe's shoulder wound. It wasn't long before he and Ian were headed for the bridge. Out in the corridor Ian asked, "Do you know where she is, Captain?"

Harlowe kept walking on toward the nearest blinker, stretching his neck, still looking as if he needed to be on a med table with Riverstone and Simon. "I have an idea," he replied.

They blinked to the bridge together. Once on the bridge, Harlowe gave Prigg the coordinates to follow.

108

The Hunch

A LIGHT DRIZZLE sprayed the forward windows as Mille descended in a slow drift toward the escarpment base where they had begun their assault the previous day. The long, spindly landing arms of the ship extended fully before they touched the wet ground. Harlowe and Ian, flanked by the cats, blinked to the perimeter of the ship and walked to the base of the massive cliff. To Harlowe it seemed like an eternity ago, not yesterday, that they were standing there about to climb the four-mile-high vertical cliff.

"Why are we here again, Captain?" Ian asked, as he watched the cats acting peculiar. Molly was moaning, sniffing the ground in an odd circular movement as Rhud sat back on his haunches, testing the air like a direction finder searching for a broadcast beam.

Harlowe's eyes narrowed, piercing the mist. "A hunch," he replied, then after a moment of study, called out. "There!" He was still in his skin, without the head cover and bugeyes. Water beads formed on his damp head and flowed down the side of his face in small rivulets. "Come on," he waved, and set out on a fast trot.

Ian looked in the direction Harlowe pointed. He couldn't figure out what Harlowe saw that he was missing as they marched toward a massive tree. The only thing unusual about the tree was its giant size and the thick, heavy, hundred-foot-long vines that touched the ground under its spreading canopy. One rebellious vine, however, seemed to defy gravity by reaching out in a 60-degree angle upward for the cliff wall. Ian wondered how that was possible without support. It was like an unruly hair jutting from the top of someone's head. From the canopy, the vine reached out for hundreds of feet and came just ten feet short of touching the cliff wall.

Harlowe removed his pistol and reloaded his empty magazine. Then he guided Ian away from under the vine. With three precise shots, Harlowe blasted the long finger of the vine, which fell to the ground with a heavy crash. Ian jumped back, staring at the vine in amazement. Two hundred feet overhead, the vine appeared thin and delicate, but close up, it was nearly a foot thick.

Harlowe reached down and retrieved the end of the wispy-thin filament that was wrapped around the vine.

Ian knew right away what it was. "How'd the dura-line get there?"

"Quay," Harlowe replied.

Ian tilted his head up the side of the escarpment wall. "You think she pulled a cliff-drop on Unikala?"

Harlowe had no doubt. "I know she did."

Ian whistled with incredulity. "That's sick, pard, even for her."

"Big-time. She got her first lesson when we jumped off Anor's building. Sizzle got one too when Rerun took her for a spin."

Ian turned back to Harlowe, worried. "Quay's lesson didn't go so well."

Harlowe was confident she'd made it. "The com would have found remains."

"So now what? If they made it, where are they?"

Harlowe hadn't filled in that blank yet. "They could be anywhere on the planet, with SIBAs."

They both knew that with SIBAs, the girls could cover a hundred miles a day without breaking a sweat. Before Harlowe ventured a guess on what to do next, a loud roar came from out of the jungle, startling them both.

"That was Rhud," Ian gasped.

Harlowe and Ian broke into a run across the clearing and into the thick underbrush. The dense growth cut off their direct line of sight, but above, birds and small treetop animals took flight, racing away in a mass exodus. Whatever was going on, they wanted no part of it.

Ian wanted to call the ship, but it was obvious that Harlowe wasn't going to waste any time with added protection. Harlowe leaped like a broken-field high hurdler over a dead tree in his path as Molly flew by them both as if they were standing still. Ian had never seen her move so fast.

They broke through the undergrowth into another wide clearing just in time to see Molly launch herself at a large, gibbon-like beast that had dropped from a high branch for Rhud's back. Rhud, for his part, didn't see him. He was busy with three others. The gibbons had heavily muscled long arms with hairless, burnt-orange-colored bodies. They had human-like faces with big, yellow eyes and huge jaws. Ian swallowed hard when he saw one of them unhinge its jaws wide and display its three rows of razor-sharp teeth. Ian had thought grogans were ugly until he saw these fearsome creatures.

Several dark shadows suddenly emerged out of nowhere from the high branches about to join the free-for-all. Harlowe pulled his pistols and quickly shot three of the shadows. The first he caught mid-flight, sizzling its brain with an incinerating bolt of plasma. Ian had to jump back as the three-hundred-pound body fell like a dead weight at his feet.

The crack of Harlowe's pistols and three more dead bodies dissuaded the circling horde in the treetops, their dark silhouettes withdrawing and hovering a healthy distance away from the jungle clearing. When Ian turned to the cats, they, too, had everything under control. Molly was doing her usual, ripping them apart, while Rhud feasted on gibbon limbs as if he were eating chicken wings.

"Where'd they come from?" Ian asked.

Harlowe shrugged. "They weren't here the first time."

Cringing with disgust, Ian sidestepped the beast at his feet. "They must rove the forest in packs." The beast had a crackling plas-shot through its forehead. He quickly glanced at the other two gibbons lying nearby with like penetrations. Even tired, Harlowe didn't miss.

"See any more?" Harlowe asked, combing the canopy.

Ian saw movement in the shadows. "Yeah, they're still up there," he replied, pointing.

Harlowe moved toward the cats to check up on their condition. Just to be sure, Ian called Prigg, who had seen the action on the outside visuals. There were over 150 in the pack, but as Ian had observed, they were keeping their distance.

While Ian was searching the area with his com, Harlowe examined the cats for injuries. Rhud, for all that he went through, had only a couple of minor scratches and a few missing tufts of white fur. Her Highness's paw was bleeding from a broken claw. Otherwise, she was okay. Harlowe patted her on the back of her mane. "We'll get you a manicure as soon as we get back, girl," he told her. She fired back an unhappy snarl.

Ian joined them. "What were you doing over here, Rhud?" he asked the big cat. His file-like tongue was out, catching his breath. "That's not like him to go wandering off like that, Dog," he added to Harlowe.

Harlowe scanned the clearing. "Whatever it was, it was important enough for him to wander this way." He patted the massive, chest-high head. "What did you find, big guy?"

Rhud growled approvingly and lumbered into the underbrush following a narrow animal path. They walked for twenty minutes until they came to an ancient temple of black stone that had been swallowed up centuries earlier by the forest.

"Quay couldn't be in there...could she?" Ian asked in a low whisper.

Harlowe said nothing. He didn't want to think about that possibility as he approached the structure, studying the ancient carvings in the ornamental niches along the walls. They continued across what had once been an outer courtyard of a temple.

"Reminds me of poison darts and Indiana Jones being chased by natives with bones in their noses," Ian said softly, pulling out his com.

Harlowe kept to himself, focused on any hidden traps. Ian might have been half-joking about Indiana Jones, but his reasoning had merit. In places like this, fiction was reality. Harlowe placed his SIBA headgear back around his head as Rhud led them through a dark portal in the side of the temple.

"What's it saying?" Harlowe asked, referring to the com readouts on Ian's screen.

Ian's eyes widened in amazement. "Ten thousand years old, give or take. There's a bunch of rats scampering around, but none of those orange dudes. Nothing threatening yet. Nothing human, either."

As long as there weren't any four-foot-long bats or yellow-eyed gibbons, Harlowe wasn't too concerned. He removed a light torch from his utility belt and began cutting away the undergrowth into the structure. The pathway he made allowed just enough light to see inside a great room on the other side of the entryway. In the center of the room was a twenty-foot statue made of the black stone. The eons of time had been easy on it. It was a statue of a gibbon beast.

The figure looked like an important personage, maybe a king. Its large, fierce eyes peered down on them behind its wide mouth and rows of long, razored teeth, Thousands of skeletal bones were piled high around the black stone pedestal at the base of the statue.

Nothing in the room seemed to have anything to do with the girls. Ian sighed, exasperated, as he returned to the com screen. Harlowe put his hands on his hips, shaking his head at another apparent deadend.

While Molly guarded the exit, Rhud parked himself on the stone ledge below the gibbon king's broken foot.

Harlowe shook his head in disappointment as he stared at the slothful cat. "Why'd you bring us here, Rhud?"

A low whistle came from Ian. "These bones date back thousands of years, Dog!"

Harlowe glared at Ian. He didn't care about bones.

"Nothing recent, though," Ian added.

Harlowe kept searching the ruins with his bugeyes at full power. Neither he nor Ian could find a single clue as to why Rhud had brought them to the temple, except perhaps to find a place to lick his paws.

"Anything, Wiz?"

Ian replaced the com on his belt. "Maybe we should let Millie in on the hunt."

"I'm down with that." He followed Molly out of the entrance and called back to Ian. "WIZ! Let's go!" he demanded.

Ian hurried to the portal entrance. "I think you should see this, Captain."

With a look of hope in his eyes, Harlowe rushed quickly back into the temple room. Ian walked over to the black stone base at the foot of the gibbon king statue and pointed to the spot were Rhud had been licking his paws. Harlowe's mouth dropped open, his face a mask of disbelief. There before them, drawn out with the chalky end of a bone, was a symbol scratched on the shiny surface of the stone.

"Is that what I think it is?" Harlowe asked, staring closely at the symbol.

"That's my guess," Ian concurred. "It's recent, too," he added, looking at his com.

Harlowe and Ian bolted out of the temple room into the clearing. Rhud and Molly sat, waiting for the next command. Harlowe walked up to Rhud, who paused with his tail between his legs. He bent down and held the great white head in his hands. "I apologize, big guy. You da man!"

Rhud returned a low snarl of "apology accepted." Then they were off, back to the ship as fast as their legs could carry them.

109

My Captain

SEVERAL HOURS LATER, the Ship came to a quiet stop at the edge of a clear green ocean. This was the seventh time it had stopped on a wide white beach with waves since leaving the gibbon king's temple. The timid residents along its shores seemed undisturbed by the Ship's presence. *Millawanda* had traveled over five thousand miles in her search, nearly a quarter of the distance around the planet. The great Consortium fortress escarpment had disappeared long ago beyond the horizon. The thick conifer forests and high jagged mountains around the escarpment had been replaced by equatorial tropical palms, lush hardwood canopies, and brightly colored birds that squawked in ceaseless banter, much like on #2 but on a much smaller scale. Three of Og's moons hung like pale yellow circles over the water, their reflections twinkling like jeweled spheres on the glassy water. A fourth moon, high in the sky behind them, was bright in the pre-dawn heaven. The large orange sun that had been high over the escarpment was now beginning another new day over the peaceful, crescent beach. Sets of slow-moving waves, beginning at a far rocky point, glistened like glass, lazily rolling onto shore in throaty rumbles over the sand.

Harlowe stepped off the blinker and walked beyond the perimeter rim of the ship into the morning sun. He looked out across the water and felt the warm winds blow against his face. He was alone. He felt it was best that way. If someone were to ask him why, he would have no answer except his insides were telling him that this was the place. Not even the cats were allowed to come with him. He wanted to be the first to know if... well, if the clue left at the temple was correct, that Quay and Sizzle had traveled to an ocean of waves. Og was not a planet of oceans like Earth. The oceans here were small seas, but the constant push and pull of its five moons created enough tidal forces for even a small sea to make some good waves. They had made several stops on these small seas. None had proved successful so far. Either they were too rocky or the waves were too flat. Most were hardly a place Quay would have chosen. But watching the small, perfect waves break along this sandy shore in long, right tubes and feeling the warm freshness of the salty air, he nodded approvingly. *Yes, this was the place Quay would have chosen.*

Harlowe wore a plain, loose-fitting, light blue shirt and matching long pants. No shoes. The warm, white sand was his sandals. He wore no weapons or 54th-century devices. The area was free of predators. A football field away sat a small hut made of palm leaves and hardwood sticks. Nearby, grey smoke from a small fire drifted up through the overhanging palms. An obvious sign of inhabitants, he knew. Clothes hung outside the hut's entrance. He trembled at the thought of another dead end and closed his eyes. It was time to go forward and ring the doorbell.

As he approached the huts, the whirring sound of the rover came up from behind him. He was starting to become angry. His orders had been explicit. No one but him. He turned angrily and was about to lash out at whoever was driving until he saw the passenger the clicker was carrying.

"I need to know too, Skipper," Simon said with pleading eyes. It had been only a few hours since Unikala shot him in the stomach.

He held his right arm tight to his side as though he was fighting against the pain of his wound. With another full day in the med unit, he would be good as new. But he had to know Sizzle's fate. Simon had forced himself out of bed in spite of his condition. He wore a dark blue T-shirt and short gold pants. His hair was sticking out on his head in several directions, his face white. He definitely needed bed rest.

Harlowe helped him out of the rover.

"Thanks, Skipper."

Harlowe lifted Simon's good arm over his own shoulder and they hobbled along the beach toward the lone beach hut, looking like wounded soldiers coming home from the war.

They were still fifty yards from the hut when Simon stopped. He hesitated, staring at the hut as if he didn't want to find the answer inside. "I'm afraid, Dog." His eyes began welling up. "I've come this far. I don't want a bad ending."

Harlowe stared anxiously with Simon. "I'm scared, too," he admitted. Yet they both knew there was no turning back. They had to continue. "Come on. We're writing our own script now, Rerun," Harlowe assured him. He lifted him up and pushed forward. "It will be okay."

Emerging from the hut was a black-haired woman in a garment of woven vines and leaves. The hair was right. It was long and golden like Sizzle's, but it wasn't Sizzle. The girl was thinner and tanner than the girl Simon knew before.

Harlowe and Simon stopped dead in their tracks. Together, looking like a theater act, they rubbed their eyes and leaned forward, peering closely at the girl, making sure she was real.

"It's her, Captain!" Simon wheezed, almost choking on his words. "Oh, it's her..."

It *was* Sizzle, and she was very much alive.

The shock on Simon's face was enough to register as a seismic event on the Ship's sensors.

Sizzle turned, her eyes suddenly catching the two visitors. At first she was startled by the intrusion. Then her eyes met Simon's, and with her mouth slightly open she began to visibly tremble from her overwhelming joy at seeing him again. She appeared to lose her balance. Simon saw her wavering and forgot his pain. He ran to her and caught her in his arms, their lips finding each other's, locking, kissing everywhere, shaking with disbelief that they were finally together again.

Unable to control his waiting any longer, Harlowe practically dove for the door of the hut. Inside was a bed of palms, whole coconuts, fruit and small berries, crude eating utensils, shells for bowls, and rags for clothes, but no Quay.

Harlowe came out of the hut, looking to Sizzle for answers.

"Quay is gone, Captain," Sizzle informed him, her eyes displaying her sadness. She went inside the hut and returned with a dried husk of a coconut palm and handed it to him. "She left this for you thirty-one sunrises ago and has not returned. I cannot read it. She said her mission was unfinished. That you would understand. It is written in a language I do not understand. I'm sorry, Captain."

Harlowe thanked her, then went solemnly to a nearby tree. He sat and read the letter from Quay, written in perfect English.

> *My Captain,*
> *I wake, as every day since I met you, filled with your heart, your touch, your thoughtfulness for my people and their freedom. I know you are coming for me! You are not far. By now our enemies have tasted the power of the*

Gamadin. What an effect you have had on me! I tremble with delight in telling you I have set out to bring the reality of your Declaration to others. This is our destiny! They will know of the brave Gamadin at every corner of the quadrant. Please, do not be angry with me for going on without you. Freedom cannot wait for a Sorcerer's night. We shall meet again one day. Of this I am certain. Until then, my Captain, you are my heart and reason for being.

Quay

* * *

For two long days Harlowe searched the planet with *Millawanda's* powerful sensors, and for two long days the Gamadin found no sign of Quay. As he stood on the shoreline of the beach where she was last seen, one thing was clear in Harlowe's mind—that if Quay wanted a way off the planet, she would have found it. She had a clear vision of a new freedom for her quadrant. How long would she wait on the beach for her quadrant's liberty? How long would he have waited? Was she any different than he? Was she their quadrant's Washington, Jefferson or Madison? Actually, more like Paine, Harlowe mused, a radical, intellectual and tough-minded revolutionary. She had the "right stuff" for the job. He laughed inwardly at the thought of anyone standing in her way.

Yes, he concluded, he would have gone on without her. After all, hadn't that been his promise, too, to free Neeja regardless of the personal sacrifice? Like he, she had her destiny to follow. Their paths would cross again one day. But not today. Today they had a bigger calling—a call to arms against all that opposed freedom and justice for all in the Omini quadrant!

He sucked in a lungful of heartache and pride. "Go girl!" he told her. He tossed a stone across the water, an old habit. "Make it happen..."

He then turned back to *Millawanda*, climbing the long rampway without a blinker, leaving Og for the last time.

110

Tomar

THE YELLOW TOMARIAN sun had barely peeked above the wide, ocean-covered horizon when hundreds of brilliant balls of intense blue light shot skyward from *Millawanda*'s perimeter and streaked through the morning clouds as they headed for deep space. Parked miles away on a wide stretch of deserted beach, Millie was polished and clean, waiting for the warm sun. After leaving Og, *Millawanda* returned Prigg to his home, his loving wife, and nine little Priggs. Following a tearful farewell, the Ship had carried the Gamadin to Tomar. It had been here on the beach for more than a week.

Miles away, Harlowe and Riverstone stood together on a lower balcony of Anor Ran's lavish palace on Tomar. They were admiring the view. From here, they could see practically forever. Only Ian remained behind in the Ship, preferring his own room and bed to the palace amenities.

To many throughout the quadrant, the Gamadin ship had become a symbol of freedom for Omini Prime. The word spread to the four corners of the quadrant about the total destruction of the Fhaal and the Consortium. Commerce was allowed to flourish everywhere in the quadrant unimpeded. The Rights of Passage was abolished forever. With the end of the Consortium, the monopoly over thermo-grym crystals ended and the price tumbled as more supplies were released from the vast Erati vaults. Prosperity was once again the way of the quadrant.

The Tomarian palace was situated on a hill at the base of a tower-ing range of snow-capped mountains that towered over a wide, green valley and a blue ocean. Near the tops of the tall peaks, strategically positioned across the ridgelines, were batteries of the most advanced sensors and plascannons in the quadrant. The castle fortress was a powerful testament to Tomarian wealth. Two cascading rivers fed by melting snow joined just below the mighty bronze gates of the castle and meandered through the gentle foothills led down to a plain of rolling meadows, wildflowers, and tall green grasses. Not far, perhaps a few miles beyond that, the river emptied out through a pristine coastline of flat sandy beaches, coves, and land points jutting out into the sea. On days when the wind was calm and the currents warm, the land points produced long, tubular lines of waves that the surfers back on Earth would call "sweet," "narly," and "rad." The palace was built to last the ages from pink and white stone. It was not colossal on a grand scale like the office structures on Gibb were. Nevertheless, in Earth terms, it was grand and massive. Built over a thousand passings before and protected by the four-mile-high mountains that cradled the valley, the main structure was a mixture of fluted columns, tall spires, and open-air balconies. All the great rooms, master suites, and banquet halls and the places where beings gathered, talked, and haggled over quadrant commercial concerns for centuries had views of the vast countryside and the meandering cold-water rivers that flowed through the plains and out to the wide, endless ocean beyond.

"We did good, huh, Dog?" Riverstone said, feeling proud and important over what they had accomplished. They looked below at Sizzle and Simon walking together and Monday giving Sharlon a lesson in golf. To everyone's relief, especially Riverstone's, Sharlon had survived the attack on the Gibbian office building. The story was that Anor Ran found her in time to save her from the fire and tend her wounds, a fact that had not surfaced during the short encounter between Harlowe and Anor on Roshmar.

Harlowe nodded. "Yeah, not so bad for a couple of surfer dudes from Lakewood."

"Have they found Anor yet?"

"No sign."

"Maybe the Fhaal got him before Og," Riverstone suggested.

Harlowe found that amusing. "I doubt it. Anor's a survivor. Toadface will turn up somewhere. Bank on it."

"Sharlon says she'll kill him herself for what he did to her daughters."

Harlowe shrugged indifferently. He made it a rule from now on to stay away from family disputes. "Whatever."

"What about Quay?"

The question raised the hairs on Harlowe's neck. "What about her?"

"Think she'll turn up?"

Harlowe shifted around uneasily. "If I had a crystal ball, I couldn't tell you." They enjoyed the view a while longer before Harlowe broke the silence. "So you're staying?" he asked straight out, shifting the uneasiness to his first officer.

"That obvious, huh?"

"Yeah, that obvious. Back to Erati?"

There was a sadness in Riverstone as he saw the path before him. The muscles in his jaws moved, not out of tension or confusion, but of what he must do next on his journey. He yearned to be on the ship that was going home. Harlowe knew that, but Riverstone's struggle had a greater need and it was why he had to stay behind. Harlowe had fought the same struggle every day he was captain of the most powerful ship in the galaxy. It was a struggle that lay between the need to be a young man again and the need to be the guardian of an ancient pledge—to save the galaxy from the evil that was still out there, waiting for the Gamadin to slay.

"Sharlon and I are going to clean it up," Riverstone finally replied.

Harlowe laid a heartfelt hand on his best friend's shoulder. It would be just as difficult to leave without him. He would miss Riverstone terribly.

"Ela would be so proud of you, pard."

"It's okay, then?"

"We won't be gone that long. There are still battles to be fought."

"Yeah, it's a big galaxy," he sighed, "with lots of trouble."

Riverstone looked down at Sharlon, who had just stroked another four hundred yard drive as Monday stood by in stunned disbelief, staring at the results. The golf ball landed a foot from the makeshift hole next to a half-dozen other well-placed shots. "How old do you think she is?"

Harlowe tried to conjure up a guess. Sharlon appeared younger than his mom. He would never divulge his mother's age, however, under penalty of certain death. "Twenty-seven," he replied, thinking it wise to guess low.

Riverstone grinned. "A hundred and thirty-one . . . earth time."

Harlowe nearly fell over the terrace wall. "I wonder what that makes Sizzle?" was Riverstone's second question. The mention of Quay went unsaid.

Harlowe forced himself to breathe, his mind still on the first question. "Don't tell Rerun. It might disturb his dream."

Riverstone smiled back, raising his eyebrows up and down. "Gamadin swear, pard." He would keep silent about a lot of things, including Quay.

To help Harlowe recover from the shock, Riverstone asked, "When's blast-off?"

Harlowe blinked, coming out of his daze. "Tomorrow," he replied. He nodded down at the garden. "Rerun's bringing Sizzle, too," he added, feeling as melancholy as he had ever been in his life. Besides his mom and his little brother, whom he figured by now was not so little, an unexplainable, nagging ache in his heart drew him home.

Riverstone then asked the most important question of all. "What about Neeja and your promise to Mrs. M? That's still not finished."

Harlowe's gaze drifted along the stone walls. He marveled at the gilded and jeweled fixtures that hung on thick chains, the tall tapestries made of the rarest threads from all over the quadrant, then up, up, up at the salmon-colored spires and the singing birds diving and gliding on gentle winds. It was straight out of a Disney fairy tale.

"It's being handled," he replied calmly as his eyes never blinked, now staring coldly at the water.

* * *

In an orbital holding pattern high above the planet Neeja, the remains of the Fhaal Imperial Fleet in the Omini Prime quadrant was preparing its final retreat back across the frontier. The great star-class battleships of the Fhaal armada that had invaded the Omini Prime quadrant many passings ago had been wiped out. There were no survivors at Og, not even the great and magnificent Commander Sar himself. Orders from the Imperial High Command were to evacuate the quadrant immediately and to proceed at flank speed back to the home world in preparation for a possible retaliatory attack. Five cycles earlier, at Sar's invitation, Commissars Keraada and Methota had traveled from the Fhaal home world to join Sar in the capture of the Gamadin mothership. Sar had envisioned sharing the glory with the Imperial High Command to solidify his standing inside the Central Council. But as Paradon had so rightly feared, without the destruction of the mothership, the wrath of the Gamadin would doom the Empire.

"Launch status?" Commissar Methota asked his ship's captain as he stared out from his Imperial Starship's bridge at all that remained of the once-invincible fleet. There were fewer than a hundred ships of various sizes and shapes left from Sar's two-thousand-ship armada, and only one star-class battleship left in the group...the Commissar's Imperial Starship!

"We are waiting for three thermo-grym shipments from the surface, Commissar," the captain replied. Before Commissar Methota could voice his displeasure, the captain added, "Without them, our ship will not make it to the frontier, Sire."

Commissar Methota turned away angrily at the apparent incompetence of the ship's crew. Standing nervously nearby with the communications officer was Commissar Keraada. "Any messages from the Imperial High Command?" the Commissar asked.

"No, Sire. All contact with the home planet has been severed," the young officer replied.

"Explanation?"

"None, Sire. Ship's communications have been checked and are in proper working order. We should be in contact with the home world."

The Commissars traded frightened glances when the ship's automatic defensive shields suddenly snapped on.

On the overhead screens, hundreds of fast-moving objects were racing toward their orbital position above Neeja.

"What are they?" Commissar Methota inquired.

The ship's captain reconfirmed his readouts, leaping from station to station before answering. "Unknown, Sire. They're headed right for the fleet!"

"Destroy them!" Commissar Keraada cried out.

"All defensive batteries are retaliating, Sire," the Commander stated.

Flying hot and true, the bright blue objects continued for the fleet unimpeded. Weapons were useless. From the bridge, Commissars Methota and Keraada watched in horror as the fleet was obliterated before their eyes. Finally, a single ball of intense blue light twisted away from the pack and headed straight for the Commissars' Imperial Starship. Neither its light cannons nor its shields would save them.

* * *

For the first time in its long, malicious history, the Fhaal home world was under assault. The Fhaal Supreme Leader, Paradon, had been rushed to his impenetrable underground bunker deep inside the Imperial High Command Center. From the far-off Andonian Cluster to the frontier of the Omini Prime quadrant, the Fhaal Imperial Fleets were being systematically destroyed . . . every last ship. On the master holo-screen, what was once a vast and mighty empire that stretched across hundreds of light passings and engulfed many quadrants was crumbling. Paradon watched in a helpless daze as, one by one, the tiny yellow lights of his battle groups winked out of existence. There was nothing he could do about it. The destruction was total. Soon there would be no more lights to contemplate.

A subordinate charged in, yellow eyes round with dread. "Your Majesty, the heavens above the home world are on fire! Unknown missiles are destroying our defenses, Sire!"

Paradon nodded, resigned to his fate. He dismissed the subordinate without reply. The Supreme Leader sat back in his chair and stared unemotionally at the intense blue light charging down from the heavens toward the Imperial Bunker. As the ball of light grew larger in the screen, he recalled the passage he had read from the ancient scrolls many passings ago from Hiit: *The wrath of the Gamadin will be felt throughout the stars and lo, while some people trembled in despair still more rejoiced; for the wrath of the Gamadin cleansed the stars for all…*

* * *

Harlowe leaned forward, eyeing the glassy lines of waves rolling in on the beach and wishing he had spent more time catching tubes before leaving Tomar.

"You'll bring them here next time when you come?" Riverstone asked, speaking of his parents.

"You know I will. In a few months, after I've had a roomful of In-N-Outs."

"Animal style!" they laughed together.

"Bring me back a franchise," Riverstone joked.

Harlowe pointed at the beach. "We'll put it there, between the left and right breaks."

Riverstone was all-in with that as he looked down at Simon, holding hands with Sizzle. "Rerun says he's going to write his next movie on the way back to Earth."

Harlowe laughed. "Between Sizzle and cleaning the cat box, he won't have much time."

Riverstone went on. "He says he's going to tone it down a little because no one would believe it."

"He's got that right!"

They laughed together as they continued toward the garden. Halfway down the stairway, Riverstone turned thoughtful again. It was one of those kinds of days, spilling your guts, tying up loose ends before saying goodbye. "I'm sorry, Harlowe."

Harlowe stopped and wondered why Riverstone was acting so strangely. It was unlike him. "Oh yeah, for what? Did you eat my last double-double?"

"Nah, Monday got that one." Harlowe's eyes rolled as Riverstone continued: "Well...when you get back to Earth I just want you to know, I...I...I wish I could have said something sooner."

Harlowe was dumbfounded. "Sorry for what? I should be apologizing to you for all that's happened."

"I know, but just leave it at that, okay?" Riverstone asked. "You'll understand soon enough."

Harlowe nodded, still at a loss as to why Riverstone was so apologetic. That wasn't like him. How long had they been away from home? Nearly a year? So many waves had come to shore without him. What did it matter now?

"Okay, pard. Your call," he replied, shrugging it off, leaving the matter in limbo as they continued down the long outer stairway toward the garden and Quincy, who was waiting patiently in the hovering rover to chauffeur them back to the Ship. "Will I be surprised?" Harlowe asked, before climbing into the shotgun side of the rover.

Riverstone forced a grin. "Ride some tubes at 42nd Street for me."

A moment later, Quincy was speeding Harlowe down the hill, following the river out to the beach and his golden ship. All the way, Harlowe's insides churned with twisted curiosity and foreboding as to what Riverstone had hinted at.

111

42nd Street

Iᴛ ᴡᴀs ᴍɪᴅ-Sᴇᴘᴛᴇᴍʙᴇʀ at 42nd Street. The air was hot and dry from the mild Santa Ana wind blowing offshore. School was back in session and the tourists had all left the SoCal beaches for home, taking their brown summer tans with them. Except for a couple of beach walkers and diehard joggers, the beach and waves were all Harlowe's and Dodger's. The sky was the bluest blue Harlowe had ever seen. After the red skies of #2, the desert rust of Roshmar and Gibb, the green domes over Palcor, and the eye-watering grey smog of Naruck, the earthly blue was heaven-sent. Adding to the perfect day was an end-of-the-summer south swell that was pumping in lines of ten-footers from a recent Baja storm. The lifeguards had closed the beach earlier, but Harlowe and Dodger were already out, defying the signs before dawn. Too many big days had already passed for such formalities. It was time to catch up.

"Go right, Harlowe!" Dodger called, treading water, watching the giant face coming toward them.

"Aye, aye, Captain," Harlowe saluted as he kicked, positioning himself for takeoff. They had been out for over an hour. The water was warm and glassy. One could easily see the sandy bottom below. It felt as if they were floating on air with SIBA wings.

Harlowe turned, stroking to meet the wave, when a vision caught his eye and sent a jolt through his heart. The girl was walking along the shore with her small dog with big ears. She was tall and blond and walked with such a delicate step that her toes seemed to hardly touch the sand. She wore grey workout clothes, obviously imported and high fashion. Her long blond hair flowed down over her shoulders in gentle waves, hiding her face for a moment. With sandals in hand, she played tag with the surf. After eons of time and hundreds of light-years, he knew that classy stride anywhere, that teasing tilt of the head, that posh and confident gait. When she finally turned toward him, his heart went to hyperlight. Even if he had been standing at the edge of the Mons, he would have seen her bright green eyes flashing his way, with her big-eared dog leaping and jumping beside her with unfettered joy. He laughed. The undog was still narly as ever.

She threw him a loving wink as if to say, "Hello stranger." She was even hotter than his dreams imagined. He rubbed his eyes, his vision obviously affected by the salt water.

He'd never thought he would see her again and understood now why Riverstone apologized that last day on Tomar. Riverstone had known all along that Lu was alive and they would meet again, and here at 42nd Street too, for what other place would there be?

He figured Lu had made Riverstone promise to keep her contrived death a secret. It was the only explanation. Riverstone would have told him for sure if she hadn't. *I should have left him on Erati,* he swore playfully. If their roles were switched, though, he would have done the same. She knew him best, and so did Riverstone. Harlowe would have gone after her if he knew she was alive. She had sacrificed their love for the planet, the quadrant, *Millawanda,* and the Gamadin. They had *all* risked their lives, but was there a more noble cause than a new beginning?

"Harlowe!" Dodger yelled. "Watch out!"

Dodger kicked once and was gone before the wave struck, shooting down the twelve-foot face like a flying dolphin. Harlowe never saw the wave coming.

He tumbled over and over as the force of the wave slammed him hard against the bottom, rolled him, pushed and pulled him in ten different ways like a rag doll. There was no up or down, only a swirling mass of darkness.

From out of nowhere, a gentle touch took his hand and guided him toward the light. Harlowe broke the surface, grateful for a lungful of air. Before his eyes cleared, the vision beside him asked, "Are you okay, soldier?"

He brushed back her long sun-struck hair to see her better. He was awestruck as if she were a dream. The Sorcerer was at it again, he knew, his magic all-powerful and great, a master's touch. *Please let her stay,* he pleaded with the Wizard.

They came together, rising and falling over the waves...alone and one again as they always had been and always would be. He squeezed the joy from his eyes as she rested peacefully in his arms. He didn't know how much longer they had together. Until the next "house call," he figured.

Harlowe returned a boyish grin, seeing her green eyes sparkle his way. "I am now," he replied.

Coming Fall, 2011

Book IV

GAMADIN

GAZZ

Harlowe was surfing in the South Pacific with his little brother, Dodger, and Simon was accepting his Oscar from Phoebe Marleigh for his performance in *Distant Galaxy*, when Riverstone called in a panic from the Omini Prime quadrant. All life on the planet Gazz was about to be wiped out by a lethal gamma ray burst in eleven days. According to Wiz, saving the planet with *Millawanda's* forcefield was a "slam dunk." The plan was going smoothly until hostile forces dropped out of hyperspace moments before the lethal rays struck. Battling two forces at once, Millie saves the planet, but at a cost: her power is sucked dry! Unable to maintain orbit, *Millawanda* plunges into the planet's ocean. Adding to the tragedy, Riverstone, Lu and Sizzle have vanished and a second gamma ray burst will hit the planet in 37 days. There is a source of thermo-grym, but Gazz is a 15th Century planet of wind-powered ships and slithering beasts called "traas." In a race against time, Harlowe must commandeer a pirate galleon and find the yellow crystals that will power *Millawanda* back to to life before his girl, his crew, his ship, the planet and his own life are lost . . .